Anne of Austria and Buckingham

The Three Musketeers

THE THREE MUSKETEERS

ALEXANDRE DUMAS

Translated by Isabel Ely Lord

DESIGNED FOR MODERN READING

Illustrated by Daniel Rasmusson

GARDEN CITY, N. Y.

Doubleday & Company, Inc.

ILLUSTRATIONS

The Three Musketeers

CHAPTER 1

ON THE FIRST MONDAY OF THE MONTH OF APRIL 1625, the town of Meung looked as if it were in as complete a state of revolution as if the Huguenots had just made a second La Rochelle of it. Many citizens, seeing the women fleeing in the direction of the main street and hearing the children crying out from doorsteps, hastened to don their cuirasses. Then, supporting their somewhat uncertain courage by grasping a musket or a pike, they directed their steps toward the tavern of The Jolly Miller. There a compact group, growing larger by the minute, had gathered, vociferous and full of curiosity.

In that period panics were frequent, and few days passed without some French city's registering in its archives an event of that sort. There were the nobles making war against one another; there was the King making war against the Cardinal; there was Spain making war against the King. Then, besides these wars—hidden or public, secret or patent—there were also robbers, beggars, Huguenots, wolves, and lackeys who made war on everybody. The citizens always took up arms against thieves, wolves, or lackeys, often against the nobles and the Huguenots, sometimes against the King—but never against the Cardinal or Spain. So on this first Monday of the month of April 1625, since such was their custom, the citizens of Meung, hearing the clamor and seeing neither the red-and-yellow standard of Spain nor the livery of the Duc de Richelieu, rushed toward The Jolly Miller. When they reached it, everyone could see plainly what was causing all this hubbub.

It was a young man—let us sketch his portrait with the pen. Imagine a Don Quixote of eighteen, a Don Quixote without a corselet, coat of mail, or thigh pieces, a Don Quixote clad in a woolen doublet with its blue faded into an indefinite shade between that of the lees of wine and a heavenly azure. His face was long and tanned; his cheekbones were prominent, a sign of shrewdness; the muscles of his jaws were enormously developed, an infallible clue to a Gascon, even when he wore no beret—and our young man did wear a beret, adorned with some sort of feather. His eyes were candid and intelligent, his nose hooked but finely chiseled. Too tall for an adolescent, too short for a grown man, by an experienced observer he might well be taken for a farmer's son on a journey had it not been for the long sword dangling from a leather belt. The sword kept hitting against its owner's calves as he walked and against the rough flank of his steed as he rode.

Our young man's steed was the observed of all observers. It was a Béarn nag twelve or fourteen years old, with a yellow coat and a tail without a single hair, but it was not without sores on its legs. As it always walked with its head below its knees, there was no need for a martingale, but it nevertheless managed to make its eight leagues a day. Unfortunately the good qualities of this horse were so well concealed under its bizarre coat and its incongruous gait that at a period when everybody was a connoisseur in horseflesh, the appearance of the said nag at Meung aroused feelings that were far from favorable, and which naturally included the man who rode it.

These feelings inflicted all the more pain on D'Artagnan—that was the name of the Don Quixote of this second Rosinante—because he could not fail to see how ridiculous such a steed made him, good horseman as he was. Indeed he had sighed deeply as he accepted the gift from his father. He was not unaware that such a beast was worth at least 20 livres, and the words that accompanied the gift were priceless.

"My son," said the old Gascon gentleman in that pure Béarn patois that Henry IV had never succeeded in losing, "my son, this horse was born in your father's house something like thirteen years ago, and here it has remained ever since. That ought to make you love it. Never sell it —let it die peacefully and honorably of old age. If you make a campaign with it, take as good care of it as you would of an old servant. At Court, if you ever have the honor to go there—an honor to which your time-honored rank as a nobleman gives you the right—uphold worthily the name of gentleman that has been borne worthily by your ancestors for more than half a century. Suffer nothing from any man except the Cardinal and the King. It is by his courage, remember, by his courage alone, that a gentleman makes his way nowadays. The man who trembles for even a second perhaps allows the bait to escape him that Fortune was holding out to him at that very second.

"You are young. You ought to be brave for two reasons: first, because you are a Gascon, and second, because you are my son. Never be afraid to seize an opportunity, and seek out adventures. I have taught you how to handle a sword; you have thews of iron and a wrist of steel. Fight at every opportunity, all the more willingly because duels are forbidden and consequently it takes twice as much courage to fight one.

"I have nothing to give you, my son, save fifteen crowns, my horse, and the counsels you have just heard. Your mother will add to these the recipe for a certain balsam that she got from a gypsy woman. It has the miraculous virtue of healing all wounds that do not reach the heart.

Take advantage of everything that happens to you, and live happily and long!

"I have but one word to add, and that is to propose an example for you—not my own, for I have never appeared at Court, and I took part in the Religious Wars only as a volunteer. I mean Monsieur de Tréville, who was once my neighbor, and who as a boy had the honor of being the playfellow of our King, Louis XIII, whom God preserve! Sometimes their games degenerated into battles, and in those battles the King was not always the victor. The blows he received from Monsieur de Tréville gave the King great esteem and friendship for that gentleman. Later, Monsieur de Tréville fought against many other men, perhaps a hundred times. And in spite of ordinances and edicts against dueling, there he is today, Captain of the Royal Musketeers, which is saying that he is the leader of a legion of Caesars that the King holds in high esteem and whom Monsieur le Cardinal fears—he who fears nothing, as everyone knows. Moreover, Monsieur de Tréville earns ten thousand crowns a year, therefore he is a very great nobleman. He began as you are beginning. Go to him with this letter, and make him your model, in order that you may accomplish what he has accomplished."

Thereupon Monsieur d'Artagnan the elder girded his own sword around his son, kissed him tenderly on both cheeks, and gave him the precious letter and his blessing.

On leaving his father's room, the young man went to find his mother, who was waiting for him with the famous recipe. The paternal advice we have just recorded would necessitate its rather frequent use. The mother's farewells were longer and more tender than the father's. Madame d'Artagnan wept abundantly, and to do justice to Monsieur d'Artagnan the younger, we must say that notwithstanding the efforts he made to be as firm as a future musketeer should be, nature prevailed and he shed many tears, and only with great difficulty did he succeed in concealing half of them.

The same day the young man set out on his journey, fitted out with his father's three gifts, consisting, as has been noted, of 15 crowns, the horse, and the letter to Monsieur de Tréville, the advice, naturally, being thrown into the bargain; and with his mother's recipe for balsam.

With such a vade mecum D'Artagnan was, both morally and physically, an exact replica of Cervantes' hero, to whom we have already compared him so appropriately. Don Quixote took windmills for giants and sheep for armies; D'Artagnan took every smile for an insult and every stare for a challenge. Accordingly all the way from Tarbes he kept his fist clenched, or he put his hand on the hilt of his sword, ten times a day. Yet his fist did not come down on any jaw nor did his sword leave its scabbard. The sight of the ill-starred yellow nag certainly lighted the faces of observers with many a smile, but as up on the nag a sword of respectable length was rattling, and as above that sword there gleamed an eye that was ferocious rather than proud, said observers restrained their hilarity. Therefore D'Artagnan remained majestic and irreproachable until he came to this ill-omened town of Meung.

But there, as he was alighting from his horse at the gate of The Jolly Miller without anyone—host, waiter, or hostler—having come to hold his stirrup, D'Artagnan, glancing through a half-open window on the ground floor, espied a gentleman with a good figure and a proud look, though rather a morose one. He was talking with two men who seemed to be listening to him with the greatest respect. D'Artagnan quite naturally, since such was his habit, thought that he was the subject of their conversation, and he listened intently. This time D'Artagnan was only partly mistaken; he himself was not their subject, but his horse was. Apparently the gentleman was enumerating all the horse's qualities for the benefit of his audience, and since the audience, as has been noted, seemed to have great deference for the narrator, they burst into roars of laughter at every moment. Now since even a half-smile was enough to arouse the wrath of our young man, it is easy to guess how this vociferous mirth affected him.

Nevertheless, before he took action, D'Artagnan wanted to read the countenance of this insolent fellow who was making fun of him. He stared haughtily at the stranger and saw a man between forty and forty-five years old, with piercing black eyes, pale skin, a nose well worthy of notice, and a black mustache that was trimmed to perfection. He was dressed in doublet and hose of violet with points of the same hue and with no other ornament except the customary slashes through which the shirt appeared. The doublet and hose, though new, looked rumpled, as if they were traveling clothes packed for a long time in a portmanteau. D'Artagnan noted all these details with the rapidity of the most meticulous observer and also, perhaps, with an instinctive feeling that this stranger was destined to have a great influence upon his future life.

While D'Artagnan was staring at the gentleman in the violet doublet the gentleman was uttering one of his most masterly and most profound expositions, and his two auditors were laughing even more uproariously than before. The speaker himself allowed a pale smile—if I may be permitted to use such an expression—to appear on his lips. This time there could be no doubt. D'Artagnan was really being insulted. Finally convinced of that now, he pulled his beret down over his eyes, and, endeavoring to copy some of the Court ways that he had picked up in Gascony from traveling noblemen, he stepped forward with one hand on the hilt of his sword and the other planted on his hip. Unfortunately, as he advanced his anger blinded him more and more at every step, so that instead of the dignified and lofty speech he had prepared as his challenge, he found nothing at the tip of his tongue except an unmannerly personal remark that he accompanied with a furious gesture.

"You, monsieur, you, monsieur, who are hiding behind that shutter—yes, you! Tell me what you are laughing at and we will laugh together!"

The gentleman turned his eyes slowly away from the horse to its rider, and in a tone of irony and insolence impossible to describe he replied:

"I was not speaking to you, monsieur."

"But I am speaking to you, monsieur, I am!" cried the young man, exasperated by this combination of insolence and good manners, of decorum and disdain.

The stranger looked at him again with his pale smile, left the window, frowned slightly, and came out of the inn slowly. He took his stand in front of the yellow horse within two paces of D'Artagnan. The Gascon drew his sword a foot out of its scabbard.

"Decidedly, this horse is, or rather was in his youth, a buttercup," the stranger went on, addressing his audience at the window. Apparently he had not noticed D'Artagnan's exasperation, although the young Gascon was standing between him and his audience. "This color is well known to botany, but up to now it has been very rare among horses."

"There are men who laugh at a horse who would not dare laugh at his master!" cried the young emulator of an angry Tréville.

"I do not laugh often, monsieur," replied the stranger, "as you can see from the cast of my countenance. But nevertheless I hold to my privilege of laughing whenever I please."

"And I," cried D'Artagnan, "I will allow no man to laugh when it offends me!"

"Really, monsieur?" the stranger continued, calmer than ever. "Well, that's all right with me," and turning on his heel, he started to go back into the inn by the front gate, where D'Artagnan had already noticed a saddled horse was standing.

But D'Artagnan was not a youth to allow to escape him like that a man who had had the insolence to make fun of him. He drew his sword and ran after the stranger, crying:

"Turn around, turn around, Master Jester, lest I strike you in the back!"

"Strike *me!*" said the stranger, turning and looking at the young man with both astonishment and contempt. "Come, come, my dear fellow, you must be insane!" Then, in a low tone, as if talking to himself, he went on: "This is annoying. What a find for His Majesty this chap would be! He's always looking everywhere for such fine fellows to recruit the Royal Musketeers!"

He had barely finished speaking when D'Artagnan made such a furious lunge at him that if he had not leaped back nimbly, he might well have jested for the last time. The stranger perceived then that more than a jest was in question, drew his sword, saluted his adversary, and placed himself on guard soberly. But at the same moment his two auditors, accompanied by the innkeeper, fell upon D'Artagnan with cudgels, shovels, and tongs. This interruption of D'Artagnan's attack was so rapid and so complete that while the young Gascon turned to face this shower of blows his adversary sheathed his sword. Having just missed being an actor in the fight, now he became a spectator, a role that he played with his habitual impassivity, nevertheless muttering:

"A plague on these Gascons! Put him back on his orange horse and send him off!"

"Not before I kill you, you poltroon!" cried D'Artagnan, meeting the attack as best he could and not giving back a step before his three assailants, who were raining blows on him.

"Another Gascon boast!" murmured the gentleman. "Upon my honor, these Gascons are incorrigible! Keep up the dance, then, since he will have it so. When he is tired he'll say that he's had enough."

But the stranger did not know as yet what a headstrong man they had to deal with. D'Artagnan was not a man to ask for quarter in any circumstances. So the fight went on a few seconds longer. But at last D'Artagnan, exhausted, dropped his sword, which the blow of a cudgel had broken in two. Another blow struck him in the forehead and brought him to the ground, covered with blood and unconscious.

It was at this point that people came flocking to the scene of action from every direction. Mine host, fearing a scandal, aided by his servants, carried the wounded man into the kitchen. As for the gentleman, he had gone back to his place at the window and stood watching the crowd with some impatience, obviously annoyed that they did not disperse.

"Well, how goes it with that madman?" he asked, turning as the opening door announced the innkeeper.

"Your Excellency is safe and sound?" inquired mine host.

"Yes, perfectly safe and perfectly sound, my dear host. I'm asking you what has happened to our young hothead."

"He's getting better. He fainted dead away. But before he fainted he gathered all his strength to challenge you and defy you."

"Why, the merry fellow must be the Devil in person!" cried the stranger.

"Oh no, Your Excellency, he isn't the Devil," mine host answered with a scornful grimace. "While he was in a faint we searched his person and his belongings, and he has nothing but one shirt, and twelve crowns in his purse. But that didn't keep him from saying as he was swooning that if a thing like that had happened in Paris, you would have been sorry for it at once, whereas now you will not be sorry for it until later."

"Perhaps," said the stranger coldly, "he's some prince of the blood in disguise."

"I have told you this, monsieur, so that you may be on your guard."

"Didn't he name any name in his rage?"

"Yes, he did. He tapped on his pocket and said, 'We shall see what Monsieur de Tréville will think of this insult to his protégé.' "

"Monsieur de Tréville?" the stranger said, his attention aroused. "He tapped on his pocket and spoke of Monsieur de Tréville? Come, my dear host, while your young man was unconscious I'm sure you did not fail to look into that pocket. What was in it?"

"A letter addressed to Monsieur de Tréville, Captain of the Royal Musketeers."

The stranger left his place at the window and frowned uneasily.

"The devil!" he muttered between his teeth. "Can Tréville have sent this Gascon after me? He is very young. Still, a sword thrust is a sword thrust, whatever the age of the one who gives it. And one does not suspect a lad as much as a grown man. A slight obstacle is enough to thwart a great plan." And the stranger fell into a reverie that lasted several minutes.

"Come, mine host," he said at last, "aren't you going to get rid of this crazy boy for me? As a matter of conscience, I can't kill him, and yet," he added with a coldly menacing expression, "yet he is in my way. Where is he?"

"In my wife's room on the second floor. They are dressing his wounds."

"Are his clothes and the bundle he had with him there too? He hasn't taken off his doublet, has he?"

"All his belongings are downstairs in the kitchen. But if he is in your way, the young fool——"

"He certainly is. Go upstairs, please, and make out my bill, then summon my lackey. I bade you have my horse saddled. Isn't it ready?"

"Yes indeed, and as Your Excellency may have noticed, it is standing by the gate, quite ready for you to ride away."

"Good! Do as I have told you, then."

"Dear me," said the host to himself, "can he be afraid of that boy?" He bowed humbly and withdrew.

"Milady* must not be seen by this rascal," the stranger said to himself. "She should not be long in coming now; she's already late. I'd better get on my horse and go to meet her. . . . If only I knew what is in this letter to Tréville!" And the stranger made his way to the kitchen, still muttering.

In the meantime the host, certain that it was only the presence of the youth that was driving the stranger from his hostelry, had gone up to his wife's room, and had found D'Artagnan in his right mind again. Giving him to understand that the police might deal with him rather roughly

*This unusual form of "my lady" is the one Dumas used, and the name has become a traditional one for this woman.

for having picked a quarrel with a great lord—for in the innkeeper's opinion the stranger could be nothing less—he insisted that D'Artagnan, despite his weakness, should get up and go on his way. D'Artagnan, half-stupefied, without his doublet and with his head swathed in bandages, rose and, shoved along by the host, began to go down the stairs. But when he reached the kitchen, he glanced through the window and saw his antagonist standing on the step of a heavy carriage drawn by two large Norman horses. He was chatting quietly with a woman whose head was framed by the carriage window. She was apparently about twenty, or perhaps a year or two older. D'Artagnan was an adept at reading faces. He saw at a glance that this woman was young and beautiful. Her beauty was all the more striking because it was entirely different from that of the Midi, where he had always lived until now. She was pale and fair, with long golden curls falling in profusion over her shoulders; she had large blue, languishing eyes, rosy lips, and hands of alabaster. She was talking eagerly with the stranger.

"So His Eminence orders me——" said the lady.

"To return to England at once, and to let him know immediately if the Duke leaves England."

"And my further instructions?" asked the fair traveler.

"They are in this box, which you are not to open until you are on the other side of the Channel."

"Very well. And you—what are you going to do?"

"I am going back to Paris."

"Without chastising that insolent boy?" the lady asked.

The stranger was about to reply, but just as he was opening his mouth D'Artagnan, who had heard everything they said, dashed across the threshold of the inn.

"This insolent boy chastises others," he shouted, "and I have good hope that the man he means to chastise will not escape him as he did before!"

"Will not escape him?" the stranger repeated, frowning.

"No, will not. In the presence of a woman, you would not dare to run away, would you?"

As she saw the stranger grasp the hilt of his sword, Milady cried: "Remember that the least delay will ruin everything!"

"You are right!" cried the gentleman. "Be off on your way, then, and I will go on mine."

Bowing to the lady, he sprang into his saddle, and at the same time the coachman lashed his horses vigorously, and the stranger and Milady went off at a gallop in opposite directions.

"Hey, your reckoning!" yelled mine host.

"Pay him, clodhopper!" the horseman shouted to his lackey, galloping on. The lackey halted long enough to throw two or three pieces of silver at the feet of the innkeeper and galloped off after his master.

"Oh, you coward, you miserable wretch, you sham gentleman!" shouted D'Artagnan, springing forward in his turn after the lackey. But his wounds had left him too weak to bear up under such an effort. Scarcely had he taken ten steps when his ears began to ring, he was seized with dizziness, a cloud of blood veiled his eyes, and he fell in the middle of the street, still crying, "Coward, coward, coward!"

"He is indeed a coward!" muttered the innkeeper.

"Aye, he is the worst of cowards," murmured D'Artagnan. "But she, how beautiful she was!"

"Who is *she?*" asked the innkeeper.

"Milady," faltered D'Artagnan. And he fainted again.

"All right," the innkeeper said to himself, "I've lost two guests, but I still have this one."

But mine host had reckoned without his guest. The next morning D'Artagnan rose at five o'clock, went down to the kitchen without help, and asked for several ingredients the properties of which have not come down to us. He asked also for wine, oil, and rosemary. With his mother's recipe in his hand, he made up a balsam with which he anointed his various wounds. He renewed his bandages himself, refusing positively the assistance of any doctor. Thanks, doubtless, to the efficacy of the gypsy balsam, D'Artagnan was on his feet that evening, and was virtually cured on the morrow.

But when the time came to pay for the rosemary, the oil, and the wine —the only expense the master had incurred, since he had fasted while the yellow horse, as the innkeeper said, had eaten three times as much as a horse of his size could reasonably be supposed to consume—then D'Artagnan found in his pocket only his little purse of threadbare velvet and the 11 crowns it contained. The letter addressed to Monsieur de Tréville had disappeared.

The young man began to search for that letter with the greatest patience, turning every one of his pockets inside out over and over again, rummaging in his bundle and then rummaging there again, opening and closing his purse many times. Then when he was convinced that the letter was not to be found, he flew into a rage for the third time, such a rage as almost cost him a fresh expenditure for wine and aromatic oils. Mine host saw the young hothead fuming and threatening to destroy everything in the tavern if his letter was not found. He seized a spit, his wife grasped a broom, and the waiters got the cudgels they had used two days before.

"My letter of recommendation!" shouted D'Artagnan. "Find my letter of recommendation or by God's blood I will run a spit through all of you as though you were ortolans!"

Unfortunately there was one circumstance that prevented the youth from carrying out his threat. His sword, the reader will remember, had been broken in two in his first conflict, a fact that he had entirely forgotten. Consequently when D'Artagnan tried to draw that sword, he found that he was armed with nothing but a fragment of it some eight or ten inches long, which the innkeeper had carefully replaced in the scabbard.

"Where is my letter?" D'Artagnan thundered. "I warn you that that letter is addressed to Monsieur de Tréville and it *must* be found, and if it isn't found, he will know how to have it found, Monsieur de Tréville will!"

That threat completed the intimidation of mine host. After the King and the Cardinal, Monsieur de Tréville was the man whose name was most often spoken among soldiers and even among civilians. Throwing down his spit and ordering his wife to do likewise with her broom and the waiters with their cudgels, the innkeeper set the example by beginning the search for the missing letter.

"Was there anything valuable in that letter?" he demanded, after a few minutes of futile attempts.

"Zounds," cried the Gascon, "I should say there was!" He was reckoning on that letter to make his way smooth at Court. "It contained my whole fortune!"

"Drafts on the Spanish Treasury?" asked the worried innkeeper.

"Drafts on the Privy Treasury of His Majesty the King of France," answered D'Artagnan. He had counted on entering the King's service, thanks to that recommendation, so he thought he might hazard that statement without being a liar.

"The devil!" said the innkeeper, now quite disheartened.

"It doesn't matter," said D'Artagnan, with true Gascon assurance. "It doesn't matter. Money is nothing to me, but that letter meant *everything*. I would rather have lost a thousand pistoles than to have lost that letter."

Suddenly a ray of light illumined mine host's mind, just as he was committing himself to the Devil for finding nothing.

"That letter is not lost!" he exclaimed.

"What do you mean?" D'Artagnan asked.

"It isn't lost. It was stolen from you."

"Stolen! Who stole it?"

"The gentleman who was here yesterday. He went down to the kitchen, where your doublet was. He was alone there for some time. I'll bet he's the one who stole it."

"Do you think so?" replied D'Artagnan. He was far from being convinced, for he knew better than anyone else how purely personal the importance of that letter was, and could think of nothing in it that would tempt a thief. "You say that you suspect that impertinent gentleman?"

"I tell you I am sure he took it. When I told him that your lordship was the protégé of Monsieur de Tréville, and that you even had a letter for that illustrious gentleman, he seemed very much disturbed. He asked me where the letter was and went straight down to the kitchen, where he knew your doublet was."

"Then he's the thief who robbed me," said D'Artagnan. "I will complain to Monsieur de Tréville, and Monsieur de Tréville will complain to the King."

Then, with a majestic air, he took 2 crowns from his purse, gave them to the innkeeper, who accompanied him to the gate, hat in hand, mounted his yellow horse, and rode off. His steed bore him without any further mishap to the Porte Saint-Antoine of Paris, where its owner sold it for 3 crowns—a very good price, considering that D'Artagnan had ridden it hard from Meung.

Thus D'Artagnan entered Paris on foot, carrying his little bundle under his arm. He walked around until he found a room to rent that suited his scanty means. It was a sort of attic situated in the Rue des Fossoyeurs, near the Luxembourg.

As soon as he took possession of his lodging, D'Artagnan spent the rest of the day sewing on his doublet and hose some ornamental braid that his mother had cut off an almost new doublet of Monsieur d'Artagnan the elder and had given her son secretly. Then he went to the Quai de la Ferraille to have a new blade put in his sword, and walked back toward the Louvre, asking the first musketeer he met with where Monsieur de Tréville's house was. It proved to be in the Rue du Vieux-Colombier, which was near the place where D'Artagnan had taken his attic. This circumstance seemed to him a happy augury for the success of his journey.

After that, quite content with the way he had conducted himself at Meung, with no remorse for the past, confident as to the present, and full of hope for the future, our young Gascon went to bed and slept the sleep of the brave.

This sleep of one who was still a provincial lasted until nine o'clock the next morning, at which hour he rose and got ready to repair to the residence of the illustrious Monsieur de Tréville, the third personage in the kingdom of France in his father's estimation.

CHAPTER 2

MONSIEUR DE TROISVILLE, THE FAMILY NAME ALWAYS
used in Gascony, or Monsieur de Tréville, as he had at last styled himself in Paris, had really begun life in Paris as D'Artagnan was now doing
—without a sou in his pocket, but with that stock in trade of audacity,
shrewdness, and intelligence that often leads the poorest Gascon lordling
to derive more in hope from his paternal inheritance than the richest of
gentleman of Périgord or Berry derives from his in reality. Monsieur de
Tréville's insolent bravery, his still more insolent success at a time when
blows showered down on him like hail, sent him up to the top of that
difficult ladder that is called Court favor. He had gone up that ladder
four rungs at a time. He was a friend of King Louis XIII, who, as everyone knows, revered the memory of his father, Henry IV. Monsieur de
Tréville's father had served Henry IV so loyally in the Religious Wars
that the monarch, since he always lacked ready money, authorized his
faithful servant to assume as his coat of arms a golden lion passant upon
gules, with the motto *Fidelis et Fortis*—Loyal and Brave. This was a great
honor, but a very small contribution to a life of ease. So when the illustrious companion of the great Henry died, the only inheritance he left his
son consisted in his sword and his motto. Thanks to this double gift and
to the spotless name that accompanied it, Monsieur de Tréville was admitted into the household of young Prince Louis, whom he served so
well with the sword, proving so faithful to his motto, that Louis XIII,
one of the best swordsmen in his kingdom, often said that if he had a
friend who was about to fight a duel, he would advise him to choose as a
second in the first place himself, next, Tréville—or perhaps Tréville even
first.

Moreover, Louis XIII felt real affection for Tréville—royal affection,
selfish affection, it is true, but nevertheless true affection. At that unhappy
period men in high places sought to surround themselves with men of
Tréville's stamp. Tréville's was one of those rare natures endowed with
obedient intelligence like that of a dog, with blind valor, with a quick
eye and a prompt hand. Apparently sight had been given him only that
he might see when the King was displeased with someone, and a hand

only that he might strike down the culprit. In short, up to now Tréville had lacked nothing save the right opportunity; but he was always on the watch for it, and he promised himself that he would seize it by three hairs of its head if it came within reach of his hand. It came at last, and Louis XIII made Tréville Captain of the Royal Musketeers, a corps that in devotion, or rather in fanaticism, was to Louis XIII what his Ordinaires had been to Henry III and his Scots Guards to Louis XI.

On his side, the Cardinal was not far behind the King in this respect. When he saw the redoubtable elite with which Louis XIII surrounded himself, this second—or shall we say the first?—real ruler of France determined to have his own guards. So he had his own musketeers—though they were called guards—as Louis XIII had his. These two rival powers vied with each other in recruiting the most celebrated swordsmen, not only from all the provinces but also from all foreign nations. Richelieu and Louis XIII often argued as to the merits of their respective soldiers while they were playing their evening game of chess. Each praised the steadiness and the courage of his own men. They denounced duels and riots authoritatively and loudly, but secretly they incited their musketeers and guardsmen to quarrel, suffering real sorrow when they were defeated and feeling real joy when they were victors.

Tréville understood the weak side of his master. It was to his skill in exploiting it that he owed the long and steadfast favor of a monarch who has not left us the reputation of a man particularly faithful in his friendships. The King paraded his musketeers before Armand Duplessis, Cardinal and Duc de Richelieu, with a bantering air that made His Eminence's gray mustaches bristle with anger. Tréville was a master of the war methods of that period, when if soldiers could not live at the expense of the enemy, they must live at the expense of their fellow countrymen. His men made up a legion of daredevils absolutely without discipline save for that they accepted from him.

Loose-living, heavy drinkers, tough, the King's musketeers, or rather Monsieur de Tréville's, were to be seen all over the city—in the taverns, in the public walks, at the public sports—shouting, twisting their mustaches, rattling their swords, and taking great pleasure in jostling Monsieur le Cardinal's guardsmen whenever they met with them. Then they would draw their swords in the open street, uttering a thousand jests. Sometimes they were killed, but they were sure that if they died, they would be both mourned and avenged. Often they were the killers, but then they were sure that they would not vegetate in a prison, since Monsieur de Tréville was lauded to the skies by these men who adored him and who, ruffians though they were, trembled before him like schoolboys before their schoolmaster. Obedient to the least word that he said, they were ready to suffer death to wipe out his lightest reproach.

In no one of the memoirs of that period which has left us so many memoirs, even in those of his enemies—and he had many enemies among men of the pen as well as among men of the sword—is this worthy gentleman accused of deriving personal advantage from the co-operation of his henchmen. Endowed with a rare genius for intrigue that made him the peer of the ablest intriguers, he remained a man of integrity. He had become one of the most gallant frequenters of bedside levees of his day, one of the most cunning squires of dames, and one of the most subtle phrasers of pretty compliments. The Captain of the Royal Musketeers was therefore admired, feared, and loved, a condition that is the apogee of human good fortune.

From six o'clock in the morning on in summer and from eight o'clock on in winter the courtyard of Monsieur de Tréville's house in the Rue du Vieux-Colombier looked like an armed camp. Fifty or sixty musketeers, who seemed to relieve one another constantly in order always to present an imposing number, strolled about continuously, armed to the teeth and ready for anything. On one of those immense staircases within the space of which our modern civilization would build a whole house, ascended and descended the petitioners of Paris who were in quest of some favor or other. There were gentlemen from the provinces eager to be enrolled in the Royal Musketeers, and lackeys bedizened in all sorts of liveries who were bringing and taking back messages between their masters and Monsieur de Tréville. In the antechamber the elect—those who had been summoned—were sitting on long circular benches. A constant buzzing was to be heard in that room from morning to night while in his office adjoining the antechamber Monsieur de Tréville received visits, listened to complaints, and gave his orders.

The day D'Artagnan presented himself there, the assemblage was certainly impressive, particularly for a provincial just arriving from his province. True, this provincial was a Gascon, and, especially at that period, D'Artagnan's compatriots enjoyed the reputation of being very difficult to intimidate. After he had stepped through the massive door, D'Artagnan found himself in the midst of a troop of swordsmen who were crossing one another as they passed to and fro, calling out, quarreling, and playing tricks on one another.

Our young man advanced through this tumult and confusion with a heart beating fast, holding his long rapier against his lanky leg and keeping one hand on the brim of his felt beret with that half-smile of the embarrassed provincial who is trying to look confident. Having got by one group, he breathed more easily, but he realized that people were turning round to stare at him, and for the first time in his life D'Artagnan, who up to now had entertained a pretty good opinion of himself, felt that he was ridiculous.

When he reached the staircase matters were still worse. On the lower steps four musketeers were amusing themselves by fencing, while ten or a dozen of their comrades were standing on the landing waiting to take their turn at the sport. One of the four stood on a step a little above the others, sword in hand, preventing, or at least trying to prevent, the others from coming up. These three others were fencing with agile swords. At first D'Artagnan took these weapons for foils, and thought they had the buttons on, but he soon realized by the scratches they inflicted that every weapon was as pointed and as sharp as any swordsman could wish. At every one of those scratches not only the spectators but even the actors themselves laughed like so many madmen.

The musketeer who was standing on the upper step was keeping his adversaries in check admirably. The rules of this game prescribed that when one of the players was hit he must give up his place, and the man who hit him was allowed another round. In five minutes, the defender of the upper stair touched the three men lower down lightly, one on the hand, one on the chin, and one on the ear. He himself remained untouched, and his dexterity won him three extra rounds, according to the rules.

However difficult it might be—or rather however difficult he pretended it was—to astonish the young Gascon, this pastime really did astonish him. In his own province, that land where heads get hot so easily, he had seen more elaborate preliminaries of duels, and he thought the gasconade—the boastful bravado—of the four fencers surpassed any that he had witnessed, even in Gascony. But our young man had not yet reached his goal; he still had to get past the landing and the antechamber.

The musketeers on the landing were not fighting; they were telling stories about women. In the antechamber stories about the Court were being told. On the landing D'Artagnan blushed; in the antechamber he shuddered. His lively and adventurous imagination, which in Gascony had made him formidable to young chambermaids, and sometimes even to their young mistresses, had never, even in moments of delirium, pictured half the amorous wonders or a quarter of the feats of gallantry he heard then, enhanced by the loftiest names and by details that were but lightly veiled.

But if his moral sense was shocked on the landing, his feeling of respect for the Cardinal was scandalized in the antechamber. There, to his amazement, D'Artagnan heard the policy that made all Europe tremble criticized freely, as well as the private life of the Cardinal. Many high-placed and powerful nobles had brought down punishment on themselves for trying to find out about that private life. That great man, so revered by Monsieur d'Artagnan the elder, was an object of ridicule to Monsieur de Tréville's musketeers, who cracked jokes about his bandy legs and his crooked back. Some of them sang ditties about Madame d'Aiguillon, his mistress, and Madame de Combalet, his niece; others were making plans to harass the pages and the guardsmen of the Cardinal-Duc.

"Certes, these fellows will be either imprisoned or hanged," thought D'Artagnan, terrified, "and I no doubt with them, for now that I have been listening to them and have heard what they were saying, I shall of course be considered their accomplice. What would my good father say if he knew that I was in the society of such heathen?"

It is therefore needless to say that D'Artagnan did not dare join in the conversation. But he looked with both his eyes and listened with both his ears, straining all his five senses in order to miss nothing. Despite his confidence in his father's admonitions, he felt himself urged by his tastes and led by his instincts to praise rather than blame the unheard-of things that were being said there.

However, as D'Artagnan was a perfect stranger to the throng of Monsieur de Tréville's courtiers, and this was the first time he had been seen in that place, a lackey came to ask him what he wanted. D'Artagnan gave his name very modestly, emphasized his statement that he was a fellow countryman of Monsieur de Tréville, and asked the lackey to request a moment's audience for him with that gentleman. The lackey promised him, with a rather patronizing air, that he would transmit the request in due season.

D'Artagnan, having recovered a little from his first surprise, now had leisure to examine the persons and the costumes around him. The central figure of the most lively group was a very tall musketeer with a haughty bearing and a costume so fantastic that it attracted everyone's attention. He was not wearing the cloak belonging to the musketeer uniform, but instead a sky-blue doublet, somewhat faded and threadbare, and over this a magnificent baldric with gold embroidery that glittered like rippling water under sunlight. A long cloak of crimson velvet fell in graceful folds from his shoulders, disclosing the front of the magnificent baldric, from which hung a gigantic rapier.

This musketeer had just come off guard. He complained of having caught a cold, and now and then he coughed affectedly. His cold was the reason he had put on his cloak, he explained to those about him, and while he spoke with a lofty air, twisting his mustache disdainfully, everyone was admiring his embroidered baldric enthusiastically, D'Artagnan more than anyone else.

"After all," said the musketeer, "it's the fashion now. It's an extravagance, I admit, but it's the fashion. Besides, a man must use in some way the money that he inherits."

"Come, Porthos," cried one of his listeners, "don't try to make us believe that that baldric comes from your father's generosity! I'll wager it was given you by the veiled lady I met you with one Sunday near the ·Porte Saint-Honoré."

"No, 'pon honor and by the faith of a gentleman, I bought it myself, with my own money," answered the man who had been called Porthos.

"Yes," commented another musketeer, "just as I bought this new purse with the money my mistress put in my old one."

"It's true, though," Porthos declared, "and the proof is that I paid twelve pistoles for it. Didn't I, Aramis?" he added, turning to another musketeer.

This musketeer offered a perfect contrast to his questioner, who had just called him Aramis. He was a young man not more than twenty-two or twenty-three years old, with a rather mild, ingenuous countenance, gentle black eyes, and cheeks as rosy and downy as an autumn peach. His delicate mustache marked a perfectly straight line over his upper lip. He seemed to be afraid to let his hands drop lest their veins swell, and from time to time he pinched his earlobes to preserve their delicate pink transparency. Habitually he spoke little and that slowly; he bowed frequently and laughed noiselessly, showing his beautiful teeth, which he seemed to take the greatest care of, as he did of the rest of his person. He answered his friend's appeal with an affirmative nod.

This affirmation seemed to settle all doubts as to the baldric. The others continued to admire it, but said no more about it, and the subject of the conversation was changed.

"What do you think of the tale Chalais's esquire tells?" asked another musketeer.

"And what does he say?" asked Porthos in a consequential tone.

"He says that at Brussels he met Rochefort, the *âme damnée* of the Cardinal, disguised as a Capuchin monk, and that this accursed Rochefort, thanks to his disguise, had tricked Monsieur de Laigues, simpleton that he is."

"A simpleton that man certainly is," said Porthos. "But is what the esquire says true?"

"Why, you know it is, Porthos," said Aramis. "I told you all about it yesterday. Let's drop the subject."

"Drop the subject!" retorted Porthos. "That's your opinion, is it? Drop the subject! Plague take it, you draw your conclusions quickly. What! The Cardinal sets a spy on a gentleman, has his letter stolen from him by a traitor, a brigand, a gallows bird? With the help of this spy and thanks to those letters he has Chalais's head cut off and while we are all gaping with wonder at the news you say, 'Drop the subject'!"

"Oh well, let's talk about it, since you wish to," replied Aramis patiently.

"That Rochefort!" cried Porthos. "If I were the esquire of poor Monsieur Chalais, Rochefort would have a bad time of it with me for a minute or two."

"And as for you, you would have a bad quarter of an hour of it with the Red Duke."

"Oho! The Red Duke! Bravo, bravo! The Red Duke is a wonderful name. I will spread that sobriquet about everywhere, my dear fellow, you may be sure of that. Isn't he a wit, our Aramis! What a pity that you didn't follow your vocation, my dear Aramis, what a delightful abbé you would have made!"

"Oh, that's only postponed temporarily," Aramis replied. "Someday I shall be an abbé. You know very well, Porthos, that I am continuing my theological studies."

"Aramis is only waiting for one thing to decide him finally to put on the cassock that is hanging under his uniform," said another musketeer.

"What's he waiting for?" asked another.

"For the Queen to produce an heir to the Crown of France."

"Don't jest on that subject, gentlemen," said Porthos. "Thank God the Queen is still of an age to produce one."

"They say the Duke of Buckingham is in France," Aramis continued with a sly smile that gave this simple statement a tolerably scandalous meaning.

"Aramis my friend, this time you are wrong," Porthos broke in. "Your wit is always leading you beyond the limits of decency. If Monsieur de Tréville heard you, you would be very sorry you said that."

"Do you think you are going to teach me better?" cried Aramis, a flash of lightning blazing in his usually gentle eyes.

"My dear Aramis, be either a musketeer or an abbé, but not both at once," Porthos answered. "Come, you know what Athos told you the other day—you eat from everybody's trencher. Don't be angry with me, I beg of you, it would be futile. You know perfectly well what we agreed on, you and Athos and I. You certainly visit Madame d'Aiguillon and you pay court to her, you visit Madame de Bois-Tracy and you pay court to her, you visit Madame de Chevreuse and you are reputed to be well to the front in that lady's good graces . . ."

A lackey threw open the office door and interrupted the conversation. "Monsieur de Tréville is ready to see Monsieur d'Artagnan," he announced.

Since the office door remained open, at that announcement all talk ceased, and amid the general silence the young Gascon crossed the antechamber and entered the office of the Captain of the Royal Musketeers, congratulating himself with all his heart on having escaped this extraordinary quarrel in the nick of time.

CHAPTER 3

MONSIEUR DE TRÉVILLE WAS IN A VERY BAD HUMOR AT the moment; nevertheless he greeted the young man courteously. D'Artagnan bowed to the ground and De Tréville smiled at the Béarn accent with which he paid his respects. It reminded the older man both of his youth and of his province, a twofold remembrance that makes any man smile, whether he is old or young. But he stepped toward the antechamber, gesturing to D'Artagnan as if to ask permission to finish with others before he began with him. He called out three names, his voice growing louder for each name, so that it ran through all the tones from that of command to that of anger.

"Athos! Porthos! Aramis!"

The two musketeers who answered to the last two names, whose acquaintance we have already made, left their group at once and went to the office. Though they did not look quite at ease, their bearing, nonchalant and full of dignity and submissiveness at the same time, aroused D'Artagnan's admiration. He saw them as demigods, and their commander as an Olympian Jupiter armed with all his thunderbolts.

When the two musketeers had entered the office and the door had shut behind them, the buzzing murmur in the antechamber revived. In his office, Monsieur de Tréville paced up and down the room three or four times in silence, with a frowning brow, passing in front of Porthos and Aramis each time. They stood at attention as if on parade. Suddenly Monsieur de Tréville stopped in front of them, eying them angrily from top to toe.

"Do you know what the King said to me, and that no longer ago than last night?" he demanded. "Do you know, gentlemen?"

"No," one of the musketeers replied after a moment of silence, "no, monsieur, we do not know." And the other echoed him.

"But I hope that you will do us the honor to tell us, monsieur," Aramis said in his most courteous tone and with his most gracious bow.

"He told me that henceforth he would recruit his musketeers from among the guardsmen of Monsieur le Cardinal!"

"The guardsmen of Monsieur le Cardinal! And why, monsieur?"
Porthos asked indignantly.

"Because His Majesty realizes that his watery wine needs to be in-
vigorated by mixing some good wine in it. Yes, yes," Monsieur de Tréville
went on, growing more excited as he spoke, "His Majesty was quite right,
for upon my honor it is true that the musketeers cut a sorry figure at
Court. When Monsieur le Cardinal was playing chess with the King last
evening he told him, with an air of commiseration that irritated me very
much, that day before yesterday those damned musketeers, those daredevils—and he emphasized those words with an ironical tone that irritated me still more—that those bullies, he added, looking at me with
those tiger cat's eyes of his, had rioted last night in a tavern in the Rue
Férou and that a patrol of his guards—I thought he was going to laugh
in my face—had been forced to arrest those disturbers of the peace.

" 'Sdeath! You must know something about it! Arrest musketeers!
You were among them, you three. Don't deny it, you were recognized,
and the Cardinal named you. But it's all my own fault, yes, it's all my
fault, because it is I myself who choose my men. You now, Aramis, why
the devil did you ask me for a musketeer's uniform when a cassock would
have fitted you much better? And you, Porthos, do you wear such a fine
baldric embroidered in gold just to hang a sword of straw from it? And
Athos! I don't see Athos. Where is he?"

"Monsieur," replied Aramis in a sorrowful tone, "he is ill, very ill."

"Ill, very ill, say you? With what disease?"

"We're afraid it's chickenpox," Porthos answered, "and if it is, it
would be a great pity, for it would spoil his good looks."

"Chickenpox! That's a pretty story to tell me, Porthos! Sick with the
chickenpox at his age! No, no—but doubtless wounded, perhaps killed.
Ah, if I only knew! 'Sblood, gentlemen of the musketeers, I will not have
my men haunting places of evil repute this way, being caught quarreling
in the streets, indulging in sword play at every crossroads. Above all, I
will not have them the laughingstock of Monsieur le Cardinal's guardsmen, who are brave, peaceful, and skillful, and who don't get themselves
into a position to be arrested, and who moreover would never allow
themselves to be arrested, those fellows! I'm sure of that. They would
rather die on the spot than give back one step. To run away, to decamp,
to flee—that's a fine thing to be said of His Majesty's Musketeers!"

Porthos and Aramis were quivering with rage. They would have
strangled Monsieur de Tréville gladly if they had not felt that it was the
great love he had for them that made him speak thus. They stamped on
the carpet, they bit their lips till they drew blood, and they grasped the
hilts of their swords with all their strength. Everyone in the antechamber
had heard Athos, Porthos, and Aramis summoned, and had guessed
from the tone of Monsieur de Tréville's voice that he was boiling with

rage. At least ten heads full of curiosity were bending close to the tapestry curtain, and they were growing pale with wrath, for their ears, glued against it, did not miss a syllable of what was said in the office, and their mouths repeated the insults of the Captain of the Musketeers to every-one in the antechamber.

"Aha! So the King's Musketeers are arrested by the Cardinal's Guards, are they!" Monsieur de Tréville went on, as furious as his soldiers, but flinging out his words and plunging them one by one, so to speak, into the breasts of the men he was castigating. "Oho! Six of His Eminence's guardsmen arrest six of His Majesty's Musketeers! 'Sdeath! I know what I'll do! I will go straight to the Louvre, I will hand in my resignation as Captain of the Royal Musketeers and ask for a lieutenancy in the Car-dinal's Guards. And if he will not accept me, 'sdeath! I'll turn abbé!"

"Well, Captain," said Porthos, quite beside himself, "it is the truth that we were six against six, but they set on us treacherously, and before we had time to draw out swords, two of our party were dead and Athos, grievously wounded, was in little better case. You know Athos, Captain. Well, Athos tried to get to his feet twice, and twice he fell down again. But we did not surrender, we did *not!* They dragged us away by force. On the way to the jail we escaped. As for Athos, they thought he was dead and they left him in peace on the field of battle, thinking it wasn't worth the trouble to carry off a corpse. That's the whole story. Devil take it, Captain, no man ever won all his battles!"

"And I have the honor to assure you, monsieur, that I killed one of them with his own sword," said Aramis. "Mine was broken at the first parry. Killed him or stabbed him, monsieur, whichever way of putting it you prefer."

"I did not know all this," said Monsieur de Tréville in a somewhat softened tone. "Monsieur le Cardinal exaggerated a little, apparently."

"But pray, monsieur," Aramis continued—now that his commanding officer was more calm, he hazarded a plea—"do not say that Athos was wounded. He would be desperately unhappy if the King should learn it. And as the wound is a very serious one, since after the blade went through his shoulder it entered his chest, it is to be feared that——"

At that instant the tapestry hanging in front of the door was raised and a noble and fine head appeared.

"Athos!" cried both the other musketeers.

"Athos!" echoed Monsieur de Tréville himself.

"You sent for me, monsieur," said Athos in a feeble but perfectly calm voice. "You asked for me, so my comrades have told me, and I am hastening to obey your orders. Here I am, monsieur. What is it you want of me?"

As he said this the musketeer, in impeccable uniform, belted according to regulations, entered Monsieur de Tréville's office with a firm step.

Monsieur de Tréville, deeply moved by this proof of Athos's courage, sprang toward him.

"I was just telling these gentlemen," he said, "that I forbid my musketeers to risk their lives needlessly. Brave men are very dear to the King, and the King knows that his musketeers are the bravest men on this earth. Your hand, Athos!"

And without waiting for the newcomer to reply to this proof of his affection, Monsieur de Tréville seized Athos's right hand and pressed it with all his might, without noticing that Athos, great as his self-control might be, could not restrain a spasm of pain and was growing even paler than before.

The door still stood open and Athos's arrival had created a sensation. Despite the care taken to keep his wound a secret, everyone there knew of it. An uproar of satisfaction greeted the Captain's last words. But suddenly he felt Athos's hand stiffen, and looking at the wounded man, he saw that he was about to faint. At that moment Athos, who had gathered all his strength to fight against pain, was at last overcome by it and fell to the floor like a dead man.

"A surgeon!" cried Monsieur de Tréville. "Mine, the King's, the best there is! 'Sblood! A surgeon, or my brave Athos will die!"

At Monsieur de Tréville's cries the whole assemblage in the antechamber rushed into the office. It didn't occur to Monsieur de Tréville to shut the door against them, and they all crowded around the wounded man. All this eager attention might have proved useless if the physician so loudly called for had not chanced to be in the house. He elbowed his way through the throng and approached Athos, who was still unconscious. As all this noise and commotion inconvenienced the physician very much, the first thing he asked, and urgently, was that Athos be taken to an adjoining room. Monsieur de Tréville immediately opened a door and led the way for Porthos and Aramis, who carried their comrade in their arms. Behind this group walked the surgeon, and behind the surgeon the door was closed. Then Monsieur de Tréville's office, usually a place held so sacred, became an annex to the antechamber. Everybody was chattering, haranguing, vociferating, swearing, cursing, and consigning the Cardinal and his guardsmen to all the devils.

An instant later, Porthos and Aramis came back, leaving Monsieur de Tréville and the surgeon alone with the wounded man. At last Monsieur de Tréville himself returned. Athos had regained consciousness, the surgeon had declared that the musketeer's condition was such that his friends had no need to worry, his weakness being due entirely to loss of blood. Then Monsieur de Tréville waved his hand and everyone withdrew except D'Artagnan, who did not forget that he had an audience and with the tenacity of a Gascon had stayed where he was.

When all the others had gone out and the door was closed, Monsieur de Tréville turned and found himself alone with the young man. The exciting event that had just taken place had broken the thread of his thoughts. He asked his persistent visitor what he wanted. D'Artagnan gave his name again and Monsieur de Tréville, suddenly recalling all his remembrances of the past and the present, remembered what this was all about.

"Pardon me," he said, smiling, "pardon me, my dear fellow country-man, but I had forgotten all about you. What can you expect! A captain is nothing but a father charged with an even greater responsibility than the father of an ordinary family. Soldiers are only big children, but as I insist on the orders of the King, and especially the orders of Monsieur le Cardinal, being carried out——"

D'Artagnan could not hide a smile, and noting that smile, Monsieur de Tréville judged that it was no fool he was dealing with, and he changed the subject of their conversation at once.

"I was very fond of your father," said he. "What can I do for his son? Tell me quickly, for my time is not my own."

"Monsieur," said D'Artagnan, "when I left Tarbes to come here, it was my intention to request you, in remembrance of the friendship you have not forgotten, to grant me the uniform of a musketeer; but after all I have seen here during the last two hours, I understand what a tremendous favor that would be, and I fear I do not deserve it."

"It is certainly a great favor, young man," Monsieur de Tréville replied, "but it may not be so far above your hopes as you believe—or you seem to believe. At all events, one of His Majesty's rulings has anticipated such a case, and I regret to inform you that no one is admitted to the musketeers until he has been through the ordeal of several campaigns or has performed certain brilliant feats or served at least two years in some regiment less favored than ours."

D'Artagnan bowed without replying. He was still more eager to don the musketeer's uniform when he learned that it was so difficult to obtain one.

"However," Tréville continued, fixing so piercing a glance on his companion that he seemed to be trying to read his most secret thoughts, "for the sake of your father, my old comrade, I want to do something for you, young man, as I have intimated. Our youths from Béarn are usually far from rich, and I have no reason to think things have changed very much since I left the province. I dare say you haven't brought any too much money with you."

D'Artagnan drew himself up proudly with a look that said plainly that he asked charity of no man.

"Very well, young man, very well," Tréville went on, "I know what those lofty airs mean. I myself came to Paris with four crowns in my pocket, and I would have fought with anyone who told me I was not in a position to buy the Louvre."

D'Artagnan drew himself up more and more proudly; thanks to the sale of his yellow nag, he was beginning his career with 4 crowns more than Monsieur de Tréville had possessed when he began his.

"You must need to husband the means you have, I say, however large the sum may be. But you also need to perfect yourself in the exercises befitting a gentleman. I will write a letter today to the Director of the Royal Academy of Arms, and tomorrow he will admit you without asking you for any fee. Our best-born and wealthiest gentlemen sometimes solicit that favor in vain. You will learn horsemanship, swordsmanship of all kinds, and dancing. You will make desirable acquaintances there, and you can call on me occasionally to tell me how you are getting along, and whether I can be of further service to you."

D'Artagnan, stranger though he was to the manners of the Court, nevertheless felt that he was being treated rather coldly.

"Alas, monsieur," said he, "I perceive now how much I need the letter of introduction that my father gave me to present to you."

"Indeed I was surprised," Monsieur de Tréville replied, "that you undertook so long a journey without that necessary viaticum, the only passport that we poor Béarnese possess."

"I had one, monsieur, and thank God, a fine one!" cried D'Artagnan. "But it was perfidiously stolen from me."

Then he related everything that had happened at Meung. He described the unknown gentleman in the most minute detail, and with a warmth and evident truthfulness that delighted Monsieur de Tréville.

"This is all very extraordinary," commented Monsieur de Tréville after reflecting a minute or two. "You mentioned my name aloud, then?"

"Yes, monsieur, I did commit that imprudence. But why not? A name like yours must needs serve me as a shield on my journey. You shall judge whether I used it often for my protection!"

Flattery was much in vogue at that period, and Monsieur de Tréville loved incense as much as any king or any cardinal. He could not restrain a smile of evident satisfaction, but that smile soon disappeared, and he returned to the adventure at Meung.

"Tell me," he said, "did this gentleman have a slight scar on his temple?"

"Yes, a scar that perhaps was made by the grazing of a bullet."

"Wasn't he a fine-looking man? Very tall?"

"Yes."

"Pale complexion? Dark hair?"

"Yes, yes, that's the man. How comes it that you know that man so well, monsieur? Oh, if ever I find him again—and I will find him, I swear, even if it's in Hell——"

D'Artagnan Leaves Home

D'Artagnan Fighting with the Cardinal's Guards

"He was waiting for a woman?" Tréville continued.

"At least he left after he had talked with one for a few minutes."

"You do not know what they talked about?"

"He gave her a little box, told her that it contained her instructions, and warned her not to open it until she reached London."

"Was this woman English?"

"He called her Milady."

"It is *he*," murmured Tréville, "it must be he! I thought he was still in Brussels!"

"Oh, monsieur, if you know who that man is," cried D'Artagnan, "I beg you to tell me who he is and where he comes from. If you do, I will release you from all your promises, even that of helping me to join the musketeers someday, for the thing I want above everything else is to avenge myself."

"Beware of attempting that, young man!" cried Tréville. "On the contrary, if ever you see him coming to meet you on one side of the street, cross over to the other side! Do not throw yourself against a rock like that; he would smash you as he would a drinking glass."

"That will not prevent me, if ever I meet him again, from——"

"In the meantime," interrupted Tréville, "take my advice—do not seek him out."

All at once Tréville stopped speaking, as if struck by a sudden suspicion. This great hatred that the young traveler proclaimed loudly for this man who had stolen his father's letter—a rather improbable story— was there some treachery hidden behind that hatred? Might not this young man be sent by His Eminence to lay a trap for Tréville? Might not this pretended D'Artagnan be an emissary whom the Cardinal was seeking to introduce into his house and to place near him in order to win his confidence and then bring about his ruin? The Cardinal had played that trick a thousand times. He looked at D'Artagnan still more intently than before. He was fairly well reassured, however, by the expression on that face sparkling with shrewd intelligence and pretended humility.

"I know he's a Gascon," he reflected, "but he may be as much of a Gascon for Monsieur le Cardinal as he is for me. Well, let's test him. My boy," he said aloud, slowly, "as the son of my old friend—for I believe your story of the lost letter is quite true—I wish to make up for the coldness you may have remarked in my welcome by revealing to you the secrets of our policy. The King and the Cardinal are the best of friends. Their apparent bickerings are only stratagems to deceive fools. I am not willing that a fellow countryman, a fine cavalier, a brave youth well qualified to make his way, should be the dupe of such artifices and fall into the trap like a simpleton, after the fashion of so many others who have done so to their ruin. Rest assured that I am devoted to both these all-powerful masters, and my earnest endeavors have no other aim than the service both of the King and of the Cardinal, who is one of the most illustrious geniuses France has ever produced.

"Now, young man, order your conduct accordingly. And if from your family, your relatives, or even your instincts, you have acquired such enmity as we are constantly discovering among gentlemen, say farewell to me and let us part. I will aid you in many ways, but without attaching you to my person. I hope that in any case my frankness will at least make you my friend, for you are the only young man I have ever spoken to like this."

D'Artagnan answered with the greatest candor: "Monsieur, I came to Paris with exactly such intentions. My father advised me to suffer nothing save from the King, Monsieur le Cardinal, and you, whom he considered the three first personages in France." D'Artagnan added Monsieur de Tréville to the other two, it is to be noted, but he thought the addition would do no harm. "I have therefore the greatest reverence for Monsieur le Cardinal," he continued, "and the greatest respect for his actions. So much the better for me, monsieur, if, as you say, you are speaking to me frankly, because in doing so you do me the honor to esteem me for sharing your opinion. But if you have any mistrust of me, as naturally you may have, I feel that I am ruining myself in speaking the truth. But still I trust that you will not esteem me any the less, and your esteem is the one thing I desire more than anything else in the world."

Monsieur de Tréville was overwhelmed with surprise. So much penetration, so much frankness, won his admiration; but it did not entirely dispel his suspicions. The more this young man showed himself superior to others, the more he was to be feared if Tréville was mistaken about him. Nevertheless he pressed D'Artagnan's hand and said:

"You are an honest lad. But at present I can do no more for you than what I just offered. My house will always be open to you. Take advantage of every opportunity, and in time you will probably obtain what you desire."

"You mean, monsieur," D'Artagnan replied, "that you will wait until I have proved myself worthy of it, don't you? Well," he added, with all the familiarity of one Gascon speaking to another, "you will not have to wait long!" And in taking his leave he bowed as if he considered the future lay in his own hands.

"Wait a minute," said Monsieur de Tréville, stopping him. "I promised you a letter to the Director of the Royal Academy of Arms. Are you too proud to accept it, young gentleman?"

"No, monsieur," said D'Artagnan, "and I assure you that this letter will not fare as my father's did. I will guard it so carefully that I swear it will arrive at its destination, and woe be to the man who tries to take it from me!"

Monsieur de Tréville smiled at this boast, and leaving his young fellow countryman standing at the window, where they had been talking together, he sat down at his desk to write the promised letter of introduction. While he was doing this D'Artagnan, having nothing better to do, began to drum a march on the windowpanes.

When he had written the letter, Monsieur de Tréville sealed it, rose, and walked toward the young man in order to give it to him. But at the very moment when D'Artagnan held out his hand to take it, to Monsieur de Tréville's amazement his protégé, fiery red with anger, made a sudden spring and rushed out of the room, crying:

"Ah, 'sblood, he shall not escape me this time!"

"Who? Who is it?" called Monsieur de Tréville.

"That man, my thief!" shouted D'Artagnan. "Ah, the traitor!"

"Devil take that madman!" murmured Monsieur de Tréville. "Unless," he added, "having failed in his purpose, this is only a clever way of making his escape!"

CHAPTER 4

D'ARTAGNAN, IN A TOWERING RAGE, CROSSED THE ANTE-
chamber in three leaps, and was darting toward the stairway expecting to
go down it four steps at a time, when in his heedless rush he ran headlong
into a musketeer who was coming out of one of Monsieur de Tréville's
private rooms. As D'Artagnan's lowered head hit the musketeer's shoulder, the latter uttered a cry, or rather a howl.

"Excuse me," said D'Artagnan, trying to be off on his way. "Excuse
me, but I am in a hurry."

Scarcely had he cleared the first step when a hand of iron seized him
by the belt.

"You're in a hurry, are you?" cried the musketeer, as white as a sheet.
"You think that's reason enough for running into me? You say 'Excuse
me,' and you think that's enough? Not at all, my boy. Do you think that
because you heard Monsieur de Tréville speak somewhat cavalierly to us
today other people can treat us the way he speaks to us? Correct your
mistake, comrade. You are not Monsieur de Tréville."

"By my faith," replied D'Artagnan, recognizing Athos, who, having
had his wounds dressed by the doctor, was going back to his lodgings, "by
my faith, I did not do it on purpose, and since I didn't do it on purpose, I
said 'Excuse me.' I should think that is apology enough. However, I tell
you once more—and perhaps once more is too much—that I am in a
hurry, a very great hurry. Let me go, then, I beg of you, let me go about
my business."

"Monsieur," said Athos, taking his hand away, "you are not very
courteous. It's easy to see that you come from somewhere far away."

D'Artagnan had already cleared three or four steps more, but Athos's
remark stopped him short.

" 'Sdeath, monsieur," he said, "I may have come far, but you are not
the man who can give me a lesson in good manners, I warn you."

"Perhaps," said Athos.

"Oh, if I were not in such a hurry, if I were not chasing somebody——"

"Monsieur the Man in a Hurry, you can find *me* without running after me. Do you get what I mean?"

"And where, if you please?"

"Near the Carmes-Déchaux, the Carmelite monastery."

"At what time?"

"About noon."

"About noon. Very well, I'll be there."

"Try not to keep me waiting, because at quarter-past twelve I am going to cut your ears off as you run away."

"Good!" cried D'Artagnan. "I'll be there at ten minutes to twelve."

And he set off running again as if the Devil was bearing him along, still hoping to overtake the man he had seen passing by with a slow step that could not have taken him very far as yet.

But at the street gate Porthos was chatting with the soldier on guard. D'Artagnan thought there was room enough between them for him, and he darted forward like an arrow. But he had reckoned without the wind. As he was about to pass, a gust of wind blew out Porthos's long cloak, and D'Artagnan ran straight into the middle of it. Doubtless Porthos had his own reasons for refusing to abandon that essential part of his costume, for instead of letting go of the fold of it he held in his hand, he pulled it toward him, so that D'Artagnan was rolled up inside the velvet.

Hearing the musketeer swear, D'Artagnan tried to get out from under the cloak, which was blinding him, and sought to find a way out among its folds. He was particularly anxious not to mar the freshness of that magnificent baldric we know about, but as he opened his eyes timidly, he found his nose glued between Porthos's shoulders—that is to say, directly on the baldric.

Alas! Like most of the things in this world that have nothing in their favor but their appearance, the baldric was glittering with gold in front but at the back was common buff. Vainglorious as he was, if Porthos could not afford a baldric covered all over with gold, he would have at least half of one. The necessity for his cold and the pressing need for the cloak were easy to understand now.

"Ye gods," cried Porthos, trying hard to get rid of D'Artagnan, who was wriggling about against his back, "you must have gone mad to bang into people like that!"

"Excuse me," said D'Artagnan, reappearing from under the giant's shoulder, "but I am in a great hurry. I'm running after someone and——"

"Do you always forget you have eyes when you're running, by any chance?" Porthos demanded.

"No," replied D'Artagnan, somewhat nettled. "No, and thanks to my good eyes, I can even see things that other people don't see."

Whether Porthos understood this or not, he gave way to his anger.

"Monsieur," he said, "you'll get your hide tanned, I warn you, if you push musketeers about that way."

"My hide tanned!" repeated D'Artagnan. "That's rather strong language."

"It's language that befits a man accustomed to looking his enemies in the face."

"Aha! By the Lord, I know full well that you don't turn your back to yours, you don't!" And the young man, delighted at his jest, started off, laughing heartily. Porthos, foaming with rage, was about to fall upon him.

"Later, later!" cried D'Artagnan. "When you're not wearing your cloak."

"At one o'clock, then, behind the Luxembourg."

"Very well, at one o'clock."

D'Artagnan turned the corner of the street. But neither in the first street, nor in the one he now scanned eagerly, could he see the man he was looking for. Slowly as the stranger was walking, he must have outdistanced D'Artagnan. Perhaps he had entered some house. D'Artagnan inquired about him of everyone he met with, he went down to the ferry, he came up again by the Rue de Seine and the Rue de la Croix-Rouge, but he found absolutely no trace of him.

He began to reflect on all the events that had occurred; they were numerous and of evil omen. It was barely eleven o'clock in the morning and already the morning had brought him into disgrace with Monsieur de Tréville, who could not fail to think that the way D'Artagnan had left him was a little cavalier. Besides that, he had picked up two fine duels with two men, each of whom was capable of killing three D'Artagnans, with two musketeers—in short, with two of those beings whom he admired so much that in his heart and in his mind he set them above all other men. The outlook was a sorry one. Sure that he would be killed by Athos, the young man, as one can easily understand, didn't worry much about Porthos. Nevertheless, as hope is the last thing to be extinguished in the heart of man, D'Artagnan ended by hoping that he would survive both these duels.

As he arrived within a few steps of the Hôtel d'Aiguillon D'Artagnan saw Aramis standing in front of it chatting gaily with three gentlemen of the Royal Guards. Aramis, for his part, noticed D'Artagnan, but as he had not forgotten that it was in this young man's presence that Monsieur de Tréville had been in such a rage at him and his comrades that morning, and a witness of the rebukes they had received was not a very pleasing sight for him, he pretended not to see him. D'Artagnan, on the other hand, full of his plans for conciliation and courtesy, approached the four young men and saluted them with a low bow accompanied by a most gracious smile. Aramis bowed slightly but did not smile. Moreover, all four of them immediately stopped talking.

D'Artagnan was not so stupid as not to perceive that he was unwelcome, but he was not yet familiar enough with the ways of the fashionable world to know how to extricate himself gallantly from a false position. He was trying to think of the least awkward way to retreat when he noticed that Aramis had dropped his handkerchief and, doubtless by mistake, had set his foot on it. This seemed to D'Artagnan a good chance to make up for his breach of good manners. With the most courteous air he could call to his help, he stooped and pulled the handkerchief out from under the musketeer's foot, in spite of the efforts Aramis made to keep it there, and gave it to him, saying:

"I believe, monsieur, that this is a handkerchief you would be sorry to lose."

The handkerchief was indeed richly embroidered, and one of the corners bore a coronet and a crest. Aramis blushed hotly and took, or rather snatched, the handkerchief from the Gascon's hands.

"Aha!" cried one of the guardsmen. "Will you persist in saying, O discreet Aramis, that you are not on good terms with Madame de Bois-Tracy when that gracious lady is kind enough to lend you her handkerchief?"

Aramis shot at D'Artagnan one of those glances that tell a man he has acquired a mortal enemy, then, resuming his usual gentle air, he replied:

"You are mistaken, gentlemen. That handkerchief is not mine, and I can't imagine why this gentleman took it into his head to give it to me rather than to one of you. As a proof of what I say, here's mine in my pocket."

As he spoke he pulled out his own handkerchief, which was also a very elegant one of fine linen, but a handkerchief without embroidery, without a crest, and ornamented only with a single initial, that of its owner.

This time D'Artagnan was not so hasty. He perceived his mistake. But Aramis's friends refused to be convinced by his denial and one of them, speaking to the young musketeer with affected seriousness, remarked:

"If things were as you pretend, I would be forced, my dear Aramis, to ask you to give the handkerchief to me, for, as you know, Bois-Tracy is an intimate friend of mine, and I cannot allow his wife's property to be sported as a trophy."

"You put your request badly," retorted Aramis, "and while I recognize the justice of your claim, I refuse it because of its form."

"The fact is," hazarded D'Artagnan timidly, "I did not see the handkerchief fall from Monsieur Aramis's pocket. He had his foot on it, that's all, and since he had his foot on it, I thought it was his."

"And you were mistaken, my dear monsieur," Aramis replied coldly, disregarding this attempt at reparation. Then, turning to the guardsman who had declared himself to be the friend of Monsieur de Bois-Tracy, he went on: "Moreover I think, my dear intimate friend of Bois-Tracy, that I am a friend of his whom he loves no less dearly than he can possibly love you. In any event, strictly speaking, that handkerchief is as likely to have fallen out of your pocket as out of mine."

"No, it didn't, upon my honor!" cried the guardsman.

"You are going to swear upon your honor, and I upon my word, and then it will be pretty evident that one of us is lying. Come, let's do better than that, Montaran, let's each take half of it.

"Absolutely just," cried one of the other guardsmen, "the judgment of King Solomon. Really, Aramis, you are full of wisdom."

They all burst out laughing, and as may be supposed, the affair had no other consequence. In a moment or two the conversation ended and the three guardsmen and the musketeer, after shaking hands cordially, separated and started off in different directions.

D'Artagnan had stood aside a little during the latter part of this conversation. Now he thought to himself:

"Here's my chance to make my peace with this gallant man." And with this good idea he approached Aramis, who was going off without paying any attention to him.

"Monsieur," he said, "you will excuse me, I trust."

"Ah, monsieur," Aramis replied, "allow me to observe that you have not behaved in this case as a gentleman should."

"What, monsieur!" cried D'Artagnan. "Do you suppose that——"

"I suppose, monsieur, that you are not a fool," interrupted Aramis, "and that you know very well, even though you have just come from Gascony, that people don't step on handkerchiefs without a reason."

"Monsieur, you are wrong in trying to humiliate me," said D'Artagnan, whose aggressive spirit was beginning to speak more loudly than his pacific resolutions. "I come from Gascony, it is true, and since you know that, I do not need to tell you that Gascons are not very patient. When they have begged to be excused once, even for a foolish act, they are convinced that they have done already at least more than half as much as they should have done."

"Monsieur," Aramis replied, "what I said to you was not in order to pick a quarrel with you. Thank God I am not a bravo, and since I am a musketeer only temporarily, I fight only when I am forced to, and always with great repugnance. But this time the affair is serious, because you have compromised a lady."

"Because *we* have compromised her!" cried D'Artagnan.

"Why were you so clumsy as to give the handkerchief back to me?"

"Why were you so clumsy as to drop it?"

"I have said, monsieur, and say again, that the handkerchief did not come from my pocket."

"Well, monsieur, you have lied about it twice now, for I myself saw it fall from there."

"Ha! So you are taking that tone, are you, Master Gascon? Very well, I'll teach you how to behave yourself."

"And I'll send you back to your Mass, Monsieur l'Abbé! Draw, if you please, and instantly."

"No, no, if you please, my fine friend—not here, at least. Don't you see that we are in front of the Hôtel d'Aiguillon, which is full of the Cardinal's henchmen? How do I know that it is not the Cardinal who has charged you to get my head for him? Now I am ridiculously fond of my head; it seems to me to fit so neatly on my shoulders. I intend to kill you, don't worry about that, but very quietly, in a snug secret retreat where you can't boast about your death to anybody."

"I'm quite willing, monsieur, but don't be too confident. And bring your handkerchief with you, whether it belongs to you or not. Perhaps you may need to use it."

"Monsieur is a Gascon?" inquired Aramis.

"Yes, and one who never postpones a rendezvous through prudence."

"Prudence, monsieur, is a virtue of very little use to musketeers, I know, but it is indispensable for ecclesiastics, and as I am a musketeer only temporarily, I have every intention of remaining prudent. At two o'clock I shall have the honor of waiting for you at the Hôtel de Tréville. There, I will acquaint you with the best place to meet."

The two young men bowed, then Aramis went off up the street leading to the Luxembourg while D'Artagnan, having noticed that the hour of his appointment was drawing near, took the road to the Carmes-Déchaux, saying to himself:

"Decidedly, I can't draw back now. But at least if I am killed, I shall be killed by a musketeer!"

CHAPTER 5

D'ARTAGNAN KNEW NO ONE IN PARIS. HE WENT TO HIS
rendezvous with Athos, therefore, without a second, resolved to be content with the seconds Athos would have chosen. Besides, he had determined to offer all the proper apologies to the brave musketeer—though
without any sign of weakness—for he feared the usual result of an affair
of this sort when a young, vigorous man fights with an adversary who is
wounded and therefore weak. If he is conquered, he doubles the triumph
of his opponent; if he is the victor, he is accused of taking unfair advantage of a wounded man, and of having courage that is easy under
such circumstances.

Now our readers must already have noted that D'Artagnan was not an
ordinary man. Therefore while he kept telling himself that his death was
inevitable, he did not resign himself to dying as tamely as a man less
courageous and less self-controlled than he might have done in his place.
He reflected on the different characteristics of the men he was to fight,
and his situation began to be more clear to him. By offering sincere
apologies, he hoped to make a friend of Athos, whose lordly ways and
austere bearing he admired so much. He flattered himself that he could
frighten Porthos with the adventure of the baldric, which, if he were not
killed on the spot, he could tell everybody, a story that, cleverly managed,
would cover Porthos with ridicule. As to the crafty Aramis, D'Artagnan
had little fear of him, and if he should survive to get to Aramis, he would
dispatch him in fine style.

Moreover, D'Artagnan possessed that invincible stock of determination that the counsels of his father had implanted in his heart, counsels
the substance of which was: "Suffer nothing from anyone save the King,
the Cardinal, and Monsieur de Tréville." So he flew rather than walked
toward the monastery of the Carmes-Déchaux. It was a building without
windows and surrounded by barren fields that usually served as a dueling
ground for men who had no time to lose.

When D'Artagnan arrived in sight of the stretch of bare ground lying
along the foot of the monastery wall, Athos had been waiting only five
minutes, and twelve o'clock was striking. D'Artagnan was, then, punctual,

and the most rigorous casuist as to duels could have nothing to say.
Athos, who was still suffering grievously from his wound, though it had
been freshly dressed by Monsieur de Tréville's surgeon, was sitting on a
stone and awaiting his adversary with that placid countenance and noble
look which never deserted him. At sight of D'Artagnan he rose and came
courteously a few steps to meet him. D'Artagnan, for his part, approached his adversary hat in hand, its plume sweeping the ground.

"Monsieur," said Athos, "I have engaged two of my friends as seconds,
but they have not yet arrived."

"I have no seconds, monsieur," replied D'Artagnan, "for as I arrived
in Paris only yesterday, as yet I know no one except Monsieur de Tréville,
to whom I was recommended by my father, who has the honor to be a
rather close friend of his."

Athos reflected a moment, then said: "Monsieur de Tréville is the
only person you know?"

"Yes, monsieur, the only one."

"Well, now," Athos went on, half to himself and half to D'Artagnan,
"well now, if I kill you I shall look like a child-killer!"

"Not too much so, monsieur," answered D'Artagnan, with a bow that
did not lack dignity, "since you do me the honor to draw your sword
against me when your wound must be troubling you very much."

"Very much, upon my word, and you hurt me devilishly when you
ran into me, I can tell you. But I will use my left hand—I usually do in
such circumstances. Don't imagine that I'm doing you a favor. I use both
hands equally well. Indeed you will be at a disadvantage—a left-handed
man can be very troublesome to people who are not used to one."

"Truly, monsieur," said D'Artagnan, bowing again, "your courtesy is
so great that I am more than grateful to you."

"You embarrass me," replied Athos, with his usual gentlemanly air.
"Pray let us talk of something else. . . . Ah, 'sblood, how you did hurt
me! My shoulder is on fire."

"If you would allow me——" said D'Artagnan, somewhat timidly.

"Allow what, monsieur?"

"I have a miraculous balsam for wounds—a balsam my mother gave
me. I have tried it on myself. I am sure that in less than three days this
balsam would cure you. And after three days, when you are cured, it
would still be a great honor for me to be your man."

D'Artagnan said this with a simplicity that did honor to his courtesy
without arousing the least doubt as to his courage.

"By the Lord, monsieur," said Athos, "there's a proposal that pleases
me! Not that I accept it, but only a gentleman born could have made it.
That is the way the gallant knights of Charlemagne's day spoke and
acted, and every knight ought to look to them for his model. Unfortunately we live in the times of Monsieur le Cardinal, and however well

guarded the secret might be, three days from now everyone would know we were going to fight, and our duel would be prevented. . . . Aren't those dawdlers ever coming?"

"If you are in a hurry, monsieur," said D'Artagnan, with the same simplicity with which a moment before he had proposed to postpone the duel for three days, "and if you would like to dispatch me at once, don't stand upon ceremony, I beg of you."

"Again you please me," said Athos, with a gracious nod to D'Artagnan. "That statement did not come from a brainless man, and certainly not from a heartless man. Monsieur, I like men of your kidney, and I see plainly that if we don't kill each other, later I shall take much pleasure in conversing with you. We will wait for my friends, if you please. I have plenty of time, and it will be more correct to wait. . . . Ah, here is one of them, I think."

In fact, at the end of the Rue de Vaugirard the gigantic form of Porthos appeared.

"What!" cried D'Artagnan. "Is Monsieur Porthos one of your seconds?"

"Yes. Does that annoy you?"

"No, not in the least."

"And here comes the other one."

D'Artagnan turned toward the direction in which Athos was looking and saw Aramis.

"What!" he cried, in a tone of even greater astonishment than before, "Is your other second Monsieur Aramis?"

"Of course. Don't you know that one of us is never seen without the others, and that by musketeers and guardsmen at the Court and in the city, we are called Athos, Porthos, and Aramis, or the three inseparables?"

"By my faith, you are well named!" said D'Artagnan.

In the meantime Porthos had come up. He waved his hand to Athos and then, turning to D'Artagnan, stood stock-still in surprise. Incidentally, he had changed his baldric and left off his cloak.

"Aha!" he said. "What does this mean?"

"This is the gentleman I am to fight with," replied Athos, pointing to D'Artagnan and saluting him with the gesture.

"Why, I am going to fight with him too!" said Porthos.

"But not until one o'clock," said D'Artagnan.

"And I too am going to fight with this gentleman," announced Aramis as he too arrived.

"But not until two o'clock," said D'Artagnan, as calmly as before.

"What are you fighting him about?" asked Aramis.

"By my faith, I really don't know. He hurt my shoulder, of course. How about you, Porthos?"

"By my faith, I'm fighting because I'm fighting," answered Porthos, growing red.

Athos, whose keen eye missed nothing, saw a shy smile on the Gascon's lips as he said:

"We had an argument about dress."

"And you, Aramis?"

"Oh, ours is a theological quarrel," replied Aramis, making a sign to D'Artagnan to keep the reason for their duel a secret.

Athos saw a second smile on D'Artagnan's lips.

"And now that we are all here, gentlemen," said D'Artagnan, "allow me to offer you my apologies."

At the word "apologies" a cloud shadowed Athos's brow, a haughty smile curled Porthos's lips, and a sign of refusal was Aramis's response.

"You do not understand me, gentlemen," protested D'Artagnan, tossing his head. At that moment a ray of sunlight played about that head and gave a golden hue to its fine, bold lines. "I am apologizing in case I cannot pay my debt to all three of you, Monsieur Athos has the first right to kill me, and that fact deprives your claim of much value, Monsieur Porthos, and makes yours almost worthless, Monsieur Aramis. And now, gentlemen, I ask you once more to excuse me, but on that account only. Now, on guard!"

Whereupon, with the most knightly gesture, D'Artagnan drew his sword. The blood had rushed to his head, and at that moment he would have drawn his sword against all the musketeers in France as willingly as he had just drawn it against Athos, and hoped to draw it against Porthos and Aramis. It was quarter-past twelve. The sun was at the zenith and its fiery heat beat down on the scene of the duel.

"It's very hot," said Athos, drawing his sword in his turn, "and yet I cannot take off my doublet, for just now I felt my wound beginning to bleed again, and I should not like to annoy Monsieur by the sight of blood he had not drawn from me himself."

"That is true, monsieur," replied D'Artagnan. "But whether drawn by myself or by another, I assure you I shall always view with regret the blood of so gallant a gentleman. I will therefore fight in my doublet, as you do."

"When you please, monsieur," said Athos, putting himself on guard.

"I was awaiting your word," said D'Artagnan, crossing swords.

But hardly had the two rapiers clashed when a squad of His Eminence's Guards, with Monsieur de Jussac in command, came round the corner of the monastery.

"The Cardinal's Guards!" cried Porthos. "Sheathe your swords, gentlemen, sheathe your swords!" And Aramis echoed him.

But it was too late. The two duelists had been seen in a position that left no doubt of their intentions.

"Oho!" cried Jussac, advancing toward them and making a sign to his men to do likewise. "Oho, musketeers, so you're fighting here, are you? And the edicts about dueling, what has become of them?"

"You are very generous, gentlemen of the guards," said Athos, full of acrimony, for Jussac was one of the aggressors of two days before. "If we saw you fighting, I assure you we would take good care not to interfere. Leave us alone, then, and you will enjoy a little amusement without any cost to yourselves."

"Gentlemen," said Jussac, "it is with great regret that I declare to you that that is impossible. We must do our duty. Sheathe your swords, then, if you please, and follow us."

"Monsieur," retorted Athos, parodying Jussac, "it would afford us great pleasure to accept your gracious invitation if it depended upon ourselves. But unfortunately that is impossible—Monsieur de Tréville has forbidden it."

This raillery exasperated Jussac, and he said: "We shall charge you, then, if you disobey."

"There are five of them," said Athos, speaking low, "and only three of us. We shall be beaten again, and we must die right here, for I swear I will not go before the Captain again a vanquished man."

Athos, Porthos, and Aramis drew together as Jussac marshaled his soldiers. This brief interval was enough for D'Artagnan to determine the part he would play. This was one of those events which decide a man's whole life. He must choose between the King and the Cardinal, and once his choice was made, he must abide by it. To fight was to disobey the law, to risk his head, to make by a single act an enemy of a Minister more powerful than the King himself. The young man perceived all this and, be it said to his credit, he did not hesitate a second. He turned toward Athos and his friends.

"Gentlemen," he said, "pray allow me to correct you. You said you were but three, but it seems to me that there are four of us."

"But you are not one of us," said Porthos.

"It is true," replied D'Artagnan, "that I am not wearing a musketeer's uniform, but I have the same spirit. My heart is a musketeer's, I am sure of that, gentlemen, and that makes me almost one of you."

"Withdraw, young man!" shouted Jussac. "You may withdraw, we will allow you to. Save your skin—get away at once."

D'Artagnan did not move.

"Upon my word, you're a fine lad," said Athos, pressing D'Artagnan's hand.

"Come, come, make up your minds," Jussac went on.

"See here," said Porthos, "we must do something about this." And Aramis agreed.

"Monsieur is most generous," said Athos. But all three of them were thinking that D'Artagnan was very young and they dreaded his lack of experience.

"We would still be only three, one of whom is wounded, plus a boy," Athos went on, "and yet everybody will say that we were four men."

D'Artagnan understood their hesitation. "Gentlemen," he said, "try me nevertheless. I swear to you on my honor that I will not leave this spot if we are vanquished."

"What is your name, my brave fellow?" asked Athos.

"D'Artagnan, monsieur."

"Well, then, Athos, Porthos, Aramis, and D'Artagnan, forward!" cried Athos.

"Come, gentlemen, have you made up your minds to make up your minds?" cried Jussac.

"We have, gentlemen," Athos replied.

"And what are you going to do?" demanded Jussac.

"We are going to have the honor of charging you," replied Athos, lifting his hat with one hand and drawing his sword with the other.

"Oh, you're resisting, are you?" cried Jussac.

" 'Sblood! Does that surprise you?"

And the nine combatants rushed to do battle with a fury that did not lack a certain amount of method. Athos took on one Cahusac, a favorite of the Cardinal's, Porthos took on Bicarat, and Aramis found himself facing two adversaries.

As for D'Artagnan, he sprang at Jussac himself. The young Gascon's heart was beating as if it would burst, not from fear—thank God he hadn't a shadow of that—but from emulation. He fought like an infuriated tiger, circling his adversary again and again and changing his ground and his guard constantly. Jussac was a fine swordsman and had had much practice, yet it took every bit of his skill to defend himself against an agile and energetic adversary who broke all the rules every moment. He attacked on all sides at once, yet parried like a man with the greatest respect for his own epidermis.

At length the struggle exhausted Jussac's patience. Furious at being held in check by one he had looked at as no more than a boy, he grew angry and began to make mistakes. D'Artagnan might lack experience, but he was well grounded in theory, and he redoubled his agility. Jussac, determined to finish the young man, sprang forward and aimed a terrible thrust at his adversary, lunging as far as he could reach. D'Artagnan parried in prime, and while Jussac was drawing back, slipped his own blade like a snake under Jussac's and passed it through his body. Jussac fell like a dead tree.

Now D'Artagnan cast an uneasy glance swiftly over the field of battle. Aramis had already killed one of his men and was pressing the other one hard. Bicarat and Porthos had just hit each other at the same moment.

Porthos had received a thrust through the arm, and Bicarat one through the thigh; but neither of the wounds was serious and they were fighting all the more stubbornly because of them. Athos had been wounded afresh by Cahusac and was growing visibly paler and paler, but he was not giving way an inch. He had, however, changed the hand holding his sword and was fighting now with it in his left hand.

According to the laws of dueling at that period, D'Artagnan was at liberty to assist whichever man he pleased. While he was looking about to see which of his companions needed his help most, he caught a glance from Athos, a glance of sublime eloquence. Athos would have died rather than call for help, but he could look, and with the look ask for support. D'Artagnan divined what Athos meant, and sprang to Cahusac's side with one terrible leap, crying:

"Here I am, monsieur! On guard! I'm going to kill you!"

Cahusac turned—it was time, for Athos, whose great courage alone had been sustaining him, fell on one knee at that moment.

" 'Sblood," Athos cried to D'Artagnan, "don't kill him, young man! I have an old affair to settle with him when I am sound again. Just disarm him, make his sword useless. That's it! Good, very good!"

Athos uttered this last exclamation as he saw Cahusac's sword fly twenty paces from him. D'Artagnan and Cahusac sprang forward at the same time, the latter to recover it, the former to get possession of it. D'Artagnan, being the more nimble, reached it first and put one foot on it. Cahusac ran to the body of the guardsman who had been killed, seized his rapier, and started back toward D'Artagnan. But on the way he met Athos, who during the brief respite D'Artagnan had afforded him had recovered his breath. Fearing that D'Artagnan might kill this enemy of his own, he was determined to resume the fight.

D'Artagnan understood that he would be disobliging Athos not to leave him alone, and a few minutes later Cahusac fell, a sword thrust through his throat. At the same instant Aramis placed the point of his sword on the breast of his fallen adversary and forced him to ask for mercy. Now only Porthos and Bicarat were left fighting. Porthos was swaggering and jesting without ceasing, but jest as he might, he was making no progress.

But they must stop fighting. The watch might come up at any moment and arrest all the combatants, whether they were wounded or not, whether they were royalists or cardinalists. Athos, Aramis, and D'Artagnan surrounded Bicarat and called upon him to surrender. Like D'Artagnan, Bicarat was a Gascon. Although he was now one against four and a sword had pierced his thigh, he was determined to hold out, but Jussac, pushing himself up on one elbow, called out to him to surrender.

"You are my brigadier," Bicarat replied, "it is my duty to obey you."

Then, springing back, he broke his sword across his knees, threw the pieces over the monastery wall, crossed his arms, and whistled a cardinalist air. Bravery always commands respect even in an enemy. The musketeers saluted Bicarat with their swords and returned them to their scabbards. D'Artagnan followed suit, then, assisted by Bicarat—the only guardsman left standing—he carried Jussac, Cahusac, and the guardsman Aramis had wounded to the porch of the monastery. The fourth guardsman was dead, as has been said. They rang the bell at the door and, leaving there three out of four of the guardsmen's swords, they went their way, fairly intoxicated with joy, toward Monsieur de Tréville's.

Arm in arm they went, taking up the whole width of the street and calling to every musketeer they met to follow them, so that in the end they were making a triumphal march. D'Artagnan was mad with delight; he marched between Athos and Porthos, clasping their arms fondly.

"If I'm not a musketeer yet," he told his new friends as they went through the gateway of the Hôtel de Tréville, "at least I've begun my apprenticeship, haven't I?"

CHAPTER 6

THE AFFAIR MADE A GREAT SENSATION. MONSIEUR DE Tréville scolded his musketeers in public and congratulated them in private. But as no time must be lost in informing the King and winning his approval, Monsieur de Tréville hastened to the Louvre. He was too late; the King was closeted with the Cardinal, and Monsieur de Tréville was told that the King was busy and could not receive him just then. In the evening Monsieur de Tréville went to the King's gaming table. The King was winning, and as His Majesty was very covetous, he was in an excellent humor. As soon as he saw Monsieur de Tréville he said:

"Come here, Monsieur le Capitaine, come here, so that I may reprimand you. Do you know that His Eminence has just been complaining to me about your musketeers and he's so stirred up about it that he's been almost sick all evening? Why, those musketeers of yours are devils incarnate, very gallows birds!"

"No, Sire," replied Tréville, who saw at first glance the turn things would be taking, "no, they are good creatures, as gentle as lambs, and they have but one desire, I'll be their guarantee for that, and that desire is never to draw their swords except in Your Majesty's service. But what are they to do? Monsieur le Cardinal's guardsmen are forever picking quarrels with them, and if only for the honor of the corps, the poor young fellows are obliged to defend themselves."

"Hearken to Monsieur de Tréville," said the King, "hearken to him! Wouldn't anyone say he was talking about members of a religious order? But don't think I am going to take you at your word. I am called Louis the Just, Monsieur de Tréville, and by and by—by and by we shall see."

"It is because I rely on your justice, Sire, that I will wait patiently and quietly the good pleasure of Your Majesty."

"Wait then, monsieur, wait," said the King. "I will not keep you waiting long."

Luck was turning, and as the King began to lose what he had won, he was not sorry to leave the table. So he rose after a moment and putting in his pocket the money still before him on the table—the major part of his winnings—he called:

"La Vieuville, take my place. I must speak with Monsieur de Tréville about important business. Oh, I had eighty louis on the table. Put the same amount there, so that those who have lost may have nothing to complain about. Justice above everything else!" Then, turning to Monsieur de Tréville and walking with him toward a window, he went on: "Well, monsieur, you say that His Illustrious Eminence's guardsmen picked a quarrel with your musketeers?"

"Yes, Sire, as they're always doing."

"How did it happen? Tell me, for as you well know, a judge must hear both sides."

"Oh, good Lord, it happened in the most simple and natural way possible! Three of my best soldiers, whom Your Majesty knows by name and whose devotion you have found of value more than once—Athos, Porthos, and Aramis—had made up a pleasure party with a young chap from Gascony whom I had introduced to them that morning. This party was to take place at Saint-Germain, I believe, and they had agreed to meet at the Carmes-Déschaux. There they were molested by De Jussac, Monsieur Cahusac, Monsieur Bicarat, and two other guardsmen, who certainly did not come there in such numbers without some evil intent against the edicts on dueling. I do not accuse them, Sire, but I leave it to Your Majesty to judge what five armed men could be going to do in such a deserted spot as the environs of the Carmes-Déchaux."

"Yes, you're right, Tréville, you're right."

"Then when they saw my musketeers they changed their minds, they forgot their private hatred in their hatred for the corps. For Your Majesty must know that the musketeers, who belong to the King, and only to the King, are the natural enemies of the guardsmen, who belong to the Cardinal."

"Yes, Tréville, yes," said the King in a melancholy tone. "And it is very sad, believe me, to see two parties in France, two heads to one kingdom. But that will come to an end, Tréville, it will come to an end. You say that the guardsmen picked a quarrel with the musketeers? But they were not alone, your musketeers, they had a boy with them, didn't they?"

"Yes, Sire, so that three of the King's musketeers, one of whom was wounded, and a youth not only held their ground against five of the most formidable of the Cardinal's guardsmen but also felled four of them."

"But that is a victory, that is!" cried the King, beaming. "A complete victory! Four men, you say, one of them wounded, and a boy?"

"A boy barely old enough to be called a young man. But he behaved so well on this occasion that I will take the liberty of recommending him to Your Majesty."

"What is his name?"

"D'Artagnan, Sire. He is the son of one of my oldest friends—the son of a man who served under your father of glorious memory in the Religious Wars."

"And you say he behaved well, this young man? Tell me about it, Tréville. You know how much I like tales of war and fighting."

"Sire," replied Tréville, "as I told you, Monsieur d'Artagnan is little more than a boy, and as he has not the honor of being a musketeer, he was in civilian dress. Monsieur le Cardinal's guardsmen, seeing how young he was and moreover that he did not belong to the musketeers, asked him to withdraw before they attacked. But he answered that he was a musketeer at heart, and that he was entirely devoted to Your Majesty, and therefore he would stay with the King's Musketeers."

"Brave young man!" murmured the King.

"Well, he did stay with them, and Your Majesty has so resolute a champion in him that it was he who gave that terrible sword thrust that has made the Monsieur le Cardinal so angry."

"He was the one who wounded Jussac!" cried the King. "He, a mere boy! That is not possible, Tréville. Jussac, one of the first swordsmen in France! I want to see this young man, Tréville, I must see him. And if anything can be done for him—well, we will attend to it."

"When will Your Majesty deign to receive him?"

"Tomorrow at noon, Tréville."

"Shall I bring him alone?"

"No, bring all four of them. I want to thank them all at the same time. Devoted men are rare, Tréville, and their devotion must be rewarded."

"At noon, Sire, we will be at the Louvre."

"Oh—by the back staircase, Tréville, the back staircase. It isn't worth while to let the Cardinal know——"

"As you say, Sire."

"You understand, Tréville—an edict is an edict, and after all, dueling is forbidden by law."

"But this encounter, Sire, was nothing like a duel, it was a brawl, and the proof of that is that five of the Cardinal's guardsmen attacked my three musketeers and Monsieur d'Artagnan."

"Exactly," said the King. "But all the same, Tréville, come by the back staircase."

Tréville smiled. But as he had already accomplished something in making this child revolt against his master, he said no more, but bowed to the King and took his leave. That evening the three musketeers were informed of the honor that had been granted them. As they had long been acquainted with the King, they were not much excited by it.

But when D'Artagnan was told of it, his Gascon imagination pictured his fortune as made by this honor, and he spent the night dreaming golden dreams. So at eight o'clock the next morning he was at Athos's rooms. He found the musketeer dressed and ready to go out. As the hour they were to wait on the King was at twelve, Athos had agreed to play tennis now with Porthos and Aramis on a court near the Luxembourg stables. He invited D'Artagnan to join them, and though he knew nothing about the game, never having played it, D'Artagnan accepted the invitation. He could think of no other way of spending the time from ten o'clock to twelve.

Porthos and Aramis were already on the court and playing against each other. Athos, who was expert at all athletic exercises, took D'Artagnan with him to one court and challenged the other pair. But although Athos played with his left hand, at his first stroke he realized that his wound was too recent to allow him to exert himself like that. D'Artagnan was left to play alone, and as he declared that he knew too little about the game to play it properly, they just sent balls to one another without keeping score. Then one of the balls, sent by Porthos's herculean hand, passed so near D'Artagnan's face that he decided that if instead of passing close, it had smashed into his face, his audience would probably have been lost, since it would have been quite impossible to present himself before the King. Now as in his Gascon imagination his whole future depended on that audience, he bowed courteously to Porthos and Aramis, declared that he would not try to play tennis again until he could hold his own with them, and went to take a seat on the raised platform overlooking the court.

Unfortunately for Monsieur d'Artagnan, among the spectators there was one of His Eminence's guardsmen, one who, still enraged over the defeat his comrades had suffered only the day before, had promised himself to seize the first opportunity to avenge it. He thought he saw that opportunity now and addressed his neighbor.

"It's nothing astonishing," he remarked, "that this young man should be afraid of a tennis ball. Doubtless he's a prentice musketeer."

D'Artagnan turned as if a snake had fixed its fangs in him and stared at the guardsman.

"Good Lord!" the latter continued, twirling his mustache. "Look at me as long as you like, my little gentleman. What I have said I have said."

"And as what you have said is too clear to need any explanation," retorted D'Artagnan in a low voice, "I beg you to follow me."

"When?" asked the guardsman, with the same jeering air.

"Immediately, if you please."

"And you know who I am, of course?"

"I don't know in the least, and I care less."

"You are wrong, for if you knew my name, perhaps you wouldn't be in such a hurry."

"What is your name?"

"Bernajoux, at your service."

"Very well, Monsieur Bernajoux. I will wait for you at the gate."

"Go along, monsieur. I will follow you."

"Don't be in too great a hurry, monsieur. We mustn't be seen going away together. You realize that for what we are going to do too much of a crowd would be a nuisance."

"All right," said the guardsman, astonished that his name had made so little impression on the young man.

Indeed the name of Bernajoux was known to everyone, probably, except D'Artagnan, for he was one of the men who figured most often in the daily brawls that all the edicts of the King and the Cardinal could not suppress.

Porthos and Aramis were so busy with their game, and Athos was watching them so intently, that no one of them even noticed their young companion leave. D'Artagnan stopped outside the gate, and a minute later His Eminence's guardsman came out. As D'Artagnan had no time to lose, in view of his audience with the King, he looked all around, and seeing that the street was deserted, said to his adversary:

"By my faith, it's lucky for you, even though your name is Bernajoux, that you have only a prentice musketeer to deal with. But rest easy, I will do my best. On guard!"

"But this seems to me a bad place for a duel. We would be better off behind the Abbaye Saint-Germain or in the Pré-aux-Clercs."

"What you say makes good sense," D'Artagnan replied. "But unfortunately I have very little time to spare, as I have an appointment at twelve sharp. On guard, then, monsieur, on guard!"

Bernajoux was not a man to have such a request made to him twice. In an instant his sword glittered in his hand and he rushed at his adversary, hoping to intimidate him, thanks to his youth.

But D'Artagnan had served his apprenticeship the day before. Fresh from his decisive victory, elated by hopes of future favors, he was determined not to give back a single inch. So the two swords crossed hilt to hilt, and as D'Artagnan stood fast, it was his adversary who took the first step in retreat. As Bernajoux did so, his sword left a straight line, and D'Artagnan seized his chance, freed his blade, lunged, and pinked Bernajoux on the shoulder. Immediately D'Artagnan took one step back in his turn and raised his sword in salute. But Bernajoux cried out that the wound was nothing, lunged blindly at D'Artagnan, and actually spitted himself on D'Artagnan's sword.

However, as Bernajoux did not fall, as he did not declare that he was vanquished, as he kept retreating in the direction of the house of the Duc de La Trémouille, where one of his relatives was a servitor, D'Artagnan did not know how serious the guardsman's wounds were. He kept pressing Bernajoux hard, and without doubt would soon have finished him with a third thrust. But two of Bernajoux's friends who had been near the tennis court and had seen him exchange some words with

D'Artagnan, and then follow him out, heard the noise in the street. They rushed out, sword in hand, and fell upon the victor. Then close behind them came Athos, Porthos, and Aramis, and just as the two guardsmen were attacking their young companion, they forced the guardsmen to turn to face them. At that moment Bernajoux fell, and as the guardsmen were only two against four, they began to shout: "To the rescue, Hôtel de La Trémouille!" At their shouts everyone in the house rushed out and fell on the four comrades, who began to shout in their turn: "To the rescue, musketeers!"

This cry was usually heeded, for the musketeers were known to be enemies of His Eminence, and were very popular because of their hatred for the Cardinal. Usually in such quarrels the guardsmen of other companies than those of the Red Duke, as Aramis had called him, sided with the Royal Musketeers. Two of these guardsmen of Monsieur des Essarts's company who were passing came to the assistance of the four companions. The other one ran toward the Hôtel de Tréville, shouting: "To the rescue, musketeers, to the rescue!" As usual, that house was full of musketeers; they ran to support their comrades, and the melee became general. But strength was with the musketeers. The Cardinal's guardsmen and Monsieur de La Trémouille's people withdrew into the house and shut the door just in time to keep their enemies from invading it as they themselves entered. As to the wounded man, he had been carried in at once; he was in a critical condition.

Excitement was at its height among the musketeers and their allies. They were already considering setting fire to the house as a punishment for the insolence Monsieur de La Trémouille's servitors had shown in daring to make a sortie on the King's Musketeers. The suggestion had been made, and was being received with enthusiasm, when eleven o'clock struck. D'Artagnan and his friends remembered their audience with the King and set off for Monsieur de Tréville's house, where he was waiting for them. He was already informed of their latest exploit.

"Quick, to the Louvre," he said, "to the Louvre without losing a second! We must try to see the King before he is prejudiced by the Cardinal. We will describe today's affair as a consequence of yesterday's and the two will pass off together."

Accordingly Monsieur de Tréville and the four young men started off for the Louvre. But there, to the great astonishment of the Captain of the Musketeers, he was told that the King had gone to hunt stags in the forest of Saint-Germain. Twice he asked to have this information repeated, and each time his companions saw his brow darken more.

"Had His Majesty," he asked, "any intention yesterday of going on this hunt?"

"No, Your Excellency," the King's valet replied. "The head huntsman came this morning to tell His Majesty that he had marked down a stag for His Majesty's benefit. At first he said he would not go, but he could not resist the pleasure of the hunt, and after dinner he left."

"Did the King see the Cardinal?"

"Most probably," replied the valet. "I saw His Eminence's carriage horses here this morning, and when I asked where he was going, they told me, 'To Saint-Germain.' "

"He's got ahead of us," said Monsieur de Tréville to his companions. "Gentlemen, I will see the King this evening, but I do not advise you to venture to do so."

This advice was too reasonable, coming as it did from a man who knew the King only too well, for the young men to question it. Monsieur de Tréville bade them go home and wait for news from him.

As he entered his own house, Monsieur de Tréville thought it would be best for him to be first in offering his complaints. He sent one of his servants to Monsieur de La Trémouille with a letter in which he begged the Duc to drive the Cardinal's guardsmen out of his house and to reprimand his people for their audacity in having attacked the musketeers. But Monsieur de La Trémouille, already prejudiced by his squire, a relative of Bernajoux's, replied that neither Monsieur de Tréville nor the musketeers had any cause for complaint. On the contrary, he, Monsieur de La Trémouille, had such cause, since the musketeers had attacked his servitors and had intended to burn his house. The debate between the two noblemen might have lasted a long time, since each naturally persisted in his own opinion. But Monsieur de Tréville thought of an expedient that might end it quickly—he would go to call on Monsieur de La Trémouille. He repaired there immediately and had himself announced.

The two noblemen greeted each other courteously, for though there was no friendship between them, there was at least esteem. Both were men of courage and honor. As Monsieur de La Trémouille, a Protestant, saw the King seldom, and belonged to no party, generally he brought no bias to his social relations. This time, however, his greeting, though courteous, was colder than usual.

"Monsieur," said Monsieur de Tréville, "each of us thinks he has cause for complaint against the other. I have come here myself so that we may try together to clear up any misunderstanding."

"I am quite willing, monsieur, but I warn you that I have gone into the matter carefully, and all the fault lies with your musketeers."

"You are too just and reasonable a man, monsieur, not to accept a proposal I am about to make."

"Make it, monsieur. I am listening."

"How is Monsieur Bernajoux, your squire's relative?"

"Why, monsieur, he is very ill. Besides the wound in his arm, which is not dangerous, one lung was pierced, and the doctor has nothing good to say about that."

"Is he conscious?"

"Certainly."

"Can he talk?"

"Yes, but only with difficulty."

"Very well, monsieur. Let us go to him and beseech him to tell us the truth, in the name of the God before whom he may soon be summoned to appear. I will accept him as judge of his own cause and I will believe everything that he has to say."

Monsieur de La Trémouille reflected a moment, then consented. They went together to the room where the wounded man was lying. When he saw these two noble lords coming to visit him, Bernajoux tried to sit up, but he was too weak and, exhausted by the effort he had made, he fell back, almost fainting. Monsieur de La Trémouille made him snuff up some smelling salts, and he recovered full consciousness. Then Monsieur de Tréville, unwilling to have it thought that he was attempting to influence the wounded man, asked Monsieur de La Trémouille to question him.

What Monsieur de Tréville had anticipated actually happened. Bernajoux, hovering between life and death as he was, did not think for a moment of concealing the truth. He described everything to the two noblemen exactly as it had happened. That was all Monsieur de Tréville wanted. He wished Bernajoux a speedy recovery, took leave of Monsieur de La Trémouille, went home, and immediately sent word to the four friends asking them to dine with him.

It's easy to guess that all through the dinner the conversation kept returning to the two defeats the Cardinal's Guards had suffered. As D'Artagnan had been the hero of both fights, all the congratulations fell to him. Athos, Porthos, and Aramis left them to him, not only as good comrades, but as men who had had their turn so often that they could well afford him his.

Toward six o'clock, Monsieur de Tréville announced that it was time to go to the Louvre, but as it was past the hour for the audience granted by His Majesty; when there, instead of claiming entrance by the back staircase, he went to the antechamber with the four young men. The King had not yet returned from the hunt. Our young men, mingling with the throng of courtiers, had been waiting barely half an hour when all the doors were thrown open and His Majesty was announced. At that announcement D'Artagnan found himself trembling to the very marrow of his bones. The next few minutes would probably decide his whole future life.

Louis XIII appeared, coming in first. He was in hunting dress that was still covered with dust, with high boots, and he held a riding crop in his hand. At the first glance D'Artagnan decided that the King was in a stormy humor. His Majesty's displeasure, evident though it was, did not

prevent the courtiers from forming lines for his passage. In royal ante-
chambers it is far better to be looked at with angry eyes than not to be
looked at at all. The three musketeers, therefore, did not hesitate to step
forward, and D'Artagnan concealed himself behind them. But although
the King knew Athos, Porthos, and Aramis perfectly well, he passed by
them without looking at them or speaking to them, as if he had never seen
them before. As to Monsieur de Tréville, when the King's eyes rested on
him for an instant, he bore the look with such steadiness that it was the
King who looked away. Then His Majesty, grumbling, entered his apartment.

"Things aren't going so well," remarked Athos, smiling. "We shall
not be appointed Knights of the Royal Order this time."

"Wait here ten minutes," said Monsieur de Tréville. "If you do not
see me come out then, go back to my house. It will be useless to stay
here after that."

The young men waited ten minutes, fifteen, twenty. Then, as Monsieur
de Tréville did not appear, they left, very uneasy over what might happen. Monsieur de Tréville entered the King's closet very boldly, and he
found His Majesty in a very bad humor. He was sitting in an armchair,
beating his boots with the handle of his riding crop. That did not prevent
Monsieur de Tréville from inquiring, quite coolly, after His Majesty's
health.

"Bad, monsieur, bad," replied the King. "I'm bored."

Indeed boredom was the malady Louis XIII suffered from most often.

"What! Your Majesty is bored!" said Monsieur de Tréville. "Didn't
you enjoy the hunt today?"

"A fine pleasure, monsieur. Upon my soul, everything is getting worse.
I don't know whether it's because the game leaves no scent or because the
dogs have no noses. We start a stag of ten branches, we chase him for
six hours, and when we are about to take him, without any warning the
whole pack goes off on the wrong scent, darts after a two-brancher. I
shall be forced to give up the hunt. Oh, I am a very unhappy king, Monsieur de Tréville! There is Monsieur le Cardinal always near, and he
never gives me a minute's rest, talking to me about Spain, about Austria, about England! By the way, speaking of the Cardinal, I am very
much vexed with you."

This was what Monsieur de Tréville had been waiting for. He had
known the King a long time, and he realized that all these complaints
were only a preface—a means of spurring himself to anger—and now he
had at last come to the point.

"How have I been so unfortunate as to displease Your Majesty?"
asked Monsieur de Tréville, feigning the greatest astonishment.

"Is this the way you do your duty, monsieur?" the King asked. "Was it
for this that I made you Captain of the Musketeers—to have your men

assassinate a guardsman, disturb a whole quarter, and try to set fire to Paris, without your saying a word? But after all," the King went on, "perhaps I am too hasty in accusing you. Doubtless those disturbers of the peace are in prison, and you have come to tell me that justice has been done."

"Sire," replied Monsieur de Tréville calmly, "on the contrary, I have come to ask you for justice."

"On whom?" cried the King.

"On slanderers," replied Monsieur de Tréville.

"Well, well, this is something new," said the King. "Do you mean to tell me that those three damned musketeers of yours, Athos, Porthos, and Aramis, and your cadet from Béarn, did not fall on poor Bernajoux like so many madmen, and did not handle him so roughly that probably he is dying this very minute? Do you mean to tell me they didn't lay siege to the Hôtel de La Trémouille, and that they didn't try to burn it? That might not have been a great misfortune in time of war, seeing that it's a hotbed of Huguenots, but in peacetime it's an inopportune example. Tell me, can you deny all that?"

"And who told you this fine story, Sire?"

"Who told me this fine story? Who should it be but the one who watches while I sleep, who labors while I amuse myself, who guides everything at home and abroad—in France and in all Europe?"

"Your Majesty is doubtless speaking of God," replied Monsieur de Tréville, "for I know of no one but God who is so far above Your Majesty."

"No, monsieur, I mean the prop of the state, my only real servant, my only friend—Monsieur le Cardinal."

"His Eminence is not His Holiness, Sire. Only the Pope is infallible, and that infallibility does not extend to Cardinals."

"Do you mean to say that the Cardinal is not telling me the truth, that he is deceiving me? You are accusing him, are you? Come, speak, confess frankly that you are accusing him."

"No, Sire, I am not accusing him. But I say that he is mistaken, that he has been misled. I say that he has been too hasty in accusing Your Majesty's musketeers, to whom he is always unjust, and that he did not get his information from the right sources."

"The accusation comes from Monsieur de La Trémouille, from the Duc himself. What have you to say to that?"

"I might answer, Sire, that he has too personal an interest in the matter to be an impartial witness. But I shall not do that, for I know that the Duc is a loyal gentleman. Therefore I refer the whole matter to him, but on one condition, Sire."

"What condition?"

"That Your Majesty will ask him to come here and will question him yourself without witnesses, and that I may see Your Majesty after you have seen the Duc."

"If you wish it," said the King. "And you will abide by what Monsieur de La Trémouille says?"

"Yes, Sire."

"You will accept his decision?"

"Without question."

"And you will agree to any amends he demands?"

"Absolutely."

"La Chesnaye!" the King called, "La Chesnaye!" Louis XIII's confidential valet, who never left the door, entered the room. "La Chesnaye," said the King, "send someone immediately to find Monsieur de La Trémouille. I wish to speak with him this evening."

"Your Majesty promises me that you will see no one after Monsieur de La Trémouille until you have seen me?"

"No one, on the word of a gentleman."

"Till tomorrow, then, Sire."

"Till tomorrow, monsieur."

"At what time, may it please Your Majesty?"

"At any hour you choose."

"But I would be afraid of awakening Your Majesty if I came too early."

"Awaken me! Do I ever sleep? I no longer sleep, monsieur. Sometimes I dream, that's all. So come as early as you like—at seven o'clock, perhaps. But woe to you if your musketeers are guilty."

"If my musketeers are guilty, Sire, the guilty shall be given into Your Majesty's hands to dispose of them at your good pleasure. Does Your Majesty require anything further? Speak, I am ready to obey."

"No, monsieur, no. I am not called Louis the Just without cause. Till tomorrow, then, monsieur, till tomorrow."

"May God guard Your Majesty until then!"

However badly the King slept, Monsieur de Tréville slept still worse. He had notified his three musketeers and their companion to come to him at half-past six in the morning. He took them with him to the Louvre, but gave them no encouragement and made no promises, nor did he attempt to conceal from them that their favor, and even his own, depended on a throw of the dice. At the foot of the back stairs, he asked them to wait. If the King was still angry at them, they could leave without being seen; if the King consented to see them, it would be easy to summon them.

In the King's antechamber Monsieur de Tréville found La Chesnaye, who informed him that they had not been able to find the Duc de La Trémouille at his house the night before, that he had come home at too late an hour to present himself at the Louvre, that he had only just arrived and was now with the King. This last circumstance was welcome news to Monsieur de Tréville, for he was certain now that no alien suggestion could be insinuated between Monsieur de La Trémouille's testimony and his own audience with the King. In fact, barely ten minutes had passed when the door of the King's closet opened and the Duc de La Trémouille came out. He went straight to Monsieur de Tréville and said:

"Monsieur de Tréville, His Majesty has just sent for me in order to inquire into the occurrences at my house yesterday morning. I have told him the truth—that the fault lay with my servitors, and that I was ready to offer you my apology. Since I have the good fortune to meet you here, I beg you to forgive me, and to count me always as one of your friends."

"Monsieur le Duc," Monsieur de Tréville replied, "I was so confident of your integrity that I asked for no other defender before His Majesty. I see that I was not mistaken. I thank you, and I am gratified that there is still one man in France of whom one can say what I have said of you."

"Well put, well put!" called the King, who had heard this conversation through the open door. "But since he claims to be a friend of yours, Tréville, pray tell him that I too would like to be his friend, but he neglects me. It's almost three years since I saw him, and I never see him except when I send for him. Tell him all that for me, since that's not the sort of thing that a king can say for himself."

"My thanks, Sire, my warmest thanks," said the Duc. "But Your Majesty knows very well that it is not those whom Your Majesty sees at all hours of the day—I don't mean to include Monsieur de Tréville—who are the most devoted to you."

"So you heard what I said? So much the better, Your Grace, so much the better," said the King, coming to the door. "Ah, it's you, Tréville! Where are your musketeers? I told you day before yesterday to bring them to me. Why haven't you done so?"

"They are below, Sire, and with your permission La Chesnaye will bid them come up."

"Yes, yes, have them come at once. It must be eight o'clock, and I expect a caller at nine. Go now, Monsieur le Duc, and come back to see me sometimes. Come in, Tréville."

The Duc bowed and withdrew. As he opened the antechamber door the three musketeers and D'Artagnan, led by La Chesnaye, appeared at the top of the stairway.

"Come in, my brave fellows," said the King, "come in. I'm going to scold you."

The musketeers advanced, bowing low, D'Artagnan following close.

"What the devil!" the King went on. "Seven of His Eminence's guardsmen downed by you four within two days! That's too many, gentlemen, too many. At that rate His Eminence will have to recruit a fresh company every three weeks, and I'll have to enforce the edicts against dueling with the utmost rigor. One man now and then I don't say much about, but seven in two days—I repeat what I said, that's too many, far too many."

"Sire, Your Majesty sees that therefore these contrite and repentant men have come to offer their apologies."

"Perfectly contrite and perfectly repentant, are they? Hm," said the King, "I have no confidence in their hypocritical faces—especially that one yonder with a Gascon look. Come here, monsieur."

D'Artagnan, realizing that this compliment was addressed to him, came forward, assuming a most despondent expression.

"Why, Tréville," said the King, "you told me that he was a young man, didn't you? This is a boy, Monsieur de Tréville, a mere boy! Do you mean to say that it was he who gave that fierce thrust to Jussac?"

"And those two equally fine thrusts to Bernajoux."

"Surely he's a very devil, this lad from Béarn. *Ventre-saint-gris!* Monsieur de Tréville, as my father used to say. That sort of work must mean slashing many doublets and breaking many swords. Now Gascons are always poor, are they not?"

"Sire, I assure you that they have not yet discovered gold mines in their mountains, though the Lord owes them a miracle like that as a reward for the way they supported the claims of the King your father."

"Which means that the Gascons made a king of me too, doesn't it, Tréville? since I'm the son of my father. Well, all right, I don't say nay to it. La Chesnaye, go rummage in all my pockets and see whether you can find forty pistoles. If you find them, bring them to me. And now come, young man, on your conscience, how did all this happen?"

D'Artagnan related the adventure of the day before in minute detail: how he had been unable to sleep for joy over the audience he was to have with His Majesty; how he had joined his three friends three hours before the time set for the audience; how they had gone to the tennis court together; how when he had been afraid of being struck in the face by a tennis ball, Bernajoux had jeered at him; how Bernajoux had just missed paying for his jeers with his life and Monsieur de La Trémouille, who had had nothing to do with the affair, had almost lost his house.

"That's it," murmured the King. "Yes, that's just the story the Duc told me. Poor Cardinal! Seven men in two days—and his very best men, too! But that's enough, gentlemen, do you hear? That's quite enough. You have taken your revenge for the affair in the Rue Férou, and even more than that. You ought to be satisfied."

"If Your Majesty is satisfied," said Tréville, "so are we."

"Oh yes, I am satisfied," returned the King. He took a handful of gold from La Chesnaye and put it in D'Artagnan's hand. "Here," he said, "is a proof of my satisfaction." Then he continued, looking at his watch, "There now, it's half-past eight, and you may retire. I told you I was expecting someone at nine. My thanks for your devotion, gentlemen. I may continue to rely on it, may I not?"

"Oh, Sire," cried the four companions with one voice, "we would let ourselves be cut to pieces in Your Majesty's service!"

"Good, good—but keep whole. That will be better, and you will be more useful to me." As the others were withdrawing, the King added in a low voice: "Tréville, since you have no room in the musketeers, and anyway we decided that a novitiate was necessary before entering the corps, put this young man in the company of the Royal Guards commanded by your brother-in-law Monsieur des Essarts. By the Lord, Tréville, I'm already enjoying the face the Cardinal will make. He will be furious, but I don't care. I am doing what is right."

The King waved a farewell to Tréville, who went out to rejoin his musketeers. He found D'Artagnan giving each of them a share of the forty pistoles.

The Cardinal, as His Majesty had foreseen, was really furious, so furious that he kept away from the King's gaming table for a whole week. That did not prevent the King from being as amicable as possible to him whenever he saw him, or from asking in his most affectionate tone:

"Well, Monsieur le Cardinal, how fares it with that poor Bernajoux of yours, and that poor Jussac?"

CHAPTER 7

WHEN D'ARTAGNAN WAS OUTSIDE THE LOUVRE, HE CON-
sulted his friends on what use he should make of his own share of the
forty pistoles. Athos advised him to order a good dinner at The Sign of
the Fir Cone, Porthos that he engage a lackey, and Aramis that he provide himself with a suitable mistress. The good dinner took place that
very day, and the lackey waited on them. The meal had been ordered by
Athos, and the lackey had been furnished by Porthos.

The lackey was from Picardy. The boastful musketeer had picked him
up on the Pont de la Tournelle, where he was spitting in the river to make
rings. Porthos contended that this occupation was a proof of a reflective
and contemplative character, and he had engaged him without any other
recommendation. The majestic bearing of Porthos, who he supposed was
to be his master, charmed Planchet—the man from Picardy—and he was
a little disappointed when he was told that Porthos was already supplied
with a lackey, one Mousqueton, and that he, Planchet, was to enter
D'Artagnan's service.

However, when he served as waiter at the dinner his master was giving
and saw D'Artagnan take out a handful of gold when he paid for it, he
thought his fortune was surely made, and he gave thanks to Heaven for
having given him service with such a Croesus. But when he made his
master's bed that evening Planchet's chimeras vanished into thin air. The
bed was the only one in the apartment, which consisted of an antechamber and a bedroom, Planchet slept in the antechamber on a coverlet
taken from D'Artagnan's bed.

Athos had a valet named Grimaud whom he had trained in a decidedly original way. He was a very taciturn man, this dignified nobleman
Athos. During the five or six years he had been living in the closest in-
timacy with Porthos and Aramis, they could remember having seen him
smile often, but they had never heard him laugh. His words were few
and expressive, always conveying all that they meant, and no more—no
embellishment, no embroidery, no arabesque. His conversation consisted
of facts, without any flourishes.

Although Athos was barely thirty and was very handsome, very intelligent, no one knew of his ever having had a mistress. He never spoke of

The Musketeers Fighting a Duel

Bonacieux Asks D'Artagnan's Help in Finding His Wife

women. However, he did not prevent others from speaking of them in his presence, although it was obvious that he found that kind of talk, in which he joined only with bitter remarks and misanthropic opinions, was most disagreeable. His reserve, his lack of sociability, and his silence almost made an old man of him. In order not to disturb his habits, he had trained Grimaud to obey his least gesture or just the movement of his lips. He spoke to him only when it was absolutely necessary.

Porthos, as we have already seen, was in character the exact opposite of Athos. He not only talked much, he also talked loudly, though, to do him justice, he cared little whether anybody listened to him or not. He talked for the pleasure of hearing himself talk, on every subject except the sciences, explaining this exception by saying that from his childhood he had always hated learned men. He lacked the air of distinction so evident in Athos, and at the beginning of their friendship the consciousness of his inferiority often caused him to be unjust toward that gentleman, whom he sought to eclipse by his own resplendent costumes. But in his simple musketeer's uniform, with only his way of tossing his head or advancing his foot, Athos instantly took the place that was his due, and consigned the ostentatious Porthos to the second rank. Porthos consoled himself by filling Monsieur de Tréville's antechamber and the guardroom of the Louvre with tales of his exploits in lady-killing.

An old proverb says, "Like master, like man." Porthos's lackey was Mousqueton, a Norman whose pacific name of Boniface Porthos had changed to the infinitely more sonorous Mousqueton. He had entered Porthos's service on condition that he be paid only by being clothed and lodged, but that handsomely. He asked only to be given three hours a day in which to devote himself to employment that would provide for his other wants. Porthos accepted the bargain; it suited him to a *t*. He had doublets made for Mousqueton from his own old clothes and his cast-off cloaks, and thanks to a very skillful tailor, who made the cloaks look as good as new by turning them, Mousqueton made a fine appearance when he was in attendance on his master.

As for Aramis, his lackey was named Bazin. Thanks to the hope his master entertained of someday taking Holy Orders, Bazin always dressed in black, as is befitting for the servant of an ecclesiastic. He came from Berry, a man of from thirty-five to forty, mild, peaceable, and plump, using the leisure his master allowed him to read pious works. When necessary, he could get up a dinner for two, with few dishes but excellent ones. In addition, he was dumb, blind, deaf, and of unimpeachable loyalty.

Athos lived in the Rue Férou, within two steps of the Luxembourg. His apartment consisted of two rooms, attractively furnished, in a lodging house kept by a woman still young and very handsome who cast tender glances at him in vain. A few traces of past splendor appeared here and there on the walls of this modest lodging. For example, there was a richly damascened sword of a fashion that went back to the age of Francis I. Its hilt alone, studded with precious stones, was probably worth 200 pistoles, and yet in times of his greatest need Athos had never been willing either to pawn it or to sell it.

In addition to this sword, there was a portrait of a nobleman of the time of Henry III, who was dressed with the greatest elegance and wore the Order of the Holy Ghost. Certain of his features were like those of Athos, indicating that this great noble, a Knight of the same Order as the King, was an ancestor of Athos's. Finally there was a magnificent casket of gold bearing the same coat of arms as the sword and the portrait. It was the central ornament on the mantelpiece, and was quite out of keeping with the other ornaments there. Athos always carried the key of this casket on his person.

Porthos lived in a very large and apparently very sumptuous apartment on the Rue du Vieux-Colombier. Every time he walked by it with a friend, Mousqueton was sure to be at one of its windows, and Porthos would look up and wave his hand and say, "There's where *I* live!" But nobody ever found him at home, so that nobody could form any idea of what real riches this seeming sumptuousness contained.

Aramis lived in a little ground-floor apartment consisting of a boudoir, a dining room, and a bedroom. The bedroom looked out on a little fresh, green, shady garden, into which his neighbors could not look.

D'Artagnan, who was very curious, like most people gifted in intrigue, tried in every way he could think of to discover the real names that Athos, Porthos, and Aramis were concealing by their pseudonyms, especially that of Athos, whose noble lineage was evidenced in so many ways. He tried to get information about Athos and Aramis from Porthos, and about Porthos from Aramis. Unfortunately Porthos knew no more about the life of his taciturn comrade than what was obvious. There was a rumor that Athos had suffered much unhappiness from some love affair, that some terrible treachery had poisoned this gallant man's existence. What could that treachery be? No one knew.

As to Porthos, except for his real name, which no one but Monsieur de Tréville knew, his life was easy to read. Vain and indiscreet, he was as transparent as a crystal.

As to Aramis, though he seemed to be anything but secretive, he was a man of mystery. He answered the questions asked him only very tersely, and he answered evasively any that concerned himself.

Despite all the pains he took, D'Artagnan was unable to learn anything more about his new friends. He therefore decided to believe for the present everything that was said about their past while hoping for more definite and more extensive revelations in the future. In the meantime, he looked upon Athos as an Achilles, Porthos as an Ajax, and Aramis as a Joseph.

The life the four young men led was merry enough. Athos gambled, and always with bad luck. Yet he never borrowed a sou from his friends, though his own purse was always at their service, and when he played on his word, he always awakened his creditors at six o'clock the next morning to pay his debts.

Porthos indulged in passionate fits of gambling. On the days he won, he was insolent and exhibitionist; when he lost, he disappeared completely for several days, appearing again with a wan face and a downcast look, but with money in his pockets.

As for Aramis, he never gambled. He was the worst musketeer and the most unconvivial companion imaginable. He always had something he must do. Sometimes in the middle of a dinner, when what with the influence of wine and friendly conversation, all the others were expecting to enjoy themselves at table for two or three hours, Aramis would look at his watch, rise with a gracious smile, and take leave of the company. He had an appointment, so he said, with a casuist he must consult. Or he would say he must go home to write a treatise, and begged his friends not to disturb him. Then Athos would smile that charming, melancholy smile of his that lighted up his face so happily and Porthos would go on drinking, swearing that Aramis would never be anything but a village curé.

Planchet, D'Artagnan's lackey, bore his master's prosperity nobly. He received 30 sous a day, and for the first month he would come back to D'Artagnan's lodgings as gay as a chaffinch and most affable to his master. When the wind of adversity began to blow on the household in the Rue des Fossoyeurs—that is, when the forty pistoles from Louis XIII were gone, or nearly gone—he began to complain in a way that Athos thought nauseous, Porthos indecent, and Aramis ridiculous. Athos advised D'Artagnan to dismiss the fellow. Porthos agreed, but thought Planchet ought to be soundly thrashed first. Aramis contended that a master should never heed anything but the compliments paid to him.

"That's very easy for you to say," D'Artagnan remarked. "You, Athos, live in silence with Grimaud, you forbid him to speak, and consequently you never have words with him. You, Porthos, with that magnificent way of yours, are a god to your lackey Mousqueton. Finally, you, Aramis, are always buried in your theological studies and you inspire the profoundest respect in your lackey Bazin, who is a mild and pious man. But I, who have no permanent place, and no resources, who am neither a musketeer nor even a guardsman—what do you think I can do to inspire Planchet with affection, or terror, or respect?"

"The matter is a serious one," said Athos. "This is a family affair. Lackeys, like wives, must be put at once in the place they are to keep. Think it over." The other two agreed with him.

D'Artagnan did think about it. He decided to thrash Planchet as a precautionary measure, and he did it conscientiously, as D'Artagnan did everything. Having thrashed him well, he forbade Planchet to leave his service without his own permission, and said to him:

"My future cannot fail to be more prosperous. I look forward with perfect confidence to better times. So your fortune is made if you stay with me, and I am too good a master to let you lose your fortune by granting you the dismissal you ask for."

This procedure gave D'Artagnan's three friends great respect for D'Artagnan's judgment. Planchet admired it quite as much, and said no more about quitting D'Artagnan's service.

The life of the four young men was life in common now. D'Artagnan, coming fresh from his province to a world quite new to him, had no settled habits, and he fell in easily with those of his friends. They rose about eight o'clock in winter, about six o'clock in summer, and went to Monsieur de Tréville's to get their orders and to see what was on foot. Although D'Artagnan was not a musketeer, he performed the duties of one with touching punctuality. He was always mounting guard, because he always went with the one of his friends who was on duty. Everybody at the headquarters of the musketeers knew him, and they all considered him a good comrade. Monsieur de Tréville, who had liked him at first glance, and who now felt real affection for him, never ceased to commend him to the King.

The three musketeers were very proud of their young comrade. The friendship that united these four men, and their need to see each other three or four times a day, whether for dueling, for some business or other, or for pleasure, kept them constantly running after one another like shadows. They were always being met with looking for each other, from the Luxembourg to the Place Saint-Sulpice or from the Rue du Vieux-Colombier to the Luxembourg.

Meanwhile Monsieur de Tréville's promises were on the way to fulfillment. One fine morning the King ordered Monsieur le Chevalier des Essarts to admit D'Artagnan to his company of Royal Guards as a cadet. D'Artagnan sighed as he donned his guardsman's uniform. He would have given ten years of his life to exchange it for that of a musketeer. But Monsieur de Tréville assured him that he would receive that favor after a novitiate of two years, and the time might be even shorter if an opportunity should present itself for D'Artagnan to do some signal service to the King, or to distinguish himself by some brilliant exploit.

Now it was Athos, Porthos, and Aramis who took turns in mounting guard—with D'Artagnan when he was on duty. By admitting D'Artagnan Monsieur le Chevalier des Essarts's company got four new men instead of one.

CHAPTER 8

BUT THE FORTY PISTOLES FROM KING LOUIS XIII, LIKE everything else in this world, after having had a beginning also came to their end, and that end found our four companions very short of funds. At first Athos supported the group for a time with his own means. Porthos succeeded him, and thanks to one of his habitual disappearances, he was able to provide for their needs for a fortnight. Then it was Aramis's turn, and he carried on with good grace, managing it, so he said, by selling some theological books for a few pistoles. Next they had recourse, as they had done so often, to Monsieur de Tréville, who advanced them some money on their pay, but those advances did not go very far with three musketeers who were already heavily in debt and one guardsman who as yet had received no pay at all.

At last, when they realized that they would soon be quite penniless, by a final effort they succeeded in scraping up 8 or 10 pistoles for Porthos to gamble with. Unfortunately he had a streak of bad luck; he lost all of it, together with 25 pistoles for which he pledged his word. Then inconvenience became actual want. The four hungry men, followed by their four hungry lackeys, could be seen haunting the quays and the guardrooms, picking up among their friends all the dinners they could find, following the advice of Aramis, who said that it was well to sow meals right and left in the days of prosperity in order to reap a few in the days of misfortune.

Athos was invited four times, and each time he took his friends and their lackeys with him. Porthos had six invitations and took along his friends to enjoy them. Aramis had eight invitations and his friends shared them. D'Artagnan, who as yet knew few other people in Paris, chased down one breakfast with chocolate at the house of a priest from his own province and one dinner at the house of a cornet of the Royal Guards. He took his little army to the priest's, where they devoured provisions that would have lasted the ecclesiastic for two months, and to the cornet's, who did wonders. But as Planchet said, people don't eat once for all, even though they eat a good deal.

D'Artagnan felt humiliated at having procured only one meal and a half for his companions—for he reckoned the priest's breakfast as only half a meal—in return for all the feasts Athos, Porthos, and Aramis had procured for him. He fancied himself a burden on the group—forgetting in his quite youthful good faith that he had provided food for them for a whole month—and he spurred his troubled mind into activity. He reflected that this coalition of four young, brave, enterprising, and active men ought to have some other object than swaggering about, taking fencing lessons, and playing practical jokes that were more or less ingenious.

In fact, four men such as they were, four men devoted to one another with both their purses and their lives; four men always supporting one another, never yielding ground and carrying out together the resolutions they had made in common; four arms threatening the four points of the compass or concentrating on a single point—these four men must inevitably, either by open or by underground means, by a mine or by a trench, by cunning or by force, open a way toward their goal, however hotly that goal might be defended and however distant it might be.

He was thinking seriously one day about this when someone rapped lightly on the door. D'Artagnan awakened Planchet and ordered him to open it. A man of unpretending appearance entered, evidently a bourgeois. Planchet, as a sort of dessert, would have liked to listen to the conversation, but the bourgeois told D'Artagnan that as what he had to say was both important and confidential; their interview must be private. D'Artagnan dismissed Planchet and asked his visitor to be seated. There was a moment of silence while the two men looked at each other as if to decide what the other was like, then D'Artagnan bowed, to indicate that he was ready to listen.

"I have heard Monsieur d'Artagnan spoken of as a very brave young man," said the bourgeois, "and his well-deserved reputation has determined me to confide a secret to him."

"Speak, monsieur, speak," said D'Artagnan, instinctively scenting something that might prove advantageous.

The bourgeois paused again, then continued:

"I have a wife who is a seamstress to the Queen, monsieur. She is not without either virtue or beauty. Though she had but a small dowry, I was led to marry her about three years ago because Monsieur de La Porte, the Queen's cloak-bearer, is her godfather and protects her."

"Well, monsieur?"

"Well," the bourgeois continued, "well, monsieur, my wife was abducted yesterday morning as she was leaving her workroom."

"Who was your wife's abductor?"

"I know nothing for certain, monsieur, but there is someone I suspect."

"And who is it you suspect?"

"A man who has been pursuing her for a long time."

"The devil you say!"

"But allow me to tell you, monsieur, that I am convinced that there is less love than politics in this affair."

"Less love than politics," D'Artagnan said, looking thoughtful. "And what is it you suspect?"

"I don't know whether I ought to tell you what I suspect."

"Monsieur, I beg you to observe that I am asking absolutely nothing of you. It is you who came to me. It is you who told me you had a secret to confide to me. Do what you like, then. There is still time for you to withdraw."

"No, monsieur, no. You look to me like an honest young man and I will trust you. I believe, then, that it is not because of any love affair that my wife has been taken, but because of the love affair of a lady far more highly placed than she."

"Aha! Could it be because of the amours of Madame de Bois-Tracy?" asked D'Artagnan, who wished to seem to this bourgeois to be familiar with Court affairs.

"Higher, monsieur, higher."

"Of Madame d'Aiguillon, or Madame de Chevreuse?"

"Higher still, monsieur, much higher."

"Of the——?" and D'Artagnan stopped there.

"Yes, monsieur," the terrified bourgeois replied, in a tone so low that it was scarcely audible.

"And with whom?"

"With whom can it be save the Duke of——?"

"The Duke of——" D'Artagnan repeated.

"Yes, monsieur," said the bourgeois, in an even lower tone than before.

"But how do you know all this? No half-confidences now or—you understand?"

"I know it through my wife, monsieur, she told me herself."

"And how did she know it?"

"Through Monsieur de La Porte. Didn't I tell you she is his god-daughter? And isn't he the Queen's confidential valet? Well, Monsieur de La Porte got my wife a place near Her Majesty so that our poor Queen might at least have someone near her whom she could trust, abandoned as she is by the King, spied upon by the Cardinal, and betrayed by everybody."

"Aha! The pattern is beginning to appear," said D'Artagnan.

"Now my wife came home four days ago, monsieur. One of her conditions on accepting the post was that she might come to see me twice a week, for my wife loves me dearly. Well, she came home, and she confided to me that at that very moment the Queen was in great fear. It seems that His Eminence is harassing her and persecuting her more than ever. And the Queen thinks——"

"Well, what does the Queen think?"

"She thinks that someone has written to the Duke of Buckingham in her name in order to induce him to come to Paris, and when once he is here to entice him into some trap."

"The devil you say! But your wife, my dear man, what has she to do with all this?"

"Her devotion to the Queen is well known, and somebody wishes either to get her away from her mistress, or to intimidate her so that she will tell Her Majesty's secrets, or to bribe her and use her as a spy."

"That sounds probable," said D'Artagnan. "But what about the man who abducted her. Do you know who he is?"

"As I told you, I think I know."

"His name?"

"That I do not know. What I do know is that he is one of the Cardinal's creatures, the one they call His Eminence's *âme damnée!*"

"But have you seen him?"

"Yes, my wife pointed him out to me one day."

"Is there anything unusual about him that would lead you to recognize him?"

"Oh, certainly. He's a nobleman who bears himself proudly, he has black hair, a pale complexion, piercing eyes, very white teeth, and a scar on one temple."

"A scar on one temple!" cried D'Artagnan. "And very white teeth, piercing eyes, pale complexion, black hair, and a proud look—why, that's my man of Meung!"

"That's your man, you say?"

"Yes, yes, but that has nothing to do with this affair. . . . No, I'm wrong—on the contrary, that simplifies things a good deal. If your man is mine, I can avenge two wrongs at one blow, that's all! But where can I meet with this man?"

"That I cannot tell you."

"Don't you know where he lives?"

"No, I don't. One day when I was taking my wife back to the Louvre he came out of the palace just as she was about to go in, and she pointed him out to me."

"Devil take it," muttered D'Artagnan, "all this is very vague! . . . Who told you your wife had been abducted?"

"Monsieur de La Porte."

"Did he give you any details?"

"He didn't know any."

"Did you learn anything from anyone else?"

"Yes, I did. I received——"

"What?"

"Why, I'm afraid I'm being very indiscreet——"

"You seem to think a lot about discretion. I beg leave to observe to you that it is too late for you to retreat now."

" 'Sdeath, I'm not retreating!" cried the bourgeois, blaspheming to keep his courage up. "Besides, by the faith of Bonacieux——"

"Your name is Bonacieux?" interrupted D'Artagnan.

"Yes, monsieur."

"Pardon me for interrupting you, but it seems to me I have heard that name before."

"That's quite possible, monsieur. I am your landlord."

"Aha!" said D'Artagnan, half rising and bowing. "So you're my landlord?"

"Yes, monsieur, I am. And as you have lived here three months, and have—I suppose because you have been busy with important affairs—forgotten to pay me my rent, and as I have not bothered you about it, I thought you would appreciate my being so considerate."

"Of course, my dear Monsieur Bonacieux," replied D'Artagnan. "I assure you that I am most grateful to you for your consideration. As I told you, if I can be of any service to you——"

"I believe you, monsieur, I believe you. And as I was about to say, by the faith of Bonacieux, I trust you absolutely."

"Go on with what you were about to tell me, then."

The bourgeois took a paper from his pocket and gave it to D'Artagnan.

"A letter?" asked the young man.

"One I received this morning."

D'Artagnan opened it, and as daylight was beginning to fade, he went to a window to read it, and the bourgeois followed him. This is what he read:

Do not try to find your wife. She will be restored to you when she is no longer needed. If you take a single step to try to find her, you will be ruined.

"That's pretty positive," D'Artagnan commented. "But after all it's only a threat."

"True, but that threat terrifies me, monsieur. I am no soldier, and I am afraid of the Bastille."

"Hm," murmured D'Artagnan, "I don't like the Bastille any more than you do. If it were only a question of dueling, I wouldn't mind it."

"But I've been counting on you, monsieur. Seeing you constantly surrounded by musketeers, and recognizing that they were Monsieur de Tréville's musketeers and therefore enemies of the Cardinal, I thought that you and your friends would be delighted to do justice to our poor Queen and to do His Eminence an ill turn at the same time."

"Undoubtedly we would be."

"And also I thought that since you owe me three months' rent and I have said nothing about that——"

"Yes, yes, you have already used that argument, and I find it an excellent one."

"Moreover, reckoning that as long as you do me the honor to live in my house, I would never mention your unpaid rent to you . . . And furthermore, I planned, if it should prove necessary, to offer you something like fifty pistoles, if by any chance you should be short of funds at the present moment, though I don't think that likely."

"Admirable! So you are rich, my dear Monsieur Bonacieux!"

"I'm in comfortable circumstances, that's all, monsieur. I have scraped together an income of something like two or three thousand crowns a year in the haberdashery business. So you realize, monsieur, that—— But look, look, monsieur!" cried the bourgeois.

"Where?"

"Who's that over there—in the street, opposite your windows—in that doorway. A man wrapped in a cloak."

"That's the man!" shouted D'Artagnan. "Oho! This time he shall not escape me!" and he sprang to seize his sword.

Drawing his sword from its scabbard, he dashed out of the room. On the staircase he met Athos and Porthos. They separated to let D'Artagnan fly between them like an arrow.

"What's up? Where the devil are you going?"

"The man of Meung!" shouted D'Artagnan as he disappeared.

D'Artagnan had told his friends more than once about his adventure with the nameless man and the apparition of the beautiful woman to whom that man had confided some important missive. The two musketeers therefore understood from the four words that D'Artagnan had shouted out what D'Artagnan was about, and as they thought that when D'Artagnan had overtaken his man or had lost sight of him, he would return home, they went on up to his apartment. When they entered it, they found it empty. The landlord, fearing the consequences of the encounter of the young man and the nameless man, which he was sure was inevitable, had judged it prudent to decamp.

CHAPTER 9

AS ATHOS AND PORTHOS HAD ANTICIPATED, D'ARTAGNAN returned some half-hour later. Once more he had missed his man, who had vanished as if by magic. Sword in hand, D'Artagnan had run through all the neighboring streets, but he had found nobody who looked like the man he was seeking. Then he did what he should have done in the first place—he knocked at the door against which the nameless man had been leaning. But he banged down the knocker ten or twelve times running in vain; no one answered it. Some of the neighbors, roused by the noise he made, stuck their heads out of their windows or came to their doors, and one of them assured him that the house had been vacant for six months.

While D'Artagnan was running through the streets and knocking at doors Aramis had joined his companions, so that when he came home D'Artagnan found their group complete.

"Well?" cried each of the musketeers as D'Artagnan came in, his expression dark with anger.

"Well," cried he, throwing his sword on the bed, "that man must be the Devil in person! He vanished like a phantom, like a ghost, like a specter. Man or devil, human body or ghost, illusion or reality, that man was born for my damnation. His flight has caused us to lose a glorious piece of business, gentlemen, one that meant earning a hundred pistoles, and perhaps more."

"How?" cried Porthos, then Aramis.

Athos, faithful to his method of silence, was content to question D'Artagnan with a look.

"Planchet," D'Artagnan ordered his lackey, who had just poked his head through the half-open door, "go down to my landlord, Monsieur Bonacieux, and tell him to send us half a dozen bottles of Beaugency wine. It's the wine I like best."

"Oh, so you've established credit with your landlord, have you?" said Porthos.

"Yes," D'Artagnan answered, "beginning today. But don't worry. If the wine isn't good, we will send for something better."

"I have always said that D'Artagnan has the longest head of the four of us," said Athos. Then he relapsed into his habitual silence.

"Come, what does all this mean?" Porthos asked.

"Yes," said Aramis, "tell us all about it, my dear friend—unless the honor of some lady is involved, in which case you would do better to keep it to yourself."

"Rest easy, Aramis," D'Artagnan replied. "No one's reputation will be compromised by what I'm going to tell you."

Then he told his friends every word that had passed between his landlord and himself, including the fact that the man who had abducted Madame Bonacieux and the man he had quarreled with at The Jolly Miller were one and the same.

"This isn't a bad bit of business," remarked Athos, after having tasted the wine like a connoisseur and nodded to signify that it was good. "You may be able to get fifty or sixty pistoles out of this worthy man. Now we have to decide whether fifty or sixty pistoles are worth the risk of four heads."

"But remember," cried D'Artagnan, "that there is a woman in the case—a woman who has been abducted, a woman who is doubtless being threatened, perhaps tortured, and all because she is faithful to her mistress!"

"Beware, D'Artagnan, beware!" said Aramis. "In my opinion you're getting too excited about what has happened to Madame Bonacieux. Woman was created for our destruction, and it is from her that all our afflictions come."

As Aramis said this Athos frowned and bit his lips.

"It isn't Madame Bonacieux that I'm worried about," cried D'Artagnan, "but the Queen! The King abandons her and the Cardinal persecutes her, and she sees the heads of all her friends fall one after the other."

"Why does she love what we hate most in all the world—the Spaniards and the English?"

"Spain is her fatherland," D'Artagnan replied, "and it is quite natural that she should love the Spaniards. As for your second reproach, I have heard it said that she does not love the English, but only one Englishman."

"Eh, by my faith," said Athos, "we must confess that this Englishman is worthy of being loved. I have never seen a man with a nobler look."

"Without reckoning that he dresses better than anyone else on earth," commented Porthos. "I was at the Louvre the day he scattered his pearls, and by the Lord, I picked up two of them that I sold for ten pistoles apiece. Do you know him, Aramis?"

"Quite as well as you do, gentlemen. I was among the guests when they arrested him in the garden at Amiens, and the affair seemed to me a cruel blow for the King."

"If I knew where the Duke of Buckingham was," announced D'Artagnan, "that wouldn't stop me from taking him by the hand and leading him to the Queen, if only in order to enrage Monsieur le Cardinal. For our real, our only, our eternal enemy, gentlemen, is the Cardinal, and if we could find a way to play him a cruel trick, I confess I would willingly risk my head to do it."

"Didn't the haberdasher tell you, D'Artagnan," asked Athos, "that the Queen believes that Buckingham is coming to Paris because of a forged letter?"

"She is afraid so."

"Wait a minute," said Aramis. "I'm trying to recall certain circumstances."

"I am convinced," said D'Artagnan, "that the abduction of the Queen's serving-woman is connected in some way with the events we have been talking about, and perhaps with the presence of the Duke of Buckingham in Paris."

"Gentlemen," said Aramis, "listen to me. Yesterday I went to call on a learned doctor of theology whom I sometimes consult about my studies." Athos smiled. "He lives in a quiet quarter; his tastes and his profession require it. Now just as I was leaving his house——" There Aramis stopped.

"Well, just as you were leaving his house——"

Aramis seemed to be making a great effort to control himself, like a man who, well started in a lie, finds himself stopped by some unforeseen obstacle. But his three friends were staring at him, their ears were wide-open, and he saw no way to retreat.

"This doctor has a niece," he continued, "a very respectable lady." His three friends began to laugh. "Oh, if you laugh, or if you doubt my word," protested Aramis, "you shall hear no more."

"We are as faithful believers as the Mohammedans and as silent as tombs," said Athos.

"I will go on, then. This niece comes to see her uncle sometimes, and by chance she was there yesterday at the same time I was, and I could do no less than offer to see her to her carriage."

"Aha!" interrupted Porthos, one of whose faults was that he couldn't hold his tongue. "So this niece of the doctor has a carriage. A very desirable acquaintance my friend."

"Porthos," said Athos, "I have had occasion to observe to you more than once that you are a fool."

"Gentlemen, gentlemen," cried D'Artagnan, who was beginning to glimpse what might be coming, "this is a serious matter. Let's try not to jest about it. Go on, Aramis, go on."

"Suddenly a tall, dark man, evidently a gentleman—now I come to think of it, very much like your gentleman of Meung, D'Artagnan——"

"Perhaps he was my man."

"It's possible," Aramis went on. "Well, he came toward me, with five or six men following some ten paces behind him, and said in the most courteous tone, 'Monsieur le Duc, and you, madame'—this to the lady on my arm—'monsieur, madame, will you be good enough to get into this carriage without offering any resistance or making the slightest noise?'"

"He took you for Buckingham!" exclaimed D'Artagnan.

"I think so," said Aramis.

"But the lady?" asked Porthos.

"He took her for the Queen!" said D'Artagnan.

"Precisely," said Aramis.

"That Gascon is the Devil," cried Athos. "Nothing escapes him."

"As a matter of fact," said Porthos, "Aramis is about the height of the handsome Duke, and something like him in build. But it seems to me that the uniform of a musketeer——"

"I was wearing an enormous cloak," said Aramis.

"I can understand," commented Athos, "that the spy, if that's what he was, may have been mistaken as to your person, Aramis, but your face——"

"I was wearing a hat with a very broad brim."

"Good Lord!" cried Porthos. "What precautions you take when you study theology!"

"Gentlemen, gentlemen," D'Artagnan said, "don't waste our time jesting. Let us separate and each of us look for the haberdasher's wife. She is the key to the plot."

"A woman of such humble standing! Do you really believe that, D'Artagnan?" asked Porthos scornfully.

"She is the goddaughter of La Porte, the confidential valet of the Queen. Didn't I tell you that, gentlemen? Moreover, on this occasion perhaps Her Majesty thought it best to look to such a lowly person for support. The heads of those of high rank can be seen from afar, and the Cardinal is farsighted."

"Anyway," said Porthos, "let's make our bargain with the haberdasher first, and a good bargain, too."

"That's useless," D'Artagnan replied, "for if he doesn't pay us, I'm sure we shall be well paid by another party."

At that moment they heard the sound of hurried footsteps on the staircase, then the door crashed open and the unhappy haberdasher rushed into the room.

"Save me, gentlemen, save me!" he cried. "There are four men below who have come to arrest me. Save me, save me!"

Porthos and Aramis started to draw their swords.

"One moment," said D'Artagnan, motioning to them to sheathe their swords. "It isn't courage that is needed now, but prudence."

"But," cried Porthos, "we cannot allow——"

"You will allow D'Artagnan to do as he thinks best," Athos interrupted. "He has, I repeat, the longest head of the four of us, and for my part, I vow I will obey him. Do whatever you think best, D'Artagnan."

Just then the four policemen appeared at the door of the antechamber, but seeing three musketeers and a guardsman standing there wearing their swords, they were hesitant to enter.

"Come in, gentlemen, come in," said D'Artagnan. "This is my apartment, and all of us here are faithful servants of the King and of Monsieur le Cardinal."

"Then, gentlemen, you will not prevent us from carrying out our orders, I take it."

"On the contrary, we would assist you if that should be necessary."

"But you promised me——" the poor haberdasher murmured.

"We can save you only if we remain free ourselves," D'Artagnan replied quickly in a whisper. "If we act as if we were defending you, we shall be arrested too." Then he said aloud: "Come, gentlemen, come, I have no reason to defend Monsieur here. I saw him today for the first time. He came here to collect his rent. Isn't that true, Monsieur Bonacieux?"

"It's the exact truth!" cried the haberdasher. "But Monsieur has not told you——"

"Hold your tongue about me, man," murmured D'Artagnan, "hold it about my friends too, and above all about the Queen, or you will ruin everybody without saving yourself! Here, gentlemen, take this man away!" and D'Artagnan pushed the half-stupefied haberdasher into the arms of the policemen, saying: "You're a scoundrel, my dear man. You come to ask me for money—me, a musketeer! Gentlemen, once more I beg you to take him away. Take him to prison, and keep him under lock and key as long as possible. That will give me time to pay him."

The myrmidons of the law were profuse with their thanks and took away their prey. Just as they were about to go down the stairs D'Artagnan tapped their leader on the shoulder.

"May I not have the pleasure of drinking to your health, and will you not drink to mine?" he said, filling two glasses with the Beaugency wine he owed to Monsieur Bonacieux's generosity.

"That will be a great honor for me," the leader replied. "I accept with thanks."

"Then here's to your health, monsieur."

"Here's to yours, monsieur."

"And above all others," cried D'Artagnan, as if carried away by enthusiasm, "here's a toast to the King and the Cardinal!"

The leader of the policemen might have doubted D'Artagnan's sincerity if the wine had been bad, but the wine was good and he was convinced that the sincerity was genuine.

"What diabolical villainy have you been up to?" said Porthos, when the policeman had joined his companions and the four friends were alone. "Shame on us, shame! An unfortunate devil begs us for help and we four soldiers allow him to be arrested right in front of us! And a gentleman drinks with a common policeman!"

"Porthos," said Aramis, "Athos has already told you you are a fool, and I agree with him. D'Artagnan, you are a great man, and when you are Monsieur de Tréville's successor, I shall ask you for your influence to get me an abbey."

"Well, I'm certainly confused," said Porthos. "Do you mean to say you approve of what D'Artagnan has just done?"

"Good Lord, of course I do," retorted Athos. "I not only approve of what he has done but I also congratulate him on it."

"And now, gentlemen," said D'Artagnan, without troubling to explain his conduct to Porthos, "All for One and One for All—that's our motto, isn't it?"

"But——" said Porthos.

"Hold up your hand and swear!" Athos commanded. And Aramis echoed him.

Overcome by the example of his comrades, but grumbling to himself, Porthos lifted his hand, and the four friends repeated with one voice the slogan dictated by D'Artagnan.

"All for One and One for All!"

"Fine!" said D'Artagnan. "Now let each of us go to his own home," he added, as though he had never done anything all his life but give orders. "And remember—from this moment on we are at war with the Cardinal!"

CHAPTER 10

WHEN, LONG AGO, HUMAN SOCIETIES IN THE PROCESS OF formation invented the police, the police invented the mousetrap. As perhaps our readers are not familiar with the cant of the Rue de Jérusalem, let us see what a mousetrap is.

When an individual suspected of any crime is arrested in a house, whatever kind it be, the arrest is kept secret. Four or five men are posted in ambush in the front room of the ground floor. The door is opened to all who knock, but as it closes behind them, they are arrested. Thus within two or three days the police have in their power almost all those who visit the house regularly. That is what a mousetrap is.

Monsieur Bonacieux's house now became a mousetrap. Everyone who came there was seized and questioned by the Cardinal's men. As was usual then, a stairway at the side gave access to the second floor, where D'Artagnan's rooms were, so that his callers were exempt from molestation. Besides, no one but the three musketeers ever came there.

They had all been searching and inquiring independently, and they had found nothing, discovered nothing. Athos had even gone so far as to question Monsieur de Tréville, something that, considering the habitual taciturnity of the dignified musketeer, had surprised his Captain very much. But Monsieur de Tréville knew nothing except that the last time he had seen the Cardinal, the King, and the Queen, the Cardinal had looked very anxious, the King seemed worried, and the Queen's red eyes indicated that she had either been sleepless the night before or had been weeping. But this last circumstance had not made much impression on him. Since her marriage the Queen had lain awake many nights and had wept much.

As to D'Artagnan, he did not stir from his quarters. He turned his room into an observatory. From his windows he saw all who came and were caught in the mousetrap. Also he had pried up some of the tiles of the floor and cleared away the planking under them so that there was nothing but the ceiling of the room below between him and the room where the inquisitions were held, and he could hear every word that passed between the inquisitors and the defendants.

Those arrested were first searched thoroughly, then the questioning began. Almost all the inquisitions went like this:

"Has Madame Bonacieux given you anything to take to her husband, or to any other person? Has Monsieur Bonacieux given you anything to take to his wife, or to any other person? Has either of them ever confided anything to you by word of mouth?"

"If they knew anything, they wouldn't be questioning people like that," D'Artagnan told himself. "Now what are they trying to find out? Whether the Duke of Buckingham is in Paris or not and whether he has had or is to have an interview with the Queen?"

D'Artagnan stopped there, as, judging by what he had heard, that idea seemed the most probable.

Meanwhile, the mousetrap was always at work, and so was D'Artagnan's vigilance. On the evening of the day after poor Bonacieux's arrest, just as Athos had left D'Artagnan to go to Monsieur de Tréville's, just as nine o'clock had struck and Planchet, who had not yet made the bed, was beginning that task, there was a knock at the street door. The door was opened immediately and shut quickly. Someone had been caught in the mousetrap.

D'Artagnan flew to his hole in the floor and lay down flat on the tiles to listen. Soon cries rang out, then moans that someone seemed to be trying to stifle.

"What the devil!" D'Artagnan thought. "That sounds like a woman. . . . They are searching her. . . . She's resisting. . . . They're using force. . . . The scoundrels!"

In spite of his prudence, D'Artagnan restrained himself with great difficulty from taking part in the scene below.

"But I tell you I am the mistress of this house, gentlemen," the unhappy woman was saying. "I tell you I am Madame Bonacieux, I tell you I belong to the Queen!"

"Madame Bonacieux!" murmured D'Artagnan. "Have I been lucky enough to find the woman all of us have been looking for?"

"You are just the one we were waiting for," said one of her inquisitors.

Her voice kept growing harder to hear. Then there were convulsive movements that shook the wainscoting. Evidently the victim was resisting as much as one woman could resist four men.

"Pardon me, gentlemen, par——" murmured the voice. Then D'Artagnan could hear nothing but inarticulate sounds.

"They are gagging her, they are going to drag her away!" exclaimed D'Artagnan, rising as if he had been shot up by the release of a spring. "Where's my sword? Good, it's here by my side. Planchet!"

"Monsieur?"

"Run to find Athos, Porthos, and Aramis. One of the three is sure to be at home, and perhaps they all are. Tell them to come here at once, armed, and to come fast. . . . Oh, I remember now—Athos is at Monsieur de Tréville's."

"But where are you going yourself, monsieur?"

"I'm going down by way of the window, so as to get there quicker. Put back the tiles, sweep the floor, go out by the door, and hurry off."

"Oh, monsieur, monsieur, you'll be killed!" cried Planchet.

"Shut up, you fool!"

Then D'Artagnan, holding onto the outer sill of the window, let himself drop from the second story to the ground, and as fortunately that was not very far away, he was not hurt in the least. He went straight to the street door and knocked, murmuring:

"Now it's my turn to get caught in the mousetrap, and Heaven help the cats who pounce on a mouse like me!"

His knock had barely sounded when the tumult within ceased, steps approached, and the door opened. D'Artagnan, sword in hand, rushed into Master Bonacieux's apartment and the door, doubtless furnished with a spring, shut behind him.

Then those who were still in that unfortunate house, and also the nearest neighbors, heard loud cries, much stamping of feet, the clashing of swords, and the smashing of furniture. Then a moment later those who, startled by the uproar, had rushed to their windows saw the street door open and four men dressed in black come out, or rather fly out like so many frightened crows, strewing the ground with feathers from their wings—in other words, with bits of their clothes and fragments of their cloaks.

D'Artagnan had been the victor without much difficulty, it must be confessed, for only one policeman was armed, and he defended himself only for form's sake. True, the other three had tried to knock the young man down with chairs, stools, and crockery, but two or three scratches from the Gascon's blade terrified them. Ten minutes was a long enough time to complete their defeat.

Those neighbors who had opened their windows with the customary composure of Parisians in times of perpetual rioting and brawls closed them again as soon as they saw the four men in black flee. Their instinct told them that for the moment it was all over.

Left alone with Madame Bonacieux, D'Artagnan turned toward her. The poor woman was lying back in an armchair, half fainting. D'Artagnan surveyed her with a swift glance. She was a charming woman of twenty-five or twenty-six, a brunette with blue eyes, a slightly retroussé nose, admirable teeth, and a complexion of mingled rose and opal. There, however, ended any likeness she might have to a lady of rank. Her hands were white, but without delicacy, her feet were not those of a woman of quality. But fortunately D'Artagnan had not yet reached the point of noticing such details.

While D'Artagnan was standing near Madame Bonacieux and looking her over, he noticed a handkerchief of fine linen on the floor at her feet, and after his habit he picked it up. On one corner of it he recognized the same monogram he had seen on the handkerchief that had nearly caused him to have his throat cut by Aramis. Ever since that day D'Artagnan had mistrusted handkerchiefs with crests on them, so without saying a word he tucked into Madame Bonacieux's pocket the one he had just picked up.

At that moment Madame de Bonacieux opened her eyes, looked about her terrified, and saw that she and her liberator were alone in the room. She held out her hands to him with a smile—and Madame Bonacieux had the sweetest smile in the world.

"Ah, monsieur," she said, "you have saved me! Permit me to thank you."

"Madame," replied D'Artagnan, "I have only done what any gentleman in my place would have done. You owe me no thanks."

"Oh yes I do, monsieur, I certainly do, and I hope to prove to you that you have not done this service to an ingrate. But what could those men—I took them at first for robbers—want with me? And why isn't Monsieur Bonacieux here?"

"Madame, those men were far more dangerous than any robbers could be, for they are agents of Monsieur le Cardinal. As for your husband, he isn't here because he was arrested yesterday and taken to the Bastille."

"My husband in the Bastille!" cried Madame de Bonacieux. "Oh, my God! What has he done? Poor dear man, he is innocence itself!" And something like a smile broke out on the young woman's face, though she was still terrified.

"What has he done, madame?" returned D'Artagnan. "I think his only crime consists in having at once the good fortune and the misfortune to be your husband."

"But monsieur, then you know——"

"I know that you were abducted, madame."

"Who did it, monsieur? Do you know? Oh, if you do, tell me who it was!"

"It was a man of forty or forty-five who has black hair, a pale complexion, and a scar on his left temple."

"That's right, that is the man! But what is his name?"

"Oh, his name? That I do not know."

"And did my husband know that I had been abducted?"

"He was informed of it by a letter that the abductor himself sent him."

"Does he suspect the reason for it?"

"I believe he attributed it to some political motive."

"I did not think so at first, but now I agree with him. Then my dear Bonacieux did not suspect me for a moment?"

"Far from it, madame. He was very sure of your virtue, and especially of your love for him." A second smile, almost imperceptible, stole over the lips of the beautiful young woman. "But how did you escape?" D'Artagnan asked.

"I took advantage of a moment when I was left alone. I tied the sheets of my bed together and let myself down from the window. Then, thinking my husband would be at home, I hurried here."

"To put yourself under his protection?"

"Oh no! Poor dear man, I knew perfectly well that he was incapable of defending me. But he could be useful in other ways, so I wanted to talk to him."

"About what?"

"Oh, that is not my secret, so I cannot tell you."

"In any case, madame," said D'Artagnan, "I think this is no place to talk confidentially. The men I put to flight will return with reinforcements. If they find us here, we are lost. I have sent word to three of my friends, but who knows whether my messenger can find them?"

"Yes, yes, you are right!" cried Madame Bonacieux, terrified again. "Let us fly, let us escape!"

She put her arm through D'Artagnan's arm and pushed him along briskly.

"But where shall we fly to?" asked D'Artagnan. "Where escape to?"

"First let's get away from this house, then we shall see."

Without taking the trouble to shut the street door, the young woman and the young man walked quickly along the Rue des Fossoyeurs, turned into the Rue des Fosses-Monsieur-le-Prince, and did not stop until they reached the Place Saint-Sulpice.

"And now what are we to do?" queried D'Artagnan. "Where do you wish me to take you?"

"I am quite at a loss how to answer," replied Madame de Bonacieux, "I intended to send my husband to Monsieur de La Porte to tell him about it, so that Monsieur de La Porte could let us know what has been happening at the Louvre for the last three days, and whether it would be safe for me to go back there."

"But I can go to Monsieur de La Porte and tell him."

"Doubtless you could. But there is one difficulty about that. They know Monsieur Bonacieux at the Louvre, so they would let him enter, but they do not know you and they would close the gate against you."

"Bah!" said D'Artagnan. "Surely there is a gatekeeper at some gate to the Louvre who is devoted to you, and who at the password would——"

Madame Bonacieux, looking earnestly at the young man, interrupted him.

"And if I give you the password, will you promise to forget it as soon as you have used it?"

"Upon my word of honor, by my faith as a gentleman," answered D'Artagnan, in accents so sincere that it was impossible to doubt him.

"Very well, I believe you. You seem to be an honest young man. Besides, your services may well make your fortune."

"Without any promise of a reward, I swear I will do all I can to serve the King and to please the Queen."

"But I—where shall I go meanwhile?"

"Haven't you any friend to whose house Monsieur de La Porte can go to get you?"

"No. There's no one I dare trust."

"Wait a minute," said D'Artagnan, "we are near Athos's door. Yes, that's it!"

"Who is Athos?"

"One of my friends."

"But what if he is at home and sees me?"

"He isn't at home, and I will lock the door and take the key with me."

"Suppose he comes home?"

"He will not come home. Besides, if he did, he would be told that I had brought a woman there and that she was in his apartment."

"But that will compromise me sadly, you realize."

"What does that matter? Nobody knows you. Besides, in our situation we can ignore certain conventions!"

"Come, then, let's go to your friend's house. Where does he live?"

"Rue Férou, only a little way from here."

"Come, then!"

As D'Artagnan had foreseen, Athos was not at home. D'Artagnan got the key, which was always given him, since he was almost a member of the family, and took Madame Bonacieux to Athos's little apartment.

"Make yourself at home," he said. "Listen—bolt the door and do not open it unless you hear three raps like this." He rapped three times. "Two raps close together, and the third, a much softer rap, after an interval."

"Very well," said Madame Bonacieux. "Now it is my turn to give you instructions."

"I am all attention."

"Go in at the gate to the Louvre on the Rue de L'Echelle and ask for Germain, the gatekeeper. When Germain asks what you want, say 'Tours and Brussels.' He will immediately place himself at your orders."

"And what shall I order him to do?"

"Tell him to go fetch Monsieur de La Porte, the Queen's valet, and when Monsieur de La Porte comes, you will send him to me."

"Very well. But where and how shall I see you again?"

"Do you wish very much to see me again?"

"Certainly I do."

"Well, leave that to me, and don't worry."

D'Artagnan bowed to Madame Bonacieux, darting at her the most loving glance he could possibly concentrate on her charming little person. As he went down the stairs he heard the door being closed, double-locked, and bolted. In two bounds he was at the Louvre. As he was entering the gate on the Rue de L'Echelle the clock struck ten. All the events we have described had taken place within one half-hour.

Everything went as Madame Bonacieux had said it would. When he heard the password, Germain bowed. Ten minutes later La Porte was at the gatekeeper's lodge. In a few words D'Artagnan told him everything, including where Madame Bonacieux was then. La Porte made sure of the address by getting D'Artagnan to repeat it twice, then set off on a run. But he had taken no more than ten steps before he came back.

"Young man," he said to D'Artagnan, "I have a piece of advice to give you."

"Yes?"

"You may get into trouble over what has just happened. Have you by any chance a friend whose clock is sometimes slow?"

"Why?"

"Go call on him, so that he can testify that you were with him at half-past nine. In a law court that is called an alibi."

D'Artagnan found this advice prudent. He took to his heels and ran to Monsieur de Tréville's. But instead of going to the salon, where most of the visitors were, he asked to be shown into the Captain's office. A servant went to inform Monsieur de Tréville that his young fellow countryman had something important to tell him and solicited a private audience. Five minutes later Monsieur de Tréville was asking D'Artagnan what he could do to be of service to him, and why he was calling at so late an hour.

"Pardon me, monsieur," said D'Artagnan, who had taken advantage of the few minutes he was left alone to put back Monsieur de Tréville's clock three-quarters of an hour, "but I thought as it was only twenty-five minutes past nine, it was not too late to wait upon you."

"Twenty-five minutes past nine!" exclaimed Monsieur de Tréville, looking at the clock. "But that's impossible!"

"But you see the clock, monsieur. That tells the truth."

"True," said Monsieur de Tréville. "But I certainly thought it was much later. But tell me, what can I do for you?"

D'Artagnan proceeded to tell his Captain a long story about the Queen. He revealed all the fears he entertained with respect to Her Majesty, he told everything he had heard about the Cardinal's schemes with regard to Buckingham, and all that with such calm and such assurance that

Monsieur de Tréville was duped, and all the more easily because he had already noticed something new in the wind between the Cardinal, the King, and the Queen.

As ten o'clock was striking D'Artagnan left Monsieur de Tréville, who thanked him for the information he had brought and enjoined him to have the service of the King and Queen always at heart. But at the foot of the stairs D'Artagnan remembered that he had forgotten his cane, so he went upstairs again very fast, entered Monsieur de Tréville's office again, and with a turn of the finger set the clock right. Then, sure that now he had a witness to prove his alibi, he went downstairs again and soon found himself in the street.

CHAPTER 11

IN A THOUGHTFUL MOOD, D'ARTAGNAN TOOK THE LONG-
est way home. What was he thinking about when he strayed from his
path, gazed at the stars, sometimes sighing, sometimes smiling?

He was thinking of Madame Bonacieux. To an apprentice musketeer,
the young woman was almost the ideal of love. Comely, mysterious, initiated in almost all the secrets of the Court, and her beautiful face reflecting such charming gravity, presumably she was not heartless—and that
is an irresistible allurement to novices in love. Moreover, D'Artagnan had
delivered her from the hands of the demons who had searched her and
maltreated her, and this important service had established a bond of gratitude that might so easily assume a more tender character.

So swiftly do dreams soar on the wings of imagination that D'Artagnan
already saw himself being accosted by a messenger from the young
woman bringing him a note appointing a rendezvous, or a gold chain, or
a diamond. Young cavaliers accepted gifts from their King without shame,
and in those days of easy morals, they felt no more shame in accepting
them from their mistresses.

Men made their way in the world by the help of the mistresses without
a blush. The women who had nothing but beauty gave that, whence
doubtless the proverb arose: "The most beautiful girl in the world can
give no more than she has." Those who were rich gave some of their
money also, and a goodly number of heroes of that gallant period would
neither have won their spurs in the first place nor won their battles afterward without the more or less well-filled purses their mistresses fastened
to the saddlebows.

D'Artagnan possessed nothing. The diffidence of a provincial—that
slight patina, that ephemeral blossom, that down on the peach—soon
evaporated under the breath of the far from orthodox counsels the three
musketeers gave their friend. D'Artagnan, following the strange custom
of the times, considered himself to be fighting the campaign of Paris
exactly as if he were fighting on the field of battle, in Flanders fighting
Spaniards, in Paris fighting women. Everywhere there was an enemy to
fight and taxes to be levied.

But we must say that at this moment D'Artagnan was moved by much more noble and disinterested sentiments. The haberdasher had told him that he himself was rich, the young man had easily divined that with a simpleton like Monsieur Bonacieux it was the wife who kept the key to the purse. But all this in no way influenced the feelings the very sight of Madame Bonacieux roused in him, and his own interests were almost forgotten in the love he was beginning to feel for her. We say "almost" forgotten because the idea that a young, beautiful, graceful, and intelligent woman is rich as well does not detract in the least from the charm of awakening love, but on the contrary, it strengthens it.

But what about Monsieur Bonacieux, whom D'Artagnan had pushed into the arms of the myrmidons of the law while renouncing him aloud after having promised softly to save him? We must confess that D'Artagnan did not give him a thought, or if he did, it was only to tell himself that Bonacieux was very well where he was, wherever that might be. Love is the most selfish of all the passions.

Meditating on his future amours, discoursing to the night, smiling up at the stars, D'Artagnan turned into the Rue du Cherche-Midi (Chasse-Midi, it was then). As Aramis lived in this quarter, he suddenly decided to pay his friend a visit in order to explain why he had sent Planchet to him with a request to come immediately to the mousetrap.

"Now if Aramis had been at home when Planchet went there, he would of course have hurried to the Rue des Fossoyeurs, and when he found no one there except perhaps Athos and Porthos, no one of them would have known what all this meant. This mystery certainly calls for an explanation."

That is what D'Artagnan said aloud, then he thought to himself that this would give him a chance to talk about lovely little Madame Bonacieux, of whom his head, if not his heart, was full.

For the last two hours Paris had been dark, and the streets were almost deserted now. All the clocks in the Faubourg Saint-Germain were striking eleven. The weather was mild. D'Artagnan inhaled the fragrance from the Luxembourg Gardens, freshened by the dews of evening and the breeze of night.

When he came to the foot of the lane where the Rue d'Assas is now, D'Artagnan turned left, for the house where Aramis lived was between the Rue Cassette and the Rue Servandoni. He had just passed the Rue Cassette and could see the door of his friend's house, which was almost hidden by a cluster of sycamores and clematis, when he noticed something like a shadow emerging from the Rue Servandoni. This shadow was wrapped in a cloak, and D'Artagnan thought at first that it was a man, but by the slenderness of the figure, the hesitancy and nervousness of the gait, he soon recognized a woman. As if she were not certain of the house she was looking for, this woman kept looking about to make out where she was, stopped, retraced her steps, and again came back. D'Artagnan was puzzled.

"Should I go offer my services?" he thought. "Judging by the way she walks, I can see that she is young; perhaps she is pretty. Oh yes, but a woman who runs about the streets at night never does that unless she is going to meet her lover. Plague on it! To disturb a lovers' rendezvous wouldn't be the best way to get to know her!"

Meanwhile the young woman kept on coming nearer, counting the houses and the windows of each one. This was neither a long nor a difficult task, since there were only three houses in that part of the street and only two windows looking out on it, one in the pavilion alongside Aramis's home, and the other Aramis's own window.

"By the Lord," said D'Artagnan to himself, recalling the doctor's niece, "it would be droll if this late-flying dove were looking for my friend's house! But upon my soul, it looks like it. Aha, my dear Aramis, this time I mean to find you out!"

Making himself as thin as he could, he took shelter on the darkest side of the street. The young woman kept on coming, betraying herself not only by her light step but also by a little cough that suggested a sweet voice. D'Artagnan thought the cough was a signal. Whether this cough had been answered by a similar signal that settled the doubts of the nocturnal adventurer or whether without that aid she had recognized that she had reached the end of her journey, she went resolutely to Aramis's shutters and rapped three times, at equal intervals.

"It *is* Aramis she wants," murmured D'Artagnan. "Aha, Monsieur l'Hypocrite, so I've caught you studying theology!"

The three raps had barely sounded when the window was opened and light shone through the slats of the shutters.

"Aha!" cried our eavesdropper. "Not through doors, but through windows. So the visit was expected. Now the shutters will open and the lady will climb in! Very pretty!"

But to D'Artagnan's great astonishment, the shutters remained closed, the light that had shone out for an instant disappeared, and all was darkness once more. D'Artagnan thought that this could not last long, and he continued to look with both his eyes and listen with both his ears. He was right. After a few seconds two sharp raps were heard inside, the young woman in the street replied by a single rap, and the shutters were opened a little way. The reader may judge whether D'Artagnan looked and listened with avidity. Unfortunately the light had been moved into another room, but the young man's eyes were accustomed to the night. Besides, the eyes of Gascons, like those of cats, possess the faculty of seeing in the dark, so it is said.

Then D'Artagnan saw the young woman take a white object from her pocket. She unfolded it quickly into the shape of a handkerchief, held it up, and showed one corner of it to the person within. D'Artagnan recalled at once the handkerchief he had found lying at Madame Bonacieux's feet, which in turn had reminded him of the one he had pulled out from under Aramis's foot. What the devil could be the meaning of this handkerchief?

Standing where he was, D'Artagnan could not see Aramis's face—we say Aramis's because D'Artagnan had no doubt that it was his friend who was holding this dialogue of raps and gestures with the lady without. Curiosity prevailed over prudence. Taking advantage of the preoccupation of the pair over the handkerchief, he stole out of his hiding place and as swift as lightning, but stepping with the utmost caution, he took his stand, pressed close to an angle of the wall, whence he could see into Aramis's room.

As he looked in, he almost cried out in surprise. It was not Aramis who was conversing with the nocturnal visitor, but a woman. However, D'Artagnan could see only enough to recognize the shape of her clothing, not enough to distinguish her features.

Just then the woman in the room took a handkerchief out of her pocket and exchanged it for the one the visitor had shown her. The two women said a few more words, then the shutters closed. The woman outside the window turned and passed within four paces of D'Artagnan, pulling down the hood of her cloak. But the precaution was too late— D'Artgnan had already recognized Madame Bonacieux.

Madame Bonacieux! The suspicion that it was she had flashed across D'Artagnan's mind when she had taken the handkerchief from her pocket. But was it likely that Madame Bonacieux, who had sent for Monsieur de La Porte in order to be escorted back to the Louvre, was running about the streets of Paris alone at half-past eleven at night, at the risk of being abducted a second time?

This must be some business of great importance. And what is the most important business for a woman of twenty-five? Love. But was she exposing herself to such hazards on her own account, or for the sake of someone else? This was the question D'Artagnan asked himself. The demon of jealousy was already gnawing at his heart as cruelly as if he were no more and no less than her accepted lover.

But there was a very simple means of finding out where Madame Bonacieux was going—to follow her. The means was so simple that D'Artagnan made use of it at once. But when she saw the young man detach himself from the wall like a statue walking out of its niche, and heard the sound of his steps behind her, Madame Bonacieux uttered a little cry and fled. D'Artagnan ran after her. It was not a difficult task to overtake a woman encumbered by a long cloak. He came up to her before she was a third of the way down the street. The unhappy woman was exhausted, not by fatigue but by terror, and when D'Artagnan put his hand on her shoulder she sank on one knee, crying in a choking voice:

"Kill me if you will! You will learn nothing!"

D'Artagnan put his arm around her waist and lifted her to her feet, but when he felt by her limp weight that she was on the point of fainting, he made haste to reassure her by protestations of his devotion. These protestations meant nothing to Madame Bonacieux, for such protestations may be made with the most evil intentions in the world. But the voice that uttered them meant everything. The young woman opened her eyes, cast one glance at the man who had frightened her so badly, and, recognizing D'Artagnan, gave a cry of joy.

"Oh, it is you, it is you! Thank God, thank God!"

"Yes, it is I," said D'Artagnan. "It is I, whom God has sent to watch over you."

"Was that your purpose when you followed me?" the young woman asked, with a smile full of coquetry. All her fears had vanished the moment that she saw a friend in the man she had taken for an enemy.

"No," D'Artagnan replied. "I confess it was chance that led me to cross your path. I saw a woman rapping at the window of one of my best friends, Aramis."

"Aramis! Who is he?"

"Come now, do you mean to tell me that you don't know Aramis?"

"This is the first time I ever heard his name."

"So it's the first time you've ever been to his house?"

"Certainly."

"And didn't you know that a young man lived there—a musketeer?"

"No."

"Then he's not the one you were looking for?"

"Not in the least. Besides, you surely saw that the person I was talking to was a woman."

"Yes, I did. But that woman may be one of Aramis's little friends."

"I know nothing about that. It's none of my business."

"But who is she?"

"Oh, that is not my secret."

"My dear Madame Bonacieux, you are charming, but at the same time you are the most mysterious woman I——"

"Do I lose much by that?" she interrupted.

"No. On the contrary, you are adorable."

"Then give me your arm and be my escort."

"Where are you going?"

"You will see, since you will leave me at the door."

"Shall I wait for you?"

"That will not be necessary."

"You will go home alone, then?"

"Perhaps I shall, perhaps not."

"Well, if someone accompanies you, will that person be a man or a woman?"

"I don't know yet."

"But I will find out! I'll wait until you come out."

"If that's the case, farewell!"

"But you asked me to——"

"I asked for the assistance of a gentleman, not for the watchfulness of a spy."

" 'Spy' is rather harsh, isn't it?"

"What is the name for those who follow people who don't want them to?"

"They are indiscreet."

"That's too mild a word."

"Well, madame, I promise to do whatever you wish if you will allow me to accompany you where you are going."

"And you will leave me afterward and will not wait until I come out? On your word of honor?"

"By my faith as a gentleman."

"Give me your arm, then, and let us go."

D'Artagnan offered his arm to Madame Bonacieux, she took it, half laughing, half trembling, and they went on up the Rue de La Harpe. At the end of that street the young woman seemed to be in doubt again. But apparently she recognized one door by some sign or other, and she went toward it.

"Now, monsieur," she said, "this is the place where I have business to do. A thousand thanks for your honorable company. It has saved me from all the dangers to which I would have been exposed had I been alone. But the moment for you to keep your word has come. I have reached my destination."

"You are sure you will have nothing to fear on your way home?"

"I shall have nothing to fear but robbers. What could they get from me? I haven't a sou with me."

"You forget that beautiful embroidered handkerchief with the crest— the one I found lying at your feet and put back into your pocket."

"Hush, you wretch, hush!" cried the young woman. "Are you trying to ruin me?"

"You know very well you are still in danger, since a single word makes you tremble, and you admit that you would be ruined if anyone overheard that word. Oh come, madame," cried D'Artagnan, seizing her hand and gazing at her ardently, "come, be more generous! Trust yourself to me. Have you not read in my eyes that there is nothing but sympathy for and devotion to you in my heart?"

"Yes, I have," Madame Bonacieux replied. "If you ask me my own secrets, I will tell them to you, but the secrets of others—that is quite another thing."

"Very well," said D'Artagnan, "I shall discover them. Since these secrets may have an influence on your life, they must become mine too."

"Beware of doing that!" cried the young woman, so gravely that D'Artagnan shivered involuntarily. "Oh, I beg you not to get entangled in anything that concerns me. Do not seek to aid me in what I am doing. I ask this of you in the name of the service you have rendered me, which I shall never, never forget. Rather, believe implicitly all that I have told you. Feel no more concern for me. For you, I no longer exist; let it be as if you had never seen me."

"If you could see into my bared heart," said D'Artagnan, "you would read there so much curiosity that you would take pity on me, and so much love that you would instantly satisfy my curiosity. No woman has anything to fear from a man who loves her."

"You speak of love very suddenly," said the young woman, shaking her head.

"That is because love has come to me so quickly, and for the first time, and because I am not yet twenty." The young woman stole a look at him. "Listen to me, madame," D'Artagnan went on. "I am already on the scent. About three months ago I came near fighting a duel with Aramis over a handkerchief like the one you showed that woman in Aramis's house, a handkerchief marked in the same way, I am certain. But you, madame, think—if you were to be arrested with that handkerchief on you and the handkerchief seized, wouldn't you be compromised?"

"In what way? Aren't the initials mine? C. B., for Constance Bonacieux."

"Or for Camille de Bois-Tracy."

"Silence, monsieur! Once more I bid you be silent. Oh, if the dangers I fear for myself do not stop you, think of those *you* may be facing! Through knowing me you are in danger of imprisonment, perhaps of death!"

"Then I will not leave you."

"Monsieur," the young woman said, clasping her hands in supplication, "in the name of Heaven, upon honor of a soldier and the courtesy of a gentleman, go your way! Listen! That is midnight striking—that is the hour at which I am expected."

"Madame," said the Gascon, bowing, "I cannot refuse you when you put your request that way. Be content, I am going."

"But you will not follow me, you will not spy on me?"

"I will go home at once."

"Ah, I was sure of it! I knew you were a gallant young man!" cried Madame Bonacieux, offering him one hand and with the other seizing the knocker of a little door almost hidden in the wall.

D'Artagnan grasped the hand she offered him and kissed it ardently.

"Ah, I wish I had never seen you!" he cried, with that artless brutality which women often prefer to the affectation of courtesy, because it betrays the depths of a man's thought and proves that feeling is outweighing reason.

"Well," Madame Bonacieux said in a tone that was almost caressing as she pressed D'Artagnan's hand, which had not let go of hers, "well, I will not say as much about you! What is lost today is not lost forever. Who knows whether someday, when I am free to speak, I may not satisfy your curiosity?"

"And will you make the same promise to my love?" cried D'Artagnan, beside himself with joy.

"Oh, as to that I'm not willing to commit myself. That will depend on the feelings you are able to inspire in me. Today, monsieur, I have got no further than gratitude."

"Ah, you are too enchanting!" said D'Artagnan sadly. "And you are taking unfair advantage of my love."

"No, I am profiting by your generosity, that is all. But pray believe me—with certain people, everything comes right in the end."

"Oh, you are making me the happiest of men! Do not forget this evening, do not forget that promise."

"Rest easy. In due time and in the right place I will remember everything. So go now, go, in Heaven's name! I was expected at midnight on the hour and I am late."

"I'm going, I'm leaving. I mean to earn what's due me for my devotion, even if that devotion may be stupid. Adieu, madame, adieu!"

Apparently it was only by a great effort that he released the hand he was holding, then he dashed off on a run while Madame Bonacieux was knocking as she had knocked on Aramis's shutters, three slow raps equally spaced. When he reached the corner of the street, D'Artagnan turned. The door had opened and closed, the haberdasher's lovely wife had disappeared. D'Artagnan went on his way. He had given his word not to spy on Madame Bonacieux. Five minutes later he was in the Rue des Fossoyeurs.

"Poor Athos!" he said to himself. "He cannot have guessed what this is all about. He has probably fallen asleep waiting for me, or else he has gone home, in which case he was told some woman had been there. A woman in Athos's apartment! Well, after all, there was certainly one at Aramis's. All this is very strange, and I'd like very much to know how it will end."

"Badly, monsieur, badly," replied a voice that his master recognized as Planchet's. Soliloquizing aloud, as people often do when they are preoccupied, D'Artagnan had turned into the passage that led to his own staircase.

D'Artagnan and Madame Bonacieux after the Rout of the Black Men

D'Artagnan and Constance Bonacieux

"What do you mean by 'badly,' you imbecile?" he demanded. "What's happened?"

"All sorts of misfortunes. In the first place, Monsieur Athos has been arrested."

"Arrested! Athos arrested! What for?"

"He was found in your rooms, and they took him for you."

"Who arrested him?"

"Police brought by those men in black you put to flight."

"Why didn't he tell them his name? Why didn't he tell them he knew nothing whatever about this affair?"

"He took good care not to, monsieur. On the contrary, he said to me: 'It's your master who needs his liberty now, since he knows all about this business and I know nothing. The police will think they have arrested him, and that will give him time. In three days I will tell them who I am, and they'll have to let me go.' "

"Bravo, Athos, noble heart!" murmured D'Artagnan. "That's just like him. And what did the policemen do?"

"Four of them took him away, I don't know where—probably to the Bastille or to For-l'Evêque. Two of them stayed with the black men, who rummaged everywhere and seized all your papers. There were two more of them, who mounted guard at the street door while this search was going on. When it was finished, all of them went away, leaving the house empty and wide-open."

"What about Porthos and Aramis?"

"I couldn't find them, so they didn't come."

"But they may come at any moment. You left word that I was expecting them, didn't you?"

"Yes, monsieur."

"Well, don't you budge from here. If they come, tell them what happened and that they're to wait for me at the Fir Cone tavern. It would be dangerous to meet here—the house may be watched. I will hurry to Monsieur de Tréville's to let him know about all this, then I will join them at the tavern. But you stay here, now. You aren't afraid to, are you?"

"Don't you worry, monsieur," Planchet said. "You don't know me very well yet. I am brave enough when I put my mind on it—that's all I need to do. Besides, I am a Picard."

D'Artagnan hurried off to the Hôtel de Tréville. Monsieur de Tréville was not home; his company was on guard at the Louvre and he was with his men. D'Artagnan must find the Captain; it was imperative that he be informed of what was going on. The Gascon decided to try to get into the Louvre somehow. His uniform as a guardsman in Monsieur des Essarts's company would surely serve him as a passport.

He took the Rue des Petits-Augustins and came up on the quay to take the Pont-Neuf. For a minute he thought of taking the ferry over the Seine, but when he put his hand automatically into his pocket, he found that he had not the wherewithal to pay the fare.

As he reached the corner of the Rue Guénégaud he saw two persons coming out of the Rue Dauphine, a man and a woman. The woman looked very much like Madame Bonacieux and the man was the very image of Aramis. Moreover the woman wore that black cloak which D'Artagnan could still see outlined against the shutters on the Rue de Vangirard and against the door in the Rue de La Harpe. The man wore the uniform of a musketeer. The woman's hood was pulled down and the man was holding a handkerchief to his face.

They took the bridge, and since that was D'Artagnan's road to the Louvre, he followed them. He had not taken twenty steps before he became convinced that the woman was Madame Bonacieux and the man Aramis. He felt himself doubly betrayed, by his friend and by the woman he already loved as if she were his mistress. Madame Bonacieux had sworn by all she held holy that she did not know Aramis, and a quarter of an hour later here she was arm-in-arm with him!

D'Artagnan did not stop to consider that he had known the haberdasher's lovely wife for only three hours, that she owed him nothing save a little gratitude for saving her from the men in black, and that she had promised him nothing. He considered himself to be an outraged, betrayed, and ridiculed lover. His face flushed with anger, and he determined to solve this mystery. The young man and the young woman suddenly realized that they were being followed, and they redoubled their speed. D'Artagnan ran ahead of them, and turned back to meet them just in front of the Samaritaine in the light of a street lamp.

"What do you want, monsieur?" demanded the musketeer as he recoiled a step or two. He spoke with a foreign accent that proved to D'Artagnan at once that he had been mistaken in one part of his conjectures.

"It isn't Aramis!" he cried.

"No, monsieur, it isn't Aramis. From your exclamation I gather that you have mistaken me for someone else, and so I pardon you."

"You pardon me!" cried D'Artagnan.

"Yes," replied the stranger. "Allow me, then, to pass you, since I am not the one you have some business with."

"You are right, monsieur," D'Artagnan replied. "My business is not with you, but with Madame here."

"With Madame! But you do not know her."

"You're mistaken, monsieur. I know her very well."

"Ah," said Madame Bonacieux in a reproachful tone, "ah, monsieur, you gave me your word as a soldier and your faith as a gentleman. I hoped I could rely on that!"

"And I, madame," returned D'Artagnan, a little troubled, "you promised me——"

"Take my arm, madame," said the stranger, "and let us go on."

But D'Artagnan, dazed, dejected, almost annihilated by all that was happening to him, stood stock-still in front of the musketeer and Madame Bonacieux. The musketeer took two steps forward and pushed D'Artagnan aside. D'Artagnan sprang backward and drew his sword. At the same moment, swift as lightning, the stranger drew his.

"In the name of Heaven, Your Grace!" cried Madame Bonacieux, throwing herself between the combatants and seizing the swords with her bare hands.

"Your Grace!" cried D'Artagnan, suddenly enlightened. "Your Grace! Pardon me, monsieur, but is it possible you are——"

"His Grace the Duke of Buckingham," said Madame Bonacieux in an undertone. "And now you may ruin all of us."

"Your Grace, madame, I ask a hundred pardons. But I love her, my lord, and I was jealous. You know what it is to love, my lord. Pardon me, and then tell me how I may risk my life to serve Your Grace."

"You're a gallant young man," said Buckingham, holding out a hand that D'Artagnan pressed with great respect. "You offer me your services and I accept them. Follow us at a distance of twenty paces until we reach the Louvre. If anyone shadows us, kill him!"

D'Artagnan put his naked sword under his arm, allowed Madame Bonacieux and the Duke to go twenty steps further, then followed them, ready to carry out the instructions of the noble and elegant Minister of Charles I. But fortunately he found no occasion to give the Duke proof of his devotion, and the young woman and the handsome musketeer entered the Louvre by the Rue de L'Echelle gate without being molested.

D'Artagnan immediately repaired to the Fir Cone tavern, where he found Porthos and Aramis waiting for him. He gave them no explanation of the trouble he had put them to, telling them only that he had finished by himself the business for which he had thought for a moment he might need their help.

CHAPTER 12

MADAME BONACIEUX AND THE DUKE ENTERED THE Louvre without difficulty, for Madame Bonacieux was known to belong to the Queen, and the Duke wore the uniform of the Royal Musketeers, who were on guard that evening. Besides, Germain, the gatekeeper, was on the Queen's side.

Once they had entered the courtyard, the Duke and the young woman skirted the palace wall for some twenty-five paces, then Madame de Bonacieux pushed at a small service door that was open by day but usually closed at night. The door opened and they went in to find themselves in complete darkness. But Madame Bonacieux knew all the turnings and windings of this part of the Louvre, which was used by the servitors of the royal household. She closed the door behind her, took the Duke's hand, felt her way along, got hold of a banister, and began to go up a staircase. The Duke counted two stories, then his guide turned to the right, followed a long corridor, went down a staircase to the first story, and a few steps farther on she put a key into a lock, opened a door, and pushed the Duke into a room lighted only by a night lamp.

"Stay here, Your Grace," she said. "Someone will come." Then she went out by the same door, which she locked, so that now the Duke was literally a prisoner.

Nevertheless, locked in though he was, the Duke of Buckingham did not experience an instant of fear. One of his most salient characteristics was his search for adventure, his love of the romantic. Brave, rash, and enterprising as he was, this was not the first time he had risked his life in such an affair. He had learned that the message purporting to come from Anne of Austria which had brought him to Paris was a trap, and instead of going back to England, he had sent word to the Queen that he positively would not go without having seen her. At first the Queen had absolutely refused to receive him, but then she grew afraid that the Duke, exasperated, might commit some folly. Therefore she had decided to receive him, and to urge him to leave Paris at once, when, on the very evening she had made this decision, Madame Bonacieux, who was to meet the Duke and lead him to the Louvre, was abducted. For two days nobody knew what had become of her, so everything remained in suspense. But once Madame Bonacieux was free again and in touch with La Porte, matters resumed their course, and now she had accomplished the perilous enterprise.

When he was alone, Buckingham went to a mirror. His musketeer's uniform was wonderfully becoming to him. At thirty-five, he passed, and with good reason, for the most handsome gentleman and the most gallant cavalier in either France or England. The favorite of two English kings, immensely rich, all-powerful in a kingdom that he turned upside down at any whim and calmed again as capriciously, George Villiers, Duke of Buckingham, led one of those fabulous lives which through the centuries have continued to amaze posterity. Sure of himself, convinced of his own power, certain that the laws which governed other men could not touch him, he went straight to any goal he aimed at, even if the goal was so high and so splendid that any other man would have been insane to have even contemplated reaching it. Hence it was that, having succeeded several times in gaining access to the beautiful and proud Anne of Austria, he had won her love by dazzling her. Standing before the mirror, George Villiers restored the waves of his beautiful blond hair that his hat had disordered and twisted his mustache. His heart swelling with joy, happy and proud at being so close to the moment he had yearned for so long, he smiled at his image with pride and hope.

Suddenly a door concealed in the tapestry opened and a woman appeared. In the mirror Buckingham saw this apparition and he uttered a cry. It was the Queen!

Anne of Austria was then some twenty-six or twenty-seven—that is, she was in the full splendor of her beauty. Her bearing was that of a queen or a goddess. Her eyes, sparkling like emeralds, were wonderfully beautiful and full of both sweetness and majesty. Her mouth was small and rosy, and though her underlip, like that of all the members of the Royal House of Austria, protruded a little, that mouth was notably gracious when she smiled, though as profoundly disdainful when she scorned. Her skin was much admired for its velvety softness, her hands and arms were of surpassing beauty—all the poets of her time sang of them as incomparable. Her hair, which had been golden in her youth, had become a lovely chestnut. She wore it curled very simply and well powdered, and it framed her face so admirably that the most severe critic could only have wished for a little less rouge, and the most exacting sculptor only for a nose a little more delicately chiseled.

Buckingham was dazzled for a moment. Never had Anne of Austria seemed to him so beautiful at Court balls and fetes and at tournaments as she seemed to him at this moment dressed in a simple gown of white satin. She was accompanied by Doña Estefana, the only one of her Spanish women who had not been driven from her by the King's jealousy or the Cardinal's persecution. Anne of Austria took two steps forward, Buckingham threw himself at her feet, and before the Queen could prevent him he had kissed the hem of her gown.

"Your Grace, you must already know that it was not I who wrote you."

"Oh yes, madame, yes, Your Majesty!" cried the Duke. "I know that I was a fool, a madman, to think that snow might come to life, that marble might grow warm. But what will you, madame? It is easy for a lover to believe in love. Besides, my journey is not a complete loss, since at least I am seeing you."

"Yes," Anne replied, "but you know why and how I am seeing you. Indifferent to all my sorrows, you have persisted in remaining in a city where you risk your life and cause me to risk my honor. I am receiving you in order to tell you that everything keeps us apart—the depths of the sea, the enmity of kingdoms, the sanctity of marriage vows. It is sacrilege to struggle against so many obstacles, my lord. In short, I am seeing you to tell you that we must never meet again."

"Speak on, madame, speak on, O Queen!" said Buckingham. "The sweetness of your voice makes up for the harshness of your words. You speak of sacrilege, but surely it is sacrilege to separate two hearts that God made for each other."

"Your Grace," cried the Queen, "you forget that I have never told you that I loved you!"

"But you have never told me that you did *not* love me, and in truth to speak such words to me would be far too ungrateful on Your Majesty's part. For tell me, where will you find a love like mine, a love that neither time nor absence nor despair can destroy, a love content with a lost ribbon, a stray glance, a chance word? It is three years, madame, since I saw you for the first time, and for three years I have loved you thus.

"Shall I tell you how you were dressed that day, every detail of the ornaments you wore? Indeed I can see you now as I saw you then. You were sitting on cushions of the Spanish fashion. You wore a gown of green satin embroidered with gold and silver, with long sleeves that were fastened up over those lovely arms with large diamonds. You wore a full ruff, a little cap of the same color as your gown, and in that cap a heron feather. Oh, madame, madame, I can shut my eyes and I see you as you were then. I open them again and I see you as you are now—a hundred times more beautiful!"

"What folly!" murmured Anne of Austria, who had not the courage to rebuke the Duke for having kept her portrait in his heart so faithfully. "What folly to feed a fruitless passion with such memories!"

"And on what do you wish me to live? I have nothing but memories. They are my happiness, my treasure, my hope. Every time I see you is one more diamond to shut into the casket of my heart. This is the fourth diamond you have let fall and I have picked up. For in three years, madame, I have seen you but four times. The first one I have just described, the second was at the house of Madame de Chevreuse, the third in the garden at Amiens."

"Your Grace," said the Queen, blushing, "do not speak of that evening."

"On the contrary, madame, let us speak of it, for it was the one happy and radiant evening of my life. Do you remember what a beautiful night it was? How soft and balmy the air was, how blue the sky studded with silver stars! Ah, that night for one moment I succeeded in being alone with you, that night you were ready to tell me everything—the loneliness of your life, the sorrows of your heart. You were leaning on my arm, do you remember?—on this very arm. As I bowed my head I could feel your hair brush my cheek, and every time it touched me I trembled from head to foot. O my queen, my queen, you do not know what heavenly happiness, what paradisiacal joy such a moment holds! Believe me, I would give all my possessions, my whole fortune, all my glory, all the days I have yet to live, for another moment like that, for another night like that! For that night, madame, that night you loved me, I swear it."

"Your Grace, it is possible, yes, that the influence of that lovely garden, the enchantment of that beautiful night, the fascination of your gaze—oh, the thousand and one circumstances that sometimes unite to destroy a woman—that all these crowded around me on that fatal night. But you saw it yourself, my lord—at the first word you dared speak, at the first rash words to which I must reply, the Queen came to the rescue of the faltering woman and I summoned my attendants."

"Yes, yes, that is true, and any other love than mine would have perished under that ordeal, but my love emerged from it more ardent and more eternal. You thought to escape me by returning to Paris, you thought I would not dare quit the treasure over which my master had charged me to watch. Ah, what do all the treasures of the world, all the kings on the earth, matter to me? A week later I was back again, madame. That time you had nothing to say to me. I had risked my King's favor and my life to see you for one second. I did not even touch your hand, and you forgave me when you saw me so submissive and so repentant."

"Yes, but calumny seized on all those follies, in which I took no part, as you know very well, my lord. The King, instigated by Monsieur le Cardinal, made a terrible outcry. Madame de Vernet was driven from me, Madame de Chevreuse fell into disfavor, and remember, my lord, that when you sought to return as Ambassador the King himself refused to accept you."

"Yes, and now France is about to pay with a war for her King's refusal. Now I may no longer see you, madame. Very well, I mean to have you hear my name every day. What is the purpose, think you, of this expedition to the Ile de Ré, and this league with the Protestants of La

Rochelle? It is the pleasure of my seeing you once more. I cannot hope to make my way into Paris sword in hand, I know that very well. But this war will end in a peace, and peace calls for a negotiator, and that negotiator will be I. No one will dare refuse me then, and I shall return to Paris, I shall see you again, and I shall be happy for a moment. It is true that thousands of men will have to pay for my happiness with their lives, but what does that matter to me provided I see you once more? Perhaps all that is folly, madness, but tell me, what woman ever had a lover more deeply in love, what queen ever had a more ardent servant?"

"My lord, my lord, you call to your defense arguments that accuse you still more. Your Grace, all these proofs of love you invoke are little better than crimes."

"Because you do not love me, madame. If you loved me, how differently you would look at all this! If you loved me—oh, but if you loved me, I would be too happy, and I would go mad. Ah, Madame de Chevreuse, of whom you spoke just now, Madame de Chevreuse was less cruel than you. Lord Holland loved her, and she returned his love."

"Madame de Chevreuse was not a queen," murmured Anne of Austria, overcome in spite of herself by the expression of so deep a love.

"Would you love me, then, if you were not a queen—tell me, would you love me then? You mean that I may believe that only the dignity of your rank makes you cruel to me? I thank you for those sweet words, I thank my beauteous sovereign, a hundred times I thank her."

"My lord, you have misunderstood me. I did not mean to say——"

"Do not say it, I beg of you!" cried the Duke. "If my happiness is an illusion, do not be so cruel as to deprive me of it. You have told me yourself that I have been lured into a trap, and it may be that I shall lose my life in it. Though it may seem strange to you, for some time I have had a presentiment that I am soon to die." And the Duke smiled a smile that was both sad and charming.

"Oh, my God!" cried Anne of Austria in a tone of terror that revealed how much greater interest she took in the Duke than she was willing to put into words.

"I do not tell you this to frighten you, madame. No—what I said is even ridiculous, and believe me, I take no heed of such dreams. But the words you have spoken, the hope you have almost given me, would pay richly for everything, even were it my life."

"But I too, Your Grace, have had presentiments, I too have had dreams. I dreamed once that I saw you lying wounded and bathed in blood."

"Wounded in the left side, was I not, and by a knife?" interrupted Buckingham.

"Yes, it was so, my lord, it was so—in the left side by a knife. Who can possibly have told you that I had had that dream? I confessed it only to God, and in my prayers."

"I ask for no more. You love me, madame. All is well with me."

"I love you, *I?*"

"Yes, you. Would God send the same dreams to you that He sends to me if you did not love me? Would we have the same presentiments if our two lives were not made one by our hearts? You love me, madame, and you will weep for me!"

"O my God, my God," cried Anne of Austria, "this is more than I can bear! In the name of Heaven, Your Grace, I beg you to go. I do not know whether I love you or do not love you, but I do know that I will not swear falsely. Take pity on me, then, and go. Oh, if you were struck down in France, if you were to die in France, and I supposed that your love for me was the cause of your death, nothing could console me, I should go mad. Go, then, go, I beseech you."

"Oh, how beautiful you are now! Oh, how I love you!"

"Go, go, I implore you. Come back later, come back as Ambassador, come back as Minister, surrounded by guards who will defend you, by servitors who will watch over you. Then I shall no longer fear for your life, and I will find happiness in seeing you."

"Oh, is what you are saying really true?"

"It is."

"Then give me some token of your indulgence, some object that comes from you and will assure me that I am not dreaming—something that you have worn on your person and that I may wear in my turn—a ring, a necklace, a chain."

"And will you go then, will you go if I give you what you ask for? This very instant? You will leave France? You will go back to England?"

"I will, I swear to you that I will."

"Wait, then, wait." Anne of Austria went back to her bedroom and returned almost immediately with a small rosewood casket that bore her initials in gold. "Here, my lord, here," she said. "Keep this in memory of me." Buckingham took the casket and knelt for a second time. "You promised me that you would go," said the Queen.

"And I keep my word. Your hand, your hand, madame, and I go."

Closing her eyes, Anne of Austria offered him one hand, and pressed the other one down on Doña Estefana's shoulder, for she felt her strength about to give way. Buckingham pressed his lips passionately to that beautiful hand, then said as he rose:

"Within six months, if I am not dead, I shall see you again, madame, if I have to upset the whole world to do it."

Then, faithful to his promise, he rushed out of the room. In the corridor he met Madame Bonacieux, who was waiting for him, and with the same precautions and the same good fortune as in coming, she guided him out of the Louvre.

CHAPTER 13

THE POLICEMEN WHO HAD ARRESTED MONSIEUR BONA-
cieux took him straight to the Bastille, where, trembling with fear, he was
marched past a platoon of soldiers who were loading their muskets. Then
he was taken down to a subterranean corridor, where his conductors submitted him to the grossest insults and the roughest treatment. They saw
that he was not a gentleman, and they treated him like a mere peasant.

After half an hour or so, a registrar came to put an end to his torment,
though not to his uneasiness, by giving orders to lead Monsieur Bonacieux to the Investigation Section. Two guards grabbed the haberdasher
and marched him across a courtyard and into a corridor guarded by three
sentinels, opened a door, and pushed him into a low-ceilinged room with
one table, one chair, and a Commissioner. The Commissioner was seated
in the chair and busy writing at the table. The two guards led the prisoner
toward the table, and at a gesture from the Commissioner drew back out
of hearing. The Commissioner, who had been bending his head low over
his papers, looked up to see what sort of person he had to deal with. He
was a crabbed-looking man with a pointed nose, sallow and prominent
cheekbones, small but piercing eyes, and an expression that had something of the weasel and something of the fox.

He began by asking Monsieur Bonacieux to give his family name, his
Christian name or names, his age, his occupation, and his address. The
accused replied that his name was Jacques Michel Bonacieux, he was
fifty-one, he was a retired haberdasher, and he lived at No. 11 Rue des
Fossoyeurs. Then the Commissioner, instead of questioning him further,
made a long speech about the danger an obscure bourgeois runs in
meddling with public affairs. He complicated this exordium by an ex-
position in which he related the power and the deeds of Monsieur le
Cardinal, that incomparable Minister, that conqueror of previous Ministers, that exemplar of future Ministers—deeds and power that no one
could thwart with impunity.

After this second part of his discourse, fixing his hawk's eyes on poor
Bonacieux, he bade him reflect on the seriousness of his situation. The
haberdasher had already reflected and had consigned to the Devil the

moment when Monsieur de La Porte had conceived the idea of marrying him to his goddaughter, and especially the moment when that goddaughter had been accepted as the Queen's seamstress.

Monsieur Bonacieux's character was one of profound selfishness mixed with sordid greed and seasoned with arrant cowardice. His love for his young wife was a quite secondary emotion; it could not overpower the primary emotions just enumerated. He thought over carefully what had just been said to him, then he remarked coolly:

"But Monsieur le Commissaire, I beg you to believe that I know and admire more than anyone else the merit of His Incomparable Eminence by whom we have the honor to be governed."

"Really?" said the Commissioner in a doubting tone. "If that is true, how comes it that you are in the Bastille?"

"How I am here, or rather why I am here, is something it is quite impossible for me to tell you, because I don't know myself. But certainly it is not for having displeased Monsieur le Cardinal in any way—not consciously, at least."

"Nevertheless you must have committed some crime, since you were brought here accused of high treason."

"High treason?" cried Bonacieux, terrified. "High treason! And how do you think a poor haberdasher who hates the Huguenots and abhors the Spaniards can be accused of high treason? Consider, Monsieur—that's absolutely impossible!"

"Monsieur Bonacieux," said the Commissioner, staring at the accused man as if his little eyes could read the very depths of his heart, "you have a wife, have you not?"

"Yes, monsieur," replied the haberdasher, shaking all over, and sensing that this was where he was going to get into trouble. "At least I *had* one."

"What! You *had* one! What have you done with her if you no longer have her?"

"They took her away, monsieur."

"*They* took her away, eh?" said the Commissioner. "And do you know who abducted her?"

"I think I do."

"Who?"

"Remember that I'm not accusing anyone, Monsieur le Commissaire. I only have suspicions."

"Whom do you suspect? Come now, answer me frankly!"

Monsieur Banacieux was in a quandary. Should he deny everything or tell everything? If he denied everything, he might be suspected of knowing too much to confess it. If he told everything, he would prove his good will. So he decided to tell the whole story.

"I suspect," he bgan, "a tall dark man of lofty bearing—he looks like a great lord. I think he's the man who followed us several times when I

used to wait for my wife at one of the Louvre gates to take her home."
The Commissioner seemed to be uneasy. "And his name?" he asked.

"Oh, his name—I don't know it. But if ever I were to see him again,
I'd recognize him at once, even if he were one among a thousand."

The Commissioner frowned. "So you could pick him out of a thousand, could you?"

"I mean, monsieur," stammered Bonacieux, who sensed that he had
gone wrong somehow. "I mean——"

"You have said that you would recognize him," said the Commissioner. "Very well, that's enough for today. Before we proceed further, I
must tell a certain person that you know who abducted your wife."

"But I didn't tell you I knew him!" cried Bonacieux in despair. "On
the contrary, I told you——"

"Take the prisoner away," the Commissioner said to the two guards.

"Where are we to take him?"

"To a cell—the first one you come to if it has a good lock," the Commissioner replied with an indifference that horrified poor Bonacieux.

"Woe is me!" he said to himself. "Misfortunes hang over my head. My
wife must have committed some terrible crime. They think I am her accomplice, and they will punish me along with her. She must have talked,
she must have vowed that she told me all about it. A woman is so weak!
A cell, the first one they come to! I see it all—one night that will pass
quickly, and tomorrow torture, then the gallows! O God, God, have
mercy on me!"

The guards, quite accustomed to hearing the lamentations of prisoners,
paid no heed to Master Bonacieux's, and led him away, while the Commissioner was hurriedly writing a letter that his clerk was waiting to take.

Bonacieux did not close his eyes, not because the cell was too disagreeable, but because his anxiety was too great to allow him to sleep. All
night he sat on his stool, trembling at the slightest noise, and when the
first rays of the sun stole into his cell, the very dawn seemed to him to
have taken on a funereal color. Suddenly he heard the bolts of his cell
door drawn back, and he gave a fearful start. He was sure they were coming to take him to the scaffold. When he saw only the Commissioner and
the clerk of the day before, he was ready to embrace both of them.

"Your affair has become much more complicated since last night, my
good man," said the Commissioner, "and I advise you to tell the whole
truth. Only your contrition can avert the Cardinal's anger."

"But I am ready to tell everything," pleaded Bonacieux, "at least
everything I know. Question me, monsieur, I beg of you."

"In the first place, where is your wife?"

"Why, I told you she was abducted."

"You did, but at five o'clock yesterday afternoon, thanks to you, she
escaped."

"My wife escaped!" cried Bonacieux. "Oh, the poor woman! If she escaped, I swear to you that it is no fault of mine."

"What was your business, then, when you visited your neighbor Monsieur d'Artagnan that day and had a long conference with him?"

"Ah yes, Monsieur le Commissaire, I did visit Monsieur d'Artagnan, and I admit that I was wrong in doing that."

"What was the purpose of your visit?"

"To beg him to help me find my wife. I thought I was right in trying to get her back. Apparently I was mistaken, and I beg your pardon humbly."

"What was Monsieur d'Artagnan's answer?"

"Monsieur d'Artagnan promised to help me, but I soon realized that he was deceiving me."

"You are deceiving the law! Monsieur d'Artagnan made an agreement with you, and in pursuance of that agreement he put to flight the police officers who had arrested your wife and he hid her somewhere where they could not find her."

"Monsieur d'Artagnan carried off my wife! Whatever do you mean?"

"Fortunately Monsieur d'Artagnan is in our hands, and you're going to be confronted with him."

"By my faith, I ask for nothing better!" cried Bonacieux. "I shall not be sorry to see the face of someone I know."

"Bring in Monsieur d'Artagnan," ordered the Commissioner, and the two guards produced Athos.

"Monsieur d'Artagnan," said the Commissioner, "make a full statement of what passed yesterday between you and Monsieur here."

"But this isn't Monsieur d'Artagnan!" cried Bonacieux.

"What! This is not Monsieur d'Artagnan?"

"Never in the world," Bonacieux replied.

"Then what is this gentleman's name?"

"I cannot tell you. I don't know him."

"What! You don't know him? Have you never seen him?"

"Yes, I have seen him, but I don't know what his name is."

"What is your name?" demanded the Commissioner.

"Athos," replied the musketeer.

"That is not a man's name, that is the name of a mountain!" the poor questioner cried, beginning to feel bewildered.

"It is *my* name," Athos answered quietly.

"But you said your name was D'Artagnan."

"*I* said so?"

"You certainly did."

"No, Monsieur le Commissaire. Somebody said to me, 'You are Monsieur d'Artagnan,' and I said, 'Do you think so?' The guards cried out that they were sure I was. I didn't wish to contradict them. Besides, I might be mistaken."

"Monsieur, you are insulting the majesty of the law. You are Monsieur d'Artagnan."

"There, you see, you are telling me that again."

"But I tell you, Monsieur le Commissaire," Monsieur Bonacieux cried, "that there's not the least doubt about it. Monsieur d'Artagnan is a lodger of mine, and though he does not pay his rent, or rather *because* he doesn't pay it, I ought to know him. Monsieur d'Artagnan is a youth of no more than nineteen or twenty, and Monsieur here is at least thirty. Monsieur d'Artagnan is in Monsieur des Essarts's company of the Royal Guards, and this gentleman belongs to Monsieur de Tréville's musketeers. Just look at his uniform, Monsieur le Commissaire, look at his uniform!"

"That's true," muttered the Commissioner. "By the Lord, that's true."

Just then the door was opened quickly and one of the gatekeepers of the Bastille ushered in a messenger, who gave the Commissioner a letter.

"Oh, the unhappy woman!" cried the Commissioner as he finished reading the letter.

"What's that? What do you mean? Who is it you're speaking of? Not my wife, I hope."

"Exactly—of her. You're getting into trouble now, let me tell you."

"But see here, monsieur," cried the haberdasher, growing angry, "be good enough to tell me how I can get into trouble because of what my wife is doing while I am in prison!"

"Because what she is doing is to carry out a plan you two agreed on, a diabolical plan!"

"I swear to you, Monsieur le Commissaire, that you are absolutely mistaken. I know nothing whatever about what my wife was to do. I don't know anything about what she has done, and if she has committed any follies, I renounce her, I abjure her, I curse her!"

"Come now," Athos said to the Commissioner, "if you have no further need of me, pray send me somewhere else. Your Monsieur Bonacieux bores me."

"Take the prisoners back to their cells," ordered the Commissioner, "and see that they are guarded more closely than ever."

"Nevertheless," said Athos, with his customary calmness, "if it's Monsieur d'Artagnan you're interested in, I don't see any too clearly how I can take his place."

"Do as I bade you," said the Commissioner to the guards. "And solitary confinement for them. You understand!"

Athos shrugged his shoulders and followed the guards without a word, while Monsieur Bonacieux uttered lamentations that would break the heart of a tiger. The haberdasher was taken back to the same cell he had occupied the night before. All day he sat there weeping like a real haberdasher. About nine in the evening, he heard steps in the corridor. The steps drew near his cell, the door was thrown open, and the guards appeared, with an officer close behind them.

"Follow me," said the officer.

"Follow you?" cried Bonacieux. "Follow you at this hour? Where, in the name of God?"

"Where we have orders to take you."

"But that is no answer."

"It is the only answer we can give you."

"Oh, my God, my God," murmured the poor haberdasher, "now I am lost indeed!"

He followed the guards like an automaton, offering no resistance. He passed through the same corridor as before, crossed a courtyard, and at last went out the gate to find a carriage surrounded by four guards on horseback. He was pushed into the carriage, the officer took his place beside him, the door was locked, and the prison on wheels moved off as slowly as if it were a hearse.

Through the locked windows the prisoner could see houses and sidewalks, no more, but true Parisian that he was, Bonacieux could recognize every street by its pavements, its signs, and its street lamps. As the carriage approached Saint-Paul, where prisoners from the Bastille are usually executed, he almost fainted, and he crossed himself twice. He thought the carriage was to stop there but it went on. Further on, as the carriage passed the Cimitière Saint-Jean, where state criminals were buried, again he was filled with great terror. One thing reassured him a little: he remembered that their heads were usually cut off before their burial, and his head was still on his shoulders.

But when he saw by the pointed roof of the Hôtel de Ville that the carriage was going toward the Place de Grève, he was sure it was all over with him. He tried to confess his sins to the officer, and when the officer refused to listen, he uttered such piteous screams that the officer declared that if Bonacieux went on deafening him that way, he would gag him. This threat reassured Bonacieux a little. If they were going to execute him on the Place de Grève, they wouldn't bother to gag him, since they were almost there. The carriage crossed the fatal spot and rolled on.

Now there was only the Croix-du-Trahoir to fear, and the carriage was on the way there. This time there was no longer any doubt, for all lesser criminals were executed there. Bonacieux had flattered himself when he had thought he was worthy of Saint-Paul or the Place de Grève. It was the Croix-du-Trahoir that was to be the end of his journey and his life! He could not yet see that awful cross, but he could almost feel it advancing to meet him. Twenty paces from it, he heard the sound of many voices, and the carriage stopped. This was more than poor Bonacieux could stand. Crushed by the emotions he had experienced, one after the other, he gave a feeble groan that anyone would have thought the last sigh of a dying man, and really fainted.

CHAPTER 14

THE CROWD THAT HAD GATHERED THERE HAD NOT COME
expecting to see a man hanged, but to contemplate a man already hanged.
The carriage stopped only a moment, then resumed its way along the
Rue Saint-Honoré, turned into the Rue des Bons-Enfants, and stopped
before a low door. The door opened, two guards took Bonacieux between
them, the officer helped to hold him erect, they pushed him along a corridor, marched him up a stairway, and deposited him in an antechamber.

Bonacieux was put through all these motions as if he were a machine.
He had walked along like a man in a dream, he caught glimpses of
the objects about him as though through a fog, his ears heard sounds
without identifying them. He might have been executed at that moment
without his making a single gesture in his defense or uttering one cry for
mercy. He stayed sitting on a bench, his back against the wall and his
arms hanging at his sides, in exactly the spot where the guards had set
him.

But when he looked about him he could see no sign of danger. The
bench was comfortably upholstered, the walls were hung with beautiful
Cordovan leather, and great red damask curtains, fastened by gold clasps,
floated before the windows. Gradually he realized that his fears had
been exaggerated, and he began to move his head right and left, up and
down. As nobody offered any objection to these motions, he gathered a
little courage, and ventured to draw up one leg and then the other. Finally,
with the help of both hands, he lifted himself from the bench and found
himself on his feet.

At that moment an officer who looked quite pleasant opened a door,
exchanged a few words with someone in the next room, and then turned
toward the prisoner.

"Is your name Bonacieux?" he asked.

"Yes, Monsieur l'Officier," stammered the haberdasher, more dead
than alive, "at your service."

"Come in here," said the officer.

Bonacieux obeyed without a word. He found himself in a large room,
its walls hung with weapons offensive and defensive. The atmosphere

was stifling; there was a fire on the hearth, though it was only late September. A square table standing in the center was covered with books and papers, and over them was spread a map of the city of La Rochelle.

Standing with his back to the fire was a man of medium height. His mien was proud and haughty, his eyes were piercing, his forehead high, and his face thin and made to seem longer by an imperial, as the short, pointed beard was called, above which was a mustache. Although this man was thirty-six, or at most thirty-seven, his hair, mustache, and beard were already growing gray. Except that he wore no sword, he looked every inch a soldier.

This man was Armand-Jean Duplessis, Cardinal-Duc de Richelieu. Not the Richelieu we see pictured today—a broken-down old man, suffering like a martyr, his body bent, his voice all but gone, his person buried in an armchair as if in a tomb, still alive only by the vigor of his genius and maintaining his struggle with all Europe only by the never-ceasing labor of his mind. This is Richelieu as he really was at that period—an adroit and gallant cavalier, frail in body, but sustained by that moral power which made him one of the most extraordinary men who ever lived. This was the one who had captured Nîmes, Castres, and Uzès, and who now was preparing to drive the English from the Ile de Ré and to lay siege to La Rochelle. At first glance, nothing in his look denoted the Cardinal; it was impossible for those who did not know his face to guess who the man was in whose presence they were.

The poor haberdasher remained standing by the door while the man by the fire concentrated on him, seeming to mean to penetrate the very depths of his past life. After a moment of silence, he asked:

"Is this that man Bonacieux?"

"Yes, Monseigneur," the officer replied.

"Good. Give me those papers, and go."

The officer took the papers Richelieu had pointed to, gave them to him, bowed very low, and left the room. Bonacieux recognized those papers as the transcript of his examination at the Bastille. From time to time the man by the fireside raised his eyes from the record and plunged them like daggers into the poor haberdasher's heart. After ten minutes of reading and ten seconds of scrutiny, the Cardinal had made his decision.

"That head there never conspired," he murmured. "But no matter, let's see all the same." Then the Cardinal said slowly to Bonacieux, "You are accused of high treason."

"So I have been told, Monseigneur," said Bonacieux, giving his questioner the title he had heard the officer use, "but I swear to you that I know nothing about it."

"You have conspired with your wife," said the Cardinal, repressing a smile, "with Madame de Chevreuse, and with His Grace the Duke of Buckingham."

"No Monseigneur, I have not. But I have heard my wife mention those names."

"On what occasion?"

"She said once that the Cardinal de Richelieu had lured the Duke of Buckingham to Paris in order to ruin both the Duke and the Queen."

"She said that?" cried the Cardinal fiercely.

"Yes, Monseigneur. But I told her she was wrong to talk about such things. I said His Eminence was incapable——"

"Hold your tongue. You are an imbecile," thundered the Cardinal.

"That's just what my wife said, Monseigneur."

"Do you know who abducted your wife?"

"No, Monseigneur."

"But you have your suspicions, haven't you?"

"Yes, Monseigneur, but my suspicions seemed to annoy Monsieur le Commissaire, so I no longer have them."

"Your wife has escaped. Did you know that?"

"No, Monseigneur, I didn't until I was told of it by Monsieur le Commissaire, a very kindly man."

Again the Cardinal repressed a smile. "Then you do not know what has become of your wife since her escape?"

"Absolutely not, Monseigneur. But doubtless she has returned to the Louvre."

"At one o'clock this morning she had not returned there."

"Good God! What can have happened to her?"

"We shall find out, I assure you. No one can conceal anything from the Cardinal. The Cardinal knows everything."

"In that case, Monseigneur, do you think the Cardinal will be kind enough to tell me what has happened to my wife?"

"Perhaps he may. But first you must confess everything you know about your wife's relations with Madame de Chevreuse."

"But, Monseigneur, I know nothing at all about them. I have never seen that lady!"

"When you went to call for your wife at the Louvre, did you always go straight home with her?"

"Almost never. She always had some business at the linen shops, and I took her there."

"How many are there of these linen shops?"

"Two, Monseigneur."

"Where are they?"

"One in the Rue de Vaugirard, the other in the Rue de La Harpe."

"Did you go into these shops with her?"

"Never, Monseigneur. I waited at the door."

"And what reason for her going in alone did she give you?"

"She didn't give me any. She just told me to wait and I waited."

"You're a very obliging husband, my dear Monsieur Bonacieux," said the Cardinal.

"He calls me his dear monsieur," the haberdasher said to himself. "The deuce! Things are going well."

"Do you know the street numbers of these shops? If so, what are they?"

"No. 25 Rue de Vaugirard, No. 75 Rue de La Harpe."

"Good," said the Cardinal. He picked up a little silver bell and rang it. The officer came back, and Richelieu said in an undertone: "Go find Rochefort, if he is here, and send him to me."

"The Comte is here," said the officer, "and asking for an immediate audience with Your Eminence."

"Let him come in, then, let him come in!"

The officer hurried out of the room with the celerity all the servitors of the Cardinal displayed in obeying him. Five seconds later the door opened again and a new personage entered.

"That's the man!" cried Bonacieux.

"What man?" demanded the Cardinal.

"The one who carried off my wife."

The Cardinal rang again. The officer appeared again. "Take this man back to his guards, and have him wait there until I send for him again."

"No, Monseigneur, no, that is *not* the man," cried Bonacieux. "No, I made a mistake. This is a different man, he isn't like my man at all. Monsieur here is an honorable man."

"Take this imbecile away!" said the Cardinal.

The officer tucked Bonacieux under his arm and carried him back to the antechamber and the two guards. The newcomer watched Bonacieux's departure impatiently, and as soon as the door closed, he turned to the Cardinal and said:

"They have seen each other."

"The Queen and the Duke?" cried Richelieu. "Where?"

"At the Louvre."

"Are you sure?"

"Perfectly sure."

"Who told you?"

"Madame de Lannoy. She is devoted to Your Eminence's interests, as you know."

"Why did she not let me know sooner?"

"Either by chance or from mistrust, the Queen made Madame de Surgis sleep in her own bedchamber, and kept her with her all day."

"Well, we've been beaten. Now we must get our revenge."

"I will assist you wholeheartedly, Monseigneur, you may be sure of that."

"How did it happen?"

"At half-past twelve the Queen was with her women in her bed-chamber. Someone came in and brought her a handkerchief from her seamstress. At once the Queen evidenced strong emotion, and despite the rouge on her face, she turned very pale. Then she rose, and said, her voice trembling, 'Ladies, wait here for me ten minutes.' Then she went out of the room."

"Why didn't Madame de Lannoy let you know of this at once?"

"She wasn't sure of anything yet. Besides, the Queen had said, 'Ladies, wait here for me,' and she did not dare disobey the Queen."

"How long was the Queen away?"

"Three-quarters of an hour."

"Did none of her women go with her?"

"Only Doña Estefana."

"And when she came back?"

"She picked up a little rosewood casket that had her monogram on it and went out again."

"When she came back again, did she bring that casket with her?"

"No."

"Does Madame de Lannoy know what was in the casket?"

"Yes—the diamond tags His Majesty gave the Queen."*

"Then Madame de Lannoy thinks she gave them to Buckingham?"

"She is certain of it. In the course of the day, Madame de Lannoy, as Lady of the Bedchamber to the Queen, looked for the casket, seemed worried when she didn't find it, and at last asked the Queen about it. The Queen grew very red, and answered that she had broken the setting of one of the tags the day before and had sent it to her goldsmith to be repaired."

"We must send someone there at once and find out whether that is or is not true."

"I have already been there. The goldsmith says he knows nothing whatever about it."

"Good, good, Rochefort! All is not lost, and it may be—it may be that all this is for the best!"

"Indeed I have no doubt that Your Eminence's genius——"

"Will repair the blunders of his agent. Is that what you were going to say?"

"That is precisely what I was going to say if Your Eminence had allowed me to complete my sentence."

"Do you know where the Duchesse de Chevreuse and the Duke of Buckingham were in hiding?"

*The French word *ferret* usually appears in former translation as "stud." Its real meaning is "tag," the bit of metal, with or without precious stones, fastened to ends of lace—in this case, ends of ribbon. "Tag" is used here as the more accurate translation.

"No, Monseigneur. My people have not been able to tell me anything certain as to that."

"But *I* know."

"You do, Monseigneur?"

"Yes—or at least I have my suspicions. One of them was staying at No. 25 Rue de Vaugirard and the other at No. 75 Rue de La Harpe."

"Does Your Eminence wish me to have both of them arrested?"

"It is too late. They will have left by now."

"At least we can make sure of that."

"Very well, take ten of my guardsmen and search both houses thoroughly."

"I shall go there at once, Monseigneur." And Rochefort rushed out of the room.

Left alone, the Cardinal reflected for an instant, then rang his bell a third time. The same officer appeared again.

"Bring the prisoner in," said the Cardinal.

Master Bonacieux was introduced once more, and at a sign from the Cardinal the officer withdrew.

"You have deceived me," said the Cardinal sternly.

"I!" cried Bonacieux. "*I* deceived Your Eminence?"

"When your wife went to the Rue de Vaugirard and the Rue de La Harpe, she did not go to see the linen drapers."

"Then what did she go there for, in God's name?"

"She went to visit the Duchesse de Chevreuse and the Duke of Buckingham."

"Yes," Bonacieux replied, recalling what he could remember about these visits, "yes, Your Eminence is right. Several times I told my wife that it was surprising to find linen drapers living in such houses—in houses that had no signs at the door—and she always laughed at me. Ah, Monseigneur," Bonacieux went on, throwing himself at His Eminence's feet, "how truly you are the great Cardinal, the man of genius the whole world reveres!"

The Cardinal, petty as was his triumph over so mean a creature as Bonacieux, enjoyed it none the less for an instant. Then almost immediately, as if a new idea had occurred to him, he smiled a little and offered his hand to the haberdasher.

"Rise, my good friend," he said. "You are an honest, worthy man."

"The Cardinal has touched my hand! I have touched the hand of the great man!" cried Bonacieux. "The great man has called me his friend!"

"Yes, my friend, yes," said the Cardinal in that paternal tone he knew how to assume on occasion, but which deceived only those who did not know him. "And as you have been suspected unjustly, well, you shall be indemnified. Here, take this purse—there are a hundred pistoles in it— and pardon me."

"*I* pardon *you*, Monseigneur," said Bonacieux, hesitating to take the purse, doubtless fearing that what pretended to be a gift might be a jest. "But you were quite within your rights to have me arrested, it is within your rights to have me tortured, even hanged! You are the master, and I wouldn't have a word to say against it. *I* pardon *you*, Monseigneur! Come now, you cannot mean that!"

"My dear Monsieur Bonacieux, you are acting very generously, and I thank you. So take this purse, and you will go away not too dissatisfied, will you not?"

"I shall go away delighted, Monseigneur."

"Farewell, then, or rather au revoir, for I hope we shall meet again."

"Whenever Monseigneur wishes. I am always at Your Eminence's orders."

"We shall see each other often, I assure you, for I have enjoyed our conversation very much."

"Ah, Monseigneur!"

"Au revoir, Monsieur Bonacieux, au revoir!" And the Cardinal motioned to him to leave.

Bonacieux answered by bowing to the ground, then he went out backward, and when he was in the antechamber, the Cardinal heard him shouting: "Long live Monseigneur! Long live His Eminence! Long live the great Cardinal!" Richelieu listened with a smile to this vociferous manifestation of Bonacieux's enthusiasm. Then when Bonacieux's shouts were fading into the distance, the great man said:

"Good! There's a man who would lay down his life for me."

Then the Cardinal began to examine with the greatest intentness the map of La Rochelle on his table. With a pencil he traced on it the line of the famous dike that, eighteen months later, was to block the port of the beleaguered city. While he was deep in his meditations on strategy the door opened and Rochefort entered.

"Well?" said the Cardinal eagerly, rising with a promptness that proved how important he thought the Comte's errand was.

"Well," said Rochefort, "a young woman of some twenty-six or twenty-eight and a young man of from thirty-five to forty certainly stayed in the houses Your Eminence named to me, the first for four days and the other for five. But the woman left last night and the man this morning."

"It was they!" cried the Cardinal. He looked at the clock. "And now it's too late to catch up with them. By this time the Duchesse is at Tours and the Duke is at Boulogne."

"What are Your Eminence's orders?"

"Not a word about what has happened. Let the Queen believe that she is perfectly safe. She must not learn that we know her secret. Let her believe that we are ferreting out some other conspiracy. Send me the Keeper of the Seals, Séguier."

"And what has Your Eminence done with that fellow Bonacieux?"

"I have done all that could be done with a man like that. I have made him a spy on his wife."

The Comte de Rochefort bowed low like a man acknowledging the great superiority of his master and withdrew. When he was alone again, the Cardinal wrote a letter, sealed it with his private seal, and rang the bell. The young officer entered once more.

"Send Vitray to me," said Richelieu, "and tell him to be ready for a journey." An instant later the man he had summoned stood before him, booted and spurred. "Vitray," said Richelieu, "you are to leave immediately for London. You must not stop a moment on the way. You will deliver this letter to Milady. Here is an order for two hundred pistoles; go to my treasurer and get the money. You shall have as much again if you are back within six days and have accomplished your mission."

Without speaking a word, the messenger bowed, took the letter and the order for two hundred pistoles, and withdrew. The letter read:

Milady:
Go to the first ball at which the Duke of Buckingham will be present. He will be wearing on his doublet a knot of ribbon with twelve diamond tags. Get close to him and cut off two of them. As soon as you have the tags in your possession, let me know.

CHAPTER 15

THE NEXT DAY, AS ATHOS HAD NOT APPEARED, D'ARTA-
gnan and La Porte reported his disappearance to Monsieur de Tréville.
As for Aramis, he had asked for a leave of absence for five days, and
rumor had it that he had gone to Rouen on family affairs.

Monsieur de Tréville was a father to his soldiers. As soon as a man
donned the musketeer's uniform the humblest and most obscure of them
was as certain of his aid and support as his own brother could be. Accordingly he went straight to the Lieutenant Provost, the highest police
magistrate. The officer in command of the Croix-Rouge district was summoned, and after much questioning it was learned that Athos was temporarily in custody in the For-l'Evêque prison.

Athos had been through all the ordeals that Bonacieux had undergone, and he had been confronted with the haberdasher, as we know. He
had refused to say anything because he was afraid that D'Artagnan
would not have the time he presumably needed to carry out his plans. But
when he thought D'Artagnan had been given time enough, he declared
that his name was Athos, not D'Artagnan. He added that he did not
know either Monsieur or Madame Bonacieux, that he had never spoken
to either, that at about ten in the evening he had called on his friend Monsieur d'Artagnan, but that until that hour he had been at Monsieur de
Tréville's, where he had dined. Twenty witnesses, he said, could testify
to that effect, and he named several distinguished gentlemen, among
them Monsieur le Duc de La Trémouille. This Commissioner was as
much bewildered as the first one had been by the plain and firm statement
the musketeer made, though men of the long robe always revenge themselves on men of the sword when they can. But the names of Monsieur de
Tréville and the Duc de La Trémouille commanded respect.

Athos was then sent to the Cardinal, but unfortunately the Cardinal
was with the King at the Louvre. It was precisely at this moment that
Monsieur de Tréville, after leaving first the magistrate and then the governor of For-l'Evêque without finding Athos, arrived at His Majesty's
palace. As Captain of the Musketeers he had the privilege of entrée there
at all times.

It is common knowledge how greatly the King was prejudiced against the Queen. The Cardinal, who in matters of intrigue distrusted women much more than men, encouraged the King's prejudice. One of the principal causes of this prejudice was the friendship of Anne of Austria for Madame de Chevreuse. These two women disturbed His Majesty's peace more than the war with Spain, the quarrels with England, and the financial difficulties of France. He was absolutely convinced that Madame de Chevreuse was serving the Queen not only in her political intrigues but also in what tormented him still more—her amorous intrigues.

At the first thing Monsieur le Cardinal said—that Madame de Chevreuse, though she had been exiled to Tours and was supposed to be in that city, had come to Paris, and in the five days she had been there had escaped the notice of the police—the King flew into a furious rage. Then the Cardinal added that not only had Madame de Chevreuse been in Paris, but that moreover the Queen had renewed relations with her by means of one of those mysterious connections at that time called a cabal. He asserted that he, the Cardinal himself, was on the point of unraveling the most carefully hidden threads of this intrigue when, just as he was armed with all the proofs and was about to arrest the Queen's emissary to the exiled Duchesse *in flagrante delicto,* a musketeer had dared to interrupt the course of justice with violence by falling, sword in hand, on the honest men of the law charged with investigating the whole affair. Then Louis XIII could contain himself no longer. He started toward the Queen's apartment, his face pale with that silent indignation which when it burst out drove this prince to commit the most ruthless cruelties. And yet, so far, the Cardinal had said no word of the Duke of Buckingham.

It was then that Monsieur de Tréville entered, cool, courteous, and impeccably attired. Warned of what had just occurred by the Cardinal's presence and the King's angry countenance, Monsieur de Tréville nevertheless felt himself as strong as Samson was before the Philistines. Louis XIII already had his hand on the doorknob. At the sound of Monsieur de Tréville's entrance he turned.

"You have come at the right time, monsieur," said the King angrily, for when he lost his temper badly he could not dissemble. "I have just learned some pretty things about your musketeers."

"And I," said Monsieur de Tréville coolly, "I have some pretty things to tell Your Majesty about your men of the law."

"Pray what do you mean?" the King replied haughtily.

"I have the honor to inform Your Majesty," Monsieur de Tréville continued with the same coolness as before, "that a party of agents, commissioners, and policemen—very estimable men, but apparently very rabid enemies of those who wear the King's uniform—took it on themselves to arrest one of my musketeers in a certain house, took him away through the public streets, and threw him into the For-l'Evêque prison. They re-

fused to show me the warrant—if they had one. One of my musketeers,
I said. Rather, one of *your* musketeers, Sire, one of irreproachable conduct and almost illustrious repute. Your Majesty knows him, and favor-
ably—Monsieur Athos."

"Athos," the King repeated mechanically. "Yes, certainly I know that
name."

"Your Majesty may remember," said Monsieur de Tréville, "that Monsieur Athos is the musketeer who had the misfortune to wound Monsieur
de Cahusac so grievously in that vexatious duel you know of. By the way,"
De Tréville continued, turning to the Cardinal, "Monsieur de Cahusac is
quite recovered, is he not?"

"He is, thank you," the Cardinal answered, pinching his lips together
angrily.

"Monsieur Athos, then, went to call on one of his friends who was
out," Monsieur de Tréville resumed. "The friend is a young man from
Béarn, a cadet in His Majesty's Guards—in Monsieur des Essarts's company. But scarcely had he arrived, and picked up a book to while away
the time until his friend's arrival, when a flock of bailiffs and soldiers
arrived, laid siege to the house, broke down several doors——"

The Cardinal made a sign to the King that evidently meant "That's
the affair I was telling you about."

"Oh, we know all about that," replied the King, "it was all done in
our service."

"Then," said De Tréville, "it was also in Your Majesty's service that
one of my musketeers, an innocent man, was seized, put between two
guards like a malefactor, and that this gallant man, who has shed his
blood a dozen times in serving Your Majesty, and is ready to do so again,
was marched through the insolent rabble for them to jeer at?"

"Bah!" said the King, somewhat shaken. "Is that what really happened?"

"Monsieur de Tréville did not tell you," observed the Cardinal with
the greatest phlegm, "that this innocent musketeer, this gallant man, an
hour before had struck down with his sword four agents sent by me to
inquire into a matter of the greatest importance."

"I defy Your Eminence to prove that!" cried Monsieur de Tréville,
with his Gascon frankness and soldierly bluntness. "Monsieur Athos,
who, I tell Your Majesty in strict confidence, is a man of very high rank,
did me the honor to dine with me, and after dinner he chatted in my
drawing-room with Monsieur le Duc de la Trémouille and Monsieur le
Comte de Châlus."

The King looked at the Cardinal.

"An official report is trustworthy," said the Cardinal, replying aloud
to the silent question of His Majesty, "and the officers of the law who
were so maltreated drew up this one, which I have the honor to present
to Your Majesty."

"And is the written report of men of the law as good as the word of men of the sword?"

"Come, come, Tréville, be quiet!" said the King.

"If Your Eminence entertains any suspicion against one of my musketeers," said Tréville, "the justice of Monsieur le Cardinal is well enough known for me to demand an investigation."

"In the house where this police raid was made," the Cardinal went on impassively, "a Béarnese lives, a friend of the musketeer, I believe."

"Your Eminence means Monsieur d'Artagnan."

"I mean the young man who is your protégé, Monsieur de Tréville."

"Yes, Your Eminence, that same man."

"Don't you suspect this young man of giving bad advice to——"

"To Monsieur Athos, to a man twice his age?" interrupted Monsieur de Tréville. "No, Monseigneur. Besides, Monsieur d'Artagnan spent the evening with me."

"Well, well," said the Cardinal. "Did everybody spend the evening with you?"

"Does His Eminence doubt my word?" asked Tréville, his face red with anger.

"No, God forbid!" replied the Cardinal. "But pray tell me, what time was he at your house?"

"Oh, I can tell Your Eminence that exactly, for as he came in I happened to notice that it was half-past eight by the clock, though I had thought it was later."

"And at what time did he leave your house?"

"At half-past ten—an hour after the event."

"Well, after all," replied the Cardinal, who did not doubt Monsieur de Tréville's integrity for an instant, but felt that the victory was slipping through his fingers, "after all, Athos *certainly* was caught in that house on the Rue des Fossoyeurs."

"Is one friend forbidden to visit another one? Is a musketeer of my company forbidden to fraternize with a guardsman of Monsieur des Essarts's company?"

"Yes, when the house where he goes is suspect."

"That house is really suspect, Tréville," said the King. "Perhaps you did not know that."

"Indeed, Sire, I did not know it. Anyway, though the house may be suspect, I deny that Monsieur d'Artagnan's apartment is. For I can swear to you, Sire, that if I can believe what he says—and I do—Your Majesty has no more devoted servant, and Monsieur le Cardinal no greater admirer."

"Isn't this the D'Artagnan who wounded Jussac in that unfortunate encounter near the monastery of the Carmes-Déchaux?" asked the King, glancing at the Cardinal, who grew red with vexation.

"And the next day Bernajoux. Yes, Sire, yes, that's the man. Your Majesty has an excellent memory."

"Come, how are we to decide?" said the King.

"That concerns Your Majesty more than it concerns me," said the Cardinal. "I would declare him guilty."

"And I deny it!" Tréville retorted. "But His Majesty has judges, and those judges will make the decision."

"That's right," said the King. "Let us refer the case to the judges. It is their business to judge, and judge they shall."

"Only," replied Tréville, "it's a pity that in these unhappy times the purest life, the most indisputable virtue, do not exempt a man from ignominy and persecution. The Army will resent being subjected to such harsh treatment at the hands of the police, I can tell you."

The words were foolhardy, but Monsieur de Tréville knew what he was doing. He hoped for an explosion, because an exploded mine gives forth fire, and fire sheds light.

"At the hands of the police!" cried the King. "And what do you know about the police, monsieur? Mind your own business, the musketeers, and don't annoy me by saying things like that. To hear you talk one would think that if by ill fortune some musketeer is arrested, all France is in danger! Eh, what a to-do about one musketeer! By God, I'll have ten of them arrested—a hundred, the whole corps—and I'll allow no one to say a word."

"The moment they are suspect in Your Majesty's eyes," said Tréville, "the musketeers are guilty. Therefore, Sire, I am ready to surrender my sword, for after accusing my soldiers, Monsieur le Cardinal will, I am sure, go on to accuse me. So it seems best for me to constitute myself a prisoner along with Monsieur Athos, who is already under arrest, and Monsieur d'Artagnan, who doubtless soon will be."

"You Gascon hothead, will you have done?" said the King.

"Sire," replied Tréville without lowering his voice in the least, "either order my musketeer to be restored to me or to be tried in a court of justice."

"He shall be tried," said the Cardinal.

"Very well. So much the better, for in that case I shall ask His Majesty to allow me to plead on his behalf."

The King, fearing a public scandal, said: "If His Eminence had not certain personal motives——"

The Cardinal saw what the King was about to say, and forestalled him: "Pardon me," he said, "but the moment Your Majesty considers me a prejudiced judge, I withdraw."

"Come now, Tréville," said the King, "will you swear by my father that Monsieur Athos was at your house during the event and that he took no part in it?"

"By your glorious father and by yourself, whom I love and revere above all else in the world, I swear it!"

"Pray stop to consider, Sire," observed the Cardinal. "If we release the prisoner, we shall never be able to discover the truth."

"Monsieur Athos will always be there," returned Monsieur de Tréville, "ready to answer whenever the men of the long robe care to question him. He will not desert, Monsieur le Cardinal, you may rest easy as to that."

"Of course he will not desert," said the King. "He can always be found, as Monsieur de Tréville says. Besides," he added, lowering his voice and giving His Eminence a beseeching glance, "let us give them apparent security. That is good policy."

Louis XIII's idea of policy made Richelieu smile.

"Order it as you please, Sire," he said. "You possess the right of pardon."

"The right of pardon applies only to the guilty," protested Tréville, who meant to have the last word, "and my musketeer is innocent. It is not an act of mercy you are about to do, but an act of justice."

"He is now in For-l'Evêque?" asked the King.

"Yes, Sire, in solitary confinement like the lowest of criminals."

"The devil, the devil!" muttered the King. "What must I do?"

"Sign the order for his release, and that will be the end of the business," the Cardinal replied. "I believe with Your Majesty that Monsieur Tréville's guarantee is more than sufficient."

Tréville bowed respectfully, with a joy not unmixed with fear. He would have preferred obstinate resistance on the part of the Cardinal to this sudden compliance. The King signed the order for release and Tréville accepted it. As he was leaving the Cardinal smiled at him amicably.

"Now he'll play me some nasty trick or other," thought Tréville. "You can't ever have the last word with a man like that. But I must make haste —the King may change his mind at any moment. Anyway, it's more difficult to send back to the Bastille or the For-l'Evêque a man who has been released than it is to keep a prisoner who is already there."

Monsieur de Tréville made a triumphant entry into the For-l'Evêque and liberated the musketeer, whose tranquil indifference had not deserted him. As soon as he saw D'Artagnan, Athos remarked:

"You've had a narrow escape. Your wounding Jussac has been paid for now, but there's still Bernajoux. You'd better not be too confident."

Indeed Monsieur de Tréville had good reason to mistrust the Cardinal, and to think that all was not over yet. The Captain of the Musketeers had scarcely closed the door when His Eminence said to the King.

"Now that we are at last alone, we can talk seriously, if it please Your Majesty. . . . Sire, the Duke of Buckingham has been in Paris five days. He left only this morning."

CHAPTER 16

IT IS IMPOSSIBLE TO PICTURE THE IMPRESSION THOSE FEW words made on Louis XIII. He flushed, then grew pale. The Cardinal saw at once that at one blow he had recovered all the ground he had lost.

"Buckingham in Paris!" cried the King. "And what did he come here for?"

"Doubtless to plot with your Huguenot and Spanish enemies."

"No, by God, no! He came to plot against my honor with Madame de Chevreuse, Madame de Longueville, and the Condés."

"Oh, Sire, how can you think that? The Queen is too discreet, and moreover she loves Your Majesty too dearly."

"Women are weak, Monsieur le Cardinal," replied the King. "And as for her loving me much, I have my own opinion as to that."

"Nevertheless I maintain," said the Cardinal, "that the Duke of Buckingham came to Paris because of some purely political scheme."

"And *I* am sure that he came for another purpose, Monsieur le Cardinal. But if the Queen is guilty, let her tremble!"

"As a matter of fact," said the Cardinal, "as much as I hate to think about such a betrayal, Your Majesty makes me think of one point. Madame de Lannoy, whom I questioned several times in accordance with Your Majesty's orders, did tell me this morning that two nights ago Her Majesty sat up very late, that the next morning she wept for a long time, and that she spent the day writing."

"That's it!" cried the King. "She was writing to *him,* I'm sure. Monsieur le Cardinal, I must have the Queen's papers."

"But how are you to get them, Sire? It seems to me neither you nor I can undertake such a mission."

"How did they go about it with the Maréchale d'Ancre?" cried the King, now in a towering rage. "They searched, searched everywhere in her apartment, and then they searched her person."

"The Maréchale d'Ancre was only the Maréchale d'Ancre, a Florentine adventuress, Sire, and the august spouse of Your Majesty is Anne of Austria, one of the greatest princesses in the world."

"She is all the more guilty for that very reason, Monsieur le Duc! The more she has forgotten the exalted position she has been given, the lower has she fallen. Besides, long ago I determined to put an end to all these petty political and amorous intrigues. She has a certain La Porte in her household, has she not?"

"She has, and I confess that I believe he is the mainspring of all this affair," said the Cardinal.

"Then you believe as I do—that she is betraying me?"

"I believe, and I tell Your Majesty so again, that the Queen is plotting against the political power of her King, but I have not said she was plotting against his honor."

"And I tell you she is plotting against both. I tell you the Queen does not love me, I tell you she loves another, I tell you she loves that villain of a Buckingham! Why did you not have him arrested while he was in Paris?"

"Arrest the Duke! Arrest the Prime Minister of King Charles I! Could you think of it, Sire? What a scandal! And if Your Majesty's suspicions proved to be justified—and I still doubt that—what a terrible explosion, what a hopeless scandal!"

"But since he behaved like a vagabond and a thief, he should have been——"

Louis XIII checked himself, frightened at what he had been about to say, while Richelieu, listening eagerly, waited in vain for the words that had died on the King's lips.

"He should have been——"

"Nothing," said the King, "nothing. But all the time he was in Paris, you didn't lose sight of him?"

"No, Sire."

"And you are sure he did not meet the Queen?"

"I believe the Queen has too high a sense of duty to allow that, Sire."

"But they corresponded. It was to *him* that the Queen was writing all day. Monsieur le Duc, I *must* have those letters!"

"But I beg Your Majesty to observe——"

"Are you betraying me too, Monsieur le Cardinal, that you always oppose my will in this way? Are you too in league with the Spaniards and the English, with Madame de Chevreuse, and with the Queen?"

"Sire," replied the Cardinal with a sigh, "I thought I was safe from such suspicions."

"Monsieur le Cardinal, you heard me—I *will* have those letters."

"There is but one way to get them."

"What is that?"

"To charge with that mission Monsieur de Séguier, the Keeper of the Seals. It is quite within the duties of his post."

"Let him be sent for instantly."

"Your Majesty's orders shall be carried out, but—the Queen may per-

haps refuse to obey them if she does not know that the orders come from
the King."

"Well then, so that she may have no doubt on that head, I will go tell
her myself."

"Your Majesty will not forget that I have done everything in my power
to prevent a misunderstanding between Her Majesty and yourself."

"No, Your Grace, I know you are very indulgent to the Queen—perhaps too indulgent—and I warn you that we shall find occasion to talk
about that later."

"Whenever it shall please Your Majesty. Meanwhile I shall always be
happy and proud, Sire, to sacrifice myself to ensure the perfect harmony
I wish to see between you and the Queen of France."

"Good, Monsieur le Cardinal, good! But in the meantime send for the
Keeper of the Seals. As for me, I go to the Queen." And Louis XIII
opened a door and took the corridor that led to the apartments of Anne
of Austria.

The Queen was surrounded by her women, Madame de Guitaut,
Madame de Montbazon, and Madame de Guéménée. In one corner sat
the Spanish Lady of the Bedchamber, Doña Estefana, who had come
from Madrid with the Queen. Madame de Guéménée was reading aloud,
and everybody was listening attentively except the Queen, who had suggested the reading in order that she might follow the threads of her own
thoughts while she pretended to listen.

These thoughts, golden though they were from a last ray of love, were
nevertheless sad. Anne of Austria, deprived of her husband's confidence,
pursued by the Cardinal's hatred—he had never forgiven her for spurn-
ing a more tender sentiment on his part—recalled the Queen Mother,
Marie de Medici, whom Richelieu's hatred had tormented all her days.
The Queen Mother had once returned his love, but Anne of Austria always refused to give him hers. Anne of Austria had seen her most devoted servitors, her most intimate confidants, her dearest favorites, struck
down around her. Like those unhappy beings endowed with a deadly
gift, she brought misfortune to everything she touched. Her friendship
was doomed to be a signal to call down persecution on anyone she be-
friended. Madame de Chevreuse and Madame de Vernet were in exile,
and now La Porte did not conceal from his mistress that he expected to
be arrested at any moment.

It was when she was plunged in the deepest and darkest of these reflections that the door opened and the King entered. Madame de Guéménée
stopped reading at once, all the ladies rose, and there was a deep silence.
As for the King, he made no pretense of courtesy. Stopping in front of
the Queen, he said:

"Madame, you are about to receive a visit from Monsieur le Chance-

Madame Bonacieux and the Duke of Buckingham

Louis XIII and Cardinal Richelieu

lier, who will communicate to you certain matters with which I have charged him."

The unhappy Queen, ceaselessly threatened with divorce, exile, and even a legal sentence, turned pale under her rouge and could not refrain from saying:

"But why this visit, Sire? What can Monsieur le Chancelier tell me that Your Majesty cannot tell me yourself?"

The King turned on his heel without answering and at almost the same instant the Captain of the Royal Guards, Monsieur de Guitaut, announced Monsieur le Chancelier. As Monsieur Séguier, Chancellor and Keeper of the Seals, entered, the Queen was still standing, in deference to the King. As soon as she saw Séguier, she sat down in her armchair and motioned to her women to be seated again.

"What do you wish, monsieur?" Anne of Austria asked in a supremely haughty tone. "What is your purpose in presenting yourself here?"

"I come in the name of the King, madame, and with all the respect I have the honor to owe Your Majesty, to make a thorough examination of all your papers."

"What, monsieur! An examination of my papers—mine! But this is outrageous!"

"I beg you to pardon me, madame, but in this instance I am only the instrument of the King. Has not His Majesty just left you? And did he not tell you himself to be ready for my visit?"

"Search, then, monsieur. I am a criminal, it seems. Estefana, give monsieur the keys of my drawers and my desks."

For form's sake the Chancellor inspected these, but he knew very well that the Queen would not put so important a letter in drawer or desk. When he had opened and closed the various drawers a score of times, whatever hesitation he might feel, he was forced to carry on to the end— that is, to search the person of the Queen herself. He therefore stepped toward Anne of Austria, and in a tone of great perplexity and with an air of great embarrassment, he said:

"Now, madame, it only remains for me to make the most important search."

"What is that?" asked the Queen, who did not understand, or rather was unwilling to understand.

"His Majesty is certain that you wrote a letter today, madame, and he knows that that letter has not been dispatched as yet. That letter is not in any of your drawers or in your desk, but it must be somewhere."

"Would you dare lay hands on your Queen?" said Anne of Austria, drawing herself up to her full height.

"I am a faithful subject of the King, madame, and everything His Majesty commands I shall do."

"Very well," said Anne of Austria. "Monsieur le Cardinal's spies serve him well. It is true that I wrote a letter today and that it has not been sent. The letter is here." And the Queen put her beautiful hand on her breast.

"Pray give me that letter, madame," said the Chancellor.

"I will give it to no one but the King, monsieur," Anne declared.

"If the King had wished to have that letter given to him, madame, he would have asked you for it himself. But I repeat that it is I whom he has charged to request it from you, and if you refuse to give it to me——"

"Well?"

"My orders go far, madame. I am authorized to search for the suspicious paper even on Your Majesty's person. I therefore beg you, madame, to comply with the King's order."

"Such conduct is infamous! Do you realize that, monsieur?"

"The King commands, madame. I beg you to forgive me."

"I will not suffer it!" cried the Queen, in whom the imperious blood of Spain and Austria began to boil. "No, I would rather die!"

The Chancellor bowed very low. It was quite evident that he did not intend to draw back one step in the accomplishment of his mission. As an executioner's assistant might have done in a torture chamber, he stepped forward toward Anne of Austria. Tears of rage were welling in her eyes.

The Queen was, as we have said, a woman of great beauty. Séguier's task might well be considered a delicate one. But the King was so violently jealous of Buckingham that he had reached the point where he was jealous of no one else. Doubtless Chancellor Séguier looked about in distress, but he summoned all his resolution and stretched out his hand toward the place where the Queen had acknowledged that the letter lay. Anne of Austria recoiled one step, as pale as if she were at the point of death. Then, supporting herself by her left hand on a table behind her, with her right hand she drew a paper from her breast and held it out to the Keeper of the Seals.

"Here, monsieur, here it is, that letter," the Queen cried, her voice broken and tremulous. "Take it, and relieve me of your odious presence."

The Chancellor, who for his part was trembling with an emotion easily guessed, took the letter, bowed to the ground, and withdrew. The door had barely shut behind him when the Queen fell half-fainting into the arms of her women. The Chancellor took the letter to the King without reading a word of it. The King took it with a trembling hand, looked for the address, which was lacking, turned very pale, and opened the letter slowly. Then when he saw from the first words that it was addressed to the King of Spain, he read it rapidly.

What he read was a complete plan for an attack against the Cardinal. The Queen was inviting her brother and the Emperor of Austria— offended as they were by Richelieu's policy, the constant purpose of which was the humiliation of the House of Austria—to threaten war against France and to make one condition of peace the dismissal of the Cardinal. But of love there was no word anywhere in the letter.

The King, full of joy, asked whether the Cardinal was still at the Louvre, and was told that His Eminence was awaiting His Majesty's orders in the audience room. The King went to him at once.

"There, Your Grace," he said, "you were right and I was wrong. The whole intrigue is political; there is no question whatever of love in this letter. But there's plenty about you."

The Cardinal took the letter and read it most attentively once, then read it a second time.

"Well, Your Majesty," he said, "you see how far my enemies go. They threaten you with two wars if you do not dismiss me. Really, if I were in your place, Sire, I would yield to such powerful pressure, and for my own part, it would be real happiness to retire from public affairs."

"What do you mean, Your Grace?"

"I say, Sire, that my health is giving way under this burden of too many struggles and endless labor. I say that in all likelihood I shall not be able to undergo the fatigues of the siege of La Rochelle, and that you would do far better to appoint Monsieur de Condé or Monsieur de Bassompierre or some other valiant professional soldier to conduct the war rather than myself, who am an ecclesiastic constantly diverted from my vocation to look after matters for which I have no aptitude. You will be the happier for it at home, Sire, and I do not doubt that you will be all the greater for it abroad."

"Monsieur le Duc," replied the King, "I understand you. Rest easy, all the persons named in this letter shall receive the punishment they deserve, including the Queen herself."

"What are you saying, Sire? God forbid that the Queen should suffer the slightest annoyance on my account! She has always believed me to be her enemy, Sire, although Your Majesty can bear witness that I have always taken her part warmly, even against you. Oh, if she were betraying Your Majesty's honor, that would be quite another thing, and I would be the first to say to you, 'No mercy, Sire, no mercy for the guilty woman!' Happily there is no question of that now, and Your Majesty has just acquired fresh proof of that."

"True, Monsieur le Cardinal," said the King, "and you were right, as you always are. Nevertheless the Queen merits all my wrath."

"It is you, Sire, who have incurred hers now, and if she should be seriously offended with Your Majesty, I could well understand it. Your Majesty has treated her with a severity that——"

"So shall I always treat my enemies and yours, Your Grace, however lofty their positions and whatever danger I may incur in treating them severely."

"The Queen is my enemy, but she is not yours, Sire. On the contrary, she is a devoted, submissive, and irreproachable wife. Pray allow me, then, to intercede with Your Majesty in her behalf."

"Let her humble herself, then, and come to me first."

"On the contrary, Sire, I beg you to set the example yourself. You were in the wrong first, since you suspected the Queen."

"What! *I* make advances!" cried the King. "Never! Besides, how could I do it?"

"By doing something that you know will please her."

"What?"

"Give a ball. You know how much the Queen likes to dance. I assure you that her resentment will not hold out against an attention like that."

"Monsieur le Cardinal, you know that I do not care for worldly pleasures."

"The Queen will be all the more grateful to you, since she knows of your antipathy to such pleasures. Besides, it will give her an opportunity to wear those beautiful diamond tags you gave her the other day on her birthday. She has not worn them as yet."

"We shall see, Monsieur le Cardinal, we shall see," the King answered. His joy in finding the Queen guilty only of a crime he cared little about, and innocent of a fault he had dreaded, made him quite ready for a reconciliation. "We shall see," he repeated, "but upon my honor, you are too indulgent."

"Sire," replied the Cardinal, "leave severity to your Ministers; clemency is the royal virtue. Exercise it and you will find that you feel the better for it."

Whereupon the Cardinal, hearing the clock strike eleven, bowed low and asked the King's permission to withdraw, beseeching His Majesty to effect a reconciliation with the Queen.

The next day, Anne of Austria, who after the seizure of her letter had expected reproach of some sort, was amazed when the King came to make overtures for a reconciliation. Her first instinct was to repel them; both her pride as a woman and her dignity as a queen had been so cruelly hurt that she could not recover so suddenly. But at last, persuaded by the advice of her women, she seemed to be beginning to forget all that. The King took advantage of this propitious moment to tell her that he meant to give a fete in the near future.

A fete of any kind was so rare a thing for poor Anne of Austria that at this announcement, as the Cardinal had foreseen, the last traces of her resentment disappeared, if not from her heart, at least from her countenance. She asked what day the fete was to take place, but the King replied that he would have to consult the Cardinal. Indeed, every day now the King asked the Cardinal the same question, but every day the Cardinal gave one pretext or another for delaying to fix the day. Ten days went by like that. On the eighth day after the scene just described, the Cardinal received a letter with a London postmark containing these few lines.

I have them, but I cannot leave London for want of money. Send me five hundred pistoles and four or five days after I receive them I will be in Paris.

The day the Cardinal received this letter the King asked his usual question. Richelieu counted on his fingers, murmuring to himself:

"She will be here, she says, four or five days after receiving the money. It will take four or five days for the money to get to her, and four or five days for her to get back. That makes ten days, say. Now, allowing for head winds, accidents, and the frailty of women, let's call it twelve days."

"Well, Monsieur le Duc," said the King, "can you set the date?"

"Yes, Sire. Today is the twentieth of September. The Aldermen of the City are giving a fete on October 3. That will suit us perfectly, for you will not seem to have gone out of your way to please the Queen." Then he added: "By the way, Sire, do not forget to tell Her Majesty the day before the fete that you wish to see how well her diamond tags look on her."

CHAPTER 17

THIS WAS THE SECOND TIME THE CARDINAL HAD SPOKEN of the diamond tags to the King. Louis XIII was impressed by this insistence, and began to think it concealed some mystery.

The Cardinal's police had not attained the perfection of the police of our time, but they were very good. More than once the King had been humiliated by the realization that the Cardinal was better informed than he was himself as to what went on in the royal household. Now he hoped that a talk with Anne of Austria might throw some light on the subject. Then he could return to His Eminence with some secret that the Cardinal knew, or one he did not know, and in either case that would enhance him greatly in the eyes of his Minister.

Therefore he went to the Queen, and as usual he accosted her with fresh threats against her servitors. Anne of Austria bowed her head, and without saying a word let the torrent flow on, hoping that it would stop soon. But this was not what Louis XIII wanted. Louis XIII wanted a discussion from which light of some kind would flash out. He was convinced that the Cardinal was keeping something back and planning one of those terrible surprises His Eminence knew so well how to prepare. He attained his end by his persistent accusations.

"But Sire," cried Anne of Austria, worn out by these vague attacks, "you are not telling me all you have in your heart. What have I done? Tell me, what crime have I committed? It isn't possible that Your Majesty is making all this to-do over a letter I wrote to my brother."

The King, attacked in his turn so directly, knew not what to reply. He decided that this was the moment to voice the desire that he had been advised to express only on the day before the fete.

"Madame," he said with great dignity, "shortly there will be a ball at the Hôtel de Ville, given by our good Aldermen. In order to do honor to them, I wish you to appear in ceremonial dress, and above all I ask you to wear the diamond tags I gave you on your birthday. That is my answer."

The answer was a terrible one. Anne of Austria thought that Louis XIII knew everything, and that the Cardinal had persuaded him to dissimulate for these long seven or eight days. Moreover, such dissimulation was quite characteristic. She turned white, one wonderfully beautiful hand grasped a table for support, a hand like wax, and she gazed at the King with terror in her eyes, and without one word of reply.

"You understand, madame," said the King, who was enjoying her embarrassment to the full, but without guessing what caused it. "You understand?"

"Yes, Sire, I understand," stammered the Queen.

"You will appear at the ball? And wearing your diamond tags?"

"Yes."

The Queen's pallor increased, if possible. The King noted it, and enjoyed it with that cold cruelty which was one of the worst sides of his character.

"Then that's agreed," said the King. "That is all I had to say to you."

"But what day will the ball take place?" asked Anne of Austria.

The Queen asked this in so very faint a voice that Louis XIII felt instinctively that he ought not to answer too much.

"Oh, very shortly, madame," he said. "I don't remember the exact date. I'll ask the Cardinal."

"It was the Cardinal, then, who told you of this fete?"

"Yes, madame," replied the King, somewhat astonished. "But why do you ask?"

"It was he who suggested that you request me to wear my diamond tags?"

"What does it matter whether it was he or I who suggested it? Is the request a crime?"

"No, Sire."

"Then you will appear wearing them?"

"Yes, Sire."

"Good," said the King, "good! I shall count on it."

The Queen curtsied, less out of etiquette than because her knees were giving way under her. The King went away delighted.

"I am lost," murmured the Queen, "lost! The Cardinal knows everything, and it is he who is prompting the King, who as yet knows nothing but will soon learn everything. Oh, my God, God, my God!"

She knelt on a cushion and prayed, her head buried in her trembling hands. Her plight was terrible indeed. Buckingham had returned to London, Madame de Chevreuse was in Tours. More closely watched than ever, the Queen sensed that one of her women was betraying her, but she could not guess which one. La Porte could not leave the Louvre; there was not one soul in the world whom she could trust. Contemplating the catastrophe that menaced her and her own helplessness, she burst into sobs. Suddenly she heard a voice full of sweetness and compassion say:

"Can I not be of some service to Your Majesty?"

The Queen turned round quickly. There was no mistaking the tone of that voice; it was a friend who had spoken. At one of the doors to the Queen's apartment the lovely Madame Bonacieux was standing. When the King entered, she had been busy arranging gowns and linen in a closet; she could not come out while His Majesty was there, and she had heard everything. The Queen gave a sharp cry of surprise on seeing her, for in her confusion she did not recognize immediately the young woman La Porte had brought to her.

"Oh, have no fear, madame," said the young woman, clasping her hands, and weeping herself for the Queen's anguish. "I am Your Majesty's body and soul. Moreover, far as I may be below you, lowly as my place may be, I think I have found a way to get Your Majesty out of your difficulty."

"You! Great heavens, *you!*" cried the Queen. "Come, look me in the face. I am betrayed on every side. Can I trust you?"

"Oh, madame," cried the young woman, falling on her knees, "upon my soul, I am ready to die for Your Majesty!" The cry came from the very bottom of her heart; its sincerity was unmistakable. "Yes," Madame Bonacieux went on, "yes, there are traitors here! But by the holy name of the Blessed Virgin I swear that there is no one more devoted to Your Majesty than I am. Those diamond tags the King asks for, you gave them to the Duke of Buckingham, did you not? They were in a little rosewood box that he kept under his arm? Am I mistaken? Wasn't it like that?"

"Oh, my God, my God!" murmured the Queen.

"Well, we must get those diamond tags back, madame."

"Yes, of course we must!" cried the Queen. "But what can we do? How can we succeed?"

"We must send someone to the Duke."

"But who? Who? Whom can I trust?"

"Put your trust in me, madame. Do me that honor, my Queen, and I will find a messenger myself!"

"But I must write the message."

"Ah yes, of course you must. A few words in Your Majesty's handwriting and your own private seal."

"But those few words may mean that I will be pronounced guilty, divorced, exiled!"

"Yes, if they fall into the wrong hands. But I promise you that those few words will be delivered to the address you give."

"Oh, my God! Must I put my life, my honor, and my reputation in your hands?"

"Yes, yes, madame, you must. And I will save them all, I promise you."

"But how? At least tell me that."

"My husband was set free two or three days ago; I have not had time to see him yet. He is a good, honest man who neither hates nor loves anyone. He will do anything I wish. When I tell him to, he will set out for London at once without knowing what it is he is carrying, and he will deliver the letter from Your Majesty to its address without even knowing that it is from Your Majesty."

In a burst of emotion, the Queen grasped the young woman's hands and gazed at her as if to read her very heart. Then, seeing nothing but sincerity in her beautiful eyes, Anne of Austria embraced her tenderly.

"Do that," she cried, "and you will have saved my life, you will have saved my honor!"

"Give me that letter, then, madame—time presses."

The Queen hurried to a little desk and wrote two lines, sealed the letter with her private seal, and gave it to Madame Bonacieux.

"And now," said the Queen, "we are forgetting one very necessary thing—money."

Madame Bonacieux blushed. "Yes, that's true," she said, "and I confess to Your Majesty that my husband is very miserly—that's his worst fault. But Your Majesty must not worry. We will find some way."

"The fact is that I haven't any money," said the Queen. "But wait a minute." Anne of Austria hurried to her jewel case. "Here," she said, "this is a ring of great value, I am told. It was given me by my brother the King of Spain, so I can dispose of it as I wish. Take this ring, get money for it, and let your husband set off at once."

"You shall be obeyed within an hour, Your Majesty."

"You generous child!" cried Anne of Austria.

Madame Bonacieux kissed the Queen's hands, hid the letter in her bodice, and disappeared. Ten minutes later she was at home. As she had told the Queen, she had not seen her husband since he was released from custody, so she did not know of the change in his opinion of the Cardinal. That change had been intensified by two or three visits from the Comte de Rochefort. The Comte had become Bonacieux's best friend, and had had no difficulty in convincing him that his wife's abduction was not a criminal act, but merely a political move.

She found her husband alone. The poor man was having difficulty in restoring order in his house. Most of the furniture was broken, and most of the closets were empty. Justice is not one of the three things King Solomon named as leaving no traces of their passage. As for the maidservant, she had fled as soon as her master was arrested.

Immediately after he came home, the worthy haberdasher had notified his wife of his happy return. She had replied by sending her congratulations and telling him that the earliest moment she could steal from her duties would be devoted to paying him a visit. This earliest moment had been delayed for five days, which under any other circumstances would have seemed a long time to Master Bonacieux. But the visit he had paid to the Cardinal and those Rochefort had paid to him gave him plenty of food for thought.

For her part, Madame Bonacieux too had been thinking, but, it must be acknowledged, on quite another subject than ambition. In spite of herself, her thoughts constantly reverted to that handsome young man who was so brave and who seemed to be so much in love with her. Married at eighteen to Monsieur Bonacieux, always living among her husband's friends—people hardly capable of inspiring any sentiment whatever in a young woman whose heart was far above her social position—Madame Bonacieux had remained virtuous. But the word "gentleman" had a great influence over the bourgeoisie at that period, and D'Artagnan was a gentleman; furthermore, he wore the uniform of the Royal Guards, which, next to that of the musketeers, was most admired by the ladies. He was, we repeat, handsome, young, and adventurous; he spoke of love like a man who loves and is eager to be loved in return. All this was enough to turn a head only twenty-three years old, and Madame Bonacieux had just reached that happy age.

Husband and wife, although they had not seen each other for more than a week and during that week serious events had occurred in which both were involved, met that day with some preoccupation on both sides. Nevertheless Monsieur Bonacieux manifested real joy as he advanced toward his wife with open arms. Madame Bonacieux presented her brow for his kiss.

"Let us talk a little," said she.

"What!" Bonacieux exclaimed in astonishment.

"Yes, we must. I have something of the greatest importance to tell you."

"As a matter of fact, I have some rather serious questions to put to you. First, explain your abduction a bit, I beg of you."

"That's of no importance just now," said Madame Bonacieux.

"What is important, then? My arrest?"

"I heard of that the day it happened, but as I knew you were not guilty of any crime and were not capable of any intrigue—in short, that you knew nothing that could compromise you or anyone else—I attached no more importance to your arrest than it warranted."

"You speak of it very lightly, madame," said Bonacieux, hurt because his wife showed so little interest. "Do you realize that I spent a whole day and a whole night in a cell in the Bastille?"

"A day and a night are soon gone. Let's forget your time in prison and return to the matter that brings me here."

"What? The matter that brings you here? Aren't you here because you want to see a husband you've been separated from for a week?" asked the haberdasher, wounded to the quick.

"For that first, of course. And afterward for something else—something of the greatest interest, something on which our good or ill fortune depends."

"The aspect of our fortunes has changed a good deal since I saw you, Madame Bonacieux, and I shouldn't be surprised if in a few months, our fortunes would excite the envy of a great many people."

"Yes indeed! Especially if you obey the instructions I am about to give you."

"*You*—give *me?*"

"Yes, *you.* There is a good and blessed deed to be done, monsieur—and a good deal of money to be made by doing it!"

Madame Bonacieux knew that in speaking of money she was attacking her husband's weak spot. But a man, even a haberdasher, who has talked ten minutes with the Cardinal de Richelieu is no longer the same man.

"A good deal of money to be made!" said Bonacieux.

"Yes, a great deal. A thousand pistoles, perhaps."

"Then what you are going to ask of me is momentous? What am I to do?"

"You must set out immediately. I will give you a paper that you must not part with on any pretext whatever. You are to deliver the paper into the proper hands."

"And where am I to go?"

"To London."

"*I* go to London! Come now, you're joking. I have no business to do in London."

"Others require you to go there."

"Who are those others? I warn you I will never again work in the dark. I must know not only what risks I run but for whose sake I run them."

"An illustrious person is sending you, an illustrious person awaits you. The reward will exceed your expectations, that is all I can promise you."

"More intrigues, always intrigues! Thank you, I mistrust them now. Monsieur le Cardinal has enlightened me on that head!"

"The Cardinal!" cried Madame Bonacieux. "You have seen the Cardinal?"

"He sent for me," the haberdasher answered proudly.

"And you went? You rash man!"

"Well, I can't say I had much choice as to going or not going, for I was taken there between two guards. I must also confess that, since I did not know His Eminence then, if I could have declined the invitation, I would have been delighted to do so."

"So he ill-treated you? He threatened you?"

"He gave me his hand and called me his friend—his friend, do you hear that, madame? I am a friend of the great Cardinal!"

"The great Cardinal!"

"Do you by any chance dispute his right to that title, madame?"

"I would dispute his right to nothing. But I tell you that the favor of a Minister is fleeting. A man must be mad to become attached to one. There are powers far higher than his, and they do not depend on the caprice of a man or on the outcome of one event. It is around those powers that we ought to rally."

"I am sorry, madame, but I recognize no other power than that of the great man I serve."

"You serve the Cardinal?"

"I do, madame, and as his servant I will not permit you to have any part in plots against the security of the state, or to assist in the intrigues of a woman who is not French and whose heart belongs to Spain. Fortunately we have the great Cardinal. His vigilant eye watches over us and penetrates to the depths of our hearts."

Bonacieux was repeating word for word a sentence he had heard the Comte de Rochefort give forth. His poor wife, who had counted on her husband and vouched for him to the Queen, shuddered at the danger she had escaped so narrowly, and at her own helplessness. Nevertheless, as she knew her husband's weakness and more particularly his cupidity, she did not despair of bringing him round to her purpose.

"So you're a cardinalist, monsieur!" she cried. "You serve the party that mistreats your wife and insults your Queen, do you?"

"Private interests count for nothing in face of the interests of all. I am for those who preserve the state," said Bonacieux pompously.

This was another of the Comte de Rochefort's pronouncements that he had remembered and now found an occasion to use.

"And have you any idea what this state you talk about is?" asked Madame Bonacieux, shrugging her shoulders. "Be content to be a plain, straightforward bourgeois, and turn toward the side that offers you the greatest advantages."

"Eh, eh," said Bonacieux, slapping a plump bag that jingled as he did so, "what do you say to that, my dear preacher?"

"Where does that money come from?"

"Can't you guess?"

"From the Cardinal?"

"From him and from my friend the Comte de Rochefort."

"The Comte de Rochefort! Why, it was he who kidnapped me!"

"That may be true, madame."

"And you accept money from that man?"

"Didn't you tell me yourself that you were kidnapped for some political reason?"

"Yes, I did. But I was abducted in order to force me to betray the Queen. They hoped by torturing me to wrest from me confessions that would jeopardize the honor and perhaps the very life of my august mistress."

"Madame," said Bonacieux, "your august mistress is a perfidious Spaniard, and what the Cardinal does is always rightly done."

"Monsieur," retorted the young woman, "I knew very well that you were a coward, a miser, and a fool, but I did not know you were a villain!"

"Madame," said Bonacieux, who had never seen his wife in a passion and recoiled before this outburst of anger, "madame, what are you saying?"

"I am saying that you are a wretched creature," replied Madame Bonacieux, who saw that she was regaining some of her influence over her husband. "Ah, you meddle with politics, do you? And with cardinalist politics at that! Why, you are selling yourself to the Devil, body and soul—for money!"

"No, it's the Cardinal."

"It's the same thing!" cried the young woman. "He who says Richelieu says Satan."

"Hold your tongue, madame, hold your tongue! We may be overheard."

"Yes, you're right. I should be ashamed to have anyone know of your cowardice."

"But just what is it you require from me? Come now!"

"I have told you. I ask you to set out instantly, monsieur, to carry out faithfully the mission I condescend to charge you with. If you do that, I will forgive everything, and what is more"—she held out her hand to him—"I will give you my love again."

Bonacieux was a coward, and he was a miser, but he loved his wife. He was deeply moved. A man of fifty cannot hold a grudge for long against a wife of twenty-three.

"Come, have you made up your mind?" she asked.

"But my love, consider what you are asking of me! London is a long way from Paris, a very long way, and perhaps the mission you are talking about is not without dangers."

"What does that matter if you avoid them?"

"No, Madame Bonacieux," said the haberdasher, "I won't do it. I positively refuse to. Intrigues terrify me. I have seen the Bastille, I have. Brr! It's a frightful place, that Bastille, the very thought of it makes my flesh creep. They threatened me with torture. No, I won't go, positively not! 'Sdeath, why don't you go yourself? Verily, I think I've been mistaken about you. I really think you're a man, and a madman at that!"

"And you—you're a woman, a miserable woman, stupid and besotted.

So you are afraid, are you? Well, if you do not leave at once, I will have you arrested by order of the Queen and have you shut up in that Bastille you dread so much."

"If you have me arrested by order of the Queen," retorted Bonacieux, "I will appeal to His Eminence, I will. "

Madame Bonacieux saw that she had gone too far, and she was appalled that she had said so much. For a moment, she was afraid as she contemplated that stupid countenance and saw on it the invincible resolution of a fool who is overcome by fear.

"Well, so be it," she said. "Perhaps you are right, after all. A man knows more about political matters than a woman, especially a man like you, Monsieur Bonacieux, who have talked with the Cardinal. And yet it is very hard," she added, "to have my husband, a man on whose affection I thought I could count, treat me so unkindly, and be unwilling to gratify one of my whims."

"That is because your whims may carry one too far," Bonacieux replied triumphantly, "and I mistrust them."

"I'll give it up, then," said the young woman with a sigh. "All right, let's say no more about it."

"Suppose you at least tell me what I was to do in London," suggested Bonacieux, who remembered a little late that Rochefort had enjoined him to try to discover his wife's secrets.

"There's no point in your knowing that," she replied, her instinctive mistrust causing her to retreat. "It was a question of a trifling matter such as women enjoy—a purchase that would mean a good profit."

But the more his young wife evaded his questions, the more Bonacieux was sure that the secret she refused to confide to him was important. Therefore he decided to hasten to the Comte de Rochefort on the instant and tell him that the Queen was seeking a messenger to send to London.

"Pray pardon me for leaving you, my dear Madame Bonacieux," he said, "but I did not know you would be coming to see me, so I made an appointment with one of my friends. I'll not be long, and if you will wait, I'll see you to the Louvre, as it's getting late."

"Thank you, monsieur," replied Madame Bonacieux, "but you are not brave enough to be of any use whatever. I will return to the Louvre quite safely by myself."

"As you please, Madame Bonacieux Am I to see you again soon?"

"Doubtless. Next week I hope my duties will allow me a little free time, and I will take advantage of it to come here and get things into some sort of order. They are certainly in a mess."

"Very well, I will expect you. You are not angry with me?"

"Who, I? Not the least in the world."

Bonacieux kissed his wife's hand and set off at a brisk pace.

"Well, well!" Madame Bonacieux murmured as soon as her husband had shut the street door. "All that man needed to make a complete fool of himself was to become a cardinalist! And I vouched for him to the Queen, I promised my poor mistress—— Oh, my God, my God, she will take me for one of those wretches the palace swarms with who have been put there to spy on her! Ah, Monsieur Bonacieux, I never did love you much and now things are worse than ever—I hate you, and I swear you shall pay for this!"

Just then she heard a rap on the ceiling and she raised her head. Then she heard a voice that came through the plaster and cried:

"Dear Madame Bonacieux, open the side door for me and I will come downstairs."

CHAPTER 18

"AH, MADAME," SAID D'ARTAGNAN AS HE ENTERED, "PER-mit me to tell you that you have a pretty mean husband!"

"So you heard our conversation?" asked Madame Bonacieux anxiously.

"Every word of it."

"But, my God, how could you do that?"

"By a method known to me alone, the same one I used to overhear the more lively conversation you had with the Cardinal's police."

"And how much did you learn from what we were saying?"

"A thousand things. First, I learned that your husband is a simpleton and a fool, which is fortunate for me. Next, that you were in trouble, which I'm very glad for, because it gives me an opportunity to be of service to you, and God knows I'm ready to risk hellfire to do that. Finally, I learned that the Queen has need of a brave, intelligent, devoted man to go to London for her. I possess at least two of the necessary qualities—and here I am."

Madame Bonacieux made no reply, but her heart leaped for joy and a secret hope shone bright in her eyes.

"And what guarantee will you give me," she asked, "if I entrust this mission to you?"

"My love for you. Come, speak, command! What am I to do?"

"My God, my God," murmured the young woman, "ought I to confide such a secret to you, monsieur? You are a mere boy!"

"I see you must have someone you trust who will vouch for me."

"I acknowledge that that would reassure me greatly."

"Do you know Athos? Porthos? Aramis?"

"No, none of them. Who are these gentlemen?"

"Three of the King's Musketeers. Do you know Monsieur de Tréville, their Captain?"

"Oh yes, I know him—not personally, but from having heard the Queen speak of him more than once as a brave and loyal gentleman."

"You're not afraid that he would betray you to the Cardinal, are you?"

"Oh no, certainly not."

"Very well, tell him your secret, and ask him whether you can trust me with it, however important, however precious, however terrible it may be."

"But the secret is not mine, and I cannot reveal it like that."

"You were about to confide it to Monsieur Bonacieux," said D'Artagnan resentfully.

"The way one trusts a letter to the hollow of a tree, the wing of a pigeon, or the collar of a dog."

"And yet you know very well that I love you."

"So you say."

"I am an honorable man!"

"I believe that."

"I am brave!"

"Oh, I'm sure of that."

"Then put me to the proof."

Madame Bonacieux looked intently at the young man, hesitating once more. But there was such ardor in his eyes, such conviction in his voice, that she felt that she could surely trust him. Besides, in her present circumstances she must risk all or lose all. The Queen might be ruined by too much caution as well as by too much trust. But we must admit that it was the affection she was beginning to feel for the young champion which decided her to speak.

"Listen," she said. "I yield to your protestations and your assurances. But I swear to you before God Who hears us that if you betray me I will kill myself and dying, will accuse you of being responsible for my death."

"And for my part, I swear before God, madame," said D'Artagnan, "that if I am arrested while I am carrying out your orders I will die without doing one thing or uttering one word that might compromise anyone."

Then the young woman told him the terrible secret that chance had already partially revealed to him in front of the Samaritaine. This was in fact the declaration of their love for each other. D'Artagnan was radiant with joy and pride. This secret he now possessed, this woman he loved! Confidence and love made him a very giant.

"I go," he said, "I go at once."

"How can you go at once?" cried Madame Bonacieux. "What about your regiment, your Captain?"

"Upon my soul, you have made me forget all that, dear Constance! Yes, you're right. I must get a furlough immediately."

"One more obstacle," murmured Madame Bonacieux sorrowfully.

"Oh, not a bad one!" cried D'Artagnan after a moment's reflection. "I'll get over it somehow. Don't you worry. I will go to Monsieur de Tréville this very evening and request him to obtain this favor for me from his brother-in-law, Monsieur des Essarts."

"But there's one thing more——"

"What is that?" asked D'Artagnan as he saw Madame Bonacieux hesitate to finish her sentence.

"Perhaps you have no money?"

"You don't need the 'perhaps'," said D'Artagnan, smiling.

"Then," said Madame Bonacieux, opening a cupboard door and taking out the bag that her husband had been fondling so lovingly half an hour before, "take this bag."

"The Cardinal's money!" cried D'Artagnan, roaring with laughter. Thanks to the tiles he had taken up he had not lost a syllable of the conversation between the haberdasher and his wife.

"Yes, the Cardinal's money," replied Madame Bonacieux. "You can see there's quite a lot of it."

"By the Lord," cried D'Artagnan, "it will be doubly amusing to save the Queen with His Eminence's money!"

"Hush!" said Madame Bonacieux.

"What's the matter?"

"Someone is talking in the street—it's my husband's voice, I recognize it."

D'Artagnan ran to the door and bolted it. "He shall not come in until I am off," said he. "When I am gone you can let him in."

"But I must leave too. How can I explain the disappearance of that money if he finds me here?"

"You're right. We must both leave."

"How can we leave the house? He will see us."

"Then you must come upstairs with me."

"Oh," cried Madame Bonacieux. "You say that in a tone that frightens me."

There were tears in her eyes. D'Artagnan saw them and, troubled and much touched, he fell on his knees.

"In my rooms," he declared, "you will be as safe as in a church, I give you my word as a gentleman."

"Let us go, then," she said. "I trust you, my friend."

D'Artagnan drew back the bolt cautiously and, as light as shadows, both of them stepped into the passage and went as quietly as possible up the stairs to D'Artagnan's apartment. Once they were there, for greater safety the young man barricaded the door. They went to the window, and through a slit in the shutter they saw Monsieur Bonacieux talking with a man wearing a long cloak. At the sight of this man D'Artagnan gave a leap, and, half drawing his sword, sprang toward the door. It was the man of Meung.

"What are you going to do?" cried Madame Bonacieux. "You will ruin both of us."

"But I have sworn to kill that man!"

"Your life belongs to a promise now, it does not belong to you. In the

Queen's name I forbid you to risk any danger other than that of your journey."

"And do you give me no orders in your own name?"

"In my own name," Madame Bonacieux replied with great emotion, "I beg you to listen. I think they are talking about me."

D'Artagnan drew closer to the window and listened attentively. Monsieur Bonacieux had entered the house, then, finding his own apartment empty, he had rejoined the man in the street.

"She's gone," he said. "She must have gone back to the Louvre."

"Are you sure," the stranger asked, "that she did not suspect your intention when you left her?"

"Yes," replied Bonacieux arrogantly. "She's too shallow-minded a woman for that."

"Is the young guardsman at home?"

"I don't think so. His shutters are closed, as you see, and I see no light through the openings."

"All the same, we must make sure. Go knock on his door."

"I will ask his lackey."

"Go do so."

Bonacieux went into the house again, took the same stairway the fugitives had taken, and knocked at D'Artagnan's door. No one answered. Porthos had borrowed Planchet that evening in order to cut more of a dash than usual. As for D'Artagnan, he took good care to show no sign of life. As Bonacieux's knock sounded, the two young people felt their hearts beat fast.

"There's nobody there," Bonacieux announced.

"All right, let's go to your apartment. We'll be safer there than in the doorway."

"Oh, my God!" murmured Madame Bonacieux. "Now we can't hear any more."

"On the contrary," replied D'Artagnan, "we shall hear all the better."

He took up the three or four tiles he had loosened, spread a rug on the floor near the place, knelt on it, and motioned to Madame Bonacieux to kneel too and to bend over to the listening post as he was doing.

"You're sure there is nobody here?" asked the nameless man.

"I will answer for it," Bonacieux replied.

"And you think your wife——?"

"Has gone back to the Louvre."

"Without speaking to anyone but you?"

"I am sure of it."

"That is an important point, you understand that, don't you?"

"So the news I brought you has some value?"

"Great value, my dear Bonacieux. I tell you that frankly."

"Then the Cardinal will be pleased with me?"

"Of course he will. Are you sure that your wife mentioned no names?"

"I don't think she did."

"She did not name either Madame de Chevreuse, the Duke of Buckingham, or Madame de Vernet?"

"No. She only said she wanted to send me to London in the interests of an illustrious person."

"The traitor!" murmured Madame Bonacieux.

"Hush!" whispered D'Artagnan, grasping a hand that she suffered him to keep.

"Never mind," the man in the cloak went on. "You're a simpleton not to have made a pretense of accepting the mission—you would be in possession of the letter now, the state, which is being threatened, would have been saved, and you——?"

"What about me?"

"Well, the Cardinal would be giving you some title or other as a nobleman."

"Did he tell you so?"

"Yes, I know he intended to surprise you with it."

"Never fear," replied Bonacieux. "My wife adores me, and there is still time."

"The idiot!" murmured Madame Bonacieux.

"Hush!" whispered D'Artagnan, pressing her hand still harder.

"What do you mean by saying there is still time?" asked the man with the cloak.

"I will go to the Louvre and ask for Madame Bonacieux. I will tell her I have been thinking it over and I'll take it on. I shall get the letter, and I will hasten to the Cardinal."

"Well, go quickly, I will return shortly to hear the result." And the nameless man left the room and the house.

"The villain!" murmured Madame Bonacieux.

"Hush!" D'Artagnan whispered once more, pressing her hand still harder.

A terrible howling interrupted D'Artagnan and Madame Bonacieux. Her husband had just discovered the disappearance of his money bag and was shrieking "Thieves! Stop thief!"

"Oh, my God," cried Madame Bonacieux, "he'll rouse the whole neighborhood!"

Bonacieux kept on howling for a long time, but such cries were heard so often in the Rue des Fossoyeurs that no one paid any attention to them. Besides, the haberdasher's house had been in ill repute for some time. Seeing that no one was coming, Bonacieux left the house, still howling, his cries growing fainter and fainter as he went toward the Rue du Bac.

"Now that he's gone it is your turn to go," said Madame Bonacieux.

"Courage, my friend, but above all, caution! Remember that you belong to the Queen."

"To her and to you!" cried D'Artagnan. "Rest easy, my lovely Constance, I shall come back worthy of Her Majesty's gratitude. But shall I come back also worthy of your love?"

The young woman's only reply was a deep blush. A few minutes later, D'Artagnan left the house, like his enemy wrapped in a great cloak, its folds lifted in knightly fashion by his long sword. Madame Bonacieux' eyes followed him with that lingering look of fondness which a woman gives the man she loves. But when he had turned the corner she fell on her knees and prayed, clasping her hands.

"O God," she cried, "watch over the Queen, watch over me!"

CHAPTER 19

D'ARTAGNAN WENT STRAIGHT TO THE HÔTEL DE TRÉ-
ville. He realized that within a few minutes the Cardinal would be informed of everything by that damned nameless man, evidently his agent,
and he thought with good reason that he had not a moment to lose.

The young man's heart overflowed with joy. He was being given an
opportunity both to win glory and to make money, and as its chief in-
spiration a bond had just been created between the woman he adored and
himself. Here at the very beginning chance was doing more for him than
he had dared to ask of Providence.

Monsieur de Tréville was in his drawing-room with his usual coterie
of gentlemen. D'Artagnan, who was well known there, went straight to
the office and sent the Captain word that he was waiting to see him on
a matter of great importance. He had been there barely five minutes
when Monsieur de Tréville came. At the first glance at the young man's
radiant face he saw that there was something quite new afoot.

All the way there D'Artagnan had been asking himself whether he
should tell Monsieur de Tréville everything or ask for carte blanche in a
matter of the greatest secrecy. But Monsieur de Tréville had always been
so wholehearted a friend to him and so completely devoted to the King
and the Queen, and he hated the Cardinal so cordially, that the young
man decided to tell him everything.

"You asked for me, my young friend?" said Monsieur de Tréville.

"Yes, monsieur, I did," replied D'Artagnan. "You will pardon me for
disturbing you, I trust, when you learn how important the matter is that
brings me here. It concerns nothing less," he went on, "than the honor
and perhaps the life of the Queen."

"What are you saying?" demanded Monsieur de Tréville, looking all
about to make sure they were alone.

"I am saying, monsieur, that chance has put me in possession of a
secret——"

"That you will guard with your very life, I trust," interrupted Monsieur de Tréville.

"But one that I must confide to you, monsieur, for you alone can help me in the mission I have just been given by Her Majesty."

"Is this secret your own?"

"No, monsieur, it is the Queen's."

"Are you authorized by Her Majesty to confide it to me?"

"No, monsieur. On the contrary, I have been enjoined to keep it absolutely secret."

"Then why are you about to betray it to me?"

"Because, as I told you, without your help I can do nothing, monsieur, and I feared you would not grant me the favor I came to request of you unless you knew my reason for asking it. I beg you to ask Monsieur des Essarts to grant me a fortnight's furlough, beginning tonight."

"Are you leaving Paris?"

"I am going on a mission."

"Can you tell me where you are going?"

"To London."

"Is there someone who will try to prevent you from reaching your destination?"

"I believe that the Cardinal would give anything in the world to stop me."

"Are you going alone?"

"I am."

"In that case, I tell you upon the word of a Tréville that you will not get any farther than Bondy. You will be murdered before that."

"Then I shall die doing my duty."

"But your mission will not be accomplished. Believe me, in undertakings of this kind, if one is to arrive, there must be four who set out."

"You're right, monsieur," D'Artagnan replied. "But you know that Athos, Porthos, and Aramis would do anything that I ask."

"And you wouldn't need to tell them your secret?"

"We four have sworn to be all for one and one for all, to trust one another blindly and devotedly. Besides, if you tell them that you trust me, they will trust me too."

"I can give each of them a fortnight's furlough, no more—to Athos, whose wound still bothers him, to go to take the waters at Forges, to Porthos and Aramis to go with their friend, as they are not willing to abandon him while he is suffering so much. Giving them furloughs will be proof that I authorize their journey."

"My thanks, monsieur. You are most kind."

"Go to them at once, then, and make all your arrangements tonight. Wait a minute—first write out your request to Monsieur des Essarts. Perhaps some spy was at your heels, and in that case the Cardinal already knows of your visit to me. You can make it seem a legitimate one by going from me to Monsieur des Essarts."

D'Artagnan drew up his request. When Monsieur de Tréville took it, he assured D'Artagnan that by two o'clock in the morning the four papers granting furloughs would be at the respective domiciles of the would-be travelers.

"Be good enough to send mine to Athos's, monsieur," said D'Artagnan. "I might run into something unpleasant if I went home."

"Don't worry, I will. Farewell, and bon voyage! By the way, have you any money?" D'Artagnan jingled the bag he had in his pocket. "Is it enough?"

"Three hundred pistoles."

"That's good. You could go to the end of the world with that. Be off, then."

D'Artagnan bowed, Monsieur de Tréville held out his hand, and D'Artagnan pressed it with respect mingled with gratitude. His first visit was to Aramis; he had not called on his friend since that fateful evening when he had trailed Madame Bonacieux. He had not seen the young musketeer often, and every time he did see him, he had noted that Aramis seemed very sad. This evening he found Aramis awake, but gloomy and pensive. D'Artagnan ventured a question or two about this deep melancholy. Aramis pleaded as his excuse a commentary on the eighteenth chapter of Saint Augustine's *Confessions*. He had to write it in Latin by the next week, and was preoccupied with it. After the two friends had chatted for a few moments, one of Monsieur de Tréville's lackey's entered with a sealed envelope in his hand.

"What's that?" Aramis asked.

"The leave of absence Monsieur requested."

"But I didn't ask for a leave of absence."

"Stop talking and take it," said D'Artagnan. Then he said to the lackey: "As for you, my good man, here's a half-pistole for your trouble. Tell Monsieur de Tréville that Monsieur Aramis thanks him very much. Now go." The lackey bowed and went out.

"What does all this mean?" asked Aramis.

"Pack up all you need for a fortnight's journey and follow me."

"But I cannot leave Paris just now without knowing——" There Aramis stopped.

"Without knowing what has become of her, isn't that it?" said D'Artagnan.

"Who?"

"The woman who was here once, the woman of the embroidered handkerchief."

"Who told you a woman had been here?" retorted Aramis, turning deathly pale.

"I saw her."

"And do you know who she is?"

"I think I can make a pretty good guess."

"See here, D'Artagnan, since you know so many things, do you know what has become of her?"

"I suppose she went back to Tours."

"To Tours? Yes, that's right—you know her. But why did she go back to Tours without letting me know?"

"Because she was afraid she would be arrested."

"Why didn't she write me?"

"Because she was afraid of compromising you."

"D'Artagnan, you restore me to life!" cried Aramis. "I thought I had been scorned, betrayed. I was so happy to see her again! I could not believe that she would risk her liberty for my sake, yet why else would she have come to Paris?"

"For the same reason that is sending us to England tonight."

"What is that reason?" demanded Aramis.

"You shall learn it someday, Aramis, but for the moment I will adopt the discretion of 'the doctor's niece.' "

Aramis smiled as he remembered the tale he had told his friends on a certain evening. "Very well. Since she has left Paris and you are sure she has, D'Artagnan, there's nothing to keep me here and I am ready to follow you. You say we are going——?"

"To Athos's first, and if you want to come with me, I beg you to make haste, for we've already wasted a lot of time. By the way, warn Bazin."

"Is Bazin to go with us?"

"Perhaps. Anyway, he'd better follow us to Athos's."

Aramis summoned Bazin and ordered him to follow them to Athos's. "Let's be off, then," he said. He took his cloak, his sword, and his three pistols and opened three or four drawers in the hope of finding a stray coin or two. When he was convinced that this was a vain hope, he followed D'Artagnan. As they went out, he laid his hand on D'Artagnan's arm and looked at him earnestly. "You haven't spoken of this woman to anyone, have you?" he asked.

"To no one on earth."

"Not even to Porthos or Athos?"

"I haven't breathed a syllable to either of them."

"That's fine!"

His mind at rest on this important point, Aramis went his way with D'Artagnan, and shortly they arrived at Athos's lodgings. They found Athos holding his leave of absence in one hand and a letter from Monsieur de Tréville in the other.

"Can you explain the meaning of this leave and this letter?" asked the astonished Athos, and he read the letter aloud.

My dear Athos:

Since I know that your health absolutely requires it, I wish you to rest for a fortnight. Go to take the waters at Forges, then, or at any other spa you prefer, and get well quickly.

Yours affectionately

De Tréville

"Well," said D'Artagnan, "that leave and that letter mean that you must come with me, Athos."

"To the waters at Forges?"

"There or somewhere else."

"On the King's service?"

"Either the King's or the Queen's. Are we not servants of both Their Majesties?"

Just then Porthos came in. "By the Lord," he said, "here's an odd thing! Since when are furloughs being granted to musketeers without their asking for them?"

"Since the moment they have friends to ask for them in their behalf," said D'Artagnan.

"Aha!" cried Porthos. "Apparently there's something new in the wind. Am I right?"

"Yes. We are setting out," said Aramis.

"For what part of the country?" demanded Porthos.

"By my faith, I don't know anything about that," observed Athos. "Ask D'Artagnan."

"For London, gentlemen," said D'Artagnan.

"For London!" cried Porthos. "And what the devil are we to do in London?"

"That is something I am not at liberty to tell you, gentlemen. You will have to trust me without knowing that."

"But to go to London," said Porthos, "we must have money, and I haven't any."

"Neither have I," said Aramis.

"Nor I," said Athos.

"I have," said D'Artagnan, pulling his treasure, or rather Monsieur Bonacieux's, from his pocket and putting it on the table. "There are three hundred pistoles in that bag. Each of us will take seventy-five. That's quite enough to get us to London and back. Besides, don't you worry—all of us will not reach London. In all probability, some of us will be left by the wayside."

"What is this, then, we're undertaking—a campaign?"

"And a most dangerous one, I warn you."

"Aha!" cried Porthos. "If we are going to risk being killed, I would at least like to know what for."

"Does the King usually give you his reasons? He just tells you quite simply, 'Gentlemen, there's fighting in Gascony—or in Flanders. Go there and fight!' and you go. Why? You don't bother about that."

"D'Artagnan is right," said Athos. "Here are our three furloughs from Monsieur de Tréville, and here are three hundred pistoles from I don't know where. So let's go and get killed wherever we're told. Is life worth the trouble of asking so many questions? D'Artagnan, I am ready to follow you."

"So am I," said Porthos.

"And I too," said Aramis. "All the more because I'm not sorry to leave Paris. I need a little recreation."

"Well, you'll get plenty of recreation, gentlemen, don't worry about that!" said D'Artagnan.

"When are we to leave?" Athos queried.

"Immediately," D'Artagnan replied. "We haven't a minute to lose."

"Holà! Grimaud! . . . Planchet! . . . Mousqueton! . . . Bazin!" cried the four young men to their lackeys, bidding them go home to polish their masters' boots and fetch their horses. The lackeys started off at full speed.

"Now for our plan of campaign," said Porthos. "Where do we go first?"

"To Calais," D'Artagnan replied. "That's the shortest route to London."

"Well," announced Porthos, "here is my advice. Four men traveling together would arouse suspicion, so we should go by different roads. D'Artagnan should give each of us his instructions."

"Porthos's plan doesn't seem feasible to me," said D'Artagnan, "inasmuch as I myself do not know what instructions I can give you. All I can say is that I have a letter to deliver. I cannot make three copies of the letter, because it is sealed. Therefore in my opinion we should all travel together. The letter is in this pocket." He touched his breast pocket. "If I am killed, one of you will take it and ride on; if that one is killed, another of you will take the letter, and so on. One thing only is imperative—one of us must arrive."

"Bravo, D'Artagnan! I agree with you," said Athos. "Besides, we must be consistent. I was to go to take the waters at Forges, but I will go to the waters of the sea instead, as I am free to do. If anyone tries to stop us, I will show Monsieur de Tréville's letter and you will show your furlough papers. If we are attacked, we will defend ourselves; if we are court-martialed, we will stoutly maintain that we had no other intention than to take dips in the sea a certain number of times. Four men alone would be only too easily disposed of, but four men together form a troop. We will arm our four lackeys with pistols and musketoons. If an army is sent out against us, we will give battle, and as D'Artagnan said, the survivor will deliver the letter."

"Right you are!" cried D'Artagnan. "You don't speak often, Athos, but when you do, you speak like Saint John of the Golden Mouth. I say we should adopt Athos's plan. How about you, Porthos?"

"I'm with you," replied Porthos, "if that suits D'Artagnan. As the bearer of the letter, D'Artagnan is naturally the leader of our enterprise. Let him make the decisions and we will carry them out."

"Very well," said D'Artagnan, "my decision is that we adopt Athos's plan, and that we set off within half an hour."

"Agreed!" shouted the three musketeers in chorus.

Then each one plunged his hand into the money bag, took seventy-five pistoles, and went off to make his own preparations to set out at the appointed time.

CHAPTER 20

AT TWO O'CLOCK THE NEXT MORNING OUR FOUR ADVEN-
turers left Paris by the Porte Saint-Denis. As long as it was black night
they were silent. They could not help feeling the influence of the awesome
darkness, and they imagined ambushes everywhere. With the first rays of
daylight their tongues were loosened, and with the sun their gaiety revived. As on the eve of battle, their hearts beat high, their eyes sparkled,
and they felt that the life they were perhaps about to lose was a good
thing, after all.

The appearance of the caravan was indeed formidable. The black
horses of the musketeers, their martial air, and that squadron training
which makes those noble companions of the soldier keep in perfect step
—these would have betrayed the most strict incognito. Their lackeys rode
behind them, armed to the teeth.

All went well until they reached Chantilly at about eight in the morning. They were ready for breakfast, and they dismounted at an inn with
a sign picturing Saint Martin giving half his cloak to a beggar. They enjoined the lackeys to keep the horses saddled, water them, and be ready
to set off again immediately.

The four friends entered the common room of the inn and sat down
at a table. A gentleman who had just arrived was breakfasting at the same
table. He opened the conversation by talking about rain and fine weather,
the travelers replied; he drank to their good health, the travelers returned
the courtesy. But just as Mousqueton came to announce that the horses
were ready and they were rising from the table, the stranger proposed to
Porthos that they drink a toast to the Cardinal. Porthos said that he
would like nothing better provided the stranger would also drink to the
King. The stranger shouted that he recognized no other king than His
Eminence. Porthos told him he was drunk; the stranger drew his sword.

"You've done a foolish thing," said Athos. "Never mind, you can't
draw back now. Kill the fellow, and join us as soon as you can."

The three others mounted their horses and rode off at full speed while
Porthos was promising his adversary to puncture him with all the thrusts
known to fencing.

"There's one of us out," said Athos presently.

"But why did the fellow attack Porthos rather than any other of us?" asked Aramis.

"Because Porthos was talking louder than the rest of us, he took him for our leader," D'Artagnan replied.

"I've always said this Gascon cadet was a well of wisdom," murmured Athos.

At Beauvais they stopped to give their horses a breathing spell as well as to wait for Porthos. After two hours, as Porthos had neither arrived nor sent word to them, they resumed their journey.

A league from Beauvais, at a place where the road narrowed between two high banks, they came upon eight or ten men who, taking advantage of the fact that the road was not paved there, seemed to be busy digging holes and opening muddy ruts. Aramis, afraid that he would muddy his boots in this artificial trench, apostrophized them sharply. Athos tried to restrain him, but it was too late. The workmen began to jeer at the travelers. Their insolence made even the phlegmatic Athos lose his head, and he urged his horse against one of them. At that every man of them retreated to the ditch and seized a hidden musket. The result was that our seven travelers were literally showered with bullets. Aramis received one through his shoulder, Mousqueton another in the fleshy parts that prolong the small of the back. Mousqueton was the only one to fall from his horse —not because he was severely wounded, but because, not being able to see the wound, he thought he was more seriously hurt than he was.

"This is an ambush," said D'Artagnan. "Don't waste a shot! On our way at once!"

Aramis, wounded though he was, clung to his horse's mane and was borne along with the others. Mousqueton's horse had joined the other lackeys' and galloped off in the proper place all by itself.

"That will give us a remount," observed Athos.

"I'd rather have a hat," said D'Artagnan. "Mine was carried away by a bullet. My faith, it's mighty fortunate the letter wasn't in it."

"See here, they'll kill poor Porthos when he comes up," said Aramis.

"If Porthos were on his legs, he would have caught up with us by now," replied Athos. "My opinion is that when they got to the dueling ground the man Porthos called drunk sobered up."

They galloped on for another two hours, though their horses were so fatigued that it was to be feared that they would give out entirely soon. They had been taking side roads, hoping to avoid further molestation, but at Crèvecœur Aramis declared he could go no farther. As a matter of fact, it had taken all the courage hidden beneath his elegant figure and his polished manners to get him that far. He grew paler and paler by the minute, and had to be held up on his horse. They lifted him down at the door of an inn, and helped him inside, left Bazin with him, and set forward again, hoping to sleep that night at Amiens.

"'Sdeath," said Athos when he and D'Artagnan were once more on their way, their numbers reduced to two masters, Grimaud, and Planchet, "I swear I won't be fooled by them again. From here to Calais, no one shall make me open my mouth or draw my sword. I swear by——"

"Let's waste no time in swearing," interrupted D'Artagnan. "Let's gallop—if our horses will let us."

The travelers dug their spurs into their horses' flanks and the horses, stimulated so vigorously, recovered their strength. They reached Amiens at midnight, and dismounted at the inn called The Golden Lily. The host looked as if he were the most honest man on earth. He received them with a candle in one hand and his cotton nightcap in the other. He wanted to assign them each in a delightful bedroom, but unfortunately these delightful bedrooms were at opposite ends of the inn, and D'Artagnan and Athos refused them. The host declared that he had no other rooms worthy of Their Excellencies, but his guests declared in their turn that they would sleep on mattresses laid on the floor of the public room. The host insisted but the travelers held their ground and he was forced to do as they wished.

They had just prepared their beds and barricaded their door when someone knocked on the courtyard shutters. They asked who was there, and when they recognized the voices of their lackeys, opened the shutters.

"Grimaud can watch over the horses by himself," said Planchet. "If you gentlemen are willing, I shall sleep across your door. Then you will be certain that no one can get at you."

"And what will you sleep on?" asked D'Artagnan.

"Here's my bed," Planchet answered, producing a bundle of straw.

"Come now, you're right," said D'Artagnan. "I don't like mine host's face at all; it's too amiable."

Planchet climbed through the window and settled himself across the doorway. Grimaud went off to lock himself into the stable, announcing that at five in the morning he and the four horses would be ready.

The night passed off quietly enough, except for two incidents. At about two o'clock, somebody tried to open the door. Planchet woke and started up crying, "Who goes there?" The somebody answered that he had made a mistake and went away. At four o'clock in the morning there was a terrible uproar in the stables. Grimaud had tried to waken the stableboys and the stableboys had set upon him and were beating him. When they opened the window, Athos and D'Artagnan saw the poor lad lying senseless on the ground, his head cut badly by a blow from the handle of a pitchfork.

Planchet went to the courtyard intending to saddle the horses. The horses were foundered. Only Mousqueton's horse, which had trotted riderless for five or six hours the day before, was fit to continue the journey. However, it seemed that by some inconceivable error, the veterinary who had been sent for to bleed the host's horse had bled Mousqueton's instead.

All this was beginning to be disturbing. All these accidents, one after the other, might possibly have happened by chance, but it was quite as probable that they might be the fruits of a plot. Athos and D'Artagnan went back to the inn while Planchet tried to discover whether there might be three horses for sale in the neighborhood. At the gate he saw two horses, fresh, strong, and fully equipped. These would be just right. He asked where their owners were and was told that they had spent the night at the inn and were now settling their accounts with the innkeeper.

Athos went to pay the reckoning while D'Artagnan and Planchet waited by the street door. The innkeeper was in a low-ceilinged back room, and Athos was asked to go there. He entered the room without the least mistrust and took two pistoles from his pocket to pay the bill. Mine host was alone and sitting at his desk, one of the drawers of which was half-open. He took the money Athos offered him, turned it over and over in his hands, then suddenly shouted that it was counterfeit, and he would have Athos and his companions arrested as coiners.

"You scoundrel!" cried Athos, stepping toward him. "I'll cut your ears off!" At that very instant four men, armed to the teeth, entered by side doors and fell upon Athos.

"I'm in a trap!" shouted Athos with all the power of his lungs. "Get away, D'Artagnan! Spur, spur!" And he fired two pistol shots.

D'Artagnan and Planchet needed no repetition of that command. They untied the horses that were waiting at the gate, leaped onto them, buried their spurs in the horses' flanks, and set off at full gallop.

"Do you know what happened to Athos?" D'Artagnan asked Planchet as they were galloping along.

"Well, monsieur," the lackey replied, "I saw one man fall at each of his shots, and as I glanced through the glass in the door, it looked as if he were using his sword on the other two."

"My brave Athos!" murmured D'Artagnan. "And to think that we must abandon him! Ah well, perhaps the same fate awaits us a few paces from here! Forward, Planchet, forward! You're a brave fellow yourself!"

"I told you, monsieur," replied Planchet, "that I was a Picard, and you find out what a Picard is when you need him. Besides, I'm in my own country here, and that puts me on my mettle."

Spurring on harder than ever, master and lackey reached Saint-Omer without drawing rein. There they rested their horses, keeping their bridles over their arms for fear of some mishap, and ate a little food standing in the road. Then they set off again.

At a hundred paces from the gate of Calais, D'Artagnan's horse sank

Louis XIII Asks the Queen to Wear the Diamond Tags

The Man in the Cloak

under him, and nothing could be done to get it up again; blood was flowing from both its eyes and its nose. There was still Planchet's horse, but it had stopped for good, and there was nothing to be done about that one either. Fortunately, as has been said, they were only a hundred paces from the city. They left their mounts on the highway and hurried to the port.

Planchet called his master's attention to a gentleman and his lackey only fifty paces ahead of them. They caught up with the gentleman quickly. He seemed to be in great haste; his boots were covered with dust. He was asking whether he could get passage to England at once.

"Nothing easier," said the captain of a vessel just ready to sail, "except that this morning orders came to allow no one to cross the Channel without express permission from Monsieur le Cardinal."

"I have that permission," the gentleman said, taking a paper from his pocket. "Here it is."

"Get it countersigned by the Governor of the Port," said the captain, "and give me first choice to take you over."

"Where shall I find the Governor?"

"At his country house, about a quarter of a league out of town. Look, you can see it from here—the one at the foot of a little hill—that slate roof."

"I see it," said the gentleman, and he set off toward the Governor's country house, followed by his lackey.

D'Artagnan and Planchet followed them five hundred paces to the rear, but once out of the city, D'Artagnan accelerated his pace, and overtook the gentleman just as he was entering a little wood.

"Monsieur," said D'Artagnan, "you seem to be in a great hurry."

"I couldn't be in a greater hurry, monsieur."

"I'm very sorry to hear that," said D'Artagnan. "I'm in a great hurry myself, and I wanted to ask you to do me a favor."

"What favor, monsieur?"

"To allow me to go ahead of you."

"Impossible," said the gentleman. "I have come sixty leagues in forty-four hours, and I must be in London by noon tomorrow."

"I have covered the same distance in forty hours, and I must be in London tomorrow by ten in the morning."

"I'm most sorry, monsieur, but I got here first and I will not take second place."

"I'm most sorry, monsieur, but I got here second and I *will* take first place."

"I am on the King's service!" said the gentleman.

"I'm on my own service!" retorted D'Artagnan.

"But this is a needless quarrel you are seeking, it seems to me. What is it you want?"

"Well, I want that permission you have. I haven't one myself, and I absolutely have to have one."

"You are jesting, I presume."

"I never jest."

"Let me pass!"

"You shall not pass."

"My fine young man, I'm going to blow your brains out. Holà, Lubin, my pistols!"

"Planchet," said D'Artagnan, "you take care of the lackey. I'll look out for the master."

Planchet, emboldened by his first exploit, sprang upon Lubin, and being strong and vigorous, threw him down flat on his back and planted his knee on Lubin's chest.

"Go ahead with your own business, monsieur," he called. "Mine is finished."

Then the gentleman drew his sword and lunged at D'Artagnan, but he had a powerful adversary to deal with. In three seconds, D'Artagnan wounded him three times, announcing as he dealt each thrust:

"One for Athos! One for Porthos! One for Aramis!"

At the third thrust the gentleman fell like a log. D'Artagnan thought he was dead, or at least unconscious, and stooped over him to seize the Cardinal's permission. But just as he stretched out his hand to search him, the wounded man, who had not dropped his sword, plunged the point into D'Artagnan's breast, crying:

"And one for you!"

"And one for me!" shouted D'Artagnan, nailing him to the earth with a fourth thrust through the body.

This time the gentleman closed his eyes and fainted. D'Artagnan felt in the pocket in which he had seen the gentleman put the order and seized it. It was made out to the Comte de Wardes. Then, casting a last glance at the handsome young man lying unconscious or perhaps dead, D'Artagnan heaved a sigh over that strange fate which drives men to destroy one another in the interests of people who are strangers to them, and who often do not even know that their champions exist.

But he was soon aroused from these reflections by Lubin, who was howling and screaming for help with all his might. Planchet grasped Lubin by the throat and bore down as hard as he could.

"Monsieur," he said, "as long as I hold him like this he won't make a sound, I'm certain of that. But as soon as I let go, he will begin to howl again as loud as ever. I can see he's a Norman, and Normans are pig-headed."

"Wait a minute," D'Artagnan replied, and he pulled out his handkerchief and gagged Lubin.

"Now," said Planchet, "let's tie him up against a tree."

They made a thorough job of that, then drew the Comte de Wardes's body close to his lackey. As night was drawing near and the wounded man and the gagged and bound lackey were at some little distance within the wood, it was evident that they were likely to stay there until the next day.

"And now," said D'Artagnan, "to the Governor's!"

"But you are wounded, aren't you, monsieur?"

"Oh, that's nothing. Let's attend to our most urgent business, then we can attend to the wound. It's not a dangerous one."

They both set forward as fast as they could toward the country house of the worthy official. Then the Comte de Wardes was announced. D'Artagnan entered and made his request.

"Have you an order signed by the Cardinal?" the Governor asked.

"Yes, monsieur," replied D'Artagnan. "Here it is."

"I see—quite regular and explicit," said the Governor.

"Naturally," said D'Artagnan. "I am one of his most faithful servants."

"Apparently His Eminence is anxious to prevent someone from crossing to England."

"Yes, monsieur, a certain D'Artagnan, a gentleman from Béarn who left Paris with three of his friends, intending to go to London."

"Do you know him personally, this D'Artagnan?"

"Very well."

"Describe him to me, then."

"Nothing could be easier." And D'Artagnan thereupon described the Comte de Wardes in the most minute detail.

"Is there anyone with him?"

"Yes, his lackey, Lubin by name."

"We will keep a sharp lookout for them, and if we lay hands on them, His Eminence may be sure that they will be sent back to Paris under proper guard."

"By doing so, Monsieur le Gouverneur, you will deserve well of the Cardinal."

"Will you be seeing him on your return, Monsieur le Comte?"

"Of course."

"Tell him, I beg you, that I am his humble servant."

"I will not fail to do so."

Delighted with this assurance, the Governor countersigned the passport and gave it to D'Artagnan. D'Artagnan lost no time in idle compliments; he bowed to the Governor, thanked him, and departed. Once outside, he and Planchet set off as fast as they could go, and by making a long detour they avoided the wood and went back to Calais by another gate. At the port they found the vessel still ready to sail and the captain was waiting on the quay.

"Well?" he said when he saw D'Artagnan.

"Here is my pass, duly countersigned," replied D'Artagnan.

"And that other gentleman?"

"He will not leave today," said D'Artagnan.

"In that case, let's go."

D'Artagnan leaped at once into the dory, Planchet followed him, and five minutes later they were aboard the vessel. It was high time, too, for they were only half a league out to sea when D'Artagnan saw a flash and heard a detonation of a cannon announcing the closing of the harbor.

Now it was time to see about his wound. Fortunately, as he had thought, it was not a very dangerous one. The point of the sword had struck a rib and glanced along the bone, his shirt had stuck to the wound at once, and he had lost very little blood. But he was quite exhausted, and when a mattress was spread out on the deck for him, he threw himself down on it and fell fast asleep.

At daybreak he learned that the vessel was only three or four leagues from the English coast. At ten o'clock the anchor was dropped in Dover Harbor. At half-past ten D'Artagnan set foot on English soil, crying:

"Here I am at last!"

But that was not all—he must get to London. In England the post was well organized. D'Artagnan and Planchet procured post horses, a postilion rode before them, and in a few hours they were at the gates of the capital. D'Artagnan did not know London at all, nor did he know a word of English, but he wrote the name Buckingham on a scrap of paper, and everyone to whom he showed it pointed out the way to the Duke's palace.

The Duke was at Windsor hunting with the King. D'Artagnan asked for the Duke's confidential valet Patrick, who had accompanied him in all his travels and spoke perfect French. The valet came, and D'Artagnan told him that he had just come from Paris on a matter of life and death, and must speak to his master immediately.

The assurance with which D'Artagnan spoke convinced Patrick at once. The Minister's minister ordered two horses saddled, and undertook to act as guide to the young guardsman. As to Planchet, he had been lifted from his horse as stiff as a ramrod; the poor lad's strength was almost exhausted. D'Artagnan seemed to be made of iron.

They reached Windsor Castle, and were told that the King and Buckingham were hawking in the marshes three or four leagues from there. In twenty minutes they reached the place, and presently Patrick recognized his master's voice calling a falcon back to him.

"Whom shall I announce to His Grace?" asked Patrick.

"The young man who challenged him one evening in front of the Samaritaine."

"That's rather a peculiar introduction!"

"You will find that it's as good as any other."

Patrick galloped off, reached the Duke, and announced that a messenger was awaiting him, identifying that messenger as he had been told to. Buckingham realized at once that the messenger was D'Artagnan. Suspecting that something important was going on in France that he was bringing news of, he rode off at once toward the spot where Patrick said the messenger was waiting. Recognizing from afar the uniform of the Royal Guards, he put his horse to the gallop and rode straight to D'Artagnan. Patrick kept discreetly in the background.

"No mishap has befallen the Queen?" Buckingham asked, in a voice betraying all his fear and all his love.

"I do not think so. But I believe she is in some great danger from which only Your Grace can rescue her."

"I?" cried Buckingham. "God knows I would be only too happy to be of service to her, any service whatever! Speak, man, speak!"

"Pray take this letter, Your Grace," said D'Artagnan.

"This letter! A letter from whom?"

"From Her Majesty, I think."

"From Her Majesty!" repeated Buckingham, turning so pale that D'Artagnan thought he was about to faint. The Duke broke the seal.

"How did this tear come to be here?" he said, pointing to a place where the paper was pierced through.

"Oh," said D'Artagnan, "I didn't notice that. It was the Comte de Wardes's sword that made that hole when he ran it into my chest."

"Are you wounded?" asked Buckingham as he opened the letter.

"Oh, it's nothing!" said D'Artagnan. "A mere scratch."

"Good heavens, what do I read here?" cried the Duke. "Patrick, stay here, or rather find the King wherever he may be and tell His Majesty that I beseech him to excuse me but that a matter of the utmost importance calls me to London." Then to D'Artagnan. "Come with me, monsieur, come!" And both of them set off toward the capital at full gallop.

CHAPTER 21

ALONG THE WAY THE DUKE DREW FROM D'ARTAGNAN not all that had happened, but all that D'Artagnan himself knew. By adding all that he heard from the young Gascon to what he himself recalled, he was able to form a pretty exact picture of the state of affairs. The Queen's letter, though short and giving few details, told him how serious the situation was. But what astonished him most was that the Cardinal, so keenly interested in preventing the young man from setting foot in England, had not succeeded in stopping him en route. When he saw the Duke's astonishment, D'Artagnan told him the precautions that had been taken; how devoted his three friends had been; how he had left them scattered along the road, covered with blood; how he had managed to get away with only the sword thrust that had gone through the Queen's letter; and with what terrible coin he had repaid Monsieur de Wardes.

As he listened to this story, told so ingenuously, the Duke looked at the young man from time to time with fresh astonishment, as if he could not understand how to reconcile so much prudence, courage, and devotion with the barely twenty years D'Artagnan's face revealed.

The horses went like the wind, and in a few minutes they were in London. Buckingham rode on at top speed, regardless of anyone who crossed his path. When they entered the courtyard of his palace, he leaped from his horse and rushed toward the entrance. D'Artagnan followed him.

The Duke walked so fast that D'Artagnan had some trouble in keeping up with him. They passed through several rooms furnished with an elegance that even the greatest nobles of France could not have imagined, and at last reached a bedchamber that was a miracle of both taste and splendor. In a recess of this room there was a door hidden in the tapestry. The Duke unlocked it with a small gold key that he wore around his neck on a chain of the same precious metal. Out of discretion, D'Artagnan held back, but as Buckingham was passing through the door he turned, and noting the young man's hesitation, said:

"Come in, and if you have the good fortune to be admitted to Her Majesty's presence, tell her what you have seen."

Encouraged by this invitation, D'Artagnan followed the Duke, who closed the door behind them. They were in a small chapel hung with tapestry of Persian silk embossed in gold and brilliantly illuminated by a great number of candles. Above what looked like an altar, under a canopy of blue velvet topped by white and red plumes, hung a life-sized portrait of Anne of Austria. It was so perfect a likeness that D'Artagnan gave a cry of surprise. The Queen looked as if she were about to speak.

On the altar, beneath the portrait, lay the casket that contained the diamond tags. The Duke went to the altar, knelt as a priest would kneel before the Sacrament, then opened the casket.

"Here," he said, taking from the casket a large knot of blue ribbon sparkling with diamonds, "here are those precious tags which I have vowed shall be buried with me. The Queen gave them to me, the Queen is taking them back. Her will be done, like that of God Almighty, in all things."

He began to kiss one by one those tags with which he must part. Suddenly he uttered a terrible cry.

"What is it?" asked D'Artagnan anxiously. "What is the matter, Your Grace?"

"The matter is that all is lost!" cried Buckingham, deathly pale. "Two of the tags are missing. There are only ten here."

"Has Your Grace lost them, or do you think they have been stolen?"

"They have been stolen," replied the Duke, "and it is the Cardinal who has dealt me this blow. Here, look, the ribbons that held them have been cut with scissors."

"If Your Grace suspects anyone—well, perhaps that person still has them."

"Wait a minute, wait!" cried the Duke. "The only time I have worn these tags was at a ball given by the King a week ago at Windsor. Lady Clark, with whom I had had a quarrel once, stood close by me at that ball, offering to make it up. That pretense of reconciliation was nothing but a jealous woman's revenge. I have never seen her since. That woman is an agent of the Cardinal's."

"Does he have agents all over the world?" cried D'Artagnan.

"Oh yes, yes," said Buckingham, gnashing his teeth with rage. "He is a terrible antagonist. But tell me, when is this ball to take place?"

"Next Monday."

"Next Monday! We still have five days, that's more time than we need. Patrick!" shouted the Duke, opening the chapel door. "Patrick!" His confidential valet appeared. "Fetch my jeweler and my secretary."

The valet went out with a promptness and a silence that showed that he was accustomed to obey blindly and without a word. But although the jeweler had been named first, it was the secretary who appeared first, as he lived in the ducal palace. He found Buckingham seated at a desk in his bedchamber, writing orders with his own hand.

"Mr. Jackson," said the Duke, "you are to call on the Lord Chancellor at once and charge him with the execution of these orders. I wish them to be issued immediately."

"But Your Grace, if the Lord Chancellor asks me what reasons led you to take such an extraordinary measure, what shall I answer?"

"That such is my good pleasure and I account for my wishes to no man."

"Is that the answer he is to send to His Majesty," asked the secretary, smiling, "if perchance His Majesty should wish to know why no vessel may leave any port in Great Britain?"

"You're right to ask, sir," replied Buckingham. "In that case he will tell the King that I have determined on war and that this measure is my first act of hostility against France." The secretary bowed and withdrew. "We are safe on that score," Buckingham said to D'Artagnan. "If the tags have not yet left for France, they will not get there before you do."

"How so, Your Grace?"

"I've just laid an embargo on all vessels at present in His Majesty's ports. Without express permission, not one of them can weigh anchor."

D'Artagnan stared with stupefaction at this man who was using in the service of his amours the limitless powers with which Charles I trusted him. Buckingham saw by the young man's expression what he was thinking, and he smiled.

"Yes," he said, "yes, Anne of Austria is my true Queen. At one word from her I would betray my country, I would betray my God. She asked me not to send the Protestants of La Rochelle the aid I had promised them, and I have not done so. I broke my word, but what matters that? I obeyed her wishes. Have I not been richly rewarded for my obedience, tell me? For it is to that obedience I owe her portrait!"

D'Artagnan wondered at the fragile and hidden threads on which the destinies of a nation or a life sometimes hang. He was lost in these reflections when the goldsmith entered. He was an Irishman, and one of the most skillful of his craft. He said himself that he earned a hundred thousand pounds a year from the Duke of Buckingham's commissions. The Duke led him into the chapel and opened the casket.

"Mr. O'Reilly," he said, "look at these diamond tags and tell me what they are worth apiece."

The goldsmith cast one glance at the elegant mounting of the diamonds, calculated the value of each tag, and answered without hesitation:

"Fifteen hundred pistoles apiece, my lord."

"How much time do you need to make two tags to match these? You can see that two are missing."

"A week, my lord."

"I will give you three thousand pistoles for each of the two if I can have them by the day after tomorrow."

"My lord, you shall have them!"

"You're a jewel of a man, Mr. O'Reilly. But that isn't all of it. Those tags cannot be entrusted to anyone—the work must be done here in this palace."

"Impossible, my lord. No one but myself can make new tags exactly like the others."

"Therefore, Mr. O'Reilly, you are now my prisoner. If you wanted to leave my palace now, you could not, so make the best of it. Name any of your craftsmen you will need, and tell me what tools they must bring with them."

The goldsmith knew the Duke; he realized that any objection would be futile, and he made up his mind at once.

"May I let my wife know?" he asked.

"Oh, you may even see her if you like, my dear Mr. O'Reilly. Your captivity will be a pleasant one, rest assured, and since every inconvenience calls for some compensation, here—in addition to the price of the tags—here is an order for a thousand pistoles to make you forget the trouble I am giving you."

D'Artagnan could not get over his surprise at the way this Minister juggled with men and millions. As to the goldsmith, he wrote to his wife, enclosing the order for one thousand pistoles and bidding her to send his most skillful apprentice, an assortment of diamonds—specifying the names and weights—some gold, the tools he needed, sending a list of these, and his personal necessities. Buckingham took him to the room allotted to him, and within half an hour it was transformed into a workshop. He stationed a sentinel at each of its doors with orders to allow no one to enter, and no one to go out, except Patrick.

Having arranged all this, the Duke returned to D'Artagnan. "Now, my young friend," said he, "all England is yours and mine. What would you like? Tell me and it shall be yours."

"A bed, Your Grace," D'Artagnan replied. "I confess that's the thing I stand in most need of at the moment."

Buckingham assigned D'Artagnan a bedchamber adjoining his own. He wanted to keep the young man close at hand—not because he mistrusted him, but in order to have someone to whom he could talk constantly about the Queen.

An hour later an ordinance was proclaimed in London forbidding the departure from any British port of any vessel bound for France. Even the mail packet was to be held up. Everyone in England took this for a declaration of war between the two kingdoms.

Two days later, at eleven in the morning, the new diamond tags were finished, and they were so perfect a match that Buckingham could not tell the new ones from the old ones, and the greatest experts would have been in like case. The Duke attached the tags to their ribbons, then summoned D'Artagnan.

"Look," he said, "here are the diamond tags you came to fetch. Be my witness that I have done everything that human power could do."

"Have no fear, my lord. I will tell what I have seen. But is Your Grace giving me the tags without the box?"

"The casket would only be a bother to you. Besides, the casket is all the more precious to me because it is all I have left. You will tell Her Majesty that I am keeping it."

"I will deliver your message word for word, my lord."

"And now," said Buckingham, looking intently at the young man, "how can I ever pay my debt to you?"

D'Artagnan blushed to the roots of his hair. He saw that the Duke was trying to find a way to get him to accept some reward, and the idea that his comrades' blood and his own were to be paid for in English gold was strangely repugnant to him.

"Let us understand each other, my Lord," he said, "let us consider the facts now, so that there may be no misunderstanding. I am in the service of the King and Queen of France. I am a guardsman in the Royal Guards, in the company of Monsieur des Essarts. My captain, like his brother-in-law Monsieur de Tréville, is particularly devoted to Their Majesties. Moreover, perhaps I would not have done all this had I not wished to please someone who is my own lady, as the Queen is yours."

"I see," said the Duke, smiling. "And I think I even know who that other lady is. She is——"

"My lord, I have not spoken her name."

"True," said the Duke. "It is to this lady, then, that I owe a debt of gratitude."

"You are right, my lord. Indeed at this moment, when war is threatening between our two countries, I confess I can see nothing in Your Grace but an Englishman, consequently an enemy. I would have much greater pleasure in meeting that enemy on the field of battle than in Windsor Forest or the halls of the Louvre. But that will not keep me from carrying out my mission punctiliously, or from laying down my life, if needs be, to do so. But I tell Your Grace again that I will accomplish it without your having any more reason to thank me at this second meeting than you had at our first meeting."

"We English have a saying, 'As proud as a Scot,' " murmured Buckingham.

"And we French say, 'As proud as a Gascon,' " retorted D'Artagnan. "The Gascons are the Scots of France."

D'Artagnan bowed to the Duke and started to withdraw.

"Come now, are you going off like that? Where? And how?"

"True, I had forgotten that England is an island and you are its king."

"Go to the port, ask for the brig *Sund,* and give this letter to the captain. He will take you to a little French harbor where you certainly are not expected. Only fishing boats use it ordinarily—Saint-Valéry. But listen carefully. When you land there, go to a mean-looking tavern that has no name and no sign—just a sailors' hovel. You can't mistake it—there's only one such place. Ask for the host, and say one word—Forward! That means *En avant!* in your tongue—it is the password.

"The man will give you a horse already saddled and show you what road to take. In the same way, you will find four relays on your route. If you will give your Paris address at each posting house, the four horses will follow you thither. You already know two of them, and as a lover of horseflesh, you seemed to appreciate them—they are those we rode from Windsor—and I give you my word that the others are just as good. These horses are fully equipped for campaigning. However proud you may be, you will not refuse to accept one of them for yourself and to get your companions to accept the others. After all, you can use them in the war against us. The end justifies the means, as you Frenchmen say, does it not?"

"Yes, my lord, I accept them," said D'Artagnan, "and please God, we will make good use of your gift!"

"Now your hand, young man. Perhaps we shall meet soon on the battlefield. Meanwhile, we part good friends, I trust."

"Yes, my lord, but with the hope of becoming enemies soon."

D'Artagnan bowed low to the Duke, and hastened to the port. Opposite the Tower of London he found the *Sund* and gave the captain his letter. The captain had it countersigned by the Governor of the Port, and weighed anchor at once.

Fifty vessels were ready to sail and waiting for the embargo to be lifted. As the *Sund* passed close alongside one of them, D'Artagnan thought he recognized the woman of Meung, the one the nameless gentleman had called Milady and whom he, D'Artagnan, had thought so beautiful. But thanks to the strong tide and a fair wind, the *Sund* passed so quickly that he caught only a glimpse of her.

The next morning at about nine D'Artagnan landed at Saint-Valéry. He went instantly in search of the tavern he had been told of, and easily identified it by the rowdy noise issuing from it. Already there was talk of war between England and France as near and inevitable, and the sailors were carousing to celebrate it. D'Artagnan made his way through the mob, found the host, and said "Forward!" The host instantly motioned D'Artagnan to follow him, and went to a stable where a horse already saddled was waiting. He asked whether D'Artagnan needed anything more.

"I want to know what road I am to take," said D'Artagnan.

"Go from here to Blangy and from there to Neufchâtel. At Neufchâtel go to the Golden Harrow inn, give the password to the innkeeper, and you will find a horse already saddled, just as you did here."

"Do I owe you anything?" asked D'Artagnan.

"Everything is paid," the host replied, "and generously. On your road now, and may God guide you safely!"

"Amen!" cried D'Artagnan as he set off at full gallop.

Four hours later he was in Neufchâtel. There, as at Saint-Valéry, he found a saddled horse awaiting him.

"Your address in Paris?"

"Hôtel des Gardes, Des Essarts company."

"Right!" said his questioner.

"Which road am I to take?"

"Rouen road, but don't enter the city, keep to the right of it. At your next stop, the little hamlet of Ecouis, there is only one inn, the French Arms. Don't judge it by its looks; it will have a horse as good as this one in its stables."

"Same password?"

"Exactly."

D'Artagnan set off at top speed. At Ecouis, the same scene was repeated. He found a host equally accommodating and a fresh horse. He left his address and set off again at the same pace for Pontoise. There he changed horses for the last time, and at nine in the evening he galloped into the courtyard of the Hôtel de Tréville. He had ridden nearly sixty leagues in twelve hours.

Monsieur de Tréville received him as calmly as if he had seen him that very morning. But as he shook hands with him a little more warmly than usual, he told D'Artagnan that Monsieur des Essarts' company was on guard at the Louvre, and he might repair at once to his post.

CHAPTER 22

ON THE MORROW, THE ONE SUBJECT OF CONVERSATION in Paris was the ball the Aldermen of the City were to give in honor of the King and Queen. Their Majesties were to dance the famous Merlaison ballet, the King's favorite dance.

For a week preparations for this great occasion had been stirring up the whole Hôtel de Ville. The municipal carpenters had erected stands to seat the feminine guests; the municipal grocer had furnished the various rooms with two hundred white wax candles, a touch of luxury unheard-of at that period; twenty violinists had been engaged, and they were to be paid double their usual wage, rumor had it, if they played all night.

At eleven o'clock, Duhallier, Captain of the Royal Guards, arrived with archers, who went at once to the posts assigned to them at the doors. At three o'clock, two companies of guards arrived, one French, the other Swiss. Half the French company was comprised of Monsieur Duhallier's men, half of Monsieur des Essarts' men.

At nine o'clock, came Madame la Première Présidente, wife of the President of the Aldermen. After the Queen she was the most important woman at the fete, and was received by the city officials and seated in a box opposite the one the Queen was to occupy. At ten o'clock, the King's collation, consisting of confections and other delicacies, was made ready in the small hall on the side toward the Church of Saint-Jean, opposite the sideboard holding the silver service belonging to the city, which was guarded by four archers.

At midnight, loud cries and many cheers were heard. They were for the King, who was making his way from the Louvre to the Hôtel de Ville through streets illuminated with colored street lamps. Immediately the Aldermen of the City, dressed in their broadcloth robes and preceded by six constables, each of whom bore a torch, came out to attend upon the King. They met him on the steps, where the Provost of the Guilds offered him the civilities of welcome, to which His Majesty replied with apologies for his late arrival, for which he blamed Monsieur le Cardinal, who had detained him until eleven o'clock to discuss affairs of state.

His Majesty, in full ceremonial dress, was accompanied by His Royal Highness Monsieur, Duc d'Orléans; the Comte de Sossoins; the Grand Prior; the Duc de Longueville; the Duc d'Elbeuf; the Comte d'Harcourt; the Comte de La Roche-Guyon; Monsieur de Liancourt; Monsieur de Baradas; the Comte de Cramail; and the Chevalier de Souveray. Everybody noted that the King looked melancholy and preoccupied.

A dressing-room had been provided for the King, and another for Monsieur. There was a masquerade costume in each, and the Queen and Madame la Présidente had been provided for in the same way. The lords and ladies of Their Majesties's suites were to dress two by two in rooms made ready for that purpose. Before entering his dressing-room, the King gave orders that he was to be notified as soon as the Cardinal appeared.

Half an hour after the King's entrance, fresh cheers announced the arrival of the Queen. The Aldermen of the City, as before, preceded by the constables, went to meet their illustrious guest. The Queen entered the Great Hall. It was remarked that, like the King, she looked melancholy, and above all, weary. Just as she entered, the curtains of a small balcony, which had been closed until then, were drawn aside and the pale face of the Cardinal appeared. He was dressed as a Spanish cavalier. His eyes were fixed on those of the Queen, and a smile of terrifying joy passed over his lips—the Queen was not wearing the diamond tags.

The Queen stood for some time receiving the compliments of the city officials and replying to the greetings of the ladies. Suddenly the King and the Cardinal appeared at one of the doors of the hall. The Cardinal was speaking to the King in an undertone, and His Majesty was very pale. Louis XIII wore no mask, and the points of his doublet were carelessly tied. He went straight to the Queen and said in a sullen tone:

"Madame, pray why are you not wearing your diamond tags when you know that I wished to see how they became you?"

The Queen glanced around and saw the Cardinal behind the King, smiling a diabolical smile.

"Sire," she answered with a faltering voice, "I feared some mishap might befall them in the midst of so great a throng."

"And you were in the wrong, madame. If I gave them to you, it was because I wished you to wear them. I tell you that you were in the wrong."

The King's voice was tremulous with anger. Those about them looked and listened in astonishment, understanding nothing of what was going on.

"Sire," said the Queen, "I can send for them. They are at the Louvre, and Your Majesty's wish can be realized very soon."

"Pray do so, madame, pray do so, and as quickly as possible. The ballet will begin within an hour."

The Queen bowed in token of submission. She followed the ladies who were to conduct her to her dressing-room, and the King returned to his.

A few minutes of disorder and confusion ensued in the hall. Everyone had noticed that something had gone wrong between the King and the Queen, but both of them had spoken so low that as the others had all drawn back out of respect, no one had heard a word. The violinists began to play with all their might, but nobody paid any attention to them.

The King was the first to come out of his dressing-room. He was attired in a hunting costume of great elegance, and Monsieur and the rest of his party were dressed as he was. It was the costume that became the King best, and when he wore it he really looked his part as the first gentleman of his kingdom. The Cardinal went to him and gave him a box. The King opened it and found two diamond tags.

"What does this mean?" he asked the Cardinal.

"Oh, nothing," replied His Eminence. "But if the Queen wears the tags—and I doubt that she will—count them, Sire, and if you find there are only ten, ask Her Majesty who can have stolen the two that are here."

The King looked at the Cardinal as if he were about to question him, but before he had time to do so a cry of admiration rose on all sides. If the King looked to be the first gentleman of his kingdom, the Queen was undoubtedly the most beautiful woman in France. Certainly her hunting costume was wonderfully becoming to her. She wore a felt hat with blue plumes, a coat of pearl-gray velvet fastened with diamond clasps, and a skirt of blue satin heavily embroidered with silver. On her left shoulder the diamond tags sparkled on a knot of ribbon of the same color as her skirt and the plumes in her hat.

The King trembled with joy and the Cardinal with anger, but they were still too far from the Queen to count the tags. The Queen was wearing them—but were there ten or twelve of them?

Just then the violins gave the signal for the ballet. The King advanced toward Madame la Présidente and His Highness Monsieur went to the Queen. They took their places and the ballet began. His Majesty danced opposite the Queen, and every time he passed her he devoured those tags with his eyes, but he could not count them. Cold sweat was pearling the Cardinal's brow. The ballet lasted for an hour; there were sixteen figures. When it ended, the whole assembly burst into applause. Each gentleman led his lady back to her place, except that the King took advantage of his privileges to leave his lady where she was and advanced eagerly toward the Queen.

"I thank you, madame," he said, "for the deference you have shown to my wishes, but I believe two of your diamond tags are missing, and I am bringing them back to you." With which he held out to the Queen the two tags Richelieu had given him.

"How is that, Sire?" cried the young Queen, feigning surprise. "You are giving me two more? But then I shall have fourteen."

The King could count them now, and found twelve tags on Her Majesty's shoulder. He summoned the Cardinal.

"Well, Monsieur le Cardinal, what does this mean?" he asked sternly.

"It means, Sire," replied the Cardinal, "that I wished to present these two tags to Her Majesty, and not venturing to offer them to her myself, I adopted this means of inducing Her Majesty to accept them."

"I am the more grateful to Your Eminence," said Anne of Austria, with a smile that proved she was not duped by this ingenious show of gallantry, "because I am sure that these two tags cost you more than the twelve others cost His Majesty."

Then, having bowed to the King and the Cardinal, she went back to her dressing-room.

The Queen had just gone, and D'Artagnan was about to withdraw, when he felt a light touch on his shoulder. Turning, he saw a young woman who was motioning him to follow her. The young woman's face was covered with a black-velvet mask, but despite this precaution—taken against others rather than against him—he recognized at once his former guide, the lightfooted and lively Madame Bonacieux.

The evening before, they had seen each other for only a moment at Germain's quarters. The young woman was in such haste to take to the Queen the good news of her messenger's return that the two lovers had had time to exchange but a few words. As D'Artagnan followed Madame Bonacieux now, he was moved by two emotions, love and curiosity. All the way through the corridors, now becoming more and more deserted, he tried to stop the young woman, to grasp her, to look into her eyes for only an instant. But, swift as a bird, she always slipped through his hands. When he tried to speak, the finger she placed on his lips in an imperious gesture full of charm reminded him that he was subject to a power that he must obey blindly and without the slightest protest. At last, after turning down one corridor after another, Madame Bonacieux opened a door and ushered the young man into a small room that was completely dark. Again she motioned to him to be silent, then she opened a second door that was hidden by a tapestry, through the interstices of which a brilliant light spread through the room, and disappeared, leaving the door a little ajar.

D'Artagnan stood motionless for a moment, asking himself where he was, but presently a ray of light that stole into the room, the warm and perfumed air that reached him, the voices of two or three women he heard using language at once respectful and elegant, and the word "Majesty" repeated several times—all these were clear indications that he was in a room adjoining the Queen's dressing-room. He waited quietly in the half-darkness.

The Queen seemed to be cheerful and happy, and that seemed to astonish the ladies with her, for they were accustomed to see her almost always anxious. The Queen attributed her joyous feeling to the beauty of the fete and the pleasure she had taken in the ballet.

Although D'Artagnan did not know the Queen, he soon distinguished her voice from the others, at first by a slight foreign accent, then by that tone of domination natural to sovereigns. He heard her approach and then go away from the partly open door, and two or three times he saw the shadow of a body block the ray of light.

Suddenly a hand and an arm of adorable form and whiteness appeared through the tapestry. D'Artagnan, understanding that this was his reward, fell on his knees, grasped the hand, and pressed his lips to it deferentially. Then the hand was withdrawn, leaving in his own hand an object that he could feel was a ring. The door was immediately closed, and D'Artagnan again found himself in complete darkness.

He slipped the ring onto his finger and again waited; evidently all was not yet over. After the reward of his devotion the reward of his love was to come. Besides, though the ballet was over, the festivities had barely begun. Supper was to be served at three, and the clock of Saint-Jean had struck a quarter of three some time ago. The sound of voices in the next room grew gradually fainter and fainter, then he heard footsteps going away, the door to the corridor opened, and Madame Bonacieux darted in.

"You! At last!" cried D'Artagnan.

"Hush!" said the young woman, pressing her hand to his lips. "Hush! And go away at once by the way you came."

"But when and where shall I see you again?"

"You will find a note at home to tell you that. Begone, begone!"

With that she opened the door to the corridor and pushed D'Artagnan out of the room. He obeyed like a child, without the least resistance or protest—proof that he was indeed in love with Madame Bonacieux.

CHAPTER 23

D'ARTAGNAN HURRIED HOME IMMEDIATELY, AND though it was three in the morning and he had to go through some of the most dangerous quarters of Paris, he met with no misadventure. He found the door to his passage ajar, sprang up the stairway, and knocked softly in a sequence he and his lackey had agreed on. Planchet, whom he had sent home from the Hôtel de Ville two hours before, bidding him wait for his own arrival, opened the door.

"Has anyone brought a letter for me?" asked D'Artagnan eagerly.

"Nobody has *brought* a letter, monsieur," replied Planchet. "But there is one that came by itself."

"What do you mean, you fool?"

"I mean to say that when I came home, though I had the key to your apartment in my pocket—and that key had never been out of it—I found a letter on the green tablecover in your bedroom."

"And where is that letter?"

"I left it where it was, monsieur. It isn't natural for letters to come to people's houses like that. If the window had been open, or even half-open, I should say nothing. But no, everything was shut tight. Beware, monsieur! There's certainly some magic about it."

While Planchet was talking, the young man was rushing into his bedroom and opening his letter. It was from Madame Bonacieux, and read as follows:

There are many thanks to be offered you and passed on to you. This evening about ten o'clock be at Saint-Cloud, opposite the pavilion standing at the corner of Monsieur d'Estrées's house.

C. B.

Reading this letter, D'Artagnan felt his heart dilate and contract with the delicious spasms that torture and caress the hearts of lovers. It was the first note from her he had received, the first rendezvous she had granted him.

"Well, monsieur," said Planchet, who had seen his master first flush, then grow pale, "didn't I guess right? Isn't this some nasty business or other?"

"You're mistaken, Planchet," replied D'Artagnan, "and to prove it, here's a crown for you to drink my health."

"I'm much obliged to Monsieur for the money, and I promise to follow his instructions exactly. All the same, letters that arrive like that in locked houses——"

"Fall from Heaven, my friend, fall from Heaven."

"Then Monsieur is happy?"

"My dear Planchet, I am the happiest of men!"

"May all the blessings of Heaven fall upon Monsieur. But all the same that letter——" And Planchet withdrew, shaking his head.

Left alone, D'Artagnan read the note and reread it, then he kissed a score of times the lines written by his lovely mistress's hand. At last he went to bed, fell fast asleep, and enjoyed golden dreams. At seven the next morning he rose and called to his lackey.

"Planchet," said D'Artagnan, "I am going out, perhaps for all day, so you are free until seven this evening. But at seven be in readiness with two horses."

"Well, so it seems that we are to get our skins run through in several places!"

"You will take along your musketoon and a pair of pistols."

"Very well," said Planchet, "what did I say? I was sure of it. Damn that letter!"

"Take comfort, you imbecile. There's nothing in hand but a pleasure party."

"Oh yes, like the one we went on the other day, when it rained bullets and produced a crop of traps!"

"Well, if you're afraid, Monsieur Planchet, I'll go without you. I'd rather go alone than with a companion who's trembling with fright."

"Monsieur will see that on occasion I do have courage."

"Do you think you have enough for tonight?"

"I hope so. I will be ready on the hour. But I thought Monsieur had only one horse in the Royal Guards stables."

"There may be only one now, but by tonight there will be four."

"So our journey is to be by relays?"

"Right," said D'Artagnan, and he went out.

Monsieur Bonacieux was at the street door. D'Artagnan had meant to go out without speaking to him, but the worthy haberdasher greeted him with such cordial friendliness that his lodger felt obliged not only to return the greeting but also to chat with him for a moment. Besides, how could he help experiencing a little condescension toward a husband whose wife had given him a rendezvous for that very evening? D'Artagnan approached him with the most amiable air he could assume.

The subject of the conversation, quite naturally, was the poor man's imprisonment. Monsieur Bonacieux, who did not know that D'Artagnan had overheard his conversation with the man of Meung, told his young lodger of all the persecutions he had suffered, and expatiated at great length upon the Bastille, its locks, its gates, its loopholes, its gratings, and its instruments of torture. D'Artagnan listened with exemplary courtesy, and when Bonacieux had finished he asked:

"And Madame Bonacieux, have you found out who abducted her? I do not forget that I owe the pleasure of your acquaintance to that unhappy circumstance."

"Ah," said Monsieur Bonacieux, "they took good care not to tell me that, and my wife has sworn to me by all that's sacred that she doesn't know. But you yourself?" he went on in the most genial tone. "What have you been doing these last few days? I haven't seen either you or your friends, and I don't think you could pick up on the sidewalks of Paris all that dust I saw Planchet brushing from your boots yesterday."

"You're right, my dear Monsieur Bonacieux. My friends and I have been on a little journey."

"Far from here?"

"Oh, Lord, no—only about forty leagues. We took Monsieur Athos to the waters at Forges, and my friends stayed on there."

"But you came back, didn't you?" Monsieur Bonacieux went on, with his most knowing look. "A handsome fellow like you doesn't get long leave from his mistress. And someone in Paris was waiting for you impatiently, wasn't she?"

"By my faith," said the young man, laughing, "I must confess that's true, the more readily, my dear Monsieur Bonacieux, because I see there is no concealing anything from you. Yes, I was expected, and very impatiently, I assure you."

"And Monsieur is to be rewarded for his diligence?" the haberdasher went on, with a slight change of tone that D'Artagnan did not note.

"Ah, you're turning prophet now," said D'Artagnan, laughing again.

"No," replied Bonacieux. "I said that only to find out whether you will be coming home late."

"Why do you want to know, my dear landlord?" asked D'Artagnan. "Do you mean to wait up for me?"

"No. But since my arrest and the robbery in my house I am frightened every time I hear a door open, especially at night. What the deuce do you expect? I'm no swordsman!"

"Well, don't be alarmed if I come in at one or even two or three in the morning. Indeed, don't be alarmed if I do not come at all."

This time Bonacieux turned so pale that D'Artagnan could not help seeing it, and asked him what was the matter.

"Nothing," Bonacieux replied, "nothing. But ever since my misfortune I have been subject to feeling faint. It comes over me all at once, and I just felt a cold shiver. Pay no attention to it; the only thing you have to occupy yourself with is your own happiness."

"Then I shall be busy, for I am surely happy."

"Not yet—wait a bit. You said this evening you——"

"Well, this evening will come, thank God! Perhaps you are looking forward to it as impatiently as I am. Perhaps Madame Bonacieux is to visit the conjugal domicile tonight."

"Madame Bonacieux is not at liberty this evening," her husband replied gravely. "Her duties keep her at the Louvre."

"So much the worse for you, my dear landlord, so much the worse for you! As for me, when I am happy I wish everybody to be so, but apparently that is not possible." And the young man went off laughing over a joke he thought he alone could understand.

"Have a good time!" Bonacieux answered in a sepulchral tone.

But D'Artagnan was too far away to hear that, and if he had heard it, in his present mood certes he would not have paid any attention to it. He went his way toward Monsieur de Tréville's. His visit of the day before had been short and had told him little.

He found Monsieur de Tréville joyful. The King and the Queen had been charming to him at the ball. True, the Cardinal had been quite ill-tempered; at one o'clock he had left, on the pretext that he was feeling ill. But Their Majesties had not returned to the Louvre until six o'clock in the morning.

"Now," said Monsieur de Tréville, lowering his voice and looking at every corner of the room to make sure they were alone, "now let us talk about you, my young friend, for it is evident that your happy return has something to do with the King's joy, the Queen's triumph, and the Cardinal's humiliation. You'll have to take good care of yourself."

"What have I to fear," replied D'Artagnan, "as long as I have the good fortune to enjoy the favor of Their Majesties?"

"Everything, believe me. The Cardinal is not the man to forget that he has been mystified without settling accounts with the mystifier. And the mystifier looks to me like a certain young Gascon of my acquaintance."

"Do you think the Cardinal knows as much as you do? Do you think he knows I have been to London?"

"The devil! You have been to London, then? Was it from London that you brought that beautiful diamond I see sparkling on your finger? Beware, my dear D'Artagnan. A gift from an enemy isn't anything good. There's some Latin verse about that. Wait a minute. . . . Ah, I've got it!— the meaning is 'I fear the Greeks, even bringing gifts.' "

"This diamond does not come from an enemy, monsieur," D'Artagnan answered. "It comes from the Queen."

"From the Queen! Aha!" said Monsieur de Tréville. "Indeed it is truly a royal jewel, one worth a thousand pistoles if it's worth a sou. By whom did the Queen send you this gift?"

"She gave it to me herself."

"Where?"

"In the little room next her dressing-room at the Hôtel de Ville."

"How did she do it?"

"While she was giving me her hand to kiss."

"You kissed the Queen's hand!" cried Monsieur de Tréville, looking earnestly at D'Artagnan.

"Her Majesty did me the honor to grant me that favor."

"In the presence of witnesses? Indiscreet woman, thrice indiscreet!"

"No, monsieur, do not be troubled. No one saw her," replied D'Artagnan. And he told everything that had happened.

"Oh, women, women!" cried the old soldier. "Who can fail to recognize them by their romantic imagination? Everything that savors of mystery charms them. So you saw an arm, that's all. If you met the Queen you would not recognize her. If she met you, she would not know who you were."

"No, but thanks to this diamond——" said the young man.

"See here," interrupted Monsieur de Tréville, "do you want me to give you a piece of advice, good advice, the advice of a friend?"

"I would be honored, monsieur," said D'Artagnan.

"Well then, go to the nearest jeweler and sell that diamond for whatever he will give you. However much of a cheat he may be, you will surely get eight hundred pistoles for it. Pistoles have no name, young man, and that ring has a terrible one. It may betray whoever wears it."

"Sell this ring! A ring that came to me from my Queen! Never!"

"Then at least turn the diamond inward, you poor foolish fellow. Everybody knows that a Gascon cadet doesn't find a jewel like that in his mother's jewel case."

"You think, then, that I have something to fear?"

"I mean that you are about as safe as a man sleeping on a mine with a lighted fuse."

"Devil take it," said D'Artagnan, whom Monsieur de Tréville's positive tone was beginning to make uneasy. "What am I to do?"

"Be on your guard every moment. The Cardinal has a tenacious memory and a long arm. Believe me, he will play you some nasty trick."

"But what trick?"

"Eh, how can I tell? Hasn't he all the Devil's tricks at his command? The least you can expect is to be arrested."

"What! Would anyone dare to arrest a man in His Majesty's service?"

"Good Lord, they didn't hesitate much in Athos's case. At all events, young man, take the word of a man who has been at Court for thirty years. Do not lull yourself into security, or you are done for. On the contrary, I tell you, look for enemies everywhere. If someone seeks a quarrel with you, even a child of ten, avoid it. If you are attacked, by day or by night, beat a retreat without feeling ashamed. If you cross a bridge, test every plank of it, lest one may give way under you. If you pass near a house being built, look up, lest a stone fall on your head. If you are out late, have your lackey with you and have him armed—at least if you are sure you can trust him. Suspect everyone, your friend, your brother, your mistress—especially your mistress."

D'Artagnan blushed. "My mistress," he repeated mechanically. "And why suspect her rather than another?"

"Because a mistress is one of the favorite means the Cardinal uses; he has no agent who works more quickly. A woman will sell you for ten pistoles, witness Delilah. You read the Scriptures, don't you?"

D'Artagnan thought of the rendezvous Madame Bonacieux had given him for that very evening. But we must say, in praise of our hero, that the bad opinion Monsieur de Tréville had of women in general did not make him in the least suspicious of his lovely landlady.

"By the way," Monsieur de Tréville went on, "what has become of your three companions?"

"I was about to ask you whether you had news of them."

"None whatever, monsieur."

"Well, I left them on the way—Porthos at Chantilly with a duel on his hands, Aramis at Crèvecœur with a bullet in his shoulder, and Athos at Amiens, accused of being a counterfeiter."

"There you have it!" said Monsieur de Tréville. "And how did *you* get away?"

"By a miracle, monsieur, I must acknowledge. Monsieur le Comte de Wardes thrust his sword into my chest, and I nailed him down in a Calais side road like a butterfly on a tapestry."

"There it is again! De Wardes, one of the Cardinal's men, a cousin of Rochefort's. . . . Wait, my dear friend, I have an idea. . . . If I were you, I would do this: While His Eminence was looking for me in Paris I would take the Picardy road, without drums or trumpets, and I would go to make inquiries about my three companions. Devil take it, they richly deserve that little attention on your part."

"Your advice is good, monsieur, and I set out tomorrow."

"Tomorrow! And why not tonight?"

"Tonight, monsieur, I am kept in Paris by most important business."

"Ah, young man, young man! Some love affair, eh? Be careful, I tell you again. It was a woman who was the ruin of us all in the Garden of Eden, so frail are we, and woman will ruin us all as long as the world endures. Take my advice—set out tonight."

"Impossible, monsieur!"

"Have you given your word, then?"

"Yes, monsieur."

"Then the question is a different one. But promise me that if you're not killed tonight, you will set out tomorrow."

"I promise, monsieur."

"Do you need money?"

"I still have fifty pistoles. I think that's all I shall need."

"How about your friends?"

"I don't think they need any. Each of us had seventy-five pistoles in his pocket when we left Paris."

"Shall I see you again before you leave?"

"I don't think so, monsieur, unless something new turns up."

"Well, bon voyage!"

"Thank you, monsieur." And D'Artagnan left Monsieur de Tréville more than ever touched by his fatherly solicitude for his musketeers.

He went in turn to the lodgings of Athos, Porthos, and Aramis. No one of them had returned. Their lackeys too were absent, and there was no news of either masters or servants. He would have asked about them at their mistresses', but he did not know who either Porthos's or Aramis's was. As to Athos, he had none. Passing the Hôtel des Gardes, he glanced into the stables. Three of the four English horses had already arrived there. Planchet, much impressed, was engaged in grooming them, and had finished with two of them.

"Ah, monsieur," said Planchet, "how glad I am to see you!"

"Why, Planchet?"

"Do you trust Monsieur Bonacieux, our landlord, monsieur?"

"I? Not the least in the world."

"How right you are, monsieur."

"But why do you ask?"

"Because while you were talking with him I watched you both without hearing what you said, monsieur, and his face turned pale, then red, two or three times. Monsieur didn't notice it; Monsieur was preoccupied by the letter he had just received. But the strange way the letter had got into the house had put me on my guard, and I didn't miss one of the expressions on his face. They were treacherous, monsieur. Moreover, as soon as you had turned the corner Monsieur Bonacieux got his hat, shut the street door, and hurried down the street the other way."

"Indeed you're right, Planchet. I find all that suspicious, and you may be sure we will pay no rent until we've got to the bottom of it."

"Monsieur jests, but Monsieur will see."

"Never mind, Planchet. What is to be is to be."

"Then Monsieur isn't giving up tonight's excursion?"

"Quite the contrary, Planchet. The more I suspect Monsieur Bonacieux, the more I'll go to that rendezvous, so be ready here at the Hôtel des Gardes at nine o'clock. I will come for you."

CHAPTER 24

AT NINE O'CLOCK D'ARTAGNAN WAS AT THE HÔTEL DES Gardes, and found Planchet there. The fourth horse had arrived. Planchet was armed with his musketoon and a pistol. D'Artagnan had his sword, and slipped two pistols into his belt. They mounted and rode off quietly, Planchet some ten paces behind his master. Night had fallen, and no one saw them leave.

D'Artagnan crossed the quays, left town by the Porte de la Conférence, and took the road to Saint-Cloud. As long as they were in the city Planchet kept at a respectful distance; but as soon as the road began to be darker and more deserted he quietly moved nearer, so that when they entered the Bois de Boulogne he was riding beside his master as a matter of course. It must be confessed that the waving of the branches of the tall trees and the gleam of moonlight on the dark thickets made him very uneasy.

"Are we going to ride like this all night?" he asked presently.

"No, Planchet, for you are staying here. I'm going a little farther. If you feel cold, you can go into one of the taverns yonder. Be waiting for me at the door at six sharp tomorrow morning."

"Monsieur, I respectfully ate and drank the crown you gave me this morning, and I haven't a sou left in case I should need something hot."

"Here's half a pistole. Good-by until tomorrow at six."

D'Artagnan dismounted, tossed his horse's bridle to Planchet, wrapped himself in his cloak, and went off quickly. As soon as he was out of sight, Planchet, in a hurry to get warm, went straight to a building that looked like a typical suburban tavern and knocked at the door.

Meanwhile D'Artagnan plunged into a bypath and followed it until he reached Saint-Cloud. There, instead of taking the main street, he turned behind the castle into a retired lane, and presently found himself in front of the pavilion he was looking for. The place where it stood was very lonely. On one side of the lane rose the high wall of the house, on the other side a hedge shielded a little garden from passers-by, and at the end of this was a shabby hovel. As he had not been told to announce his presence, he waited.

No noise was to be heard; D'Artagnan might imagine he was a hundred leagues from the capital. He glanced behind him, then leaned against the hedge. Beyond that hedge, that garden, and that hovel, dense fog covered the vast area where Paris was sleeping, a gaping void where a few lights gleamed, the sinister stars of that hell. But for D'Artagnan every prospect had a happy shape, every idea had a smiling look, every shadow was transparent. The hour of the rendezvous was about to strike. In fact, almost at once the bells of the church of Saint-Cloud let fall slowly from their sonorous jaws ten strokes.

D'Artagnan stood staring at the little pavilion. All its windows were shuttered, except for one on the second story. Through that window shone a dim light that turned to silver the foliage of two or three linden trees that rose in a group beyond the garden. Surely behind that little window with so friendly a light Madame Bonacieux was waiting for him.

Lost in this enchanting thought, D'Artagnan waited patiently for half an hour, staring up at the part of the ceiling that he could see, with its gilded moldings that were witness to the elegance of the room. The belfry of Saint-Cloud rang half-past ten. This time, without understanding why, D'Artagnan shivered. Perhaps he was beginning to feel cold, and mistook a purely physical sensation for a mental impression.

Then it occurred to him that he might have misread the letter, and the rendezvous was for eleven o'clock. He drew close to the window, stood in a ray of its light, took the letter from his pocket, and read it again. He had made no mistake; the rendezvous was for ten o'clock. He went back to his post, beginning to be rather troubled by the silence and the solitude.

Eleven o'clock struck. Now he began to be really afraid that something had happened to Madame Bonacieux. He clapped his hands three times, the usual signal of lovers, but there was no answer, not even an echo. Then he thought with some annoyance that perhaps the young woman had fallen asleep while she waited for him. He went to the wall and attempted to climb up it, but he could get no hold on it.

Then he bethought himself of the trees, their leaves turned to silver by the light from the room above, and he decided that from one of the branches of one of them, he might see into the room. In an instant he was up among its branches, and through the window he saw a scene that made him shudder.

One window was broken, the door to the room had been forced and, half-broken, hung on its hinges. A table that he could see had held an elegant supper was lying overturned on the floor. Broken glass and crushed fruits were scattered over the floor. Everything in that room testified to a violent and desperate struggle. D'Artagnan even thought he detected fragments of clothing, and a few traces of blood on tablecloth and curtains.

He climbed hastily down to the street, his heart thumping terribly. There he saw something he had not noticed before—the ground, trampled here and rutted there, showed confused traces of men, horses, and carriage wheels. Finally, as he continued his search, he found a woman's glove. It was torn, but immaculate—the kind of perfumed glove that lovers delight to snatch from a pretty hand. As D'Artagnan went on with his investigation, more and icier sweat broke out in beads on his forehead, his heart was oppressed with horrible anguish, he panted for breath. Yet he told himself that perhaps this pavilion had nothing to do with Madame Bonacieux, that she had given him a rendezvous opposite the pavilion, not inside it, that she might have been kept in Paris by her duties, or perhaps by her husband's jealousy.

But all this reasoning was attacked, destroyed, overthrown, by that feeling of personal pain which sometimes takes possession of a man's being and cries out from everything he is fated to hear that a great misfortune is hanging over him. Then D'Artagnan became almost insane. He ran down the highway, took the path he had taken before, reached the ferry, and questioned the ferryman.

At seven o'clock that evening, the ferryman said, he had brought over the river a woman wrapped in a black cloak. She seemed to be anxious not to be recognized, but for that very reason he had looked at her attentively, and he had discovered that she was young and pretty. D'Artagnan did not doubt for an instant that it was Madame Bonacieux whom the boatman described.

D'Artagnan took advantage of the lamp in the ferryman's hut to read Madame Bonacieux's letter again, to make sure that he had not made a mistake, that the rendezvous was at Saint-Cloud, in front of Monsieur d'Estrées's pavilion. His presentiments were confirmed; some terrible misfortune had happened. He ran back to the house, thinking that perhaps there had been some new development at the pavilion and that he would get fresh information there.

The lane was still deserted and the same calm, soft light shone from the window. Then he remembered the dark, silent hut at the end of the garden. Someone there might have seen what happened and perhaps could tell him about it. The garden gate was shut, but he vaulted over the hedge, and paying no attention to the barking of a chained dog, went to the hut.

To his first knocks there was no reply. Deathlike silence reigned in the hut, as it had in the pavilion. But the hut was his last resort, and he kept on knocking. Presently he thought he heard a slight noise within, a timid noise as if someone were trembling lest anyone hear it.

D'Artagnan stopped knocking and begged to be admitted, in a voice so full of anxiety and promises, of terror and cajolery, that it would have reassured even the most fearful listener. At length an old worm-eaten shutter opened, or rather half-opened, and closed again when the light from a wretched lamp shone on D'Artagnan's baldric, sword hilt, and the holsters of his pistols. Swift as the movement was, D'Artagnan had nevertheless caught a glimpse of an old man's head.

"In the name of Heaven," he cried, "listen to me! I have been waiting for someone who has not come; I am dying of anxiety. Has some mishap occurred around here? Tell me, I implore you."

The window slowly opened again and the same face appeared again, even paler than before. D'Artagnan told his story simply, without mentioning any names—how he had a rendezvous with a young woman in front of the pavilion; how, when he did not see her come, he had climbed the linden tree; and how he had seen from there the disorder in the room. The old man listened attentively, merely gesturing that it was all true. When D'Artagnan had finished, he shook his head with an air that augured nothing good.

"What do you mean?" cried D'Artagnan. "In the name of Heaven, tell me everything."

"Ah, monsieur," said the old man, "do not ask me anything, for if I told you what I had seen, certainly what would happen to me would be nothing good."

"Then you saw something?" said D'Artagnan. "If you did, in Heaven's name speak, tell me what you saw"—he tossed the old man a pistole— "and I pledge the faith of a gentleman that I will not repeat one word of it."

The old man read so much sincerity and so much suffering in D'Artagnan's expression that he motioned to him to listen, and said in a low voice:

"It was almost nine o'clock. I had heard a noise in the street, and was wondering what it could be when as I went to my door I saw that somebody was trying to get into the garden. As I am a poor man and am not afraid of being robbed, I went to open the gate, and I saw three men standing there. In the shadows yonder stood a carriage and three saddle horses, which evidently belonged to the three men.

" 'Ah, my fine gentlemen,' I cried, 'what do you want?'

" 'Have you a ladder?' asked the one who seemed to be the leader of the party.

" 'Yes, monsieur, the one I use to pick my fruit.'

" 'Lend it to us, and go back to your house. Here's a crown for your trouble. But remember that if you breathe one word of what you see or hear—for however much we may threaten, I am sure you will look and listen—you will be ruined.' With these words he flung me a crown, I picked it up, and he took the ladder.

"After I had shut the hedge gate behind them I pretended to go back home, but I went right out through the back door and stole through the shadows to that clump of elder bushes yonder. From there I could see everything without being seen myself. The three men had brought the carriage up quietly, and pulled out of it a little man who was fat, short, growing gray, and meanly dressed in dark clothes. He climbed the ladder very cautiously, looked slily into the room, came down quietly, and murmured in a low tone: 'It is she!'

"Immediately the man who had spoken to me went to the door of the pavilion, opened it with a key he had with him, shut the door, and disappeared. Meanwhile the two others climbed the ladder. The little old man stayed near the carriage door, the coachman took care of his horses, and the lackey held the saddle horses.

"All at once screams rang out in the pavilion. A woman rushed to the window and opened it as if to throw herself out of it, but as soon as she saw the other two men she drew back. The two men came into the room through the window in a flash.

"Then I saw no more, but I heard the furniture being smashed. The woman screamed and called for help, but soon her cries were smothered. The three men came to the window with the lady in their arms. Two of them carried her down the ladder and into the carriage, and the little old man got in it too. The man who had stayed in the pavilion shut the window and an instant later came out of the front door and made sure that the woman was in the carriage. His two companions were already on their horses, the lackey took his place by the coachman, the carriage went off at a gallop with the three horsemen for escort."

Overcome by such terrible news, D'Artagnan stood stock-still and silent while all the demons of anger and jealousy howled in his heart.

"But my good gentleman," said the old man, "come, don't take on so. They didn't kill her, that's the important thing."

"Do you know anything about the leader of this devilish expedition?"

"Nothing whatever."

"But you spoke to him, you saw him."

"Oh, you are asking me what he looked like? Well, he was a tall, thin, swarthy man with a black mustache and black eyes. He looked like a gentleman."

"That's the man!" cried D'Artagnan. "Once again he, forever he! My demon, it seems. And the other man—the little one?"

"Oh, he was no nobleman, I vouch for that! Besides, he didn't wear a sword, and the others showed him no consideration."

"Some lackey," murmured D'Artagnan. "Poor woman, poor woman, what have they done with you?"

"You promised to keep my secret, monsieur," said the old man.

"And I repeat my promise. Have no fear, I am a gentleman. A gentleman has only his word, and I have given you mine."

With a heavy heart, D'Artagnan went back to the ferry. Sometimes he

could not believe that the unfortunate woman had been Madame Bonacieux, and he hoped to find her at the Louvre on the morrow. Sometimes
he feared that she had had an affair with some other man and that in his
jealousy that man had taken her by surprise and carried her off. His mind
wavered, he was heartbroken, he was in despair.

"Oh, if only my friends were here!" he cried. "At least I would have
some hope of finding her. But who knows what has become of them!"

It was almost midnight. Now he must find Planchet. One after the
other, D'Artagnan called at all the taverns that showed a light, but found
Planchet in none of them. He had told his lackey where to meet him at
six in the morning, and wherever he was now, he was in the right. Moreover, he thought that by remaining near the spot where the tragedy had
occurred, he might perhaps obtain some light on this mysterious affair.

D'Artagnan stopped at the sixth tavern, asked for a bottle of the best
wine, and settled himself in the darkest corner of the room, determined
to wait until daybreak. When he had drunk the wine, he made himself as
comfortable as he could in his corner and fell asleep.

Toward six o'clock in the morning, he awakened with the discomfort
that usually follows a bad night. He was not long in making his toilet. He
looked to see if anyone had taken advantage of his sleep to rob him. Having found his diamond still on his finger, his purse in his pocket, and his
pistols in his belt, he rose, paid for his wine, and went out to see whether
he would have better luck this morning in his search for his lackey than
he had had the night before. As a matter of fact, the first thing he saw
through the damp grayish mist was honest Planchet, waiting, two horses
in hand, at the door of a dark little tavern that D'Artagnan had passed
the night before without even suspecting its existence.

CHAPTER 25

INSTEAD OF GOING STRAIGHT HOME, D'ARTAGNAN DIS-
mounted at Monsieur de Tréville's door and went up the stairway quickly.
This time, he had determined to tell everything that had happened. Monsieur de Tréville would doubtless give him good advice, and besides, as
he saw the Queen almost every day, he might perhaps find out from Her
Majesty something about the poor woman who was surely paying dearly
for her devotion to her mistress. Monsieur de Tréville listened to the
young man's story with a gravity that proved that he saw something more
in the matter than a love affair, and when it was finished, he said:

"Hm! All this smacks of His Eminence."

"But what is to be done?" D'Artagnan asked.

"Nothing, absolutely nothing, for the present except to leave Paris as
soon as possible, as I told you before. I will see the Queen and tell her all
about the disappearance of that poor woman. Probably she doesn't know
of it. On your return, perhaps I shall have some good news for you."

D'Artagnan knew that, although he was a Gascon, Monsieur de Tréville wasn't given to making promises, and that when he did promise, he
kept his word, and more. Full of gratitude for both past and future
favors, he bowed low as he took leave of his Captain.

Determined to follow Monsieur de Tréville's advice immediately,
D'Artagnan started for the Rue des Fossoyeurs to superintend the packing of his luggage. He found Monsieur Bonacieux standing in his doorway, in morning dress. All that the prudent Planchet had said the night
before about the sinister character of his landlord now recurred to D'Artagnan, and he looked at his landlord more closely than he had ever done
before. The man's yellowish, jaundiced pallor indicated an excess of bile
in the blood. That might be accidental, but D'Artagnan noted something
especially crafty and perfidious in his wrinkled countenance. To D'Artagnan it seemed that Monsieur Bonacieux was wearing a mask, and a very
ugly one. He felt such repugnance for the man that he was about to pass
him without speaking, but Monsieur Bonacieux accosted him, as he had
done the day before.

"Well, young man," he said, "we seem to have made a night of it, eh?

Seven o'clock in the morning, plague on it! It seems to me you're turning things upside down. You come home when other people are going out. Where the deuce have you been all night, my young master? It wasn't very clean in the byroads, was it?"

D'Artagnan glanced down at his boots, all covered with mud. But that same glance fell on the haberdasher's shoes and stockings. They looked as if they had been dipped in a mud puddle. A sudden idea came to him. That little elderly man, short, growing gray, that sort of lackey dressed in dark clothes, who got no consideration by the swordsmen who were his escort—that was Bonacieux himself! The husband had actually superintended the kidnapping of his wife!

D'Artagnan was seized with a terrible desire to leap at the haberdasher's throat and strangle him. But we have said he was a prudent lad, and he controlled himself. Yet his change of expression was so easy to see that Bonacieux was frightened by it. He stepped back, but as the door behind him was closed, he was forced to stand where he was.

"Come, my good man, you are joking," said D'Artagnan. "It seems to me that if my boots need cleaning, your shoes and stockings could do with a brush! Have you been gadding about too, Master Bonacieux? Devil take it, that's unpardonable in a man of your age, and one moreover who has a pretty young wife like yours."

"Good lord, no!" said Bonacieux. "I went to Saint-Mandé yesterday to ask about a servantmaid, and the roads were so bad that I brought back all this mud."

To D'Artagnan, the place named by Bonacieux as his destination was a fresh proof of his own suspicions. Bonacieux had said Saint-Mandé because Saint-Mandé was far from Saint-Cloud in the opposite direction. This fact offered his first consolation to D'Artagnan. If Bonacieux knew where his wife was, somehow the haberdasher might be forced to reveal the secret. Now it was only a question of changing a probability into a certainty.

"Pardon me, my dear Monsieur Bonacieux, if I don't stand on ceremony with you," said D'Artagnan. "Nothing makes a man so thirsty as lack of sleep. I'm parched with thirst. May I drink a glass of water in your kitchen?"

And without waiting for his landlord's permission, D'Artagnan entered the house quickly. As he went through the apartment, a swift glance at the bed told him that no one had slept in it. Bonacieux must have returned only an hour or two ago; therefore he must have accompanied his wife to the place where she had been taken, or at least as far as the first relay.

"Thank you, Master Bonacieux," said D'Artagnan, draining his glass. "That is all I wanted of you. Now I'll go up to my place and have Planchet

D'Artagnan Looking for Constance at the Window

Porthos

clean my boots. When he's done I'll send him to brush your shoes, if you like. One good turn deserves another."

And he left the haberdasher much astonished at their unusual farewell and asking himself whether he hadn't got himself into trouble. At the top of the staircase D'Artagnan found Planchet in a great fright.

"Ah, monsieur," cried Planchet as soon as he saw his master, "here's more trouble! I thought you'd never get home!"

"What's the matter now?" asked D'Artagnan.

"Oh, I'll give you a hundred guesses, a thousand. Who do you think called while you were away? . . . Monsieur de Cavois!"

"The Captain of His Eminence's Guards? Did he come to arrest me?"

"I suspect he did, monsieur, for all his wheedling manner. He was as sweet as honey. He said he came on behalf of His Eminence, who feels most friendly toward you, to beg you to go with him to the Palais Royal."

"What did you tell him?"

"That it was impossible, since you were not at home, as he could see for himself."

"What did he say then?"

"That you must not fail to call on the Cardinal in the course of the day. Then he added, very low: 'Tell your master that His Eminence is very well disposed toward him, and that his fortune may perhaps depend on this interview.' "

"The trap is a pretty clumsy one to be the Cardinal's," the young man said with a smile.

"Yes, I saw the trap myself, and I answered that you would be sadly disappointed on your return. 'Where did he go?' asked Monsieur de Cavois. 'To Troyes in Champagne,' said I. 'And when did he leave?' 'Last night.' "

"Planchet my friend," said D'Artagnan, "you're really a jewel of a man!"

"You see, monsieur, I thought if you really want to see Monsieur de Cavois you could always give the lie to me by saying that you hadn't left yet. As I'm not a gentleman, I can tell lies, I can."

"Don't you worry, Planchet. You shall keep your reputation as a truthful man. We are leaving in a quarter of an hour."

"That's just the advice I was about to give you, monsieur. And where are we going, if I may ask without being too curious?"

"By the Lord, in the direction opposite to the one you told him I had taken. Besides, aren't you as eager to get news of Grimaud, Mousqueton, and Bazin as I am to learn what has happened to Athos, Porthos, and Aramis?"

"Indeed I am, monsieur," said Planchet, "and I'll start as soon as you like. I think the air of the provinces will do us more good just now than the air of Paris. So then——"

"So then, get the packing done and we'll be off. I'll leave first, with my hands in my pockets so that no one will suspect anything. Meet me at the Hôtel des Gardes. By the way, Planchet, I think you're right about our landlord—certainly he's a frightful scoundrel."

D'Artagnan went out first, as arranged. Then, so that he might not have to blame himself for any neglect, he went once more to the lodgings of his three friends. No news of them had been received, but a perfumed letter in a delicate and elegant handwriting had come for Aramis, and D'Artagnan took charge of it. Ten minutes later, Planchet joined him at the stables of the Hôtel des Gardes. So that no time would be lost, D'Artagnan had saddled his own horse.

"Good!" he said to Planchet. "Now saddle the three other horses and we'll be off."

"Do you think we'll travel faster with two horses apiece?" asked Planchet, with his shrewdest look.

"No, Master Jester," D'Artagnan answered. "But with four horses we can bring our three friends back, provided we find them still alive."

"Which would be unexpected good luck," replied Planchet. "But we must not despair of the mercy of God."

"Amen!" said D'Artagnan as he mounted his horse.

They separated after leaving the Hôtel des Gardes, one to leave Paris by La Villette, the other by the Porte Montmartre. They had agreed to meet beyond Saint-Denis, a strategic move executed punctually and with the most fortunate results.

Our two travelers reached Chantilly without any mishap and alighted at the Grand-Saint-Martin inn, where they had stopped on their first journey. When he saw a young man with a lackey and two remounts, to show his respect the innkeeper came to the door to welcome them. As they had already ridden eleven leagues, D'Artagnan thought it was well to stop at the inn, whether Porthos was there or not. Moreover, perhaps it would be prudent not to ask at once what had become of the musketeer. Without asking any questions at all, D'Artagnan dismounted, told his lackey to look after the horses, and went into a small private room. He bade his host bring him a bottle of his best wine and as good a breakfast as he could, and was served with miraculous celerity.

The regiments of the Royal Guards were recruited from among the first gentlemen of the kingdom, and D'Artagnan, with a lackey and four magnificent horses, could not fail to make a great impression, despite his uniform as a private. Mine host himself waited on him, and D'Artagnan asked him to bring two glasses.

"By my faith, my good host," said D'Artagnan as he filled both glasses, "I asked for your best wine, and if you have cheated me, you shall be punished for your own sin. As I hate to drink alone, you are going to drink with me. Take your glass, then, and let us drink. What shall we drink a toast to that can hurt no one's feelings? Let's drink to the prosperity of your establishment. I have passed through Chantilly perhaps ten times, and I have stopped at your place four or five times. As a matter of fact, I was here again some ten or twelve days ago, with some friends of mine, some musketeers. One of them got into an argument with a complete stranger, who picked a quarrel with him, why I don't know."

"Yes indeed," said the innkeeper, "I remember it perfectly. Isn't it Monsieur Porthos your lordship is referring to?"

"Right—that's my traveling companion's name. Good Lord, my dear host, tell me, has any misfortune befallen him?"

"But your lordship must have remarked that Monsieur Porthos was unable to continue his journey."

"Right. He promised to join us farther on, and we haven't seen him since."

"He has done us the honor to remain here, monsieur. We have advanced a good deal of money to Monsieur Porthos, and this very morning the surgeon swore that if Monsieur Porthos didn't pay him, he would look to me for payment, since it was I who sent for him."

"Porthos is wounded, then?"

"I cannot tell you, monsieur. Men in my position cannot tell all they know, monsieur, especially when they are told that their ears will answer for what their tongues say."

"Well, may I see Porthos?"

"Certainly, monsieur. Go upstairs one story and knock at No. 1. But be sure to tell him who you are. Monsieur Porthos might take you for one of the inn servants, and in his anger he might run his sword through you or blow out your brains."

"Whatever have you done to him?"

"We asked him for money, that's all. True, he had been gambling the night before with a gentleman who happened to be here."

"I see. I suppose the foolish fellow lost all his money he had with him."

"And even his horse, monsieur. When the stranger was about to leave, we saw his lackey saddling Monsieur Porthos's horse."

"Is Mousqueton here too?"

"Yes, monsieur, and he's turning everything upside down, and because he thinks we might refuse something he asks for, he just takes everything he wants without ever asking us."

"Porthos will pay you. He is the favorite of a very great lady. She will not permit him to be inconvenienced for the paltry sum he owes you."

"If I may venture to say so, I know all about that great lady. You see, monsieur, Monsieur Porthos gave me a letter for this Duchesse, and instead of putting it in the mail, which is never very safe, I took advantage of the fact that one of my lads was going to Paris and ordered him to give the letter to the Duchesse in person. Well, monsieur, do you know who this supposed Duchesse is?"

"No, I have merely heard Porthos speak of her."

"Well, monsieur, she's only the elderly wife of an attorney at the Châtelet. Her name is Coquenard. She's at least fifty and still pretends to be jealous. When she read the letter, she flew into a great rage and said that Monsieur Porthos was a philanderer, and that he had received his wound in a duel over some woman."

"So he was wounded, was he?"

"Yes, but he forbade me to say so."

"Why?"

"By Our Lady, monsieur, because he had boasted that he would pierce the stranger through, and it was the stranger who laid Monsieur Porthos low, for all his boasting. Now Monsieur Porthos is a very vainglorious man, and he doesn't want anyone to know he's been wounded—except the Duchesse. He thought he could arouse her concern by telling her of his bad luck."

"So it's a wound that's keeping him in bed?"

"A masterly sword thrust, monsieur. I saw the fight. When Monsieur Porthos acknowledged himself beaten, the stranger asked his name, and when he discovered that it wasn't D'Artagnan, he helped Monsieur Porthos back to the inn and rode off."

"So it was Monsieur D'Artagnan the stranger wanted to fight with?"

"Apparently it was."

"And do you know what has become of him?"

"No. I had never seen him before and I haven't seen him since."

"Very well. Did you say Porthos was one flight up, in No. 1?"

"Yes, monsieur, the best room in the house. I could have rented it ten times over."

"Bah, don't worry about it," said D'Artagnan laughing. "Porthos will pay you with the Duchesse de Coquenard's money."

"But you see, monsieur, she said she wouldn't sent him a sou."

"Porthos can't owe you much."

"What, not much! A score of pistoles already, without counting the doctor."

"Never mind. If his mistress deserts him, I assure you he will find friends."

"Monsieur promises me not to say a word about the attorney's wife, or about the wound?"

"Quite so. You have my word for it."

"Oh, he would kill me if you did!"

"Have no fear. He's not as much of a devil as he looks."

Thereupon D'Artagnan went up the stairs, leaving his host somewhat reassured. At the top of the stairs, he saw that on the most conspicuous

door in the corridor a gigantic "No. 1" was inscribed in black ink. D'Artagnan knocked, and was invited to enter.

Porthos was in bed, playing a game of lansquenet with Mousqueton to
keep his hand in. A spit loaded with partridges was turning before the
fire, at either side of a wide chimney piece. The bubbling saucepans of
two chafing dishes exhaled the fragrant odors of a fricassee of rabbit and
a fish stew. The top of a desk and the marble of a chest of drawers were
covered with empty bottles. When he saw his friend, Porthos cried out
joyfully:

"By the Lord, it's you! Welcome, and excuse me for not getting up."
Then, looking at D'Artagnan somewhat uneasily, he added, "Do you
know what's happened to me?"

"No."

"The host didn't tell you anything?"

"I asked for you, then came right up." Porthos seemed to breathe more
easily. "And what did happen to you, my dear Porthos?" D'Artagnan
went on.

"It chanced that as I was lunging at my adversary—I had already
given him three thrusts and I was about to finish with a fourth—my foot
tripped on a stone and I strained my knee. That was lucky for the scoundrel, I tell you, for I should have left him dead on the spot, I assure you.
He had had enough, and was off without asking for more. But how about
you, my dear D'Artagnan?"

"So this strained knee keeps you abed, my dear Porthos," remarked
D'Artagnan.

"Oh, Lord yes, that's all. I shall be up again in a few days."

"Why didn't you go back to Paris? You must be desperately bored
here."

"I meant to, but my dear friend, I must confess I really was desperately
bored, and as I had the seventy-five pistoles you gave me, to amuse myself, I invited a gentleman who was staying here to play a game of dice.
And by my faith, my seventy-five pistoles got out of my pocket and into
his, to say nothing of my horse, which he won into the bargain."

"My dear Porthos," said D'Artagnan, "you know the proverb—'Unlucky at play, lucky in love.' You are too fortunate in your love affairs
not to have gambling take its revenge. What do reverses in fortune matter
to you? Your Duchesse will not fail to come to your rescue."

"Well, you see, my dear D'Artagnan, bad luck pursues me," Porthos
replied with the most nonchalant air in the world. "I wrote to her to send
me fifty louis that I needed badly. She must be at her country place, for
she hasn't answered. So yesterday I sent her a second letter, one much
more urgent than the first. But here you are, my very dear friend. What
about you? I was beginning to be a little worried on your account."

"But your innkeeper seems to be treating you very well, my dear

Porthos," said D'Artagnan, pointing to the full saucepans and the empty bottles.

"So-so," replied Porthos. "Three or four days ago the impertinent fellow presented his bill to me, and I had to throw him and his bill out of the door. So now I am something of a victor."

"But," said D'Artagnan, "apparently you make sorties from time to time." And he pointed to the bottles and the saucepans.

"Not I, unfortunately," said Porthos. "This wretched knee keeps me in bed, but Mousqueton forages a bit and brings back the provisions. Friend Mousequeton," Porthos went on, "you see that we have been reinforced, and we must have more food."

"Thank you, my friend. Unfortunately I have just breakfasted," said D'Artagnan.

"Very well," said Porthos. "Set the table, Mousqueton, and while you and I are breakfasting D'Artagnan will tell us what has been happening to him these last ten days."

"Gladly," said D'Artagnan.

And while Porthos and Mousequeton ate, D'Artagnan told how Aramis, wounded, had been forced to stop at Crèvecœur; how he had left Athos at Amiens fighting four men who accused him of being a counterfeiter; and how he himself had been forced to run the Comte de Wardes through the body in order to reach England. But there D'Artagnan's confidences stopped. He merely added that when he returned from Great Britain he had brought back four magnificent horses, one for himself and one for each of his friends, and that the one that was destined for Porthos was already in the stables of the inn.

Just then Planchet entered to inform his master that their horses had rested long enough, and that they could sleep at Clermont that night. As D'Artagnan was fairly reassured about Porthos, and as he was anxious to obtain news of his two other friends, he shook hands with the invalid and told him that he was resuming his search for the other musketeers. Bidding Mousqueton to take good care of Porthos, he settled his bill at the inn and went on his way with Planchet, now relieved of one led horse.

CHAPTER 26

D'ARTAGNAN HAD SAID NOTHING TO PORTHOS ABOUT HIS wound or about his lawyer's wife. Our Béarnese, young as he was, was very wise. He had therefore pretended to believe everything the vainglorious musketeer had said. And yet all along his way a profound melancholy weighed heavily on his heart. He was thinking of the young and lovely Madame Bonacieux who was to give him the reward of his devotion.

Nothing makes time pass more quickly and shortens the journey more than thoughts that absorb every faculty of the thinker. D'Artagnan rode the six or eight leagues to Chantilly at whatever gait his horse liked. Not until he reached the village and saw the inn where he had left Aramis, without remembering anything he had seen on the way, did he put his horse to the gallop. He pulled up at the inn door. This time it was not a host but a hostess who greeted him. D'Artagnan was a good physiognomist, and he took in at one glance the plump, cheerful countenance of the mistress of the place, and understood at once that he need not dissemble and that he had nothing to fear from anyone with so merry a face.

"My good lady," he said, "can you tell me what has become of one of my friends whom we were obliged to leave here about twelve days ago?"

"A handsome young man of twenty-three or twenty-four, gentle, amiable, and well built? And wounded in one shoulder?"

"Precisely."

"Well, monsieur, he's still here."

"Ah, by the Lord, my dear lady," said D'Artagnan, leaping from his horse and throwing the bridle to Planchet, "you restore me to life. Where is my dear Aramis, that I may embrace him? I tell you I am in great haste to see him again."

"I beg your pardon, monsieur, but I doubt whether he can receive you just now."

"Why? Has he a woman with him?"

"Jesus Christ, what are you saying? The poor lad! There's no woman with him. He's with the curé of Montdidier and the Superior of the Jesuits of Amiens. After his illness the grace of God touched him, and he has decided to take Holy Orders."

"I see," said D'Artagnan. "I had forgotten he was a musketeer only temporarily."

"Does Monsieur still insist on seeing him?"

"More than ever."

"Well, Monsieur has only to go up the right-hand stairway from the courtyard to the third floor and knock at No. 5."

D'Artagnan rushed off in the direction she had pointed out and found one of those outer stairways that may be seen still in the courtyards of old inns. But it was not easy to get to the future abbé. Bazin was stationed in the corridor, and he barred his passage all the more intrepidly because after years of trial, he now found himself near the goal he had hoped for years to attain. It had always been Bazin's dream to serve an ecclesiastic, and he had waited impatiently for the day when at last Aramis would throw the uniform to the dogs and don the cassock. Only Aramis's promises that the moment was drawing near had kept Bazin in the service of a musketeer.

It is easy to understand that under these circumstances nothing could be more unwelcome to Bazin than D'Artagnan's arrival, which might well throw his master back into the vortex of mundane thoughts that had swept him on for so long. He resolved to defend the door bravely, and since, betrayed by the hostess, he could not say that Aramis was not home, he tried to prove to the newcomer that it would be the height of indiscretion to disturb his master during a pious conference. D'Artagnan simply pushed Bazin aside with one hand and with the other turned the doorknob of No. 5.

Aramis, in a black gown, his head covered with a flat round cap very much like a priest's calotte, was sitting at an oblong table covered with rolls of paper and huge volumes in folio. At his right sat the Superior of the Jesuits, at his left the curé of Montdidier. All the worldly objects that usually meet the eye in a young man's room—especially when that young man is a musketeer—had disappeared as if by enchantment.

At the sound of the opening door, Aramis looked up and recognized his friend. But to D'Artagnan's great astonishment, his appearance seemed to make little impression on Aramis, so completely was his mind detached from things of this world.

"Good day to you, my dear D'Artagnan," said Aramis. "Believe me, I am very happy to see you."

"And I am delighted to see you," said D'Artagnan, "although I'm not yet quite sure that this is Aramis I'm speaking to."

"It is, my friend—he himself. What makes you doubt it?"

"I was afraid I had mistaken your room and walked in on some ecclesiastic. Then when I saw these two gentlemen with you, I was afraid you were dangerously ill. Perhaps I am disturbing you, my dear Aramis, for from what I see I judge you are making your confession to those gentlemen."

Aramis blushed almost imperceptibly.

"Disturbing me, you? Quite the contrary, my dear friend, I swear to you. I am rejoiced to see you safe and sound."

"Ah, he's coming round," D'Artagnan said to himself. "Not so bad."

"Monsieur is a friend of mine who has just escaped great danger," Aramis continued unctuously, addressing the two priests.

"Praise be to God, monsieur," they said in unison, bowing to D'Artagnan.

"I did not fail to praise Him, Your Reverences," said the young man, returning their bow.

"You arrive at the right time, dear D'Artagnan," said Aramis. "By taking part in our discussion, you may shed some light of your own on the subject. Monsieur le Principal of Amiens, Monsieur le Curé de Montdidier, and I are arguing about certain theological questions that have long fascinated us. I would be delighted to get your opinion about them. I myself start from this simple syllogism: First, the world does not lack attractions. Second, I am quitting the world, therefore I am making a sacrifice. Now the Scriptures say positively, 'Make a sacrifice unto the Lord.' My resolution is irrevocable. Tomorrow I hope to satisfy you, Reverend Fathers."

For some time longer the priests and Aramis discussed theological questions, using much Latin that D'Artagnan did not understand, and then the two priests decided to leave.

"Work slowly," said the curé. "We are leaving you in an excellent frame of mind."

"Yes, the ground is well seeded," said the Jesuit.

"Farewell, my son," said the curé, "until tomorrow."

"Till tomorrow, my young friend," said the Jesuit. "You promise to become one of the lights of the Church. God grant that this light may not become a consuming fire!"

The two men in black rose, bowed to Aramis and D'Artagnan, and went toward the door. Bazin, who had been standing near and listening with pious jubilation, sprang toward them, picked up the breviary the curé had left on a chair and the Jesuit's missal, and respectfully walked out first to lead the way.

When they were alone, the two friends at first looked at each other in embarrassed silence. One of them must perforce break it, and as D'Artagnan seemed determined to leave that honor to his friend, Aramis at last said:

"You see that I have returned to my original ideas. My plans to retire from the world were formed long ago. You've heard me talk about them, haven't you, my friend?"

"Of course, but I confess I thought you were jesting."

"Jesting about such a subject? Oh, D'Artagnan!"

"What the deuce! People jest even about death."

"And people are wrong, D'Artagnan, for death is the gate that leads to perdition or salvation."

"Granted. But if you please, let's not talk theology, Aramis, you must have had enough of it today. As for me, I confess I have eaten nothing since ten o'clock this morning, and I am devilish hungry."

"We will dine shortly, my dear friend. But I must remind you that it is Friday, so that I cannot eat meat or see it eaten. If you can eat my humble dinner——"

"I'll put up with it for the sake of your company. . . . So, Aramis, you have decided to go into the religious life. What will our two comrades say? What will Monsieur de Tréville say? They'll look on you as a deserter, I warn you."

"I am not *going into* the religious life, I am *going back* to it. I deserted the Church for the world. I violated my own nature when I put on the uniform of a musketeer. The time has come for me to return to the bosom of Mother Church."

"But why today rather than tomorrow? What has happened to give you such melancholy ideas?"

"This wound, my dear D'Artagnan, has come to me as a warning from Heaven."

"Your wound! Bah! It's almost healed, and I know well that it is not your wound that is giving you the greatest pain today. You have a wound in your heart, Aramis, a deeper and a bloodier one, a wound given you by a woman."

In spite of himself, Aramis's eyes flashed. "Ah," he said, concealing his feelings under feigned indifference, "don't speak of such things. What! I think of such things and suffer the pangs of love? For whom? For some light-o'-love, some chambermaid, that I toyed with in some garrison! Fie on you!"

"I crave your pardon, Aramis, but I thought you aspired to something higher."

"Higher? And who am I to be so ambitious? A poor musketeer, a beggar and a nobody who detests slavery of any sort, and a sorry misfit in this world! Dust I am, and to dust I shall return. Life is full of humiliations and sorrows," he continued, growing more and more melancholy. "All the threads that attach a man to life break one after the other in his hand, especially the golden ones.

"Oh, my dear D'Artagnan," Aramis went on in a somewhat bitter tone, "believe me, if you have wounds, conceal them well. Beware of letting anyone, whoever it may be, get a clue to your sorrows. The curious suck on tears as flies suck the blood of a wounded deer."

"Alas! my dear Aramis, it's my own story you are telling."

"How so?"

"Yes, a woman I loved, a woman I adored, has just been taken from me by force, I do not know where she is, where she has been taken. She may be a prisoner, she may be dead."

"But at least you have the consolation of telling yourself that she did not leave you of her own free will, that if you have no news of her, it is because she has been forbidden to communicate with you. While I——"

"While you——?"

"Nothing," replied Aramis, "nothing."

"So you are renouncing the world forever, then. Your resolution is irrevocable, the die is cast?"

"Forever and ever. Today you are my friend, tomorrow you will be no more to me than a shadow, or rather you will not even exist. As for the world, it is a tomb, nothing more."

"The devil! All you are saying is very sad."

"What do you expect? My vocation commands, it calls me away." D'Artagnan smiled, but made no answer. Aramis went on: "And yet, while I am still of this earth, I would like to talk about you, about our friends."

"And I," said D'Artagnan, "would like to talk about you yourself, but I find you are so completely detached from everything. Love you scorn, your friends are shadows, the world is a tomb."

"Alas! You will find it so yourself," said Aramis with a sigh.

"Let's say no more about it, then," said D'Artagnan, "and let's burn the letter I have here."

"What letter?" Aramis cried eagerly.

"One that was delivered at your rooms during your absence, and was given to me to take to you."

"Who wrote it?"

"Oh, some heartbroken servantmaid or some light-o'-love in despair —perhaps Madame de Chevreuse's chambermaid who, in order to seem chic, stole some of her mistress's perfumed paper and sealed it with a duchess's coronet. . . . Wait! I must have lost it," D'Artagnan said teasingly as he pretended to search for it. "But never mind. Fortunately the world is a tomb, men, and consequently women, are shadows, and love is an emotion that you scorn."

"Ah, D'Artagnan, D'Artagnan, you are killing me!"

"Here it is at last," said D'Artagnan, pulling the letter out of his pocket.

Aramis sprang up, seized the letter, and read it, or rather devoured it, his face radiant.

"Thank you, D'Artagnan, thank you!" cried Aramis, almost delirious with joy. "She was forced to return to Tours. She is not unfaithful to me, she loves me still. Come, my dear friend, let me embrace you. My happiness almost takes my breath away! My dear D'Artagnan, let us drink, 'sdeath, let us drink while the wine is cool, drink mightily, and while we do, tell me a little about what is happening in the world yonder."

CHAPTER 27

"NOW WE HAVE TO GET NEWS OF ATHOS," SAID D'ARTA-
gnan after he had told Aramis everything that had happened in the capital
since they had left it.

"Do you think some misfortune has befallen him?" asked Aramis.
"Athos is so cool, so brave, and such a skillful swordsman."

"Yes, of course, and no one has a higher opinion than I of Athos's
courage and his skill. But I prefer to have my sword clanging against
lances rather than against staves. I fear Athos has been struck down by
a mob of lackeys. That is why I confess I would like to set out again as
soon as possible."

"I will try to go with you," said Aramis, "though I hardly feel well
enough to get onto a horse. When are you leaving?"

"Tomorrow at daybreak. Sleep as soundly as you can tonight and tomorrow, if you are all right, we will set out together."

"Till tomorrow, then," said Aramis. "Your nerves may be made of
iron, but even so you must be in need of rest."

When D'Artagnan entered Aramis's room the next morning he found
his friend standing at the window.

"Whatever are you staring at?" he asked.

"My word, I am admiring those three magnificent horses the stableboys are holding. What a princely pleasure it must be to ride such
steeds!"

"Well, my dear Aramis, that pleasure will be yours, for one of those
horses belongs to you."

"I can't believe it. Which one?"

"The one you choose. I myself have no preference."

"And is the sumptuous caparison mine too?"

"Of course."

"Do you mean to say that those gilded holsters, that velvet horsecloth,
and that saddle studded with silver are all mine?"

"They are all your own, just as the horse that is pawing the ground
is mine and that other horse prancing is Athos's."

"The deuce! They are superb animals."

"I am very glad you like them so much."

"Was it the King who gave you a present like that?"

"It certainly wasn't the Cardinal. But don't worry about where they came from. Just remember that one of them is yours."

"I choose the one the redheaded boy is holding."

"That's a fine choice."

"God be praised!" cried Aramis. "He is wiping out all my sorrow. I could ride that horse with thirty bullets in my body. Bless my soul, what handsome stirrups! Holà, Bazin, come here this instant."

A dull and dispirited Bazin appeared in the doorway. "Rub up my sword, get my hat ready, brush my cloak, and load my pistols!" ordered Aramis. Bazin heaved a sigh. "Come, Master Bazin, don't take it so hard. People in every state of life win the Kingdom of Heaven."

"Alas!" sighed Bazin. "I know very well, monsieur, that everything in the world is topsy-turvy nowadays."

The two young men and the lackey went down to the courtyard.

"Hold my stirrup, Bazin," said Aramis, and he sprang into the saddle with his usual agility and grace. But after a few leaps and curvets of the noble animal, its rider felt such unbearable pain that he grew very pale and swayed in his seat. D'Artagnan, foreseeing such a possibility, had kept an eye on him, and sprang toward him at once, caught him in his arms, then helped him to his bedroom.

"It's all right, my dear Aramis," he said. "Take good care of yourself. I will go alone in search of Athos."

"You are a man of bronze," said Aramis.

"No, I'm lucky, that's all. But tell me what you're going to do while I'm gone. No more theological theses, eh?"

Aramis smiled and said: "I'll write a little poetry."

"Yes, I dare say—verses fragrant with the perfume of the letter from Madame de Chevreuse's chambermaid. As for the horse, ride him a little every day, so that you get accustomed to riding."

"Oh, don't worry about that," said Aramis. "You will find me ready to go with you."

They took leave of each other, and ten minutes later D'Artagnan, having charged Bazin and the hostess of the inn to take good care of Aramis, was trotting along the road to Amiens, pondering his problem. In what condition would he find Athos—and would he even be able to find him? The position in which he had left his friend was a serious one. Athos might well have been killed. At this thought he frowned, and sighed more than once, then made several vows of vengeance.

Athos was the oldest of the four friends, and apparently the most unlike D'Artagnan in tastes and interests. Yet D'Artagnan cared for that gentleman far more than for the other two. Athos's noble and distinguished bearing, the flashes of greatness that from time to time burst out from the shadows in which he preferred to remain, his unfailing equanimity, which made him the pleasantest companion in the world, his forced and rather bitter gaiety, his courage that might be called rash if it had not been for its unusual coolness—these qualities aroused in D'Artagnan more than esteem, more than friendship, they aroused admiration.

Athos was only middling tall, but so well built and so well proportioned that more than once in wrestling with Porthos he had thrown him, though that giant's physical strength was proverbial among the musketeers. Athos's head, with its keen eyes, its straight nose, and the finely chiseled chin, had an indefinable character of grandeur and grace. His hands, of which he took no care, were the envy of Aramis, who gave his own great attention, with the help of much almond paste and perfumed oils.

Athos's voice was both penetrating and melodious. Moreover, no one could understand how Athos, always keeping himself modestly in the background, could have such knowledge of the world and the customs of the most brilliant society. That look of a thoroughbred, though he seemed unconscious of it, showed in everything he did or said. Still further, in an age when soldiers compromised so easily with their religion and their conscience, lovers with the strict delicacy of our own day, and the poor with the Seventh Commandment,* Athos's probity was unassailable. He was an extraordinary man, this Athos.

And yet this distinguished nature, this wonderful person, this fine type, was sometimes to be seen turning insensibly toward the material side of life. Then the demigod vanished and Athos was hardly a human being. His head hanging, his eyes dull, his speech thick and difficult, Athos would sit for hours at a time looking at his bottle and his glass. He drank enough for four men, and that without seeming to be affected by it except by showing a heavier frown or a deeper melancholy.

D'Artagnan, with that keen and probing mind of his, however much he wished to satisfy his curiosity, had not been able to account for these fits of melancholy or to find out how often they occurred. But he did note that June and July were terrible months for Athos.

For the present Athos seemed to feel no concern; when anyone spoke of the future, he shrugged his shoulders. His secret, then, must be in the past, as D'Artagnan had heard vaguely from one or another. The mystery that surrounded his whole personality only made more interesting the man whose eyes and mouth, even when he was completely drunk, had never revealed anything about himself, however skillfully he had been questioned.

At about eleven o'clock that morning D'Artagnan and Planchet were at Amiens, and at half-past eleven they were at the door of that accursed inn. D'Artagnan had often meditated on the vengeance he would take on

*Eighth except in the Roman Catholic Church: "Thou shalt not steal."

that perfidious host, one of those fine revenges that offer some consolation in the mere hope of it. His hat drawn low over his eyes, his left hand on the hilt of his sword, and his right hand cracking his riding crop, he entered the inn.

"Do you recognize me?" he asked the host, who came to greet him.

"No, I have not that honor, my lord," the host replied, his eyes dazzled by the brilliant style in which D'Artagnan traveled.

"Well, let me refresh your memory. Something like a fortnight ago you had the audacity to accuse a gentleman of offering you counterfeit money. What have you done with him?"

Mine host grew deathly pale, for D'Artagnan's attitude was very menacing.

"Ah, my lord, don't speak of that!" cried mine host in his most lachrymose tone. "Ah, God, I have paid dearly for that mistake, unhappy wretch that I am!"

"But the gentleman—what has become of him?"

"Be good enough to listen to me, my lord, and be merciful. Be seated, I beg of you!" D'Artagnan, mute with anger and anxiety, took a seat, looking as menacing as a judge. "Here's the whole story, my lord," the host went on, trembling all over. "I recognize you now—you are the gentleman who left when I was having that unfortunate difference with the gentleman you're talking about."

"Yes, I am he. So you see you have no mercy to expect if you do not tell me the whole truth."

"Be good enough to listen to me and you shall know all about it. . . . I had been warned by the authorities that a notorious counterfeiter would arrive at my inn with several companions disguised as musketeers or guardsmen. They furnished me with a description of your horses, your lackeys, your persons—everything."

"Go on, go on!" said D'Artagnan, who knew very well from what source such an exact description had come.

"The authorities sent me a reinforcement of six men and, acting on their orders, I took all the measures I thought necessary to secure the persons of the supposed counterfeiters. The authorities had terrified me, and you know that an innkeeper must keep on good terms with the authorities."

"But I ask you once more—where is that gentleman? What has happened to him? Is he dead? Is he alive?"

"Patience, my lord, we are coming to that. You remember what happened, and your precipitate departure seemed to authorize what happened next. That gentleman, your friend, defended himself desperately. Unfortunately, through some misunderstanding, his lackey had quarreled with some of the men belonging to the authorities, who were disguised as stableboys——"

"You scoundrel!" interrupted D'Artagnan. "You were all in the plot. I don't know what keeps me from exterminating all of you!"

"Oh no, my lord, we were not in any plot, as you shall see. Monsieur, your friend—forgive me for not calling him by the honorable name he doubtless bears, but I do not know it—your friend, after putting two men out of action with his two shots, retreated defending himself with his sword. He disabled one of my men and stunned me with a blow from the flat of the blade."

"You infernal villain, will you have done?" cried D'Artagnan. "Athos —what happened to Athos?"

"When he retreated as I told you he did, my lord, he backed up against the door to the cellar, and as the door was open, he took the key, stepped onto the cellar stairs, and locked himself in. As we were sure the authorities could find him there, we left him alone."

"I see," said D'Artagnan. "As you did not especially wish to kill him, you made him your prisoner."

"Good God, our prisoner, my lord? He imprisoned himself, I swear he did! And he had done a fine job of work first—one man killed on the spot and two others severely wounded. The dead man and the two who were wounded were carried away by the comrades, and I have heard nothing of any of them since. As for me, when I came to my senses I called on Monsieur le Gouverneur, told him everything that had passed, and asked him what I should do with the prisoner. But Monsieur le Gouverneur said he didn't know what I was talking about. The orders I had received had not come from him, and if I had the audacity to mention his name in connection with this brawl, he would have me hanged. It seems that I had made a mistake, monsieur. I had arrested the wrong man."

"But Athos!" cried D'Artagnan. "What has happened to Athos?"

"As I was anxious to right the wrong I had done the prisoner," the innkeeper answered, "I went to the cellar to set him free. Monsieur, he was no longer a man, he was a devil! When I offered him his liberty, he declared it was nothing but a trap, and that before he came out he would impose his own conditions. I told him humbly—for I realized what a scrape I was in for laying hands on one of His Majesty's musketeers—I told him I was quite ready to accept his conditions.

" 'First,' said he, 'I want my lackey sent down here fully armed.' We hastened to obey this order, for you can understand, monsieur, that we were willing to do everything your friend wished. Monsieur Grimaud was therefore sent to the cellar, wounded though he was. Then his master, having admitted him, barricaded the door again, and ordered us to stay in our own place."

"But where is he now?" cried D'Artagnan. "Where is Athos?"

"In the cellar, monsieur."

"What, you wretch! Have you been keeping him in the cellar all this time?"

"Good God, no, monsieur. *We* keep him in the cellar! Do you know what he's doing there? Oh, if you could persuade him to come out, monsieur, I would be grateful to you the rest of my days."

"So he is still in your cellar? I shall find him there?"

"Certainly you will, monsieur; he has insisted on staying there. Every day we pass down some bread on a pitchfork, and some meat when he asks for it. But alas! it is not bread and meat that he consumes most. Once when I tried to go down with two of my lads he flew into a towering rage. I heard the sound as he cocked his pistol and the servant cocked his musketoon. When I asked what they meant to do, the master replied that they had forty bullets to fire between them and they would fire every one of them before he would permit a single one of us to set foot in the cellar. Then, monsieur, I went to complain about it to the Governor, and he told me that I had got just what I deserved, and it would teach me not to insult noble and honorable gentlemen who came to stay in my inn."

"What has happened since?" asked D'Artagnan, who could not help laughing at mine host's woebegone expression.

"Since then, monsieur, we have been leading the most miserable existence you can imagine. You see, monsieur, all our supplies are in that cellar—our bottled wine and our wine in casks, our beer, our oil and spices, our bacon and hams and sausages. And as we are not permitted to go down there, we are forced to refuse food and drink to our guests. Our inn is losing money day by day. If your friend stays another week in the cellar I shall be a ruined man."

"And that will be justice, you stupid fellow. Couldn't you tell by our looks that we were people of quality and not counterfeiters?"

"Yes, monsieur, yes, you are right," said the host. "But hark, hark! There he is in a passion again!"

"Doubtless somebody disturbed him," said D'Artagnan.

"But it's absolutely necessary to disturb him. Two English gentlemen have just arrived. The English like good wine, as you know, monsieur, and these two have ordered the best we have. My wife probably asked Monsieur Athos's permission to go to the cellar, and as usual he refused it. Ah, God in Heaven, listen! The hullabaloo is louder than ever!"

Indeed D'Artagnan could hear a great uproar rising from the cellar and, preceded by the host wringing his hands and Planchet with his musketoon cocked, started for the scene of action. The two English gentlemen were exasperated; they had ridden far and were dying of hunger and thirst.

"But this is an outrage!" cried one of them, in French that was excellent, though with a foreign accent. "This lunatic will not allow these good people access to their own wine. Nonsense! We'll break down the door, and if he gets too wild, all right, we'll kill the fellow!"

"Softly, gentlemen!" said D'Artagnan, drawing his pistols from his belt. "Nobody is to be killed, if you please."

"Good, good!" Athos's calm voice said from the other side of the door. "Let them just come in, these devourers of little children, and we shall see."

Brave as they seemed to be, the two English gentlemen looked at each other hesitatingly. You might have thought that in that cellar was one of those ravenous and gigantic ogres, the heroes of popular legends, into whose cavern no man ventured to force his way with impunity. There was a moment of silence, but the Englishmen were ashamed to retreat, and the more dogged of the two went down the five or six steps leading to the cellar and kicked at the door savagely.

"Planchet," said D'Artagnan, cocking his pistols, "I'll take on the one up here, you take care of the one down there. Now, gentlemen, if it's a fight you want, you shall have it."

"God above!" cried Athos's cavernous voice. "It's D'Artagnan I hear, I do believe."

"You're right," said D'Artagnan, raising his voice. "I'm here, my friend."

"Good, then," said Athos, "we'll give these breakers of doors a little exercise!"

The Englishmen had drawn their swords, but they found themselves between two fires. They hesitated again, but, as before, their pride prevailed, and a second kick split the door from top to bottom.

"Stand aside, D'Artagnan, stand aside!" cried Athos. "I'm going to shoot!"

"Gentlemen," said D'Artagnan, whose common sense never deserted him, "pray stop to think! Patience, Athos. Gentlemen, you're heading into bad trouble, and you will be riddled with bullets. My lackey and I have three shots apiece for you, and a like number will come from the cellar. After that we have our swords, and I assure you that my friend and I handle them pretty well. Allow me to settle your business and my own. Presently you shall have something to drink, I give you my word."

"If there's any wine left," growled the jeering voice of Athos.

The host felt cold sweat trickle down his back.

"Devil take it, there must be plenty left," said D'Artagnan. "Keep calm, mine host, the two of them can never have drunk the cellar dry. Gentlemen, sheathe your swords."

"Very well, if you will return your pistols to your belt."

"Gladly." And D'Artagnan set the example. Then he motioned to Planchet to uncock his musketoon. The Englishmen sheathed their swords, grumbling a little. "Now, gentlemen, go back to your rooms and I give you my word that in ten minutes everything you want shall be brought to you." The Englishmen bowed and withdrew.

"Now that I am alone, my dear Athos," said D'Artagnan, "open the door, I beg of you."

"Certainly, this minute," said Athos.

Then there were loud noises of fagots knocking against each other and posts groaning as the beleagured Athos demolished his counterscarp and bastions. An instant later the broken door was set aside, the pale face of Athos appeared, and he made a quick survey of the situation. D'Artagnan embraced him tenderly. Then he tried to drag his friend out of his damp abode, but to his surprise he saw that Athos was staggering.

"Are you wounded?" he asked.

"No, not at all. I am dead-drunk, that's all, and never did a man make a better job of it. Blessed be God, mine host! I must have drunk at least a hundred bottles all by myself."

"God help me!" cried the host. "If the lackey has drunk only half as much as his master, I am a ruined man!"

"Grimaud is a well-bred lackey. He would never think of drinking the same wine as I—he drank only from the casks. Listen—I think he has forgotten to put the bung back. Don't you hear the wine running out?"

D'Artagnan burst into peals of laughter that turned the host's chill into a burning fever. Grimaud appeared behind his master, his musketoon on his shoulder and his head wavering like some tipsy satyr in a Rubens painting. The procession crossed the public room and went up to the best room in the inn, commandeered by D'Artagnan. In the meantime the host and his wife, armed with lamps, rushed down to the cellar, where a frightful spectacle awaited them.

Beyond the fortifications Athos had breached in order to get out, here and there bones of the hams he and Grimaud had eaten were swimming in pools of olive oil and wine. One corner of the cellar was heaped with a pile of broken bottles. Out of fifty large sausages that had been hanging from the beams, barely ten were left. The shrieks of the host and his wife rose from the cellar vault until D'Artagnan himself was much moved. Athos did not even turn his head. But grief followed rage. The host armed himself with a spit and in his desperation rushed to the room the two friends occupied.

"Some wine!" ordered Athos when he saw the host.

"Some wine!" cried the host in amazement. "Why, you have already drunk more than a hundred pistoles' worth! I am ruined, lost, destroyed."

"Bah!" said Athos. "We were dry all the time."

"You shall pay for all this!" cried the exasperated host.

"You triple ass!" said Athos, rising. But he sank back into his chair immediately. He had taxed his strength to the utmost. D'Artagnan came to his rescue, raising his riding crop. The host drew back and burst into tears.

"That will teach you," said D'Artagnan, "to treat more courteously the guests God sends you."

"God! Better say the Devil."

"My dear friend," said D'Artagnan, "if you keep on deafening our ears like that, all four of us will go and shut ourselves up in your cellar and discover whether the damage is as great as you say it is."

"Oh indeed, gentlemen, I am in the wrong, I admit it. But every sin finds forgiveness. You are noblemen and I am a poor innkeeper—surely you will have pity on me."

"Oh, if you talk like that," said Athos, "you'll break my heart. We are not the devils we seem. Come here and let us talk things over." The host drew near uneasily. "Come, I tell you," continued Athos, "have no fears. . . . As I was about to pay your bill, I put my purse on the table."

"Yes, my lord."

"That purse contained sixty pistoles. Where is it now?"

"Deposited in the Registrar's office. I had been told the money was counterfeit."

"Well, get my purse back and keep the sixty pistoles."

"But your lordship knows perfectly well that the Registrar never gives up anything he once lays hands on. If the money had been counterfeit, there might be some hope, but unfortunately your coins are good."

"Settle all that with him, my good man. It's no concern of mine, all the more because I haven't a sou left."

"Come," said D'Artagnan, "where is Monsieur Athos's horse?"

"In the stables."

"How much is it worth?"

"Fifty pistoles at the most."

"It's worth eighty," said D'Artagnan. "Keep it, mine host, and let us forget the whole matter."

"What! You're selling my horse, my Bajazet? And what shall I ride on in my next campaign? On Grimaud?"

"I have brought you another horse," said D'Artagnan.

"And a magnificent one it is!" cried the innkeeper.

"Very well. If I am to have a finer and younger mount, keep the old one, and let us have some wine."

"What wine shall I fetch?" asked the host, quite cheerful once more.

"Some of that at the back of your cellar. There are twenty-five bottles of it left; all the rest were broken when I fell. Bring six of them."

"And don't forget," said D'Artagnan, "to take four bottles of the same sort to the two English gentlemen."

"Now," said Athos, "while we're waiting for the wine tell me, D'Artagnan, what has become of our comrades."

D'Artagnan told him how he had found Porthos in bed with a sprained knee and Aramis sitting at a table between the two theologians. As he was finishing his tale, the host entered with the wine and a ham that, fortunately for him, had not been kept in the cellar.

"Good!" said Athos, filling his own glass and D'Artagnan's. "So much for Porthos and Aramis. But what about you, D'Artagnan? What has happened to you personally? You don't look happy."

"Alas! I am the most unhappy of all of us!"

"You unhappy, D'Artagnan! Why are you unhappy? Tell me."

D'Artagnan related his adventure with Madame Bonacieux. Athos listened without a change of expression, and when his friend had finished he commented:

"Trifles, all that, mere trifles!"

"That sounds just like you, my dear Athos," said D'Artagnan, "and that comes very ill from you, who have never been in love."

Athos's glazed eyes suddenly flashed, but only for an instant, then they became dull and vacant again. "That's true," he said quietly. "I have never been in love, have I!"

"Acknowledge, then, you stony-hearted man, that you have no right to be so hard on those of us who are tenderhearted."

"A tender heart means a broken heart. Love is a lottery in which he who wins, wins death! You are very fortunate in having lost, believe me, my dear D'Artagnan, and if I have advice to give you it is—always lose in that lottery."

"She seemed to love me so dearly!"

"Seemed to, did she?"

"Oh, she *did* love me."

"Child that you are! There's not a man alive who hasn't believed as you do that his mistress loved him, and not a man alive who has not been deceived by his mistress."

"Except you, Athos, who never had one."

"True," said Athos after a moment's silence, "I have never had a mistress. . . . Well, let's drink!"

"Philosopher as you are," said D'Artagnan, "it is your duty to instruct me, to sustain me. I need to be taught and to be consoled."

"Consoled! For what?"

"For my unhappiness."

"Your unhappiness makes me laugh," said Athos, shrugging his shoulders. "I wonder what you'd say if I were to tell you a real love story."

"One that happened to you?"

"Or to a friend of mine. What difference does it make?"

"Tell me the story, Athos, please."

"Let us drink instead. We'll be better off."

"Do both—drink and tell your story."

"Really, that's not a bad idea," said Athos, draining his glass and filling it again. "The two amusements go together wonderfully well."

Athos collected himself, and as he did so D'Artagnan saw him grow more and more pale. He was at that stage of intoxication where vulgar drinkers fall on the floor and sleep. He held himself erect and dreamed without sleeping.

"You insist on hearing the story?" he asked.

"I beg you to tell it."

"Then you shall have your wish. One of my friends—one of my friends, please note, not I," said Athos, interrupting himself with a melancholy smile, "one of the Comtes in my province, Berry, one as nobly born as a Dandolo or a Montmorency, a man of twenty-five, fell in love with a girl of sixteen, a girl as beautiful as love itself. Through the naïveté natural at her age there beamed an ardent spirit, the spirit not of a woman but of a poet. She did not merely please a man, she intoxicated him. She was living in a small town with her brother, who was a curé. Nobody knew where they had come from, but seeing her so beautiful and her brother so pious, nobody ever asked. It was rumored, however, that they were well-born. My friend, who was the seigneur of that place, might have seduced her, or might have taken her by force, for he was the master. Who would have come to the help of two strangers, two people nobody knew? Unfortunately he was an honorable man; he married her. The fool, the ass, the imbecile!"

"How so, if he loved her?"

"Wait. One day when she was out hunting with her husband," Athos went on, speaking in a low voice and very rapidly, "she fell from her horse and fainted. The Comte rushed to help her, and as she seemed to be stifling, cut her bodice open with his dagger, baring her shoulder. Can you guess what he found on her shoulder, D'Artagnan?" asked Athos, with a loud burst of laughter.

"How could I know?"

"A fleur-de-lis," said Athos. "She had been branded as a criminal!" And Athos drained his glass with one gulp.

"Horrors!" said D'Artagnan. "What are you saying?"

"The truth. My friend, the angel was a devil. The wretched girl had been a thief!"

"And what did the Comte do?"

"The Comte was a great nobleman; on his own estate he had the right to administer both high and low justice. He tore her clothes off the Comtesse, tied her hands behind her, and hanged her on a tree."

"Good heavens, Athos, a murder!" cried D'Artagnan.

"Yes, a murder, no more and no less," said Athos, as pale as death. "But I seem to have no wine." He seized by the neck the last of their bottles and drained it at a single draught as though it were only a wineglass. Then he sank his head into his hands while D'Artagnan stood before him horror-stricken. "That cured me of beautiful, poetical, and loving women," he said, rising, and forgetting to keep up the fiction of his friend the Comte. "God grant you as much enlightenment! Come, let us drink!"

"So she is dead?" D'Artagnan stammered.

"By the Lord, she is! But hold out your glass. Oh, there's no more wine. Have some ham, man, since we can't drink!"

"And her brother," asked D'Artagnan timidly—"the priest?"

"Oh, I made inquiries about him so that I could have him hanged too, but he had got ahead of me, he had left his curacy the day before."

"Did anyone ever find out who this wretch was?"

"Oh, probably the first lover and the accomplice of my beauty, a fine fellow who had perhaps pretended to be a priest in order to marry off his mistress and provide for her future. I hope he has been drawn and quartered by now."

"Oh, my God, my God!" exclaimed D'Artagnan, quite stunned by the relation of this horrible adventure.

"Try some of this ham, D'Artagnan; it is delicious," said Athos, cutting a slice and putting it on the young man's plate. "What a pity that there weren't four more like it in the cellar. Then I might have drunk fifty bottles more!"

D'Artagnan could endure this conversation no longer; it would have driven him mad. He let his head sink into his hands and pretended to fall asleep.

"Young fellows don't know how to drink any more," said Athos, looking at him pityingly. "And this lad is one of the best of them, too!"

CHAPTER 28

D'ARTAGNAN WAS ASTOUNDED BY THE TERRIBLE SECRET
Athos had revealed. Yet many things in this partial revelation still seemed
to him obscure. In the first place, it had been made by a man who was
quite drunk to a man who was only half-drunk, and yet despite the vague-
ness that the fumes from three or four bottles of Burgundy had sent to
his brain, when he woke the next morning, D'Artagnan remembered every
word Athos had said. All his own doubts only increased his desire to
arrive at certainty, and he went to his friend's room firmly resolved to
renew the conversation of the evening before. But he found Athos quite
himself again—that is, the shrewdest and most impenetrable of men.
Moreover, after they had shaken hands the musketeer broached the matter first.

"I was pretty drunk yesterday, my dear D'Artagnan," he said. "I could
tell that this morning by the feel of my tongue, which is still very thick,
and by my pulse, which is very fast. I wager I talked a fearful lot of
nonsense." And he gazed at his friend with an earnestness that embarrassed D'Artagnan.

"Not at all," said D'Artagnan. "If I remember right, you said nothing
out of the ordinary."

"You surprise me very much. I thought I had told you a most mourn-
ful tale."

And he looked at the young man as if to read the very depths of his
heart.

"By my faith," said D'Artagnan, "I must have been even drunker than
you were, for I remember nothing of the kind."

Athos was not deceived, and went on: "You cannot have failed to
notice, my dear friend, that every man has his particular kind of drunken-
ness, sad or gay. In my own case, I am melancholy when I am drunk,
and when I am in my cups I am possessed by a mania to tell all the
lugubrious tales my foolish nurse stuffed my brain with."

Athos spoke so naturally that D'Artagnan's conviction was shaken.

"Oh, so that's it," replied the young man. "Now I remember, as one
remembers a dream, that we talked about people being hanged."

"Ah, you see how it is," said Athos, growing still paler and yet attempting a laugh. "I was sure of it—hanging people is my particular nightmare."

"Yes, yes," D'Artagnan answered. "I remember now. . . . Yes, you told me about—wait a minute—yes, about a woman———"

"That's it," replied Athos, now almost livid. "That's my fine story of the blonde woman. When I tell that one, I am indeed dead-drunk."

"Yes, that's it," said D'Artagnan. "The story about a blonde woman who was beautiful and had blue eyes."

"Yes, and who was hanged."

"By her husband, who was a nobleman of your acquaintance," D'Artagnan continued, looking intently at Athos.

"Well, you see how a man can compromise another when he himself doesn't know what he is saying," answered Athos, shrugging his shoulders. "I don't mean to get drunk again, D'Artagnan, it's a very bad habit."

D'Artagnan said nothing. Suddenly Athos changed the subject. "By the way," said he, "many thanks for the horse you brought me. But it isn't a horse for hard work."

"You're mistaken there. I've ridden it twenty leagues in less than an hour and a half, and it seemed no more distressed than if it had merely gone around the Place Saint-Sulpice once."

"Now you begin to awaken my regret. You see, I have parted with it."

"How did that happen?"

"Well, this morning I woke at six. You were sleeping like a log, and I didn't know what to do with myself. As I went into the public room, I saw one of our Englishmen bargaining with a horse-dealer over a mount. I drew near, and found he was offering a hundred pistoles for a burned-chestnut horse. 'By the Lord, monsieur,' said I, 'I too have a horse for sale.'

" 'And a very handsome one,' said he. 'I saw it yesterday.'

" 'Do you consider it worth a hundred pistoles?'

" 'Yes. Will you sell it to me for that price?'

" 'No, but I'll play you for it at dice.' No sooner said than done, and I lost the horse. By the way," he added, "I won back the caparison."

D'Artagnan looked rather sour. "Does that vex you?" asked Athos.

"Well, I confess it does," D'Artagnan replied. "That horse was one of the four that were to make us men of mark on the battlefield. It was a pledge—a remembrance. You were wrong to gamble it away, Athos."

"Well, my dear friend, put yourself in my place," the musketeer replied. "I was bored to death, and anyway, upon my honor, I don't like English horses. Come, if it's only a question of being recognized by somebody, the saddle will suffice for that; it is remarkable enough! As for the horse, we'll find some excuse to explain its disappearance."

D'Artagnan looked as sour as ever. "I'm very sorry," Athos continued, "that you seem to be so much attached to these beasts, for I haven't finished my story."

"What else have you done?"

"After losing my own horse by a throw of nine against ten I had an idea—I would stake yours."

"An idea all right, but I hope that you stopped at the idea."

"No, I didn't. I put it into execution at once." D'Artagnan looked very anxious. "I threw the dice, and I lost."

"You lost my horse?"

"Your horse, by seven against eight—one point short."

"Athos, you're not in your right mind. I swear you're not."

"My dear fellow, you should have told me that yesterday, when I was telling you silly stories, not this morning. I lost your horse, then, and every bit of its equipment. . . . Wait a minute—we still had that diamond sparkling on your finger."

"My diamond!" cried D'Artagnan, putting his hand quickly on the ring.

"And as I am a connoisseur, having owned a few myself once, I estimated it at one thousand pistoles."

"I hope," said D'Artagnan, half-dead with fear, "that you didn't mention my diamond."

"On the contrary, my dear friend. You must realize that your diamond was now our only resource. With it I might win back our horses and their equipment, and perhaps money to get us home. So I mentioned your diamond to my fellow dicer; he had noticed it too. What the devil, my friend, do you think you can wear a star from heaven on your finger and no one will notice it?"

"Go on, my dear fellow, go on!" said D'Artagnan. "Upon my honor, you are killing me with your sangfroid!"

"Well, we divided your diamond into ten parts of a hundred pistoles each."

"Ah, you are jesting!" cried D'Artagnan, anger seizing him as violently as Minerva seized Achilles' hair in the *Iliad*.

"Hear the rest of it. I lost my thirteenth throw, and now I had lost everything. Thirteen has always been my unlucky number."

"God's body!" interrupted D'Artagnan, rising from the table.

"Patience now," said Athos. "I had a plan. The Englishman was an odd man. I had seen him talking with Grimaud that morning, and Grimaud had told me that the gentleman had made him proposals to enter his own service. I staked Grimaud, the mute Grimaud, divided into ten parts."

"What a stake!" said D'Artagnan, who could not help laughing.

"Grimaud himself, you understand! And with the ten parts of Grimaud, which altogether aren't worth a ducatoon, I won back the diamond. Now tell me that persistence isn't a virtue!"

"By my faith, that's very funny!" cried D'Artagnan, somewhat consoled and holding his sides for laughter.

"You'll understand that now that I was having good luck, I immediately staked the diamond again."

"The devil you did!" said D'Artagnan, blowing gloomy again.

"I won back your harness, then your horse, then my harness, then my horse, and then I lost both horses again. In short, I ended up with your harness, then my own. That's where we stand now. I had made superb throws, so I called quits."

"But of what use is the equipment without the horses?"

"I have an idea about that. Listen. You haven't gambled for a long time, have you?"

"No, and I have no desire to."

"Well, the Englishman and his companion are still here. I noticed that he regretted his loss of the harness very much. As for you, you seem to think a lot of your horse. Now if I were in your place, I would stake your harness against your horse."

"But he wouldn't be interested in one harness, would he?"

"Stake both of them, by the Lord. I'm not as selfish as you are!"

"What if I lose?"

"You will win."

"But if I *do* lose?"

"Well, you'll give up the harness."

"All right. Here goes for one throw!" said D'Artagnan.

Athos went in search of the Englishman, whom he found in the stables looking at the harness with a covetous eye. It was the right moment. Athos decided the conditions—the two harnesses against either one horse or one hundred pistoles, as the winner chose. D'Artagnan threw the dice with a trembling hand and rolled a trey. His pallor frightened Athos, but he merely commented:

"That's an unfortunate throw, comrade. . . . You will have the horses fully equipped, monsieur."

Triumphant, the Englishman did not bother to shake the dice, but threw them onto the table without looking down, so sure was he of the victory. D'Artagnan had turned away to hide the fact that he had lost his temper.

"Hullo, look at that!" said Athos in his usual calm tone. "That's an extraordinary throw of the dice! I have seen it only four times in my life. Two aces!"

The Englishman looked and was astounded. D'Artagnan was overcome with delight.

"So Monsieur gets his horse back," said the Englishman.

"Certainly," said D'Artagnan.

"And there is no revenge to be had?"

"Our conditions said no revenge, you remember?"

"Right. Your horse will be given to your lackey, monsieur."

"One moment," said Athos. "With your permission, monsieur, I would like to have a word with my friend."

"You may do so, monsieur."

Athos drew D'Artagnan aside.

"Well," D'Artagnan said, "what more do you want of me, tempter? You want me to throw again, don't you?"

"No, I just want you to consider the situation carefully. You want your horse back, don't you?"

"Of course I do."

"You are wrong. I would take the hundred pistoles. As you know, you have your choice. For my part, I wouldn't hesitate a moment, I would take the hundred pistoles. We need the money to get back to Paris."

"I care a lot for that horse, Athos."

"There again you are wrong. A horse shies or slips and breaks his knees. There's a horse—or rather a hundred pistoles—lost. A master must feed his horse, whereas on the contrary, a hundred pistoles will feed its master."

"But how shall we get back to Paris?"

"On our lackeys' horses, by the Lord! People can always tell by our looks that we are persons of quality."

"Pretty figures we'll cut on nags while Aramis and Porthos caracole on their war horses!"

"Aramis! Porthos!" cried Athos, and he began to laugh.

"What are you laughing at?" asked D'Artagnan, at a loss to understand his friend's hilarity.

"All right, all right, let's decide."

"So your advice is——?"

"To take the hundred pistoles, D'Artagnan. With a hundred pistoles we can live in luxury for a month. We have undergone a great deal of fatigue, remember, and it will be good to rest a little."

"Rest—I? Oh no, Athos. As soon as I am in Paris I shall go in search of that unhappy woman."

"Well, do you think your horse would be as useful to you in that as the good golden coins would be? Take the hundred pistoles."

D'Artagnan needed only one reason in order to give in, and this last reason seemed convincing. Besides, he feared he would seem selfish in Athos's eyes if he resisted any longer. He therefore acquiesced and chose the hundred pistoles, which the Englishman paid forthwith. Then they thought of nothing but their departure. To make their peace with their host, in addition to Athos's old horse, cost 6 pistoles. D'Artagnan and Athos took the nags of Planchet and Grimaud, the lackeys following on foot with the saddles on their heads.

Badly as the two friends were mounted, they were soon far ahead of their lackeys and reached Crèvecœur ahead of them. From afar they espied Aramis leaning out of his window in deep melancholy to look for dust on the horizon.

"Holà, Aramis!" D'Artagnan shouted. "What the devil are you doing there?"

"So it's you, D'Artagnan, and you, Athos," the young man said. "I was meditating on the rapidity with which the good things of this world leave us. My English horse has just vanished in a cloud of dust and has furnished me with a living image of the fragility of earthly things."

"What do you mean?" asked D'Artagnan.

"I mean that I have just made a fool of myself. I got only sixty louis for a horse that, judging by his gait, can cover at least five leagues an hour." D'Artagnan and Athos burst out laughing. "My dear D'Artagnan," said Aramis, "don't be too angry with me, I beg of you. Necessity knows no law. Besides, I am the one most severely punished, since that rascal of a horse-dealer cheated me out of at least fifty louis. Ah, you two are good managers; you ride your lackeys' nags and have your own splendid horses led by hand gently and in easy stages."

Just then a market cart that had appeared on the Amiens road a few minutes before pulled up at the inn and they saw Grimaud and Planchet get out of it with the saddles on their heads. The cart was returning empty to Paris, and the two lackeys, in return for their transportation, had agreed to quench the carter's thirst along the road.

"What's this?" said Aramis when he saw them. "Nothing but saddles?"

"Do you understand now?" Athos asked.

"My friends, that's just what I did. Some instinct told me to keep my harness. Ho, Bazin, bring my new saddle and carry it alongside those of these gentlemen."

"And what have you done with your priests?" D'Artagnan asked.

"My dear friend, I invited them to dine with me the next day," said Aramis. "They have some capital wine here, by the way. I did my best to get them drunk, then the curé forbade me to quit my uniform and the Jesuit begged me to get him into the musketeers. Since that time I have been living very agreeably."

D'Artagnan and Athos stayed an hour to rest their horses; Aramis paid his bill and sent Bazin to ride in the cart with his comrades. Then they set forth to join Porthos. They found him up, paler than D'Artagnan had left him, sitting at a table that, though he was alone, was set for four. The dinner consisted of nicely dressed meats, choice wines, and superb fruits.

"Ha, by the Lord," said Porthos, rising, "you come in the nick of time, gentlemen. I was just beginning with the soup, and now you must dine with me."

"This dinner wasn't meant for you alone, was it, Porthos?" asked Aramis.

"No," Porthos replied. "I was expecting some gentlemen of the neighborhood, but they have just sent me word that they cannot come. You will take their places, and I shall not lose by the exchange."

"Do you know what we're eating here?" asked Aramis, after they had been enjoying the food for some ten minutes.

"By the Lord," said D'Artagnan, "I'm eating some delicious veal larded with cardoons and marrow."

"As for me," said Porthos, "I have some fine fillets of lamb."

"And I'm eating savory breast of chicken," said Aramis.

"You are mistaken, gentlemen, all of you," said Athos gravely. "You are eating horseflesh, aren't we, Porthos? And perhaps harness with it."

"No, gentlemen, I kept the harness," cried Porthos.

"Upon my word," Aramis declared, "we are all alike. Anyone might think we had agreed on it."

"What could you expect?" said Porthos. "That horse made my visitors ashamed of theirs, and I didn't like to humiliate them!"

"And then your Duchesse is still taking the waters, isn't she, Porthos?" D'Artagnan went on.

"Yes, she is," Porthos replied. "Now by my faith, the Governor of the province—one of the gentlemen I expected today—took such a shine to my horse that I gave it to him."

"*Gave* it to him!" cried D'Artagnan.

"Oh, Lord, yes—'gave' is the right word," said Porthos. "For it was certainly worth a hundred and fifty louis, and the stingy fellow would pay me only eighty."

"Without the saddle?" Aramis asked.

"Yes, without the saddle."

"You will observe, gentlemen," said Athos, "that Porthos has made the best bargain of any of us."

Then there was a roar of laughter that astonished poor Porthos, but when the reason for the hilarity was explained to him, he joined in with his usual vociferous sounds of mirth.

"So we're all in funds now, aren't we?" said D'Artagnan.

"Not I," said Athos. "I found Aramis's Spanish wine so good that I had sixty bottles of it put in the cart with our lackeys. That has pretty well emptied my purse."

"And not I," said Aramis. "You see, I have given practically my last sou to the church of Montdidier and the Jesuits of Amiens."

"And not I," said Porthos. "Do you think my sprained knee cost me nothing? After I settle my account, I shall have perhaps thirty crowns left."

"And I about ten pistoles," said Aramis.

"Well, well," said Athos, "it seems that we are as rich as Croesus. How much have you left of your hundred pistoles, D'Artagnan?"

"My hundred pistoles? Why, first of all, I gave you fifty."

"So you did, I remember now. In brief, how much have you now?"

"Twenty-five pistoles," D'Artagnan replied.

"Now then, let's calculate how much we possess all together. Porthos? 'Thirty crowns.' Aramis? 'Ten pistoles.' And you, D'Artagnan? 'Twenty-five pistoles.' How much does that make, all told?"

"Four hundred and seventy-five livres," said D'Artagnan.

"When we get to Paris, we shall still have four hundred," said Porthos, "plus the harnesses. Come, let's eat our dinner; it's getting cold."

When he reached Paris, D'Artagnan found a letter from Monsieur de Tréville informing him that the King had granted him the favor of being admitted to the Royal Musketeers in the near future. As this was the height of D'Artagnan's ambition in this world—except of course for his desire to find Madame Bonacieux—he ran, full of joy, to find his friends. He had left them perfectly happy only a half an hour before, but now he found them very sad and deeply preoccupied. Monsieur de Tréville had just notified them that His Majesty had decided to open the campaign on May 1, and they must get all their equipment ready immediately. The four philosophers looked at one another in bewilderment. Monsieur de Tréville never jested in matters of discipline.

"How much do you think all our equipment will cost?" D'Artagnan asked.

"Oh, there's no telling," Aramis answered. "We have just made our calculations with Spartan niggardliness, and each of us needs fifteen hundred livres."

"Four times fifteen makes sixty—six thousand livres," Athos remarked.

"For my part," said D'Artagnan, "I think that with a thousand livres apiece——"

"Wait," said Porthos. "I have an idea!"

"Well, that's something. As for me, I haven't the shadow of one," said Athos calmly. "But as to D'Artagnan, gentlemen, his happiness at becoming one of us as a musketeer has driven him mad. A thousand livres! I vow I need two thousand for myself alone."

"Four times two makes eight," Aramis put in. "We need eight thousand livres for horses and equipment, though to be sure we have our saddles."

Athos waited until D'Artagnan, who was going off to thank Monsieur de Tréville, had shut the door, and then announced:

"Plus the beautiful diamond that sparkles on our friend's finger. Devil take it, D'Artagnan is too good a comrade to leave his brothers in need when he wears a king's ransom on his ring finger."

CHAPTER 29

THE MOST PREOCCUPIED OF THE FOUR FRIENDS WAS CERtainly D'Artagnan. But our Gascon cadet was of a provident, almost an avaricious, nature, and yet—explain the paradox if you can—almost as vain as Porthos. Preoccupied by his vanity as he was, he was stirred by a far more unselfish anxiety. Despite all the inquiries he had made about Madame Bonacieux, he had discovered nothing. Monsieur de Tréville had asked the Queen about her. The Queen knew nothing of the young woman's whereabouts, but she promised to have a search made for her. But this promise was all too vague, and it did nothing to reassure D'Artagnan.

Athos would not leave his apartment; he was determined not to take a single step to provide for his equipment.

"We still have a fortnight," he told his friends. "Well, if at the end of a fortnight I have found nothing—or rather if nothing has come to find me—as I am too good a Catholic to blow out my brains, I will pick a fine quarrel with four of His Eminence's guardsmen, or with eight Englishmen, and I will fight until one of them kills me—that, given the odds, cannot fail to happen. Then it will be said that I died for the King, so I shall have done my duty without the expense of the equipment."

Porthos continued to walk about, his hands behind his back, tossing his head and repeating: "I shall follow up an idea of mine."

Aramis, apprehensive and for once disheveled, said nothing. From these disastrous details it is easy to understand that despair reigned in the group. The three friends—for as we have said, Athos had sworn not to take a single step to provide for his equipment—would go out early in the morning and return very late. When they met, they all had the same desolate look, one that meant "Haven't you found anything?"

Porthos was the first to act. One day D'Artagnan saw him making his way to the Church of Saint-Leu and followed him instinctively. Porthos entered the church and took his stand against a pillar. D'Artagnan, whom Porthos had not seen, leaned against the other side of it. D'Artagnan noted a lady sitting on the bench nearest the pillar, a lady with a sort of ripe beauty. She was rather yellow, and rather dry, but erect and haughty

Athos Tells D'Artagnan of His Marriage

Kitty Gives D'Artagnan Milady's Note to De Wardes

under her black hood. Porthos kept looking at this lady furtively, then let his eyes wander over the nave.

On her side, the lady, blushing from time to time, kept darting lightning glances toward the fickle Porthos, and immediately Porthos's eyes looked away. Evidently this behavior piqued the lady in the black hood, for she bit her lips fiercely and fidgeted nervously. Porthos, seeing all this, twisted his mustache, stroked his goatee, and began to make signs to a beautiful lady sitting near the choir—a lady not only beautiful, but doubtless a great lady, for she was attended by a little Negro boy who had brought the red cushion on which she was kneeling, and by a maidservant who was holding the bag with a coat of arms that held her prayer book.

The lady with the red cushion, who was really very beautiful, evidently made a deep impression on the lady with the black hood, who saw in her a rival very much to be feared, and a deep impression on Porthos, who found her much more lovely than the lady with a black hood, and a deep impression on D'Artagnan, who recognized in her the lady of Meung, Calais, and Dover, the one his persecutor, the man with the scar, had called Milady.

Leaving Porthos with the lady in the black hood, who he was sure was Madame Coquenard, D'Artagnan followed Milady out of the church without her seeing him, saw her step into her carriage, and heard her order the coachman to drive to Saint-Germain. It was futile to try to follow on foot a carriage that was drawn by two powerful horses. In the Rue de Seine he met Planchet and ordered him to go to Monsieur de Tréville's stables, get their two horses, and bring them to Athos's lodgings.

D'Artagnan went to the Rue Férou and found Athos at home, and told his friend what he had seen in the Church of Saint-Leu. Suddenly Planchet poked his head meekly through the half-open door and announced that the two horses were there.

"Au revoir, my dear Athos," said D'Artagnan, and he and Planchet got into the saddle and took the road to Saint-Germain.

All along the way D'Artagnan thought about Madame Bonacieux. Although he was not given to sentimentality, the haberdasher's lovely wife had made a deep impression on his heart. He was ready to go to the ends of the earth in search of her. But the earth, being round, has many ends, so he did not know which way to turn. Meanwhile he was going to try to find out who Milady was. She had talked with the man in the black cloak, therefore she must know him. Now D'Artagnan felt certain that it was this man who had carried off Madame Bonacieux the second time, as he had the first time. So when D'Artagnan told himself that by going in search of Milady he was also going in search of Constance, he was only half lying, which is lying but little.

D'Artagnan reached Saint-Germain shortly. He was riding along a quiet street, looking to right and left to see whether he could find any

trace of the beautiful Englishwoman, when as he came to an attractive
house that had no window looking out on the street, he thought he saw
someone he knew, and he pulled up. This person was walking about on
a flower-decked terrace. Planchet recognized him first.

"Look, monsieur," he said, "don't you remember that vacant-looking
face over there? It's that wretched Lubin, the lackey of the Comte de
Wardes you took such good care of a month ago at Calais."

"So it is," said D'Artagnan. "I recognize him now. Do you think he'd
recognize you?"

"My word, monsieur, he was having such a hard time of it that I don't
think he'll remember me very clearly."

"Well, go talk to the fellow and see if you can find out whether his
master is dead or alive."

Planchet dismounted and went straight to Lubin, who as a matter of
fact did not recognize him. The two lackeys began to chat in the most
friendly way while D'Artagnan turned the two horses into a lane and
came back to listen to the conference behind a hedge of hazel bushes.
After listening a minute or two, he heard the sound of a carriage and then
saw Milady's coach draw up in front of him. D'Artagnan crouched down
in order to see without being seen.

Milady put her charming blond head out of the carriage window and
gave some order to her lady's maid. The maid, a pretty girl of twenty or
twenty-two—the very soubrette for a lady of fashion—jumped from the
carriage step on which she was sitting, according to the custom of the
times, and made her way to the terrace where D'Artagnan had caught
sight of Lubin. By chance someone within the house had summoned
Lubin, so that Planchet, left alone, was looking all about him to find out
in which direction his master had disappeared. The maid went up to
Planchet, whom she took for Lubin, and holding out a small note to him,
said:

"This is for your master. The message is very urgent. Take it quickly."

Thereupon she ran back to the carriage and jumped onto the step, and
the carriage drove off. Planchet looked at the note on one side, then on
the other. Then he jumped down from the terrace, ran toward the lane,
and twenty paces away met D'Artagnan, who had seen everything and
was coming to meet him.

"For you, monsieur," Planchet said, holding out the note.

"For *me?* Are you sure?"

"Of course I'm sure, monsieur. The soubrette said, 'For your master.'
I have no master but you, so——"

D'Artagnan took the letter, opened it, and read these words:

A woman who takes more interest in you than she is willing to confess
wishes to know on what day you will be well enough to walk in the forest. To-

morrow, at the inn of the Field of the Cloth of Gold a lackey in black and red livery will await your reply.

"Oho!" D'Artagnan said to himself, "here's something that sounds rather ardent. It seems that Milady and I are anxious about the health of the same person. Well, Planchet, how is our good Monsieur de Wardes? Evidently he's not dead."

"No, monsieur, he's as well as a man can be with four sword thrusts in his body. I told you Lubin wouldn't recognize me. He didn't, and he told me our adventure from start to finish."

"Well done, Planchet, you are the king of lackeys! Now to horse again and we'll overtake the carriage."

That was soon done; five minutes later they saw the carriage drawn up by the roadside, and a richly dressed cavalier standing by the window. The conversation between Milady and the cavalier was so animated that D'Artagnan stopped on the far side of the carriage without being noticed by anyone but the pretty soubrette. Milady and the cavalier were conversing in English, a language D'Artagnan did not understand. But by the intonation of her voice our young man divined that the beautiful Englishwoman was furiously angry. She interrupted the conversation with a gesture that left no doubt of that—she struck the cavalier with her fan so hard that the delicate feminine weapon flew into a thousand pieces. The cavalier roared wtih laughter, which seemed to exasperate Milady still more. D'Artagnan, thinking this was the moment for him to intervene, drew up at the window on his side and, taking off his hat respectfully, said:

"Madame, will you allow me to offer my services? Apparently this gentleman has incurred your anger. Speak but one word, madame, and I will undertake to chastise him for his lack of courtesy."

At his first words Milady had turned toward him, looking at him in astonishment; when he had finished, she said, in excellent French:

"Monsieur, I would gladly put myself under your protection if the person who is quarreling with me were not my brother."

"Pray excuse me, then," said D'Artagnan. "You must realize that I did not know that."

"What is that simpleton interfering for?" cried the cavalier, bending low to look through the carriage window. "And why doesn't he go on his way?"

"Simpleton yourself!" said D'Artagnan, in his turn bending down to look through the window on his side. "I am not going because it is my good pleasure to stay here." The cavalier said a few words to his sister in English. "I am talking French to you, I am," said D'Artagnan. "Pray do me the favor of answering in the same language. You may be Madame's brother, but you are not mine, I'm happy to say."

It might be thought that Milady would interfere to prevent the quarrel from going too far. On the contrary, she threw herself back in the carriage and called coolly to the coachman:

"Home, at once!"

The carriage drove off and left the two men face to face. The cavalier made a move as if to follow the carriage, but D'Artagnan caught at his bridle and stopped him. Angry as he was, he was further enraged by recognizing in this man the Englishman who had won his horse at Amiens, and had only just missed winning his own diamond from Athos.

"Eh, monsieur," he said, "you seem to be even more of a simpleton than I, for you seem to have forgotten that we have begun a little quarrel we haven't settled yet."

"Oh, so it's you, my man, is it?" said the Englishman. "Must you always be playing some game or other?"

"Yes, and that reminds me that I have a revenge to take. We shall see, my dear monsieur, whether you can handle a sword as skillfully as you handle a dicebox."

"You can see perfectly well that I carry no sword. Do you enjoy playing the braggart with a man who is not armed?"

"I trust you have a sword at home," D'Artagnan replied. "Anyway, I have two, and I'll dice with you for one of them if you like."

"That is unnecessary," said the Englishman. "I am well supplied with such playthings."

"Very well, monsieur," D'Artagnan replied. "Pick out the longest one you have and show it to me this evening."

"Where?"

"Behind the Luxembourg. That's a delightful place for little excursions of the kind I am suggesting. Shall we say six o'clock?"

"All right with me. I'll be there."

"By the way, you'll doubtless have one or two friends with you?" said D'Artagnan.

"I have three who will be honored to join me in the sport."

"Three! Wonderful! Just right," said D'Artagnan. "That's exactly the number I'll have."

"Now pray tell me who you are," said the Englishman.

"I am Monsieur d'Artagnan, a Gascon gentleman serving in the Royal Guards, Monsieur des Essarts's company."

"I am Lord Winter, Baron of Sheffield."

"Well, your servant, Monsieur le Baron, though I find your names hard to remember." With that D'Artagnan spurred his horse and galloped back to Paris.

CHAPTER 30

AT THE APPOINTED HOUR THE FOUR FRIENDS REPAIRED with their lackeys to a spot behind the Luxembourg. Soon another party of four arrived and joined the musketeers. Then, following an English custom, introductions were made. The Englishmen, all men of high rank, were not only surprised but disturbed by the queer names of their adversaries. When Athos, Porthos, and Aramis announced their appellations, Lord Winter said:

"But we still do not know who you are. We cannot fight with men bearing names like those—they are nothing but shepherds' names."

"As you have guessed, my lord," said Athos, "they are names we have assumed."

"That only makes us the more desirous to learn your real names," the Englishman answered.

"You were quite willing to gamble with us without knowing our names," said Athos. "Isn't the fact that you won two of our horses proof of that?"

"True, but we risked only our money; now we are risking our lives. A gentleman gambles with anybody, he fights only with his equals."

"That is only fair," said Athos, and he drew aside the man he was to fight and whispered his real name. Porthos and Aramis followed suit. "Are you satisfied?" Athos asked his adversary. "Do you consider me of sufficiently high rank to do me the honor of crossing swords with me?"

"Yes, monsieur," said the Englishman, bowing.

"Well, then, may I tell you something else?" asked Athos frigidly. "You would have been wiser not to insist on my telling you who I am."

"Why so?"

"Because I am supposed to be dead, and I have my reasons for wishing no one to know that I am alive, therefore I shall have to kill you to keep my secret from being told." The Englishman thought Athos was jesting, but he meant exactly what he said. "Are we ready, gentlemen?" said Athos to his friends and his foes.

"Yes," Englishmen and Frenchmen replied together.

"On guard, then!" cried Athos.

Immediately eight swords flashed in the rays of the setting sun and the combat began with a fury natural to men who had double reason to be enemies. Athos fenced as calmly and methodically as he would have at practice in a fencing school. Porthos, without doubt less confident because of his adventure at Chantilly, handled his sword with finesse and prudence. Aramis fought as if in haste to get it over and return to his own affairs.

Athos was the first to kill his adversary. He had given him only one thrust, but, as he had prophesied, the thrust was a mortal one; it pierced the Englishman's heart. Porthos was the second to finish his man, who fell on the grass wounded in the thigh. The Englishman cried quits then and surrendered his sword. Porthos, taking him up in his arms, carried him back to his carriage. Aramis went for his man so vigorously that after retreating some fifty paces the Englishman took to his heels and disappeared, followed by the jeers of the lackeys.

As for D'Artagnan, at first he fought purely and simply on the defensive, then when he saw that his adversary was pretty well exhausted, with a twist of his wrist he sent the Englishman's sword flying through the air. Lord Winter, finding himself disarmed, retreated a few steps, but his foot slipped and he fell on his back. One leap and D'Artagnan stood over him, the point of his sword at the Englishman's throat.

"I could kill you, monsieur," said he. "You are completely at my mercy. But for the sake of your sister I spare your life."

D'Artagnan was highly elated, and the Englishman was delighted over having such a kindly gentleman to deal with. He rose, embraced D'Artagnan, and said a thousand kind words to the other three musketeers. Then, since Porthos had already installed his adversary in the carriage, and Aramis's had made off, they had no one to consider but the dead man. As Porthos and Aramis took off his clothes, hoping that his wound was not a mortal one, a heavy purse fell from his belt. D'Artagnan picked it up and held it out to Lord Winter.

"What the devil do you expect me to do with that?" the Englishman asked.

"You can give it to his family," replied D'Artagnan.

"His family isn't interested in a trifle like that. They will inherit fifteen hundred louis from him. Give the purse to your lackeys." D'Artagnan put the purse in his pocket.

"And now, my young friend—I hope you will allow me to call you so—" Lord Winter continued, "if you like, I will present you to my sister-in-law, Lady Clark, this very evening. I would like to have her feel as cordial toward you as I do. She is not in bad favor at the Court, and perhaps a word from her may be of service to you someday."

D'Artagnan blushed with pleasure and bowed in assent. Meanwhile Athos had come up to him.

"What do you mean to do with the purse?" he whispered.

"Why, I was counting on giving it to you, my dear Athos."

"To me? Why to me?"

"Bless me, you killed him, didn't you? These are the spoils of victory."

"Do you think I'd despoil an enemy? What do you take me for?"

"Then," said D'Artagnan, "let us give the money to the lackeys, as Lord Winter bade us."

"Yes," said Athos, "we'll give the money to the lackeys, but not to ours—to the Englishmen's." Athos took the purse and threw it to the coachman. "For you and your comrades," he said.

Such grand ways in a man who was penniless struck even Porthos dumb, and such French generosity, reported throughout Paris by Lord Winter and his friend, made a fine impression everywhere except on Messieurs Grimaud, Bazin, Mousqueton, and Planchet.

In taking leave of him, Lord Winter gave D'Artagnan Milady's address—No. 6 Rue Royale, then the fashionable quarter of the city—and offered to call for him. D'Artagnan thanked him, and asked him to come to Athos's house at eight o'clock.

This coming introduction to Milady quite filled our young Gascon's mind. He recalled the strange way in which this woman had already been concerned with his destiny. He was convinced that she was some creature of the Cardinal's, and yet he felt invincibly drawn to her by one of those feelings no one can account for. His one fear was that Milady would recognize him as the man she had seen at Meung and at Dover. Moreover, she knew he was one of Monsieur de Tréville's friends, and consequently that he belonged heart and soul to the King. That would make him lose part of his present advantages, but knowing Milady as he did now, he could play the game as well as she could. He began it by going home to don the most flamboyant raiment he possessed. Then he went to call on Athos and as usual with him told his friend everything. Athos listened attentively to his plans, then he shook his head and advised him to be very careful.

"What!" said Athos. "You have just lost one woman you say was good, charming, perfect, and here you are running after another!"

D'Artagnan felt the truth of this reproach. "I love Madame Bonacieux with my heart," he said, "whereas I love Milady with my head. In being presented to her I am trying chiefly to get some light on the part she plays at Court."

"What part she plays! Good heavens, that is not hard to guess from what you have told me. She is some emissary of the Cardinal's, a woman who will entice you into a trap in which you'll probably leave your head."

"The devil you say, my dear Athos! You're looking at the dark side of things, methinks."

"My dear fellow, I mistrust women. What can you expect? I have paid dearly for my experience—especially with blondes. You said Milady was a blonde, didn't you?"

"She has the most beautiful golden hair imaginable."

"Oh, my poor D'Artagnan!" said Athos.

"Listen, I want to find out the truth about her. When I have done that, I will leave her alone."

"Go ahead and find out all about her," said Athos phlegmatically.

Lord Winter arrived at the hour appointed and Athos, warned in good time, disappeared into the adjoining room. As it was almost eight, my lord escorted the young man to the street. An elegant carriage was waiting there, and as it was drawn by two fine horses, they were at the Place Royale in no time at all. Lady Clark received D'Artagnan ceremoniously. Her house was remarkably sumptuous, and though most of the English had left France, or were about to leave it, because of the war, Milady had recently spent a goodly sum on her furnishings. Evidently the general measures that had sent the English home did not concern her.

"Here," said Lord Winter in presenting D'Artagnan to his sister, "is a young gentleman who held my life in his hands and refused to take advantage of his victory, although we were doubly enemies—I had insulted him, and I am English. So thank him, madame, if you have any affection for me."

Milady frowned a little, an almost imperceptible cloud shadowed her brow, and so peculiar a smile appeared on her lips that when the young man saw these three signs he almost shuddered.

"You are welcome, monsieur," Milady said in a voice of singular sweetness that contradicted the symptoms of ill humor that D'Artagnan had just remarked. "Today you have won an everlasting right to my gratitude."

Then the Englishman told the story of the duel, omitting no detail. Milady listened with the greatest attention, yet however great the effort she made to hide what she felt, it was easy to see that the recital irked her. The blood rose to her face, and her little foot tapped impatiently. Lord Winter noticed none of this. When he had finished his story, he went to a table where a bottle of Spanish wine and some glasses were set out on a salver. He filled two glasses and gestured to D'Artagnan to drink.

D'Artagnan knew that to refuse to drink to an Englishman was to offend him, so he went to the table and took the second glass. However, he did not lose sight of Milady, and in a mirror on the wall he saw her expression change. Now that she thought that no one was watching her, something like ferocity blazed on her countenance, and she gnawed at her handkerchief savagely.

The pretty little soubrette D'Artagnan had noticed before entered and said a few words to Lord Winter in English. Thereupon my lord asked

D'Artagnan's permission to retire, excusing himself on the ground of urgent business. D'Artagnan shook hands with Lord Winter and went back to Milady. With surprising mobility her face had resumed its gracious expression; only a few little spots of blood on her handkerchief told that she had bitten her coral lips until they bled. The conversation took a cheerful turn. Milady seemed to be herself once more. She explained that Lord Winter was only her brother-in-law, not her blood brother; she had married a younger brother who left her a widow with one child. This child was Lord Winter's only heir, unless Lord Winter were to marry. All that she said made D'Artagnan feel that a veil of mystery covered her, but as yet he could not see under the veil. But a half-hour conversation convinced him that Milady was of his own country; she spoke French with a purity and an elegance that left no doubt as to that.

D'Artagnan was profuse in gallant speeches and lavish with protestations of devotion. Milady smiled benevolently at all the nonsense our Gascon uttered. When it was time for him to withdraw, D'Artagnan took leave of Milady and left her drawing-room the happiest of men. On the stairway he met the pretty soubrette. She brushed against him lightly as she passed him; she blushed and begged his pardon for having touched him, in a voice so sweet that D'Artagnan instantly granted it.

On the morrow D'Artagnan called on Milady again and was received even better than before. Lord Winter was not there and it was Milady who did the honors of the house. She seemed to take a great interest in him. Where did he come from, she asked, who were his friends, and had he ever thought of entering Monsieur le Cardinal's service? D'Artagnan, who was exceedingly prudent for a lad of twenty, remembered now his suspicions of Milady. So he launched into a fine eulogy of His Eminence, and told her he would not have failed to join the Cardinal's Guards if he had happened to know Monsieur de Cavois instead of Monsieur de Tréville.

Milady changed the subject quite naturally, asking D'Artagnan in the most casual way whether he had ever been in England. He replied that he had been sent there by Monsieur de Tréville to negotiate for some horses and that he had brought four back as specimens. Two or three times in the course of their conversation Milady pinched her lips together hard. She was dealing with a Gascon who played a careful game.

At the same hour as the night before D'Artagnan withdrew. In the hall he met the pretty soubrette, Kitty by name. She looked at him with an unmistakably friendly expression, but D'Artagnan was so preoccupied with Milady that he noticed nothing whatever except what came from her.

CHAPTER 31

IN SPITE OF THE CRIES OF HIS OWN CONSCIENCE AND THE wise counsels of Athos, D'Artagnan grew more enamored of Milady hour by hour. He never missed a day in his courtship of her. Our adventurous Gascon was convinced that someday, sooner or later, she would respond.

One evening when he arrived with head held high, his heart as light as that of a man who expects a shower of gold, he found the soubrette at the gateway to the house. This time pretty Kitty was not content with touching him as he passed her—she took him gently by the hand.

"Good!" thought D'Artagnan. "Her mistress has charged her with some message to me."

"May I have two words with you, Monsieur le Chevalier?" Kitty stammered.

"Speak, my child, speak," said D'Artagnan. "I am listening."

"Here? Impossible. What I have to say is too long, and above all, too secret. If Monsieur le Chevalier would follow me?" added Kitty timidly.

"Wherever you please, you beautiful child."

"Come, then." And Kitty, who had not let go of D'Artagnan's hand, led him up a little dark winding stairway, then up some fifteen steps, and opened a door. "Come in here, Monsieur le Chevalier," she said. "Here we shall be alone and can talk safely. This is my own room, monsieur; it communicates with my mistress's by that door. But have no fear, she will not hear what we say—she never goes to bed before midnight."

D'Artagnan cast a glance around him. The little room was charming, both tasteful and neat, but in spite of himself his eyes were fixed on that door to Milady's chamber. Kitty divined what he was thinking and heaved a deep sigh.

"So you love my mistress dearly, Monsieur le Chevalier!" she said.

"Oh, more than I can say! I'm mad about her, Kitty!"

"Alas! monsieur," Kitty said, "that's a great pity!"

"Why the devil do you find it so pitiable?"

"Because my mistress, monsieur, does not love you in the least," Kitty replied.

"What!" cried D'Artagnan. "Did she charge you to tell me so?"

"Oh no, monsieur. Because of the regard I have for you, I resolved to tell you myself."

"Thanks, my good Kitty, but for the intention only. For you must agree with me that your information is hardly agreeable."

"You mean you don't believe what I've said?"

"I confess that until you deign to give me some proof——"

"What do you think of this?" Kitty demanded, pulling out a little note from her bosom.

"For me?" asked D'Artagnan, snatching the letter.

"No, for someone else."

"His name! Tell me his name!" cried D'Artagnan.

"Read the address."

"Monsieur le Comte de Wardes." The memory of the scene at Saint-Germain flashed across the mind of the presumptuous Gascon. With a motion as quick as thought he tore open the letter, in spite of Kitty's cry when she saw what he was about to do, or rather what he had already done.

"Oh, my God, Monsieur le Chevalier," she cried. "what are you doing?"

"Who—I?" said D'Artagnan. "Nothing, nothing." Then he read:

You have not answered my first note. Are you ill, then, or have you forgotten the glances you favored me with at Madame de Guise's ball? You have an opportunity now, Monsieur le Comte, do not allow it to escape you.

"Poor dear Monsieur D'Artagnan," said Kitty in a voice full of compassion and pressing the young man's hand again.

"So you pity me, you kind child," said D'Artagnan.

"That I do, with all my heart, for I know what it is to be in love."

"You know what it is to be in love?" said D'Artagnan. "Well, then, instead of pitying me, you would do much better to help me to avenge myself on your mistress. I want to triumph over her and supplant my rival."

"I will never help you to do that, Monsieur le Chevalier."

"Why not?" D'Artagnan asked.

"For two reasons. The first is that my mistress will never love you."

"How do you know that?"

"You have cut her to the heart."

"I? How can I have offended her, I who ever since I have known her have lain at her feet like a slave? Tell me, I beg of you."

"I will never confess that to any man save the one who can read to the very depths of my soul!"

D'Artagnan looked at Kitty. Many a duchess would have given her coronet for the maid's youthful beauty and freshness.

"Kitty," he said, "I myself will read to the depths of your soul whenever you like. Don't you worry about that, my dear child." And he gave her a kiss that made the poor girl turn as red as a cherry.

"Oh no!" cried Kitty. "You do not love *me*, it is my mistress you love. You told me so just a moment ago."

"Does that prevent you from telling me your second reason?"

"My second reason, Monsieur le Chevalier," said Kitty, emboldened by D'Artagnan's kiss, "is that in love, each for herself."

Then only D'Artagnan recalled the languishing glances Kitty had given him when they had chanced to meet in the corridor or on the stairs. Absorbed in his desire to please the great lady, he had disdained the soubrette—he who hunts an eagle does not bother about the sparrow. But this time our Gascon saw at a glance the advantages he might gain from the love that Kitty had just confessed so innocently—or so boldly. She could intercept letters addressed to the Comte de Wardes, act as his secret agent on the spot, give him access to Kitty's room next her mistress's whenever he wanted it. Obviously the perfidious man was already thinking of sacrificing the poor girl in order to obtain Milady at any cost.

"Well, my dear Kitty," he said, "would you like to have me give you a proof of this love you seem to doubt?"

"What love?" the young girl asked.

"The love I am beginning to feel for you."

"And what is the proof you want?"

"Will you let me spend with you tonight the hours I usually spend with your mistress?"

"Oh yes," said Kitty, clapping her hands, "gladly!"

"Well then, my dear child," said D'Artagnan, settling down in an armchair, "come here and let me tell you that you are the prettiest soubrette I ever saw!"

And he said so much, and said it so well, that the poor child, who asked for nothing better than to believe him, did believe him. Yet to D'Artagnan's great astonishment pretty Kitty resisted his advances resolutely. Times passes quickly when it is devoted to offensive and defensive maneuvers. Midnight struck, and at almost the same moment Milady's bell rang in the next room.

"Good heavens," cried Kitty, "there's my mistress calling me! Go, go at once!"

D'Artagnan rose and took his hat as if he meant to obey her, but instead of opening the door leading to the stairway, he threw open the door to a large closet and plunged into the midst of Milady's gowns and dressing-gowns.

"What are you doing?" cried Kitty.

D'Artagnan, who had taken possession of the key, locked himself into the closet without answering.

"Well," called Milady sharply, "are you asleep that you don't come when I ring?"

D'Artagnan heard the communicating door open violently.

"Here I am, Milady, here I am!" cried Kitty.

The two women went into Milady's bedroom, and as the door to it stayed open, D'Artagnan could hear Milady scolding her maid for some time. At last she calmed down, and while Kitty was helping her mistress get ready for bed the conversation turned upon him.

"Well, I haven't seen our Gascon tonight," Milady remarked.

"What, madame, didn't he come?" asked Kitty. "Can he possibly be inconstant before he has been made happy?"

"Oh no. He must have been detained by Monsieur de Tréville or perhaps by Monsieur des Essarts. I know what I'm doing, Kitty, and I hold him in my hand, that one!"

"What will Madame do with him?"

"What will I do with him? Have no fear, Kitty. There is something to be settled between that man and me that he knows nothing of—he almost ruined my credit with His Eminence. Oh, I'll have my revenge for that!"

"I thought Madame loved him."

"*I* love *him?* I detest him. A simpleton who held Lord Winter's life in his hands and didn't kill him, and so lost me an income of three hundred thousand louis!"

D'Artagnan shuddered to the marrow of his bones as he heard that suave creature reproaching him because he had not killed a man he had seen showering her with friendship.

"And," Milady went on, "I would have had my revenge on him already if the Cardinal, for some reason I don't know, hadn't asked me to be kind to him."

"Yes, but Madame has not been kind to that little woman he was so fond of."

"Oh, the haberdasher's wife. Hasn't he already forgotten that she ever existed? A fine revenge, my word!"

A cold sweat broke out on D'Artagnan's brow. This woman was truly a monster. He resumed his eavesdropping, but unfortunately Milady was now ready for bed.

"That will do," said Milady. "Go to your room, and tomorrow try to get an answer to the letter I gave you."

"The letter for Monsieur de Wardes? Now there's a man," said Kitty, "who looks to me like just the opposite of that poor Monsieur d'Artagnan."

"Go to bed, mademoiselle," said Milady. "I don't care for your comments."

D'Artagnan heard the door close, then the sound of two bolts as Milady locked herself in. On her side, but as softly as possible, Kitty turned the key in the lock. Then D'Artagnan pushed open the closet door.

"Oh, good Lord," Kitty whispered, "what is the matter with you? How pale you are!"

"The abominable creature!" murmured D'Artagnan.

"Hush, monsieur, hush!" said Kitty. "Please go! There's nothing but a thin wooden partition between Milady's bedroom and mine; every word said in one can be heard in the other."

"That's exactly why I will not go," said D'Artagnan. "Or at least why I'll go—later."

He drew Kitty to him. She could offer no resistance, for resistance would have made too much noise. Accordingly Kitty yielded. D'Artagnan's love-making was meant as a vengeance upon Milady, and he found there was good reason to say that vengeance is the pleasure of the gods. With a little more heart, he might have been content with this new conquest, but his chief characteristics were pride and ambition. However, to give his due, it must be confessed that the first use he made of his influence over Kitty was to try to find out what had become of Madame Bonacieux. But the poor girl swore on the crucifix that she knew nothing at all about that except that she believed she could say that Madame Bonacieux was not dead.

As to the circumstance that had almost made Milady lose her credit with the Cardinal, Kitty was equally ignorant. But in this instance D'Artagnan was better informed than she. He had seen Milady on board a ship just as he was leaving England, and he suspected that it was the affair of the diamond tags that had put her out of favor. But the clearest thing of all was that the hatred, the deep and inveterate hatred, that Milady felt for him was aroused by the fact that he had not killed her brother-in-law.

The next day D'Artagnan returned to Milady's, and finding her in a very bad humor, he felt sure that it was the failure of an answer from Monsieur de Wardes that made her so irritable. Toward the end of the evening, however, the beautiful lioness grew more gentle, smiled while she listened to D'Artagnan's sweet speeches, and even gave him her hand to kiss.

D'Artagnan departed, no longer knowing what to think, but as he was a lad who did not lose his head easily, he had thought up a little plan while he was paying his court to Milady. He found Kitty at the door, and again accompanied her to her room. Kitty had been accused of negligence, and roundly scolded. Milady could not understand at all why the Comte de Wardes was still silent, and she had ordered Kitty to come to her the next morning at nine to get a third letter. D'Artagnan made Kitty promise to bring him that letter the next morning. The poor girl promised everything her lover asked of her.

Things went as they had gone the night before. D'Artagnan hid in the closet, Milady summoned Kitty, got ready for bed, dismissed Kitty, and shut her door again. As on the night before, D'Artagnan did not go home until five o'clock in the morning.

At eleven the next morning, he saw Kitty coming, holding in her hand Milady's new letter. This time the poor girl did not even try to argue with D'Artagnan; she let him do what he would; she belonged body and soul to her handsome soldier. D'Artagnan opened the note and read as follows:

This is the third time I have written you to tell you that I love you. Beware lest I write you a fourth time to tell you that I detest you.

If you repent of the way you have acted toward me, the young girl who gives you this note will tell you how a man of spirit may obtain his pardon.

D'Artagnan flushed and grew pale several times as he read the note.

"Oh, you love her still!" exclaimed Kitty.

"No, Kitty, you are mistaken. I no longer love her. But I mean to avenge myself for her contempt of me."

"Yes, I know the vengeance you plan; you told me about it."

"What does it matter to you, Kitty! You know very well that I love only you."

"How can I be sure of that?"

"By the contumely I shall visit on that woman."

Kitty sighed. D'Artagnan took a pen and wrote:

Madame:

Until now I could not believe that your first two letters were addressed to me, so unworthy did I consider myself of such an honor. Besides, I was so seriously indisposed that I would have hesitated to reply to them in any case.

But today I am forced to believe in your excessive graciousness, since not only your letter but also your servant assure me that I have the good fortune to be favored with your love.

You do not need to teach me the way in which a man of spirit may obtain his pardon. I will come to ask for mine at eleven o'clock tonight. To delay a single day would in my eyes be committing a fresh offense.

He whom you have made the happiest of men,

Comte de Wardes

In the first place, this note was a forgery; next, it was an indelicacy; it was even, according to our customs today, something like an infamy. But at that period people were less scrupulous than they are today. Besides, D'Artagnan knew from Milady's own avowals that she was guilty of treachery in far more important matters, and he had very little respect for her. And yet, despite this lack of respect, he felt an uncontrollable passion for this woman boiling in his veins. It was passion intoxicated by scorn—passion or thirst, as you will.

D'Artagnan's plan was very simple. From Kitty's bedroom he would gain access to that of her mistress. He would take advantage of the first moment of surprise, shame, and terror to triumph over her. He might perhaps fail, but something must be left to chance. In a week the campaign would open; D'Artagnan had no time to prolong his siege of love.

"There," the young man said, addressing and sealing the letter and giving it to Kitty, "give this to Milady. It is Monsieur de Wardes's reply."

CHAPTER 32

SINCE THE THREE FRIENDS HAD BEEN SEARCHING EACH for his own equipment, they had had no fixed meetings. Each dined alone wherever he chanced to be. However, they had agreed to meet once a week at about one o'clock with Athos as host. The day Kitty had gone to D'Artagnan was the day they were to meet, and as soon as Kitty had left him, he set off for the Rue Férou, where he found Athos and Aramis discussing philosophy. Porthos arrived a minute after D'Artagnan, and the four friends were together once more.

The four countenances expressed four dissimilar moods. Porthos looked tranquil, D'Artagnan hopeful, Aramis uneasy, and Athos indifferent. After a moment's conversation in which Porthos hinted that a lady of high rank had been good enough to undertake to relieve him from his embarrassment, Mousqueton entered. He begged Porthos to return at once to his lodgings, where he said his presence was urgently called for. Porthos rose, bowed to his friends, and followed Mousqueton. A few seconds later, Bazin appeared at the door.

"What do you want with me?" asked Aramis.

"A man is waiting for Monsieur," Bazin replied. "A beggar, I think."

"Give him alms, Bazin, and bid him pray for a poor sinner."

"But this beggar insists on speaking to you, and he claims that you will be very glad to see him."

"Did he give you any particular message for me?"

"Yes, he did. 'If Monsieur Aramis hesitates to come,' he said, 'tell him I am from Tours.' "

"From Tours!" cried Aramis. "A thousand pardons, gentlemen, but no doubt this man brings me news that I was expecting." And rising in his turn, he set off at a quick pace.

"I think those fine fellows have everything they need," said Athos. "What do you think, D'Artagnan?"

"I know Porthos was in a fair way to get his," D'Artagnan replied. "As to Aramis, to tell you the truth, I have never worried much about him. But you, my dear Athos, you who gave away so generously the Englishman's pistoles, which were your legitimate property, what are you going to do?"

"I am quite content with having killed that scoundrel, my lad, seeing that it is consecrated bread to kill an Englishman. . . . To change the subject, what do you think Monsieur de Tréville told me when he did me the honor of calling on me yesterday? That you were frequenting those suspect English protégés of the Cardinal's."

"Well, I do visit an Englishwoman, the one I told you about."

"Ah yes, the blonde woman about whom I gave you some advice, which of course you took care not to follow."

"I gave you my reasons. I have obtained sure information that this woman had something to do with the abduction of Madame Bonacieux."

"Yes, I understand now—in order to find one woman you are paying court to another. It's the longest way round, but undoubtedly the most amusing one."

D'Artagnan was on the point of telling Athos the whole story, but one consideration stopped him; Athos was a punctilious gentleman where honor was concerned, and in the little plan our man in love had devised with regard to Milady, there were certain things that he knew beforehand would not obtain the assent of that puritan, so he said nothing.

We have seen with what alacrity Aramis followed, or rather preceded, Bazin when he heard that the man who wished to speak to him came from Tours; he ran without stopping from the Rue Férou to the Rue Vaugirard. Entering his apartment, he found a very short man with intelligent eyes, but dressed in rags.

"You asked for me?" said the musketeer.

"I wish to see Monsieur Aramis. Is that your name, monsieur?"

"Yes. You have brought me something?"

"Yes, if you will show me a certain embroidered handkerchief."

Aramis took a small key from his breast pocket and unlocking a little ebony box inlaid with mother-of-pearl, drew out the handkerchief.

"Here it is," he said, "look!"

"Right," said the beggar. "Send your lackey away."

Aramis motioned to Bazin to retire. When he was gone, the beggar looked quickly around the room to make sure that no one could either see or hear him. Then, opening his ragged vest, scarcely held together by a leather belt, he began to rip a seam in the upper part of his doublet, from which he pulled out a letter. Aramis gave a cry of joy at the sight of the seal, kissed the superscription with almost religious reverence, and opened the letter, which read as follows:

My friend, it is the will of fate that we should be separated for some time yet, but the beautiful days of youth are not lost beyond return. Do your duty in the camp; I will do mine elsewhere.

Accept what the bearer brings you; make your campaign like the brave and handsome gentleman you are, and think of me, who kiss your black eyes tenderly.

Adieu, or rather au revoir!

The beggar was still ripping seams. From one of his dirty garments he took out 150 Spanish double pistoles, which he laid in golden rows on the table. Then he opened the door, bowed, and disappeared before the young musketeer, stupefied, had ventured to address a word to him. Now Aramis reread the letter, and saw that there was a postscript:

P.S. You may behave courteously to the bearer, who is a Count and Grandee of Spain.

"Golden dreams!" cried Aramis. "Oh, beautiful life! Yes, we are young! Yes, we shall yet know happy days! Oh, my love, my blood, my life, all, all are thine, my beautiful mistress!" And he kissed the letter passionately without even looking at the gold that gleamed on the table.

Bazin scratched at the door, and Aramis bade him enter. Bazin was so astounded at the sight of the gold that he forgot he had come to announce D'Artagnan, who, curious to know who the beggar might be, had come straight to Aramis on leaving Athos. Now as D'Artagnan never stood on ceremony with Aramis, seeing that Bazin had forgotten to announce him, he announced himself.

"The devil, my dear Aramis!" he said. "If these are the plums people send you from Tours, please give my compliments to the gardener who picks them."

"You are mistaken, my friend," said Aramis, circumspect, as he always was. "These coins are from my publisher. He has just sent me my fee for a poem that I began when I was in Touraine."

"Oh, really!" said D'Artagnan. "Well, your publisher is generous, my dear Aramis, that's all I can say."

"What, monsieur," cried Bazin, "a poem sells for as much money as that! Oh, monsieur, it's unbelievable! A poet is almost as good as an abbé. Ah, Monsieur Aramis, turn poet, please do!"

"Bazin, my friend," said Aramis. "I believe you are interfering with our conversation." Aware that he was at fault, Bazin bowed and went out.

"Well," said D'Artagnan with a smile, "the productions you sell are evidently worth their weight in gold. You are very lucky, my friend. But take care or you will lose that letter peeping out of your doublet, which also no doubt is from your publisher."

Aramis blushed to the roots of his hair, pushed the letter in, and buttoned up his doublet over it.

"My dear D'Artagnan," said he, "let us go to find our friends, if you please, and since I am rich now, today we will begin to dine together again, until you are all rich in your turn."

Having put 3 or 4 double pistoles in his pocket for present needs, Aramis locked the rest in the little ebony box inlaid with mother-of-pearl containing the embroidered handkerchief that had served him as a talisman. The two friends repaired first to Athos, who, faithful to his vow that he would not go out, undertook to have the dinner brought to his apartment. Then they went to fetch Porthos.

CHAPTER 33

THAT EVENING, D'ARTAGNAN CALLED ON MILADY AS usual about nine. He found her in a delightful mood; never had she received him so pleasantly. Our Gascon saw at first glance that his letter had been delivered, and that it had done its work. Kitty entered bringing sherbets. Her mistress smiled on her most graciously, but the poor girl was in such low spirits that she did not even notice Milady's kindliness.

By ten o'clock Milady began to seem uneasy, and D'Artagnan knew what that meant. She kept looking at the clock, got up, sat down again, smiled at D'Artagnan as if to say: "You are very amiable, of course, but you would be charming if only you would go!" D'Artagnan rose and took his hat; Milady gave him her hand to kiss. He felt it press against his lips and realized that the pressure was not inspired by coquetry, but by gratitude for his departure.

"She's desperately in love with him," he murmured as he left.

This time Kitty was not waiting for him anywhere. D'Artagnan had to find his way himself to the back stairway and her bedroom. Kitty was sitting with her face buried in her hands, weeping. She heard D'Artagnan enter, but she did not look up, and when he went to her and took her hands in his, she burst into sobs. As D'Artagnan had conjectured, when Milady received the letter, in a delirium of joy she had told her maid everything. When D'Artagnan caressed her, the poor girl raised her head. D'Artagnan was frightened by her ravaged face. She clasped her hands in a gesture of supplication, but without venturing to speak.

However hard D'Artagnan's heart might be, he was deeply touched by this mute sorrow; but he held too tenaciously to his plans, and especially to this one, to make any change in the program he had determined on. He therefore allowed Kitty no hope of softening him, but told her that his action was merely one of vengeance. Moreover, this vengeance was to be easier now, because Milady, doubtless to hide her blushes from her lover, had ordered Kitty to put out all the lights in the room, and even in her own room. Monsieur de Wardes was to leave just before daybreak, while it was still dark.

Presently they heard Milady come to her room. D'Artagnan plunged into his closet at once, and had hardly hidden himself there before Milady's bell rang. Kitty answered it, taking care to shut the door, but the partition was so thin that D'Artagnan could hear every word the two women said. Milady seemed to be intoxicated with joy. She made Kitty repeat the most minute details of her sham interview with De Wardes— how he had received the letter, what he had said, what the expression on his face had been, whether he had seemed very much in love. To all these questions poor Kitty, forced to assume a pleasant expression, replied in a choked voice, but so selfish is happiness that her mistress did not remark its doleful tone.

Finally, as the hour for her meeting with De Wardes drew near, Milady had all the lights in her chamber extinguished, bade Kitty go back to her own room, and to admit De Wardes as soon as he arrived. Kitty did not have long to wait. The moment that D'Artagnan saw through the key-hole of his closet door that all was darkness, he darted out from his hiding-place just as Kitty was closing the door to Milady's room.

"What is that noise?" Milady demanded.

"It is I," said D'Artagnan, in a low tone, "the Comte de Wardes."

"Well, why don't you come in?" said Milady in a tremulous voice. "Come, Monsieur le Comte. You know very well that I am expecting you."

At this appeal D'Artagnan pushed Kitty aside and darted into Milady's bedroom. If rage and suffering can torture the soul in many ways, surely the worst way is when a lover receives under a name that is not his own protestations of love meant for his happy rival. D'Artagnan found himself in a painful situation that he had not foreseen. Jealousy gnawed at his heart, and he suffered almost as much as poor Kitty.

"Yes, Monsieur le Comte," said Milady in her sweetest voice as she pressed his hand tenderly in her own, "I am happy in the love that your glances and your words have expressed each time we have met. I too love —I love you. Oh, tomorrow, yes, tomorrow, I must have some token from you that will prove you are thinking of me, and lest you might forget me, take this pledge of my love." And she took a ring from her own finger and slipped it onto one of D'Artagnan's. D'Artagnan remembered that he had seen that ring on Milady's hand; it was a magnificent sapphire encircled with diamonds. His first instinctive thought was to return it to her, but Milady said: "No, no. Keep this ring for love of me. Besides," she added in a voice full of feeling, "by accepting it you will do me a greater service than you can possibly imagine. Poor angel," she went on, "that monster of a Gascon only just missed killing you. Are your wounds still painful?"

"Oh, very," said D'Artagnan, who did not know what he ought to say.

"Rest easy," murmured Milady. "I will avenge you myself—and cruelly!"

"Plague on it!" D'Artagnan said to himself. "The moment for confidences has not come yet."

It took some time for D'Artagnan to recover from the effects of this brief dialogue, but all the ideas of vengeance that he had brought with him had completely vanished. This woman exerted an unbelievable power over him; he hated her and adored her at the same time.

But one o'clock had just struck; they must part. As he left Milady, D'Artagnan's only feeling was one of sharp regret that he must go. While they exchanged passionate farewells they agreed on another meeting in the following week. Poor Kitty had hoped to say a few words to D'Artagnan when he went through her room, but Milady herself guided him out through the darkness and did not leave him until they reached the stairway.

The next morning D'Artagnan hurried to Athos. He was involved in so strange an adventure that he wanted his friend's advice. He told Athos everything. Athos frowned several times as he did so.

"Your Milady," he said, "seems to me to be an infamous creature. Nevertheless you were wrong to deceive her. Here you are, for one reason or another, with a terrible enemy on your hands."

As he spoke Athos was staring at the sapphire ring that D'Artagnan now wore on the finger where once had sparkled the Queen's ring, now safely stored in a jewel box.

"Are you looking at my ring?" asked the Gascon.

"Yes," said Athos. "It reminds me of a family heirloom."

"It is beautiful, isn't it?"

"Magnificent! I did not think two sapphires of such fine water existed. Did you trade your diamond for it?"

"No," said D'Artagnan, "it is a gift from my beautiful Englishwoman, or rather my beautiful Frenchwoman, for although of course I didn't ask her, I am convinced that she was born in France."

"Then Milady gave you that ring?" cried Athos in a tone evincing great emotion.

"She did; she gave it to me last night."

"Let me see it," said Athos. He examined the ring carefully and grew very pale. Then he tried it on the third finger of his left hand; it fitted perfectly. A shadow of wrath and vengefulness darkened his usually serene brow. "It couldn't possibly be that ring," he said. "How could it have come into Lady Clark's hands? And yet however could two jewels look so much alike?"

"Do you know that ring?" asked D'Artagnan.

"I thought I did, but doubtless I was mistaken," Athos replied, and he gave the ring back to D'Artagnan, but without ceasing to stare at it. Then after a pausing moment he went on: "Come, D'Artagnan, either take off that ring or turn the stone around. It recalls such cruel memories that I wouldn't be able to keep my head cool enough to talk with you. But didn't you come to ask my advice, didn't you tell me that you didn't know what to do? . . . But stop! Let me see that sapphire again. The one I was speaking of has a scratch on one of its facets—the result of an accident."

D'Artagnan took off the ring again and gave it to Athos. Athos started. "Look there!" he said, showing D'Artagnan the scratch that he had remembered. "Isn't that strange?"

"How did you get this ring, Athos?"

"From my mother," Athos replied, "my father's wedding present to her. I told you it was a family heirloom; it was never to leave the family."

"And you—sold it?" asked D'Artagnan hesitatingly.

"No," answered Athos with a strange smile. "I gave it away in a night of love, exactly as it was given to you." D'Artagnan grew pensive in his turn, wondering what secrets lay in the dark, mysterious abyss of Milady's soul. He put the ring not on his finger, but in his pocket.

"Come," said Athos, taking his friend's hand, "you know that I love you, D'Artagnan. If I had a son I could not love him more than I do you. Come, take my advice. Give up this woman. I do not know her, but some instinct tells me that she is a lost soul, and that there is something fatal about her."

"And you are right," said D'Artagnan. "I will have done with her. I confess she terrifies me."

"Will you have the courage to do it?" asked Athos.

"I will," D'Artagnan replied. "And I'll do it instantly."

"Good! Truly, you will be right, my lad," said Athos, pressing the Gascon's hand with almost fatherly affection. "God grant that this woman, who has only just come into your life, will not leave a terrible trace in it!" And Athos nodded dismissal to D'Artagnan like a man who wishes to make it clear that he is not sorry to be left alone with his thoughts.

On reaching home D'Artagnan found Kitty waiting for him. A month of fever could not have ravaged the poor child's face more than her night of sleeplessness and sorrow. She had been sent by her mistress to the supposed De Wardes. Her mistress was mad with love, intoxicated with joy; she wanted to know when her lover would give her a second night.

Athos had great influence over the young man. The counsels of his friend, together with the cries of his heart, had determined him that now that his pride was salvaged and his vengeance satisfied, he would not see Milady again. Accordingly as his only answer he wrote the following letter:

Do not count on me for another rendezvous, madame. Since my convalescence I have been so busy with affairs of this sort that I have had to put them in some sort of order. When your turn comes, I shall have the honor to let you know.

I kiss your hands,

Comte de Wardes

Not a word about the sapphire ring. Did the Gascon expect to keep it as a weapon against Milady? Or, to speak frankly, was he keeping it as a last resource to provide his equipment?

D'Artagnan showed the letter to Kitty. When she read it first, she could not understand its purport, but when she read it again she was almost wild with joy. She could not believe in such happiness. D'Artagnan had to renew in spoken words the assurances the written words had given her. Whatever the danger—in view of Milady's violent character—the poor child ran in giving her mistress that letter, she ran to the Rue Royale as fast as her legs would carry her. Milady opened the letter with an eagerness as great as Kitty's in delivering it. But at the first word she read she grew livid. She crushed the paper in her hand and turned on Kitty with blazing eyes.

"What is this letter?" she demanded.

"The answer to Madame's," said Kitty, all in a tremble.

"Impossible!" cried Milady. "Impossible! No gentleman could write such a letter to a woman!" Then suddenly she shuddered and said: "My God! Can it be——"

And there she stopped. She ground her teeth, her face ashen pale; she tried to get to the window for air. But she could do no more than stretch out her arms; her legs gave way, and she sank into an armchair. Kitty, fearing she was about to faint, rushed to her to loosen her bodice, but Milady started up, pushing Kitty away.

"What are you trying to do?" she said. "How dare you touch me?"

"I thought Madame was going to faint. I was only trying to help Madame," replied the servant, terrified at Milady's fierce expression.

"*I* faint, I, I? Do you take me for a silly schoolgirl? When I am insulted I do not faint, I avenge myself, do you hear me?" And she motioned to Kitty to leave the room.

CHAPTER 34

THAT EVENING MILADY GAVE ORDERS TO ADMIT MON-
sieur d'Artagnan at once if he came as usual. But he did not come. The
next morning Kitty went to see the young man again and told him all that
had happened the day before. D'Artagnan smiled; Milady's jealous anger
was his revenge. That evening Milady was even more impatient than she
had been the evening before; she gave the same order concerning the
Gascon, but once again she waited for him in vain.

The next day when Kitty appeared at D'Artagnan's rooms, she was no
longer joyous and lively, as she had been the two preceding days, but on
the contrary as sad as if she were dying. D'Artagnan asked the poor girl
what the matter was, but her only answer was to take a letter from her
pocket and give it to him. The letter was in Milady's handwriting, only
this time it was addressed not to Monsieur de Wardes, but to Monsieur
d'Artagnan. He opened it and read as follows:

Dear Monsieur d'Artagnan:
   It is very wrong of you to neglect your friends this way, particularly at the
moment when you are about to leave them for so long. My brother and I expected you yesterday and the day before, but in vain. Will it be the same this
evening?

Your very grateful
Lady Clark

"How easy it all is!" said D'Artagnan. "I was expecting that letter. My
credit rises as that of the Comte de Wardes falls."

"Will you go?" Kitty asked.

"Listen, my dear child," said the Gascon, who was trying to justify
himself in his own eyes for breaking the promise he had made Athos,
"you must know that to decline so positive an invitation would not be
good policy. If Milady did not see me come back, she would not understand why I had interrupted my visits. She might suspect something, and
who can say how far a woman of her character would go to get her revenge?"

"Oh, my God!" said Kitty. "You know how to put things in such a way that you are always in the right. But you're going to pay court to her again, and if you succeed in pleasing her this time in your own name and with your own face, it will be much worse than it was before."

Instinctively the poor girl guessed some part of what was going to happen. D'Artagnan reassured her as best he could, and promised her that he would remain deaf to Milady's seductions. As nine o'clock struck he was at the house in the Rue Royale. The servants had obviously been warned, for as soon as D'Artagnan appeared, before he had even asked for Milady, one of them ran to announce him.

"Show him in," said Milady quickly, in a tone shrill enough for D'Artagnan to hear it in the hall. As he was ushered in Milady said to the lackey: "I am at home to no one. You understand? To no one."

The lackey bowed and withdrew. D'Artagnan cast a questioning glance at Milady. She was pale and her eyes were red, either from tears or from lack of sleep. D'Artagnan went toward her with his usual gallantry and she made an extraordinary effort to receive him well, but never did a more ravaged face give the lie to a more amiable smile. To D'Artagnan's questions concerning her health she replied:

"I feel ill, quite ill."

"Then my visit is ill-timed," said D'Artagnan. "No doubt you are in need of rest, so I will intrude no longer."

"No, no," replied Milady. "On the contrary, do stay, Monsieur d'Artagnan. Your agreeable company will divert me."

"Oho!" thought he. "She has never been so charming before. I must be on my guard."

Milady assumed the most affectionate air she could, and conversed with the greatest brilliancy possible to her. At the same time the fever that had left her for an instant returned to give luster to her eyes, color to her cheeks, and vermilion to her lips. D'Artagnan saw once more the Circe who had woven her spells around him. His love for her, which he had thought was dead and which was only dormant, awoke once more in his heart. Milady smiled, and D'Artagnan thought he would be willing to be damned for that smile. For a moment he felt something like remorse.

Little by little Milady became more communicative. She asked D'Artagnan whether he had a mistress.

"Alas!" he said, with the most sentimental air he could assume, "how can you be so cruel as to put such a question to me—to me who from the moment I saw you have breathed and sighed only through you and for you!"

Milady smiled a strange smile. "Then you do love me?" she asked.

"Do I need to tell you so? Have you not seen it?"

"Yes, I have. But you know that the prouder a woman's heart is, the more difficult it is to win it."

"Oh, difficulties do not frighten me," said D'Artagnan. "Nothing appalls me save impossibilities."

"Nothing is impossible to true love," replied Milady.

"The devil you say!" thought D'Artagnan. "She has changed her tune. Is this capricious woman about to fall in love with me by any chance? Can she be thinking of giving me another sapphire like the one she gave me when she took me for De Wardes?"

"Come," said Milady, "what would you be willing to do to prove this love you talk about?"

"Anything whatever!" cried D'Artagnan, who knew that he had little to risk in making such a pledge.

For a moment Milady remained pensive and as if undecided, then, as if she had come to a decision, she said:

"I have an enemy."

"You, madame!" cried D'Artagnan, feigning surprise. "How in God's name is that possible? You, good and beautiful as you are!"

"A mortal enemy. An enemy who has insulted me so cruelly that it is war to the death between us. May I count on you as an ally?"

D'Artagnan understood immediately what the vindictive creature was driving at.

"You may indeed, madame," he said emphatically. "My arm and my life belong to you, as does my love."

"Then," said Milady, "since you are as generous as you are loving——" She paused.

"Well?" demanded D'Artagnan.

"Well," Milady continued after a moment of silence, "from this moment on stop talking about impossibilities."

"Do not overwhelm me with happiness!" cried D'Artagnan, throwing himself on his knees and covering with kisses the hands she surrendered to him.

"Avenge me on that infamous De Wardes," Milady muttered to herself between her teeth, "and I'll know very well how to get rid of you, you double fool, you living and breathing swordblade!"

Meanwhile D'Artagnan was saying to himself: "Fall willingly into my arms after having abused me so shamelessly, you hypocritical and dangerous woman, and then I will laugh at you with the man you wish me to kill!" He raised his head and said aloud: "I am ready!"

"So you have understood me, dear Monsieur d'Artagnan," said Milady.

"I could divine your meaning from a single one of your glances."

"Then that arm of yours which has already won so much renown—you would use it in my behalf?"

"Instantly!"

"But on my part," said Milady, "how am I to repay such a service? I know what lovers are. They don't do anything for nothing."

"You know the only answer I long for," said D'Artagnan, "the only one worthy of you and of me!"

He drew her gently toward him; she barely resisted.

"You think of only your own interests," she said with a smile.

"Ah," cried D'Artagnan, really swept away by the passion this woman had the power to kindle in him, "ah, that is because my happiness seems to me so improbable, and I have such fear that it may fly away from me like a dream that I long to make it a reality!"

"Well then, deserve this pretended happiness!"

"I am at your orders, madame. Name the scoundrel who has brought tears to your beautiful eyes."

"Remember, his name is my own secret," said Milady.

"Yet I must know it."

"Yes, you must. See what confidence I have in you!"

"You overwhelm me with joy. What is his name?"

"You know him," said Milady.

"Surely he is not one of my friends?" said D'Artagnan, affecting hesitation in order to make her believe him ignorant.

"If it were one of your friends, would you hesitate?" cried Milady, a menacing gleam in her eyes.

"No, not if he were my own brother!" cried D'Artagnan, as if carried away by enthusiasm.

"I love your devotion," said Milady.

"Alas! Is that the only thing you love in me?"

"I love you too, you yourself," she declared, grasping his hand. The burning pressure of her hand made D'Artagnan shiver as if in that touch the fever that was consuming Milady had been communicated to him.

"You love me—*you!*" he cried. "Oh, if that were really so, I would go mad!"

He clasped her in his arms. She made no effort to turn her lips away from his kisses but she did not respond to them. Her lips were cold; it seemed to D'Artagnan that he was embracing a statue. But he was none the less drunk with joy, electrified by love. He almost believed in Milady's tenderness; he almost believed that De Wardes was the criminal. If De Wardes had stood before him at that moment, D'Artagnan would have killed him. Milady took advantage of the moment.

"His name is——" she paused.

"De Wardes, I know it!"

"And how do you know it?" demanded Milady, seizing both his hands and trying to look through his eyes to the very bottom of his soul. D'Artagnan realized that he had allowed himself to be carried away and had made a blunder. "Tell me, tell me, tell me, I say," repeated Milady, "how do you know his name?"

"Why, I know it because yesterday I was in a salon where De Wardes was displaying a ring that he said he had from you."

"The wretch!" cried Milady. "Well?"

"Well, I will avenge you on this wretch," D'Artagnan declared.

"My thanks, my brave friend!" cried Milady. "And when shall I be avenged?"

"Tomorrow . . . immediately . . . when you please!"

Milady started to cry out "Immediately!" but she checked herself, reflecting that such precipitation would not be very courteous to D'Artagnan. Besides, she had a thousand precautions to take, and a thousand counsels to give her champion, so that he might avoid any argument with the Comte before witnesses. The matter was settled by a few words from D'Artagnan.

"Tomorrow," he said, "you will be avenged or I shall be dead."

"No!" she cried. "You will avenge me, but you will not die. He is a coward."

"A coward with women, perhaps, but not with men. I know something of him. . . . But would it be just to allow me to go to a possible death without having given me something more than hope?"

Milady answered with a glance that meant "Tell me, is that all?" Then she added an explanation of the glance: "What you ask is no more than just," she said tenderly.

"Oh, you are an angel!" exclaimed the young man.

"Then all is agreed on?" she asked.

"Except what I ask of you, dear love."

"But I have told you that you could rely on my affection. . . . Hush! I hear my brother. There is no point in his finding you here." She rang the bell and Kitty appeared. "Go out this way," she said to D'Artagnan, opening a small secret door, "and come back at eleven. We will finish our conversation then. Kitty will show you to my apartment." The unhappy maid almost fainted. "Well, mademoiselle, what are you doing, standing there like a statue? Come, show Monsieur le Chevalier out. And tonight at eleven—you heard what I said." Milady held out her hand to him and D'Artagnan kissed it tenderly.

"Come," he said to himself as he withdrew quickly so as to avoid listening to Kitty's reproaches, "come, don't be a fool. Decidedly this woman is a consummate villain. Look out for yourself!"

CHAPTER 35

DESPITE THE ENTREATIES KITTY HAD MADE EARLIER, INstead of going up to her room, D'Artagnan left the house. He had two reasons for doing so: first, he could escape Kitty's reproaches, recrimination, and prayers; second, he was not sorry to examine his own thoughts a little, and, if possible, to fathom the thoughts of this woman.

The two facts that were clearest in all this were that D'Artagnan loved Milady to the point of madness, and that she did not love him in the least. At once D'Artagnan saw what he had best do. He must go home and write Milady a long letter confessing that he and De Wardes were, up to the present moment, one and the same, and consequently he could not undertake to kill De Wardes without committing suicide. On the other hand, a ferocious desire for vengeance spurred him on; he wanted to possess this woman in his own name.

He walked around the Place Royale five or six times, turning after every ten steps to look at the light shining through the shutters of Milady's bedchamber. It was evident that this time she was not in such haste to repair there as she had been at their first tryst. At last the light went out, and with it the last spark of irresolution in D'Artagnan's heart was extinguished. He recalled all the details of that first night, and with his heart pounding and his head on fire, he went back to the house again and rushed up to Kitty's room. The poor girl, deathly pale and trembling in every limb, tried to stop her lover. But Milady was listening for every sound and heard D'Artagnan enter. She opened her door.

"Come," she said.

She was so incredibly brazen, so monstrously brazen, that D'Artagnan could hardly believe what he saw and heard. He felt as if he were being drawn into one of those fantastic situations that one gets into only in dreams. However, that did not keep him from rushing to Milady, drawn to her by that irresistible attraction which draws iron to a magnet.

As the door closed after them, Kitty darted toward it. Jealousy, rage, offended pride, in short all the passions that contend for the heart of a woman in love, urged her to reveal the truth. But she reflected that she would be undone if she confessed that she had assisted in such a scheme, and above all, that D'Artagnan would be lost to her forever.

D'Artagnan, for his part, had attained the summit of all his desires. It was no longer a rival who was loved in his person, now it was he himself who was apparently the loved one. A secret voice in the depths of his heart whispered that he was nothing but the tool of Milady's vengeance, to be caressed only until he had dealt the death she longed for. But pride, self-conceit, and madness silenced that voice, stifled that feeble murmur.

He gave himself over entirely to the sensations of the moment. For him, Milady was no longer the woman whose fatal intent had terrified him for an instant; now she was the ardent, passionate mistress who abandoned herself to a love that she seemed to return in full measure. When, two hours later, the transports of the two lovers calmed somewhat, Milady, who had not the same motives for forgetfulness as D'Artagnan, was the first to come back to reality. She asked the young man whether he had planned how he would bring about the duel between himself and De Wardes.

But D'Artagnan, whose thoughts had taken quite a different course, forgot himself, fool that he was, and replied gallantly that it was too late at night to think about duels. This indifference toward the only interest that occupied her mind alarmed Milady, and her questions became more pressing.

D'Artagnan, who had never thought seriously about this impossible duel, tried to change the subject, but he did not succeed. Milady kept him firmly within the limits she had outlined in advance with her irresistible spirit and her iron will. D'Artagnan thought he was very crafty in advising Milady to forgive De Wardes and renounce her impetuous plans. But at his first words the young woman trembled and drew away from him.

"Are you perchance afraid, dear D'Artagnan?" she asked in a shrill, jeering tone that rang out strangely.

"You cannot think that, dear love," D'Artagnan answered. "But what if this poor Comte de Wardes were less guilty than you imagine?"

"In any case," said Milady gravely, "he has deceived me, and from the moment he deceived me he has deserved death."

"He shall die then, since you condemn him!" D'Artagnan declared with a decisiveness that Milady took for the expression of his absolute devotion. And she drew close to him again.

It would be difficult to say how long that night seemed to Milady, but D'Artagnan felt that he had been with her barely two hours when dawn gleamed through the shutters. Milady, seeing that D'Artagnan was about to leave her, reminded him of his promise to avenge her on De Wardes.

"I am quite ready," said D'Artagnan, "but first I should like to be certain of one thing—that you really love me."

D'Artagnan and Milady

Porthos, Athos, and Aramis Eavesdropping on Richelieu and Milady

"I have given you proof of that, have I not?"

"Yes, you have, and I am yours, body and soul."

"My thanks, my brave lover! But as I have just proved my love for you, you will in your turn give proof of your love for me, will you not?"

"Of course I will," D'Artagnan answered. "But if you love me as much as you say, have you no fear of what may happen to me?"

"What have I to fear?"

"Well, I might be dangerously wounded—even killed."

"Impossible!" Milady protested. "Are you not a valiant man and a fine swordsman?"

"You would not prefer," suggested D'Artagnan, "some means that would avenge you as effectively without the necessity of a duel?"

Milady looked at her lover in silence. "I do believe," said she, "that you are beginning to hesitate."

"No, I'm not hesitating. But I really feel sorry for that poor Comte de Wardes now that you no longer love him. It seems to me that a man so cruelly punished by the loss of your love needs no further chastisement."

"Who told you that I ever loved him?" demanded Milady.

"At least I can believe without being too fatuous that you have loved some other man," D'Artagnan said in a caressing tone, "and I repeat that I am concerned for the Comte."

"And why are *you* so concerned?" asked Milady.

"Because I alone know that he is far from being—or from having been—as guilty as you think."

"Indeed!" said Milady, looking somewhat uneasy. "Tell me what you mean, for I really do not understand you." D'Artagnan was holding her close, and she looked up at him with eyes that blazed brighter and brighter.

"Yes, I am a man of honor, I am," D'Artagnan declared, determined to settle the matter. "And since your love is now mine and I am sure of it—I can be sure of it, can I not?"

"Yes, it is wholly yours. Go on."

"Well, I am in ecstasies—and a confession weighs on my conscience. If I had the least doubt of your love, I would not make that confession. But you do love me, my beautiful mistress, don't you?"

"Of course I do."

"Then if through loving you too much I have been guilty toward you, you will forgive me?"

"Perhaps!" D'Artagnan, assuming his most winning smile, tried to press his lips on Milady's, but she pushed him away. "The confession!" she said, turning pale. "What is that confession?"

"You gave a rendezvous to De Wardes last Thursday, here in this room, did you not?"

"I did? No, that is not true," said Milady in a tone so steady and a face so much angered that D'Artagnan would have doubted had he not been certain of the truth.

"Do not lie to me, my beautiful angel," said D'Artagnan, smiling. "That would be futile."

"What do you mean. Speak! You are killing me."

"Rest easy, my dear, you are not in the least guilty toward me. I have already forgiven you."

"What next, what next?"

"De Wardes has nothing to boast of."

"Why? You told me yourself that the ring——"

"That ring, my love—it is I who have it. The Comte de Wardes of last Thursday and the D'Artagnan of today are one and the same man."

The rash youth expected to see surprise mingled with shame, a little storm that would resolve itself into a flood of tears. But he was completely mistaken, and he did not persist in his error long. Pale and trembling, Milady sat up, and pushing D'Artagnan back with a violent blow on the chest, she leaped out of bed. It was almost broad daylight now. D'Artagnan held her back by her nightdress of fine India muslin, imploring her pardon, but with a powerful jerk she tried to get free. The frail muslin was torn, baring her shoulders, and on one of those beautiful white, exquisitely rounded shoulders D'Artagnan was inexpressibly shocked to see the fleur-de-lis, that indelible mark branded on criminals by the degrading hand of the public executioner.

"Great God!" cried D'Artagnan, losing his hold of her nightgown and lying back on the bed, mute, motionless, and icy-cold.

Milady read her denunciation in D'Artagnan's terror. Of course he had seen everything, he knew her secret, that terrible secret that was hidden from all the world save from him. She turned on him, no longer a furious woman now but a wounded panther.

"Ah, wretch," she said, "you have betrayed me, dastard that you are. Moreover, you know my secret! You shall die!"

She flew to her dressing-table and took a little inlaid casket, flung the lid up with a feverish hand, seized a small dagger with a gold handle and a sharp, thin blade, and in one leap threw herself on D'Artagnan, half-naked as he was. Though D'Artagnan was brave, as we know, he was terrified by those distorted features, those horribly dilated pupils of her eyes, and those bleeding lips. He recoiled into the space between the bed and the wall as he would have done had he seen a snake crawling toward him. His sword swung against his hand cold with sweat and he drew it.

Milady, paying no heed to the sword, tried to step up on the bed to get at him, and she did not stop until she felt the point of the sword at her throat. Then she tried to seize the blade, but D'Artagnan kept it out of her grasp, leveling it now at her eyes, now at her breast. He slipped around to the foot of the bed, hoping to retreat through the door to Kitty's room.

Meanwhile Milady continued to strike at him with horrible fury, shrieking like a maniac. All this looked much like a duel, and D'Artagnan gradually recovered his poise.

"Well, well, beautiful lady," he said. "For God's sake calm yourself or I shall have to trace a second fleur-de-lis on those lovely cheeks."

"You wretch! You villain!" howled Milady.

But D'Artagnan, still trying to get to the door, remained on the defensive. At the uproar they made, Milady upsetting furniture to get at him and D'Artagnan moving it to barricade himself against her, Kitty opened the door. D'Artagnan had kept maneuvering to reach that door, and was now only three steps from it. With one leap he was in Kitty's room, and quick as lightning he slammed the door, then leaned his whole weight against it while Kitty bolted it. With a strength and a violence far beyond those of a normal woman, Milady tried to break down the buttress that imprisoned her in her room. When she found that to be impossible she kept stabbing at the door with her dagger, piercing through the wood time after time. At every blow she shouted fearful curses.

"Quick, Kitty, quick!" D'Artagnan whispered as soon as the door was bolted. "Get me out of the house. If we give her time to think, she will have me killed by her lackeys."

"But you can't go out like that," said Kitty. "You are almost naked."

"That's true," said D'Artagnan, only then realizing that he had but a nightshirt on. "Get me something to wear, anything you have. But hurry, my dear girl. Think—it's a question of life or death."

Kitty understood that only too well. In a turn of the hand she muffled him up in a flowered gown, a large hood, and a short cloak, and gave him some slippers for his bare feet. Then she helped him down the stairway. It was time—Milady had already aroused the whole household. The gatekeeper opened the gate for him just as Milady, half-naked, screamed from her window.

"Don't open the gate, I tell you!"

CHAPTER 36

THE YOUNG MAN FLED DOWN THE STREET WHILE MILADY was still menacing him with impotent gestures. As soon as she lost sight of him she fell back into her bedroom in a swoon.

D'Artagnan was so completely bewildered that, without worrying about what would become of Kitty, he ran at full speed across half Paris, and did not stop until he came to Athos's door. The utter confusion of his mind, the terror that spurred him on, the cries of some patrols who started in pursuit of him, the hooting of people who were going to their work despite the early hour—all these only made him run all the faster.

Crossing the courtyard, he ran up the two flights to Athos's apartment and pounded at the door like mad. Grimaud opened it, his eyes swollen with sleep. D'Artagnan sprang into the room so violently that he almost knocked the lackey down. In spite of poor Grimaud's disciplined muteness, this time he found his tongue.

"Hey, there," he cried, "what do you want, you streetwalker? What are you after, you hussy?"

D'Artagnan threw off his hood and got his hands out of the cloak. At the sight of his mustache and his naked sword poor Grimaud saw that he had to deal with a man, and concluded he was some assassin.

"Help! To the rescue! Help!" he yelled.

"Hold your tongue, you stupid fellow! I am D'Artagnan, don't you know me? Where is your master?"

"Grimaud," said Athos, emerging from his bedroom clad in a dressing-gown, "did I hear you permitting yourself to speak?"

Grimaud contented himself with pointing his finger at D'Artagnan. Athos recognized his comrade and, phlegmatic though he was, burst into laughter that was certainly justified by the bizarre masquerade he had before his eyes. D'Artagnan stood there with hood askew, skirts falling down to his slippers, sleeves tucked up, and mustache bristling with agitation.

"Don't laugh, my friend," cried D'Artagnan. "For heaven's sake don't laugh, for upon my soul I swear to you that this is no laughing matter."

He uttered the words with so solemn an air and with such real terror that Athos seized his hand, crying:

"Are you wounded, my friend? How pale you are!"

"No, not wounded, but something terrible has just happened to me. Are you alone, Athos?"

"Good Lord, who do you think would be here at this hour?"

"Good, good!" And D'Artagnan rushed into Athos's bedroom.

"Come, speak!" said the latter, shutting the door, and bolting it. "Is the King dead? Have you killed Monsieur le Cardinal?"

"Athos," said D'Artagnan, getting rid of his female garments and emerging in his nightshirt. "Prepare yourself to hear an incredible, an unheard-of, story."

"Put on this dressing-gown first," the musketeer said. D'Artagnan got into the dressing-gown, still so agitated that he mistook one sleeve for the other. "Well?" asked Athos.

"Well," replied D'Artagnan, bending close to Athos's ear and speaking almost in a whisper, "Milady is branded on her shoulder with a fleur-de-lis."

"Oh!" cried the musketeer, as if he had been shot through the heart.

"Come, Athos, are you sure that *the other woman* is dead?"

"The other woman," repeated Athos, in so low a tone that D'Artagnan barely heard him.

"Yes, the woman you told me about one day at Amiens." Athos groaned and buried his face in his hands. "This one," D'Artagnan went on, "is some twenty-six or twenty-eight."

"Blonde, is she not?" asked Athos, "with light-blue eyes of a strange brilliancy, with black eyelashes and eyebrows?"

"Yes."

"Tall, slender, shapely? She has lost a tooth next to the eyetooth on the left?"

"Yes."

"The fleur-de-lis is small, reddish, and looks as if she had tried to efface it by some application or other?"

"Yes, you can hardly see it."

"But you say she is an Englishwoman?"

"They call her Milady, but she may be French. Lord Winter is only her brother-in-law."

"I must see her, D'Artagnan!"

"Be on your guard, Athos, be on your guard! You tried to kill her. She is the sort of woman to treat you the same way, and she would not fail as you did."

"She would not dare say anything, for she would be declaring herself guilty."

"She is capable of anything and everything, Athos. Have you ever seen her in a rage? She's a tigress, a panther! Ah, my dear Athos, I am very much afraid that I have called down a terrible vengeance on both of us." Then he told his friend of Milady's maniac anger and her threat of murder.

"You are right," said Athos, "my life would not be worth a sou. Fortunately we leave Paris day after tomorrow, in all probability for La Rochelle, and once we are gone——"

"If she recognizes you, she will follow you to the ends of the earth, Athos. Let her exhaust her hatred on me alone."

"Eh, my dear fellow, what does it matter if she should kill me?" said Athos. "Do you perchance think that I set any great store by my life?"

"There's some horrible mystery under all this, Athos. She is one of the Cardinal's spies, I am sure of that."

"In that case, look out for yourself, D'Artagnan. If the Cardinal hadn't a great admiration for you because of the London affair, he would hate you bitterly. But as after all he cannot accuse you openly, and hatred must be satisfied—especially a Cardinal's hatred—be on your guard! When you go out, do not go alone; when you eat, take every precaution against poison. Mistrust everything, even your own shadow."

"Fortunately," said D'Artagnan, "all this will be necessary only until the day after tomorrow, for once in the Army, I hope we shall have only men to fear."

"Meanwhile," said Athos, "I will renounce my vow of seclusion, and wherever you go I shall go with you. You must go back to the Rue des Fossoyeurs; I shall accompany you."

"But though it is not far, I cannot go like this."

"That's true enough," said Athos, and he rang the bell and unbolted the door.

Grimaud entered. In sign language Athos ordered him to go to D'Artagnan's lodgings and bring back some clothes. Grimaud replied in the same way that he understood perfectly, and departed.

"All right, but all this isn't helping you get your equipment," Athos remarked. "If I'm not mistaken, you left most of your clothes at Milady's, and I doubt very much that she will have the courtesy to return them to you. Fortunately you have the sapphire."

"The sapphire is yours, my dear Athos. Didn't you tell me it was a family heirloom?"

"Yes, my father gave two thousand crowns for it, he once told me. It was one of his wedding presents to my mother, and it was a magnificent one. My mother gave it to me, and I, fool that I was, instead of keeping it as a holy relic, gave it to that villainous woman."

"Take it back, my dear friend. I can see that it means a lot to you."

"*I* take back that ring after it has passed through the hands of that infamous creature! Never. That ring has been defiled, D'Artagnan."

"Sell it, then."

"Sell a jewel my mother gave me! I confess I would look on that as a desecration."

"Pawn it, then. You can borrow at least a thousand crowns on it. With that sum you can extricate yourself from your present difficulties, with the first money you get hold of you can redeem it, and you will get it back cleansed of its earlier stains by passing through the hands of usurers."

"You're a delightful companion, my dear D'Artagnan," said Athos with a smile. "Your never-failing cheerfulness gives a lift to poor souls in affliction. All right, let us pawn the ring, but only on one condition—five hundred crowns for you and five hundred crowns for me."

"What are you thinking of, Athos? I don't need a quarter of that sum. Selling my saddle will give me enough. What do I need? A horse for Planchet, that's all. Besides, you forget that I too have a ring."

"A ring that you apparently value more highly than I do mine. At least I thought you seemed to."

"Yes, I value it, for in some crisis it might not only get us out of considerable trouble but even out of some great danger. It is not merely a valuable diamond, it is also an enchanted talisman."

"I don't understand you, but I'll take your word for it. But to come back to my ring—or rather yours. If you refuse to accept half of what we get for it, I'll throw it into the Seine."

"Very well, then I accept."

Just then Grimaud returned, accompanied by Planchet. The latter, worried about his master and curious to find out what had happened to him, had taken advantage of the opportunity, and brought his master's clothes himself. D'Artagnan dressed; Athos did the same. When they were ready to go out, Athos made a gesture like a man taking aim, and Grimaud immediately took his musketoon from its rack and got ready to follow his master.

They reached the Rue des Fossoyeurs safely, but found Bonacieux standing in the doorway. He greeted D'Artagnan with a bantering look.

"Eh, my dear lodger," he said, "make haste. There's a very pretty girl waiting for you upstairs, and you know women don't like to be kept waiting."

"It's Kitty!" exclaimed D'Artagnan, and he darted into the passage and up the stairs.

In fact, on the landing by his room he found the poor child crouched against his door, all atremble. As soon as she saw him she said:

"You promised to protect me, monsieur. You promised to save me from her anger. Remember, it was you who ruined me!"

"Yes, to be sure," said D'Artagnan. "Don't worry, Kitty. But what happened after I left?"

"How do I know?" said Kitty. "Milady screamed . . . the lackeys rushed up . . . she was mad with anger . . . every curse there is she spit out at you. Then I thought she might remember that you had gone through my room into hers and then she would think I was your accomplice. So I took what little money I had, and my best clothes, and got away as fast as I could."

"Poor child! But what can I do with you? I am leaving for the campaign day after tomorrow."

"Do what you please, Monsieur le Chevalier. But help me to get out of Paris, even help me to get out of France!"

"But I can't take you to the siege of La Rochelle," said D'Artagnan.

"No, but you can get me a place in the provinces with some lady of your acquaintance—in your own country, for instance."

"My dear little love, in my corner of the world the ladies do without lady's maids. But stop! I think I can manage something for you. Planchet, go to Monsieur Aramis and request him to come here at once. Say I've something very important to tell him. Now, Kitty, when we are about to part, and as you are no longer jealous of me——"

"Monsieur le Chevalier," Kitty interrupted, "far away from you or near you, I shall always love you."

"And I shall always love you, too, be sure of that," said D'Artagnan. "But come, answer me. The question I am about to put to you is one of great importance to me. Have you never heard anything about a young woman who was carried off one night?"

"Wait a minute. . . . Oh, God, Monsieur le Chevalier, do you still love that woman?"

"No, it's one of my friends who loves her. You see, my child, Madame Bonacieux is the wife of that frightful baboon you saw at the door when you came in."

"Oh, my God," cried Kitty, "you remind me of all my fears! If only he didn't recognize me!"

"What, recognize you! Then you have seen that man before?"

"He came to Milady's twice."

"Did he indeed? When?"

"Somewhere about a fortnight ago. And he came again last evening, just before you came."

"My dear Athos," said D'Artagnan, "we are caught in a network of spies! . . . Do you think he recognized you, Kitty?"

"I pulled down my hood as soon as I saw him, but perhaps it was too late."

"Go down, Athos, and see if he is still at the door. He mistrusts you less than he does me."

Athos went down, and returned at once. "He's gone," he said, "and the door is locked."

"He has gone to report that all the pigeons are now in the dovecote," commented D'Artagnan.

"Well then, let us all fly away," said Athos. "All except Planchet. We'll leave him here to bring us news."

"Wait a minute. What about Aramis? I sent for him."

"Oh yes," said Athos, "we must wait for Aramis."

At that moment Aramis arrived. The friends told him all about the matter, and gave him to understand how urgent it was that he should find a place for Kitty among some of his high connections. Aramis reflected a moment, blushing.

"Will it really be doing you a favor, D'Artagnan?" he asked.

"I shall be grateful to you for it all my life."

"Well, Madame de Bois-Tracy did ask me the other day whether I knew of a trusty lady's maid—for one of her friends who lives in the provinces, I think. So if D'Artagnan can answer for Mademoiselle——"

"Oh, monsieur," cried Kitty, "please believe that I will be absolutely loyal to the lady who makes it possible for me to leave Paris."

"Everything is for the best, then," said Aramis. He sat down at a table and wrote a short note, sealed it with his ring, and gave it to Kitty.

"Now, my child," said D'Artagnan, "you know this isn't a very good place for any of us to be found. We must part. We will meet again in better days."

"Whenever we meet again and wherever it may be," said Kitty, "you will find me loving you as dearly as I love you now."

A few seconds later the three young men separated, after agreeing to meet again at four o'clock in Athos's apartment. Planchet was left to guard the house. Aramis went home, Athos and D'Artagnan hurried off to pawn the sapphire ring. As our Gascon had foreseen, they found it easy to raise 300 pistoles on the ring. Moreover, the pawnbroker told them that if they would sell it to him, he would give as much as 500 for it, since it would make a magnificent pendant.

Athos and D'Artagnan, active as soldiers and shrewd as connoisseurs, took barely three hours to buy the musketeer's equipment. Athos found a superb Andalusian horse with a jet-black coat, slender and beautifully modeled legs, and nostrils of fire. The asking price was a thousand livres. Perhaps Athos might have got it for less but while D'Artagnan was bargaining with the horse-dealer, Athos was counting out the money on the table. For Grimaud Athos bought a short, powerful cob from Picardy for which he paid 300 livres. But when the saddle and his weapons had been bought for Grimaud, he had not a sou left of his 150 pistoles. D'Artagnan offered his friend part of his own share, the loan to be repaid at Athos's convenience. Athos's only answer was to shrug his shoulders.

"What did the pawnbroker say he would give for the sapphire if we sold it?" he asked.

"Five hundred pistoles."

"In other words, two hundred pistoles more, a hundred for you and a hundred for me. Why, that's a fortune, my friend. Come on, back to the pawnbroker!"

"What! Do you mean——?" queried D'Artagnan.

"That ring would certainly recall only very bitter memories," said Athos, "and anyway we shall never be masters of three hundred pistoles to get it back, and so we'd lose two thousand livres if we didn't sell it. Go tell him the ring is his, D'Artagnan, and bring back the two hundred pistoles."

"Better think it over, Athos."

"Ready money is at a premium these days," replied Athos, "and we must all learn to make sacrifices. Go, D'Artagnan, go. Mousqueton will accompany you with his namesake musketoon."

Half an hour later D'Artagnan returned with the 2000 livres, and without having met with any mishap. So it was that Athos by staying quietly at home had found resources he did not expect.

CHAPTER 37

AT FOUR O'CLOCK THE FOUR FRIENDS MET AGAIN IN Athos's lodgings. Their anxiety over their equipment had vanished, for Porthos too had found his—through Madame Coquenard. Each face expressed no worries except the secret ones of its· owner, for behind all present happiness fear of the future always lurks.

Suddenly Planchet entered, bringing two letters for D'Artagnan. The first was a little note neatly folded lengthwise, with a pretty seal of green wax stamped with a dove bearing an olive branch. The other was a large square epistle resplendent with the fearsome coat of arms of His Eminence the Cardinal-Duc.

At the sight of the little note, D'Artagnan's heart beat fast, for he recognized the handwriting. He had seen it but once before, but he had kept the remembrance of it deep down in his heart. So he took it up first and opened it eagerly. The letter read:

Ride along the road to Chaillot next Wednesday between six and seven in the evening. Look carefully into the carriages that pass you. But if you value your own life and the lives of those who love you, do not speak one word or make one gesture that might lead any onlooker to think that you have recognized the woman who is risking everything in order to see you for but an instant.

There was no signature.

"That's a trap," said Aramis. "Don't go, D'Artagnan."

"And yet," said DArtagnan, "I think I know that handwriting."

"The note may be a forgery," Athos replied. "Between six o'clock and seven in the evening the Chaillot road is absolutely deserted. You might as well go for a ride in the forest of Bondy!"

"But suppose we all go," said D'Artagnan. "What the devil, they couldn't destroy all four of us, plus four lackeys and eight horses and our weapons!"

"But you're forgetting your second letter," Athos reminded him. "It seems to me that the seal denotes that it calls for some attention. For my part, D'Artagnan, I declare I think it is more important than the trifling note you have slipped so craftily over your heart."

D'Artagnan blushed. "Well," he said, "let us see, gentlemen, what His Eminence wants of me." And he opened the second letter and read as follows:

Monsieur D'Artagnan, of the Royal Guards, Des Essarts company, is expected at the Palais-Cardinal at eight o'clock this evening.

La Houdinière, Captain of the Guards

"The devil!" said Athos. "Here's a rendezvous far more serious than the other one."

"I'll go to the second after I've been to the first," said D'Artagnan. "I'll have plenty of time for both."

"Hm," said Aramis, "I wouldn't go to either."

"I agree with Aramis," declared Porthos.

"Gentlemen," said D'Artagnan, "I had a similar invitation from His Eminence once before, through Monsieur de Cavois. I paid no attention to it, and the next day a great misfortune befell me—Constance disappeared. Whatever may happen now, I will go."

"If you've made up your mind, all right," said Athos. "But suppose we all keep by D'Artagnan the whole evening. Each of us can wait at one of the palace gates with three musketeers behind him. If any one of us sees a carriage with suspiciously closed windows drive out, all of us will fall upon it. It's a long time since we have had a skirmish with Monsieur le Cardinal's guardsmen."

"Admirable!" the young men replied in chorus.

"I have no horse," D'Artagnan remarked, "but I will get one from Monsieur de Tréville's stables."

"That isn't necessary," said Aramis. "Take one of mine."

"One of yours! How many have you?" D'Artagnan asked.

"Three," Aramis answered with a smile. "I bought two and one was a present."

"Well, in that case we can manage famously," said D'Artagnan. "Which of the horses will you ride, one of those you bought or the one that was given you?"

"The one that was given me, of course. You understand, D'Artagnan, that I cannot offend——"

"The unknown donor," interrupted D'Artagnan. "Is one of those you bought useless to you now?"

"Virtually."

"Did you select it yourself?"

"With the greatest care."

"Good! Will you let me have it at the price it cost you?"

"My dear D'Artagnan, I was about to offer it to you, giving you all the time you may need to pay me such a bagatelle."

"How much did you pay for it?"

"Eight hundred livres."

"Here are forty double pistoles, my dear friend," said D'Artagnan, taking the sum from his pocket.

"Then you are really rich?" asked Aramis.

"Rich! I'm rolling in money, my dear fellow!" And D'Artagnan jingled the coins left in his pocket.

"Send your saddle to the Hôtel de Tréville, and your horse can be brought here with ours."

"Good! But it's almost five o'clock. Let us make haste!"

Fifteen minutes later Porthos rode up mounted on a very handsome jennet with Mousqueton behind him on a small Auvergne horse. At the same moment Aramis appeared on a superb English charger with Bazin following him on a roan, leading a powerful Mecklenberg horse that was to be D'Artagnan's. Grimaud arrived on his cob, leading Athos's mount. D'Artagnan and Athos went down to the street and vaulted into their saddles. The four friends rode off side by side, Aramis on a horse he owed to his mistress, Porthos on one he owed to the lawyer's wife, and D'Artagnan on one he owed to luck, the best mistress of all. The lackeys formed a rearguard.

A short gallop brought them to the Chaillot road by twilight. Carriages were coming and going; D'Artagnan, guarded by his friends not far behind him, darted a scrutinizing glance into every carriage, but he could discern no face he knew.

At length, after some quarter of an hour and just as twilight was turning into night, a carriage appeared driving fast along the Sèvres road. Suddenly a woman's face appeared at the window, two fingers on her mouth as if to enjoin silence or perhaps to throw a kiss. D'Artagnan gave a cry of joy. That woman, or rather that apparition—for the carriage passed him as swift as a vision—was Madame Bonacieux.

Automatically and despite the warning he had been given, D'Artagnan put his horse to the gallop and in a few seconds overtook the carriage. But now the window was hermetically closed and the vision had vanished. Then D'Artagnan recalled the injunction: "If you value your life and the lives of those who love you, do not speak one word or make one gesture." He stopped, therefore, trembling not for himself, but for the poor woman who had evidently exposed herself to great danger by appointing this rendezvous.

The carriage went on its way at the same swift pace, drove into Paris, and disappeared. D'Artagnan, dumfounded, sat perfectly still on his horse. He did not know what to think. If it was really Madame Bonacieux and she was returning to Paris, why this fugitive meeting, why this mere exchange of glances, why this lost kiss? On the other hand, if it was not Madame Bonacieux—which was quite possible, for in the dim light he might easily have been mistaken—if it was not she, might not this be the beginning of some machination against him in which this woman he was known to love was being used as a decoy?

His three companions joined him. All of them had seen perfectly well a woman's face appear at the carriage window, but none of them but Athos knew Madame Bonacieux. Athos felt sure it was she, but less pre-occupied than D'Artagnan with that lovely face, he had fancied he also saw a man's face, in the back of the carriage.

"If that is true," said D'Artagnan, "they are doubtless taking her from one prison to another. But what can they intend to do with the poor creature, and how shall I ever find her again?"

Half-past seven struck from a belfry nearby; the carriage had been twenty minutes late at the rendezvous. D'Artagnan's friends reminded him that he had a visit to pay, at the same time suggesting that he still had time to change his mind. But D'Artagnan was at once headstrong and curious. He had made up his mind to go to the Palais-Cardinal to find out what His Eminence had to say to him, and nothing could swerve him from his determination.

They reached the Rue Saint-Honoré, and then the Place du Palais-Cardinal, where they found the twelve musketeers they had summoned. There for the first time these gentlemen were told what the affair was all about. D'Artagnan was popular with the Honorable Corps of the King's Musketeers. They knew that one day he would take his place among them, and already looked upon him as a comrade. Accordingly they gladly accepted the duty assigned them. Besides, in all probability the affair would do the Cardinal and his men an ill turn, and for expeditions of that sort these worthy gentlemen were always ready.

Although he felt himself ably supported, D'Artagnan was not quite easy as he went up the great staircase, step by step. His behavior toward Milady had been very much like treachery, and he was suspicious of the political relations that existed between this woman and the Cardinal. Moreover, De Wardes, whom he had treated so ill, was one of His Eminence's henchmen, and D'Artagnan knew that His Eminence was ruthless toward his enemies and strongly attached to his friends.

"If De Wardes has told the Cardinal all about our little affair, which is almost certain, and if he recognized me, which is probable, I must consider myself a doomed man," said D'Artagnan to himself, shaking his head. "But why has he waited until now? . . . Well, that's quite simple —Milady must have made her complaint against me with all that hypo-critical grief that makes her so interesting, and my latest crime has filled the cup till it is spilling over!

"Fortunately," he added, "my good friends are down yonder, and they will never allow me to be taken away without a fight. But Monsieur de Tréville's musketeers cannot all by themselves wage a war against the Cardinal, who has at his command the armed forces of all France, and before whom the Queen is impotent and the King has no will of his own. D'Artagnan, my friend, you are brave, and you have some fine qualities, but the women will ruin you someday!"

He reached this melancholy conclusion just as he entered the antechamber. He gave his letter to the usher on duty, who took him to a waiting-room and then went into the inner rooms of the palace. In the waiting-room there were five or six of the Cardinal's guardsmen. They recognized D'Artagnan, and knowing that it was he who had wounded Jussac, they looked at him with smiles of doubtful meaning. D'Artagnan thought those smiles were a bad augury, but our Gascon was not easily intimidated—or rather, thanks to the great pride natural to the men of his province, he never betrayed what was passing through his mind when that was anything like fear. He planted himself haughtily in front of the guardsmen, one hand on his hip, in an attitude by no means lacking in majesty.

The usher returned and motioned to D'Artagnan to follow him. They followed a corridor, crossed a large drawing-room, and then D'Artagnan found himself in the presence of a man seated at a desk, writing. The usher announced him and withdrew in silence. D'Artagnan remained standing and examined the man before him.

At first he thought he had to do with some judge who was looking over his own record, but soon he saw that the man at the desk was writing, or rather correcting, lines of unequal length, tapping out the rhythm with his fingers. So he was in the presence of a poet! Suddenly the poet closed his manuscript, on the cover of which was printed: *Mirame; A Tragedy in Five Acts,* and raised his head. D'Artagnan recognized the Cardinal.

CHAPTER 38

THE CARDINAL RESTED HIS ELBOW ON THE MANUSCRIPT, his cheek on his hand, and looked at the young man for a moment. No one had a more searching eye than Cardinal de Richelieu, and D'Artagnan felt that glance run through his veins like a fever. But he kept a good countenance, standing, hat in hand, awaiting the good pleasure of His Eminence without too much assurance, but also without too much humility.

"Monsieur," said the Cardinal, "are you a certain D'Artagnan from Béarn?"

"Yes, Monseigneur," the young man answered.

"There are several branches of that family at Tarbes or near there. To which of them do you belong?"

"I am the son of the D'Artagnan who served in the Wars of Religion under the great King Henry IV of blessed memory."

"I see. You set out from your province seven or eight months ago to seek your fortune in the capital, didn't you?"

"Yes, Monseigneur."

"You passed through Meung, where something happened to you—I don't know just what, but something or other!"

"Monseigneur," D'Artagnan replied, "this is what happened——"

"You don't need to tell me," interrupted the Cardinal, with a smile that meant he knew the whole story quite as well as the youth who had started to tell it. "You were recommended to Monsieur de Tréville, were you not?"

"Yes, Monseigneur, but in that unfortunate affair at Meung——"

"Your letter was lost," His Eminence interrupted again. "Yes, I know that. But Monsieur de Tréville, being a skilled physiognomist who can judge a man at first sight, got you a place in the company of Monsieur des Essarts, his brother-in-law, leading you to hope that someday you would join the musketeers."

"Monseigneur is perfectly informed," said D'Artagnan.

"Since then many things have happened to you: you took a walk back of the Carmes-Déchaux one day when it would have been better for you to be elsewhere. Then you journeyed to Forges with your friends, and they stopped en route, but you went on. It is all quite simple—you had business in England."

"Monseigneur," began D'Artagnan, taken aback, "I was going——"

"Hunting at Windsor—or somewhere else. That is your own affair. I know all that because it is my business to know everything. On your return, you were received by an august personage, and I am glad to see that you have kept the keepsake that lady gave you." D'Artagnan turned inward the diamond of the ring the Queen had given him, but it was too late. "The day after that you received a visit from Cavois," the Cardinal continued. "He came to invite you to come here. You did not accept that invitation, and you were in the wrong."

"Monseigneur, I feared I had incurred Your Eminence's disfavor."

"Eh, why, monsieur? Could you earn my disfavor by carrying out your superior's orders with more intelligence and courage than most men would have shown? I punish those who fail in obedience, not those who obey orders, like you—shall we say too well? As a proof of that, recall the date of the day on which you were asked to call on me, and search your memory in order to recall what happened that very evening."

That evening was the one when Madame Bonacieux had been abducted. D'Artagnan shuddered.

"In short," the Cardinal continued, "as I have heard nothing of you for some time now, I wished to know what you were doing. Besides, you really owe me some thanks. You must have noticed yourself how considerately you have been treated in all these circumstances." D'Artagnan bowed respectfully. "That," the Cardinal went on, "arose not only from a spirit of pure justice, but also because of a plan I had formed for your future." D'Artagnan grew more and more astonished. "I wanted to explain my plan to you on the day you received my first invitation, but you did not come. Fortunately nothing has been lost by this delay, and today you shall hear my plan. Sit down there in front of me, Monsieur d'Artagnan; you are too well born to stand while you listen to me," and the Cardinal pointed to a chair.

"You are brave, Monsieur d'Artagnan," continued His Eminence, "and you are also prudent, which is even better. I like both men with hearts—that is, men of courage—and men with heads—that is, men who can think. But young as you are and only on the threshold of your career, you have powerful enemies. If you are not on your guard, they will destroy you!"

"Alas! Monseigneur," the young man replied, "they can do so easily, for they are strong and well supported, while I stand alone."

"True. But however much you may stand alone, you have already accomplished a great deal, and you will accomplish even more, I am sure. Yet I think you need guidance in the adventurous career you have undertaken—for if I am not mistaken you came to Paris with the ambitious intention of making your fortune."

"At my age every man has extravagant hopes, Monseigneur," said D'Artagnan.

"Only fools have extravagant hopes, monsieur, and you are an intelligent man. Come, what would you say to a commission as ensign in my guards, with a lieutenancy after the campaign? You accept it, do you not?"

"Monseigneur," began D'Artagnan, much embarrassed, "I——"

"What! You refuse?" cried the Cardinal.

"I am in His Majesty's Guards, Monseigneur, and am to be transferred soon to the Royal Musketeers. I have no reason to be dissatisfied."

"But it seems to me that my guards are also His Majesty's guards. Everyone who serves in a French corps serves the King."

"Monseigneur, Your Eminence has misunderstood me."

"You want an excuse to make the change, do you not? Well, here it is. Promotion, the campaign that is beginning, the opportunity I offer you. So much for the outside world. As for you personally, the safe protection you stand in need of, for you must know, Monsieur d'Artagnan, that I have received serious complaints against you. You do not devote your days and your nights exclusively to the service of the King." D'Artagnan blushed. "Moreover," the Cardinal went on, putting his hand on a bundle of papers, "I have here your complete dossier. But before reading it, I wished to talk to you. I know you to be a man of determination, and if you have good guidance your services may lead to something very advantageous to you instead of bringing you to ruin. Come, think it over, and make your decision."

"Your kindness overwhelms me, Monseigneur," D'Artagnan answered, "but since Monseigneur permits me to speak frankly——"

"Certainly. Speak."

"Well, I will presume to say that all my friends serve either in the Royal Musketeers or the Royal Guards, and, by some inconceivable ill turn of fortune, all my enemies are in the service of Your Eminence. Therefore if I should accept what Monseigneur offers me, I would be ill received among Your Eminence's forces and ill regarded among the King's."

"Can you be so conceited as to think that what I offer you is not as much as you deserve?" asked the Cardinal, with a disdainful smile.

"Monseigneur, Your Eminence is a hundred times too kind to me. On the contrary, I think I have as yet done nothing to be worthy of your kindness. The siege of La Rochelle is about to begin, Monseigneur. I shall be serving under the eyes of Your Eminence. If I have the good fortune to conduct myself in that siege so as to attract Monseigneur's attention there—well, then I shall feel that I have earned the protection

Your Eminence would honor me with. Everything must come in its own time, Monseigneur. Perhaps later I shall have the right to *give* myself; now I should seem to be *selling* myself."

"In other words, you refuse to serve me, monsieur," said the Cardinal in a tone of annoyance in which nevertheless some esteem was apparent. "Stay free, then, keep your hatreds and your sympathies."

"Monseigneur——"

"Well, well," said the Cardinal, "I don't hold it against you. But you must know that it is hard enough to defend and reward our friends; we owe nothing to our enemies. But I will give you one piece of advice. Be very careful, Monsieur d'Artagnan, for the moment I withdraw my protecting hand I would not give a sou for your life."

"I will try to do so, Monseigneur," the Gascon assured him.

"In the future, especially if some mischance should happen to befall you," said Richelieu meaningfully, "remember that it was I who sought you out, and that I did everything in my power to keep that mischance from befalling you."

"Whatever may happen," said D'Artagnan, putting his hand on his heart and bowing, "I shall entertain everlasting gratitude to Your Eminence for what you are doing for me now."

"Well then, so be it. As you have said, Monsieur d'Artagnan, we shall meet again after the campaign. I will keep an eye on you, for I shall be there, and on our return, well—we will cast up our accounts."

"Ah, Monseigneur," cried D'Artagnan, "spare me the burden of your disfavor! Remain neutral, Monseigneur, if you find that I act as becomes a gallant man."

"Young man," said Richelieu, "if I can repeat to you someday what I have said to you today, I promise you to do so."

Richelieu's final words conveyed a terrible doubt; they alarmed D'Artagnan more than a threat would have done, for this was a warning. So the Cardinal was seeking to preserve him from some misfortune that menaced him. D'Artagnan opened his mouth to reply, but with a haughty gesture the Cardinal dismissed him.

D'Artagnan went out, but at the door his heart almost failed him and he thought of returning. But the grave, stern countenance of Athos rose before him. If he made the pact the Cardinal had proposed, Athos would never shake hands with him again, Athos would repudiate him. It was fear of this that stopped him, so powerful is the influence of a truly great character.

D'Artagnan went down the staircase by which he had come, and found Athos and his three musketeers awaiting his return. They were beginning to be anxious, but D'Artagnan reassured them with a word and Planchet ran to tell the other sentinels that it was useless to mount guard any longer, as his master had emerged from the Palais-Cardinal safe and sound.

When the friends got back to Athos's apartment, Aramis and Porthos inquired eagerly as to the reason for this strange interview. But D'Artagnan contented himself with telling them that Monsieur de Richelieu had sent for him to propose that he enter the Cardinal's Guards with the rank of ensign, and that he had refused.

"And you were right!" cried Porthos, then Aramis. Athos fell into a deep reverie and said nothing.

All the next day was spent in preparations for departure. That night all the comrades of Monsieur des Essarts's guardsmen and of Monsieur de Tréville's musketeers convened; they had always been friends. They were parting to meet again when and if it pleased God. As may be imagined, the night was a decidedly riotous one.

As the bugles sounded reveille in the morning the friends separated, the musketeers hastening to the Hôtel de Tréville, the guardsmen to the Hôtel des Essarts. Each captain then led his company to the Louvre, where the King was to review them. The King was gloomy and looked ill, which deprived him of a little of his usual lofty bearing. Nevertheless he had determined to set out that very evening, and despite all remonstrances, he insisted on holding the review. The review over, the guards set forth alone, the musketeers waiting to escort the King.

Meanwhile D'Artagnan was marching off with his company. At the Faubourg Saint-Antoine he turned to look at the Bastille and missed seeing Milady, who, mounted on a light-chestnut horse, was pointing him out to two evil-looking men. They drew close to the ranks in order to get a good look at him. They glanced at Milady questioningly; she nodded that he was the man. Then, certain that there would be no mistake about the execution of her orders, she spurred her horse and disappeared. The two men followed Monsieur des Essarts's company, and as they left the Faubourg Saint-Antoine, they mounted two well-equipped horses that a lackey out of livery was holding in readiness.

CHAPTER 39

THE SIEGE OF LA ROCHELLE WAS ONE OF THE GREAT
political events of the reign of Louis XIII and one of the Cardinal's great
military enterprises. The political designs of the Cardinal when he undertook this siege were far-reaching. But certain private purposes perhaps
influenced His Eminence no less. A chronicler is forced to recognize the
petty aims of a man in love and a jealous rival.

As everyone knows, Richelieu had been in love with the Queen. Was
his love only a means to a political end, or was it quite simply one of
those deep passions that Anne of Austria inspired in almost all the men
who came near her? We cannot say, but at all events, we have already
recorded how Buckingham had triumphed over Richelieu, especially in
the affair of the diamond tags.

Accordingly, Richelieu meant not only to rid France of a public
enemy, but to avenge himself on a rival of his own. This vengeance,
moreover, must be a vast and striking one worthy in every way of a man
who handles the forces of a whole kingdom as if he were wielding a
sword. Richelieu knew that in fighting England he was fighting Buckingham, that in triumphing over England he was triumphing over Buckingham, and finally, that in humiliating England in the eyes of Europe he
was humiliating Buckingham in the eyes of the Queen.

On his side, Buckingham, while proclaiming that he was maintaining
the honor of England, was motivated by interests absolutely like those of
the Cardinal. Buckingham too was pursuing a private vengeance. He had
not been able, under any pretext whatever, to return to France as an
ambassador; he was determined to return as a conqueror. So the real
stake in this game which two powerful kingdoms were playing for the
good pleasure of two men in love, was merely a kind glance from Anne
of Austria.

The first advantage had been won by Buckingham. Arriving unex-
pectedly near the Ile de Ré with 90 vessels and almost 20,000 men, he
had surprised the Comte de Toirac, who was in command of the island
for the King, and after a bloody fight effected a landing. The Comte de
Toirac withdrew to the citadel of Saint-Martin with its garrison and

threw a hundred men into a little stronghold called the Fort de La Prée.

This event had hastened the Cardinal's decision. Until he and the King could assume command of the siege of La Rochelle, he had sent Monsieur, the Duc d'Orléans, the King's brother, to direct the opening operations, and had ordered all the troops he could dispose of to march to the theater of war. Our friend D'Artagnan was among the men sent as a vanguard.

The King, as has been said, was to follow, but on June 23 he was attacked by fever. Despite his illness he insisted on setting out, but as his fever rose, he was forced to halt at Villeroi. Now whenever the King halted, so did the musketeers. Thus D'Artagnan, as still a mere guardsman was separated, if only momentarily, from his good friends. This annoyed him, but he would have become seriously worried had he guessed what unknown dangers surrounded him. However, he arrived without mishap at the camp before La Rochelle on September 10, 1627.

Everything was at a standstill. The Duke of Buckingham and his Englishmen were still masters of the Ile de Ré; they were continuing to besiege the citadel of Saint-Martin and the Fort de La Prée, but without success. Hostilities against La Rochelle had begun two or three days before.

The Royal Guards under the command of Monsieur des Essarts took up their quarters in a monastery. Now we know that D'Artagnan, obsessed by his ambition to be enrolled in the musketeers, had formed few friendships with his own comrades; he was lonely, and given over to his own meditations. His reflections were not very cheerful. In the two years since he had come to Paris he had been mixed up in public affairs, but his private affairs had made little progress, whether his love affair or his making his fortune. As to love, the only woman he had really loved was Madame Bonacieux, and Madame Bonacieux had vanished without his being able to discover what had happened to her. As for making his fortune, humble as he was, he had made an enemy of the Cardinal, the man before whom the greatest men of the kingdom trembled, even the King himself.

Richelieu could easily crush him, and yet he had not. To a mind as keen as D'Artagnan's was, this forbearance of the Cardinal was a ray of light that gave him a glimpse of a happier future. But he had made another enemey, one less to be feared, he thought, but one not to be despised—Milady.

To balance all this, he had acquired the protection and the friendship of the Queen. But as things were going now, the Queen's friendship was one more cause for persecution. His clearest gain in all this was the diamond worth 5000 or 6000 livres that he wore on his finger. And even this diamond was of little value to him now. What if in his ambitious plans he kept it so that some fine day he might show it to the Queen as a pledge of her gratitude? Since he could not sell it, it was worth no more than the pebbles he trod underfoot.

As D'Artagnan thought all this he was walking alone along a pretty little road that ran from the camp to the village of Angoutin. His reflections had led him farther than he had realized, and the day was near its end, when he thought he saw the barrel of a musket glitter behind a hedge. D'Artagnan had a quick eye and a ready understanding. He realized that the musket had not come there all by itself, and that the man who carried it had not hidden behind the hedge with any friendly intention. He had just decided to take to the open when on the other side of the road, behind a rock, he saw the muzzle of another musket. Obviously, this was an ambush.

The young man cast a glance at the first musket and noted with some anxiety that it was being slowly leveled at him. As soon as he saw the muzzle come to a standstill he threw himself flat on the ground. At the same instant he heard a bullet whiz by above his head. He must lose no time. He sprang to his feet just as a bullet from the other musket scattered the gravel at the very spot where he had been lying a moment before.

D'Artagnan was not one of those foolhardy men who seek a ridiculous death in order to have it said of them that they did not retreat one step. Besides, there was no question of courage here; D'Artagnan had been ambushed.

"If there's a third shot, I'm done for!" he said to himself as he took to his heels and fled toward the camp with all the celerity of a Gascon— and Gascons are noted for their agility.

But though he ran fast, the first man who had fired had had time to reload his musket and now fired again, this time with such good aim that the bullet went through D'Artagnan's hat and sent it flying ten paces ahead of him. As he had no other hat, he picked it up on the run, and reached his quarters out of breath and very pale. He sat down without saying a word and began to reflect.

There might be three reasons for this attack. The first and the most natural explanation was that the men of La Rochelle might have laid an ambush for him. They would not be sorry to kill one of His Majesty's guardsmen. D'Artagnan picked up his hat, examined the bullet hole, and shook his head. This was no musket ball, but a bullet from a harquebus. This was not a military ambush, for the bullet was not of the caliber for a military weapon.

Second, this might be a nice little remembrance from Monsieur le Cardinal. He recalled that at the very moment when he had sighted the first musket barrel, thanks to the timely rays of the setting sun, he had been wondering again about His Eminence's forbearance. But D'Artagnan shook his head again. His Eminence rarely had recourse to such methods with people he had merely to stretch out his hand to destroy.

Third, this might be vengeance from Milady. That was the likeliest explanation. He sought in vain to recall the features or the dress of the murderers. He had escaped so rapidly that he had no time to notice anything about them.

"Ah, my dear friends, where are you now?" he murmured. "And how sorely I miss you!"

D'Artagnan spent a very bad night. Three or four times he woke with a start, imagining that he saw a man approaching his bed to plunge a dagger into him. But at last daylight appeared and darkness had brought no mishap. But he felt certain that his troubles had been only postponed. He stayed in his quarters all day, telling himself in excuse that the weather was bad.

Two days later, at nine in the morning, the drums beat to arms. The Duc d'Orléans was making an inspection. The guardsmen ran to get their arms, and D'Artagnan took his place among his comrades. Monsieur passed along the front of the line; the commanding officers approached him to pay their respects, among them Monsieur des Essarts. After a minute or two it seemed to D'Artagnan that Monsieur des Essarts was gesturing him to come forward, but fearing that he might be mistaken, he awaited another sign from his commanding officer. The Captain motioned again, and D'Artagnan left his place in the ranks and advanced to receive his orders.

"The Duc d'Orléans is about to ask for volunteers for a mission that is dangerous but one that will bring honor to those who carry it out. I summoned you because I thought you should be in readiness."

"Thank you, Captain," replied D'Artagnan, who wished for nothing better than to distinguish himself in the eyes of the Lieutenant-General.

The men of La Rochelle had made a sortie during the night and had recaptured a bastion that the Royal Army had taken two days before. The question was to ascertain by a desperate reconnaisance whether the enemy was holding the bastion. Presently Monsieur raised his voice and said:

"For this mission I want three or four men and one dependable man to lead them."

"I have the dependable man here, Monseigneur," Monsieur des Essarts said, gesturing to D'Artagnan. "As for the volunteers, Monsieur d'Artagnan has only to make his wishes known and the men will not be wanting."

"Four men of good will wanted who will risk their lives with me!" cried D'Artagnan, raising his sword in salute.

Two of his fellow guardsmen sprang forward at once, two soldiers joined them, and D'Artagnan thought the number sufficient. His mission was to get near enough to the bastion to ascertain the truth. He set out along the trench with his four companions; the two guardsmen marched abreast of him, with the privates behind them. Screened by the wall of the trench, they got within some hundred paces of the bastion, then D'Artagnan turned, and he noticed that the privates had disappeared. He decided that fear had led them to lag behind.

As the counterscarp turned they found themselves within almost sixty paces of the bastion. They saw no one; apparently the bastion had been abandoned. The three who now constituted the forlorn hope were deliberating whether they should advance further when suddenly a circle of smoke veiled the huge pile of stone and a dozen bullets came whistling around D'Artagnan and his two companions. They knew all they wanted to know—the bastion was garrisoned. To stay in that dangerous spot any longer would have been a foolish lack of caution. D'Artagnan and the two guardsmen beat a hasty retreat.

As they reached the turn in the trench that was to serve them as a rampart one of the guardsmen fell, shot through the chest. The other one, who was unhurt, ran on toward the camp. D'Artagnan, unwilling to abandon his comrade, bent over him to get him to his feet and help him back to the camp. At that moment two shots were fired; one bullet shattered the head of the wounded guardsman, the other passed within two inches of D'Artagnan's head and was flattened on a rock.

D'Artagnan turned round quickly. That attack could not come from the bastion, for it was hidden by the turn in the trench. Could it come from the two soldiers who had abandoned him? That reminded him of the murderers of two days ago. This time he determined to find out who it was he had to deal with. He fell over the body of his comrade as if he too were dead. Soon he saw two heads rise above an abandoned earthenwork some thirty paces away. They were the heads of the two privates. D'Artagnan had not been mistaken; those two men had followed him only in order to murder him, hoping that his death would be put to the account of the enemy.

But as he might be only wounded and able to proclaim their crime, they approached him to make sure, and if necessary, to finish him. Fortunately, deceived by D'Artagnan's ruse, they neglected to reload their guns. When they were within ten paces of him, D'Artagnan sprang up, sword in hand. The assassins realized that if they fled to the camp without having killed their man, he would denounce them, so now they decided to go over to the enemy. One of them grasped his gun by the barrel and, using it like a club, aimed a fearsome blow at D'Artagnan. He avoided it by leaping aside, but in doing so he left the way clear for the bandit to make for the bastion. As the men of the garrison of La Rochelle knew nothing of the intentions of the man they saw coming, they opened fire on him and he fell, his shoulder broken by a bullet.

Meanwhile D'Artagnan had attacked the second soldier with his sword, and it was no long fight. The wretch had only an empty harquebus to defend himself with. The guardsman's sword grazed the barrel of the man's useless weapon and pierced the thigh of the murderer. He fell, and D'Artagnan pressed the point of his sword against his throat.

"Oh, don't kill me!" cried the bandit. "Have mercy on me, Monsieur l'Officier, have mercy on me and I will tell you all."

"Is your secret worth enough to me to induce me to spare your life?" asked D'Artagnan.

"Yes, if you think life means something to a man of twenty like you who has everything before him, handsome and brave as you are."

"Speak quickly, you miserable wretch! Who gave you the task of murdering me?"

"A woman I don't know, but my comrade knew her, and he called her Milady. She made the bargain with him, not with me. He even has a letter from her in his pocket, a letter that is of very great importance to you, so he told me."

"And how much did she give you two for this fine enterprise?"

"A hundred louis."

"Well, all right," said D'Artagnan with a smile. "She must think I'm worth something. A hundred louis! That's a sum to tempt a pair of rascals like you two. I understand why you accepted the job and I will spare your life—but on one condition."

"What is it?" asked the soldier anxiously.

"That you will go and fetch me the letter your comrade has in his pocket."

"Why," cried the bandit, "that's only another way of killing me! How can I go to get that letter under fire from the bastion?"

"You must nevertheless make up your mind to go and get it or I swear you shall die by my hand."

"Have mercy on me, monsieur! In the name of that young lady you love and whom you perhaps think is dead but who is alive!" cried the bandit, falling on his knees.

"And how do you know that there is a young woman I love, and that I thought that woman was dead?" demanded D'Artagnan.

"By that letter my comrade has in his pocket."

"Then you understand that I must have that letter," said D'Artagnan. "So no more delay now, no more hesitation, or however reluctant I may be to soil my sword again with the blood of a rascal like you, I swear by the faith of an honest man——" And as he said this he made so threatening a gesture that the wounded man got to his feet.

"Stop, stop!" cried the man, as terror gave him fresh courage. "I will go, I will go!"

D'Artagnan took the soldier's harquebus and drove the man forward, prodding him with the point of his sword. It was a fearsome thing to see the miserable fellow trying to drag himself along without being seen from the bastion toward the corpse of his accomplice twenty paces away, leaving a trail of blood behind him. Terror was so evident on that face covered with a cold sweat that D'Artagnan took pity on him, and, looking at him with contempt, he said:

"All right, I'll show you the difference between a man of courage and a coward like you. Stay here—I will go myself."

With a nimble step and his eyes watching for every movement of the enemy, and taking advantage of every accident of the terrain, D'Artagnan eventually reached the soldier's corpse. There were two means of gaining his end: He could either search the body on the spot or he could carry it back, using it as a shield for his own body, and search it in the trench.

D'Artagnan preferred the second method, and he lifted the murderer's corpse to his shoulders at the very moment that the enemy opened fire. A slight shock, the dull sound of three bullets penetrating human flesh, a last cry and a shudder of agony, told D'Artagnan that the man who had tried to murder him had just saved his life.

D'Artagnan reached the trench safely and laid the corpse by the body of the wounded man. Then he began his search. A leather wallet, a purse in which was what was evidently part of the sum the blackguard had received, a dicebox and a pair of dice—such were the dead man's heirlooms. He left the dicebox and the dice where they had fallen, tossed the purse to the wounded man, and opened the wallet eagerly. Among various papers of no importance he found the following letter:

Since you have lost all trace of that woman and she is now safe in a convent that you should never have allowed her to reach, try at least not to miss the man. If you do, remember that my arm reaches very far, and that you shall pay dearly for the hundred louis I gave you.

There was no signature, but the letter was obviously from Milady. He kept it as evidence, and sheltered by the turn of the trench, he began to question the wounded man. The fellow admitted that with his comrade he had undertaken to carry off a young woman who was to be taken out of Paris by the Porte de La Villette. But they had stopped at a tavern to drink, and so had missed the carriage by ten minutes.

"But what were you to do with that woman?" asked D'Artagnan in a tone of anguish.

"We were to take her to a house on the Place Royale."

"Yes, yes," murmured D'Artagnan, "that's it—to Milady's."

Then he shuddered as he saw so clearly what a terrible thirst for vengeance was driving this woman to destroy not only him but all those who loved him. How well informed she was of what went on at Court! How easily she had discovered everything! Of course she had done so through the Cardinal. But he also saw clearly, and with real joy, that the Queen had finally discovered the prison where Madame Bonacieux was paying dearly for her loyalty, and had set her free. As Athos had predicted, it would be possible to find Madame Bonacieux. A convent is not impregnable.

That thought aroused D'Artagnan's pity again. He turned to the wounded man, who was watching him anxiously, and held out his arm to him.

"Come," he said, "I'm not going to leave you like this. Lean on me, and we'll go back to the camp."

"Yes," said the man, who could hardly believe in such magnanimity, "but only to have me hanged, you mean, don't you?"

"No, I give you my word. For the second time I am sparing your life."

The man fell on his knees, seeking to kiss the feet of his savior, but D'Artagnan cut short these evidences of his gratitude.

The guardsman who had returned after the first shot had reported that all four of his companions were dead, so everyone was much surprised and much delighted to see D'Artagnan return safe and sound. He explained the sword thrust his companion had received by a sortie that he improvised gaily. He told of the death of the other soldier and the perils his party had encountered. The recital was the occasion of a veritable triumph for him. For a whole day the Army talked of nothing else, and the Duc d'Orléans sent him his personal congratulations. Moreover, as every brave deed brings its own reward, D'Artagnan's fine exploit restored to him the peace of mind he had lost. In fact, he felt that since of his two late enemies one had been killed and the other was devoted to his interests, he could enjoy tranquillity—a tranquillity that proved one thing: D'Artagnan did not yet know Milady.

CHAPTER 40

AFTER MOST DISHEARTENING NEWS OF THE KING'S ILL-
ness, a report that he was convalescent was now current in the camp, and
it was said that as soon as he could mount a horse he would set out.
Meanwhile Monsieur, the Duc d'Orléans, did little, as he knew that at any
moment he might be relieved of his command by the Duc d'Angoulême
or Bassompierre or Schomberg, who were all eager for his post. He
wasted day after day in indecision, and he dared not attempt any large-
scale enterprise to drive the English from the Ile de Ré, where they were
still besieging the citadel of Saint-Martin and the Fort de la Prée, just as
the French were besieging La Rochelle.

Meanwhile D'Artagnan had become somewhat more tranquil, as always happens after a danger has passed, especially when the danger
seems to have vanished. His only anxiety now was because he had no
news of his friends. But one morning early in November everything was
explained—or seemed to be—by the following letter:

Monsieur D'Artagnan:

Messieurs Athos, Porthos, and Aramis, after having eaten a good dinner
at my place and enjoyed themselves greatly, created such a disturbance that
the provost of the castle, a very strict man, ordered them to be confined to
their quarters for several days. But I am carrying out their orders by sending
you a dozen bottles of my Anjou wine, which they found so much to their
taste. They want you to drink their healths in their favorite wine.

In obeying them I am, monsieur, with great respect,
Your most humble and obedient servant,
Godeau
Steward of the Musketeers

"That's good!" cried D'Artagnan. "They remember me in their pleasures as I remember them in my troubles. Most certainly I shall drink to
their healths, and with all my heart. But I will not drink alone."

He hurried off to invite two of the guardsmen he had come to know
the best to enjoy with him the delicious light Anjou wine he had just received from Villeroi. One of the two guardsmen had an engagement that

evening and the other had one for the next day, so the meeting was set for two days later. On his return to his quarters D'Artagnan sent the twelve bottles to the guards' canteen with orders to take good care of it. Then on the festive day, as the dinner was to be at noon, he sent Planchet to the canteen at nine in the morning to get everything ready.

Planchet, very proud of being promoted to the dignity of maître d'hôtel, determined to make all the arrangements in the most intelligent way. With this purpose he enlisted the services of the lackey of one of the guests, a lad named Fourreau, and the pretended soldier who had tried to kill D'Artagnan. That man, whose name was Brisemont, did not belong in the ranks, and since his life had been spared by D'Artagnan, had entered his service, or rather that of Planchet.

The hour of the feast arrived. The two guests took their places and the viands were put on the table. Planchet acted as waiter, Fourreau uncorked the bottles, and Brisemont decanted the wine, which seemed to have acquired a good deal of sediment as a result of its being shaken in its travels. The first bottle was a little cloudy toward the bottom. Brisemont poured the lees into a glass, and D'Artagnan told him he might drink it, for the poor devil was still very weak.

After they had eaten their soup, the guests were about to lift the first glass to their lips when suddenly the cannon of Fort Louis and Fort Neuf roared. All the guardsmen, thinking this might mean a surprise attack, either by the French in La Rochelle or by the English, sprang to their swords, and all three ran to their posts.

But they had barely left the canteen when they discovered that the cannon were firing a salute. Cries of "Long live the King!" "Long live Monsieur le Cardinal!" rang out on every side, and all the drums in the camp were beating. In his impatience to get to La Rochelle the King had proceeded by forced marches, and was arriving at that very moment, with all his household and a reinforcement of 10,000 troops, his musketeers preceding and following him. From his post in the ranks of his company D'Artagnan saluted his friends with a gesture of welcome. Their eyes met his, and so did those of Monsieur de Tréville, who was the first to recognize him. The ceremonies of the arrival over, the four friends were soon embracing each other.

"By the Lord," cried D'Artagnan, "you couldn't have come at a better time! The dinner hasn't had time to get cold yet. Isn't that right, gentlemen?" he added, turning to the two guardsmen. Then he presented them to his friends.

"Ah, ah, so we're banqueting, are we?" said Porthos.

"I trust there are no women at your dinner," remarked Aramis.

"Is there any drinkable wine in your shanty?" asked Athos.

"Why, by the Lord, this is your own wine, my dear friends," D'Artagnan replied.

"*Our* wine?" Athos asked in astonishment.

"Yes, the wine you sent me—that light wine from the slopes of Anjou."

"And so, connoisseurs in wine that we are, we sent you Anjou wine, did we?" said Porthos.

"Not exactly. You ordered the wine sent to me in your names."

"Did you send the wine, Aramis?" asked Athos. "Or you, Porthos?"

"No," answered each.

"Did you, Athos?" Porthos asked.

"No."

"Well, if it wasn't any of you, it was the steward of your mess— Godeau, the steward of the musketeers."

"By my faith, never mind where it comes from," said Porthos. "Let's taste it, and if it's good, let's drink it."

"No," said Athos, "let us drink no wine that comes from an unknown source."

"You are right, Athos," said D'Artagnan. "But did none of you order Godeau to send me wine?"

"No! Yet you say he sent you some as coming from us?"

"Here is his letter!" said D'Artagnan.

"That's not Godeau's handwriting!" declared Athos. "I know his writing because before we left Villeroi I settled the regimental accounts at the mess."

"It's a forgery," Porthos declared. "We were never confined to quarters."

"D'Artagnan," said Aramis reproachfully, "how could you possibly believe that we had created a disturbance?"

D'Artagnan grew pale and shuddered.

"Thou alarmest me!" said Athos, who never used "thee" and "thou" except on very special occasions. "What does this mean?"

"Make haste, make haste, my friends!" cried D'Artagnan. "A horrible suspicion crosses my mind! Can this be another vengeance on the part of that woman?"

It was Athos who grew pale now. D'Artagnan rushed toward the canteen, the three musketeers and the two guardsmen following him. The first thing that met D'Artagnan's eyes when he entered the canteen was Brisemont stretched out on the floor and writhing in horrible convulsions. Planchet and Fourreau, both deathly pale, were trying to help him, but it was plain that any attempt to succor him was futile. His features were distorted in agony.

"Ah," he cried when he saw D'Artagnan, "this is terrible. You pretend to spare my life and you poison me!"

"I?" cried D'Artagnan. "I, you miserable wretch! What are you saying?"

"I say that it was you who gave me that wine, you that told me to drink it."

"Don't think that for a moment, Brisemont," protested D'Artagnan. "I swear to you——"

"Oh, but God is there above, God will punish you! O God, make this man suffer someday what I am suffering now!"

"I swear to you on the Gospels," cried D'Artagnan, throwing himself down by the dying man, "that I did not know the wine was poisoned. I was about to drink it myself, as you did."

"I don't believe you!" said the soldier. Then he expired writhing in agony.

"Horrible, horrible!" murmured Athos. Porthos was breaking the bottles and Aramis was giving somewhat belated orders to fetch a confessor.

"O my friends," said D'Artagnan, "once again you have saved my life, and not only mine, but the lives of these two gentlemen. Gentlemen," he went on, addressing the guardsmen, "I ask you never to speak of this affair. Persons highly placed may have been involved in the scene you have witnessed, and if that is true, evil might befall all of us. Gentlemen, you understand that a banquet like this could only be a melancholy one after what has happened. Pray accept my excuses; we will put it off for another day."

The guardsmen accepted D'Artagnan's excuses courteously and, understanding that the four friends wished to be alone, they withdrew. When the young guardsman and the three musketeers were without witnesses, they looked at each other meaningly; all of them understood the seriousness of the situation.

"First," said Athos, "let us leave this room. A dead man is not pleasant company, especially one who died a violent death."

"Planchet," said D'Artagnan, "I commit the corpse of this poor devil to your care. See that he is buried in holy ground. He committed a crime, it is true, but he repented."

The four friends left the room. The steward gave them another room, where he served them eggs in the shell, and water that Athos went to draw from the well himself.

"Well," D'Artagnan said to Athos, "you see, my dear friend, that this is war to the death."

Athos shook his head. "Yes, yes," he said, "I see that quite plainly. But do you really think it is *she?*"

"I am sure that it is."

"Yet I confess that I still have my doubts."

"But that fleur-de-lis on her shoulder?"

"She may be an Englishwoman who committed some crime in France and was branded for it."

"Athos, it is your wife, I tell you," D'Artagnan insisted. "Don't you recall how much alike our descriptions of her were?"

"Yes," Athos agreed. "Still, I should think the other one must be dead. I hanged her so thoroughly!"

It was D'Artagnan's turn to shake his head. "But what are we to do now?" he asked.

"We certainly cannot go on with a sword hanging eternally over our heads," replied Athos. "We must get out of this situation. Listen, D'Artagnan, you must try to meet her again and get her to explain her position. Say to her: 'Is it to be peace or war? I give you my word as a gentleman that I will never say a word about you, that I will never do anything against you. On your side, I ask for a solemn oath that you will remain neutral with regard to me. Otherwise I will apply to the Chancellor, to the King, to the public executioner; I will stir up the Court against you; I will denounce you as a branded woman; I will have you brought to trial, and if you are acquitted—well, by my faith as a gentleman, I will kill you myself as I would kill a mad dog!' "

"I like that method well enough," said D'Artagnan, "but where and how can I meet her again?"

"Time, my dear friend, brings opportunity, opportunity is man's game of double or quits. The more we have at stake, the more we win when we know how to wait."

"Yes, but to wait surrounded by assassins and poisoners——"

"Bah!" said Athos. "God has preserved us hitherto, God will preserve us still."

"And besides, we are men and after all, to risk our lives is our natural lot," said D'Artagnan. "But what about Constance?"

"Oh, Madame Bonacieux," said Athos. "My poor friend, I had forgotten you are in love."

"Well," said Aramis, "didn't you find out from the letter you found on the dead ruffian that she is in a convent? One can be very comfortable in a convent. I will be responsible for finding out where she is."

"You, Aramis?" asked first one, then another. "How?"

"Through the Queen's almoner, whom I happen to know very well," answered Aramis, blushing.

On this assurance, their modest meal finished, the four friends separated, promising to meet again that evening.

CHAPTER 41

MEANWHILE THE KING, WHO SHARED THE CARDINAL'S hatred for Buckingham, but with more reason for it, was in such haste to meet the enemy that he made all necessary preparations in order first to drive the English out of the Ile de Ré and next to press the siege of La Rochelle.

Conditions were favorable. The English, who require good food above all else in order to fight well, were living on salt meat and moldy hardtack. Many of them fell sick. Moreover the sea, always very rough at that time of year along the Mediterranean coast, destroyed some little vessel or other every day. Even if the King's troops stayed quietly in their camp it was evident that Buckingham, who only held onto the island through obstinacy, would be forced to raise the siege before long. But as Monsieur de Toirac reported that preparations for a fresh assault were being made in the enemy camp, the King, judging it well to get the whole affair finished, gave the necessary orders for a decisive action.

This undertaking succeeded, to the great astonishment of the King and to the great glory of Monsieur le Cardinal. The English, driven back foot by foot, beaten in every encounter, were forced to take to their ships again, leaving 2000 men on the battlefield, as well as four cannon and sixty battle flags. Te Deums were sung in camp and throughout all France.

The Cardinal was now free to carry on the siege of La Rochelle without having anything to fear, at least for the present, from the English. But this respite was a short one. Through the capture of an envoy of the Duke of Buckingham, a certain Lord Montague, proof was obtained of a league between the Holy Roman Empire, Spain, England, and Lorraine, a league directed against France. Further, in Buckingham's quarters, which he had been forced to abandon more hurriedly than he had expected, papers were found that confirmed the existence of this league, and as the Cardinal asserts in his memoirs, they strongly compromised Madame de Chevreuse, and consequently the Queen. The whole responsibility for this affair fell on the Cardinal, for no man can be a despotic Minister without assuming responsibility. All the resources of his great genius were strained as he listened night and day for even the vaguest rumor current in any one of the great kingdoms of Europe. If the league that was threatening France were to triumph, Richelieu's influence would come to its end. Spanish policy and Austrian policy would have their representatives in the Louvre Cabinet, where as yet they had only partisans, and he, Richelieu, the French Minister, the national Minister, would be ruined. The King, while obeying him like a child, hated him as a boy hates his schoolmaster, and would abandon him to the personal vengeance of the Duc d'Orléans and Anne of Austria. He must guard against that.

So it was that in the little house by the Pont de La Pierre where the Cardinal had established his headquarters couriers arrived one after the other by day and by night, and their numbers increased constantly. There were monks who wore the frock with such ill grace that it was easy to see that they belonged to the Church Militant. There were women somewhat embarrassed by their page-boy dress, the wide breeches of which could not conceal their feminine curves. There were peasants with dirty hands but with slender legs who a league away bore the stamp of men of rank. Then there were other less agreeable visitors, for two or three times it was reported that the Cardinal had escaped assassination but narrowly. Yet these attempts did not keep the Cardinal, whose personal bravery his most inveterate detractors have never denied, from making nocturnal excursions for purposes of his own.

As for the musketeers, who had little to do during the siege, they were not under strict orders, and they led a merry life, especially our three comrades. Being friends of Monsieur de Tréville, they easily obtained his permission to be away from the camp after it was officially closed. Now one evening when D'Artagnan could not accompany them because he was on duty in the trenches, Athos, Porthos, and Aramis, mounted on their war horses, wrapped in their great cloaks, and with their hands on the butts of their pistols, were returning from a tavern called The Red Dovecote. They were riding along the road to the camp, keeping well on guard for fear of an ambush, when at a quarter of a league from the village of Boinar they fancied they heard the sound of horses coming toward them. Immediately all three halted, closed in, keeping to the middle of the road, and waited. An instant later the moon broke out from behind a cloud and they saw two horsemen at a bend in the road. When the newcomers saw them, they halted in their turn, apparently to deliberate whether they should continue their way or turn back. This hesitation aroused the suspicion of the three friends, and Athos, riding a few paces ahead of the others, called out in a firm voice:

"Who goes there?"

"Who goes there yourselves?" one of the horsemen replied.

"That's no answer," said Athos. "Who goes there? Answer **or we** charge."

"Beware of what you do, gentlemen," retorted a clear voice in what was evidently an accustomed tone of command.

"That's some officer making his night rounds," Athos murmured. Then he called out:

"What do you want, gentlemen?"

"Who are you?" replied the same voice in the same tone of command. "Answer in your turn or you may find yourselves in trouble for your disobedience."

"Royal Musketeers," answered Athos, more and more convinced that their questioner spoke with authority.

"What company?"

"Monsieur de Tréville's."

"Advance and account for what you are doing here at this late hour."

The three companions rode forward rather crestfallen, for they were all sure now that they were facing someone much more powerful than they were. One of the two horsemen, the one who had spoken last, was some ten paces ahead of his companion. Athos motioned to Porthos and Aramis to stay where they were and rode ahead alone.

"Pardon us, Monsieur l'Officier," he said, "but we did not know who it was we had to deal with, and as you can see, we were keeping good guard."

"Your name?" demanded the officer, partially covering his face with his cloak.

"But you yourself, monsieur," rejoined Athos, who was beginning to resent this inquisitor, "I beg you to give me some proof that you have a right to question me."

"Your name?" demanded the horseman a second time, letting his cloak drop to leave his face uncovered.

"Monsieur le Cardinal!" cried the musketeer in amazement.

"Your name?" His Eminence asked for the third time.

"Athos," replied the musketeer.

The Cardinal gestured to his equerry to draw near. "These three musketeers are to follow us," he said in an undertone. "I do not wish to have it known that I have left camp, and if they are with us we shall make certain that they tell no one."

"We are gentlemen, Monseigneur," protested Athos. "Ask us to give you our word and you need not worry about that. Thank God we can keep a secret!"

"You have keen ears, Monsieur Athos," said the Cardinal. "But listen to me—it is not from mistrust that I request you to follow me, but for my personal security. Your companions are doubtless Messieurs Porthos and Aramis?"

"Yes, Your Eminence," Athos replied as the two musketeers rode up, hat in hand.

"I know you, gentlemen," said the Cardinal, "I know you. I know you are not exactly friends of mine, and I am sorry for that. But I also know you are brave and loyal gentlemen, and that you are trustworthy. Monsieur Athos, pray do me the honor, you and your two friends, to accompany me. Then I shall have an escort that will excite the envy of His Majesty if we should chance to meet him."

The three musketeers bowed till their heads touched the necks of their horses.

"Very well," said Athos. "Upon my honor, Your Eminence is right in taking us with you. We saw several rascally faces on the road, and we even had a quarrel at The Red Dovecote with four of those faces."

"A quarrel?" said the Cardinal. "You know I don't like quarrels, gentlemen. What was this one about?"

"The wretches were drunk," replied Athos. "They knew a woman had arrived at the tavern this evening, and they tried to break down her door—to offer her some violence, doubtless. I had the honor to inform Your Eminence that the wretches were drunk."

"And was this woman young and good-looking?" asked the Cardinal somewhat anxiously.

"We did not see her, Monseigneur," Athos replied.

"You didn't see her? Ah well," said the Cardinal quickly, "you acted rightly in defending a woman's honor. Was the lady alone?"

"There was a cavalier with her, but despite the hullabaloo he did not appear. Evidently he was a coward."

" 'Judge not,' says the Gospel," replied the Cardinal. Athos bowed. "And now, gentlemen," the Cardinal continued, "follow me."

The three musketeers fell in behind His Eminence, who again covered his face with his cloak and rode off slowly, keeping some ten paces ahead of his companions. They soon reached the silent, solitary tavern. Doubtless the host knew what an illustrious visitor he expected and had got rid of all intruders.

Ten paces from the tavern door, the Cardinal signaled to his equerry and the three musketeers to halt. A saddled horse was tethered to a shutter. The Cardinal knocked three times in a special way. A man wrapped in a cloak came out at once and exchanged a few swift words with the Cardinal, then mounted the horse and rode off in the direction of Surgières, which was also the direction of Paris.

"Advance, gentlemen," the Cardinal commanded, turning to the musketeers. "You told me the truth, gentlemen, and it will not be my fault if our encounter this evening does not prove to be to your advantage. Meanwhile, follow me."

The Cardinal dismounted, so did the musketeers. The Cardinal tossed the bridle of his horse to the equerry, the three musketeers tethered their horses to the shutter. Mine host stood at the door. To him, the Cardinal was merely an officer coming to visit a lady.

"Have you a room on the ground floor where these gentlemen can wait for me by a good fire?" the Cardinal asked.

The host opened the door of a large room in which a rickety old stove had just been replaced by a fine large fireplace.

"I have this one, monsieur," he said.

"That will do very well," said the Cardinal. "Go in there, gentlemen, and be good enough to wait for me. I shall not be more than half an hour."

And while the three musketeers were entering the ground-floor room the Cardinal, without asking for further information, was mounting the staircase like a man who does not need to be shown the way.

CHAPTER 42

IT WAS EVIDENT THAT, WITHOUT SUSPECTING IT AND prompted only by their chivalrous and adventurous character, our three friends had recently rendered a service to someone whom the Cardinal honored with his special protection. Now who was this someone? That was the question the three musketeers put to each other first. Then, realizing that none of the answers any of them could make was satisfactory, Porthos summoned the host and asked for dice.

Porthos and Aramis sat down at a table and began to play. Athos walked about, lost in thought. While he was thinking and walking back and forth, he kept passing by the broken stovepipe, the upper end of which evidently entered the room above, and every time he did so he heard a murmur of voices that finally attracted his attention. He went close to the break in the pipe and distinguished a few words that he thought of so great interest that he motioned to his companions to be silent. He bent down with his ear close to the lower end of the break.

"Listen, Milady," the Cardinal was saying, "this business is important. Sit down and let us talk it over."

"I am listening to Your Eminence most attentively," replied a woman's voice that made the musketeer tremble.

"A small vessel with an English crew, whose captain serves me, awaits you at the mouth of the Charente, at the Fort de La Pointe. It will sail tomorrow morning."

"Then I must go there tonight?"

"Instantly—that is to say, as soon as you have received my instructions. Two men whom you will find at the door as you leave this tavern will serve as your escort. You will allow me to leave first, then half an hour later you will set out."

"Very well, Monseigneur. Now let us come back to the mission you wish to entrust to me. Since I am most desirous of continuing to merit Your Eminence's confidence, pray deign to explain it to me in the most clear and precise terms, so that I may make no mistake."

An instant of profound silence followed. It was obvious that the Cardinal was considering carefully the terms in which he was about to speak.

Athos took advantage of this moment of silence to whisper to his two companions to close the door and to motion to them to come and listen with him. The two musketeers brought chairs, and all three sat down with their heads close together and their ears on the qui vive.

"You will go to London," the Cardinal continued, "and when you get there, you will go to see Buckingham."

"I must beg Your Eminence to remember," said Milady, "that His Grace has always suspected me of being concerned in the affair of the diamond tags, and since then he mistrusts me."

"Well," replied the Cardinal, "this time it's not a question of gaining his confiidence, but of presenting yourself openly and frankly as a go-between."

"I will follow Your Eminence's instructions to the letter. I am waiting to learn what I am to do."

"You will go to Buckingham on my behalf. You will tell him that I know all the preparations he is making, but that I am not disturbed by them, because at the first move he makes I will ruin the Queen."

"Will he believe that Your Eminence is in a position to carry out that threat?"

"Yes, for I have the proofs I need."

"I must be able to present these proofs to him."

"Of course. You will tell him that I will publish the reports made by Bois-Robert and the Marquis de Beautru on the interview the Duke had with the Queen on the evening at Madame la Connétable's masquerade. To convince him that I know everything, you will tell him that he went there in the costume of the Great Mogul that the Chevalier de Guise was to have worn, and that he gave the Chevalier three thousand pistoles for it."

"Very well, Monseigneur."

"You will tell him that I know every detail of his entering and leaving the Louvre on the night when he presented himself disguised as an Italian fortuneteller. So that he cannot doubt the correctness of my information, you will tell him that under his cloak he wore a large white robe sprinkled with black tears, deathsheads, and skulls and crossbones."

"Is that all, Monseigneur?"

"Tell him I know every detail of the adventure at Amiens, that I will have a little romance written about it, one wittily turned and illustrated by a plan of the garden and portraits of the principal actors in that nocturnal drama. Tell him further that Montague is in my hands, that he is in the Bastille, that though it is true that no letter was found on his person, torture may make him tell what he knows, and even—what he does not know."

"Capital!"

"Finally, add that when His Grace left the Ile de Ré so precipitately,

he forgot and left in his quarters a certain letter from Madame de Chevreuse that thoroughly compromises the Queen, in that it proves not only
that Her Majesty can love the King's enemies but also that she is conspiring with the enemies of France. . . . You remember perfectly all
that I have said, do you not?"

"Your Eminence shall judge: the masked ball given by Madame la
Connétable; the night at the Louvre; the evening at Amiens; the arrest of
Montague; the letter from Madame de Chevreuse."

"That's right," said the Cardinal, "quite right. You have an excellent
memory, Milady."

"But what if, despite all these reasons," asked Milady, "the Duke does
not give way and continues to threaten France?"

"The Duke is in love with the passion of a madman, or rather a fool,"
Richelieu answered with great bitterness. "Like the paladins of old, he
has undertaken this war only to win one glance from his ladylove. If he
becomes certain that the war may cost the lady of his thoughts, as he calls
her, her honor and perhaps her liberty, I assure you he will think twice."

"And yet," Milady argued, "if he persists?"

"If he persists——" His Eminence paused a moment. "If he persists—
well, I shall hope for one of those events which change the destinies of
nations. In all times and in all countries, especially in those where there
are religious differences, there will always be fanatics who ask nothing
better than to become martyrs. Wait a moment—I remember now that
the Puritans of England are furious against the Duke of Buckingham.
Their preachers call him the Antichrist. Well," the Cardinal went on in
an indifferent tone, "for example, we only need to find some beautiful,
clever young woman who has her own reasons to take revenge on the
Duke. Such a woman can surely be found. The Duke has had many love
affairs. If he has aroused love in many women by promises of eternal
constancy, he must have also aroused hatred in many by his eternal in-
fidelities."

"Doubtless she could be found," said Milady coolly, "though she would
be the accomplice of an assassin."

"What do you require for your mission?"

"I require an order ratifying beforehand everything I would find it
necessary to do for the greatest good of France."

"But first we must find some woman who longs for revenge on the
Duke."

"She has been found," said Milady. "And I need that order now."

"Then we must find a miserable fanatic who will serve as the instrument of God's justice."

"He shall be found."

"Very well," said the Cardinal-Duke, "when that is done it will be time
for you to claim the order you just asked for."

"Your Eminence is right," Milady replied, "and I was wrong in seeing in the mission with which you honor me anything but what it actually is— to tell His Grace, on behalf of Your Eminence, that you know——" And she repeated everything that the Cardinal had told her to say to Buckingham. "If he still persists, in spite of all that, my mission will have been accomplished, and I shall have nothing more to do except to pray to God to perform a miracle in order to save France. That is all, is it not, Monseigneur? I have nothing else to do?"

"That is all," the Cardinal replied dryly.

"And now," said Milady, without seeming to notice the Cardinal's change of tone, "now that I have received Your Eminence's instructions concerning his enemies, will Monseigneur permit me to say a few words about mine?"

"Have you enemies, then?" asked Richelieu.

"Yes, Monseigneur, enemies against whom you owe me all your support, since I made them in serving Your Eminence."

"Who are they?"

"In the first place, there is a little scheming woman named Bonacieux."

"She is in the prison of Mantes."

"She *was* there," Milady said, "but the Queen obtained an order from the King by which she was transferred to a convent."

"What convent?"

"That I do not know. The secret has been well kept."

"But *I* will find out!"

"And Your Eminence will let me know the name of the convent where that woman is?"

"I see no reason why I should not."

"Good! But I have another enemy I fear much more than I do that little Madame Bonacieux—her lover."

"What is his name?"

"Oh, Your Eminence knows him well!" cried Milady, trembling with anger. "He is the evil genius of both of us. It was he who in an encounter with Your Eminence's guards decided the victory in favor of the Royal Musketeers. It was he who wounded your emissary De Wardes four times. It was he who caused the affair of the diamond tags to miscarry. Finally, it was he who, knowing that it was I who had had Madame Bonacieux abducted, swore that I should die. . . . I mean that scoundrel D'Artagnan."

"He is a bold fellow," said the Cardinal.

"And just because he is bold, he is only the more to be feared."

"I must have a proof of his connection with Buckingham," said the Cardinal-Duc.

"A proof!" cried Milady. "I can furnish ten proofs."

"Well then, it's the simplest thing in the world. Get me that proof and I will send him to the Bastille."

"Fine, Monseigneur. But afterward?"

"Once a man is in the Bastille, there is no afterward," declared the Cardinal in a hollow voice. "By the Lord, if only it were as easy for me to get rid of my enemies as it is to get rid of yours, and if it were only people like that you wanted to feel safe from!"

"Monseigneur," said Milady, "a fair exchange—life for life, man for man. Give me that one and I will give you the other!"

"I don't know what you mean, nor do I ever wish to know," the Cardinal answered. "But I do wish to please you, and I see no reason why I should not give you what you ask with regard to so unimportant a person, especially as you say this chap D'Artagnan is a libertine, a duelist, and a traitor."

"An infamous scoundrel, Monseigneur, infamous!"

"Give me paper, pen, and ink, then."

"Here they are, Monseigneur."

There was a moment or two of silence; the Cardinal was evidently either thinking what terms to use or writing the letter. Athos, who had not lost a word of the conversation, took his companions by the hand and led them to the far end of the room.

"Well," said Porthos, "what do you want? And why didn't you let us hear the rest of the conversation?"

"Hush!" Athos warned. "We have heard all we need to hear. Besides, I am not preventing you from listening, but I must be off."

"You must be off!" asked Porthos. "But if the Cardinal asks for you, what are we to say?"

"You are not to wait until he asks. Speak first, and tell him I have gone on the lookout because something the host said made me think the road is not safe. I'll mention it to the Cardinal's equerry. As for the rest, that's my business, don't you worry about it."

"Be careful, Athos," said Aramis.

"Be easy on that head," Athos replied. "You know I'm cool enough."

Porthos and Aramis went back to their places by the stovepipe. Athos went out quite naturally, untied his horse, convinced the Cardinal's equerry of the need for a vanguard, mounted, examined the priming of his pistols pointedly, drew his sword, and rode off on the road that led to the camp.

CHAPTER 43

IT WAS NOT LONG BEFORE THE CARDINAL CAME DOWN. Opening the door of the room where the musketeers were, he found Porthos playing a hot game of dice with Aramis. With quick glances he searched every corner of the room, and saw that one man was missing.

"What has become of Monsieur Athos?" he asked.

"Monseigneur," Porthos answered, "he went out as a scout because something the host said made him think the road was not safe."

"And what have you been doing, Monsieur Porthos?"

"I've won five pistoles from Aramis."

"And now you may both come with me!"

"We are at Your Eminence's orders."

"To horse, then, gentlemen, for it is getting late."

The Cardinal's equerry was at the door, holding the bridle of His Eminence's horse. Not far away a group of two men and three horses could be seen standing in the shadows; these men were to escort Milady to the Fort de La Pointe and see that she boarded the ship. The equerry confirmed what the musketeers had told the Cardinal about Athos. His Eminence gestured his approval and took to the road again with the same precautions he had taken when he had arrived. Athos had ridden for a hundred paces at the slow gait with which he had started, but as soon as he was out of sight of the tavern he had put his horse to the trot and turned to the right, circled, and come back within twenty paces of a high ledge to watch for the arrival of the little troop. When he recognized the gold-laced hats of his comrades and the golden fringe of the Cardinal's cloak, he waited until the horsemen had turned the corner of the road, then galloped back to the tavern. The host recognized him at once.

"My commanding officer," said Athos, "forgot to give the lady some important information. He sent me back to——"

"Go on up," said the host. "She is still in her room."

Athos availed himself of the permission, went up the stairway with his lightest step, and from the landing, through the open door saw Milady putting on her hat. He went into the room and shut and bolted the door. At the sound, Milady turned and saw Athos standing in front of the door,

wrapped in his cloak, his hat pulled down over his eyes. When she saw
that figure, silent and motionless as a statue, Milady was terrified.

"Who are you," she cried, "and what do you want?"

"Hm," murmured Athos, "it is she!" Letting his cloak drop and taking
off his hat, he went toward Milady. "Do you recognize me, madame?" he
asked.

Milady took one step forward, then recoiled as if she were seeing a
snake.

"So far, so good," said Athos. "I see that you recognize me."

"The Comte de La Fère!" murmured Milady turning pale and retreating until the wall stopped her.

"Yes, Milady, the Comte de La Fère in person, who has come ex-
pressly from the other world to enjoy the pleasure of seeing you once
more. Let us sit down and talk, as the Cardinal said." Milady, in the grip
of indescribable terror, sat down without uttering a word. "So you are a
demon from Hell sent to the earth!" Athos went on. "Your power is
great, I know; but you yourself know that with God's help men have
often vanquished the most terrible demons. Once before you crossed my
path and I thought I had sent you underground, madame, but either I was
mistaken or Hell has brought you back to life again."

At these words, which recalled frightful memories, Milady bowed her
head with a hollow groan.

"Yes, Hell has brought you back to life," Athos continued. "Hell has
made you rich. Hell has given you another name, and almost a different
face. But it has effaced neither the stains on your soul nor the brand on
your body."

Milady leaped up as if she were moved by a powerful spring, and her
eyes flashed lightning. Athos sat unmoved and went on:

"You thought me dead, did you not, as I thought you were dead? And
the name Athos concealed the Comte de La Fère just as the name Lady
Clark concealed the name Anne de Bueil! Wasn't that the one you bore
when your honorable brother married us? Our position is truly a strange
one," and Athos laughed. "We are alive now only because each believed
the other was dead."

"But tell me what brings you back to me?" said Milady. "And what do
you want of me?"

"I want to tell you that while I have remained out of your sight, I have
not lost sight of you, I assure you. I can tell you what you have been doing day by day, ever since you entered the service of the Cardinal." An
incredulous smile touched Milady's pale lips. "Listen!" Athos went on.
"It was you who cut off the two diamond tags from the shoulder of the
Duke of Buckingham. It was you who had Madame Bonacieux abducted.
It is you who, in love with De Wardes and thinking to spend the night
with him, opened your bedroom door to Monsieur d'Artagnan. It is you

who, thinking that De Wardes had betrayed you, tried to have him killed by his rival. It is you who when his rival discovered your shameful secret sought to have him killed by two assassins you sent in pursuit of him. It was you who, learning that their bullets had missed him, sent the poisoned wine with a forged letter that would make your victim think the wine came from his friends. Finally, it is you who a few minutes ago, sitting in the chair where I am sitting now, promised the Cardinal de Richelieu to have the Duke of Buckingham assassinated, in exchange for his promise to allow you to assassinate D'Artagnan."

Milady was livid. "You must be Satan!" she cried.

"Perhaps I am," Athos retorted. "But at all events listen to this: Murder the Duke of Buckingham or have him murdered, it matters little to me! I do not know him, and besides, he is an Englishman. But if you lay one finger on one hair of D'Artagnan's head, I swear by my father's soul that that crime will be your last."

"Monsieur d'Artagnan has insulted me cruelly," said Milady in a somber tone. "Monsieur d'Artagnan shall die."

"Is it really possible to insult you, madame?" asked Athos with a laugh. "He has 'insulted' you, and he must die?"

"He shall die," Milady repeated. "First that Bonacieux woman, then he."

Athos felt himself grow dizzy. The sight of this creature who had nothing womanly about her brought back terrible memories. He recalled how once, in a situation much less dangerous than now, he had tried to sacrifice her to his honor. His desire to kill her came back to him and ran through his veins like a raging fever. He rose, drew his pistol from his belt, and cocked it.

Milady, pale as a corpse, tried to cry out, but her frozen tongue could make no human sound; she could only growl like a wild beast. Athos slowly raised his pistol, stretched out his arm until the weapon almost touched Milady's forehead, and in a voice all the more terrible because it was so perfectly calm and so inflexibly resolute, said:

"Madame, you will give me this very instant the paper the Cardinal signed or upon my soul I will blow your brains out."

With any other man Milady might have preserved some doubt, but she knew Athos. Yet she stood motionless.

"You have one second in which to make your decision," said he.

Milady saw by the contraction of his features that he was about to pull the trigger. Quickly she put her hand into her bosom, drew out the paper, and held it out to Athos.

"Take it," she muttered, "and damn your soul!"

Athos took the paper, put his pistol back in his belt, went to the lamp to make sure it was the right paper, opened it, and read:

December 3, 1627

It is by my order and for the service of France that the bearer of this paper has done what he has done.

Richelieu

"And now," said Athos, resuming his cloak and putting on his hat, "now that I have drawn your fangs, you viper, sting me if you can."

He left the room without looking back once. At the outer door he found Milady's two escorts and the horse she was to ride.

"Gentlemen," he said, "you know the orders Monseigneur gave you. You are to escort this woman at once to the Fort de La Pointe and you are not to leave her until she is on the ship."

As this agreed perfectly with the orders they had received, they both nodded. As to Athos, he vaulted into his saddle and galloped off. But instead of following the road, he rode across the fields at a rapid pace, halting from time to time to listen. During one of these halts he heard the hoofbeats of several horses. He felt certain it was the Cardinal and his escort. He rode on to appear on the highway about two hundred paces from the camp.

"Who goes there?" he challenged as soon as he saw the horsemen.

"That must be our brave musketeer," said Richelieu. "Monsieur Athos, my thanks for the good guard you have kept for us. Gentlemen, we are back again. Take the gate on the left. The password is *Roi et Ré*."

The Cardinal bowed to the three friends and rode off.

"Well," said Porthos as soon as the Cardinal was out of hearing, "so he signed the paper she asked for!" And Aramis echoed him.

"I know he did," said Athos calmly, "because here it is."

The three friends did not say a word until they reached their quarters, except to give the password to the sentinels. Then they sent Mousqueton to tell Planchet that his master was urgently requested to come to their quarters as soon as he left the trenches.

Meanwhile, as Athos had foreseen, Milady found her escort and made no objection to going with them. For an instant she had felt inclined to ask to be escorted back to the Cardinal so that she could tell him all that had happened since she had seen him. But any revelation on her part would bring about a revelation on Athos's part. She might tell that Athos had hanged her, but then he would tell that she was branded. So she thought it was better to preserve silence, accomplish her difficult mission with her usual skill, and then, when everything had been done to the Cardinal's satisfaction, to go back to him and claim her vengeance.

After traveling all night, at seven in the morning she reached Fort de La Pointe. By eight she had embarked, and at nine the vessel weighed anchor and steered its course toward England.

CHAPTER 44

ON ARRIVING AT THE QUARTERS OF HIS THREE FRIENDS, D'Artagnan found them together in one of their rooms. Athos was meditating, Porthos was curling his mustache, Aramis was reading his prayers in a charming little prayer book bound in blue velvet.

"By the Lord, gentlemen," said D'Artagnan, "I hope what you have to tell me is worth the trouble of listening. If it isn't, I warn you that I will not forgive you for summoning me here instead of letting me get a little rest after a night spent in capturing and dismantling a bastion. Ah, why weren't you there, my friends! It was hot work!"

"We were somewhere else," replied Porthos, "where it was by no means cold!"

"Hush!" said Athos, frowning a little.

"Oh, oh," D'Artagnan contributed, understanding the musketeer's frown, "apparently there's something new going on here."

"Aramis," said Athos, "you dined day before yesterday at The Sign of the Heretic, didn't you?"

"I did."

"How did you fare?"

"Well, I fared very badly myself. Day before yesterday was a day of abstinence, and they had nothing but meat."

"What!" said Athos, "no fish at a seaport? But that isn't what I meant, Aramis. I want to know whether you were left alone and nobody bothered you."

"As I remember, there were not too many intruders. Indeed, Athos, we would be very comfortable at the Heretic, for what you're thinking about."

"Let's go to the Heretic, then," said Athos, "for here the walls are as thin as paper."

D'Artagnan, who was used to his friend's ways, realized immediately from a word, a gesture, or a sign from him when the situation was serious. He took Athos's arm and went out with him in silence. Porthos followed, chatting with Aramis. On their way they met Grimaud. Athos motioned him to follow, and Grimaud, as usual, obeyed in silence.

They arrived at the Heretic tavern at seven o'clock in the morning, just at daybreak. The four friends ordered breakfast and went into a room where the host said they would not be disturbed. Unfortunately they had chosen a bad hour for a private conference. Reveille had just sounded, all the troops in the camp were shaking off the drowsiness of the night and, to dispel the damp chill of the morning air, were coming to the inn for a first drink. Dragoons, Swiss mercenaries, guardsmen, musketeers, and hussars followed one another with a rapidity that might be very good business for the host but was far from welcome to the four friends.

"I see how it will be," said Athos. "We'll get into some pretty little quarrel or other, and we don't stand in need of one just now. D'Artagnan, tell us what sort of night you have had, and then we'll tell you about ours."

"Ah yes," said a man of the light cavalry, Busigny by name, "weren't you in the trenches last night, you guardsmen? You and the La Rochelle men had a bone to pick, didn't you?"

"Didn't you storm a bastion?" asked a Swiss who was drinking rum in a beer glass.

"Yes, monsieur," answered D'Artagnan with a bow, "we had that honor. We also set a barrel of powder under one of the angles, and when it blew up it made a nice little breach in the walls."

"What bastion was that?" inquired a dragoon who was sharing with a friend a goose spitted on his sword.

"The Saint-Gervais bastion," replied D'Artagnan.

"Did you have a hot time of it?"

"Yes, rather hot. We lost five men and the La Rochelle fellows lost eight or ten."

"But probably they will send sappers this morning to repair the damage," said Busigny.

"Yes, probably they will," said D'Artagnan.

"Gentlemen," said Athos, "I have a wager to propose."

"What is it?" asked the cavalryman.

"Well, Monsieur de Busigny, I wager that my three friends, Porthos, Aramis, and D'Artagnan, and myself will breakfast in the Saint-Gervais bastion and that we will stay there, watch in hand, a full hour, whatever the enemy may do to dislodge us."

Porthos and Aramis looked at each other; they were beginning to understand what Athos was planning.

"Look here," D'Artagnan whispered in Athos's ear, "You are going to get us all killed without mercy."

"We are much more likely to be killed if we do not go."

"I take your wager," said Monsieur de Busigny. "What shall the stake be?"

"You are four," Athos replied, "and there are four of us. Suppose we say a dinner for eight, with no limits on the cost. Will that do?"

"Wonderfully well," answered Monsieur de Busigny.

"Your breakfast is ready, gentlemen," announced the host.

"Bring it in then!" said Athos.

The host obeyed. Athos called Grimaud, pointed to a big basket lying in one corner and made motions as if he were wrapping food in a napkin. Grimaud understood instantly that this was to be a breakfast in the open, picked up the basket, packed the viands in it, added the bottles, and took the basket on his arm.

"Where are you going to eat my breakfast?" asked the host.

"What does it matter to you," asked Athos, "so long as we pay for it?" And he threw 2 pistoles onto the table with a lordly air.

"Shall I give you the change, Monsieur l'Officier?"

"No, mine host. Just add two bottles of champagne, and what is left will pay for the napkins."

"Monsieur de Busigny," said Athos, "will you be so good as to set your watch with mine, or to allow me to set mine with yours?"

"Certainly, monsieur," said the cavalryman, taking out his watch.

"Twenty-five minutes of eight," said Athos. "We will remember that my watch is five minutes ahead of yours, monsieur."

Bowing to the astonished men around them, the young men started off toward the Saint-Gervais bastion, followed by Grimaud carrying the basket. As long as they were in the camp area the four friends did not exchange a word. They were followed by some curious soldiers who had heard about the wager and wanted to discover what would come of it. But once they had crossed the line of circumvallation and found themselves in the open, D'Artagnan who was completely ignorant of what was going on, thought it was time to ask for an explanation.

"And now, my dear Athos," he implored, "will you be kind enough to tell me where we are going?"

"You can see plainly enough that we are going to the bastion."

"But what are we going to do there?"

"You know quite well that we are going to breakfast there."

"But why did we not breakfast at the Heretic?"

"Because we have some very important matters to discuss. It was impossible to talk for five minutes in that tavern with all those tiresome fellows coming and going, bowing to you and addressing you. Over there," Athos went on, pointing to the bastion, "at least no one can disturb us."

"But it seems to me," remarked D'Artagnan, "that we could have found some isolated spot on the downs or by the seashore."

"Where we would have been seen, all four of us, conferring together, and fifteen minutes later the Cardinal would have learned from his spies that we were holding a council. There is no spot where a bird cannot fly overhead, or a fish jump out of the water, or a rabbit come out of its burrow, and I truly believe that bird, fish, and rabbit are all spies for the Cardinal. Therefore we had best go on with our undertaking. Besides, we cannot retreat without dishonor. We made a wager that could not be foreseen, the true reason for which I defy anyone to guess. In order to win this wager we must stay in the bastion for one hour. Either we shall be attacked or we shall not be. If we are not, we shall have all the time we want to talk, and nobody will overhear us. If we are attacked, we will discuss our affairs just the same. Moreover, in defending ourselves we shall cover ourselves with glory."

"Yes," commented D'Artagnan, "and we will undoubtedly get plenty of bullets."

"Well, my dear lad," said Athos, "you know very well that the bullets that are most to be feared do not come from this enemy."

"But on an expedition like this surely we should have brought our muskets?" queried Porthos.

"You're being stupid, friend Porthos. Why should we load ourselves with a useless burden? Didn't you hear what D'Artagnan said about the attack last night—that five Frenchmen and eight or ten men from La Rochelle were killed?"

"What of it?"

"The bodies were not plundered, were they? Apparently, the victors had something more pressing to do. Well, we shall find their muskets, powder flasks, and cartridges. Instead of four musketeers—to call D'Artagnan one for the moment—and twelve bullets we shall have some fifteen guns, and a hundred charges to fire."

"O Athos," said Aramis, "truly you are a great man!"

Porthos nodded in agreement. D'Artagnan alone did not seem convinced.

When they reached the bastion, the four friends turned to look back. More than three hundred soldiers of all kinds were gathered at the camp gate, and in a separate group they could distinguish Monsieur de Busigny, the dragoon, the Swiss, and the fourth wagerer. Athos took off his hat, and hanging it on point of his sword, waved it in the air. All the spectators returned his salute, accompanying this courtesy with loud cheers. Then the four friends disappeared in the bastion, where Grimaud had preceded them.

CHAPTER 45

AS ATHOS HAD FORESEEN, THE BASTION WAS OCCUPIED
only by a dozen dead bodies, some their own French and some from
La Rochelle.

"Gentlemen," said Athos, who had assumed command of the expedition, "while Grimaud is setting the table for breakfast let us begin to collect guns and cartridges. We can talk while we are doing this necessary work. These, gentlemen," he added, pointing to the dead men, "cannot hear us."

"But we could throw them into the ditch," Porthos suggested, "after making sure that there is nothing in their pockets."

"Yes," said Athos. "That's Grimaud's job."

"Very well," said D'Artagnan, "let Grimaud search them and then throw them over the parapet."

"Have a care not to do that," said Athos. "They may be useful to us."

"Those dead men useful to us?" queried Porthos. "Nonsense! You're going mad, my dear friend."

" 'Judge not that ye be not judged,' says the Gospel and Monsieur le Cardinal," Athos answered. "How many guns, gentlemen?"

"Twelve," Aramis replied.

"How many cartridges?"

"Something like a hundred."

"That is quite as many as we need. Let us load the guns."

The four musketeers set to work. As they were loading the last musket Grimaud signaled that breakfast was ready. Athos, always by gestures, replied that that was well and pointing to a structure shaped like a pepper shaker, indicated to Grimaud that he was to stand guard there. The four friends sat down on the ground, their legs crossed like Turks or tailors.

"Now that there is no danger of being overheard," observed D'Artagnan, "I trust you are going to tell us your secret, Athos."

"I hope to procure for you at the same time amusement and glory, gentlemen," Athos began. "I have taken you for a delightful walk; here is a very delicious breakfast; and yonder five hundred persons who take us for madmen or heroes, two species of idiots that are pretty much alike."

"But the secret?" said D'Artagnan.

"The secret is that I saw Milady last night," announced Athos.

D'Artagnan was lifting his glass to his lips, but at the name of Milady his hand shook so badly that he put the glass on the ground again for fear of spilling the contents.

"You saw your wi——"

"Hush!" interrupted Athos, speaking low. "You forget, my dear fellow, that these gentlemen have not been initiated in my family secret as you have been." Then he said louder, "I saw Milady."

"Where?" asked D'Artagnan.

"About two leagues from here, at the Red Dovecote tavern."

"In that case I am a lost man," D'Artagnan said.

"No, not quite yet," replied Athos, "for by now she must have left the shores of France."

D'Artagnan breathed more easily.

"But after all, who is this Milady?" inquired Porthos.

"A charming woman," said Athos, sipping a glass of sparkling wine. "Yes, a very charming woman who was most kind to D'Artagnan. He played some dirty trick or other on her and she tried to get her revenge for it a month ago by getting him shot, a week ago by trying to poison him, and yesterday by demanding his head of the Cardinal."

"What! She demanded my head of the Cardinal?" cried D'Artagnan, pale with terror.

"Yes," said Porthos, "that's as true as the Gospel. I heard it with my own ears."

"So did I," said Aramis.

"Then it is useless to struggle any longer," said D'Artagnan, letting his arm fall to his side in discouragement. "I may as well blow my brains out and make an end of it."

"That's the last folly to commit," said Athos, "seeing that it is the only one there is no remedy for."

"I can never escape such enemies as these," D'Artagnan protested. "First, the unknown man at Meung; then the Comte De Wardes, whom I wounded four times; then Milady, whose secret I discovered; and now the Cardinal, whose revenge I thwarted."

"Well," said Athos, "that makes only four, and there are four of us—one against one. . . . By the Lord, if we can trust the signs Grimaud is making, we're going to have to deal with a far larger number than that! . . . What's up, Grimaud?" he asked. "Considering the seriousness of the situation, I permit you to speak, my friend. But be laconic, I beg you. What do you see?"

"A troop."

"How many in it?"

"Twenty men."

"What sort of men?"

"Sixteen sappers, four soldiers."

"How far away?"

"Five hundred paces."

"Good! We still have time to finish this fowl and drink a glass of wine to your health, D'Artagnan."

"To your health!" repeated Porthos and Aramis.

"Very well then, to my health! Though I don't think your good wishes will help me very much."

"Bah!" said Athos. "God is great, as the Mohammedans say so often, and the future is in His hands."

Then, draining his glass and setting it down beside him, Athos rose nonchalantly, took the first musket at hand, and went to one of the loopholes. Porthos, Aramis, and D'Artagnan followed his example. Grimaud was ordered to stand behind the four friends ready to reload their weapons. In a minute or two the troop appeared, advancing along a zigzag communication trench between the bastion and the city.

"By the Lord," said Athos, "it's hardly worth while to disturb ourselves for twenty rascals armed with pickaxes, mattocks, and shovels! Grimaud had only to motion to them to go away and I am convinced they would have left us alone."

"I doubt that," said D'Artagnan. "They are advancing very resolutely. Besides, with the sappers there are four soldiers and a corporal, all armed with muskets."

"By my faith," said Aramis, "I confess I have a great aversion to firing on those poor devils of townsmen."

"He's a bad priest who pities heretics," said Porthos.

"Really, Aramis is right," said Athos. "I'm going to warn them."

"What the devil are you doing?" cried D'Artagnan. "You'll get yourself shot, my dear fellow."

But Athos paid no heed to this admonition. He mounted the breach, musket in one hand and hat in the other, and called out to the advancing soldiers and sappers, who, amazed at this apparition, halted some fifty paces from the bastion. Bowing to them courteously, Athos said:

"Gentlemen, a few friends of mine and I are breakfasting in this bastion. Now you know that there is nothing more annoying than to be disturbed while eating breakfast. We therefore beg you, if you have any very important business here, either to wait until we have finished our meal or to come back later. Unless, of course, you have the salutary desire to quit the side of the rebels and come to drink with us to the health of the King of France."

"Look out, Athos!" cried D'Artagnan. "Can't you see that they are taking aim?"

"Of course," Athos replied. "But they are only townsmen, who are very poor marksmen, and I'm certain they won't hit me."

At that instant four shots were fired and the bullets flattened themselves against the wall all around Athos, but not one touched him. Four shots answered them almost instantaneously, but they were much better aimed than those of the aggressors. Three soldiers fell dead and one sapper was wounded.

"Grimaud, another musket!" called Athos.

Grimaud obeyed immediately. The three friends had already reloaded, and now they fired again. The corporal and two of the sappers fell dead; the rest of the troop took to flight.

"Now, gentlemen, a sortie!" said Athos.

The four friends rushed out of the fort, reached the scene of the fight, picked up the four soldiers' muskets and the corporal's short pike, and then, certain that the fugitives would not stop until they got to the city, returned to the bastion bearing the trophies of their victory.

"Reload the weapons, Grimaud," Athos ordered. "As for us, gentlemen, let us get back to our breakfast and resume our conversation. Where were we?"

"I remember," said D'Artagnan, who was much preoccupied with the itinerary Milady was following. "Where is Milady going?"

"She is going to England," Athos replied.

"For what purpose?"

"For the purpose of assassinating the Duke of Buckingham, or getting someone to assassinate him."

D'Artagnan uttered an exclamation of surprise and indignation. "But that is infamous!" he cried.

"Oh, as to that," said Athos, "I beg you to believe that I care very little. . . . Now that you have finished, Grimaud," he went on, "take the corporal's pike, tie a napkin to it, and plant it on the top of our bastion to let these La Rochelle rebels see that they have brave and loyal soldiers of the King to deal with."

Grimaud obeyed without replying. A moment later the white flag, the standard of the Bourbons, was waving over the heads of the four friends. A thunder of applause greeted its appearance. Half the men in the French camp were standing at the barrier.

"But why do you care so little whether she kills Buckingham, or has him killed?" D'Artagnan asked. "The Duke is our friend."

"The Duke is English, the Duke is waging war against us, let her do what she likes with the Duke. I care no more for him than I do for an empty bottle." And Athos threw some fifteen paces away from him a bottle he had emptied into his glass.

"Wait a minute," said D'Artagnan, "I'm not giving up Buckingham that way. He gave us some very handsome horses."

"And some very handsome saddles, too," said Porthos.

"Besides," Aramis contributed, "God wishes the conversion of a sinner, not his death."

"Amen," said Athos, "and we'll return to that subject presently, if such is your pleasure. But what was engaging my attention the most at the moment—and I am sure you will understand me, D'Artagnan—was to get back from this woman the paper with a blank endorsement that she extorted from the Cardinal and by means of which she could get rid of you, D'Artagnan, and perhaps of all of us, with impunity."

"And this blank endorsement," said D'Artagnan, "is it still in her hands?"

"No, it came into mine," Athos replied. "Here it is." And he took the priceless paper from his pocket.

D'Artagnan unfolded it with a hand the trembling of which he did not even attempt to conceal, and read:

December 3, 1627

It is by my order and for the service of France that the bearer of this paper has done what he has done.

Richelieu

"That paper must be destroyed," said D'Artagnan, who fancied he read his death sentence in it.

"On the contrary," said Athos, "we must preserve it as something very precious. I would not exchange it for as many gold pieces as would cover it."

"And what is she going to do now?" queried D'Artagnan.

"Oh, she will probably write to the Cardinal that a damned musketeer named Athos extracted her safe-conduct from her by force. In the same letter she will probably advise him to get rid of the musketeer's two friends Porthos and Aramis at the same time. The Cardinal will remember that these are the same men who are always crossing his path. So one fine morning he will have D'Artagnan arrested, and for fear he should be lonely, will send us three to keep him company in the Bastille."

"Come now," said Porthos, "it seems to me you are making very dull jokes, my friend."

"I am not joking," said Athos.

"I have an idea," said D'Artagnan.

"Let's have it."

But suddenly Grimaud shouted, "To arms!"

The young men sprang up and seized their muskets. This time a troop of some twenty-five men was advancing toward the bastion, but they were no sappers, they were all garrison soldiers.

"Come," said Aramis, "we must decide on a plan of action."

"That's very simple," Athos said. "As soon as the enemy are within range we fire. If they continue to advance, we fire again, we fire as long as we have loaded guns. If the survivors try to storm the place, we let them get as far as the ditch and then we push this strip of wall down on their heads. It's still standing only by some miracle of balance."

A moment or two later he shouted, "Fire!" The four shots roared together, four men fell. The drumbeat sounded at once and the little troop advanced at the double. Then the shots followed one another irregularly, but always with the same deadly accuracy. Nevertheless the men of La Rochelle, as if they knew the numerical weakness of the friends, continued to advance at the quickstep. At every three shots from the bastion at least two men fell, but the pace of those unscathed did not slacken. When the enemy reached the foot of the bastion, they still numbered twelve or fifteen. A last volley greeted them but did not stop them. They leaped into the ditch and got ready to scale the breach.

"Now, my friends," cried Athos, "let's finish them with one blow! To the wall, to the wall!"

And the four friends, seconded by Grimaud, pushed with the barrels of their muskets against a huge section of the wall. It leaned over as if it were battered by the wind. Then, loosened from its base, it fell with a horrifying crash into the ditch. A fearful cry rang out, a cloud of dust rose toward the heavens, and all was over.

"Can we have crushed every one of them?" asked Athos.

"By my faith, it looks like it," said D'Artagnan.

"No!" cried Porthos. "There go two or three of them limping away."

In fact three or four of these unfortunates, covered with mud and blood, were fleeing along the communication trench toward the city. Athos looked at his watch.

"Gentlemen," he said, "we have been here for an hour, and we have won the wager. But we must be good sportsmen. Besides, D'Artagnan has not told us about his idea."

"Well," said D'Artagnan. "My idea is to go to England a second time and find the Duke of Buckingham."

"You are not to do that, D'Artagnan," Athos said coldly.

"And why not? Haven't I done it once?"

"Yes, but at that time we were not at war. At that time the Duke of Buckingham was an ally, not an enemy. What you now contemplate doing would be called by an evil name—treason. Let us have your idea, Aramis."

"We must warn the Queen."

"Warn the Queen!" said Athos. "And how can we do that? Have we any connections at Court? Could we send anyone to Paris without its being known in the camp?"

"As to getting a letter to Her Majesty safely," said Aramis, blushing,

"I know a clever person at Tours——" And Aramis stopped as he saw Athos smile.

"Oho!" cried Athos. "What can be going on in the city? The drums are beating the general alarm. Mark my words, they are going to send a whole regiment against us."

"You don't expect to hold out against a whole regiment, do you?" said Porthos.

"Why not?" Athos replied. "I feel quite in the humor for it. If we had taken the precaution to bring along a dozen more bottles, I could hold out against a whole army. If we leave this place we shall never find another to suit us as well as this one. Wait a minute, gentlemen, I have it—the right idea has just occurred to me."

"Tell us what it is, then."

"First allow me to give Grimaud some indispensable orders." Athos motioned his lackey to approach. "Grimaud," he said, pointing to the bodies lying under the wall of the bastion, "pick those gentlemen up, prop them against the parapet, put their hats on the heads and their guns in their hands."

"O wonderful man!" cried D'Artagnan. "I understand now what you mean to do."

"Do you understand too, Grimaud?" asked Aramis. The lackey nodded assent.

"Now let's get back to my idea," said Athos.

"Yes, yes, your idea!" cried D'Artagnan.

"This Milady, this woman, this creature, this demon, has a brother-in-law, didn't you tell me, D'Artagnan?"

"Yes, I know him well. Also I believe that he has little affection for his sister-in-law."

"That's not bad," said Athos. "If he hates her, that's all the better for us. What is this brother-in-law's name?"

"Lord Winter."

"Where is he now?"

"He went back to London at the first rumor of war."

"Well," said Athos, "he's just the man we want. He's the man we must warn. We will let him know that his sister-in-law is planning to have someone assassinated, and we will beg him not to lose sight of her. There must be some institution for streetwalkers in London. He will have her put in one and our minds will be set at ease."

"Yes," said D'Artagnan, "until she gets out again. But who will take the letter to Tours and who the one to London?"

"I can vouch for Bazin," said Aramis.

"And I for Planchet," said D'Artagnan.

"Right. We cannot leave the camp," said Porthos, "but our lackeys can."

"Of course they can," said Aramis. "We'll write the letters this very day and send them off."

"Quick, on your guard!" cried D'Artagnan. "I see some black and red dots moving over there. Did you say a regiment, Athos? It's an army!"

"By my faith," said Athos calmly, "there they are. The sneaks are coming without beat of drum or sound of trumpet. Holà, Grimaud, have you finished?"

Grimaud nodded yes and pointed to a dozen corpses that he had set up in the most picturesque attitudes. Some were shouldering arms, others seemed to be taking aim, the rest had swords in their hands.

"Bravo, Grimaud!" cried Athos. "That does honor to your imagination."

"Let us beat a retreat," said D'Artagnan.

"Upon my word, I have no objection now to a retreat. We wagered that we would stay here an hour and we have been here an hour and a half. Let us be off, gentlemen."

Grimaud had already started, carrying the basket and what was left of the food. The four friends followed about ten paces behind him.

"Eh, what the devil are we doing, gentlemen?" cried Athos.

"Have you forgotten something?" Aramis asked.

" 'Sdeath, the white flag! We must not leave our flag in the hands of the enemy, even though that flag is only a napkin."

And Athos ran back into the bastion, stepped up on the gun platform, and took down the flag. As the men of La Rochelle had come within range, they opened a murderous fire on this man who was apparently exposing himself to it just for the pleasure of it. But Athos seemed to bear a charmed life; the bullets whistled all around him but not one of them touched him. He waved his flag, turning his back on the enemy, and saluting the men in the camp. From both sides loud shouts arose, from the enemy cries of anger, from the camp cries of enthusiasm. A second volley from the enemy followed the first one and three bullets pierced the napkin, making it a real battle flag. Cries of "Come down, come down!" were heard from the camp. Athos stepped down. His comrades, who were awaiting him anxiously, were full of joy when they saw him coming back.

Suddenly they heard a furious fusillade.

"What on earth is that?" asked Porthos. "What are they firing at now? There's no one in the bastion."

"They're firing at our dead men," Athos answered.

"But our dead men will not return their fire."

"Exactly. So those rebels will think it's an ambush, they will stop to think about it, and when they have found out that it is a joke, we shall be out of the range of their bullets."

A fresh volley sent bullets to stir the pebbles all around the four friends and to whistle close to their ears. At last the men of La Rochelle had taken possession of the bastion.

"Those fellows are bunglers," observed Athos. "But what's the matter with your hand, D'Artagnan? It's bleeding."

"It's nothing," said D'Artagnan. "A mere scratch. My fingers got caught between two stones, one in the wall and one in my ring, and the skin was broken."

"That's what comes of wearing diamond rings, my master," said Athos contemptuously.

"That's it!" cried Porthos. "We have a diamond, haven't we! And why the devil then do we complain about lack of money when we have a diamond? Let's sell it."

"But," protested D'Artagnan, "it's the Queen's diamond."

"All the more reason to sell it, D'Artagnan," returned Athos. "The Queen will be saving the Duke of Buckingham, her lover—nothing could be more fitting. The Queen will be saving us, her friends—nothing could be more ethical. Let us sell the diamond. What says Monsieur l'Abbé?"

"Why," said Aramis, blushing again, "in my opinion, since the ring is not the gift of a mistress and so not a love token, D'Artagnan may sell it."

"Very well," said D'Artagnan gaily, "we will sell the diamond and say no more about it."

"Upon my word," said Athos, "it was high time Porthos got this idea. Here we are back at the camp. Not a word more about all this. Our comrades are watching us, they are coming to meet us, probably they will carry us back on their shoulders in triumph."

Indeed the whole camp was carried away by enthusiasm. More than two thousand men had been watching the bravado of the four friends, without suspecting in the least the real reason for the exploit. On every side cries arose of "Long live the Royal Guards! Long live the Royal Musketeers!" Monsieur de Busigny was the first to come to seize Athos's hand and acknowledge that he and his companions had lost the wager. The dragoons and the Swiss followed him, then all their comrades followed them to offer their congratulations, with handshakes and embraces, and endless laughter at the expense of the men of La Rochelle.

At last the tumult grew so great that the Cardinal thought there must be a mutiny on foot and he sent La Houdinière, Captain of His Eminence's Guards, to discover what it was all about, and it was described to him with the greatest enthusiasm.

"Well?" asked the Cardinal when La Houdinière returned.

"Well, Monsiegneur, it appears that three musketeers and a guardsman wagered with Monsieur de Busigny that they would go to breakfast in the Saint-Gervais bastion. While they were breakfasting there they held the bastion for two hours against the enemy and killed I don't know how many of the men from La Rochelle."

"Did you inquire who the three musketeers were?"

"Yes, Monseigneur. They were Athos, Aramis, and Porthos."

"Always my three brave fellows!" murmured the Cardinal. "And the guardsman?"

"Monsieur d'Artagnan."

"Always my young scapegrace! Those four men must positively be mine."

That same evening the Cardinal spoke of the morning's exploit to Monsieur de Tréville, who had received an account of the adventure from the mouths of the heroes of it. He repeated every detail to His Eminence, and he did not forget the episode of the napkin flag.

"That's fine, Monsieur de Tréville," said the Cardinal. "Pray have that napkin sent to me. I will have the fleur-de-lis embroidered on it in gold and I will give it to your company as a guidon."

"Monseigneur," said Monsieur de Tréville, "that would be doing the Royal Guards an injustice. Monsieur d'Artagnan is not one of my men; he serves under Monsieur des Essarts."

"Well then, take him," said the Cardinal. "When four brave men are so attached to one another, they should not serve in different companies."

That same evening Monsieur de Tréville announced the good news to the three musketeers and to D'Artagnan, inviting all four to lunch with him the next day. D'Artagnan was beside himself with joy. We know that his lifelong dream was to become a musketeer. And his three friends were almost as joyful.

"Upon my word," D'Artagnan said to Athos, "that was a triumphant idea of yours! As you told us we would, we have acquired glory, and we were enabled to carry on a most important conversation."

"And we can resume that conversation now without anyone's being suspicious of us, for with the help of God we shall henceforth pass for cardinalists."

That evening D'Artagnan went to pay his respects to Monsieur des Essarts, and to inform him of the promotion he himself had received. Monsieur des Essarts, who was very fond of D'Artagnan, offered to assist him, as this change of corps would occasion heavy expenditure for equipment. D'Artagnan declined respectfully, but, thinking this a good opportunity, asked the Captain to have the diamond ring appraised and sold. The next morning at eight o'clock Monsieur des Essarts's lackey called on D'Artagnan and handed him a bag containing 7000 gold livres. That was the price of the Queen's diamond.

CHAPTER 46

THE LUNCHEON AT MONSIEUR DE TRÉVILLE'S WAS DE-lightfully gay. D'Artagnan was already wearing his new uniform. He and Aramis wore practically the same size, and as Aramis had been paid so generously by the publisher who had purchased his poem that he had bought double of everything, he had gladly supplied his friend with a complete outfit. D'Artagnan would have been full of joy over his fulfilled wishes had he not always seen Milady hovering like a dark cloud on the horizon.

After luncheon Athos and his friends agreed to meet that evening at Athos's lodgings to finish with the whole affair. There were now only three things to be decided upon. First, what they should write to Milady's brother-in-law; second, what they should write to the clever person at Tours; third, which two lackeys should carry the letters. As to this last point, Aramis said:

"Gentlemen, the chief consideration is not to decide which of the four lackeys is the most discreet, the strongest, the cleverest, or the bravest, but which one of them loves money most. Are our lackeys sufficiently de-voted to us to risk their lives for us? I say no."

"They will promise everything for the sake of the money, and when they are on the road fear will prevent them from acting," said Athos, who was an optimist where things were concerned and a pessimist in regard to men. "Once caught, they will be pressed; pressed, they will confess everything. Devil take it, we are not children! To reach England"—Athos lowered his voice—"a man must cross France, which is strewn with the Cardinal's spies and creatures. He must have a passport to embark. And he must know enough English to ask his way in London. Really, I find the whole thing very difficult."

"Not at all!" cried D'Artagnan, who was determined that the mission be carried out. "On the contrary, I think it is very easy. By the Lord, of course if we write Lord Winter about things beyond all reason, about the horrors the Cardinal perpetrates, about intrigues and state secrets, un-doubtedly we will all be broken on the wheel. But for God's sake don't forget, Athos, that we are writing to him about family affairs, we are writing for the sole purpose of getting him to meet Milady as soon as she gets to London and then seeing to it that she is where she has no power to injure us. I will write to him about like this: 'Monsieur and dear friend——' "

"Ah yes, 'dear friend' to an Englishman," Athos interrupted. "A fine beginning! Bravo, D'Artagnan! For that phrase alone you would be quartered instead of broken on the wheel."

"All right. Then I'll say just 'Monsieur.' "

"You may even write 'My lord,' " suggested Athos, always a stickler for good form.

" 'My lord, do you remember the little enclosure at the Luxembourg where I spared your life?' "

"My dear D'Artagnan," said Athos, "you will never be anything but a poor letter-writer. Handle the musket and the sword, my dear lad, but give the pen to Monsieur l'Abbé, that's his province."

"So be it," said D'Artagnan. "You word this letter for us, Aramis."

"I could ask for nothing better," returned Aramis, with that naïve confidence in himself that every poet has. "But tell me something about the subject matter. I have heard, here and there, that this sister-in-law is a vile woman. I got some proof of it when I overheard her conversation with the Cardinal. But the details escape me."

D'Artagnan and Athos looked at each other for some time in silence. At length Athos, after regaining command of himself and growing even more pale than usual, made a gesture of assent, and D'Artagnan understood that he was at liberty to speak.

"Well, say something like this: 'Monsieur, your sister-in-law is a villainous woman who has sought to kill you in order to inherit your wealth. But she was not really married to your brother because she had already married a Frenchman, and she was——' " D'Artagnan stopped as if he were trying to find the right word and looked at Athos, who said:

" 'Driven out of her husband's house.' "

"Because she had been branded," D'Artagnan went on.

"Nonsense!" said Porthos. "Impossible! And she tried to have her brother-in-law killed?"

"Yes."

"She was married before, in France?" Aramis inquired.

"Yes."

"And her husband discovered that a fleur-de-lis was branded on her shoulder?" cried Porthos.

"Yes." It was Athos who said "Yes" three times, in a tone that grew more gloomy for each one.

"And who has seen that fleur-de-lis?" asked Aramis.

"D'Artagnan and I, or rather, to observe the chronological order, I and D'Artagnan," replied Athos.

"And this frightful creature's husband is still alive?" Aramis asked.

"He is still alive."

"You are sure of that?"

"I am that husband." There was a moment of dead silence. Athos broke it first. "This time," he said, "D'Artagnan has given us an excellent plan for the letter. That is the right beginning."

Aramis took up the pen, reflected for a few moments, wrote eight or ten lines in a charming little hand that looked somewhat feminine, and then, speaking softly and slowly as if each word had been scrupulously weighed, he read as follows:

My lord:

The person who writes these few lines had the honor of crossing swords with you in the little enclosure off the Rue de L'Enfer. As you have several times since then been good enough to declare yourself the friend of that person, he feels it to be his duty to repay your friendship by some good advice. Twice you have just missed being the victim of a close relative of yours whom you believe to be your heir because you do not know that before contracting a marriage in England, she had already been married in France. But when she tries a third time, as she is planning to do now, she may succeed.

She sailed from La Rochelle for England last night. Watch for her arrival, for she has vast and terrible plans. If you are really determined to know what she is capable of, read her past history on her left shoulder.

"Marvelously well done, my dear Aramis!" said Athos. "You have the pen of a Secretary of State. If your letter reaches Lord Winter, he will be on his guard, and even if it should fall into the hands of His Eminence himself, we shall not be compromised. But as the lackey we send with the letter might stop at Châtellerault and pretend he had been to London and back, let us give him only half of the sum we promise him, telling him the other half will be given him in exchange for the answer. Have you your diamond with you, D'Artagnan?"

"I have something better—I have its value in money." And D'Artagnan threw the bag of coins onto the table.

"How much is there in that little bag?" Athos asked.

"Seven thousand livres in louis of twelve francs."

"Seven thousand livres!" cried Porthos.

"But gentlemen," said D'Artagnan, "in all this we are not thinking of the Queen. Let us pay some attention to the well-being of her dear Buckingham. That is the least we owe her."

"That's right," said Athos, "but that is Aramis's concern."

"Well," Aramis answered, blushing, "what do you want me to do?"

"Oh, that's quite simple," rejoined Athos. "Write a second letter for that clever person who lives in Tours."

Milady Reaches England

Milady and Felton

Aramis picked up his pen, reflected again and wrote the following lines, which he immediately submitted to his friends for their approval.

My dear cousin:

His Eminence the Cardinal, whom may God preserve for the happiness of France and the confusion of the enemies of our kingdom, is on the point of putting an end to the heretical rebellion of La Rochelle. Probably the succor of the English fleet will never even arrive in sight of the place. I will even venture to say that I am certain that the Duke of Buckingham will be prevented by some momentous event from even setting out. His Eminence is the most illustrious statesman of times past, of times present, and probably of times to come. He would extinguish the sun if the sun thwarted him.

Give these happy tidings to your sister, my dear cousin. I dreamed that this accursed Englishman was dead. I cannot remember whether it was by steel or by poison, but of this I am sure—I dreamed that he was dead. As you know, my dreams never deceive me.

You may be sure of seeing me return soon.

"Wonderful!" cried Athos. "You are the king of poets, my dear Aramis. You speak like the Revelation and you are as true as the Gospel. Now you have only to address the letter."

"That's soon done," said Aramis.

He folded the letter neatly and wrote the address:

To Mademoiselle Michon
Seamstress
Tours

The three friends looked at one another and laughed; their curiosity was not satisfied.

"Now," Aramis went on, "pray understand, gentlemen, that Bazin alone can take this letter to Tours. My cousin knows nobody but Bazin; any other person would fail to reach her."

"Very well," said D'Artagnan, "I accept Bazin gladly. But grant me Planchet. Milady had him thrown out of her house one day with sundry blows from a cudgel. Now Planchet has a good memory and I will guarantee that if he can think up any possible vengeance, he would allow himself to be beaten to death before he would relinquish it. If Tours is your affair, Aramis, London is mine. I request, then, that Planchet be chosen to go to London, especially as he has already been there with me, and can say quite correctly: 'London, sir, if you please' and 'my master, Lord d'Artagnan.' "

"In that case Planchet must be given seven hundred livres for going and seven hundred livres for coming back," said Athos, "and Bazin three hundred for going and three hundred for coming back. That will reduce our assets to five thousand livres. We will each take one thousand livres to use as each sees fit and we will leave a backlog of a thousand livres in the care of Monsieur l'Abbé here for extraordinary occasions or our common needs. Will that do?"

"My dear Athos," said Aramis, "you speak like Nestor, who as everyone knows was the wisest of the Greeks."

"Well, that's settled. Planchet and Bazin shall go. Everything considered, I am not sorry to keep Grimaud. He's used to my ways and I am exacting."

Planchet was summoned and given his instructions. D'Artagnan had already spoken of the matter to him, pointing out first how much money, second how much glory, he would get, and third how much danger he would risk.

"I will carry the letter in the lining of my coat," Planchet declared, "and if I'm caught, I will swallow it."

"But then you won't be able to fulfill your mission," D'Artagnan replied.

"You will give me a copy of it this evening and I will know it by heart by morning."

D'Artagnan looked at his friends as if to say, "Well, what did I tell you?" Then he continued, addressing Planchet: "You have eight days to get to Lord Winter and eight days to get back here—sixteen days in all. If you are not here at exactly eight o'clock in the sixteenth evening— eight o'clock, not five minutes past eight—you'll get no money."

"Then, monsieur," said Planchet, "you must buy me a watch."

"Take this one," said Athos, giving Planchet his own watch with his usual careless generosity, "and be a good lad. Remember, if you talk, if you blab, if you loiter, you are risking the head of a master who has such confidence in your loyalty that he has vouched for you. But remember also that if any evil befalls Monsieur d'Artagnan through your fault, I will find you wherever you may be for the purpose of ripping your belly open."

"Oh, monsieur!" cried Planchet, humiliated by the suspicion and terrified by the imperturbable calm of the musketeer.

"And I," announced Porthos, rolling his big eyes, "I will skin you alive!"

"And I," said Aramis in his soft, melodious voice, "I will roast you like a savage over a slow fire."

Planchet began to weep, but D'Artagnan clasped his hand, saying:

"You see, Planchet, these gentlemen say such things only out of affection for me. Really, they all like you very much."

"Monsieur," declared Planchet, "either I will succeed or I will let them cut me into quarters, and if they cut me into quarters, not one piece of me will speak."

It was decided that Planchet should leave the next morning at eight in

order to have plenty of time to learn the letter by heart. By this arrangement he gained just twelve hours; he was to be back on the sixteenth day
by eight in the evening. In the morning, just as the lackey was about to
mount his horse, D'Artagnan, who deep in his heart felt a partiality for
the Duke, drew Planchet aside and said:

"Listen to me. When you have given the letter to Lord Winter and he
has read it, say further to him. 'Watch over His Grace the Duke of Buckingham, for there are those who wish to assassinate him.' But this is so
serious and important, Planchet, that I have not been willing to tell even
my friends that I was trusting you with this secret, and I wouldn't put it in
writing for a captain's commission."

"Rest easy, monsieur," said Planchet. "You shall see whether I am to be
trusted."

Planchet, mounted on an excellent horse, set off at a gallop. Bazin set
out the next morning for Tours, and was allowed eight days for his
errand.

All the time their messengers were absent the four friends, as may well
be supposed, kept their eyes on the road, their noses to the wind, and
their ears listening. All day they were trying to catch everything that was
said, observing the Cardinal's proceedings, and spying out every courier
who came. More than once when they were called upon for special duty
they were seized by uncontrollable fears. Moreover, they had to look to
their own safety, for Milady was the kind of phantom that did not allow
those to whom it had appeared to sleep very soundly.

On the morning of the eighth day Bazin, as fresh and smiling as usual,
entered the Heretic tavern as the four friends were sitting down to breakfast, and in the terms agreed upon, said:

"Monsieur Aramis, here is your cousin's answer."

The four friends exchanged joyous glances; half the work was done.
Aramis took the letter, read it, and passed it to Athos, saying:

"See what she writes to me, Athos."

Athos glanced over the letter, then read it aloud.

My dear cousin:
My sister and I are skillful at interpreting dreams, and also we are terrified
by them. But as to yours we will be able to say, I hope, that the whole dream
is a lie. Adieu! Take care of yourself, and act in such a way now and then
we may be told what you are doing.

Marie Michon

Bazin's auspicious return had dispelled only part of the anxiety that
weighed on the four friends. Days of expectation always seem long, and
D'Artagnan would have wagered that now every one of these days had
forty-eight hours. He forgot the necessary slowness of navigation and he
exaggerated Milady's power. Moreover his confidence in the worthy

Picard lackey grew less day by day. His anxiety was so great that it affected both Porthos and Aramis. Athos alone remained unshaken. On the sixteenth day in particular, D'Artagnan, Porthos, and Aramis were so uneasy that they could not stay quietly in one place, but wandered about restlessly on the road by which Planchet was expected.

"Really," Athos said to them, "you're not men, but children, to let a woman terrify you this way. And what is it you're afraid of? Being imprisoned? Well, but someone would get us out. Madame Bonacieux got out. Being decapitated? Why, we go cheerfully into the trenches every day to expose ourselves to worse than that. A bullet may break a leg for one of us, and I'm convinced that a surgeon would give us more pain by amputating a leg than an executioner would in cutting off our heads. Wait quietly, then. In two hours, in four, in six at most, Planchet will be here. He promised to be, and I have great faith in Planchet's promises. He looks to me like a very good lad."

"But suppose he doesn't come?" queried D'Artagnan.

"Well, if he doesn't come, it will be because he has been delayed, that's all. He may have fallen off his horse, or have ridden so fast against the wind that he came down with pneumonia. Eh, gentlemen, let us reckon upon the unexpected. Be philosophers, as I am, gentlemen; sit down at the table and let us drink. Nothing makes the future look so rose-colored as to look at it through a glass of Chambertin."

The day went by, and evening came slowly, but did come at last. The taverns were crowded with topers. Athos, who had pocketed his share of the diamond, stayed on at the Heretic. In Monsieur de Busigny—who had given them a magnificent dinner—he found a partner worthy of his company. They were gambling together as usual when at half-past seven the drums sounded retreat.

"We are lost," murmured D'Artagnan in Athos's ear.

"You mean we *have* lost," said Athos calmly, taking 4 pistoles from his pocket and throwing them onto the table. "Come, gentlemen," he went on. "They are beating the tattoo, let us get to bed."

Athos left the Heretic, D'Artagnan followed him, then Aramis and Porthos arm-in-arm. Suddenly a shadow was distinguishable in the darkness, a figure that D'Artagnan knew, and a well-known voice said:

"Monsieur, I have brought your cloak. It is chilly this evening."

"Planchet!" cried D'Artagnan, beside himself with joy.

"Planchet! Planchet!" repeated Porthos and Aramis.

"Why yes, Planchet, to be sure," said Athos. "What is there so astonishing in that? He promised he would be back at eight o'clock, and there's eight just striking. Bravo, Planchet! You're a lad of your word, and if ever you leave your master, I promise you a place in my service."

"Oh no, never will I leave Monsieur d'Artagnan, never," said Planchet.

As he said this, Planchet was slipping a note into D'Artagnan's hand.

The note burned in his hand; he tried to walk faster, but Athos took his arm and forced him to walk at his own slow pace. At last they reached the tent, lit a lamp, and while Planchet stood guard at the entrance, D'Artagnan broke the seal with a trembling hand and opened the long-awaited letter. It contained just half a line in English and in a very British handwriting, and was quite spartan in its brevity:

Thank you, be easy.

Athos took the letter from D'Artagnan, carried it to the lamp, set fire to it, and did not let go of it until it was reduced to ashes. Then, calling Planchet, he said:

"Now, my lad, you may claim your seven hundred livres. But you didn't run any great risk with a note like that."

CHAPTER 47

IN THE MEANTIME MILADY, BESIDE HERSELF WITH ANGER
and roaring on the deck like a caged lioness, had been tempted to throw
herself into the sea to swim to the shore. She could not accept the thought
that she had been insulted by D'Artagnan and threatened by Athos and
that she was leaving France without being revenged on either. Soon this
thought became so unbearable to her that she implored the captain to put
her ashore, no matter what terrible risks she might run. But the captain
was in haste to escape from his bad position; his ship lay between French
and English cruisers. He must reach the English coast as soon as possible, and he stubbornly refused to obey what he took for a woman's
whim. Milady therefore perforce continued her voyage, and on the very
day that Planchet embarked at Portsmouth for France His Eminence's
lovely messenger entered that port in triumph.

The whole town was in a state of extraordinary excitement. Four large
vessels recently built had just been launched. At the end of the jetty, his
clothing richly bedecked with gold and resplendent as usual with diamonds and other precious stones, the white plume of his hat falling to his
shoulder, stood Buckingham, surrounded by a staff of officers almost as
brilliant as himself. It was one of those rare and beautiful winter days
when England remembers that there is a sun.

Milady's vessel entered the roadstead, but as the crew were about to
cast anchor a little formidably armed cutter acting as a coast guard approached the merchantman and dropped a small boat into the water. The
boat was manned by an officer, a boatswain's mate, and eight oarsmen.
The officer alone went on board, where he was received with all the deference inspired by his uniform. The officer talked with the captain a few
moments and gave him several papers to read, then, at the captain's order,
all those on the vessel, crew and passengers, were summoned on deck.

The officer inquired in a loud voice as to the brig's port of departure, its
course, and its landings. The captain answered all these questions easily
and without hesitation. Next the officer began to question all the persons
on the deck one after the other. Stopping before Milady, he surveyed her
with special care, but did not speak to her. Then he returned to the cap-

tain and said a few more words to him. The brig resumed its course, still
escorted by the little cutter, which sailed alongside, menacing it with the
mouths of its six cannon.

While the officer had been scrutinizing Milady, she on her side was
fairly devouring him with her glances, but she met with a countenance
so impassive that she learned nothing. The officer who had stopped in
front of her and studied her silently with so much care was a young man
of about twenty-five. His face was pale, his eyes were a clear blue and
rather deeply set. His strongly marked chin denoted that strength of will
which in the ordinary British type indicates only obstinacy. His brow
receded a little, as is fitting for poets, enthusiasts, and soldiers, and was
scantily shaded with thin, short hair, which, like the beard that covered
the lower part of his face, was of a beautiful deep-chestnut color.

When they entered the harbor, it was already night, and fog made the
darkness even thicker. The air they breathed was dismal, dank, and
chilly. Milady, courageous though she was, shivered in spite of herself.
The officer asked to have Milady's baggage pointed out, had it put into
the small boat, and invited her to follow it, offering her his hand. Milady
looked at him, hesitated, and asked:

"Who are you, sir, who are so kind as to give yourself so much trouble
on my account?"

"You must see by my uniform, madam, that I am an officer of the
British Navy," the young man replied.

"But is it the custom of the officers of the British Navy to place themselves at the service of their women compatriots when these land at British ports, and to carry their gallantry so far as to escort them ashore?"

"Yes, my lady, it is the custom, not through gallantry but through
prudence, that in wartime foreigners be escorted to particular hostelries,
so that they remain under the surveillance of the Government until complete information about them can be obtained."

These words were said with the most careful courtesy and with perfect
calm. Nevertheless they did not convince Milady.

"But I am not a foreigner, sir," she protested in perfect English. "My
name is Lady Clark, and this measure——"

"This measure is general, madam, and it will be vain for you to try
to evade it."

"Then I will follow you, sir."

Accepting the officer's hand, she started down the ladder at the foot of
which the small boat waited. The officer followed her. A large cloak had
been spread out at the stern. The officer requested her to be seated on
it and sat down beside her.

"Row!" he said to the sailors.

The eight oars fell into the sea with a single splash, and the boat
seemed to fly over the water. Within five minutes they reached land. The

officer sprang up onto the pier and offered his hand to Milady. A carriage was waiting nearby.

"Is that carriage for us?" asked Milady.

"Yes, madam," the officer replied.

"The hostelry is at some distance, then?"

"At the other end of town."

"Very well, let us go," said Milady, and she got resolutely into the carriage.

The officer saw that the baggage was fastened securely to the back of the carriage and then took his place beside Milady and closed the door. Immediately, without receiving any order or being told his destination, the coachman drove his horses off at a gallop.

So strange a reception naturally gave Milady plenty to think about. Seeing that the young officer seemed not at all disposed to begin a conversation, she leaned back in her corner of the carriage and reviewed one after the other all the surmises that passed through her mind. After a quarter of an hour, however, surprised at the length of the journey, she leaned forward to look out the window to try to see where she was being taken. There were no houses to be seen now; only tall trees appeared in the darkness like great black phantoms chasing each other. Milady shuddered and observed:

"But we are no longer in the town, sir." The young officer remained silent. "I will not go farther, I tell you, unless you tell me where you are taking me." This threat brought no response. "Oh, this is too much!" she cried. "Help, help!"

But no voice replied, the carriage rolled on rapidly, the young officer sat like a statue. Milady looked at him with one of her characteristically terrifying and rarely ineffective expressions. Anger made her eyes flash in the darkness. The young man sat unmoved. Milady tried to open the door and jump out.

"Take care, madam," said the young man coldly. "You will kill yourself if you jump."

She sat down again foaming with rage. The officer leaned forward, looked at her, and seemed surprised that a face so beautiful a few moments before could suddenly become so distorted and almost hideous in its rage. The artful creature realized that she was injuring herself by thus betraying her true nature. She composed her features and said in a piteous tone:

"In the name of Heaven, sir, tell me if it is to you, to your Government, or to an enemy that I must attribute the violence done me?"

"No violence is being done you, madam. What is happening to you is the result of a very simple measure that we have been forced to adopt with all who land in England."

"Then you do not know me, sir?"

"This is the first time I have the honor of seeing you."

"And upon your honor you have no reason to hate me?"

"None, I swear to you."

There was so much serenity, calmness, even mildness, in the young man's voice that Milady felt reassured.

At length, after about an hour's journey, the carriage stopped before an iron gate at the entrance to a narrow road that led to a castle severe in form, massive, and isolated. Then, as the wheels rolled over fine gravel, Milady heard a great roaring that she recognized at once as the noise of surf breaking on a rocky shore. The carriage passed under two arched gateways and at last stopped in a square, gloomy courtyard. Almost immediately the carriage door opened and the young man sprang out lightly and offered his hand to Milady, who supported herself by it and in her turn got out with tolerable calmness.

"So I am a prisoner, then," she said, glancing about her and then back at the officer with a most gracious smile. "But I am sure it will not be for long. My conscience and your courtesy, sir, are guarantees of that."

However flattering the compliment might be, the officer made no reply, but drawing a little silver whistle such as boatswains use from his belt, he blew it three times in three different keys. Immediately several men appeared, unharnessed the steaming horses, and put the carriage in a coach house.

The officer, with the same calm courtesy, invited his prisoner to enter the house. With the same smiling face Milady took his arm and passed with him under a low arched door and up a stone staircase winding around a stone pillar. Then they came to a massive door. The young man took a key from his pocket and turned it in the lock. The door turned heavily on its hinges and opened into the room Milady was to occupy. With one glance the prisoner took in the room in its minutest details. The furniture was equally appropriate for a prisoner and for one who was free, but the bars at the windows and the bolts on the outside of the door decided the question in favor of the prison.

In an instant all this woman's strength of mind forsook her. She sank into an armchair, her arms crossed, her head bowed, expecting every moment to see a judge enter to interrogate her. But no one entered except some sailors who brought in her trunks and bags, set them down in a corner, and retired without speaking. The officer superintended this with the same calmness Milady had always seen in him, never uttering a word, but giving his orders by a gesture of his hand or a note of his whistle. It was as if between this man and his inferiors no spoken language existed. At last, unable to hold out longer, Milady broke the silence.

"In the name of Heaven, sir," she cried, "what does all this mean? Put an end to my doubts, I beg you. I have courage enough for any danger I can foresee, for every misfortune I can understand. Where am I, and why am I here? If I am free, why all these bars and bolts? If I am a prisoner, what crime have I committed?"

"You are here in the room that was made ready for you, madam. I received orders to meet you on the sea and conduct you to this castle. I believe I have carried out these orders with the fidelity of a soldier and the courtesy of a gentleman. There my duty as regards you has been done. The rest concerns another person."

"And who is that other person?" Milady asked. "Can you not tell me his name?"

At that moment a loud jingling of spurs was heard on the stairway, voices passed by and faded away, then the sound of one man's footsteps approached the door.

"That person is here, madam," said the officer, stepping aside to leave the entrance clear and drawing himself up in an attitude of great respect.

The door opened, a man appeared on the threshold. He was hatless, he wore a sword by his side, and he was crumpling a handkerchief in one hand. Milady thought she recognized this shadow in the gloom; she leaned one hand heavily on one arm of the chair and thrust her head forward as if to confront a certainty. As the newcomer advanced slowly, and came into the circle of light thrown out by the lamp, she recoiled involuntarily. Then, when she no longer had any doubt, she cried, fairly dumfounded.

"What, my brother, is it you?"

"Yes, fair lady," Lord Winter answered, making a bow that was half courteous and half ironical, "it is I myself."

"Then this castle——?"

"Is mine."

"This room——?"

"Is yours."

"Then I am your prisoner?"

"Practically."

"But this is a frightful abuse of power!"

"No highfalutin words, please! Let us sit down and chat quietly, as is fitting for a brother and a sister." Then, turning toward the door and seeing that the young officer was waiting for further orders, he said: "All is well, thank you. Now pray leave us, Mr. Felton."

CHAPTER 48

WHILE LORD WINTER WAS CLOSING THE DOOR, FASTENING a shutter, and approaching his sister-in-law, Milady, deep in thought, was searching every possibility and trying to discover the plot that she had not even been able to guess at as long as she did not know into whose hands she had fallen. She knew her brother-in-law to be a true gentleman, a great huntsman, a fearless gambler, a master hand with women, but no man of unusual skill in intrigues. How had he found out that she was arriving? Why had he had her seized? Why was he holding her?

Athos had let drop some words that proved that the conversation she had had with the Cardinal had been overheard by enemy ears, but she could not believe that he had dug a countermine so promptly and so boldly. Perhaps her earlier activities in England had been discovered. Buckingham might have guessed that it was she who had cut off the two diamond tags and was avenging himself for that little perfidy. But Buckingham was incapable of persecuting a woman, especially if that woman was actuated by jealousy. At all events, she congratulated herself on having fallen into the hands of her brother-in-law, since she was sure she could easily get the better of him, instead of into the hands of a definite and intelligent enemy.

"Yes, let us chat, brother," she said with a sort of cheerfulness, determined as she was to obtain from the conversation, despite all the dissimulation Lord Winter might bring to it, the information she needed in order to regulate her future conduct.

Lord Winter adopted Milady's own tactics, thinking that since his sister-in-law employed them, they must be the best. "But tell me, my dear sister," he queried in his turn, "why have you come to England?"

"But I have come in order to see you," replied Milady, without realizing how much she was aggravating by this reply the suspicions D'Artagnan's letter had aroused in her brother-in-law's mind. Her hope was to win his goodwill by her lie.

"Ah, just to see me?" Lord Winter asked, as if he doubted her.

"Of course to see you. Why does that surprise you?"

"And you had no other object in coming to England—only to see me?

It is for my sake alone that you have taken the trouble to cross the English Channel?"

"For your sake only."

"The deuce! What affection you must have for me, my sister!"

"But am I not your nearest kin?" asked Milady in a tone of the most touching ingenuousness.

"And so my only heir, are you not?" asked Lord Winter in his turn, looking at her intently.

However great her command over herself, Milady could not help starting, and as Lord Winter had his hand on her arm, that start did not escape him. Indeed the blow was direct and severe. The first idea that flashed across Milady's mind was that Kitty had betrayed her, telling Lord Winter how she had imprudently shown in the presence of her maid how much she disliked him. She remembered too the furious and equally imprudent attack she had made upon D'Artagnan when he had spared her brother-in-law's life.

"I do not understand you, my lord," she said, to gain time to force her adversary to declare himself. "Whatever do you mean? Is there some hidden meaning in your words?"

"Oh, good Lord, no!" said Lord Winter, with apparent geniality. "You wish to see me and you come to England. I learn of your desire, or rather I guess that you feel it, and in order to spare you all the inconvenience and the fatigue of landing so late at night, I send one of my officers to meet you, I place a carriage at his orders, and he brings you to this castle of which I am governor, where I come every day, and where, so that we may satisfy our mutual desire of seeing each other, I have had a room prepared for you. What is there more astonishing in what I tell you than in what you have told me?"

"That is not what I find astonishing, but it does astonish me that you knew that I was coming."

"That is perfectly simple, my dear sister. Did you not notice that when the captain of your little vessel entered the roadstead he sent to ask permission to enter the port by a small boat that took his logbook and his passenger list? I am commandant of the port. They brought me the papers and I recognized your name. My heart told me what your words have just confirmed—that is, what your purpose was in exposing yourself to the dangers of so rough a sea, or one so difficult at the moment, and I sent my cutter to meet you. You know the rest."

Milady knew quite well that Lord Winter was not telling the whole truth, and that alarmed her still more. "My brother," she rejoined, "was it not His Grace the Duke of Buckingham whom I saw standing on the jetty this evening as I arrived?"

"He himself, undoubtedly," replied Lord Winter. "Oh, I can understand the impression the sight of him made on you. You come from a country where his name is in everyone's mouth, and I know that his war-like preparations against France are giving great concern to your friend the Cardinal."

"My friend the Cardinal!" cried Milady, perceiving that on this point too Lord Winter seemed perfectly informed.

"Why, isn't he your friend? I beg your pardon, I thought he was. But you came, I think you said, in order to see me?"

"Yes."

"Well, you shall have your wish. We shall see each other every day."

"Am I to stay here forever?" asked Milady, terrified.

"Are you uncomfortably lodged, my sister? Ask for anything you want and I'll hasten to have it given to you."

"But I have neither maids nor lackeys."

"You shall have all that, madam. Tell me how your first husband arranged your household, and although I am only a brother-in-law, I will arrange the same for you here."

"My first husband!" cried Milady, staring at Lord Winter with eyes almost starting from their sockets.

"Yes, your French husband. I am not speaking of my brother. Have you forgotten about your first one? As he is still living, I might write to him and ask him to send me information on the subject."

A cold sweat broke out on Milady's brow. "You are jesting," she said in a hollow voice.

"Do I look as if I were?" asked Lord Winter, rising and stepping back.

"Or rather you are insulting me," she continued.

"Insulting you, I!" said Lord Winter contemptuously. "Do you really think, madam, that it is possible to insult you?"

"In truth, sir," said Milady, "you are either drunk or mad. Go, and send me a woman."

"Women are very indiscreet, my sister. May I not serve you as a maid? In that way our secrets would be kept in the family."

"You insolent wretch!" cried Milady, and she sprang at Lord Winter, who stood waiting for her attack with his arms crossed, but with one hand on the hilt of his sword.

"Well, well," he said, "I know you have the habit of assassinating people, but I warn you I shall defend myself, even against you."

"Oh, you would!" said Milady. "You look to me as if you were coward enough to lift your hand against a woman."

"Perhaps I would, and I would have an excuse. My hand would not be the first to be raised against you." And Lord Winter pointed with a slow and accusing gesture to Milady's left shoulder, almost touching it with his finger.

Milady gave a deep groan and shrank back into the farthest corner of the room, like a panther that is recoiling for a leap.

"Oh, groan all you like," cried Lord Winter, "but don't try to bite, for I warn you it would not help you. There are no lawyers here to settle an estate in advance, no knights errant to challenge me for the sake of a beautiful lady I am keeping prisoner. But I have judges ready to take care of a bigamist, a shameless woman who crept into my brother's bed, and those judges, I warn you, will send you to an executioner who will make your two shoulders alike."

Milady's eyes flashed like lightning, and though he was an armed man facing an unarmed woman, Lord Winter felt cold fear penetrate his very soul. Nonetheless he went on, with rising anger:

"Yes, I know all about it. After you had inherited my brother's fortune, it would have suited you very well to inherit mine. But you might as well know that if you kill me, or have me killed, my precautions are taken. Not one penny of mine can possibly get into your hands. Were you not already rich enough, you who possess almost a million? Could you not have done with your wicked career? Or did you go on doing evil for the supreme delight of doing it? If my brother's memory were not sacred to me, you would be rotting now in a state dungeon or be a spectacle to satisfy the curiosity of sailors at Tyburn. As it is, I will be silent, but as for you, I advise you to endure your captivity quietly. Within two or three weeks I go to La Rochelle with the British Army. Before I leave, a vessel that I will watch set sail will come for you and take you to one of our colonies to the south. I assure you that you will be accompanied by a guard who will blow your brains out at the first attempt you make to return to England or to the Continent."

Milady listened with an intentness that dilated her fiery eyes.

"Yes," Lord Winter continued, "for the present you will remain in this castle. The walls are thick, the doors are strong, the bars on the windows are unbreakable. Besides, your window opens on a steep cliff over the sea. My men, who are absolutely devoted to me, mount guard around this room and watch all the passages that lead to the courtyard. And even if you could succeed in reaching the courtyard, there would still be three iron gates for you to get through. My orders are positive: one step, one gesture, one word, suggesting escape and you will be shot. If you are killed, English justice will be under an obligation to me for having saved it the task. Ah, I see that your features are regaining their calmness, your countenance is recovering its assurance. 'Two weeks, three weeks,' you are telling yourself. 'Bah! I have an inventive mind. Between now and then some idea will come to me. I have a hellish soul, and I shall find some victim to get me out of here.' All right, madam—just try it!"

Milady, seeing that he had guessed what she was thinking, dug her fingernails into her flesh to master any expression of her countenance other than that of pain. Lord Winter continued:

"The officer in command here during my absence you already know.

You must have observed that he knows how to obey orders, for I am sure you did not come here with him from Portsmouth without trying to make him talk. What have you to say about him? Could a marble statue be more impassible or more mute? You have tried your powers of seduction on many men, and unfortunately you have always been successful. But try them on this man; by the Lord, if you succeed with him I shall pronounce you the Devil himself!" He went to the door and flung it open. "Summon Mr. Felton," he said, then to Milady: "Wait a moment longer and I will recommend you to his care."

The man and the woman waited in a strange silence. Then slow regular footsteps were heard approaching, and soon the young Lieutenant we already know stopped at the door, awaiting his master's orders.

"Come in, my dear John," said Lord Winter, "come in, and shut the door." The young officer entered. "Now look carefully at this woman. She is young, she is beautiful, she possesses all earthly allurements. Very well, she is a monster who, at twenty-five, has been guilty of as many crimes as you could read in a year in the archives of our law courts. Her voice prepossesses in her favor those who hear her speak, her beauty serves as a bait for her victims, and her body pays what she promises— at least I must do her justice as to that. She will endeavor to seduce you, perhaps she will even endeavor to kill you. I rescued you from dire poverty, Felton, I had you made a Lieutenant, and once I saved your life, you know on what occasion. I am not only your protector but your friend, not only your benefactor but a father to you. This woman has come back to England to plot against my life. I now hold this snake in my hands. Well, I have had you summoned, and I say to you: Friend Felton, John my son, be on guard for me, and above all be on guard for yourself, against this woman. Swear by your own hopes of salvation to preserve her for the punishment she has deserved. John Felton, I trust in your word, John Felton, I trust in your loyalty!"

"My lord," said the young officer, his gentle countenance taking on the expression of all the hatred he could find in his heart, "my lord, I swear that all shall be done as you desire."

Milady received this speech with the look of a resigned victim; no one could imagine a more submissive or a gentler expression than the one on her beautiful face. Even Lord Winter could hardly believe that this was the tigress he had been getting ready to fight a few moments before.

"She is never to leave this room, do you understand, John? She is not to write to anyone, she is to speak to no one but you—if you do her the honor to address a word to her."

"That is enough, my lord. I have sworn to do what you wish."

"And now, madam, try to make your peace with God, for men have passed judgment on you."

Milady let her head sink as though she were crushed by that judgment.

Lord Winter went out, motioning Felton to follow him and the door was closed and locked after them. A moment later the heavy tread of a sentry was heard in the corridor, a sentry with an ax in his belt and a musket on his shoulder.

Milady sat for some moments in the same position, for she thought someone might be looking her over through the keyhole. Then she slowly raised her head, with a formidable expression of menace and defiance. She ran toward the door to listen, went to look out the window, then, returning to sink again into the armchair, she sat lost in thought.

CHAPTER 49

MEANWHILE THE CARDINAL WAS WAITING FOR NEWS from England, but no news came except what was disturbing and most threatening. Although La Rochelle was invested, however certain eventual success might appear—thanks to the precautions taken by the besiegers, especially the dike that prevented the entrance of any vessel whatever into the invested city—the blockade might still last for a long time. That would be a great affront to the King's army and a great inconvenience to the Cardinal. True, he no longer needed to embroil Louis XIII with Anne of Austria, for he had accomplished that, but he had to settle difficulties between Monsieur de Bassompierre and the Duc d'Angoulême. As to the Duc d'Orléans, who had begun the siege, he left the task of finishing it to the Cardinal.

On their side, from time to time the besiegers captured the messengers sent to Buckingham from La Rochelle, or the spies sent to La Rochelle by Buckingham. In either case, the trial was soon over. Monsieur le Cardinal pronounced tersely, "Hang him!"

Nevertheless time passed and La Rochelle did not surrender. The last spy captured was the bearer of a letter telling Buckingham that the city was in desperate straits. But instead of adding, "If succor from you does not arrive within a fortnight, we will surrender," the addition was quite simply, "If succor from you does not arrive within a fortnight, we shall all be dead of hunger when it does arrive."

Buckingham, then, was the sole hope of the men of La Rochelle; Buckingham was their Messiah. It was clear that if they should once learn certainly that they could no longer count on Buckingham, their courage would die with their hopes. Therefore the Cardinal waited impatiently for the news from England that would announce that Buckingham would not come.

The question of taking the city by storm, though often debated in the King's Council, had always been rejected. In the first place, La Rochelle seemed impregnable. Moreover the Cardinal, whatever he might have said, realized perfectly that the horror aroused by the bloodshed of that assault of Frenchmen against Frenchmen was a backward step to the policy of some sixty years before and the Cardinal was at that period what we now call a progressive man. La Rochelle, all the besieging generals argued, was impregnable save by famine.

The Cardinal could not dispel the fear he had of his terrible emissary Milady. He knew her strange dual nature—sometimes a snake, sometimes a lioness. Had she betrayed him? Was she dead? In any event he knew her well enough to know that whether acting for him or against him, as a friend or as an enemy, nothing would keep her from acting except the greatest obstacles. But who had contrived those obstacles? That he could not learn. Yet he felt he could count on Milady, and with reason. He had divined that there was something so terrible in that woman's past that only his red mantle could cover it. He felt that he had made this woman his own creature, for only in him could she find support stronger than the danger that threatened her.

He resolved now to carry on the war alone, and to look on any success that came from elsewhere as only a stroke of luck. He continued to urge the raising of the dike that was to starve La Rochelle. He had little notes thrown over the walls into the city in which he told its inhabitants how unjust, selfish, and barbarous the conduct of their leaders was. These leaders, he wrote, had wheat in abundance, yet they would not share it with the people. Their maxim—for they too had maxims—was that women, children, and the aged might die as long as those defending their walls remained healthy and strong. These notes had all the effect their writer had anticipated, since they determined a large number of the inhabitants to open private negotiations with the Royal Army.

But at the moment when the Cardinal saw this measure begin to bear fruit and was congratulating himself for using it, a citizen of La Rochelle had succeeded, God knows how,—such was the watchfulness of Bassompierre, Schomberg, and the Duc d'Angoulême, themselves watched by the Cardinal—in getting through the royal lines and entered the city. He had come from Portsmouth and reported that he had seen a magnificent fleet there ready to sail within a week. Further, Buckingham sent word to the mayor that at last the Great League against France was about to be proclaimed, and that France was soon to be invaded at the same time by English, Holy Roman Empire, and Spanish armies. Buckingham's letter was read publicly in every square in the city, and copies were posted at every street corner. Even those who had opened negotiations with the Royal Army now broke them off, resolving once more to await the succor so impressively announced.

This unexpected circumstance revived Richelieu's earlier anxieties, and forced him in spite of himself to look once more toward England.

During this interval, exempt from the anxieties of its only real leader, the Royal Army led a gay life, neither money nor provisions being wanting in the camp. All the corps rivaled one another in audacity and high spirits. To capture spies and hang them, to make hazardous expeditions out on the dike or to the sea, to contrive wild plans and to carry them out coolly—these were the pastimes that made the Army find these days all too short. For the men of La Rochelle, prey to famine and anxiety, these days were long, and they were long for the Cardinal, who was blockading them so closely.

Sometimes when the Cardinal was riding along looking thoughtfully at the dike engineers from all over France were constructing, he would meet some musketeer of Monsieur de Tréville's company. He drew near him, looked him over in an odd way, then, not recognizing him as one of our four companions, he would turn his keen glance and his profound thoughts in another direction.

One day, oppressed by deadly ennui, without hope of negotiating with the city, and without news from England, the Cardinal rode out along the beach accompanied by only Cahusac and La Houdinière. His horse took him to the top of a little hill, whence he saw seven men lying on the sand behind a hedge, surrounded by empty bottles. Four of these men were our musketeers, who were getting ready to listen to a letter one of them had just received. The letter was so important that it had made them abandon their cards and dice on the drumhead. The other three were engaged in opening a demijohn of Collioure wine.

The Cardinal, as has been noted, was in very low spirits, and when he was in that state of mind nothing increased his gloominess more than seeing others enjoying themselves. Motioning to Cahusac and La Houdinière to halt, he dismounted and walked toward these suspect merrymakers, hoping that the sand would deaden the sound of his footsteps, the hedge conceal his approach, and that he might overhear some part of the conversation that seemed to be interesting them so much.

He had taken barely ten steps when he recognized a Gascon voice, and as he already knew that these men were musketeers, he was sure the three others were those known as the inseparables: Athos, Porthos, and Aramis. Consequently he was all the more desirous of hearing what they were saying. His eyes took on a strange look, and with the step of a tiger cat he stole toward the hedge. But he had caught only a few meaningless syllables when a loud cry made him start and attracted the attention of the musketeers.

"An officer!" cried Grimaud.

"You spoke, I think, you scoundrel," said Athos, rising on his elbow and staring at Grimaud with blazing eyes. So Grimaud said no more, but contented himself with pointing with his index finger toward the hedge, announcing by that gesture the Cardinal and his escort. With one bound the musketeers got to their feet and saluted respectfully. The Cardinal looked very angry.

"It seems that musketeers keep on guard," he said. "Are the English expected by land, or do the musketeers consider themselves to be field officers?"

"Monseigneur," replied Athos, who amid the general consternation had preserved that calm and coolness of a nobleman which never left him, "when the musketeers are not on duty, they drink and dice, and for their lackeys they are decidedly field officers."

"Lackeys!" grumbled the Cardinal. "Lackeys who are ordered to warn their masters when anyone passes by are not lackeys, they are sentries."

"Yet His Eminence can see that if we had not taken this precaution, we might well run the risk of letting him pass without paying our respects and offering our thanks for the favor he has done in bringing us together. D'Artagnan," Athos went on, "just now you were hoping for an opportunity to express your gratitude to Monseigneur. Here it is, avail yourself of it."

These words were spoken with that imperturbable sangfroid which distinguished Athos in the hour of danger, and with that extreme courtesy which at certain moments made him more majestic than kings by birth. D'Artagnan stepped forward and stammered out a few words of thanks, which soon died out under the Cardinal's gloomy stare.

"No matter, gentlemen," said the Cardinal, apparently not at all diverted from his original purpose by the incident Athos had created, "I do not like to have mere soldiers play the part of great noblemen just because they happen to belong to a privileged corps. Discipline is the same for them as for everyone else."

Athos let the Cardinal finish his sentence, then bowed, and said:

"Discipline we have not forgotten in any way, Monseigneur. We are not on duty, and being off duty, we thought we could spend our time as we pleased. If we are so fortunate as to have His Eminence give us some special order, we are ready to obey him. Monseigneur can see," Athos went on, frowning, for this type of interrogation was beginning to annoy him, "that we did not come out here unarmed." And he pointed out to the Cardinal the four muskets stacked beside the drum on which the cards and the dice were lying.

"Pray believe, Your Eminence," added D'Artagnan, "that we would have gone to meet you if we could have imagined that you were coming toward us with so small an escort."

The Cardinal bit his mustache and even his lips a little. "Do you know what you look like?" he said. "Always together, always armed, always guarded by your lackeys? You look like four conspirators."

"Oh, as to that, Monseigneur, we do conspire," said Athos, "as Your Eminence may have observed the other day, but only against the men of La Rochelle."

"Well, gentlemen-politicos," replied the Cardinal, frowning in his turn, "perhaps the secret of many mysterious things might be found if one could read your minds as easily as you were reading that letter which you hid so quickly when you saw me coming."

Athos flushed, took a step toward His Eminence, and said: "We might think you really suspected us, Monseigneur, and that we're being submitted to an inquisition. If so, we trust Your Eminence will deign to explain, so that at least we may know where we stand."

"And if it were an inquisition," said the Cardinal, "others have submitted to it, Monsieur Athos, and have given their answers."

"I have told Your Eminence that you have but to ask, we are ready to answer."

"What was that letter you were about to read, Monsieur Aramis, and which you hid so promptly?"

"A letter from a woman, Monseigneur."

"Oh, I see," said the Cardinal, "we must be discreet about that kind of letter. But nevertheless it can be shown to a confessor, and you know I have taken Holy Orders."

"Monseigneur," said Athos with a calmness that was all the more terrible because he knew he was risking his head by his reply, "the letter is from a woman, but it is not signed Marion de Lorme or Madame d'Aiguillon."

The Cardinal turned deathly pale, his eyes darted lightning, and he turned to give an order to Cahusac and La Houdinière. Athos, seeing this movement, stepped toward the muskets. His three friends were staring at the weapons like men ill disposed to submit to arrest. The Cardinal's party numbered only three, the musketeers with their lackeys numbered seven. Richelieu judged that the contest would be all the more uneven if Athos and his friends were really conspiring. By one of those sudden reversals he could always command all his anger faded into a smile.

"Come, come," he said, "you are brave young men, proud in daylight, and loyal in the darkness. There is no harm in watching over yourselves when you watch so carefully over others. Gentlemen, I have not forgotten the night when you served me as an escort to the Red Dovecote tavern. If there were any danger to be feared on the road I am about to take, I would beg you to accompany me. But since there is none, stay where you are, and finish your bottles, your gambling, and your letter. Adieu, gentlemen."

And mounting his horse again, he waved his hand in farewell and rode off. The four young men stood motionless and silent until he had disappeared, then they looked at one another in consternation. In spite of His Eminence's friendly farewell they knew very well that the Cardinal went away filled with rage. Athos alone smiled, a masterful and disdainful smile. When the Cardinal was out of sight, and so out of hearing, Porthos cried:

"That Grimaud kept bad watch!" Porthos was inclined to vent his ill humor on someone.

Grimaud was about to answer, excusing himself, but Athos lifted one finger and Grimaud was silent.

"Would you have given up the letter, Aramis?" D'Artagnan asked.

"I?" said Aramis in his most flutelike tone. "Yes, I had made up my mind to. If he had insisted, I would have given him the letter with one hand and with the other I would have run my sword through his body."

"I was expecting that," said Athos. "That is why I threw myself between you and him. I must say that man is very indiscreet to talk to other men as he did to us. One would think he never had anyone to deal with but women and children."

"My dear Athos," said D'Artagnan, "I admire you. But after all we were in the wrong."

"We in the wrong?" said Athos. "Whose, then, is the air we breathe? Whose is the ocean we are looking at? Whose is the sand where we are lying? Whose is the letter about your mistress? Do any of these belong to the Cardinal? Upon my honor, that man imagines that the whole world belongs to him. There you stood before him, stammering, stupefied, annihilated! Anyone might think the Bastille was appearing before you and that gigantic Medusa was turning you to stone. Come, is being in love conspiring? You are in love with a woman the Cardinal has had imprisoned and you want to get her out of the Cardinal's hands. You're playing a game with the Cardinal. That letter is your hand of cards. Why should you let your opponent see it? That isn't done. Let him guess—very well, we will guess what cards he holds!"

"Indeed," said D'Artagnan, "what you are saying makes good sense."

"In that case, let us forget what has just happened," said Athos, "and let Aramis get on with the letter Monsieur le Cardinal interrupted."

Aramis took the letter from his pocket, his three friends drew near him, and the three lackeys went back to their places by the demijohn.

"You had only read a line or two," said D'Artagnan, "so start again at the beginning."

"Willingly," said Aramis, and he read:

My dear cousin:

I think I shall decide to leave for Béthune, where my sister has placed our little maidservant in the Carmelite convent. The poor child is quite resigned, since she knows she cannot live elsewhere without endangering the salvation of her soul. Nevertheless, if our family affairs can be arranged as we hope, I believe she runs no risk of being damned, and that she will someday return to those she regrets to have left, especially as she knows they are always thinking of her. Meanwhile she is not too unhappy. The thing she desires most is a letter from her lover. I know that such a commodity is difficult to get through a convent grating, but after all I have given you proofs, my dear cousin, that I do not lack skill, and I will undertake the commission.

My sister thanks you for your kind and never-ceasing remembrance. She was quite worried for a little, but now she is somewhat reassured, as she has sent her secretary yonder to make sure that nothing unforeseen happens.

Adieu, my dear cousin. Let me have news of you as often as you can—I mean as often as you can safely. I embrace you.

Marie Michon

"Oh, how much I owe you, Aramis!" cried D'Artagnan. "Dear Constance, at last I have news of her. She is alive, she is in safety in a convent, she is at Béthune! Where is Béthune, Athos?"

"In Lorraine, not far from the Alsace border. As soon as the siege is over we can take a trip in that direction."

"And that will not be long, it is to be hoped," said Porthos. "This morning they hanged a spy who confessed that the people of La Rochelle have been reduced to eat the leather of their shoes. Even if after eating the leather they eat the soles, I can't see that they have anything left—unless they eat each other."

"Poor fools," said Athos, draining a glass of excellent Bordeaux wine. "Poor fools! As if the Catholic religion were not the most advantageous and the most agreeable of all religions! All the same," he resumed after smacking his tongue over the wine, "they are brave fellows! . . . But what the devil are you doing, Aramis? You are squeezing that letter into your pocket!"

"Athos is right," said D'Artagnan. "The letter must be burned. And yet if we burn it, who knows whether Monsieur le Cardinal has some secret of his own with which he can read the ashes!"

"He must have one," said Athos.

"What will you do with the letter, then?" Porthos asked.

"Come here, Grimaud," said Athos. "As a punishment for having spoken without permission you are going to eat this paper. Then to reward you for the great service you did us you will drink this glass of wine. Here is the letter first. Chew it up well!"

Grimaud smiled, and with his eyes fixed on the glass of wine Athos had filled to the brim, he ground the paper between his teeth and swallowed it.

"Bravo, Master Grimaud!" said Athos. "Now take this! And I give you a dispensation for your thanks."

Silently Grimaud drained the glass of Bordeaux, but his eyes, raised heavenward all the time that this delicious occupation lasted, spoke a language that was all the more expressive for being mute.

"And now," said Athos, "unless Monsieur le Cardinal should get the clever idea of ripping Grimaud open, I think we may be pretty much at our ease about the letter."

In the meantime His Eminence was continuing his melancholy ride, murmuring under his mustaches:

"Those four men positively must be mine."

CHAPTER 50

MEANWHILE MILADY WAS STILL PLUNGED IN AN ABYSS OF dismal reflections, a dark hell at the gate of which she had almost abandoned all hope. For the first time in her life she was in doubt, for the first time she was afraid. On two occasions luck had deserted her; twice she had been exposed and betrayed, and each time it was the same fatal genius, whom God must have sent to combat her, who caused her fall. D'Artagnan had vanquished her—and her invincible evil power. He had deceived her in love, humbled her pride, thwarted her ambition, and now he was ruining her fortune, depriving her of her liberty, and even threatening her life. Furthermore, he had lifted one corner of her mask, that shield which covered her and made her so strong.

D'Artagnan had protected Buckingham—whom she hated as she hated everyone she had ever loved—from the tempest that had menaced the Duke in the person of the Queen. D'Artagnan had pretended to be De Wardes, for whom she had conceived one of those uncontrollable tigerish fancies not unusual in women of her type. D'Artagnan knew the terrible secret that she had sworn no one should know and stay alive. Lastly, at the very moment when she had just obtained from Richelieu the blanket endorsement by means of which she was to avenge herself on her enemy, it had been snatched from her hands, and it was really D'Artagnan who was now holding her captive and was about to send her to some filthy Botany Bay, some infamous Tyburn in the Indian Ocean!

All this she owed to D'Artagnan. Who else could have heaped so much shame on her head? He alone could have told Lord Winter all the frightful secrets that he had discovered one after the other by such a succession of fatal chances. He knew her brother-in-law, he must have written to him.

What hatred seethed within her as she sat motionless in her lonely room, her eyes fixed and blazing! What magnificent plans for vengeance she concocted in the lightning flashes of her tempestuous rage—against Madame Bonacieux, against Buckingham, above all against D'Artagnan —plans buried in the distance of the future! Yes, but in order to avenge herself she must be free, she must pierce a wall, loosen bars, cut through a floor—tasks that can be accomplished by a strong, patient man but before which the feverish irritation of a woman must own defeat. Besides, to do all that she needed time—months, perhaps years—and she had but ten or twelve days, as her brotherly and fearsome jailer Lord Winter had told her. Yet if she were a man, she would attempt all that, and might perhaps succeed. Why had Heaven made the fatal mistake of placing a manlike soul in that frail and delicate body!

The first moments of her captivity were terrible to her; a few paroxysms of rage that she could not suppress paid her debt of feminine weakness to nature. But little by little she subdued the outbreaks of her insane rage. The nervous tremors that shook her body vanished and she sat as if coiled in repose like a wearied snake.

"Come, come," she said to herself as she stared into the mirror that reflected her burning glance, "I must have been mad to let myself be carried away like that. No violence now, violence is a proof of weakness. Furthermore, I have never succeeded by that means. Perhaps if I employed my strength against women, I might find them weaker than I am and consequently vanquish them. But it is with men I am struggling now, and to them I am only a woman. Let me fight like a woman, then. My strength lies in my weakness."

Then, as if to take account of all the changes she could impose on her expressive and mobile countenance, she assumed one expression after the other, from that of passionate anger that distorted her features to that of the sweetest, most affectionate, and most seductive smile. Under her skillful hands her hair took on all the waves that she knew might add to the charm of her face. At length she was satisfied and murmured: "Come, nothing is lost. I am still beautiful."

It was then almost eight in the evening. Milady looked at the bed and decided that a few hours of rest would refresh not only her head and her ideas, but also her complexion. But before she lay down a better idea occurred to her. She had heard something said about supper. She had already been in this room an hour; someone would surely be bringing her food before long. Determined not to lose any time, she resolved to make some attempt that evening to find out what she had to work on by studying the characters of the men to whose guardianship she had been committed. A ray of light appeared under the door, announcing the return of her jailers. Milady, who had already left the bed, at once flung herself into the armchair, her head thrown back, her beautiful hair falling loose and disheveled, her throat half-bare under her crumpled lace, one hand on her heart and the other hanging by her side. The bolts were drawn, the door grated on its hinges, footsteps sounded in the room and drew near her.

"Put the table here," said a voice that she recognized as Felton's. His order was obeyed. "Bring lights, and then relieve the sentinel," he continued.

This double order which the young man gave to the same individuals proved to Milady that the men who served her were also her guards—that is to say, soldiers or sailors. Felton's orders were carried out with a silent rapidity that told Milady much about the discipline he maintained.

At length Felton, who had not yet looked at Milady, turned toward her.

"Ah, ah," he said, "she is asleep. Very well, when she wakes she can eat her supper." And he took a step toward the door.

"But Lieutenant," said a soldier who, less stoical than his officer, had approached Milady, "this woman isn't asleep."

"What, not asleep?" said Felton. "What is she doing, then?"

"She has fainted. Her face is very pale, and I can't hear her breathe."

"You are right," said Felton after looking at Milady from the spot where he stood, taking no step toward her. "Go tell Lord Winter that his prisoner has fainted. I don't know what to do. We had not foreseen this."

The soldier went to obey his officer's orders, Felton sat down in an armchair that chanced to be near the door, and waited, without saying a word, without making a gesture. Milady possessed the great art, so much practiced by women, of looking through her long eyelashes without seeming to open her eyelids. She watched Felton, who sat with his back to her, looking at him steadily for nearly ten minutes, and during that time her impassive guardian never turned round once.

She thought Lord Winter would come in presently, and that his presence would give fresh strength to her jailer. Her first attempt had failed. She decided to act like a woman who uses all her resources, so she raised her head, opened her eyes, and sighed a little. At that sigh Felton at last turned round.

"Ah, you are awake, madam," said he. "Then I have nothing more to do here. If you want anything, you can ring."

"Oh, my God, my God, how I have suffered!" murmured Milady in that melodious voice which, like those of the enchantresses of old, charmed all whom they wished to destroy. Then, sitting up in the armchair, she assumed a still more graceful and abandoned position than when she was lying back. Felton rose, and said:

"You will be served three times a day, madam: breakfast at nine, dinner at one, supper at six. If that does not suit you, you can tell me the hours you prefer and in that respect we will comply with your wishes."

"But am I always to remain alone in this huge, dismal room?" asked Milady.

"A woman of the neighborhood has been sent for. She will come to the castle tomorrow and will return whenever you desire her presence."

"I thank you, sir," replied the prisoner meekly.

Felton made a slight bow and went toward the door. As he was about to cross the threshold Lord Winter appeared in the hall, followed by the soldier who had been sent to inform him that Milady had fainted. He held a vial of smelling salts in his hand.

"Well, what is this? What's going on here?" he said in a jeering tone as he saw his prisoner sitting up and Felton about to leave. "Has this dead woman come to life again already? By the Lord, Felton my boy, didn't you see that she took you for a novice and that she was playing only the first act of the comedy for you? We shall doubtless have the pleasure of following all the later developments."

"I did think so, my lord, but after all the prisoner is a woman, and I wished to pay her every attention a gentleman owes a woman, if not on her own account, at least on his own."

Milady shuddered from head to foot. Felton's words ran through her veins like ice.

"Aha!" said Winter, laughing. "So that beautiful hair so artfully disheveled, that white skin, and that languishing glance have not seduced you yet, you stony-hearted man!"

"No, my lord," the young man replied indifferently. "Believe me, it takes more than the tricks and the coquetry of a woman to corrupt me."

"In that case, my gallant Lieutenant, let us leave Milady to think up something else, and go to our supper. But remember that she has a fertile imagination, and the second act of the comedy will soon follow the first one." Whereupon, laughing again, Lord Winter passed his arm through Felton's and led him out.

"Oh, I'll be a match for you yet!" Milady muttered between her teeth. "Be assured of that, you wretched would-be monk, you wretched convert of a soldier with your uniform made over into a monk's frock!"

"By the way," Lord Winter added as he was crossing the threshold, "don't let this defeat take away your appetite. Taste that chicken and that fish, I haven't had them poisoned, upon my honor. I get on very well with my chef, and as he is not my heir, I have perfect confidence in him. Do as I do! Adieu, my dear sister, until your next swoon."

Milady could endure no more. She clenched her hands, she ground her teeth, her eyes followed the motion of the door as it almost closed behind Lord Winter and Felton. The moment she was alone a fresh fit of despair seized her. Glancing at the table, she saw the glitter of a knife, reached toward it, and took it up. But her disappointment was cruel. The tip of the silver blade was round and flexible. A burst of laughter rang out from the other side of the half-closed door and the door opened again.

"Ha, ha, ha!" cried Lord Winter. "You see, my gallant Felton, it's just as I told you. That knife was for you, my son; she would have killed you. You see it's one of her eccentricities to rid herself, in one way or another, of anyone who inconveniences her. If I had listened to you, that knife would have been pointed and made of steel. That would have been the end of Felton; she would have cut your throat and then the throats of the rest of us. Look, John, see how well she handles a knife!"

Milady was still holding in her clenched hand the harmless weapon she had meant to use in attack, but at these last words, at this supreme insult, her hand, her strength, and even her will failed her. The knife fell to the floor.

"You were right, my lord," said Felton, in a tone of profound disgust that sank to the very bottom of Milady's heart, "you were right and I was wrong."

Once more both men left the room. But this time Milady listened more intently than she had the first time, and heard their footsteps die away in the distant corridor.

"I am lost!" she murmured. "Here I am in the power of men on whom I have no more influence than I would have on statues of granite or bronze. They know me perfectly, and they wear armor my weapons cannot pierce. But it is impossible that this should end as they have decreed."

She grasped instinctively at the hope in this last reflection. Fear and weakness could not survive long in that abysmal soul. Milady sat down at the table, ate from several dishes, drank a little Spanish wine, and felt all her resolution returning.

Before going to bed she considered, analyzed, turned over and over, examined in every detail, the gestures and even the silence of her interlocutors, and from this deep, skillful, and masterly study she decided that, everything considered, Felton was the more vulnerable of her two persecutors.

One expression especially recurred to her mind. "If I had listened to you," Lord Winter had said to Felton. Then Felton must have spoken in her favor, since Lord Winter had not been willing to listen to him.

"Weak or strong," mused Milady, "that man has at least a spark of pity in his soul, and I will blow that spark into flames that shall devour him. As for the other, he knows me, he fears me, and he realizes what he has to expect if ever I escape from his hands, so it is futile to attempt anything with him. But Felton, that's something else. He is young, ingenuous, and pure; apparently he is virtuous. There are ways to destroy that man."

Milady went to bed and fell asleep with a smile on her lips. Anyone who had seen her would have said she was a young girl dreaming of the wreath of flowers she would wear on her head at the next festival.

CHAPTER 51

MILADY DREAMED THAT AT LAST SHE HAD D'ARTAGNAN
in her power. She was witnessing his execution, and it was the sight of his
odious blood flowing down under the executioner's ax that brought that
charming smile to her lips. She slept the sleep of a prisoner soothed by his
first hope of freedom. When the sentinel entered in the morning she was
still in bed. Felton was standing in the corridor. He ushered in the woman
he had spoken of the night before, and she approached Milady's bed and
proffered her service. Milady was habitually pale, so that her color might
easily deceive anyone who was seeing her for the first time.

"I am feverish," Milady said. "I have not slept for a moment all night.
I am in a frightful pain. Will you be kinder to me than the others were
yesterday? All I ask is permission to stay in my bed."

"Would you like a physician called, madam?" asked the woman. Felton
stood listening in silence. Milady reflected that the more people she had
about her, the more people she could get to pity her, and also, the more
carefully would Lord Winter watch over her. Besides, the physician might
declare that Milady was only feigning illness, and now that she had lost
the first trick in her game she did not intend to lose the second one.

"Fetch a physician?" said she. "What good would that do? Yesterday
these gentlemen declared that my illness was a comedy; they would say
the same today. They have had plenty of time since last night to send for
a doctor."

"Then," said Felton, growing impatient, "will you please tell us yourself, madam, what treatment you wish to follow?"

"Eh, how do *I* know. My God, I know that I am in pain, that is all.
Give me anything you will, I don't care in the least."

"Send for Lord Winter," ordered Felton.

"Oh no, no!" cried Milady. "No, sir, do not summon him, I beseech
you. I am well, I want nothing. Do not send for him." She made her plea
with such vehemence and such persuasive eloquence that Felton, almost
won over, took a few steps into the room. "He has come in," Milady
said to herself.

"If you are *really* in pain, madam," said Felton, "a physician shall be sent for. If you are deceiving us, very well, it will be so much the worse for you. At least we shall have no cause to reproach ourselves."

Milady made no reply, but threw her beautiful head back on the pillow, burst into tears, and sobbed bitterly. Felton gazed at her for a moment with his usual impassivity, then when this hysteria threatened to continue for some time, he went out. The serving-woman followed him. Lord Winter did not appear.

"I think I'm beginning to see my way," Milady said to herself with savage joy, pulling up the bedcovers to hide her inward satisfaction from anyone who might be spying on her. Two hours went by, and Milady said to herself: "Now it's time that my illness is over. I'll get up and gain some advantage this very day. I have only ten days, and tonight two of them will be gone."

The next morning an orderly brought in a table holding her breakfast. She was sure it would not be long before he came to remove it, and then she would see Felton again. She was not mistaken. Soon Felton appeared, and without looking to see whether Milady had or had not touched the food, he motioned to the orderly to take the table away. Felton stayed, holding a book in his hand. Milady, leaning back in an armchair near the fireplace, beautiful, pale, and resigned, looked like a saintly virgin awaiting martyrdom. Felton approached and said:

"Lord Winter, a Catholic like yourself, madam, believes that you might suffer if you were deprived of the rites and ceremonies of your Church. He has therefore decided to allow you to read the ordinary of your Mass every day. Here is the book that contains the ritual."

At the manner in which Felton laid the book on the little table near Milady, at the tone in which he said "your Mass," at the disdainful smile with which he accompanied those words, Milady raised her head and looked at the officer more intently. Then, noting the severe arrangement of his hair, the exaggerated simplicity of his dress, his brow that was as smooth as marble and as hard and impenetrable, she recognized him as one of those somber Puritans whom she had so often met with both at the Court of King James and at that of the King of France, where despite memories of the St. Bartholomew's Day massacre they sometimes sought refuge.

Then there came to her one of those sudden inspirations which only geniuses receive in great crises, in supreme moments that are to decide their fortunes or their lives. Those two words "your Mass" and one glance at Felton revealed to her the importance of the reply she was about to make. With the rapidity of understanding that was characteristic of her she already had her answer on the tip of her tongue.

"*I*," she cried, in a tone of contempt that matched that of the young officer. "I sir, call it *my* Mass! Lord Winter, that corrupt Catholic, knows perfectly well that I am not of his religion. This is a trap he is setting for me!"

"Then what religion do you profess, madam?" asked Felton, with an astonishment that despite his command over himself, he could not entirely conceal.

"I will declare it," cried Milady with feigned exaltation, "on the day when I shall have suffered enough for my faith."

Felton's expression revealed to Milady the full extent of the path she had opened for herself by that one word "faith." Yet the young officer still stood silent and motionless; only his expression had spoken for him.

"I am in the hands of my enemies," she went on in that tone of enthusiasm she knew the Puritans used. "So be it. Let my God save me or let me die for Him! That is the answer I beg you to convey to Lord Winter. And as to this book," she added, pointing to the missal but not touching it, as if she feared to be contaminated by contact with it, "take it back and make use of it yourself. You are undoubtedly Lord Winter's accomplice—an accomplice in his persecution and an accomplice in his heresies."

Felton made no reply. He took the book with the same repugnance that he had shown before and withdrew, deep in thought.

Lord Winter came about five o'clock in the afternoon. Milady had had all day to draw up her plan of action. She received him with the air of a woman who has already recovered every advantage.

"It seems," said Lord Winter, seating himself in an armchair facing hers, and stretching out his legs carelessly to the hearth, "it seems that we have decided to indulge in a bit of apostasy."

"What do you mean, sir?"

"I mean that since the last time we met you have changed your religion. You haven't by any chance married a third husband, have you, and this time a Protestant?"

"Tell me what you mean, my lord," the prisoner answered majestically, "for though I hear your words, I do not understand them."

"Then you haven't any religion at all," said Lord Winter, grinning. "Well, I really like that better."

"Certainly that would be consistent with your own principles, or lack of them."

"Oh, I confess that I don't care what you believe."

"There is no need for you to avow your indifference to religion, my lord. Your debaucheries and your crimes make that only too plain."

"Oho, you speak of debaucheries, do you, Madam Messalina, Lady Macbeth! Either I misunderstand you or by the Lord you are pretty impudent."

"You say that because you know we are overheard, sir," Milady said coldly. "You are trying to prejudice your jailers and your hangmen against me."

"My jailers, my hangmen. Heyday, madam, you are getting quite poetical. Yesterday's comedy is turning into a tragedy, is it? Well, in a week you will be where you belong, and my task will be finished."

"An infamous task," cried Milady with the exaltation of a criminal provoking a judge. "An impious task!"

"On my word of honor," said Lord Winter, rising, "I believe the hussy is going mad. Come, come. Calm yourself, Madam Puritan, or I'll have you put in a dungeon. By the Lord, my Spanish wine has gone to your head, hasn't it? But don't worry, that kind of intoxication is not dangerous, and there will be no bad results."

Whereupon Lord Winter withdrew, swearing heartily, as was the Cavalier custom of the time. Felton had been standing behind the door and had missed no word of this scene.

"Yes, go, go!" she said to her brother. "But I warn you that the consequences of your wickedness are drawing near you. But you, weak fool that you are, will not see them until it is too late to avoid them."

Silence reigned again in the room. Two hours more went by. When the soldiers brought Milady's supper she was engaged in saying her prayers aloud, prayers that she had learned from hearing an austere Puritan say them, one of her second husband's servants. She seemed to be in an ecstasy, and apparently paid no attention to what was going on around her. Felton motioned to the soldiers that she was not to be disturbed and then he went out. Milady knew that she might be watched, and she went on with her prayers to the end. It seemed to her the soldier who stood guard at her door was no longer pacing to and fro but apparently was listening to her.

For the moment that was all she hoped for. She rose, sat down at the table, ate a little, and drank only water. An hour later the soldiers came to remove the table, but Milady noted that this time Felton did not come with them. Was he afraid of seeing her too often? She turned her face to the wall to smile, knowing well that such a triumphant smile would betray her real feelings.

She waited half an hour, then when all was silence in the old castle except for the never-ending murmur of the surge of the sea, she began to sing in her pure, harmonious, and vibrant voice the first verse of a hymn that was then in great favor with the Puritans:

> *"Lord, pity me because*
> *Man would upswallow me,*
> *And fighting all the day throughout,*
> *Oppress me sore doth he."*

The verses were not very good—indeed far from it—but, as is well known, the Puritans did not pique themselves on their poetry.

While she was singing, Milady listened. The soldier on guard at her door stopped and stood as if changed to stone. Milady could judge by

Milady Stabs Herself before Felton and Lord Winter

The Death of Buckingham

that the effect of her hymn. So she went on singing with inexpressible fervor and feeling. But the sentry, doubtless a zealous Catholic, seemed to be able to throw off the spell, for he shouted through the door:

"Hold your tongue, madam! Your song is as dismal as a *De profundis*. If those of us on duty have to listen to things like that, it will be more than we can stand."

"Be silent!" said a stern voice that Milady recognized as Felton's. "What business is it of yours, stupid? Has anyone ordered you to keep this woman from singing? No. You were told to guard her and to shoot her if she tries to escape. Guard her, and if she tries to flee, kill her, but don't go beyond your orders, do you hear?"

An expression of unutterable joy illumined Milady's countenance, but it was as fleeting as a flash of lightning. Without seeming to have heard this dialogue, no word of which she had lost, she began to sing again, with all the charm, all the power, and all the seduction the Devil had bestowed on her voice.

> *"Mine enemies they would*
> *Me swallow up daily,*
> *For they be many that do fight*
> *Against Thee, O Most High."*

That voice of marvelous power and sublime passion imparted to the rude uncouth poetry of the hymn a magical effect such as the most exalted Puritans rarely found in the songs of their brethren. Felton thought he was hearing the song of the angel who solaced the three Hebrews in the fiery furnace.

> *"I'll put my trust in Thee*
> *What time I am afraid,*
> *In God I'll praise His word, in God*
> *My confidence have stayed."*

This verse, into which the terrible enchantress put her whole soul, perturbed the young officer beyond endurance. He flung the door open and Milady saw him appear, pale as he always was, but with burning and almost distracted eyes.

"Why are you singing?" he cried. "And with that voice——"

"I crave your pardon, sir," said Milady meekly. "I forgot that my songs are out of place in this house. Perhaps I have offended you as to your beliefs, but I did not mean to do so, I assure you. Forgive me for an error that perhaps is a great one but which certainly was not intended."

Milady was so beautiful at that moment, her seeming religious ecstasy lent her countenace so wonderful an expression, that Felton was dazzled and fancied he was beholding the angel whose song he had just heard.

"Yes, yes," he answered, "yes, you are troubling and exciting everyone in the castle."

The poor distracted young man was not aware of the incoherence of his words, whereas Milady with her lynx's eyes was reading the very depths of his heart.

"I will keep silent, then," Milady said with all the sweetness she could give to her voice, and looking down with all the resignation she could muster.

"No, no, madam," Felton protested. "But do not sing so loud, especially at night." And with this Felton, feeling that he could no longer maintain his severity toward the prisoner, rushed out of the room.

CHAPTER 52

FELTON HAD COME TO SEE HER, BUT THERE WAS STILL another step for Milady to take. She must detain him, or rather she must be quite alone with him, and as yet she saw but dimly how to bring this about. She must do still more—she must make him speak, so that she could speak to him. Milady knew very well that her greatest charm lay in her voice, which ran so skillfully over the whole gamut of tones from human speech to celestial language.

Yet despite her powers of seduction, Milady might fail, for Felton had been forewarned against the slightest risk of that. From that moment she watched over her every action and her every word, her every gesture, from the simplest glance from her eyes to her breathing, which might be interpreted as a sigh. In fact, she studied everything as an experienced comedian studies a new role of a type he is not accustomed to.

With Lord Winter her plan of conduct was easier; she had decided on that the evening before. To be silent and dignified in his presence, now and then to irritate him by affected disdain or a contemptuous word, to provoke him to threats and violence as a contrast to her resignation—that was her plan. Felton might perhaps say nothing, but would see everything.

The next morning Felton came as usual, but Milady allowed him to superintend all the breakfast preparations without addressing a word to him. Just as he was about to withdraw she was cheered by a ray of hope, for she thought he was about to speak. But his lips moved without making any sound, and by a strong effort of his will, he sent back to his heart the words that had almost escaped his lips, and left the room.

Toward noon Lord Winter entered. It was a rather fine winter day, and rays of that pale English sun that gives light but not warmth were making their way through the barred windows of her prison. Milady was looking out the window, and pretended not to hear the door when it opened.

"Aha!" said Lord Winter. "After playing comedy and then tragedy, here we are playing melancholy, are we?" His prisoner made no reply. "Yes, yes," he went on, "I understand—you would like very much to be at liberty on that shore! You would like equally well to be on a good ship plowing the waves of that emerald-green sea. You'd enjoy greatly, whether on land or on the ocean, laying for me one of those nice little ambushes you are so expert at. Patience, patience! Only four days more and you will be allowed to set foot on the shore, the sea will be open to you—more open than you will like, perhaps—for in four days England will at last be rid of you!"

Milady clasped her hands, and raising her beautiful eyes heavenward, said with angelic meekness of gesture and tone: "O Lord, Lord, forgive this man as I myself forgive him!"

"Yes, pray, you accursed woman!" cried Lord Winter. "Your prayer is all the more generous because, and I swear it, you are in the power of a man who will never forgive you." And he left the room.

Just as he went out she felt a piercing glance reaching her through the half-open door and she saw Felton stepping quickly aside to prevent her seeing him. Then she fell to her knees and began to pray.

"O my God, my God," she cried, "Thou knowest in what holy cause I am suffering. Give me, then, the strength to endure my trials."

The door opened softly. The beautiful suppliant pretended not to hear the sound and continued in a voice full of tears: "O God of vengeance, O God Who art good, wilt Thou permit the abominable plans of this man to be carried out?"

Then only she pretended to hear the sound of Felton's footsteps. Rising as quick as thought, she blushed as if ashamed of being surprised on her knees.

"I do not like to disturb anyone who is praying, madam," Felton said gravely. "Do not interrupt your prayers on my account, I beseech you."

"How do you know that I was praying, sir?" asked Milady in a voice stifled by sobs. "You are mistaken, sir. I was not praying."

"Do you think, madam," Felton answered in the same grave voice but in a more gentle tone, "do you think that I believe I have the right to prevent a human being from bowing down before the Creator of us all? God forbid! Besides, repentance befits the guilty. Whatever crimes they may have committed, for me the guilty are sacred when they kneel at the feet of God."

"Guilty, I guilty?" cried Milady with a smile that would have disarmed the angel of the Day of Judgment. "Guilty! O God, Thou knowest whether I am guilty! Say I have been sentenced, sir, if you wish, but you know that God, who loves martyrs, sometimes permits the innocent to be condemned."

"If you have been unjustly condemned, if you are a martyr," Felton answered, "you have all the more reason to pray, and I will support you with my own prayers."

"Oh, you are a righteous man!" cried Milady, throwing herself down at his feet. "Now I can hold out no longer. I am afraid my strength will fail me at the moment when I am forced to undergo the struggle and confess my faith. I beseech you to listen to the plea of a woman in despair. You have been deceived, sir, but that is not the question now. I ask but one favor of you, and if you grant it, I will bless you both in this world and in the next world."

"Speak to my master, madam," said Felton. "Fortunately I am not charged with the power to pardon or to punish. It is one in a loftier station than mine whom God has charged with that responsibility."

"No, I will speak to you, only to you! Listen to me, sir, instead of contributing to my ruin, to my shame."

"If you have deserved that shame, madam, if you have brought this ignominy on yourself, you must submit to it, making it an offering to God."

"What are you saying? Oh, you do not understand me. When I speak of shame, you think I mean some kind of punishment—imprisonment or death! Would to Heaven it were no more than that! What do I care about imprisonment or death?"

"Now I certainly do not understand you, madam."

"Or rather you pretend not to understand me," replied the prisoner with a skeptical smile.

"No, madam, upon the honor of a soldier, upon the faith of a Christian."

"What! Do you mean you do not know what Lord Winter plans to do with me?"

"I know nothing of his plans, madam."

"But Lord Winter conceals his plans so badly that surely you guess them."

"I do not attempt to guess at anything, madam. I wait until someone confides in me, and except for what Lord Winter has said to me in your presence, he has confided nothing to me."

"Then you are not his accomplice!" cried Milady in an incredibly truthful tone. "You are not his accomplice. You do not know that he is planning a disgrace for me that is more horrible than all the other punishments in the world."

"You are mistaken, madam," said Felton, blushing. "Lord Winter is not capable of such a crime."

"Good!" Milady said to herself. "He knows nothing about it, but he calls it a crime!" Then she said aloud, "The friend of that infamous man is capable of anything."

"Whom are you calling that infamous man?" asked Felton.

"Are there two men in England to whom such a name could be given?"

"You mean George Villiers?" Felton asked, his eyes blazing.

"I mean the man pagans and godless Gentiles call the Duke of Buckingham," answered Milady. "I did not think there was a man in England who needed such a long explanation to make him understand of whom I am speaking."

"The hand of the Lord is stretched out over him," said Felton. "He will not escape the chastisement he deserves."

Felton was expressing as to the Duke of Buckingham only the execration that all the English felt for the man the Catholics themselves called the extortioner, the pillager, the debaucher, and whom the Puritans called simply Satan.

"O God, God," cried Milady, "when I supplicate Thee to send down on this man the chastisement that he has merited, Thou knowest that it is not my own vengeance I seek but the deliverance of a whole nation that I implore."

"Do you know this man, then?" Felton asked.

"At last he is questioning me," said Milady to herself, at the height of joy to have obtained such a result so quickly, then aloud she said: "Do I know him? Yes, I do, to my sorrow, to my everlasting grief."

Felton doubtless felt his strength forsake him, for he took several steps toward the door, but the prisoner had been watching him and she sprang after him and stopped him.

"Sir," she cried, "be kind and merciful, listen to my prayer! That knife which Lord Winter's fatal caution made useless to me because he knows how I would like to use it—oh, hear me to the end—oh, give me a real knife for one minute only, for mercy's sake, for pity's sake! I am at your knees. See, you may close the door, for it is not you I seek to harm. Oh, God—you, the only righteous and compassionate being I have met with here, you, who may be my savior, give me that knife but for one minute, only one, and I will give it back to you through the grating. Only one minute, Mr. Felton, and you will have saved my honor."

"You mean to kill yourself!" cried Felton, forgetting in his terror to withdraw his hands from hers.

"I have told my secret, sir," murmured Milady, sinking to the floor as if fainting. "I have told it to you. He knows all. My God, I am lost!" Felton stood motionless and uncertain. "He still doubts," thought Milady. "I didn't make it strong enough."

Footsteps sounded in the corridor and Milady recognized Lord Winter's stride. Felton recognized it too, and took a step toward the door. Milady sprang toward him.

"Oh, not one word of this, I beseech you!" she cried in a hushed voice. "Not one word to that man of what I have said or I am lost, and it will be you, you——"

Then as the steps drew nearer, fearing that she might be overheard, she pressed her beautiful hand against Felton's lips with a gesture of infinite terror. Felton pushed Milady back quickly and she sank into a chaise longue. Lord Winter passed by the door without stopping and the sound of his footsteps died away in the distance. Felton, as pale as death, stood for a few seconds listening intently, then when there was no longer any sound to be heard, he drew a long breath like a man awaking from a dream and rushed out of the room.

"Aha!" said Milady to herself as she listened to Felton's footsteps going off in the direction opposite to the one Lord Winter had taken. "At last you are mine!"

Then her brow darkened. "If he tells Lord Winter, I am lost indeed, for that man knows that I will not kill myself. He will give me the knife in Felton's presence and Felton will learn that all my great despair was only play-acting." She went to the mirror and looked at herself; never before had she been so beautiful. "True, true," she said, smiling, "but Felton will not tell him!"

That evening Lord Winter entered when Milady's supper was brought her.

"Is your presence a necessary accessory to my imprisonment, sir?" asked Milady. "Could you not spare me the added tortures that your visits inflict on me?"

"How now, my dear sister!" replied Winter. "Didn't you inform me affectionately, with those same lovely lips that are so cruel to me today, that you had come to England for the sole purpose of seeing me at your ease, a pleasure you felt the privation of so much that you risked everything to attain it—rough seas, tempests, and captivity? Well, here I am, so be content. Besides, this time my visit has a motive."

Milady shuddered—she thought Felton had told him all. Perhaps never before in her life had this woman who had experienced so various and so powerful emotions felt her heart beat so violently. She was seated. Lord Winter drew up an armchair and sat down beside her. Then he took a paper from his pocket, unfolded it slowly, and said:

"Take this, please. I want you to see the kind of passport I have drawn up for you myself. Henceforward it will serve to identify you in the life I am willing to let you live." Then, turning his eyes from Milady to the paper, he read:

Order to conduct to——

Lord Winter interrupted himself. "The name is left blank," he said. "If you have any preference, you can tell me, and provided the place is at least a thousand leagues from London, your request will be granted. I will begin again."

Order to conduct to—— the woman named Charlotte Backson, branded by order of a court of justice in the kingdom of France, but released after suffering that penalty. She is to reside permanently in the place named, and shall never be permitted to go more than three leagues away from it. In case of any attempt of escape on her part, the penalty of death shall be imposed. She shall receive 5 shillings per day for board and lodging.

"That order does not concern me," said Milady icily. "It bears some-one else's name, not mine."

"Name! Have you a name, then?"

"I bear your brother's name."

"You are mistaken. My brother was only your second husband, and your first husband is still alive. Tell me his name and I will substitute it for the name Charlotte Backson. No? You don't wish to tell me? You are silent? Very well, you will be entered on the list of prisoners as Charlotte Backson."

Milady did not speak, but this time her silence was not a pretense. She was terrified. She believed that the order was about to be carried out, that Lord Winter was hastening her departure and had doomed her to leave that very evening. For an instant she thought she was lost, but suddenly she saw that the order bore no signature. Her joy at this discovery was so great that she could not conceal it.

"Yes, yes," said Lord Winter, who read her thoughts, "you were looking for the signature, and saying to yourself: 'All is not lost, for that order is not signed. He's showing it to me only to frighten me, that's all.' You are mistaken. Tomorrow this order will be sent to His Grace of Buckingham, the next day it will come back signed by his own hand and bearing his seal, and within twenty-four hours after that it will be put into execution, I will see to that myself. Adieu, madam. That is all I had to say to you."

"And I tell you, sir, that this abuse of power, this exile under a false name, is infamous!"

"Would you prefer to be hanged under your real name, my lady? You know that our English laws about mistakes as to marriages are inexorable. Tell me frankly what you want. Although my name, or rather my brother's, would be involved, I am willing to risk the scandal of a public trial to make sure that I shall be rid of you for good."

Milady made no answer, but she grew as pale as a corpse.

"Oh, I see you prefer to travel. Fine, madam. A wise Englishman once said, 'Travel, in the younger sort, is a part of education.' By my faith, you are not wrong after all. And life is sweet. That's the reason why I take such care that you shall not deprive me of mine. Now the only question to be settled is your allowance of five shillings a day. You think that I'm rather parsimonious, don't you? The reason for that is that I don't care to have you bribing your jailers. Anyway, you will always have left your charms to seduce them with. Employ them—if your failure with Felton has not disgusted you with attempts of that sort."

"Felton has not told him," Milady told herself. "Nothing is lost, then."

"And now, madam, till we meet again. Tomorrow I will visit you to announce the departure of my messenger." Lord Winter rose, bowed to her ironically, and left the room.

Milady breathed again. She still had four days, and four days would suffice to complete the seduction of Felton. But a terrible idea flashed across her mind—perhaps Lord Winter would send Felton himself to get the order signed by Buckingham. If he did, Felton would escape her, since her success with him called for the magic of a continuous fascination. Still, one circumstance reassured her: Felton had not spoken.

As she was not willing to seem disturbed by Lord Winter's threats, she sat down at the table and ate her supper. Then, as she had done the evening before, she fell on her knees and said her prayers in a fairly loud voice, and as on the evening before, the sentinel stopped his pacing to listen to her. Soon after that she heard coming from the far end of the corridor lighter footsteps than those of the sentinel, and they stopped at her door.

"It is he, Felton," she told herself. And she began to sing the same hymn that had excited Felton so strongly the evening before.

But though her sweet, full, sonorous voice rang out more harmoniously and more piteously than ever, the door did not open. It is true that in one of the furtive glances she darted now and then at the grating in the door Milady thought she saw the ardent eyes of the young man peering through the narrow opening. But whether it was really he or only her imagination, this time he had self-control enough to refrain from entering. However, a few minutes after she had finished singing her hymn, Milady thought she heard a deep sigh, then the same footsteps she had heard approach went away again slowly and as if regretfully.

CHAPTER 53

THE NEXT DAY WHEN FELTON ENTERED MILADY'S ROOM he found her standing on a chair holding in her hands a rope of sorts. She had torn linen handkerchiefs into strips, tying them together, and had woven them together into this rope. At the noise Felton made in entering, Milady leaped lightly to the ground and tried to hide the improvised cord by holding it behind her. The young officer was even paler than usual, and his eyes, reddened by want of sleep, showed that he had spent a feverish night. Nevertheless his expression was more austerely severe than ever. He advanced slowly toward Milady, who had seated herself, and took one end of the murderous rope, which either by mistake or perhaps by design, she allowed to show.

"What is this, madam?" he asked coldly.

"That? Oh, nothing," replied Milady, smiling with that pained expression she knew so well how to give to a smile. "Boredom is the mortal enemy of prisoners. I was bored, and I amused myself by twisting this rope."

Felton looked at the wall near which he had found Milady standing on the chair, and he noticed a gilded peg fixed in the wall, one of the sort used to hang clothes or weapons on. He started, and the prisoner saw that start, for though she was looking down, nothing escaped her.

"What were you doing standing on that chair?" he asked.

"What can that possibly matter to you?" retorted Milady.

"But I wish to know," replied Felton.

"Do not question me, sir," said the prisoner. "You know very well that we Christians are forbidden to lie."

"Well then, I'll tell you what you were doing, or rather what you were about to do. You were going to carry out the fatal plan you cherish. Remember, madam, that if our God forbids us to lie, He forbids us much more sternly to commit suicide."

"When God sees one of His creatures persecuted unjustly, and forced to choose between suicide and dishonor, believe me, sir," said Milady in a tone of intense conviction, "God pardons suicide, for then suicide is martyrdom."

"You say either too much or too little. Speak, madam. In Heaven's name, tell me what you mean."

"You want me to recite my misfortunes so that you may treat them as fables. You want me to tell you all my plans so that you can denounce them to my persecutor. No, sir, I will not do it. Besides, what do you care about the life or the death of an unhappy woman who has been condemned? You are responsible for my body alone, are you not? Provided you can produce a corpse that can be recognized as mine, no one will ask any more of you. Perhaps you might even get a double reward."

"I, madam, I!" cried Felton. "Do you suppose that I would accept a reward for your death? Oh, you cannot mean what you say!"

"Let me do what I will, Felton," said Milady, growing more excited still, "let me do what I will. Every soldier should be ambitious, shouldn't he? You are a lieutenant. Well, when you follow me to the grave, you will have a captain's commission."

"What have I done to you," cried Felton, much shaken, "that you should burden me with such a responsibility before both God and man? In a few days you will be out of here, madam, and your life will no longer be under my care. And then," he added with a sigh, "then you will do what you will with it."

"So you," cried Milady, as though unable to suppress her holy indignation, "you, a pious man, you who are called a righteous man, you ask for but one thing—that you will not be accused of my death or be troubled about it!"

"It is my duty to watch over your life, madam, and I will do my duty."

"But do you understand the mission you are charged with? A mission cruel enough if I am guilty, but what name can you give it, what name will the Lord God give it, if I am innocent?"

"I am a soldier, madam, and I obey the orders that have been given me."

"Do you think that on the Judgment Day God will separate the blind executioner from the wicked judges? You will not let me kill my body, yet you are the agent of the man who means to kill my soul!"

"But I tell you again," replied Felton in great agitation, "that no danger threatens you. I will answer for Lord Winter as I would for myself."

"You poor foolish man!" cried Milady. "Who dares to answer for another man when the wisest and most Godfearing men hesitate to answer for themselves, and the man who ranges himself on the side of the strongest and the most fortunate does not hesitate to crush the weakest and the most unfortunate?"

"Impossible, madam, impossible," murmured Felton, who felt the justice of this argument to the very depths of his soul. "While you are a prisoner you shall not recover your liberty through my fault; while you are alive you shall not lose your life through my fault."

"Perhaps," cried Milady, "but I shall lose something that is dearer to me than life, Felton—I shall lose my honor. And it is you, you, that I shall hold responsible before God and man for my shame and my disgrace."

This time Felton, impassive as he was, or seemed to be, could not resist the secret influence that had already taken possession of him. To see this lovely woman, fair as an angelic vision, by turns disconsolate and threatening, to suffer at the same time the ascendancy of grief and of beauty—it was too much for the visionary, too much for a brain undermined by the ardent dreams of an ecstatic faith.

Milady saw his confusion, she felt intuitively the flame of the opposing passions that were burning in the young fanatic's blood. Like a skillful general who, seeing the enemy about to retreat, marches toward him with a cry of victory, she rose, as beautiful as a priestess of old, inspired like a Christian virgin, and with her arm stretched out, her throat uncovered, her hair disheveled, her left hand holding her gown modestly over her breast, her look filled with that fire which had already brought such perturbation to the young Puritan, she stepped toward him, crying out vehemently in her sweet voice, to which on occasion she could give such a terrible stress:

> *"Then shall my foe tremble*
> *When I cry unto Thee;*
> *This I do know assuredly*
> *Because God is for me."*

Felton stood as if petrified. "Who are you? Who are you?" he cried, clasping his hands. "Are you a messenger from God or a servant of Hell? Are you an angel or a devil? Are you called Eloa or Astarte?"

"Do you not know me, Felton? I am neither angel nor devil; I am a daughter of earth, I am your sister in the faith, that is all."

"Yes, yes," cried Felton, "I doubted still, but now I believe you!"

"You believe me, yet you are the accomplice of that son of Belial men call Lord Winter! You believe me, yet you leave me in the hands of my enemies, of the enemy of England, the enemy of God! You believe me, yet you deliver me to that man who fills and defiles the world with his heresies and his debaucheries, that infamous Sardanapalus whom the blind call the Duke of Buckingham, and true believers call the Antichrist!"

"I deliver you to Buckingham, I!" cried Felton. "What mean you in saying that?"

"Having eyes, see you not? And having ears, hear ye not?" cried Milady.

"Yes, yes," said Felton, passing his hand over his perspiring brow as if to wipe away his last doubt, "I recognize the voice that speaks to me in my dreams. I recognize the features of the angel who appears to me every night, crying to my soul, which cannot sleep. 'Strike! Save England, save thyself, or thou wilt die without having appeased thy God.' Speak, speak! I can understand you now."

A flash of terrible joy, swifter than thought, flamed from Milady's eyes. Fleeting as this murderous flash was, Felton saw it and he shuddered as though its light had revealed the abysses of this woman's heart. Suddenly he recalled Lord Winter's warnings, Milady's seductions, her first attempts on her arrival. He shrank back and his head drooped, but he continued to gaze at her as if, fascinated by this strange creature, he could not take his eyes from her.

Milady was not a woman to misunderstand the meaning of this hesitation. Under the emotions she displayed, her icy coolness never deserted her. Before Felton had time to reply and before she would be forced to resume this conversation, so difficult to sustain in the same exalted tone, she let her arms drop to her sides as if the weakness of the woman were getting the better of the enthusiasm of the inspired fanatic.

"But no!" she said. "It is not for me to be the Judith who will deliver Bethulia from Holofernes. The sword of the Eternal is too heavy for my arm. Let me escape dishonor by dying, let me take refuge in martyrdom. I do not ask you for liberty as a guilty woman would, nor for vengeance, as a heathen would. Let me die, that is all, I supplicate you, on my knees, and my last sigh will be a blessing for my savior."

Hearing that voice, so meek and suppliant, and seeing that look, so timid and downcast, Felton drew nearer. Little by little the enchantress had clothed herself with that magic which she assumed or cast aside at will—beauty, meekness, and tears, and above all the irresistible attraction of mystical voluptuousness, the most devouring voluptuousness of all.

"Alas!" said Felton, "there is but one thing I can do—to pity you if you prove to me that you are a victim. But Lord Winter accuses you of wronging him grievously. You are a Christian, you are my sister in the true faith. I feel myself drawn toward you, I who have never loved anyone but my benefactor, I who in all my life have met only traitors and impious men. But you, madam, so beautiful in reality, so pure in appearance, you must have done many evil things to make Lord Winter proceed against you in this way."

"Having eyes, see you not?" repeated Milady in a tone of unspeakable grief. "Having ears, hear you not?"

"Speak, then!" cried the young officer. "Speak, speak!"

"Confide my shame to you," cried Milady, the blush of modesty coloring her face, "for often the crime of one becomes the shame of another. Confide my shame to you, a man, and I a woman? Oh," she continued, covering her beautiful eyes with her hand, "never, never could I do that."

"Not to me, your brother?" said Felton.

Milady looked at the young officer for some time with an expression that he took to be doubting, but which actually was watchful and above all intent on fascinating him. Felton, a suppliant in his turn, clasped his hands.

"Well then," Milady said, "I will dare to trust myself to my brother. I will dare to——"

At that moment Lord Winter's footsteps were heard approaching. This time Milady's ruthless brother-in-law was not content to stop before the door and then pass on, as he had done the evening before. He stopped and exchanged a few words with the sentinel, then the door opened and he appeared. As he was saying those few words Felton drew back quickly, and when Lord Winter entered Felton was standing several paces from the prisoner. Lord Winter came in slowly, and giving a scrutinizing glance first to Milady and then to Felton, he said:

"You've been here a long time, John. Has this woman been telling you the tale of her crimes? If she has, I can understand the length of the interview."

Felton shuddered and Milady realized that unless she came to the rescue of her disconcerted Puritan she was lost.

"Ah, so you are afraid your prisoner may escape!" she cried. "Very well, ask your worthy jailer what favor I was soliciting of him just now."

"You were soliciting a favor, were you?" Lord Winter asked, growing suspicious.

"Yes, my lord," said Felton in some confusion.

"And what favor, pray?" asked Lord Winter.

"That I would give her a knife that she said she would return to me through the grating a moment after she had received it," Felton replied.

"Is there someone concealed here, then, whose throat this amiable lady would like to cut?" Lord Winter inquired in an ironical, contemptuous tone.

"There is myself," Milady answered.

"I have given you your choice between the Americas and Tyburn, Milady," said Lord Winter. "Choose Tyburn. Believe me, the rope is more certain than the knife."

Felton grew pale and took one step forward as he remembered that at the moment he entered the room Milady had held a rope in her hand.

"You are right," she replied. "I have often thought of it." Then she added in a whisper, "I will go on thinking of it."

Felton shuddered to the marrow of his bones, and Lord Winter said: "Beware, John! I have placed my trust in you, John my son. Be on your guard! I have warned you. Besides, keep up your courage, my lad, in three days we shall be rid of this creature. And where I am sending her she can harm no one."

"You hear him!" cried Milady with a vehemence that might, she thought, make Lord Winter believe that she was addressing Heaven and make Felton understand that she was addressing him.

Felton bowed his head, and meditated. Lord Winter took the young officer by the arm and led him out, turning his own head so that he would not lose sight of Milady until he went out.

"Come, come," the prisoner said to herself when the door had closed. "I haven't got as far as I expected to. Lord Winter has exchanged his natural stupidity for a prudence he did not possess before. How a desire for vengeance shapes a man's character! As to Felton, he is hesitating. Ah, he is not the man that damned D'Artagnan is. A Puritan adores only virgins, and he shows his adoration by clasping his hands. A musketeer loves women, and he shows his love by clasping them in his arms."

Milady waited impatiently, fearing that the day might pass without her seeing Felton again. But an hour later she heard someone speaking in a low voice near the door, and soon after the door opened and she saw Felton on the threshold. The young man came into the room quickly, leaving the door open. He motioned to Milady to be silent. He looked very much agitated.

"What do you want of me?" she asked.

"Listen," Felton replied in a low voice. "I have sent the sentinel away so that I could stay here without anyone's knowing that I had come and I could speak to you without being overheard. Lord Winter has just told me a horrible story." Milady again assumed the smile of a resigned victim, and shook her head. "Either you are a devil," Felton went on, "or Lord Winter, my benefactor, my father, is a monster. I have known you for four days, and I have loved him for two years. I may well hesitate as to which of you to believe. Do not be alarmed at what I am saying—I must be convinced. After midnight tonight I will come to see you, and you will convince me, will you not?"

"No, Felton, no, my brother. The sacrifice is too great, and I know what it must cost you. No, I am lost, you must not be lost with me. My death will speak for me much more eloquently than my life. The silence of the corpse will convince you more surely than the words of the prisoner."

"Hush, madam!" cried Felton. "Do not speak to me like that. I have come to beg you to promise me upon your honor, to swear by all you hold sacred, that you will make no attempt upon your life."

"I will not promise that," said Milady, "for no one has more respect than I have for an oath, and if I made a promise, I would have to keep it."

"Very well. Make your promise only for the time until you see me again. If you still persist after that, then you shall be free, and I myself will give you the weapon you have asked me for."

"Very well," declared Milady, "for your sake I will wait."

"Swear it!"

"I swear that I will, by our God. Are you satisfied?"

"I am," said Felton. "Until tonight, then."

He darted out of the room, shut the door, and waited in the corridor, the sentinel's half-pike in his hand as if he were mounting guard in his place. When the soldier returned Felton gave him back his weapon. Through the grating Milady saw the young officer cross himself with delirious fervor and go away in a transport of joy. She returned to her chair with a smile of savage contempt on her lips and, blaspheming, she repeated the awful name of the God she had sworn by without ever having learned to know Him.

"My God," she cried, "what a mad fanatic! I am my own God, I am, and that man shall help me to get my vengeance!"

CHAPTER 54

MILADY HAD WON AT LEAST A HALF-VICTIM, AND HER success doubled her strength. It was not a difficult thing to conquer, as she had done heretofore, men prompt to allow themselves to be seduced, men whom education in gallantry at Court had made them fall quickly into her snares. Milady was beautiful enough to meet little resistance on the part of the flesh, and skillful enough to overcome all the obstacles of the spirit. But this time she had to contend with an uncouth and reserved character made callous by the strong hand of austerity. Religion and penitence had made of Felton a man inaccessible to ordinary allurements.

Consequently many times during that evening she despaired of her fate and of her own powers. She did not invoke God, as we very well know, but she had faith in the genius of evil, that boundless sovereignty which reigns over every detail of human life and by which, as the Arabs say, one pomegranate seed is enough to rebuild a ruined world. By means of her sham virtue, Milady had made a breach in the opinion of a man who was horribly prejudiced against her, and by her beauty a breach in the heart of a man hitherto chaste and pure.

Quite ready to receive Felton, Milady lined up her guns for the morrow. She knew that she had only two days left. Once the order was signed by Buckingham, Lord Winter would put her aboard ship at once.

To be a woman condemned to a wretched and disgraceful punishment does not keep a woman from being beautiful, but it is an adamant obstacle to her becoming powerful. Of course she would return from her exile, she did not doubt that for a moment, but how long would that exile last? To lose a year, two years, three years, to her meant losing an eternity. Would she return to find that D'Artagnan and his friends, happy and triumphant, had received from the Queen the reward they had so richly earned in her service? Such hideous thoughts a woman like Milady could not endure.

What spurred her on even more was the remembrance of the Cardinal. What must the mistrustful, disquieted, suspicious Cardinal be thinking of her silence? He was not only her sole support, her sole prop, her one protector in the present, but he was also the chief instrument of her future fortunes and of her vengeance. She knew him well, she knew that on her return from a futile errand it would be useless to tell him of imprisonment, useless to enlarge upon the sufferings she had undergone. The Cardinal would answer with that ironic smile of the skeptical and forceful genius, "You should not have allowed yourself to be caught."

Time passed. One after the other the hours seemed to awaken the bells, and every stroke of the bronze tongues re-echoed in the prisoner's heart. At nine o'clock Lord Winter made his usual visit. He examined the window and its bars, sounded the flooring and the walls, inspected the fireplace and the doors, and during this long and minute investigation neither he nor Milady said a single word.

"Well, well," Lord Winter said as he was leaving, "you won't escape tonight!"

At ten o'clock Felton came to change sentinels, Milady recognized his step. She was as well acquainted with it now as a mistress is with that of her heart's belovèd, but at the same time she detested and despised him as a weak fanatic. This was not the appointed hour—Felton would not enter. Two hours later, as the clock struck twelve, the sentinel was changed again. Now the hour had come, and Milady waited impatiently. The fresh sentinel began to pace the corridor, and after ten minutes Felton came. Milady listened carefully.

"See here," Felton said to the sentinel, "you are not to leave this door on any pretext whatever. You know that last night my lord punished one man for having left his post for only an instant, even though I myself took his place while he was away."

"Yes, I know he did," replied the soldier.

"I warn you, therefore, to keep the strictest watch. I am going into this woman's room again. I am afraid she is planning to take her own life, and I have orders to keep my eyes on her. If I call, come in. If anyone comes, call me."

"Good!" murmured Milady. "The austere Puritan has learned to lie!"

Felton entered Milady's room. She rose.

"So you are here?" she said.

"I promised you I would come, and I am here," Felton replied.

"You promised me something else, too."

"What else? Oh, my God!" said the young man, who in spite of his iron self-command felt his knees tremble and sweat break out on his brow.

"You promised to bring me a knife, and to leave it with me after we had had our talk."

"Don't speak of that, madam," protested Felton. "There is no state of affairs, however terrible it may be, that gives any one of God's creatures the right to take his own life. I have considered the matter with care. I must never become guilty of such a sin."

"So you have been considering the matter," said Milady with a disdainful smile. "I too have been considering."

"To what purpose?"

"I have decided that I have nothing to say to a man who breaks his word."

"Oh, God——" murmured Felton.

"You may withdraw, sir," said Milady coldly. "I shall not speak."

"Here is your knife!" cried Felton, pulling it out of his pocket. He had brought it, but he had hesitated to give it to the prisoner.

"Let me see it," said Milady. "Upon my honor, I will give it back to you at once. Lay it down on this table, and you can stand between it and me." Felton held out the knife to Milady. She examined the temper of the blade carefully and tried the point on the tip of her finger. "Good," she said as she returned the knife. "That is excellent steel. You are a faithful friend, Felton." Felton took back the weapon and laid it on the table as the prisoner had just suggested he should. Milady followed his motion with her eyes and gestured her satisfaction. "Now," she said, "listen to me." The injunction was unnecessary; the young man stood erect before her, awaiting her words as if he would devour them.

"Felton," continued Milady with a solemnity full of melancholy, "suppose your own sister, the daughter of your father, said to you: 'While I was still young, and unfortunately rather beautiful, a trap was set for me and I was caught in it. I resisted. I was surrounded by snares and many kinds of violence. I resisted. The creed, the faith, whose servant I am and the God I adore were blasphemed because I called for help to that God. I resisted. Every outrage was heaped upon me, and since my persecutor could not make me lose my soul, he determined to defile my body forever. Finally——' " Milady paused, a bitter smile curved her lips.

"Finally," said Felton, "what?"

"Finally one evening he resolved to paralyze the resistance that he could not overcome. He added a powerful narcotic to the water in my glass. I had hardly finished my supper when I felt myself sinking slowly into a strange torpor. I tried to struggle against the sleep that was overtaking me. I rose to my feet, tried to get to the window and call for help, but my legs failed me. I tried to pray, but I could not move my tongue. I sank down on the floor, the prey of a sleep that was like death. What happened while I slept or how long I lay unconscious I cannot tell. I remember only that I awoke in bed in a circular room that was sumptuously furnished. Light penetrated there only through an opening in the ceiling. Moreover, there seemed to be no door to the room. It might well be called a magnificent prison.

"My mind seemed to be struggling vainly to throw off the heavy darkness of that sleep. Vaguely I remembered having been driven a long way in a carriage, but everything was dark and indistinct in my mind. My clothes were near me on a chair, but I could not remember having undressed or going to bed. Then gradually the truth began to dawn on me, a truth terrible to my modesty. I was no longer in my own home. I had fallen asleep the evening before; I must have slept for twenty-four hours. What had happened during that long sleep?

"I dressed as quickly as I could. That room had been furnished to receive a woman. Certainly I was not the first woman to be held captive in this splendid prison. Yes, it was a prison, for I tried in vain to get out. I sounded all the walls, hoping to discover a door, but everywhere the walls gave back only a dull, flat sound. Meanwhile night was falling rapidly, and with night my terror increased. No noise reached me from outside that room by which I could measure the time as it passed. I could only guess that it was probably seven or eight o'clock in the evening.

"Suddenly the noise of a door turning on its hinges made me start. A globe of fire appeared above the glazed opening in the ceiling, casting a brilliant light into the room, and I perceived with terror that a man was standing a few steps from me. A table bearing supper for two had appeared in the middle of the room as if by magic. The man was the one who had pursued me for a whole year, who had sworn my dishonor, and who by the first words he uttered gave me to understand that he had accomplished his purpose the previous night."

"The infamous villain!" muttered Felton.

"Indeed yes, the infamous villain!" cried Milady, seeing with delight the interest with which the young officer listened to this fanciful tale. "He believed that by triumphing over me in my drugged sleep, everything would be easy. He came hoping that I would accept my shame. He came to offer me his fortune in exchange for my love.

"All the proud contempt and disdainful words that a woman's heart can hold I poured out on that man. He listened to me calm and smiling, his arms crossed, then he came toward me. I sprang toward the table, seized a knife, and held the point against my breast. 'Take one more step,' I said to him, 'and you will have not only my dishonor but my death on your conscience.' Everything about me doubtless conveyed conviction, for he stopped in his tracks.

" 'Your death!' he exclaimed. 'Oh, no! You are too charming a mistress for me to consent to losing you when I have had the enjoyment of you only once. Farewell, my lovely beauty, I will wait until you are in a better humor to visit you again.' He blew a silver whistle. The globe of fire disappeared, the noise of the door opening and shutting was repeated, the globe of fire appeared again. I was alone. It was a frightful moment for me. I was in the power of a man I not only hated but also despised, a man capable of any wickedness."

"Who was that man?" demanded Felton.

"I spent the night sitting in a chair," Milady went on, ignoring his question, "but the hours passed without any fresh attempt by my persecutor. The knife I was holding was my only hope."

Milady continued to relate her fantastic experiences, how she refused the wine brought with her meals, but drank only water from the tap, and how that too had been drugged, and again she was in the villain's power. Then she told how she determined to kill her ravisher, hiding a knife under her pillow, and when the miscreant came she struck him in the chest only to find he was wearing a shirt of mail. He announced forthwith that he was not the kind of tyrant who holds women by force, and he would set her free on the morrow.

When she threatened to tell all his villainy once she was free, he declared that in that case he would not allow her to leave, and she replied that she would kill herself even if left without a weapon; she would starve herself to death. He tried again to ensure her silence by asking her to swear upon the crucifix that she would reveal nothing. On her refusal he told her he would condemn her to infamy, and when she still refused he brought in a man who branded the fleur-de-lis on her shoulder. Baring her lovely breasts, and her shoulder, she showed Felton the brand, and at last brought him to his knees asking for her forgiveness.

During this mendacious recital Felton had interrupted her many times, either to beg her to continue or to ask the villain's name. When she had modestly covered her breast and shoulder again, once more he demanded:

"Now tell me your real executioner's name, for the other man was only a tool."

"What, my brother," cried Milady, "do I need to say his name? Have you not guessed it?"

"What, *he* once more, always he, the archcriminal!"

"The archcriminal," Milady repeated. "The man who is devastating England, who persecutes the Puritans, the coward who has ravished the honor of many women, the man who, to satisfy a whim of his corrupt heart, is about to shed English blood, the man who protects the Protestants today and will betray them tomorrow."

"Buckingham!" cried Felton wrathfully. "So it is Buckingham!" Milady hid her face in her hands as if she could not bear the shame that name recalled. "Buckingham, the tormentor of this angelic creature! And Thou didst not hurl Thy thunderbolts at him, O God! Thou hast left him noble, honored, powerful, for the ruin of us all!"

"God abandons those who abandon themselves," said Milady.

"But this man will draw down upon his head the punishment reserved for the damned!" Felton went on with increasing exaltation. "He puts human justice above the justice of Heaven!"

"Men fear him and spare him."

"Not I," declared Felton. "I do not fear him, I, and I will not spare him!" Diabolical joy filled Milady's soul. "But," Felton went on, "how can Lord Winter, my protector, my father, be involved in all this?"

"Listen, Felton," answered Milady. "By the side of cowardly and despicable men, there are often found men of great and generous natures. I had a fiancé, a man whom I loved and who loved me—he had a heart like yours, Felton. I went to him and told him all; he knew me, that man did, and he did not doubt me for a moment. He was a great nobleman, a man the peer of Buckingham in every way. He said nothing, but he girded on his sword, wrapped himself in his cloak, and went straight to Buckingham's palace."

"Yes, yes," said Felton. "I understand what he meant to do. But with men like that it is not the sword one must use, it is the dagger."

"Buckingham had left England the day before, sent as Ambassador to Spain, where he was to ask for the hand of the Infanta for King Charles I, then only the Prince of Wales. My fiancé came back to me. 'Hear me,' he said. 'The man is gone, my dear, and so he has escaped my vengeance for the moment. But in the meantime let us marry as we had planned to do. Then leave it to Lord Clark to uphold his honor and that of his wife.'"

"Lord Clark!" cried Felton.

"Yes," said Milady, "Lord Clark, Lord Winter's brother. And now you must certainly understand everything. Buckingham was away for almost a year. A week before he came back, Lord Clark died suddenly, leaving me his only heir. Whence came that blow? God, Who knows all, doubtless knows. As for me, I accuse no one."

"Oh, what an abyss, what an abyss!" cried Felton.

"Lord Clark died without revealing anything to his brother. My terrible secret was to be concealed from everyone until it blazed out like a thunderbolt over the head of the guilty. Your protector had been troubled by his brother's marriage with a portionless young girl. I felt that I could not look for any support from a man disappointed in his hopes of an inheritance. I went to France, determined to live there for the rest of my days. But all my possessions were in England. When communication between France and England was interrupted by the war, I was in want of everything, and I was forced to return here. I landed at Portsmouth six days ago."

"And then?" queried Felton.

"Then doubtless Buckingham heard of my arrival in some way. He spoke of me to Lord Winter, who was already prejudiced against me, telling him that his sister-in-law was a prostitute, a branded woman. The fine, noble voice of my husband was no longer there to defend me. Lord Winter believed everything that was told him, all the more easily because it was in his interest to do so. He had me arrested, and conveyed here, where he put me under your guard. The rest you know. The day after tomorrow he is having me banished and deported. The day after tomorrow he exiles me among the infamous. Oh, the web is skillfully woven, the plot is crafty, and my honor will not survive it! You see that I must die, Felton. Felton, give me that knife!"

With these words, as if all her strength were exhausted, Milady sank back, weak and languishing, into the arms of the young officer. Intoxicated by love, anger, and voluptuous sensations that he had never known before, he received her with rapture, and pressed her against his heart, trembling all over as he felt the breath from that beautiful mouth, and distraught by the touch of her throbbing breasts against him.

"No, no," he declared, "no. You shall live honored and pure, you shall live to triumph over your enemies."

Milady put him from her with her hand very slowly but drawing him nearer with her eyes. Felton embraced her only the more closely, imploring her as if she were a goddess.

"Oh, death, death," she murmured, half-closing her eyes. "Oh, death rather than shame! Felton, my brother, my friend, I beseech you for it!"

"No!" cried Felton. "No, you shall live and you shall live avenged!"

"Felton, I bring misfortune to all who come near me! Felton, abandon me! Felton, let me die!"

"Well then, we will die together!" he cried, pressing his lips to hers.

Knocking sounded loud on the door. This time Milady pushed him away firmly.

"Listen," she said. "We have been overheard. Someone is coming. All is over, we are lost!"

"No," Felton answered. "That is only the sentinel warning me that they are about to change guard."

"Then hurry to the door and open it yourself."

Felton obeyed; this woman now commanded all his thought, his whole soul. He found a sergeant in charge of a watch patrol.

"Well, what's the matter?" the young Lieutenant asked.

"You told me to open the door if I heard anyone cry for help," the soldier on guard replied, "but you forgot to leave me the key. I heard you cry out but I could not understand what you were saying. I tried to open the door, but it was locked on the inside. So I called the sergeant."

"And here I am," said the sergeant.

Felton, bewildered, almost distracted, stood speechless. Milady perceived that she was the one who must deal with the situation. She ran to the table and seized the knife that Felton had laid there.

"And by what right will you prevent me from dying?" she demanded.

"Great God!" exclaimed Felton as he saw the knife glitter in her hand.

At that moment a burst of ironical laughter resounded through the corridor. Lord Winter, attracted by the clamor, was standing on the threshold clad in a dressing-gown, his sword under his arm.

"Aha!" he said. "Here we are at the last act of the tragedy, are we? You see, Felton, the drama has gone through all the phases I described. But don't worry—no blood will flow."

Milady saw that all was lost unless she gave Felton an immediate and a terrible proof of her courage.

"You are mistaken, my lord," she said calmly. "Blood will flow, and may that blood fall back on those who cause it to flow!"

With a cry Felton rushed toward her, but it was too late. Milady had already stabbed herself. But fortunately—or rather by Milady's skill—the blade struck the steel busk of Milady's corset, glanced down it, tearing her gown, and penetrated on a slant between her flesh and her ribs. Her gown was nevertheless instantly stained with blood. She fell back as though in a swoon. Felton wrested the knife from her hand.

"See, my lord," he said with a gloomy look, "here is a woman who was under my guard, and she has killed herself!"

"Rest easy, Felton," Lord Winter answered. "She is not dead. Demons don't die as easily as that. Rest easy, and go wait for me in my room."

"But, my lord——"

"Go, sir, I command you."

This injunction from his superior Felton obeyed, but as he went out he pushed the knife under his coat. As for Lord Winter, he contented himself with summoning the woman who waited on Milady. When she was come, he commanded the swooning woman to her care and left the two alone together. But since, everything considered, in spite of his suspicions the wound might be a serious one, he immediately sent a man on horseback to fetch a physician.

CHAPTER 55

AS LORD WINTER HAD SURMISED, MILADY'S WOUND WAS not a dangerous one. As soon as she was left alone with the woman Lord Winter had summoned, who made haste to undress her, Milady opened her eyes. But she must feign weakness and pain, which was not a difficult task for so finished an actress as Milady. The poor woman was completely duped by the prisoner, and in spite of Milady's protests she insisted on sitting by her bed all night.

But the woman's presence did not prevent Milady from thinking. There could be no doubt that she had convinced Felton now. Felton was hers. If an angel had appeared to that young man to denounce Milady, in his present state of mind he would certainly take the angel for a messenger from the Devil. Milady smiled at that thought, for Felton was now her only hope, her only means of safety. But Lord Winter might well have become suspicious of him, and Felton might be under surveillance himself.

Toward four o'clock in the morning the doctor arrived. But in the brief time since Milady had stabbed herself the wound had closed. The doctor could therefore judge neither its direction nor its depth. He took the patient's pulse as his only recourse, and from its regularity decided that the case was not serious.

In the morning, pretending that she had not slept all night and needed rest, Milady sent the serving-woman away. She had one hope—that Felton might come at breakfast time. But Felton did not come. Were her fears realized? Would Felton, suspected by Lord Winter, fail her at the decisive moment? She had only one day left. Lord Winter had told her that she was to embark on the twenty-third and it was now the morning of the twenty-second. Nevertheless she waited patiently until the hour for dinner.

Although she had eaten nothing that morning, her dinner was brought at the usual time. Milady saw with dismay that the uniforms of the soldiers who guarded her were different now. She ventured to ask what had become of Felton and was told that he had left half an hour before on horseback. She asked whether Lord Winter was still in the castle. The

soldier replied that he was, and that he had given orders to be informed
if the prisoner wished to speak with him. Milady replied that she was too
weak at the moment, and her only desire was to be left alone. The soldier
went out, leaving the table holding her dinner.

So Felton had been sent away, the marine guard had been relieved;
Felton was distrusted, then. This was the latest blow for the prisoner.

Left alone, she got out of bed. That bed, where she had remained from
prudence, and in order that they might believe her to be seriously
wounded, burned her as if it were a flaming brazier. Glancing at the door,
she saw that Lord Winter had had a plank nailed over the grating. No
doubt he was afraid that through this opening she might, by some diabolical means, succeed in corrupting her guards. Milady smiled with joy. She
was free now to give way to her transports without being observed. She
paced the room with the frenzy of a madwoman, all the fury of a tigress
caged behind iron bars. Certes, if she had still had the knife, she would
have dreamed not of killing herself, but this time Lord Winter.

At six o'clock Lord Winter came in, armed to the teeth. This man,
whom up to then Milady had looked on as only a rather simple-minded
gentleman, had become an admirable jailer. He seemed to foresee everything, divine everything, forestall everything. One look at Milady told
him what was going on in her mind.

"Well and good," he said, "But you shall not kill me today. You have
no weapon now, and besides, I am on my guard. You had begun to per-
vert my poor Felton. He was already yielding to your hellish influence.
But I will save him—he shall never see you again, it's all over. Get your
clothes together, for tomorrow you go. I had set the date of your sailing
for the twenty-fourth, but I bethought me that the sooner you leave, the
safer it will be for all of us.

"Tomorrow at noon I shall have the order for your exile, signed by
Buckingham. If you say a single word to anyone before going aboard, my
sergeant will blow your brains out; he has his orders. If when you are
aboard you speak a single word to anyone before the captain gives you
permission, the captain will have you thrown into the sea; that has been
agreed upon. Au revoir, Milady. That is all I have to say to you today.
Tomorrow I will see you again to bid you farewell!"

With that Lord Winter left the room. Milady had listened to this
menacing tirade with a disdainful smile on her lips but rage in her heart.
Her supper was served. Milady felt that she needed all her strength; she
did not know what might happen that night, which was coming on
menacingly. Great masses of clouds rolled over the heavens and distant
flashes of lightning announced a storm.

The storm burst at about ten o'clock. Milady took some consolation in
seeing nature share the disorder of her own heart. The thunder growled
in the air like the anger in her thoughts. She howled like the hurricane

and her voice was lost in the great voice of Nature, who seemed to be groaning in despair, as she was.

All at once she heard a tap on a windowpane and in a flash of lightning she saw a man's face appear behind the bars. She ran to the window and opened it.

"Felton!" she cried. "I am saved!"

"Yes," said Felton, "but hush, hush! I must have time to file through the bars. Just make sure that they do not see us through the grating."

"Oh, this is a proof that the Lord God is on our side, Felton," Milady replied. "They have covered the grating with a plank."

"Excellent! God has deprived them of their wits! Shut the window, please. Go to bed, or at least lie on the bed fully clothed. When I have finished I will rap on the pane. But are you strong enough to follow me?"

"Oh yes! My wound gives me some pain, but it doesn't keep me from walking."

"Then be ready at my first signal."

Milady shut the window, blew out the lamp, and went to crouch on the bed, as Felton had bade her. Amid the wailing of the storm she could hear the rasp of the file against the bars, and with every flash of lightning she saw the shadow of Felton behind the panes. She spent fully an hour breathless, panting, cold sweat beading her brow, her heart in the grip of frightful anguish at every movement she heard in the corridor. There are hours that seem to go on until they become a year.

After another hour had passed Felton tapped again. Milady sprang out of bed and opened the window. Two bars had been removed to make an opening through which a man or a woman could pass.

"Are you ready?" Felton asked.

"Yes. Shall I take anything with me?"

"Gold, if you have any."

"Yes. Fortunately they left me all I had."

"So much the better, for I have spent all mine to charter a vessel."

"Take this," said Milady, putting into Felton's hands a bag filled with louis d'or.

Felton took the bag and threw it to the foot of the wall. "Now will you come?" he said.

Milady mounted on a chair and passed the upper part of her body through the window. She saw the young officer suspended over the fearsome abyss on a rope ladder. For the first time in her life a feeling of terror reminded her that she was a woman. The dark emptiness terrified her.

"I expected this," said Felton.

"It's nothing, nothing at all," said Milady. "I will go down with my eyes shut."

"Do you trust me?" asked Felton.

"How can you ask me that!"

"Put your two hands together. Cross them—that's right." Felton tied her wrists together, then tied a handkerchief over them.

"What are you doing?" asked Milady, surprised.

"Now put your arms around my neck and fear nothing."

"But I shall make you lose your balance, and we shall both be dashed to pieces."

"Have no fear—I am a sailor."

There was not a second to lose. Milady put her arms around Felton's neck and let herself slip through the window. Felton began to descend the ladder slowly, rung by rung. Despite the weight of their two bodies the blast of the hurricane swung them to and fro in the air. Suddenly Felton stopped.

"What is the matter?" Milady asked.

"Ssh!" Felton answered. "I hear footsteps." There was a silence of several seconds, then he said, "No, it is nothing."

"But what is that noise, then?"

"The patrol making its rounds."

"Which way do they go?"

"Just below us."

"They will discover us!"

"No, not unless there are flashes of lightning."

"They will run against the bottom of the ladder."

"Luckily it is too short by six feet."

"There they are! My God!"

"Hush!"

Both of them remained hanging there twenty feet above the ground, motionless and breathless, while the soldiers passed below, laughing and chatting. It was a horrible moment for the fugitives. The patrol passed on. They heard the sound of footsteps and the murmur of voices die away in the distance.

"Now," declared Felton, "we are safe."

Milady breathed a deep sigh and fainted. Felton continued to descend. Reaching the foot of the ladder and finding that there was no further support for his feet, he clung to the ropes. Then he hung onto the last rung with his strong hands and touched ground. He stooped, picked up the bag of money, and held it between his teeth. Then he took Milady in his arms and set off briskly in the direction opposite to the one the patrol had taken. Soon he left the path, went down across the rocks, and when he reached the shore, blew a whistle. A similar signal answered, and five minutes later he saw a boat coming, rowed by four oarsmen.

The boat approached the shore as close as it could, but the water was not deep enough for it to touch land. Felton walked into the sea up to his waist, being unwilling to entrust his precious burden to anyone else.

Fortunately the storm was beginning to die away, but the sea was still very rough.

"To the sloop!" ordered Felton. "And row fast!"

The four men bent to their oars, but the sea was too high for the oars to get good hold of it. However, gradually they left the castle behind; that was the important thing. It was a very dark night and it was almost impossible to distinguish the shore from the boat, and even less likely that anyone ashore could distinguish the boat.

A black dot was floating on the sea; it was the sloop. While the boat was speeding on with all the strength of its four oarsmen, Felton loosed the handkerchief and untied the cords that bound Milady's hands together. Then he took some sea water and sprinkled it over her face. Milady heaved a sigh and opened her eyes.

"Where am I?" she asked.

"You are safe," the young officer replied.

"Oh, safe, safe!" she cried. "Yes, there is the sky, here is the sea. The air I breathe is the air of liberty. Thank you, Felton, thank you!" The young man pressed her to his heart. "But what is the matter with my hands?" she went on. "It feels as if my wrists had been crushed in a vise." Milady held out her hands and gazed at her bruised wrists.

"Alas!" said Felton, looking at those beautiful hands and shaking his head sorrowfully.

"Oh, it's nothing, nothing!" cried Milady. Then she looked around her as if in search of something.

"There it is," said Felton, touching the money bag with his foot.

They were drawing near the sloop now. A sailor on watch hailed the boat, and the boat replied.

"What vessel is that?" Milady asked.

"The one I chartered for you."

"Where will it take me?"

"Wherever you wish, provided you put me ashore first at Portsmouth."

"What are you going to do at Portsmouth?" Milady asked.

"Carry out Lord Winter's orders," replied Felton with a gloomy smile.

"What orders?"

"You don't understand?" asked Felton.

"No. Explain, I beg of you."

"As he distrusted me, he determined to guard you himself, so he sent me in his stead to get Buckingham to sign the order for your deportation."

"But if he mistrusted you, how could he trust you with such an order?"

"How could I be supposed to know what paper I was bearing?"

"True. And you are going to Portsmouth?"

"I have no time to lose. Tomorrow is the twenty-third and Buckingham sets sail tomorrow with his fleet."

"He sails tomorrow? For what destination?"

"La Rochelle."

"He must not sail!" cried Milady, losing her usual presence of mind.

"Rest easy. He will not sail," replied Felton.

Milady started with joy. She had read to the very depths of the young man's heart, and Buckingham's death sentence was written there in full.

"Felton," she cried, "you are as great as Judas Maccabaeus! If you die, I will die with you. That is all I can say to you."

"Silence!" said Felton. "We are here."

They were, in fact, alongside the sloop. Felton went up the ladder first, then gave his hand to Milady. A moment later they were on the deck.

"Captain," said Felton, "here is the lady I told you of. You are to convey her safe and sound to France."

"For a thousand pistoles," said the captain.

"I have paid you five hundred of them."

"That's correct," said the captain.

"And here are the other five hundred, Captain," added Milady, touching her bag of gold.

"No, madam," said the captain. "I keep my word. My agreement with this young man was that the second five hundred was to be paid me only on arrival in Boulogne."

"And we will surely reach Boulogne?"

"Safe and sound," replied the captain. "As sure as my name is Jack Butler.

"Very well," said Milady, "if you keep your word, it's not five hundred pistoles I will give you, but a thousand pistoles."

"Hurrah for you, then, beautiful lady!" cried the captain. "And may God send me often passengers like your ladyship!"

"Meanwhile," said Felton, "take us to the little bay of——near Portsmouth. You remember it was agreed that you should put in there."

The captain ordered the necessary maneuvers, and toward seven in the morning the little vessel cast anchor in the designated bay.

During the passage Felton told Milady all that he had done: how instead of going to London he had chartered the little vessel; how he had returned and scaled the wall by fastening crampons in the interstices of the stones to give him foothold, and how when he had reached the barred window he had made the ladder secure. Milady knew the rest. On her part, Milady began to encourage Felton in his project, but at the first words she uttered she saw plainly that the young fanatic needed to be restrained rather than to be urged on.

It was agreed that Milady would wait for Felton until ten o'clock. If he did not return by then she was to set sail for France. Later, if he was still at liberty, he would rejoin her at the Carmelite convent at Béthune.

CHAPTER 56

FELTON TOOK LEAVE OF MILADY AS A BROTHER ABOUT to go for a stroll takes leave of his sister, kissing her hand. His whole attitude was apparently as calm as usual. But an unwonted fire blazed feverishly from his eyes. He was paler than ever, his teeth were clenched, and his speech had a short, dry accent that spoke of something somber agitating him. As long as he was in the rowboat that bore him to the shore he kept his face turned toward Milady, who stood on the deck following him with her eyes. Both were now sure that there was no danger of pursuit. No one ever went to Milady's room before nine o'clock, and it would take three hours to get from the castle to London.

Felton jumped ashore, climbed the little rise that led to the top of the cliff, waved to Milady for the last time, and set out for the city. After a hundred paces, as the ground sloped down, he could see no more than the mast of the sloop. He ran toward Portsmouth, and soon came in sight of it some half-mile ahead of him, its towers and houses dimly seen through the morning mist. Beyond Portsmouth lay the sea, covered with vessels, and he could see their masts swaying in the wind like a forest of poplars stripped of their leaves by winter. As he hurried on Felton reviewed in his mind all the accusations, true or false, against the favorite of James I and Charles I that two years of brooding and a long residence among the Puritans had supplied him with. When he compared the crimes this Minister had committed against the public—shattering crimes, crimes against all Europe—with the private and unknown crimes with which Milady charged him, Felton was convinced that the most guilty side of Buckingham's dual character was the one the public knew little or nothing about. This first love of his, so strange, so ardent, made him see Lady Clark's imaginary shameful accusations with the magnification with which one sees through a microscope atomies that in reality are imperceptible beside an ant appear as terrifying monsters.

The rapidity of his pace heated his blood still more. He entered Portsmouth about eight o'clock, and found the whole population astir. Drums were beating in the streets and at the port; troops about to embark were marching toward the wharfs. When he reached the Admiralty Palace he was covered with dust and streaming with perspiration; his face, ordinarily so pale, was almost purple with heat and passion. The sentry tried to refuse him entrance, but Felton called to the officer in charge and, pulling out of his pocket the letter he was carrying, said:

"A pressing message from Lord Winter to His Grace the Duke of Buckingham."

On hearing the name of Lord Winter, who was known to be one of His Grace's intimate friends, and moreover seeing that Felton himself wore the uniform of a naval officer, the officer in charge of the post gave orders to allow him to pass. Felton darted into the palace. Just as he was entering the vestibule another man was entering also, covered with dust and out of breath. He had just dismounted from a post horse that had fallen on its front knees, exhausted.

This man and Felton addressed Patrick, the Duke of Buckingham's confidential valet, at the same moment. Felton named Lord Winter, whereas the stranger refused to give any name but asserted that he could make himself known only to the Duke himself. Each insisted that he must gain admission ahead of the other. Patrick, who knew that Lord Winter was in government service and in very friendly relations with the Duke, naturally gave the preference to the man who came on his behalf. The other man was forced to wait, and it was easy to see that he was cursing the delay.

Patrick led Felton across a great hall where the deputies of La Rochelle, headed by the Prince de Soubise, were waiting and ushered him into a dressing-room where Buckingham, just out of his bath, was finishing his toilet, to which he always paid the greatest attention.

"Lieutenant Felton, coming from Lord Winter," announced Patrick.

"From Lord Winter!" Buckingham repeated. "Well, show him in."

Felton entered just as Buckingham was throwing down on a couch his dressing-gown richly embossed with gold. He began to don a doublet of blue velvet heavily embroidered with pearls.

"Why did not Lord Winter come himself?" he demanded. "I expected him this morning."

"He bade me tell Your Grace," Felton replied, "that he regretted very much not to have that honor, but he was prevented by the watch he must keep at the castle."

"Yes, I know," said Buckingham. "He has a prisoner."

"It is about that prisoner I wish to speak to Your Grace."

"Well then, speak!"

"What I have to say must not be heard by anyone except yourself."

"Leave us, Patrick," said Buckingham, "but keep within sound of the bell. I will summon you presently." Patrick went out. "We are alone, sir. What is it you have to say?"

"Your Grace," said Felton, "the other day Lord Winter wrote you to

Milady Poisons Constance Bonacieux

Constance Dies in D'Artagnan's Arms

request you to sign an embarkation order for a young woman named Charlotte Backson."

"He did, sir, and I answered that if he would bring me or send me the order I would sign it."

"Here it is, my lord."

"Give it to me," said the Duke.

Taking it from Felton, Buckingham glanced over it rapidly, and seeing that it was the one he had been told of, he laid it on the table, took up a quill, and prepared to sign it.

"I beg your pardon, my lord," said Felton, stepping forward to stop the Duke, "but does Your Grace know that Charlotte Backson is not the real name of this young woman?"

"Yes, sir, I know it," the Duke replied, dipping his quill in the ink-well.

"Then Your Grace knows her real name?" Felton asked sharply.

"Yes, I know that too." The Duke put his pen to the paper. Felton grew paler still.

"And knowing her real name, Monseigneur will sign the order all the same?" he asked.

"Certainly I will," Buckingham replied, "and I'd like to sign twice instead of once."

"I cannot believe," said Felton, his voice growing even sharper, "that His Grace knows that the woman in question is Lady Clark."

"I know that perfectly well, but I am surprised that you should know it!"

"And Your Grace will sign that order without compunction?"

Buckingham stared haughtily at the young man. "See here, sir," said he, "do you know that you are asking me very strange questions, and that I am very foolish to answer them?"

"Answer them, Monseigneur," said Felton. "The circumstances are more serious than you perhaps imagine."

Buckingham supposed that as this young man came on Lord Winter's behalf, he was doubtless speaking in his master's name, and he softened a little.

"I will sign without any compunction whatever," he said. "Lord Winter knows as well as I do that Lady Clark is a great criminal, and that she is being treated mercifully in having her punishment limited merely to deportation." The Duke put his pen to the paper again.

"You will not sign that order, my lord!" cried Felton, taking a step toward the Duke.

"I will not sign that order!" Buckingham repeated. "And pray you, why not?"

"Because you will take counsel with your own conscience and you will do justice to Milady."

"It would be doing her justice to send her to Tyburn," Buckingham replied. "Milady is an infamous woman."

"Monseigneur, Milady is an angel, you know very well that she is, and I demand that you set her free."

"Come now," said Buckingham, "are you mad, man, to talk like that to me?"

"My lord, forgive me! I am speaking as well as I can, I am restraining myself. Think of what you are about to do, and beware lest you go too far."

"Whatever do you mean? Bless my soul," cried Buckingham, "I really believe the man is threatening me!"

"No, my lord, I am still beseeching you. And I say to you: One drop of water is enough to make a full vase overflow, one little mistake may bring punishment down on a head that has been spared until now despite so many crimes."

"Mr. Felton," said Buckingham, "you will leave here at once and place yourself under arrest."

"You shall listen to me to the end, my lord. You seduced this young girl, you outraged her, you defiled her. Make compensation for your crimes toward her, let her go free, and I will require nothing else of you."

"You will *require*——?" said Buckingham, gazing at Felton in astonishment and stressing every syllable of the words as he said them.

"My lord," Felton went on, growing more excited as he spoke, "my lord, beware! All England is weary of your iniquities. My lord, you have abused the royal power, you have almost usurped it, and you are held in horror by God and by men. God will punish you hereafter, but I will punish you here and now."

"Oh, this is too much!" cried Buckingham, taking a step toward the door.

Felton barred his passage, saying: "I ask you most humbly, Your Grace, to sign an order to set Lady Clark free. Remember that she is a woman you have brought to shame."

"Withdraw at once, sir," said Buckingham, "or I will call one of my attendants and have you put in irons."

"You shall not call," Felton said, throwing himself between the Duke and the bell standing on a small table inlaid with silver. "Beware, my lord! You are in the hands of God!"

"In the hands of the Devil, you mean!" cried Buckingham, raising his voice in order to attract the notice of his servitors without actually summoning them.

"Sign, my lord, sign the order to set Lady Clark free!" said Felton, holding out a paper to the Duke.

"What! By force? You are joking! Holà, Patrick!"

"Sign, my lord."

"Never! Help, help!" cried the Duke, springing toward his sword.

But Felton did not give him time to draw it. He was holding open under his shirt the knife Milady had stabbed herself with. In one bound he flung himself on the Duke.

At that moment Patrick entered, crying out: "A letter from France, my lord!"

"From France," exclaimed Buckingham, forgetting everything else in thinking who must have sent him that letter. Felton took advantage of that moment of forgetfulness and plunged the knife into Buckingham's side up to the hilt. "Ah, traitor!" Buckingham cried out. "You have killed me!"

"Murder, murder!" shrieked Patrick.

Felton looked about him for some means of escape, and seeing that the door was open, he rushed into the next room, where, as has already been noted, the deputies from La Rochelle were waiting, crossed it on the run, and precipitated himself toward the stairway. But on the first stair he encountered Lord Winter. Seeing Felton deathly pale, confused, fairly livid, his face and hands stained with blood, Lord Winter seized him, crying:

"I knew it! I guessed it only one minute too late. Oh, wretched, wretched man that I am!"

Felton offered no resistance. Lord Winter gave him over to the guards, who led him to a small terrace overlooking the sea, where they awaited further orders. Lord Winter rushed on into Buckingham's dressing-room.

At the Duke's cry and Patrick's call for help the man from France whom Felton had encountered in the vestibule dashed into the dressing-room. He found the Duke lying on a sofa, his clenched hands pressing his wound.

"La Porte," said the Duke in a faint voice, "La Porte, do you come from her?"

"Yes, Monseigneur," replied Anne of Austria's faithful cloak-bearer, "and perhaps too late."

"Hush, La Porte, someone might hear you. Patrick, let no one enter. Oh, I shall never know what she has written me! O God, I am dying!" And the Duke fainted.

Meanwhile Lord Winter, the deputies from La Rochelle and the leaders of the delegation, and the chief members of Buckingham's household had all made their way into the dressing-room. Cries of despair filled the little room. The news spread through the palace, filling it with wails and moans, and soon spread throughout the city. Presently cannon shots were announcing that something new and unexpected had happened. Lord Winter was tearing his hair in agony.

"Too late by one minute!" he cried. "Oh, my God, my God, what a mischance!"

At seven o'clock that morning he had been informed that a rope ladder was dangling from one of the castle windows. He had hastened to Milady's room and found it empty, the window open, and the bars filed through. He remembered the verbal warning D'Artagnan had sent by his messenger and he trembled for the Duke. Running to the stable, without taking time to have a horse saddled, he vaulted onto the first horse he came to, galloped at full speed to the Duke's palace, leaped down in the courtyard, mounted the stairway as fast as he could, and on the first step, as we know, he met Felton.

The Duke was not dead as yet. He recovered a little, opened his eyes. Hope revived in all the hearts of all those about him.

"Gentlemen," he said, "leave me alone with Patrick and La Porte. Ah, it's you, Winter. You sent me a strange madman this morning. See what he has done to me!"

"Oh, my lord," cried Lord Winter, "I shall never forgive myself!"

"And you would be quite wrong, my dear Winter," said Buckingham. "I know of no man who deserves to leave another man inconsolable for the whole of his life. But leave us now, I entreat you."

Lord Winter went out sobbing. The wounded Duke, Patrick, and La Porte were alone together. A doctor was being sought but so far none had been found.

"You will live, my lord, you will live," the faithful servitor of Anne of Austria kept saying as he knelt by the Duke's couch.

"What did she write me?" said Buckingham faintly, streaming with blood and overcoming his atrocious agony to speak of the woman he loved. "What did she write? Read me her letter."

"Oh, my lord!" said La Porte.

"Do as I bid you, La Porte. Don't you see that I have no time to lose?" La Porte broke the seal and held the paper before the Duke's eyes, but Buckingham tried in vain to decipher the writing. "Read it to me, then, read! I can no longer see. Soon, perhaps, I shall no longer hear, and I shall die without knowing what she has written."

La Porte made no further protest and read:

My lord:

By what I have suffered through you and for you ever since I have known you, I conjure you, if you have any regard for my peace of mind, to put a stop to those great armaments you are preparing against France, to put an end to a war of which it is openly said that religion is the ostensible cause, and whispered that the real cause is your love for me. That war may not only bring great catastrophe down on both England and France, but also on your own head, my lord, misfortunes for which I should be inconsolable.

Watch carefully over your life, which is threatened, and which will be dear to me from the moment when I am no longer forced to look on you as an enemy.

Your affectionate
Anne

Buckingham mustered all his remaining strength to listen, and when the reading was ended he said, as if he had met a bitter disappointment:

"Have you nothing further to tell me that you yourself know, La Porte?"

"Yes, my lord, I have. The Queen bade me tell you to be very careful, for she had been informed that there would be an attempt to assassinate you."

"And is that all, La Porte, is that all?" Buckingham asked impatiently.

"Her Majesty also charged me to tell you that she still loves you."

"Ah, God be praised!" cried Buckingham. "To her, my death will not be the death of a stranger." La Porte burst into tears. "Patrick," the Duke went on, "bring me the casket in which I kept the diamond tags." Patrick brought the casket, which La Porte recognized as having belonged to the Queen. "Now the little white-satin bag with her monogram embroidered in pearls." Again Patrick obeyed.

"Here, La Porte," said Buckingham, "are the only remembrances I ever received from her, this silver casket and these two letters. You will give them back to Her Majesty. And as a last remembrance," he went on looking around him for some precious object, "you will also give her——"

He was still searching, but his eyes, shadowed by death, met with nothing but the knife that had fallen from Felton's hand, its blade still hot with the Duke's blood.

"You will give her this knife with them," the Duke whispered, pressing La Porte's hand.

He still had just strength enough to place the bag in the casket and let the knife drop into it, motioning to La Porte that he was no longer able to speak. Then, in a final convulsion that he no longer had the strength to strive against, he slid from the sofa to the floor. Patrick gave a loud cry.

Buckingham tried to smile a last time, but Death checked the thought, which remained imprinted on his brow like a last kiss of love.

At that moment the Duke's physician arrived, quite distraught. They had not been able to reach him before because he was already aboard the flagship. He came to the Duke, took his hand, held it for an instant in his, then let it fall.

"All is useless," he murmured. "His Grace is dead."

"Dead, dead!" Patrick shrieked.

At this cry the crowd assembled again, and everywhere there was consternation and confusion. As soon as Lord Winter knew that Buckingham had died, he ran to Felton, still under guard on the terrace.

"You miserable wretch," he said to the young man, who now that he knew Buckingham was dead had regained the calm and self-possession that never after deserted him. "You miserable wretch! What have you done?"

"I have avenged myself!"

"Avenged yourself!" cried Lord Winter. "Say rather that you have served as the tool of that accursèd woman. But I swear to you that this crime shall be her last!"

"I do not know what you mean, my lord," Felton answered calmly. "I do not know who it is you're talking about. I killed the Duke of Buckingham because twice he refused at your own request to give me a captain's commission. I punished him for his injustice, that is all."

Lord Winter, dumfounded, watched the guards bind Felton. He knew not what to think of such callousness.

One thing alone rested like a shadow on Felton's pallid brow. At every sound he heard, the simple-minded Puritan fancied he recognized the step and the voice of Milady coming to throw herself into his arms, to accuse herself and to meet death with him. Suddenly he gave a start. His eyes became fixed on one dot far out on the sea. From the terrace where he stood he could see the whole expanse of the waters. With the eagle eye of a sailor he discerned there what another man might have thought a gull rocking on the waves—the white sail of a sloop steering for the coast of France. He grew deadly pale, put his hand on his heart, which was breaking, and suddenly he understood all Milady's treachery.

"One last favor, my lord!" he said to Lord Winter.

"What favor?"

"What time is it?"

Lord Winter took out his watch. "It lacks ten minutes to nine," he replied.

Milady had set sail an hour and a half earlier than the time they had agreed on. When she had heard the sound of the cannon that announced the fatal news, she had given orders to weigh anchor. Now the sloop was making way far from the English coast under a beautiful blue sky.

"God has so willed it," Felton said with the resignation of a fanatic, but he could not take his eyes from that vessel, on board of which he perhaps thought he could distinguish the woman for whom he had sacrificed his life.

Lord Winter followed Felton's glance, saw his suffering, and guessed the truth. "You are to be punished *alone* at first," Lord Winter said to Felton, who was being led away while his eyes were still searching the sea, "but I swear to you by the memory of the brother I loved so dearly that your accomplice will not escape."

Felton bowed his head without uttering a single word. As to Lord Winter, he descended the stairway hurriedly and went straight to the port.

CHAPTER 57

THE FIRST FEAR THAT SWEPT OVER CHARLES I, KING OF England, when he heard of Buckingham's death was lest such terrible news might discourage the defenders of La Rochelle. Richelieu says in his *Memoirs* that Charles tried to keep the news from them as long as possible. He closed all the ports of his kingdom and took the greatest care to prevent any vessel from sailing until the army Buckingham had made ready should have set out. Now that Buckingham was gone, he undertook to oversee its departure himself. He carried the strictness of this order so far that he detained in England the Danish ambassadors, who had already taken leave of him, and the regular ambassador from Holland, who was to return to the port of Flushing the Indian merchantmen Charles I was having restored to the United Provinces.

As King Charles did not think of giving these orders until five hours after Buckingham's murder—at two o'clock in the afternoon—two vessels had already sailed. One of these was taking Milady to France. She had suspected what had happened, and she was confirmed in her belief by seeing the black flag flying at the masthead of the flagship of the fleet. As to the other vessel, presently we will learn whom it was bearing and how it came to sail.

Meanwhile, nothing new was happening in the camp before La Rochelle. But the King, who was still suffering from boredom, as usual, had decided to go incognito to Saint-Germain to celebrate the festival of his patron saint, Saint Louis. He requested the Cardinal to provide him an escort of only twenty musketeers. The Cardinal, who was sometimes as bored as the King, gave his royal lieutenant leave of absence with the greatest pleasure. The King promised to return about September 15.

Monsieur de Tréville, notified of all this by His Eminence, had his baggage packed at once. Without knowing their reasons, he knew the eager desire and even the urgent need that his four friends had to get back to Paris, so naturally he named them as part of the King's escort. The four young men heard the news only a quarter of an hour later than Monsieur de Tréville. It was then that D'Artagnan appreciated fully the favor the Cardinal had conferred upon him by having him at last transferred to the

Royal Musketeers. Without that transfer, he would have been forced to remain in the camp while his companions left it.

Of course this eager desire to return to Paris was caused by the danger Madame Bonacieux would run in meeting at the convent in Béthune Milady, her mortal enemy. Therefore Aramis had written immediately, as we already know, to Marie Michon, that seamstress in Tours who had such high-placed acquaintances, asking her to obtain from the Queen authority for Madame Bonacieux to leave the convent and retire either to Lorraine or to Belgium. They did not have long to wait for the answer; a week later Aramis received the following letter:

My dear cousin:

Enclosed you will find authorization from my sister that will enable our poor servantmaid to leave the Béthune convent, since you think the air there does not agree with her. My sister sends you this authorization with great pleasure, for she is very fond of the little girl, and she intends to be of further service to her in the future.

I embrace you.

Marie Michon

The order enclosed read as follows:

The Louvre, August 10, 1628

The Superior of the convent at Béthune is instructed to deliver into the hands of the bearer of this note the novice who entered the convent on my recommendation and under my patronage.

Anne

The four musketeers had obtained what they wanted—the order to remove Madame Bonacieux from the Carmelite convent at Béthune. It is true that this order would be of no great use to them while they were in camp before La Rochelle; that is to say, at the other end of France. So Aramis was about to ask Monsieur de Tréville for a leave of absence, confiding to him quite frankly the importance of such a leave, when he and his three comrades were informed that the King was leaving for Paris with an escort of twenty musketeers, and that they had been detailed among the number. Their joy almost overwhelmed them. They sent their lackeys on ahead with their baggage, and the next morning they set out themselves.

The Cardinal accompanied His Majesty from Surgières to Mauzé, and then the King and his Minister took leave of each other with great demonstrations of friendship.

The King, however, was looking for diversion, and although he traveled as fast as possible—for he wished to reach Paris by September 23—he stopped from time to time to fly his falcons at magpies. The taste for this pastime had been taught him a long time ago by De Luynes, and he had always retained a great partiality for it. When this happened, sixteen of the twenty musketeers rejoiced over the relaxation, but the other four cursed heartily. D'Artagnan especially felt a perpetual buzzing in his ears, which Porthos explained thus:

"A very great lady told me once that when you feel that, somebody is talking of you somewhere."

At last the escort crossed Paris on the night of September 23. The King thanked Monsieur de Tréville, and gave him permission to allow his men a four-day furlough, on one condition—that no one of those thus favored should appear in any public place, under penalty of imprisonment in the Bastille. The first four leaves granted, as may be imagined, went to our four friends. Moreover, Aramis obtained from Monsieur de Tréville six days instead of four, with two nights added, for they were to leave on the twenty-fourth at five in the afternoon, and as a further kindness Monsieur de Tréville postdated the leave to the morning of the twenty-fifth.

"Good Lord," said D'Artagnan, who, as we know, never had doubts about anything, "I think we're making a lot of fuss about a very simple matter. I can get to Béthune in two days by killing two or three horses. That's a small matter to me, I have plenty of money. I deliver the Queen's letter to the Mother Superior and I bring back my long-sought belovèd treasure. I do not take her to Lorraine or to Belgium, but to Paris, where she can be hidden much better, especially while the Cardinal is at La Rochelle. Then once we come back from the campaign—well, half because of the protection of her 'cousin,' half because of what we have done for her personally, we can obtain from the Queen what we desire. So do you stay here and don't tire yourselves out needlessly. I myself and Planchet, that is all that is needed for so simple an errand."

To which Athos replied quietly: "We too have plenty of money. I have not yet drunk all my share of the diamond, and Porthos and Aramis have not eaten their shares. So we can kill four horses apiece. But consider, D'Artagnan," he added in a voice so somber that his tone made the younger man shudder, "consider that Béthune is the town where the Cardinal has appointed a meeting with a woman who brings misfortune with her wherever she goes. If you only had four men to deal with, D'Artagnan, I would allow you to go alone; as you have that woman to deal with, the four of us must go. And may God grant that together with our four lackeys there will be enough of us!"

"You alarm me, Athos!" cried D'Artagnan. "In God's name, what do you fear?"

"Everything!" Athos replied.

D'Artagnan studied the faces of his companions. Like Athos's, all of them wore expressions of deep anxiety. They rode off at full speed, without breaking silence again.

On the evening of September 25, as they were entering Arras and D'Artagnan had just dismounted at the inn, The Sign of the Golden Harrow, to drink a glass of wine, a horseman rode out of the posting yard, where he had just changed mounts. His horse was fresh, and he took the road to Paris at full gallop. As he was passing through the main gateway into the street, the wind blew open the cloak in which he was wrapped, though it was only September, and blew off his hat. He caught it just as it left his head and pulled it down quickly over his eyes. D'Artagnan, who had been staring at the man, turned deathly pale and let his glass fall to the ground.

"What's the matter, monsieur?" Planchet asked. "Oh, hurry here, gentlemen, my master is ill!"

The three friends hastened to D'Artagnan and found that instead of being ill, he was running to his horse. They blocked his way.

"Where the devil are you going?" cried Athos.

"It is *he!*" shouted D'Artagnan, pale with anger and his brow beaded with sweat. "That's the man! Let me catch up with him!"

"But who is *he?*" Athos inquired. "What man do you mean?"

"He—that man!"

"What man?"

"That damned evil genius of mine. I have seen him every time I was threatened with some calamity. He was with that horrible woman when I met her for the first time, he is the man I was trying to get at when I offended our friend Athos, and Monsieur de Tréville, the man I saw the very morning Madame Bonacieux was carried off! And now I have seen him again! I recognized him when the wind blew his hat off!"

"The devil you say!" said Athos dreamily.

"To horse, gentlemen, to horse!" shouted D'Artagnan. "Let us pursue and overtake him."

"My dear boy," said Aramis, "remember that he is going in exactly the opposite direction from ours, that he has a fresh horse and our horses are tired. Consequently we might kill our own mounts without ever getting a chance to catch him. Let the man go, D'Artagnan, and save the woman."

"Hey, monsieur!" yelled a stableboy, running after the nameless man. "Hey, monsieur, here's a paper that dropped from your pocket. Hey, monsieur, hey!"

"My friend," said D'Artagnan, "a half-pistole for that paper!"

The stableboy, delighted at earning so easily the price of his day's wage, went back to the courtyard. D'Artagnan unfolded the paper.

"Well," his friends asked eagerly, "what is it?"

"Nothing but one word," D'Artagnan answered.

"Yes," said Aramis, "but that one word is the name of some town or village."

" 'Armentières,' " Porthos read. "Armentières! I never heard of it."

"That name of a town or a village is in *her* handwriting!" cried Athos.

"Come, let us keep this paper carefully," said D'Artagnan. "Perhaps I have not wasted my last pistole. To horse, my friends, to horse!"

And the four comrades galloped off toward Béthune.

CHAPTER 58

GREAT CRIMINALS BEAR A KIND OF PREDESTINATION
that enables them to overcome all obstacles, and escape every danger, until the moment that a wearied Providence has marked out the reef on
which their impious fortunes will be wrecked. It was like that with Milady.
She had sailed through the fleets of both the nations at war, and reached
Boulogne without mishap.

When she landed at Portsmouth, Milady was an Englishwoman driven
from La Rochelle by the persecutions of the French; when she landed at
Boulogne, after a two-day crossing, she passed as a Frenchwoman persecuted at Portsmouth because of the English hatred for France. Besides,
Milady had the most effective of passports: her beauty, her noble bearing, and the liberality with which she distributed her pistoles. Freed from
the usual formalities by the affable smile and the gallant manners of the
aged Governor of the Port, she remained in Boulogne only long enough
to post the following letter:

> Boulogne, evening of September 25
> To His Eminence Monseigneur le Cardinal de Richelieu at his camp before
> La Rochelle.
> Monseigneur:
> Your Eminence may be reassured. His Grace the Duke of Buckingham
> *will not set out* for France.
>
> Lady ————
> P.S. In accordance with the wishes of Your Eminence I am going to the
> convent of the Carmelites at Béthune, where I will await your orders.

That same evening Milady began her journey. That night she slept at
an inn. The next day she set out at five in the morning, and three hours
later she reached Béthune. She inquired for the convent of the Carmelites
and went there immediately. The Mother Superior received her, and
Milady was immediately assigned a room and given breakfast.

In the eyes of this woman, all her past was already blotted out. With
her gaze fixed on the future, she beheld nothing but the high fortune the

Cardinal was reserving for her. She had served him well, and without his name's being involved in this bloody business. The passions, always new ones, that consumed her gave her life the semblance of those white clouds which float in the heavens, reflecting sometimes azure, sometimes fire, sometimes the opaque blackness of a tempest, and which leave no traces on the earth save those of destruction and death.

After breakfast the Mother Superior came to pay her a visit. There are few diversions in a convent, and the good nun made haste to get acquainted with her new guest. Milady was eager to please the Mother Superior. Now this was a very easy matter for so skillful a woman as Milady. She made herself very amiable, very charming, and she captivated the good nun with the variety of her conversation and the graciousness of her personality. The Mother Superior, who was of noble birth, took delight in hearing tales of the Court, which so seldom travel to the remote parts of the kingdom, and which especially have such difficulty in climbing over the walls of convents, the thresholds of which worldly rumors reach only to die there.

Milady, on the other hand, was quite conversant with all the aristocratic intrigues amid which she had lived constantly for five or six years. She made it her business, therefore, to amuse the good Mother Superior by relating all the worldly practices of the Court of France. She recited the scandalous chronicle of the lords and ladies of the Court, whom the Mother Superior knew perfectly well by name. She touched lightly on the love affair of the Queen and Buckingham. She talked a great deal in order to induce her listener to talk a little. But the Mother Superior was content to listen and to smile without saying a word. However, Milady saw that this type of conversation diverted the nun very much, so she continued it. Only now she began to speak of the Cardinal.

However, here she was in a difficult position. She did not know whether the Mother Superior was a royalist or a cardinalist. She decided that it was prudent to steer a middle course. But on her part, the Mother Superior maintained a still more prudent reserve, contenting herself with bowing low every time the traveler mentioned His Eminence's name.

Milady began to feel that she would soon be bored by life in a convent, so she decided to take a risk in order to find out what the situation was. Wishing to discover how far the good Mother Superior's discretion would go, she began to tell an ugly story, vague at first but afterward very circumstantial, about the Cardinal, relating his love affairs with Madame d'Aiguillon, Marion de Lorme, and several other gay ladies. The Mother Superior listened attentively, grew more and more animated, and smiled from time to time.

"Good!" thought Milady. "She is taking pleasure in what I am saying. If she is a cardinalist, at least she isn't a fanatical one!"

Then Milady went on to describe the persecutions the Cardinal inflicted on his enemies. The Mother Superior merely crossed herself, showing neither approval nor disapproval. This confirmed Milady in her opinion that the nun was royalist rather than cardinalist. Milady continued, making her tales more and more impressive.

"I am very little acquainted with all those matters," remarked the Mother Superior at last. "But however remote from the Court we may be, however untouched we are by worldly concerns in this retreat, we do have very sad examples of what you have been saying. We have a guest here now who has suffered much from the vengeance and the persecution of Monsieur le Cardinal."

"A guest of yours!" said Milady. "Oh the poor woman, how I pity her!"

"And you have good reason to, for she is certainly to be pitied. Imprisonment, threats, ill usage—she has suffered them all. But after all," the Mother Superior continued, "perhaps Monsieur le Cardinal had plausible motives for acting thus. Though this young woman looks like an angel, we cannot always judge by appearances."

"Good!" said Milady to herself. "Who knows! Perchance I am about to discover something here. I'm in luck." And she made every effort to assume an expression of perfect candor.

"Alas!" she said aloud, "I know that is true. People say that—that we must not trust others' faces. But in what can we trust, if not in the Lord God's most beautiful work? As for me, perhaps I shall be mistaken all my life, but I shall always have faith in anyone whose countenance inspires me with sympathy."

"Then you would be tempted to think this young woman innocent," said the Mother Superior.

"Monsieur the Cardinal does not pursue criminals only," said Milady. "There are certain virtues that he persecutes more severely than certain offenses."

"Permit me, madame, to express my surprise," said the Mother Superior.

"About what?" asked Milady with the utmost naïveté.

"At the language you use."

"What do you find so astonishing in my words?" asked Milady, smiling.

"You are a friend of the Cardinal, since it was he who sent you here, and yet——"

"And yet I speak ill of him," interrupted Milady.

"At least you say no good of him."

"That is because I am not his friend," declared Milady, sighing, "but his victim."

"But what about that letter in which he recommends you to me?"

"It is an order to hold me in a sort of prison that he will have some of his satellites take me from."

"But why have you not run away?"

"Where could I go? Do you think there is any spot on earth the Cardinal cannot reach if he takes the trouble to stretch out his hand? If I were a man, I might possibly be able to do it, but what do you think a woman can do? This young guest of yours, has she attempted to escape?"

"No, she has not. But her case is not like yours. I believe that she is kept in France by some love affair."

"Then," said Milady, sighing again, "if she is in love, she is not altogether unhappy."

"So you too are a poor persecuted woman?" asked the Mother Superior, looking at Milady with increased interest.

"Alas! yes," answered Milady.

The nun looked at her for a moment as though a fresh thought had crossed her mind. "You are not an enemy of Holy Church?" she stammered.

"I?" cried Milady, "I a Protestant! Oh, no! I call upon God Who hears us to bear witness that I am a devout Catholic."

"Then, madame," said the Mother Superior, smiling, "you may rest easy. This house will not be a very harsh prison, and we will do everything in our power to make you enjoy your captivity. What is more, you will have as a companion the young woman I told you of, who is doubtless persecuted because of some Court intrigue. She is amiable and courteous."

"What is her name?"

"She was sent to me by someone of the highest rank under the name Kitty. I have not tried to discover her real name."

"Kitty!" cried Milady. "What! Are you sure of that?"

"That she is called so?" answered the nun. "Yes, madame, I am sure. Do you know her?"

Milady smiled at the idea that had flashed across her mind. Could this young woman possibly be her one-time maid? Remembering her was connected with remembered anger. A desire for vengeance distorted Milady's features, but she soon resumed the calm and benevolent expression that this woman of a hundred faces had allowed them to lose for a moment.

"When may I see this young lady?" she asked. "I already feel great sympathy for her."

"This evening," said the Mother Superior, "or perhaps during the day. But you have been traveling for four days, as you told me yourself. You rose this morning at five, and you must need to rest. Lie down and go to sleep. At dinnertime we will wake you."

Although Milady could have got along very well without sleep, buoyed up as she was by all the excitement with which a new adventure filled that heart greedy for intrigues, she accepted the Mother Superior's suggestion.

For twelve or fifteen days she had experienced so many and such varied emotions that even if her frame of iron was still capable of withstanding fatigue, her mind had need of rest.

She took leave of the Mother Superior, accordingly, and went to her room to lie down, lulled gently to sleep by the thoughts of vengeance that the name Kitty had naturally aroused. She remembered the almost unlimited promise the Cardinal had made her provided she succeeded in her undertaking. She had succeeded; D'Artagnan was in her clutches!

One thing alone alarmed her—the remembrance of her first husband, the Comte de La Fère, whom she had believed to be dead, or at least no longer in France, and had found again in Athos, D'Artagnan's best friend. Moreover, as he was D'Artagnan's friend, he must certainly have aided the Gascon in all the moves he had made by which the Queen had thwarted His Eminence's plans. If he was D'Artagnan's friend, he was the Cardinal's enemy. Doubtless she could succeed in entangling him in the folds of the vengeance in which she intended to smother the young musketeer. All these hopes were sweet thoughts to Milady; so it was that, cradled by them, she soon fell asleep.

She was awakened by the sound of a sweet voice speaking from the foot of her bed. As she opened her eyes she saw the Mother Superior and with her a young woman with dark hair and a delicate complexion, who was looking at her with friendly curiosity. She had never seen the young woman's face before. They looked at each other with the greatest intentness as they exchanged the usual courtesies. Both of them were beautiful, but with very different types of beauty. But Milady smiled as she realized what an advantage she had over the younger woman as to lofty bearing and aristocratic ways. It is true that the novice's habit the younger woman was wearing did not serve her very well in a contest of that kind. After the Mother Superior had completed the formality of introducing them to each other, her duties called her to the convent chapel and she left the two young women alone together.

The novice, seeing that Milady remained in bed, was about to follow the Mother Superior, but Milady stopped her.

"Come, madame," she said, "I have barely seen you and already you mean to deprive me of your company. Yet I had counted on it a little, I confess, for the time I am to spend here."

"Pardon me, madame," replied the novice. "My only thought was that I had chosen the wrong time. You were asleep, you are very tired."

"Well," replied Milady, "what is it people who are sleeping hope for? A happy awakening, is it not? You have given me one. Allow me to enjoy it at leisure." Taking the novice's hand, Milady drew her to an armchair standing by her bed.

The novice sat down and said: "My God, but I am unlucky! Here I have been in this place six months without the slightest diversion. Then

you come, and your presence was going to give me a charming companion
—and now in all probability I shall be leaving the convent at any moment."

"What!" said Milady. "You are leaving soon?"

"At least I hope so," said the novice with a joyful expression that she
made no effort to hide.

"I think I've been told you have suffered persecution by the Cardinal,"
Milady went on. "That would be one more reason for our sympathizing
with each other."

"So what our good Mother Superior told me is true, and you too are a
victim of that wicked priest?"

"Hush!" said Milady. "Even here we must not speak of him thus.
Almost all my misfortunes come from my saying almost what you have
just said. A woman I believed to be my friend overheard me and betrayed
me. And you, are you also a victim of such a betrayal?"

"No," the novice answered, "I am the victim of my loyalty—loyalty
to a woman whom I love, one for whom I would have given my life, for
whom I would give my life even now."

"And she has abandoned you, is that it?"

"I was unjust enough to believe so, but two or three days ago I received proof that this was not true, thank God. It would have hurt me
very much to think that she had forgotten me. But you, madame," she
went on, "apparently you are free. If you wish to escape, it must be
easy for you to do so."

"Where do you think I could go when I am without friends, without
money, and I am in a part of France I know nothing of? I have never
been here before."

"Oh," cried the novice, "as to friends, you will find friends everywhere
you go, you seem so good, and you are so beautiful!"

"That," Milady replied, softening her smile so as to give herself an
angelic expression, "does not keep me from being alone and persecuted."

"Believe me," said the novice, "we must put all our trust in Heaven.
There always comes a moment when the good you have done pleads your
cause before God. Come, perhaps it is good fortune for you that you have
met with me, humble and powerless though I am. For if I leave here—
well, I have a few powerful friends, who after they have set to work on my
behalf will set to work on yours."

"Oh, when I said I was alone," said Milady, hoping that by talking of
herself she could make the novice talk of herself too, "it was not because
I have no friends of high rank. But those very friends tremble before the
Cardinal, the Queen herself does not dare oppose that terrible Minister. I
have proof that Her Majesty, despite her great courage, has been forced
more than once to abandon to His Eminence's anger persons who had
served her well."

"Believe me, madame, the Queen may seem to have abandoned those persons, but you must not judge by appearances. The more those who serve her are persecuted, the more the Queen thinks of them, and often they receive proofs of her kind remembrance when they expect it least."

"Alas! I believe that," said Milady. "The Queen is so kind and good."

"Oh, so you know her, madame, our beautiful and noble Queen, since you say that!" cried the novice enthusiastically.

"I do not mean that I have ever had the honor of being presented to Her Majesty herself," replied Milady, driven to cover, "but I know many of her most intimate friends. For example, I know Monsieur de Putange, I met Monsieur Dujart in England. I know Monsieur de Tréville."

"Monsieur de Tréville!" cried the novice. "You know Monsieur de Tréville, the Captain of the Royal Musketeers?"

"Indeed I do. I know him very well."

"Oh, you will see," exclaimed the novice, "that very soon we are going to know each other well, to be almost friends. If you know Monsieur de Tréville, you must have visited him, have you not?"

"Often!" said Milady, who, having started on that path, and seeing that her lie was successful, determined to follow the path to the end.

"And at his house you must have met some of his musketeers, surely."

"All those whom he receives regularly," replied Milady. She was beginning to take a deep interest in this conversation.

"Pray name some of those you know, madame, and we shall see whether they are friends of mine."

"Well," said Milady, somewhat at a loss, "I know Monsieur de Sauvigny, Monsieur de Courtivron, Monsieur de Férussac."

The novice let Milady go on until she saw that no more names were coming, then she asked:

"Don't you know a gentleman named Athos?" Milady turned as white as the sheets in which she was lying. Mistress of herself as she was, she could not help uttering a cry. Grasping the novice's hand, she fairly devoured the young woman with her eyes. "What is it? What is the matter? Oh, my God," said the poor woman, "Have I said anything to hurt your feelings?"

"No, no. But that name surprised me because I too know that gentleman, and it seemed so strange to meet with someone else who knows him well."

"Oh yes, I know him very well, and not only him, but also his friends Monsieur Porthos and Monsieur Aramis."

"Really! I know them likewise!" cried Milady, feeling her heart grow icy-cold.

"Well, then, if you know them, you must know what good and true gentlemen they are. Why don't you appeal to them if you need help?"

"We-ell," stammered Milady, "as a matter of fact they are not close friends of mine. I know them only because I have heard one of their friends talk about them so much—Monsieur d'Artagnan."

"You know Monsieur d'Artagnan!" cried the novice in her turn, grasping Milady's hand and devouring Milady with her eyes. Then, noting the strange expression on Milady's face, she went on: "Pardon me, madame, but how do you happen to know him?"

"Why," answered Milady, somewhat embarrassed, "only as a friend."

"You are deceiving me, madame. You have been his mistress."

"You are the one who has been his mistress," Milady retorted.

"I!" protested the novice.

"Yes, you. I know who you are now—you are Madame Bonacieux." The young woman recoiled in surprise and terror. "Oh, do not deny it," Milady continued. "Answer me."

"Well, yes, madame, I am Constance Bonacieux," said the novice. "But are we rivals?" So savage a joy lit up Milady's countenance that in any other circumstances Madame Bonacieux would have fled in terror, but now she was entirely given over to jealousy. "Come, tell me, madame," said Constance Bonacieux with a vigor that no one would have thought her capable of, "have you been his mistress? Are you his mistress now?"

"Oh no!" cried Milady with an emphasis that left no doubt of her truthfulness. "Never, never!"

"I believe you, madame. But why did you cry out that way when I said his name?"

"What! You don't understand!" replied Milady, who had already mastered her agitation and recovered her presence of mind.

"How can you expect me to understand? I don't know what you're talking about."

"Don't you understand that since Monsieur d'Artagnan is my friend, he has taken me into his confidence?"

"Indeed!"

"Don't you see that I know everything—your being carried off from the little house at Saint-Germain, D'Artagnan's despair and that of his friends, their search for you in vain up to this very moment? And how could I help being astonished when, without the least expectation of it, I meet you face to face—you whom D'Artagnan and I have talked of so often, you whom he loves with all his soul, you whom he taught me to love before I had ever seen you? Ah, my dear Constance, at last I have found you, at last I see you!"

And Milady held out her arms to Madame Bonacieux, who, convinced by what that clever woman had just said, in that woman whom an instant before she had thought her rival now saw only a sincere and devoted friend.

"Oh, forgive me, forgive me!" she cried, burying her face in Milady's shoulder. "I love him so dearly!"

The two women held each other for an instant in a close embrace. Certes, had Milady's strength been as great as her hatred, Madame Bonacieux would never have escaped alive from that embrace. But not being able to strangle Constance, Milady smiled at her.

"O you dear, pretty, good little creature!" said Milady. "How happy I am to see you at last! Let me look at you." As she said this she absolutely devoured Constance with her eyes. "Oh yes, it is really you. Indeed, from what he has told me I recognize you now, I recognize you perfectly."

The poor young woman could not possibly suspect what terribly cruel thoughts were seething behind the protection of that pure brow, behind those brilliant eyes in which she read only deep interest and compassion.

"So you know what I have suffered," said Madame Bonacieux, "since he has told you how much he has suffered. But to suffer for him is happiness for me."

Milady replied mechanically: "Yes, that is happiness for you." She was thinking of something else.

"And now," Madame Bonacieux went on, "my suffering is almost at an end. Tomorrow, mayhap even tonight, I shall see him again and then the past will no longer exist for me."

"Tonight? Tomorrow?" cried Milady, roused from her reverie by those words. "What do you mean? Do you expect news of him?"

"I expect him in person, D'Artagnan himself."

"But that's impossible! He is at the siege of La Rochelle with the Cardinal. He will not leave until the city is taken."

"You may think so, but is there anything that is impossible to my D'Artagnan, that noble and faithful gentleman?"

"Oh, I cannot believe you!"

"Very well. Read that, then!" The unfortunate young woman cried in her excess of pride and joy, handing a letter to Milady.

"Madame de Chevreuse's writing," Milady said to herself. "Ah, I was very sure they had some secret understanding!" Then she read avidly these few lines:

My dear child:

Hold yourself in readiness. *Our friend* will see you soon, and he will see you only in order to release you from the prison in which your own safety required you to be hidden. So make ready for your departure and never despair of us.

Our charming Gascon has just proved himself to be as brave and as loyal as ever. Tell him that certain persons are very grateful to him for the warning he has given them.

"Yes, yes," said Milady. "The letter is very clear. Do you know what the warning was?"

"No. I only suspect that he has warned the Queen against some fresh machination of the Cardinal's."

"Yes, doubtless that is it," said Milady, returning the letter to Madame Bonacieux and bowing her head to her breast, deep in thought.

At that moment they heard the sound of a galloping horse.

"Oh listen!" cried Madame Bonacieux, darting to the window. "Can that be he already?"

Milady was still in bed. She lay there petrified by surprise. So many unexpected things were happening to her and so suddenly that for the first time she was at a loss.

"He! He!" she murmured. "Can it be he?" and she still lay in bed, her eyes staring.

"Alas! no," said Madame Bonacieux. "It's a man I don't know, but he seems to be coming here. Yes, he is checking his horse—he is at the gate, he is ringing."

Milady sprang out of bed. "Are you quite sure it is not D'Artagnan?"

"Oh yes, quite sure."

"Perhaps you did not see him plainly."

"Oh, if I saw only the plume of his hat, the bottom of his cloak, I would recognize him, my own man!"

Milady was dressing now. "Never mind! The man is coming here, you say?"

"Yes, he has come in."

"He must be coming either for you or for me."

"Oh, good Lord, how disquieted you seem!"

"Yes, I confess I am. I am not as confident as you are. I am terribly afraid of the Cardinal."

"Hush!" said Madame Bonacieux. "Someone is coming."

The door opened and the Mother Superior entered. "Did you come from Boulogne?" she asked Milady.

"Yes, I did," replied Milady, trying to recover her sangfroid. "Who is asking for me?"

"A man who will not give his name. He says he comes from the Cardinal."

"And he wishes to speak to me?" asked Milady.

"He wishes to speak to a lady who came here from Boulogne."

"Then let him come in, madame, if you please."

"Oh, my God, my God!" said Madame Bonacieux. "Can it be that he brings bad news?"

"I'm afraid that he does."

"I will leave you alone with this stranger, madame, but as soon as he goes, I will return, if you will allow me to."

"Of course I will. Indeed, I beg you to do so."

The Mother Superior and Madame Bonacieux left the room. Milady, left alone, fixed her eyes on the door. An instant later she heard the jingle of spurs on the stairway, the sound of footsteps drew near, the door opened, and a man appeared. Milady gave a cry of joy. It was the Comte de Rochefort, the *âme damnée* of His Eminence.

CHAPTER 59

"AH," CRIED MILADY, "IT IS YOU!"

"Yes, it is I," said Rochefort.

"And where do you come from?" asked Milady.

"From La Rochelle. And you?"

"From England."

"What about Buckingham?"

"He is either dead or dangerously wounded. At the moment I was leaving without having been able to obtain anything from him a fanatic had just assassinated him."

"Aha!" said Rochefort with a smile. "That was a stroke of luck indeed. His Eminence will certainly be delighted. Have you informed him of it?"

"I wrote him from Boulogne. But what brings you here?"

"His Eminence was anxious, and sent me to search for you."

"I arrived only yesterday."

"And what have you been doing since yesterday?"

"I have not wasted my time."

"Oh, I'm sure of that!"

"Do you know whom I have met with here?"

"Of course I don't."

"Guess."

"How do you expect me to?"

"That young woman the Queen got out of prison."

"The mistress of that fellow D'Artagnan?"

"Yes—Madame Bonacieux. The Cardinal didn't know where she was in hiding."

"Well, well," said Rochefort, "that's a stroke of luck to match the first one. Monsieur le Cardinal is truly a privileged man!"

"Imagine my astonishment," Milady continued, "when I found myself face to face with this woman."

"Does she know who you are?"

"No."

"Then she looks upon you as a stranger?"

Milady smiled. "I am her best friend," she declared.

"Upon my honor," said Rochefort, "It is only you, my dear Milady, who can perform such miracles!"

"And much good has that done me, Monsieur le Chevalier," retorted Milady, "for do you know what is going on here?"

"No, naturally I don't."

"Someone is coming tomorrow or day after tomorrow to take her away by order of the Queen."

"Indeed! And who is the someone?"

"D'Artagnan and his friends."

"Really, someday those men will go so far that we shall be forced to send them to the Bastille."

"Why hasn't that already been done?"

"Can't you think why? Because Monsieur le Cardinal has a partiality for those men, though I don't understand it in the least."

"Well, tell him this, Rochefort. Tell him that those four men overheard our conversation at the Red Dovecote. Tell him that after his departure one of them came up to my room and used violence to wrest from me the safe-conduct His Eminence had given me. Tell him that they warned Lord Winter of my journey to England, that once again they only just missed thwarting my mission as they succeeded in doing in the affair of the diamond tags. Tell him that of the four, only two are to be feared —D'Artagnan and Athos. Tell him that the third, Aramis, is the lover of Madame de Chevreuse. He may be left alone; we know his secret, and it may be useful to us. As to the fourth, Porthos, he is a fool, a coxcomb, a booby, and not worth bothering about."

"But surely those four men must be at the siege of La Rochelle now."

"I thought so too, but a letter Madame Bonacieux has received from Madame la Connétable, which she was indiscreet enough to show me, leads me to believe that these four men are on their way here to take her away."

"The devil you say! What are we to do?"

"What did the Cardinal say about me?"

"That I was to get from you everything you had to communicate to him, in writing or orally, and to return posthaste. Then as soon as he learns what you have done he will consider what you are to do next."

"Must I stay here?"

"Here or in this neighborhood."

"You cannot take me with you?"

"No. My orders are explicit. Near the camp you might be recognized and your presence, as you must be aware, might compromise His Eminence."

"Then I must wait here or somewhere near here."

"But you must tell me where you will await your fresh orders from the Cardinal, so that I may know where to find you."

"But note that it is not probable that I shall be able to remain here in the convent."

"Why?"

"You forget that my enemies may arrive at any moment."

"True. So this little woman is going to escape from His Eminence's hands?"

"Bah!" said Milady, with a mysterious smile that was hers alone, "you forget that I am her best friend."

"That's true. Then I can tell the Cardinal, as far as this woman is concerned, that——"

"That he may rest easy."

"Nothing more than that?"

"He will know what that means."

"He will guess, at least. Now let's see—what had I better do?"

"Set off at once. I think the news you are taking to him makes it well worthwhile for you to make haste."

"My chaise broke down as I entered Lilliers."

"Capital!"

"What do you mean by 'Capital'?"

"I mean that I need your chaise."

"And how am I to travel?"

"Riding a horse at full speed."

"You say that as if it were easy. I've a hundred and twenty leagues to cover."

"What's that to you?"

"I'll manage them. And then?"

"When you reach Lilliers you will send me your chaise and tell your servant to obey any order I give him."

"Very well."

"You must be carrying some order of the Cardinal's."

"I have one giving me full authority."

"Show it to the Mother Superior and tell her that someone will come to fetch me either today or tomorrow, and that I am to go with the person who comes in your name."

"Very well."

"Don't forget to speak harshly of me to the Mother Superior.

"What good will that do?"

"To her, I am one of the Cardinal's victims. You see, I must inspire some confidence in that poor little Madame Bonacieux."

"True, you must. Now will you give me a report of everything that has happened?"

"But I have told you every detail. You have a good memory. Just repeat what I have told you. A paper might be lost."

"Right you are. But you must let me know where to find you. I don't want to waste time in looking all over the neighborhood for you."

"True enough. Wait a minute."

"Do you want a map?"

"Oh, I know this part of the country perfectly well."

"You do? When were you here before this?"

"I was brought up here. It's an advantage, you see, to have been brought up somewhere."

"Where will you wait for me?"

"Let me think a minute. . . . Oh, that will do—at Armentières."

"Where's that—Armentières?"

"It's a little town on the Lys. I need only cross the river to be in a foreign country."

"Fine! But we agree, don't we, that you are to cross the river only in case of danger?"

"Certainly."

"And if you do cross it, how shall I find out where you are?"

"You don't need your lackey, do you?"

"No."

"Is he trustworthy?"

"Thoroughly."

"Give him to me. Nobody knows him. I will leave him at Armentières when I leave myself and he will guide you to the place where I'll be."

"And you say you'll wait for me at Armentières? Write that name on a piece of paper or I may forget it. The name of a town isn't compromising, is it?"

"Eh, who knows whether it may be? Never mind," said Milady, writing the name on a half-sheet of notepaper, "I'll compromise myself."

"That's good," said Rochefort, taking the bit of paper from Milady, folding it, and pushing it into the lining of his hat. "Besides, to make sure that I'll remember I'll do as children do—keep repeating the name all along my way. Now is that all?"

"I think so."

"Let's make sure—Buckingham dead or dangerously wounded; your conversation with the Cardinal overheard by the four musketeers; Lord Winter warned of your arrival at Portsmouth; D'Artagnan and Athos to be sent to the Bastille; Aramis the lover of Madame de Chevreuse; Porthos a coxcomb and a fool; Madame Bonacieux discovered at last; the chaise to be sent you as soon as possible; my lackey to be placed at your disposal; you to pass as a victim of the Cardinal's so that the Mother

Superior will entertain no suspicions; Armentières on the banks of the Lys. Is that all correct?"

"Truly, my dear Chevalier, you have a perfect memory. By the way, there's one thing more."

"What is it?"

"I have noticed a very pretty piece of woods close to the convent garden. Tell the Mother Superior that I am to be allowed to walk in those woods. Who knows? Perhaps I shall need to get out by a back door."

"You think of everything, don't you?"

"And you are forgetting one thing."

"What's that?"

"You have forgotten to ask me whether I need money."

"So I have. How much do you want?"

"All the gold you have with you."

"I have something like five hundred pistoles."

"I have as much. With a thousand pistoles one can face any emergency. Empty your pockets."

"Very well. Here you are."

"Capital! When do you leave?"

"Within an hour. Just enough time to eat a few mouthfuls, and during that time I will send for a post horse."

"Excellent! Farewell, Monsieur le Chevalier!"

"Farewell, Milady."

"Commend me to the Cardinal."

"Commend me to Satan."

Milady and Rochefort smiled at each other and parted. An hour later, Rochefort set out at full gallop; five hours later he passed through Arras. Our readers already know that he was recognized there by D'Artagnan, and that this fact, by arousing fears in the minds of the four musketeers, had spurred them on to travel faster.

CHAPTER 60

ROCHEFORT HAD SCARCELY DEPARTED WHEN MADAME Bonacieux returned. She found Milady smiling, almost laughing.

"Well," said the young woman, "so what you were dreading has happened. Tonight or tomorrow the Cardinal is sending someone to take you away, isn't he?"

"Who told you that, my child?" asked Milady.

"I heard it from the messenger himself."

"Come sit here close to me. Now wait until I'm sure that no one can hear us."

"Here I am. But why all these precautions?"

"You shall learn soon." Milady rose, opened the door, looked into the corridor, closed the door again, and returned to her seat by Madame Bonacieux. "So he played his part well," she said.

"Who did?"

"The man who presented himself to the Mother Superior as a messenger from the Cardinal."

"He was playing a part, then?"

"Yes, my child."

"Then that man isn't——"

"That man," said Milady, lowering her voice, "is my brother."

"Your brother!" cried Madame Bonacieux.

"Yes, and you are the only one who knows that secret, my child. If you reveal it to anyone else in the world, I shall be lost, and perhaps you will be as well."

"Oh, my God!"

"Listen to me. Here is what happened. My brother was coming to my rescue to take me away from here, by force if that should prove necessary. He met with the Cardinal's emissary, who was coming in search of me. He followed the man and when they came to a lonely part of the road he drew his sword and forced the messenger to give him the papers the man was carrying. The messenger tried to defend himself, and my brother killed him."

"Oh!" cried Madame Bonacieux, shuddering.

"It was the only thing he could do, you must see that. Then my brother decided to substitute cunning for force. He took the man's papers and presented himself here as the Cardinal's emissary, and within an hour or two a carriage will come to take me away in His Eminence's name."

"I understand. Your brother is sending the carriage."

"Exactly. But that isn't all. The letter you received, the one you think is from Madame Chevreuse———"

"I *think*———?"

"You are mistaken. It is a forgery."

"How can that be, madame?"

"It is a forgery. It is a decoy to keep you from making any resistance when they come for you."

"But it is D'Artagnan who will come."

"Do not be deceived. D'Artagnan and his friends are detained at the siege of La Rochelle."

"How do you know that?"

"My brother met with some of the Cardinal's men wearing musketeers' uniforms. You were to be summoned to the gate, you were supposed to believe that these men were your friends, and they were to carry you off and take you back to Paris."

"Oh, my God, my senses fail me amid this chaos of wickedness! If this continues," added Madame Bonacieux, raising both hands to her brow, "I shall surely go mad!"

"Listen!"

"What is it?"

"I hear a horse's hoofs. That's my brother setting off again. I must bid him a last farewell. Come!" Milady opened the window and motioned to Madame Bonacieux to join her. The young woman did so. Rochefort was galloping by. "Farewell, brother!" cried Milady.

The Chevalier looked up at the two young women and without stopping waved his hand to Milady in friendly salute.

"Dear good Georges!" she said as she closed the window; the expression on her face was full of both affection and melancholy. She went back to sit in her chair and seemed to be plunged in purely personal reflections.

"Dear lady," said Madame Bonacieux, "pardon me for disturbing you, but what do you advise me to do? Good heavens, I'm so ignorant! You have had so much more experience than I. Speak and I will listen with gratitude in my heart."

"In the first place," Milady replied, "I may be mistaken and D'Artagnan and his friends are really coming to your rescue."

"Oh, that would be too wonderful!" cried Madame Bonacieux. "Such happiness as that cannot be for me."

"In that case, you see, it would be only a question of time, a kind of race to see who would get here first. If your friends win it by being the more speedy, you will be saved. If the Cardinal's satellites win, you will be lost."

"Oh yes, yes, lost beyond redemption! But what am I to do? What am I to do?"

"There is one quite simple, very natural way——"

"What way? Tell me."

"You can wait in hiding somewhere near here until you make sure who the men are who come to ask for you."

"But where can I wait?"

"Oh, there's no difficulty about that. I myself am going to hide a few leagues from here to wait for my brother to join me. Very well, I can take you with me. We will hide and wait together."

"But I will not be allowed to leave," Madame Bonacieux objected. "I am practically a prisoner here."

"As I am supposed to be leaving on orders from the Cardinal, no one will believe that you are anxious to go with me."

"And so?"

"So the carriage is at the gate, you are bidding me adieu, you mount the step to embrace me for the last time. My brother's servant, who has come to fetch me, has been warned. He gives a signal to the postilion and we go off full speed."

"But D'Artagnan, D'Artagnan! What if he comes?"

"Shall we not know it if he comes?"

"How?"

"That's perfectly easy. We will send my brother's lackey back to Béthune—we can trust him. He shall assume a disguise and take lodgings opposite the convent. If the first to arrive are the Cardinal's emissaries, he will stay where he is. If they are Monsieur d'Artagnan and his friends, he will meet them and bring them to us."

"Does the lackey know them, then?"

"He must know them. Hasn't he seen Monsieur d'Artagnan often at my house?"

"Oh yes, yes, you are right. Everything is going well, all is for the best. But we must not go far away from the convent."

"Seven or eight leagues at most. We will keep near the frontier, and at the first alarm we can get out of France."

"And what shall we do meanwhile?"

"Wait."

"But suppose my friends come soon?"

"My brother's carriage will be here first."

"What if I should not be with you when it comes—at dinner or supper, for instance?"

"You must tell your good Mother Superior that we wish to be together as much as possible, and therefore you are asking her for permission to take your meals with me."

"Will she give it to me?"

"What objection could she have?"

"Oh, that's fine! Then we needn't be separated for a moment."

"All right. Go down now and make your request. My head seems a little confused. I'm going to take a turn in the garden."

"Please do. And where shall I find you?"

"In this room, within an hour."

"Here, within an hour. Oh, you are so kind to me, madame, and I am so grateful!"

"How could I help being interested in you? Even if you were not so beautiful and charming, would you not still be the belovèd of one of my best friends?"

"Dear D'Artagnan, ah, how grateful he will be to you!"

"Indeed I hope so. Now then, everything is settled, so let's go downstairs."

"You're going to the garden?"

"Yes."

"Follow this corridor, then, and you'll find a little flight of steps that leads to it."

"Fine! Thank you very much." And the two women parted after smiling charmingly at each other.

Milady for once had told the truth. Her head was somewhat confused, for her ill-arranged plans were clashing together chaotically. She needed to be alone to get her thoughts in some kind of order. She foresaw her future only vaguely, but she must have a little silence and quiet to give her ideas, now so chaotic, a definite form, an ordered plan.

The most urgent matter was to get Madame Bonacieux away and to some safe place where she could hold the young woman as a hostage if she had need of one. Madame Bonacieux was D'Artagnan's very life; the life of the woman he loved was dearer to him than his own. In case of some mischance, here was a means of negotiating with him and obtaining favorable terms.

One thing was sure—Madame Bonacieux would accompany her without any misgivings. Once she was in hiding with her at Armentières, it would be easy to make her believe that D'Artagnan had not come to Béthune. In a fortnight at the latest, Rochefort would return. During that fortnight Milady could be devising plans for avenging herself on the four friends. She wouldn't be bored, thank God, because she would be enjoying the most charming pastime that circumstances could provide for a woman of her character—she would be perfecting plans for a cruel vengeance.

As she daydreamed of all this, she looked about her and made a little map of the garden in her mind. As a good general does, Milady foresaw the possibilities of both victory and defeat and was quite prepared to march forward or to beat a retreat, whichever the chances of the battle called for. After an hour, she heard a sweet voice calling her; it was Madame Bonacieux's. The good Mother Superior had of course granted all her requests, and to begin with, they were to eat supper together.

As the two young women reached the courtyard, they heard the sound of a carriage that was stopping at the gate.

"Do you hear that?" Milady asked.

"Yes—the rumble of a carriage."

"It is the one my brother is sending for me."

"Oh, my God!"

"Come now, courage!" Someone was ringing at the convent gate. Milady had not been mistaken. "Go up to your room," she said to Madame Bonacieux. "You must have some jewels that you want to take with you."

"I have *his* letters."

"Very well. Go and get them and go to my room. We will eat in haste. We may have to travel all night and we must keep up our strength."

"Oh, God Almighty," cried Madame Bonacieux, pressing her hand to her breast, "my heart is beating so hard that it chokes me. I cannot take a step."

"Courage now, courage! Remember that in one short quarter of an hour you will be safe. Remember too that what you are about to do is for *his* sake."

"Oh yes, everything is for him. You have restored my courage by a single word. Go on up. I will join you in a minute."

Milady ran up to her room at once. She found Rochefort's lackey there and gave him her instructions. He was to wait at the gate. If by any chance the musketeers appeared, the carriage was to set off at full speed, circle the convent, then go to wait for Milady at a little village on the other side of the woods back of the convent. If that happened, Milady would cross the garden and get to the village on foot. We have already learned that Milady knew this part of France perfectly well. If the musketeers did not appear, things were to go on as Milady had told her companion. Madame Bonacieux was to mount the carriage step as if to bid Milady adieu and the carriage was to drive off.

Madame Bonacieux entered Milady's room, and to rid her of any suspicion she might still have, Milady repeated to the lackey in her presence the latter part of her instructions. Milady also asked some questions about the carriage and learned that it was a chaise drawn by three horses and guided by a postilion. Rochefort's lackey would ride ahead of it as a courier.

Milady was wrong in fearing that Madame Bonacieux had any sus-

D'Artagnan and Planchet Ride to Saint-Cloud

The Execution of Milady

picions; the poor young woman was too innocent to suspect that any woman could be guilty of such treachery. Besides, the name of Lady Clark, which she had heard the Mother Superior use, was quite unknown to her. She had no idea, moreover, that a woman had played so important and so fatal a role in the misfortunes that she had suffered.

"You see," said Milady when the lackey had gone, "everything is as it should be. The Mother Superior does not suspect the truth; she believes that I am sent for by the Cardinal's order. The lackey has gone to give his last orders. Eat a mouthful or two and drink a little wine. Then let's be off."

"Yes," repeated Madame Bonacieux mechanically, "let's be off."

Milady motioned Constance to sit beside her, poured a small glass of Spanish wine for her, and served her some breast of chicken.

"See how everything is helping us," she said. "Here's night coming on, by daybreak we shall have reached our retreat, and no one will be able to guess where we are. Come, courage, my dear, eat something."

Madame Bonacieux ate a few mouthfuls automatically and just touched the wine glass with her lips.

"Come, come now," said Milady, lifting her glass to her lips. "Do as I do."

But just as she was about to drink she held the glass still. She had heard something on the road that sounded like the far-off hoofbeats of a gallop drawing nearer, and almost at the same moment she thought she heard the neighing of horses. The sound roused her from her joy as the rumbling of a storm awakens a sleeper who is dreaming a happy dream. She grew pale and ran to the window. Madame Bonacieux, rising all atremble, grasped the back of her chair to keep from falling. There was nothing to be seen as yet, but they heard the sound of galloping drawing nearer and nearer.

"Oh, my God!" said Madame Bonacieux. "What can that sound mean?"

"Our friends or our enemies," replied Milady with her frightening calmness. "Stay where you are. I'll let you know."

Madame Bonacieux stood stock-still, as mute, rigid, and pale as a statue. The sound grew louder, the horses could not be more than a hundred paces away. If it was not yet possible to see them, it was because of a bend in the road. Soon the sound became so clear that you could have counted the number of horses by the staccato beat of their hoofs.

Milady was watching as hard as ever she could. It was just light enough for her to be able to recognize those who were coming. All at once she saw at the bend in the road the glitter of gold-laced hats and the waving of plumes. She counted first two, then five, then eight horsemen. One of them was ahead of his comrades by twice the length of his horse. Milady

gave a stifled groan. In the first horseman she had recognized D'Artagnan.

"Oh, my God, my God!" cried Madame Bonacieux. "What is it? What
is it?"

"They are wearing the uniform of the Cardinal's guardsmen. There's
not a moment to lose. We must flee, we must flee!"

"Oh yes, we must flee!" echoed Madame Bonacieux, but she could
not take one step, rooted to the spot as she was by terror.

They heard the horsemen riding by under the window.

"Come, come, I tell you!" cried Milady, trying to drag the young
woman along by the arm. "Thanks to the garden, we can still escape, I
have the key. But we must make haste, in five minutes it will be too late."

Madame Bonacieux tried to walk, but after two steps she fell to her
knees. Milady attempted to lift her and carry her, but she could not
manage it. At that moment they heard the rumble of the carriage, which
as the musketeers were approaching drove off at full speed. Then they
heard the sound of several shots.

"For the last time, will you come?" demanded Milady.

"Oh, my God, my God, can't you see that my strength fails me, and
that I cannot walk? You must escape alone!"

"Escape alone and leave you here! No, no, never!" cried Milady.

Suddenly Milady stood stock-still, a livid flame flashing from her eyes.
Then she ran to the table, opened the bezel of her ring with extraordinary rapidity and dropped its contents into Madame Bonacieux's wineglass. The ring had contained a reddish granule that dissolved instantly.
Then, grasping the glass firmly, she said:

"Drink, the wine will give you strength. Drink!" She put the glass to
Constance's lips and the poor woman drank automatically. "Well, that
isn't the way I meant to get my revenge," said Milady to herself as she
smiled diabolically and set the glass on the table, "but by my faith, we
do the best we can!" And she rushed out of the room.

Madame Bonacieux watched her go without being able to follow her.
She was like a woman who dreams that she is being pursued and tries in
vain to get away. Several minutes passed, then an alarming noise was
heard at the gate. At every moment Madame Bonacieux expected to see
Milady reappear, but she did not come. In her terror she felt icy sweat
beading her burning brow. At last she heard the grating sound of the
gates as they opened, then the pound of boots and the jingling of spurs
on the stairway. There was a confused sound of voices going away and
drawing near, and she thought she heard someone speak her own name.

Suddenly she uttered a great cry of joy and darted toward the door.
She had recognized D'Artagnan's voice.

"D'Artagnan, D'Artagnan," she called, "is that you? This way! This
way!"

"Constance, Constance!" shouted the young man. "Where are you? Where are you?"

At that very moment the door sprang open as if it had been assaulted and several men rushed into the room. Madame Bonacieux had sunk back into an armchair unable to move.

D'Artagnan threw to the floor a pistol that was still smoking and fell on his knees before his mistress. Athos pushed his pistol back into his belt, Porthos and Aramis were holding their drawn swords in their hands and returned them to their scabbards.

"O D'Artagnan, my belovèd D'Artagnan, you have come at last! You have not failed me, it is really you!"

"Yes, yes, Constance, at last we are together once more!"

"Oh, she told me in vain that you would not come. I hoped in silence. I did not want to escape with her. Oh, how right I was, how happy I am!"

At the word "she" Athos, who had been sitting quietly, started up.

"*She!* Who is *she?*" asked D'Artagnan.

"Why, my companion, the lady who wanted to get me away from my persecutors out of friendship for me, the lady who fled because she thought you were some of the Cardinal's guardsmen."

"Your companion!" cried D'Artagnan, growing paler than the white novice's veil of his mistress. "What companion are you talking about, dear Constance?"

"The lady whose carriage was at the door, the lady who said she was a friend of yours and that you had told her everything."

"Her name, her name!" cried D'Artagnan. "My God, don't you know her name?"

"Yes, I do. I heard someone say it. Wait a minute. It's a strange name. . . . O God, my head is swimming, I cannot see."

"Help, my friends, help!" cried D'Artagnan. "Her hands are icy-cold. She is ill. Great God, she is losing consciousness!"

While Porthos called for help with his strong voice, Aramis ran to the table to get a glass of water, but he stopped suddenly when he saw the horrible change that had come over Athos, who was standing by the table. His hair was rising on end, his eyes were frozen in a stupor. Staring into one of the wineglasses, he seemed to be the prey of the most horrible suspicion.

"Oh," he said, "oh no, it's impossible! God would not permit such a crime."

"Water, water!" shouted D'Artagnan. "Water!"

"Oh, poor woman, poor woman!" murmured Athos in a broken voice.

Madame Bonacieux opened her eyes under D'Artagnan's kisses.

"She's coming to!" her lover cried. "O God, God, I thank Thee!"

"Madame," said Athos, "in the name of Heaven, whose was this empty glass?"

"Mine, monsieur," the young woman answered in a dying voice.

"Who poured you the wine that was in it?"

"She."

"But who is she?"

"Oh, I remember now," said Madame Bonacieux. "She is Lady Clark."

The four friends cried out as if with one voice, but Athos's cry rose above the others. At that moment Madame Bonacieux grew livid, frightful agony shook her whole body, and she sank gasping into the arms of Porthos and Aramis.

D'Artagnan seized Athos's hand with indescribable anguish. "What is it?" he pleaded. "Do you think——"

"I think this is the end," Athos replied, biting his lips till he drew blood to keep from sighing.

"D'Artagnan, D'Artagnan," gasped Madame Bonacieux, "where are you? Don't leave me. You must see that I am dying."

D'Artagnan let go of Athos's hand, which he had been holding tight in his own, and ran to her. Her beautiful face was distorted by agony, her glazed eyes were fixed in a stare, her body was trembling convulsively, sweat was running down her pallid brow.

"In the name of Heaven, run, call for help, Porthos, Aramis. Get help!"

"It is useless," said Athos, "quite useless. There is no antidote for the poison *she* pours."

"Yes, yes, help, help!" murmured Madame Bonacieux. "Help me!"

Then, gathering all her strength, she took her lover's head between her two hands, looked at him for a moment as if her whole soul was in that farewell look, and with a sobbing cry pressed her lips on his.

"Constance, Constance!" cried D'Artagnan.

A sigh escaped Madame Bonacieux, and D'Artagnan felt it touch his lips lightly. That sigh was her pure and loving soul ascending to Heaven. It was a dead woman D'Artagnan was holding in his arms. He uttered a cry and fell beside her, as pale and as icy-cold as she was. Porthos wept, Athos shook his fist toward the heavens. Aramis blessed himself with the sign of the Cross.

Just then a man appeared in the doorway, a man almost as pale as those in the room. Looking around him, he saw Madame Bonacieux dead and D'Artagnan in a swoon. He realized that he was arriving at the moment of stupefaction which follows great catastrophes.

"I have made no mistake," he said. "This is Monsieur D'Artagnan, and you are his three friends, Messieurs Athos, Porthos, and Aramis." The three musketeers he had just named looked at the newcomer in surprise, and all three thought his face was familiar. "Gentlemen," he went on, "you are come like myself in search of a woman. She must have passed this way," he added with a bitter smile, "for I see a corpse here!"

The three friends remained silent. His voice and his face reminded them of someone they had seen somewhere, but they could not recall under what circumstances.

"Gentlemen," the stranger continued, "since you do not recognize a man who probably owes his life to you twice over, I must needs introduce myself. I am Lord Winter, the brother-in-law of *that woman*."

The three friends cried out in surprise. Athos rose and held out his hand. "You are welcome, my lord," said he. "You are one of us."

"I left Portsmouth five hours after she did," Lord Winter said. "I reached Boulogne three hours after her, I missed her by twenty minutes at Saint-Omer. Finally at Lilliers I lost all trace of her. I was riding about haphazard, questioning everybody I met, when I saw you gallop past and I recognized Monsieur d'Artagnan. I shouted to you but you did not answer. I tried to overtake you but my horse was too tired to catch up with yours. And now I see that in spite of all your diligence you arrived too late."

"Yes, you see," said Athos, pointing to Madame Bonacieux's body and to D'Artagnan, whom Porthos and Aramis were trying to revive.

"Are they both dead?" asked Lord Winter icily.

"No," Athos replied. "Fortunately Monsieur d'Artagnan has only fainted."

"So much the better for him!" said Lord Winter.

At that moment D'Artagnan opened his eyes, tore himself from the arms of Porthos and Aramis, and threw himself down like a madman on the dead body of his mistress. Athos rose, walked over to his friend with a slow and solemn step, embraced him tenderly, and as D'Artagnan burst into sobs, said in his noble and persuasive voice:

"Friend, be a man! Women weep for the dead, men avenge them!"

"Oh, yes," said D'Artagnan, "yes. If it be to avenge her, I will follow where you lead, Athos."

Athos took advantage of this moment of strength which the hope of vengeance had restored to his friend to motion to Porthos and Aramis to fetch the Mother Superior. They met her in the corridor, still very much worried and quite distraught by so many strange happenings. She summoned several nuns and, against all conventual customs, they found themselves in the presence of five men.

"Madame," said Athos, drawing D'Artagnan's arm through his own, "we abandon to your pious care the body of this unfortunate woman. She was an angel on earth before becoming an angel in Heaven. We beg you to treat her as one of your own sisters. We will return someday to pray over her grave."

D'Artagnan hid his face against Athos's breast and burst into sobs.

"Weep, my son," said Athos. "Weep, O heart full of love, youth, and life! Alas! Would that I could weep as you do!" And he led his friend away, with the affection of a father, the consolation of a priest, and the magnanimity of a man who has suffered much.

All five of them, followed by their lackeys leading their horses, went on foot to the town of Béthune and stopped at the first inn they came to.

"But," protested D'Artagnan, "are we not going in pursuit of that infamous woman?"

"Later," Athos replied. "I have certain measures to take first."

"She will escape us," protested the young man, "and it will be your fault, Athos."

"She will not escape us," Athos answered. "I will see to that."

D'Artagnan had such confidence in his friend's word that he bowed his head and entered the inn without another word. Porthos and Aramis looked at each other, wondering why Athos was so confident. Lord Winter thought that Athos had spoken thus in order to soothe D'Artagnan's grief.

"Now, gentlemen," Athos went on when he had ascertained that there were five rooms available in the inn, "let us each retire to his own room. D'Artagnan needs to be alone to weep for his dead and to sleep. I will take charge of everything. The rest of you may set your minds at rest."

"But it seems to me," said Lord Winter, "that if there are any measures to be taken against Lady Clark, they concern me. She is my sister-in-law."

"And they concern me too," said Athos. "She is my wife!"

D'Artagnan smiled. He understood that Athos was sure of his vengeance, since he was willing to reveal his terrible secret. Porthos and Aramis looked at each other and grew pale. Lord Winter thought Athos had gone mad.

"I beg you to retire to your own rooms now," said Athos. "Leave it to me to act. You must see that since I am the woman's husband, the affair is my special concern. But D'Artagnan, if you have not lost it, give me the paper that fell from that man's hat—the one on which is written the name of a village."

"Ah," said D'Artagnan, "I understand—that name is in her handwriting."

"You surely see now," said Athos, "that there is a God in Heaven."

CHAPTER 61

ATHOS'S DESPAIR HAD GIVEN WAY NOW TO A CONCEN-
trated grief that made even more lucid the brilliant mind of that extraordinary man. He was obsessed by but one thought now, that of the promise
he had made and the responsibility that he had assumed. He was the last
to retire to his room. He requested the host to procure a map of the
province for him and, examining every line traced upon it, he saw that
there were four roads from Béthune to Armentières.

He sent for all four of the lackeys. Planchet, Grimaud, Mousqueton,
and Bazin appeared, and Athos gave them clear, exact, and momentous
instructions. They were to set out at daybreak and go to Armentières,
each by a different road. Planchet, the most intelligent of the four, was
to follow the road taken by the carriage at which their four masters had
fired, and which, we remember, had been accompanied by Rochefort's
lackey.

Athos sent the lackeys off first because ever since these men had been
in his service or that of his friends he had come to recognize their different and their noteworthy talents. Moreover, lackeys who ask passers-by
for information arouse less suspicion than their masters might, and are
apt to get more help. In addition, although Milady knew all four of the
friends, she knew none of the lackeys, while the lackeys knew Milady
perfectly well.

All four of them were to meet at eleven o'clock the next morning. If
they had discovered Milady's hiding-place, three would mount guard
there and the fourth would return to Béthune to report to Athos and serve
as a guide to the four friends. When this was all agreed on, the lackeys
went off.

Athos rose from his chair, girded on his sword, and left the inn. It was
then almost ten in the evening. At that hour, as everybody knows, in
provincial towns the streets are little frequented, yet Athos was obviously
trying to find someone he could question. At last he met a belated pedes-
trian, went up to him, and said a few words. The man recoiled in terror,
yet he answered the musketeer by a gesture in a certain direction. Athos
offered the man a half-pistole to accompany him, but the man refused it.

Athos plunged into the street the man had pointed out, but when he reached a crossroads he stopped again, visibly perplexed. Nevertheless, as the crossroads offered him a better chance of meeting someone than did any other place, he waited there. In a few minutes a night watchman came along. Athos asked him the same question he had asked the first man, and the night watchman evinced the same terror, refused in his turn to accompany Athos, and merely pointed to the road Athos should take.

Athos walked in the direction indicated until he came to a suburb at the side of the town opposite the side where he and his companions had entered it. Once again he seemed anxious and perplexed, and he stopped for a third time. Fortunately a beggar appeared and came up to him to ask for alms. Athos offered him a crown to accompany him to his destination. The beggar hesitated a moment, but the sight of the silver coin shining in the dim light decided him, and he started off ahead of Athos. When they reached a certain street corner, the beggar pointed out a small house in the distance, isolated, lonely, and dismal. Athos went toward the house and the beggar, having received his reward, ran off as fast as his legs could carry him.

Athos walked all around the house before he could distinguish the door amid the red paint that covered the house. No light shone through the chinks of the shutters, no sound gave reason to think that it was inhabited. It was as dark and as silent as the tomb.

Twice Athos knocked at the door without receiving any answer. At his third knock, however, he heard footsteps within. At last the door opened halfway and a tall, pale man with black hair and beard appeared. Athos and he exchanged a few words in low tones, then the tall man gestured to Athos to enter. Athos took advantage of the invitation at once and the door closed behind him.

The man whom Athos had come so far to seek and had had so much difficulty in finding ushered him into his laboratory, where he had been engaged in fastening together with wire the rattling bones of a skeleton. It had all been put together except the skull, which lay on the table. The rest of the furnishings indicated that the man who lived in this house was concerned with the natural sciences. There were big glass jars full of snakes, dried lizards set in great black frames shone like emeralds, and bunches of sweet-smelling herbs hung from the ceiling and in the corners of the room. But there was no sign of a family or of a servant. The tall man lived in this house alone.

Athos looked about coldly and uninterestedly at all the objects just enumerated and then at the other man's invitation he sat down near him. He explained the reason for his visit and told the tall man of the service he had come to ask. But he had barely finished speaking when the nameless man, who had remained standing before the musketeer, recoiled with every sign of terror and shook his head. Then Athos took from his pocket a small piece of paper on which were written two lines and a signature, and stamped with a seal. He gave it to the man who had given such premature signs of repugnance. The tall man had scarcely read these two lines, noted the signature, and recognized the seal, when he bowed to indicate that he no longer had any objection to make and that he was ready to obey.

Athos required no more. He rose, bowed, and departed, returned exactly as he had come, entered the inn, and went to his room.

At daybreak D'Artagnan came there and asked: "What do we do now?"

"Wait," Athos replied. A few minutes later the musketeers received word from the Mother Superior that the burial would take place at noon. As to the poisoner, there were no tidings whatever of her. They knew only that she had escaped by way of the garden, where her footsteps had been found in the sand. The garden gate was locked, and the key had disappeared.

At the hour appointed, Lord Winter and the four friends repaired to the convent. The bells were tolling. The chapel was open, but the grating of the chancel was closed. In the center of the chancel the body of the victim, clad in her novice's habit, lay in an open coffin. On either side of the chancel, behind the gratings that communicated with the convent, the whole community of the Carmelite convent was assembled. There they stood listening to the requiem Mass and mingling their chanting with the intoning of the priests, without seeing or being seen by the laity.

At the chapel door D'Artagnan felt his courage fail him again and he turned to look for Athos, but Athos had disappeared. Faithful to his mission of vengeance, Athos had asked to be conducted to the garden. Then, following the light tracks of that woman, who had always left a trail of blood wherever she had passed, he reached the garden gate that led to the wood, broke it open, and plunged in among the trees.

Then all his suspicions were confirmed. The road by which the carriage had disappeared encircled the wood. Athos followed the road for some time, his eyes fixed on the ground. A few drops of blood that had fallen from the wound inflicted on either the courier or one of the horses dotted the road. At the end of perhaps three-quarters of a league, within fifty paces of Festubert, he found a larger spot of blood, and the ground here had been pawed by horses. Between the wood and this accusing place, a little farther on than the trampled spot, he found footsteps like those in the garden, and the carriage had stopped here. This was the spot where Milady had come out of the wood and got into the carriage.

Satisfied with this discovery, which confirmed all his suspicions still further, Athos returned to the inn, where he found Planchet awaiting him impatiently.

Everything had gone as Athos had anticipated. Planchet had followed the road assigned him. Like Athos, he had found bloodstains, like Athos, he had noted the spot where the horses had stopped. But he had pushed on farther than Athos. Stopping at the village of Festubert, he did not have to ask questions, but learned while drinking at a tavern there that at half-past eight the evening before a wounded man who accompanied a lady traveling in a post chaise had been forced to stop there, being in no condition to go on. The mishap had been attributed to robbers who had held up their chaise in the woods. The wounded man had stayed in the village, the lady had procured fresh horses and continued her journey.

Planchet went in search of the postilion who had guided the chaise, and found him. He had taken the lady as far as Fromelles, and from Fromelles she had set out for Armentières. Planchet took the crossroad and by seven in the morning he was at Armentières. There was only one inn there, the Hôtel de la Poste. Planchet presented himself there as a lackey out of work who was looking for a place. He had not chatted with the people of the inn ten minutes before he learned that a woman had arrived there alone at eleven the night before, had engaged a room, then had sent for the innkeeper and told him that she intended to stay for some time in that neighborhood. That was all Planchet wanted to know. He hurried to the meeting-place appointed for the lackeys, found the others there and posted them as sentinels at the exits of the inn, then went back to Athos.

Athos had just received Planchet's report when his three friends returned from the convent. Every face was gloomy and disturbed, even Aramis's gentle countenance.

"What do we do now?" asked D'Artagnan.

"Wait," answered Athos.

Each of the five withdrew to his own room. At eight o'clock that evening Athos ordered the horses to be saddled and sent word to Lord Winter and to his friends to be prepared to set off. They were all ready in a few seconds. Each examined his own weapons and put them in order. Athos was the last to come down and he found D'Artagnan already mounted and growing impatient.

"Patience, my son," said Athos. "One of our party is still missing."

The four horsemen looked about in astonishment, for they could not imagine who this missing person might be. At that moment Planchet brought up Athos's horse and the musketeer vaulted lightly into the saddle.

"Wait for me," he said. "I will be back presently." And he set off at a gallop.

A quarter of an hour later he returned, accompanied by a man who was masked and wrapped in a great red cloak. Lord Winter and the three musketeers looked at one another as if to ask what this meant. No one of them could give the others any information, for they could none of them guess who this man might be. Yet they were sure it was right for him to be there, since Athos had so ordered it.

At nine o'clock, guided by Planchet, the little cavalcade rode off along the road the carriage had taken. It was a melancholy sight that those six men presented, all riding in silence, each one plunged in his own thoughts that were as dismal as despair, as somber as punishment.

CHAPTER 62

IT WAS A DARK AND STORMY NIGHT. GREAT CLOUDS WERE scudding across the sky, dimming the brightness of the stars. The moon would not be rising until midnight. Now and then a flash of lightning on the horizon lighted the road opening out before them, white and solitary. Then when the flash died down everything was pitch-dark again.

Over and over Athos had to call D'Artagnan, who was always at the head of the little troop, back to his place with the others, but after a moment he would leave it again. He was obsessed by but one thought—to go ahead as fast as he could. And go ahead he did. They passed in silence through the little village of Festubert, where the wounded courier was staying, then skirted the forest of Richebourg. At Herlier, Planchet, who was guiding the column, turned left.

Several times either Lord Winter or Porthos or Aramis tried to enter into conversation with the man in the red cloak, but each time one of them said something to him he merely bowed without replying. They soon realized that there must be some good reason why this nameless man kept silence and they did not speak to him again.

Moreover, the storm was growing worse. Flashes of lightning followed one another more and more rapidly, thunder began to growl, and the wind, precursor of a hurricane, whistled through the plumes of the horsemen's hats and through their hair. The little cavalcade rode on at full gallop.

A little way beyond Fromelles the storm burst in all its fury. They put on their cloaks. They still had three leagues to cover, and they rode them under torrents of rain. D'Artagnan took off his hat, and he had not put on his cloak. He found it pleasant to let the water trickle over his burning brow and cool his whole body, which was shaken by feverish shudders.

Just as the little troop had ridden beyond Goskal and were approaching the posting house, a man who had taken shelter under a tree left his refuge, where he had been concealed in the darkness, and stepped into the middle of the road, putting a finger on his lips. Athos recognized Grimaud.

"What is it?" Athos asked. "Has she left Armentières?" Grimaud nodded yes. D'Artagnan ground his teeth. "Be quiet, D'Artagnan," said Athos. "*I* am in charge of the whole business, and so I am the one to question Grimaud."

Grimaud pointed in the direction of the river Lys.

"How far from here?"

Grimaud held up to his master a bent forefinger.

"Is she alone?"

Grimaud nodded.

"Gentlemen," Athos said, "she is alone half a league from here, somewhere toward the river."

"Good!" said D'Artagnan. "Take us there, Grimaud."

Grimaud started off across the open country as their guide. After some fifty paces they came to a brook and forded it. A flash of lightning showed them the village of Enguinghem.

"Is that where she is, Grimaud?" Athos asked.

Grimaud shook his head.

"Silence, then!" Athos cried.

The little troop went on. Lightning flashed once more. Grimaud stretched out his arm to point and by that serpentine line of bluish light they distinguished a small house standing alone on the riverbank within a hundred paces of a ferry. They could see a light in one window.

"This is the place," said Athos.

Just then a man who had been lying in a ditch stood up; it was Mousqueton. He pointed to the lighted window and said: "She is there."

"And Bazin?" asked Athos.

"While I have been keeping watch on the window he has been watching the door."

"Fine!" said Athos. "You are good and faithful servants."

Athos sprang from his horse, gave the bridle to Grimaud, motioned to the others to go toward the door, and walked toward the window. The little house was surrounded by a quickset hedge two or three feet high. Athos jumped over it and went up to the window. It had no shutters, but there were half-curtains, carefully closed. Athos stepped up onto the stone window sill so that he could peer in over the curtains.

By the light of a lamp near her, he saw a woman wrapped in a dark-colored mantle, sitting on a stool by a dying fire. Her elbows rested on a shabby table, and she was holding her head between her ivory-white hands. Athos could not see her face, but a sinister smile twisted his lips. He could not be mistaken; here was the woman he was seeking. At that moment one of the horses neighed. Milady raised her head, saw Athos's pallid face glued to the windowpane, and screamed.

Athos realized that she had recognized him and pushed the pane in with hand and knee; the glass gave way and shivered into splinters that fell to the floor. Athos, looking like the very specter of vengeance, leaped into the room. Milady rushed to the door and flung it open. On the threshold, still paler and more menacing than Athos, stood D'Artagnan. Milady recoiled with another scream. D'Artagnan, thinking that she must have some means of flight and fearing that she might escape him, drew his pistol from his belt. But Athos raised his hand to stop him.

"Put back that weapon, D'Artagnan," he commanded. "We must bring this woman to trial, not murder her. Wait but a little, D'Artagnan, and you shall be satisfied. . . . Come in, gentlemen."

D'Artagnan obeyed, for Athos spoke with the solemn voice and the commanding gesture of a judge sent by God Almighty Himself. Behind D'Artagnan came Porthos, Aramis, Lord Winter, and the tall man in the red cloak. The four lackeys guarded the door and the window. Milady had sunk onto her chair, her hands stretched out as if to conjure away that terrible apparition. When she saw her brother-in-law she uttered a frightful cry.

"What do you want?" she shrieked.

"We want Charlotte Backson," Athos replied, "who was first called the Comtesse de La Fère and afterward Lady Clark, Baroness of Sheffield."

"I am she, I am she," murmured Milady, overwhelmed by terror. "What do you want with me?"

"We want to bring you to trial for your crimes," declared Athos. "You will be allowed to defend yourself, to justify yourself if you can. Monsieur d'Artagnan, it is for you to accuse her first."

D'Artagnan stepped forward. "Before God and before men," he said, "I accuse this woman of having poisoned Constance Bonacieux, who died last evening." He turned toward Porthos and Aramis.

"We bear witness to the truth of the accusation," said the two musketeers.

"Before God and before men," D'Artagnan continued, "I accuse this woman of having attempted to poison me too, in wine that she sent me at Villeroi with a forged letter saying that the wine came from my friends. God preserved me, but a man died in my stead, a man named Brisemont."

"We bear witness to the truth of this accusation, also," declared Aramis and Porthos.

"Before God and before men I accuse this woman of having urged me to murder the Comte de Wardes, and since no one heard her and could bear witness to the fact, I attest it myself. I have spoken." And D'Artagnan walked to the other side of the room to stand with Porthos and Aramis.

"It is your turn next, my lord," said Athos, and Lord Winter stepped forward.

"Before God and before men," he declared, "I accuse this woman of having caused the assassination of the Duke of Buckingham."

"The Duke of Buckingham assassinated?" They all cried as if with one voice.

"Yes," replied Lord Winter, "assassinated! Upon receiving the warning letter you sent me, I had this woman arrested. I placed her under the guard of a loyal servitor of mine. She corrupted this man, put a dagger in his hand, and instigated him to kill the Duke. At this very moment Felton may be paying with his life for the crime committed in reality by that Fury."

All of the judges shuddered at the revelation of these crimes they had not known of before.

"That is not all," Lord Winter continued. "My brother, who had made you his heir, my lady, within three hours after he had made his will died of a mysterious illness that left livid spots all over his body. My sister, how did your husband die?"

"Horrible!" cried Porthos, and Aramis echoed him.

"Murderess of Buckingham, murderess of Felton, murderess of my brother, I demand that justice be done you, and if it is not done by others, I swear that I will do it myself." And Lord Winter went to stand by D'Artagnan, leaving his place free for another prosecutor.

Milady let her head sink between her hands and tried to collect her thoughts, which were whirling about in a deadly dizziness.

"Now it is my turn," announced Athos, trembling as a lion is said to tremble before a serpent. "Now it is my turn. I married that woman when she was a young girl. I married her against the wishes of my whole family. I endowed her with my wealth, I gave her my name. One day I discovered that this woman was branded as a criminal, that she had been stamped on the left shoulder with the fleur-de-lis."

"Oh," cried Milady, rising to her feet, "I challenge you to find anyone that pronounced such an infamous sentence upon me. I challenge you to find the man who executed it."

"Be silent," said a hollow voice, and the man in the red cloak stepped forward in his turn.

"Who is that man, who is he?" cried Milady, choking with terror. Her disheveled hair bristled above her livid face looking as if every hair were alive.

The eyes of all the others turned toward this man, for none of them except Athos knew who he was. Even Athos looked at him with as much astonishment as the rest, for he had not the faintest idea how the tall man could be concerned in the horrible drama that was now reaching its denouement.

The nameless man approached Milady at a slow and portentous pace until only the table separated them, then he removed his mask. Milady stared for some moments at that pale face framed by black hair and beard, the only expression of which was one of icy impassiveness. Suddenly she retreated until her back rested against the wall.

"Oh no no!" she cried out. "No, no—this is an apparition from Hell!

It cannot be he! Help! help!" And she turned toward the wall as if she hoped to tear an opening through it with her hands.

"Who are you, then?" asked first one and then another of the witnesses of this scene.

"Ask that woman," replied the man in the red cloak. "You can surely see that she had recognized me."

"The executioner of Lille, the executioner of Lille!" shrieked Milady, the prey of despairing terror. She grasped at the wall with her hands to keep herself from falling. All the others drew back; the man in the red cloak was left standing alone in the middle of the room. "Oh, have mercy on me, have mercy on me!" cried the wretched woman, falling to her knees.

The nameless man waited for silence, then he went on: "I told you that she had recognized me! Yes, I am the public executioner of the city of Lille, and this is what I have to tell you."

All eyes were fixed on this man, and all listened to his words with eager intentness.

"This young woman was once a young girl, as beautiful then as she is now. She was a nun in the Benedictine convent at Templemar. A young priest with a pure and trusting heart was serving in the chapel of that convent. She determined to seduce him, and she succeeded—she would have seduced a saint.

"The vows both of them had sworn were sacred and irrevocable. Their liaison could not last long without ruining both of them. She persuaded him to leave that part of the country, but in order to get away, to escape with her to some other part of France where they could live in safety because no one would know them, they had to have money. Neither of them had any. The priest stole the sacred vessels and sold them. But just as they were preparing to go off together, both of them were arrested.

"Within a week she seduced the jailer's son and escaped. The young priest was sentenced to ten years in irons and to be branded with the fleur-de-lis. I was the public executioner of the city of Lille, as this woman has said. It was my duty to brand the guilty man—and that guilty man, gentlemen, was my brother! I swore then that the woman who had brought him to ruin, who had been his accomplice, since she had instigated him to commit the crime, that this woman should at least suffer part of his punishment. I thought I knew where she was hiding, I followed her, I caught up with her. I put handcuffs on her and stamped on her shoulder the same brand I had stamped on my brother.

"The day after my return to Lille my brother succeeded in making his escape also, and I was sentenced to prison in my brother's place until he should return to take his own punishment. My poor brother did not know of my sentence. He had joined this woman. They had fled together to the province of Berry and there he had obtained a small curacy. This woman passed as his sister. The lord of the estate on which stood the church of which my brother was curé saw his supposed sister and fell in love with her so deeply that he asked her to marry him. So she left the man she had ruined for the man she was about to ruin, and she became the Comtesse de La Fère."

All eyes turned toward Athos, whose real name they knew now, and he nodded to confirm the truth of what the executioner had said.

"Then," the man in the red cloak continued, "fairly insane, desperate, and determined to be rid of an existence that she had deprived of all honor and all happiness, my poor brother returned to Lille, and when he learned of the sentence that made me a prisoner in his stead, he gave himself up. And that same night he hanged himself on the iron bar of the window of his cell. Those who had sentenced me kept their word, and as soon as my brother's dead body was identified, I was set free. I have told you what the crime is that I accuse her of, and the reason why she was branded."

"Monsieur d'Artagnan," said Athos, "what penalty do you demand for this woman?"

"The penalty of death," replied D'Artagnan.

"Lord Winter," Athos continued, "what penalty do you demand for this woman?"

"The penalty of death," answered the Englishman.

"Messieurs Porthos and Aramis," Athos continued, "you are her judges too. What penalty do you request for this woman?"

"The penalty of death," answered one and then the other in somber tones.

Milady gave a frightful shriek. She was still on her knees, and dragged herself a little way toward her judges.

"Anne de Bueil, Charlotte Backson, Comtesse de La Fère, Lady Clark," pronounced Athos, "your crimes have wearied men on earth and God in Heaven. If you know any prayer, say it now, for you have been sentenced, and you shall die."

At these words, which left her no hope, Milady rose from her knees to her full height and tried to speak. But her strength failed her. She felt as if a powerful and implacable hand had seized her by the hair and was dragging her to her doom as irrevocably as the hand of fate drags a man where it will. She made no attempt whatever at resistance, but at a gesture from the man in the red cloak she stumbled out of the little house.

The executioner followed her, with Lord Winter, D'Artagnan, Athos, Porthos, and Aramis close behind him. The lackeys followed their masters. The room was left empty, its window broken, its door open, and the smoky lamp burning dismally on the shabby table.

CHAPTER 63

IT WAS ALMOST MIDNIGHT. THE WANING MOON, A NAR-row semicircle now, and reddened by the last traces of the storm, was rising behind the little town of Armentières. The dark silhouette of the town's houses and the skeleton of its tall belfry were outlined by its wan light. Ahead of them, the Lys rolled by, its waters like those of a river of molten lead. On the other bank rose a black mass of trees outlined against a stormy sky covered with great copper-colored clouds that created what seemed to be twilight in the black night.

To the left rose an old abandoned mill with motionless vanes, and from its ruins an owl was sending out at regular intervals its strident, monotonous cry. Here and there on the plain to the right and the left of the way the dismal procession was taking, appeared a few low, stunted trees that looked like deformed dwarfs crouched to spy on men who were walking there at this sinister hour.

From time to time a broad sheet of lightning illuminated the whole horizon, twisting over the black mass of trees like a snake and flashing down like a scimitar to cut into two parts both the heavens and the waters. Not a breath of wind came to make the atmosphere less heavy. A deathlike silence weighed down all nature, the ground was wet and slippery with the recent rain, and the refreshed vegetation gave forth its pleasant odors with renewed vigor.

Two of the lackeys were pulling Milady along, each of them holding her by an arm. The executioner walked behind them, and Lord Winter, D'Artagnan, Athos, Porthos, and Aramis were close behind him. Planchet and Bazin came last.

The other two lackeys led Milady toward the river. She uttered no word, but her eyes were speaking with their unutterable eloquence, supplicating first one, then the other. When she saw that they were a little ahead of the others, she whispered to the lackeys:

"A thousand pistoles for each of you if you will help me to escape, but if you give me up to your masters, I have friends near here who will make you pay dearly for my death."

Grimaud hesitated and Mousqueton trembled from head to foot.

Athos, who had heard Milady's voice, came up to them quickly, and Lord Winter came with him.

"We must change the lackeys," said Athos. "She has spoken to them, and we can no longer trust them."

He summoned Planchet and Bazin, who took the places of the other two.

When they reached the riverbank the executioner approached Milady and tied her hands together and her feet together. Then she broke her silence to scream:

"You are cowards, you are wretched murderers! It takes ten of you to kill one woman. Beware! If I am not saved, I shall be avenged."

"You are not a woman," said Athos icily. "You do not belong to the human species, you are a devil escaped from Hell, and we are going to send you back there."

"Aha, you virtuous gentlemen," said Milady, "remember that anyone who touches a hair of my head becomes a murderer too."

"The public executioner can kill, madame, without becoming a murderer," said the man in the red cloak, tapping his broadsword. "This is the final judge, that's all. That's what our neighbors the Germans call it —*Nachrichter.*"

As he said these words and bound her, Milady uttered two or three shrieks that produced a somber and extraordinary effect in the dark night.

"If I am guilty," she shrieked, "if I have committed the crimes you accuse me of, take me to a court of justice. You are not legal judges, you men. You cannot sentence me."

"I offered you Tyburn," said Lord Winter. "Why did you not accept it?"

"Because I do not want to die!" cried Milady, still struggling to escape her doom. "Because I am too young to die!"

"The woman you poisoned at Béthune was even younger than you, madame, and yet she is dead," said D'Artagnan.

"I will enter a cloistered order, I will become a nun," vowed Milady.

"You *were* a cloistered nun," said the executioner, "and you left the cloister to destroy my brother."

Milady uttered a cry of terror and fell on her knees once more. The executioner put his hands under her arms, lifted her, and started to carry her toward the little boat at the riverbank.

"Oh, my God, my God," shrieked Milady, "are you going to drown me?"

Her cries were so heartrending that D'Artagnan, who until now had been Milady's most implacable pursuer, sank down on the stump of a tree and bowed his head, stopping up his ears with the palms of his hands. D'Artagnan was the youngest of them all, and his courage failed him.

"Oh, I cannot bear this horrible sight!" he muttered, "I cannot consent to let the woman die like that!"

Milady heard his words and her black despair was lighted by a ray of hope.

"D'Artagnan, D'Artagnan," she cried, "remember that I loved you!"

The young man rose and took one step toward her. But Athos stepped forward, drew his sword, and barred D'Artagnan's way.

"If you take one step more, D'Artagnan," he said, "you fight with me." D'Artagnan fell on his knees and prayed. "Come, executioner," Athos went on, "do your duty."

"Willingly, Monseigneur," replied the executioner, "for as truly as I am a good Catholic, I firmly believe that I am doing justice in putting an end to this woman."

"Well and good," said Athos, and he took one step toward Milady. "I forgive you," he said, "for all the evil you have done me. I forgive you for my future blasted, for my happiness lost, for my love defiled, and for my salvation forever jeopardized by the despair into which you have plunged me. May you die in peace!"

Lord Winter stepped forward next. "I forgive you," he said, "for poisoning my brother, for causing the assassination of His Grace the Duke of Buckingham, for causing the death of poor Felton, and for your attempts on my own life. May you die in peace!"

"As for me," said D'Artagnan, "I beg you to forgive me, madame, for having provoked your anger by a trick unworthy of a gentleman. And in return, I forgive you for the murder of my beloved mistress and for your other cruel attempts at vengeance upon me. May you die in peace!"

"I am lost!" murmured Milady in English. "I must die."

Then she got to her feet without help and cast about her one of those brilliant glances that seemed to dart from her eyes like flames.

She could see nothing. She listened, and she heard nothing. She had no one near her but her enemies.

"Where am I to die?" she asked.

"On the other bank of the river," the executioner replied.

Then he put her into the boat. Just as he was about to step into it himself, Athos handed him a sum of money.

"Here," he said, "is your fee for the execution, as witness that we are acting as judges."

"That is what we agreed on," said the executioner, "and so that now this woman may know in her turn that I am not acting as the public executioner, but doing my duty as a man——" And he threw the money into the river.

The boat moved off toward the left bank of the Lys, bearing the condemned woman and the executioner. The other men remained on the right bank and fell on their knees. The boat glided along, guided by the rope of the ferry, in the reflected light of a pale mist that was hanging over the water. The friends watched the skiff touch the left bank; the two figures stood out in black against the red-hued horizon.

During the crossing Milady had managed to untie the rope that bound her feet. On reaching the bank, she jumped lightly ashore and took to flight. But the ground was wet, and as she got to the top of the slope, she slipped and fell to her knees. Doubtless a superstitious idea occurred to her and she realized that Heaven had refused to succor her. She stayed there just as she had fallen, her head drooping and her hands clasped.

Then the men on the right bank saw the executioner raise both arms slowly. A moonbeam lighted up the blade of his broadsword. His arms fell. They heard the whistle of the steel blade and the cry of the victim. Then they saw a headless body fall.

The executioner took off his red cloak, spread it out on the ground, laid the body on it, tossed in the head. He brought up the four corners of the cloak and tied them securely, lifted the burden to his shoulder, and carried it back to the boat. When he reached the middle of the Lys, he stopped rowing and held up his ghastly burden over the river.

"God's justice be done!" he cried in a loud voice.

Then he let the cloak and all it held drop into the depths of the water, which closed over it.

Three days later the four musketeers were back in Paris.

CHAPTER 64

ON THE SIXTH DAY OF THE FOLLOWING MONTH, THE KING, in compliance with the promise he had made to the Cardinal to return to the siege of La Rochelle, left his capital still fairly stunned by the news, which had spread everywhere, that Buckingham had been assassinated. The Queen, despite the fact that she had been warned that the man she loved so dearly was in great danger, would not believe it when his death was announced to her. She was even indiscreet enough to cry out:

"It is not true! He has just written to me."

But the next day she was forced to accept the fatal news as true. La Porte, who had been detained in England like everyone else by the orders Charles I had given, came back now bearing the last present Buckingham sent to the Queen as he lay dying.

The King's joy had been very great. He did not even trouble to dissemble; in the Queen's presence he let it burst forth with special delight. Louis XIII, like all weak-minded men, was sadly wanting in generosity. But soon the King grew gloomy again, and once more his health was bad; he was not a man to display an unclouded brow for very long. He knew that in returning to the camp he was returning to slavery. Nevertheless, back there he went. For him, the Cardinal was the fascinating snake and he himself was the fascinated bird that flutters from branch to branch in the vain effort to escape.

Hence the return journey to La Rochelle was most melancholy. Our four friends, in particular, amazed their comrades. They rode on side by side, their eyes somber and their heads drooping. Athos alone raised his head from time to time, his eyes flashing and his lips twisted in a bitter smile. Then, like his comrades, he sank again into reverie. As soon as the escort arrived at a town and had conducted the King to his quarters, the four friends either retired to their own quarters or went to some obscure tavern, where they neither gambled nor drank, but only conversed in low tones, looking about them carefully to make sure that no one could overhear them.

One day the King had stopped on the way to hunt magpies, and instead of joining in the sport, the four friends stopped as usual at a tavern on the highway. Presently a man arrived from the direction of La Rochelle, riding full speed, and stopped at the door to drink a glass of wine. He darted a searching glance into the room where the four musketeers were sitting at a table.

"Holà, Monsieur d'Artagnan!" he called out. "Isn't that you I see over there?"

D'Artagnan raised his head and uttered a cry of joy. It was the man he called his phantom, the nameless man of Meung, the Rue de Fossoyeurs, and Arras. He drew his sword and sprang toward the door. But this time instead of taking to his heels the nameless man leaped from his horse and came to meet D'Artagnan.

"So, monsieur," said D'Artagnan, "at last I meet you again, and this time you shall not escape me!"

"I have no intention of doing so, monsieur, for this time it was I who was looking for you. In the name of the King, I place you under arrest. I order you to surrender your sword, monsieur, and that without resistance. Your head is at stake, I warn you."

"Who are you? Tell me that," said D'Artagnan, lowering his sword but not surrendering it.

"I am the Chevalier de Rochefort," the stranger replied, "the equerry of Monseigneur le Cardinal de Richelieu. I have orders to conduct you to His Eminence."

"We are just about to go where His Eminence is, Monsieur le Chevalier," said Athos, stepping forward. "Pray be good enough to accept Monsieur d'Artagnan's word that he will go straight to La Rochelle and His Eminence."

"It is my duty to place him in the hands of guards who will take him to the camp."

"We will act as his guards, monsieur, we give you our word as gentlemen," Athos returned. "But," he added, "we also give you our word as gentlemen that Monsieur d'Artagnan shall not leave us."

The Chevalier de Rochefort cast a glance behind him and saw that Porthos and Aramis were standing between him and the gate. He understood that he was completely at the mercy of the four friends.

"Gentlemen," he said, "if Monsieur d'Artagnan will surrender his sword to me and add his word to yours, I will be satisfied with your promise to convey Monsieur d'Artagnan to the quarters of Monseigneur le Cardinal."

"You have my word, monsieur," said D'Artagnan, "and here is my sword."

"That is much better for me," said Rochefort, "for I must continue my journey."

"If that is for the purpose of joining Milady, it is a futile journey," said Athos coldly. "You will not find her."

"What has become of her, then?" asked Rochefort eagerly.

"Come back to camp with us and you shall learn that."

Rochefort reflected for a moment. Then, since Surgières, where the Cardinal had gone to meet the King, was only a day's journey away, he decided to follow Athos's advice. Besides, returning with them gave him the advantage of keeping his own eyes on his prisoner. They set out together, the four friends, their lackeys, and the equerry.

On the morrow, at three o'clock in the afternoon, they reached Surgières. The Cardinal was there, where he had awaited Louis XIII. When they met, the Minister and the King embraced each other most tenderly, congratulating each other on the happy chance that had rid France of the implacable enemy who had roused all Europe against their country. Then the Cardinal, having been informed by Rochefort that D'Artagnan was under arrest, and wishing to see him at once, took leave of the King. Returning that evening to his quarters by the Pont de La Pierre, the Cardinal found D'Artagnan standing in front of his house without his sword, and the three musketeers beside him, fully armed.

This time, as he was well attended, Richelieu looked at them sternly before beckoning to D'Artagnan with eye and hand to follow him. D'Artagnan obeyed.

"We will wait for you, D'Artagnan," said Athos, loud enough for the Cardinal to hear.

His Eminence frowned, stopped for a moment, then went on his way without a word. D'Artagnan went in after the Cardinal, the door was shut behind him, and guard was mounted before it. His Eminence went to the room that served him for an office and motioned to Rochefort to bring in the young musketeer. Rochefort obeyed and withdrew.

D'Artagnan was alone with the Cardinal. This was his second interview with Richelieu, and in after-years he confessed that he had been convinced that it would be his last. Richelieu remained standing, leaning against the chimney piece, with a table between D'Artagnan and himself.

"Monsieur," said the Cardinal, "you were arrested by my orders."

"So I have been informed, Monseigneur."

"Do you know why?"

"No, Monseigneur, how could I? The only thing that I might be arrested for is not yet known to Your Eminence."

Richelieu stared at the young man. "Holà!" he said, "What do you mean by that?"

"If Monseigneur will be good enough to tell me first what crimes I am charged with, I will then inform him what I have actually done."

"You are charged with crimes that have brought down far loftier heads than yours, monsieur!" said the Cardinal.

"What are they, Monseigneur," asked D'Artagnan with a calmness that astonished the Cardinal himself.

"You are charged with having corresponded with enemies of this kingdom, you are charged with having intercepted state secrets, you are charged with having endeavored to thwart the plans of your commander."

"And who charges me with all that, Monseigneur?" asked D'Artagnan, feeling sure that his accuser was Milady. "Is it not a woman who has been branded by the justice of our country, a woman who married one man in France and another in England, a woman who poisoned her second husband and tried to poison me?"

"Whatever are you saying, monsieur?" cried the Cardinal. "What woman are you speaking of that way?"

"Milady—Lady Clark," answered D'Artagnan. "Yes, Lady Clark. When Your Eminence honored her with your confidence, no doubt you were ignorant of all her crimes."

"Monsieur," said the Cardinal, "if Lady Clark has committed the crimes you name, she shall be punished."

"She has been punished already, Monseigneur."

"And who punished her?"

"We—my three friends and I."

"Is she in prison?"

"She is dead."

"Dead!" echoed the Cardinal, who could not believe what he heard. "Dead! Did you say she was dead?"

"Three times she attempted to kill me, and I forgave her. But she murdered the woman I loved. Then my friends and I seized her, tried her, and sentenced her."

Then D'Artagnan related the poisoning of Madame Bonacieux in the Carmelite convent at Béthune, the trial held in the lonely house, the execution on the bank of the Lys. A shudder shook the Cardinal's whole body, and he was not a man to shudder easily. But suddenly, as if influenced by a secret thought, his expression, gloomy until then, gradually cleared and at last became perfectly serene.

"So you and your friends appointed yourselves as judges," said the Cardinal in a mild tone that was a strange contrast to the severity of his words. "You set yourself up as judges without remembering that those who punish without license to punish are murderers!"

"Monseigneur, I swear to you that never for a moment have I intended to defend my life against you. I will willingly submit to any punishment that Your Eminence may please to visit me with. I do not hold life so dear as to be afraid of death."

"Yes, I know you are a brave man, monsieur," said the Cardinal, almost affectionately. "I can therefore tell you at once that you will be tried, and probably condemned."

"Another man might reply to Your Eminence that he has his pardon in his pocket. As for me, I am content to say, 'Give your orders, Monseigneur. I am ready'."

"Your pardon?" exclaimed Richelieu in surprise.

"Yes, Monseigneur," said D'Artagnan.

"A pardon signed by whom?" asked the Cardinal in an extraordinary tone of contempt. "By the King?"

"No, by Your Eminence."

"By *me?* Have you gone mad, monsieur?"

"Monseigneur will surely recognize his own handwriting." And D'Artagnan gave the Cardinal the precious paper that Athos had wrested from Milady and had given his friend for his protection. His Eminence took the paper and read slowly, stressing every syllable, the following:

December 3, 1627

It is by my order and for the service of the state that the bearer of this note has done what he has done.

Richelieu

Signed by my hand at the
camp of La Rochelle.

After he had read these few lines the Cardinal fell into a deep reverie, but he did not return the paper to D'Artagnan.

"He is meditating by what sort of torture he will have me killed," D'Artagnan murmured to himself. "Well, by my faith, he shall see how a gentleman can die!" The young musketeer was in an excellent frame of mind to meet his end heroically.

Richelieu was still deep in thought, rolling and unrolling the paper in his hands. At last he raised his head and fixed his eagle glance upon the loyal, candid, and intelligent countenance before him. He read on that face furrowed with tears all the sufferings D'Artagnan had endured for the last month. He reflected for the third or fourth time what a noble future this lad of twenty-one had to look forward to, and what the resources of his energy, his courage, and his shrewd understanding might offer to a good master. On the other hand, he remembered how the crimes, the power, and the devilish genius of Milady had more than once terrified him, and he felt as it were a secret joy at being forever rid of such a dangerous accomplice. Slowly he tore up the paper D'Artagnan had so generously entrusted to him.

"I am lost!" D'Artagnan said to himself. And he bowed low before the Cardinal, like a man who says, "Lord, Thy will be done!"

The Cardinal went to his desk and without sitting down wrote a few lines on a parchment that was already two-thirds filled and affixed his seal to it.

"That is my death sentence," thought D'Artagnan. "He is sparing me the boredom of the Bastille and the tedium of a trial. That's very kind of him."

"Here, monsieur," the Cardinal said, "I have taken one carte-blanche document from you, and I am giving you another. The name is wanting on this commission; you can write it in yourself."

D'Artagnan took the paper hesitatingly and glanced over it. It was a lieutenant's commission in the Royal Musketeers. D'Artagnan fell on his knees before the Cardinal.

"Monseigneur, my life is yours," he declared. "Use it henceforth as you will. But I do not deserve this favor you have bestowed on me. I have three friends who are all more deserving, more worthy——"

"You are a good lad, D'Artagnan," the Cardinal interrupted, tapping him on the shoulder, delighted that he had at last mastered that rebellious nature. "Do what you will with this commission. But remember that though the name is blank, it is to you that I give it."

"I shall never forget it," replied D'Artagnan. "Your Eminence may be certain of that."

The Cardinal turned and called in a loud voice, "Rochefort!" The Chevalier, who was doubtless close to the door, entered at once.

"Rochefort," said the Cardinal, "you see Monsieur d'Artagnan here. I count him as one of my friends, so embrace each other—and be good, both of you, if you want to keep your heads where they are."

Rochefort and D'Artagnan embraced each other rather coldly, but the Cardinal was watching them with his vigilant eye. They left the room together.

"We shall meet again, shall we not, monsieur?" said Rochefort.

"Whenever you please," D'Artagnan replied.

"There will surely be an opportunity," commented Rochefort.

"What's that?" asked the Cardinal opening the door of his office.

The two men smiled at each other, shook hands, and bowed to His Eminence. When D'Artagnan got outside with his three friends, Athos said:

"We were beginning to grow impatient."

"Here I am, my friends," said D'Artagnan, "not only free, but in high favor!"

"You'll tell us all about it?"

"This evening, I promise."

Accordingly that evening D'Artagnan betook himself to Athos's quarters. He found his friend in a fair way to empty a bottle of Spanish wine, an occupation to which he devoted himself religiously every night. D'Artagnan related what had passed between the Cardinal and himself and, pulling the commission out of his pocket, he announced:

"Here, my dear Athos, this naturally belongs to you."

Athos smiled one of his sweet and charming smiles. "My friend," he said, "for Athos this is too much, for the Comte de La Fère it is too little. Keep the commission, it is yours. Alas! You have bought it dearly enough."

D'Artagnan took leave of Athos and went to call on Porthos. He found that gentleman clad in a magnificent costume covered with sumptuous embroidery. He was standing before a mirror admiring himself.

"Aha!" said Porthos. "It's you, my dear friend! How do you think I look in these garments?"

"Wonderful!" answered D'Artagnan. "But I have come to offer you a costume that will be even more becoming."

"What's that?" asked Porthos.

"The uniform of a lieutenant of the Royal Musketeers." Then D'Artagnan told Porthos of his interview with the Cardinal, and again pulling the commission out of his pocket, he said: "Here, my dear fellow, write your name on this, and treat me well when you're my officer."

Porthos glanced over the document and, to the Gascon's great astonishment, handed it back to him.

"Yes," he said, "that would be very flattering, but I wouldn't have time enough to enjoy that distinction. During our expedition to Béthune my Duchesse's husband died. The coffers of the dear departed hold out their arms to me. I am marrying the widow. Look, I was just trying on my wedding clothes when you came in. Keep the lieutenancy, keep it yourself, my dear fellow." And he returned the commission to D'Artagnan.

D'Artagnan went off to Aramis's. He found him kneeling at a prie-dieu, his head bowed down on an open prayer book. Again D'Artagnan described his interview with the Cardinal and, pulling the commission out of his pocket for the third time, held it out, saying:

"Aramis, our friend, our guiding light, our invisible protector, I beg you to accept this commission. You have earned it far more than any of the rest of us by your wisdom and your counsels, which have always led to such happy results."

"Alas! my dear friend," Aramis answered, "our last adventures have disgusted me completely with the life of the world and the life of the sword. After the siege is raised, I shall enter the Order of the Lazarists. Keep the commission, D'Artagnan. The profession of arms suits you perfectly; you will be a brave and venturesome captain."

D'Artagnan, his eyes both moist with gratitude and beaming with joy, went back to Athos. He found his friend still at table, holding up his last glass of Malaga to look through it in the light of the lamp.

"Well," said D'Artagnan, "they too have refused!"

"That is because no one is more worthy of it than you, dear friend." And Athos picked up a pen, wrote D'Artagnan's name in the blank on the commission, and gave the document back to him.

"I shall no longer have any friends, then," said the young man. "Alas! I have nothing now but bitter memories." And he buried his head in his hands as two large tears rolled down his cheeks.

"You are young," Athos answered. "Your bitter memories have still time to change into sweet memories!"

EPILOGUE

LA ROCHELLE, DEPRIVED OF THE ASSISTANCE OF THE English fleet and the reinforcements promised by Buckingham, surrendered after a year's siege. On October 28, 1628, the capitulation was signed. The King made his entrance into Paris on December 23, receiving as triumphant a welcome as if he had come from conquering an enemy of France rather than fellow Frenchmen.

D'Artagnan took over his lieutenancy. Planchet obtained through Rochefort a sergeancy in the Royal Guards.

Porthos left the service and in the course of the following year he married Madame Coquenard. The coffers he had coveted so avidly contained 800,000 livres. Mousqueton wore magnificent livery and enjoyed the satisfaction of his lifelong ambition—he rode on the lackey's seat of a gilded carriage.

Aramis, after a journey into Lorraine, suddenly disappeared and wrote no more to his friends. Later they learned through Madame de Chevreuse, who told it to two or three of her suitors, that he had entered a monastery in Nancy. Bazin became a lay brother.

Athos remained a musketeer in the company D'Artagnan commanded until 1631, when, after a journey into Touraine, he too left the service under the pretext that he had inherited a small estate at Roussillon. Grimaud followed him.

D'Artagnan fought with Rochefort three times, and three times wounded him.

"I shall probably kill you the fourth time," he remarked as he gave Rochefort his hand to help him up.

"Then it's best both for you and for me to stop where we are," replied the wounded man. "By the powers, I am a better friend to you than you think. After our first duel, by saying one word to the Cardinal, I could have had your throat cut!"

This time they embraced heartily and without any mental reservation.

Monsieur Bonacieux lived on very quietly, quite ignorant of what had become of his wife and caring very little about the matter. One day he was indiscreet enough to recall himself to the Cardinal's memory. Richelieu sent word to him he would provide for Bonacieux so well that he would never want for anything in the future. In fact, the next day Monsieur Bonacieux left his house at seven o'clock in the evening to go to the Louvre, and was never seen again in the Rue des Fossoyeurs. The opinion of those who seemed to be the best informed was that he was being lodged and fed in some royal stronghold at the expense of His Generous Eminence.

THE END

D'Artagnan Fights with Lord Winter